Born rich and grow... W9-CJS-631
sexual and political conquest, nothing stops Stewart
Gansvoort. Not the beautiful women who share his
bed, nor the men corrupted in his service.

THE DARK SIDE OF THE DREAM

THE DARK SIDE OF THE DREAM

a novel by
JOHN STARR

WARNER BOOKS

A Warner Communications Company

WARNER BOOKS EDITION

Copyright © 1982 by The Estate of John Starr
All rights reserved.

Cover design by Gene Light

Cover art by Victor Gadino

Warner Books, Inc.,
666 Fifth Avenue,
New York, N.Y. 10103

 A Warner Communications Company

Printed in the United States of America

First Paperback Printing: July, 1983

10 9 8 7 6 5 4 3 2 1

"... out of reality are our tales of imagination fashioned."
—HANS CHRISTIAN ANDERSEN

"I only know that he who forms a tie is lost. The germ of corruption has entered into his soul."
—JOSEPH CONRAD

THE
DARK
SIDE OF THE
DREAM

Book One

Time: THE PRESENT
NAN KENNICOTT

From her place at the edge of the reflecting pool, the woman in the wheelchair could look past the glass and marble immensity of the Bell Tower, across the open space where the gaunt skeletal construction of the unfinished Edifice traced its pattern against the false dawn.

Beyond lay the City, sprawling down the steep hillside to the edge of the river, now almost hidden as if by the morning mist. Beyond that the foothills, just now tipped with pink as if the day were about to begin.

But it wasn't mist, and the rosy flush wasn't approaching dawn, although the sun would soon rise. It was smoke from burning buildings in the ghetto; it was the dying flames reflected from the pall of smoke. Far in the distance the muted clang of a single fire engine disturbed the tag end of the night.

None of these things meant anything to the woman in the wheelchair. She was lost in her surroundings, the vast towering awesomeness of the Mall, which for all its size had a warm intimacy for her, as though she were cuddled in her own blanket, protected from the rest of the world. Safe against the night. And the coming day.

It was to be a day like no other day for Nan Kennicott.

How curious, and yet somehow right, that she should be sitting here among the stark white buildings in the huge expanse of the Mall. For nine years it had been her life. For nine years she had watched the bills, agonized about the money spent, despaired at every setback. She felt a kinship with every square of Italian marble, every shrub and bush, that lined the Plaza. In a sense she knew the Mall more intimately than she had known a father . . . or a lover.

In the buildings of the City occasional lights pierced the drifting smoky air, the sound of starting engines rose as the City came awake. As the sun neared the rim of the earth its reflection tinted the cumulus clouds a brilliant shocking pink. Across the reflecting pool the light touched the huge Alexander Calder sculpture and turned its weathered surface into molten steel.

A pair of blue jays swooped the length of the Mall Plaza, one coming to rest on the gracefully curving shoulder of a statuesque nude by Aristide Maillol, the other, with no respect for modern art, placed its droppings on a massive bronze configuration by Henry Moore. Then, discovering the motionless woman by the pool, the jays buzzed her with raucous squawks, furious at this invasion of their turf. When their nagging produced no reaction, the birds left her to investigate another alien presence.

With that unerring instinct that allows wild things to distinguish the quick from the dead, one of the jays settled lightly on the back of the man who floated face down in the shallow water. For a moment the bird and the woman stared at each other, until the bird tired of it and took off to join its mate.

The sun climbed higher, bathing in early morning light the clean stark lines of the Plaza and the Mall, the Museum, the Bell Tower, the state office buildings, revealing every crevice of the monstrously ugly State Capitol that brooded over it all like some raddled beldame from another age. An errant breeze rippled the surface of the reflecting pool, causing the body of the man to undulate gently and recapture, for a moment, a life of its own.

The woman was conscious of the Department of Parks man with his burlap sack, the click of his pointed stick as he stabbed at papers caught in the flowering shrubbery. He stopped near her, and she heard him say, "Jesus Christ, lady!" and then his running footsteps, sharp and urgent on the marble deck of the Mall. She listened until they faded away, and she thought, *Now it begins. . . . Or is this merely the ending . . . ?*

4

The sound of howling sirens, when they came, was almost a relief. She watched the police cruiser come bounding down the shallow steps at the Capitol end of the Plaza, followed almost immediately by its twin.

No one touched her. No one spoke to her.

One of the troopers waded into the shallow water and steered the body to the side of the pool, rather like a child pushing his small boat. Others turned it over and drew it out by the arms. The dead face lay pale as the blue-white marble pavement. Death had smoothed away the arrogant edges and left innocence—the innocence of the boy-man she had first known so long ago. White-coated interns spirited the body away, and nothing was left but a wet outline on the smooth marble.

And memories. . . .

Someone said, "She hasn't said a word, Commissioner. We haven't tried to question her. I . . . thought you'd want to handle it yourself."

And then Gavin was there, standing so straight and tall, his dear familiar face now drawn with pain and worry—an island of refuge in a world grown gray and desolate.

Gavin Riordan leaned over and gently lifted the revolver from among the other things she held in her lap. A brassiere, a wisp of bikini panties, the metal braces she usually wore on her crippled legs. The dilation of her pupils made her eyes placid, blank.

Her gaze followed his hand as he passed the gun to the police captain beside him and then returned to his face. For the first time she seemed to be aware of what was happening around her. Her eyes grew large and full of fear. Her voice, when it came, was so small and far away that he leaned again to hear her—and caught the fragrance of spring flowers from her hair.

"I didn't do it, you know . . ." and then, "What will they do to me, Gavin?"

"It's all right, Nan. Don't say any more. There'll be time . . . later. Now we have to go."

He moved around behind her, his hands briefly comforting on her shoulders. Then he was pushing her wheelchair toward his waiting limousine.

5

Yes. It's time, she thought. *And then perhaps they'll let me sleep....*

She let him lift her into the deep backseat, heard him say, "Macy, put the wheelchair into the trunk of your cruiser, and then you two follow me."

A new voice, loud and importunate: "Commissioner! Commissioner! Can you tell us what happened? Who is the woman? Is she implicated? Did she do it?"

Then Gavin, sharply authoritative, "We don't know as yet. Captain Phillips will give you all we have. There'll be a statement from my office as soon as we have anything."

"Jesus, Riordan! You can't just . . ."

She heard the soft whish of the window as it closed. The car began to move and she collapsed against him. She was grateful for the gentle pressure of his arm around her. She closed her eyes and sighed deeply. Everything began to drift away....

After a moment Riordan realized she was asleep.

"Where to, Boss?"

"Gansvoort Hospital." In the rearview mirror he caught his driver's look of surprise.

"It's calm down there now. They won't look for her in the riot area. Maybe we can keep her under wraps—for a while at least. Until I know what happened . . ." Riordan passed a hand wearily over his unshaven face. "Jesus, we really didn't need this . . . not with everything else."

Sergeant Barry clucked sympathetically. "Things'll cool off, Boss. I think you got the lid on it now. Brothers all gone home for breakfast and counting their loot. Saw one cat luggin' three TV sets. *Three* of 'em. Give him a hernia."

"Yeah," Riordan said tiredly. "All buttoned up. Until the next time. And, Barry, don't lose the squad car. I'll want Macy to guard her until she's ready to talk. Only to me."

He felt the woman's deep steady breathing against his chest and was overwhelmed with pity. He couldn't bear to think of the *why*'s or the *if*'s . . . Not now. All that would come later, when the machinery of the law took over. There was no protecting her from that.

6

Now his mind was filled with what he had to do and all the implications of what had happened. They had all lived so long with Stewart Gansvoort at the center of the web. Like the Mall, huge, overwhelming, disruptive, praised and damned. Stewart Gansvoort— lauded, envied, fawned upon, hated by too many, loved by . . . ?

And now gone.

Would it come crashing down around their heads, the monstrous power structure he had built? And who would pick up the pieces, bind the wounds his death inflicted? Because, with Gansvoort dead, a lot of things were sure to surface. And Police Commissioner Gavin Riordan would be in the middle of it. Hands untied, free to act.

The thought gave him a savage pleasure.

How long before they'd have it on the air? Seconds? Minutes? He had to get to a phone. He couldn't use the police band in his car. Not for what he wanted to say.

The limousine was skirting the edge of the ghetto now, approaching the river north of the City. The smell of charred wood was strong even in the air-conditioned car. Wisps of smoke hung over gutted buildings. The streets were covered with last night's debris and awash with water from the fire hoses. The neighborhood was the inanimate victim of vandalism, shootings, stabbings, muggings, burning, years of benign neglect by the City's white politicians. Broken glass littered vacant lots, uncollected garbage everywhere. People still lived here, but there was no sign of them now. They were hiding behind closed doors and drawn window shades, invisible in their shame and guilt, nursing their rage.

Now it was over. Until the next time.

They were approaching Gansvoort Hospital, built in 1891 by Jacob Gansvoort, grandfather to the dead man in the reflecting pool. The hospital, which had started its life in a woody shaded suburb of the burgeoning City, was now in the heart of its ghetto, its patients the poor and the needy, no longer serving the rich and privileged for whom it was intended. But still supported by endless Gansvoort grants and endowments and clothed with the majesty of the Gansvoort name.

In his exhaustion Riordan found his mind wandering and pulled himself upright with a jerk. He had to keep functioning. At least until he could piece together what had happened. That is, if Nan Kennicott was capable of telling him. No way of knowing how spaced out she was. . . .

Gansvoort's Emergency Room was still crowded with last night's casualties. Riordan instructed the resident in charge in exactly what he wanted done and told Sergeant Macy to follow through. From the public phone booth in the lobby he dialed the Gansvoort home, gave his name and asked for Miss Serena, because he couldn't remember which of her married names she was using now.

When Serena came on she said, "We were up half the night watching the riot on TV. I just heard the bulletin. What the hell happened? Is it true?"

"Yes. He's dead. Serena . . . I'm sorry."

There was a moment of silence, then, "We'll let that one pass. How did it happen?"

"We don't know yet. Serena . . . does Ericka know?"

"She's still asleep."

"Keep her away from the news, if you can. I'll be out as soon as possible."

Again a silence. Serena's voice was cool. "You worry too much, Gavin. Ericka can take care of herself."

"Do it!" he said violently. "Just do it!" And hung up abruptly.

He debated momentarily whether or not to call Putnam Kennicott, Nan's father, and then decided to hell with it. Let him find out for himself.

Sergeant Macy was waiting for him in the hallway.

"Nobody talks to her. Until I'm ready. Get that resident to cooperate. Tell everybody she's in shock. Nobody. Not the DA. Not the press."

At Macy's unspoken question he hesitated, then "I'll be at Riverhaven. With his wife. But only if you have to. Keep 'em off my back if you possibly can. And have a steno here when I get back. I won't be long. And, Macy, get our lab people to run a paraffin test on her. First thing. I'll want that too when I get back.

"Now. Where's the back way out of this place? I don't want reporters on my ass. Tell Sergeant Barry to hold the limo here until I get back."

Macy pointed down the corridor.

8

"Turn right at the cafeteria. Follow the signs to the delivery entrance. And, Boss . . . what'll I tell 'em?"

"Nothing, damnit! Tell 'em nothing!"

Macy watched him as he left, and shook his head.

2

Time: THE PRESENT
THE GOVERNOR,
STEWART STUYVESANT GANSVOORT

Charlie Bishop looked at the young reporter and thought, *How right the man was—youth is wasted on the young. I should chop this asshole right now. Tell him to fuck off, call his boss and get him fired. . . .*

They were sharing breakfast at Carey's Bar & Grill. For Bishop, pickled hard-boiled eggs and a stein of beer, for the reporter, a fried egg on rye and a glass of milk. The milk had left a half-moon on his upper lip.

"We both know," the young man said, "that there *was* a report on all the crooked shit at the Mall. All I'm asking is why did the governor suppress it? You're as close to him as anybody, so I came to you first. If you can give me one good reason . . ."

Reasons? Bishop thought. *You dumb shit. There's a million reasons. If he blows the whistle, it triggers investigations. Work stops on the Mall. Which costs the taxpayers more millions. Which might cost the man the next election. To say nothing of the legisla-*

tors who backed him on it. And all because of some petty bunch of crooks trying to make a few bucks off the state. . . . I'll give you reasons, you silly bastard. . . .

But he didn't. He said, "I was a reporter once. Not here."

The young man looked dubious.

"Yep. Statehouse beat. Same as you. Let me tell you a story. Through some smart snooping I got a look at the airport log on who was flying the state planes. It turned out the governor, and the governor's wife and kids, and their friends, and his friends and the friends' friends were using those planes like they owned them. All over the state—at the taxpayers' expense.

"My editor was for the opposition, so he played it big. Front page and all, and I was a hero—for about twenty-four hours.

"Then you know what? When somebody else got around to examining those airport trip logs, they didn't show what I had seen at all. They were clean as a baby's conscience. The next thing was, I couldn't get press passes honored at all sorts of things—like the press gallery in the Capitol. All my unofficial leaks dried up. In a week I was out of business: You can't write about something you don't have access to.

"You know what my editor said when he fired me? He said, 'Charlie, if you want to report on the system, then you got to be part of the system. You don't shit on it. I thought you knew that.' "

Bishop studied the earnest young face across from him to see if he was getting through to him and found he wasn't.

"What if I told you," the young man said slowly, "that one of the O'Hare Agency detectives on the investigation was willing to talk . . . ?"

"I'd say you had a decision to make." Bishop was suddenly wary, which caused him to turn on his infectious grin. "Look, kid, I've been with the man for twenty years, and he is my friend. He's one of the finest men in government. I think he'll be president one day. In all those years I've never known him to do anything that wasn't in the best interests of the people. He's got a grand vision. He's dedicated his whole life to public service—when Christ knows he didn't need to. I tell you I know him. And I love him. If he's sitting on the report, you can bet there's a damn good reason why."

Bishop's voice rang out with sincerity because he believed what he was saying—or most of it. He *did* love the man. When he thought of all the good things he had done for so many, many people . . .

"Now," Bishop said. "You gonna take my word for it? You gonna fight City Hall? Or . . ."

"Or what?" the young man said. "Join the system?"

He was looking at the star sapphire on Charlie Bishop's ring finger, then at the twenty-four-carat Patek Philippe that peeked from under his Turnbull & Asser silk shirt, then at the seven-hundred-dollar Chipp pinstripe crafted to conceal Charlie Bishop's rounded paunch, and Charlie Bishop saw the contempt in his eyes.

"I can see the 'system's' been pretty good to you," the young man said.

At that moment they both heard the announcer's voice from the television set behind the bar.

"We interrupt this broadcast to bring you a special news bulletin. Governor Stewart Gansvoort has been assassinated. . . ."

They both ran to the bar, to see as well as hear.

The announcer's solemn dramatics went on and on as they watched an ambulance discharge the governor's body at the Harkavy Pavilion, one of the several private institutions established by the governor's grandfather.

Dear God, Charlie Bishop thought, *I left him just a few hours ago. And now he's gone. It's true. Oh, Stew, Stew . . . All the plans, the hopes . . . We had a real shot at it. . . . The top. . . . Right to the top. Oh, Christ . . . I'll miss you. Why you? Why did it have to happen to you . . . ?*

He found he was still holding his beer and put it down. His hands gripped the rounded edge of the bar because he had to hold on to something. He felt the tears roll slowly down his cheeks.

"What are you cryin' for?" the reporter said. "Because the goose is through laying eggs?"

Bishop knocked him down and made to leave, his only thought to get away, to be alone with his grief. Turning away was a mistake, because the young man got up and decked Charlie with his own beer mug.

Charlie Bishop lay with his face on the barroom floor, the salt tears mingling with the spilled beer.

Betsy Tate used a sleepshade, so she wasn't aware of what a beautiful day it was until her alarm went off at 8:20. She slept in the nude, so she stood modestly to one side as she pulled the draw string to open the curtains that covered her windows. *And so much more,* she thought deliciously. *If they only knew. How wonderful to be in love.*

As she had done most mornings for the past two months, she savored her new one-room apartment with delight. He had furnished it in muted blues and browns. Even the telephone beside the rumpled studio bed was brown. The superb Vertes nude on the far wall was pale blue with a brown frame. He said it looked like her, but she didn't believe it. Her breasts were smaller. She didn't have that delicate smudge at the *V* of her legs because he liked her pelvis shaved. But still there *was* something . . .

In the tiny bathroom, as she sat down to pee, his dark blue silk robe hanging on the door brushed her shoulder. She drank in the faint odor of English Leather lime cologne. Behind the clear glass door of the shower she soaped herself with lazy sensuality in every nook and cranny, loving the feel of her body because he loved it.

Out of the steamy bathroom she stood before the full-length closet mirror, brushing her damp blond hair, her expression dreamy, approving of what she saw. Slim ankles rising to graceful calves; molded thighs; hips slim as a boy's; the naked pudendum, innocent as a child's; small pear-shaped breasts, nipples now tumescent from her toweling; shoulders showing a faint tan, the first of summer; her skin still moist from the shower, faintly flushed with pink. The heart-shaped face, clean of makeup, lips naturally red, a soft dusting of freckles across the nose and cheekbones.

She turned sideways and struck a pose, with one hand piling her hair high, head up, chin lifted, a pose she considered regal. Which was what he would expect her to be when she became Mrs. Stewart Gansvoort. The governor's wife.

She hugged the phrase to her as though it were tangible, the most beautiful words she had ever encountered in all her nineteen years. She lost herself in a fantasy of what it would be like to have him all to herself instead of the few evening hours he gave her now.

She shook herself out of her reverie, closing her mind to it because she felt it was unlucky to think too much about it until it actually happened.

Behind the closet mirror hung a long rack of the clothes he had selected for her, dresses from Bergdorf's, suits from Halston, places she had never shopped herself. She chose a flared gray flannel skirt and a soft beige cashmere sweater with a deep cowl neck.

When she was dressed, she stood before the shelves filled with books he had told her it was her duty to read, because there wasn't time right now to complete her education and she must prepare herself to be his wife. She selected a book called *The Making of the President* by someone named Theodore White and sat down in the sunlight that flowed through the windows.

After ten minutes she had had enough. She put the book down because thoughts of him kept intruding. He was so gentle, so tender, so wise, so full of knowledge and sureness. She tasted every facet of him like delicious forbidden cakes and candies. It never occurred to her to wonder, in her adoration of her lover, if he were also the father she had never known. The father who existed only in the framed picture on her mother's mantel.

She got up and switched on the TV. That was when she heard it.

She was on the floor, the rug bristly against her cheek; someone was pounding on her head. Ringing, hollow blows. She heard the announcer say *Harkavy Pavilion* and she knew she must go to him.

She got up and with great deliberation went to her bureau and selected a scarf to cover her hair, then the huge dark sunglasses, because she mustn't be recognized. Now pain was all around her. She was drowning in pain. Her mouth was so dry that she was conscious of each distinct tooth, enormous against her lips.

In the street the sun hit her like a fist. She managed to hail a cab. All the way to the hospital the driver talked about the assassination of the governor. She listened as though he were talking about someone else, some stranger who had nothing to do with her.

The lobby of the hospital was crowded with people, police, cameras, cameramen, TV lights and cables. She hadn't expected that. She recognized the lieutenant governor standing next to the admitting desk, surrounded by reporters. She pushed her way to him and said, "I must see him, please."

The lieutenant governor turned an inquiring look at a man next to him, who moved toward her.

"I'll handle it."

"You know her . . . ?"

"I said I'd handle it!"

"I am Betsy Tate," she said clearly. "I am to be his wife."

There was a babble of voices around her. She heard the lieutenant governor's shocked voice. "Jesus Christ! Get her out of here!"

The man next to him grabbed her arms, spun her around and shoved her through the crowd and up the corridor. She found herself propelled through a door into a hospital room. The man pushed her down onto the empty bed.

"What the hell are you trying to do to him! You some kind of nut?"

"I must see him," she said. "Will you please take me to him." And then questioningly, "I don't know you. . . ."

"But I know you, baby," the man said. "I know all of 'em. It's my business to know all of you."

She stared at him. And then it broke. All the hurt, the terror. There was nothing left but the buzzing black pain at the back of her skull. She was alone. He was dead. She would never see him again. She began to keen like an animal. Her mouth was open. She twisted from side to side on the narrow bed.

"I want to die, I only want to die."

The man slapped her twice, rocking her head from side to side.

Prisoner No. 86805 didn't join the others as they beat their tin plates on the long steel mess-hall tables. The guards let the uproar go on for five or six minutes before they began to move, and the men quieted down. The man next to 86805 was laughing quietly.

"Wish I'd pulled the trigger," the man whispered. "The son of a bitch deserved it."

No, 86805 thought frantically. *Never! Not Stewart Gansvoort. He was the best friend a man ever had.*

He sat staring at the food on his plate. His head was a jumble, his

14

mind a projector flashing disconnected scenes on a wavering screen. He saw his wife and his small son. Their faces were blank. He couldn't make the images come clear. He saw the Mall as he had first seen it, a huge hole in the ground filled with earth movers, trucks, scurrying men. Everything speeded up, as though his projector had gone wild. Nine years of construction, pouring the cement platform, erecting steel, applying marble skin to the tall buildings, all of it like some insane kaleidoscope whirling before his eyes.

And last the gentle, kindly face of Stewart Gansvoort as he had last seen him, blue eyes filled with compassion, an arm reassuringly warm about his shoulders.

"Tom," the governor had said, "you're not to worry. I'll take care of you. I'll take care of everything. . . ."

And what now? he thought. *Who takes care of Tom Christie now . . . ?*

86805 got up and became part of the file moving out of the mess hall. From habit he joined his work detail, shuffling along with the rest until he came to the library, where he worked as chief librarian, a cushy job that took a lot of influence to get—and keep. He stood before the closed glass doors, unable to lift his hand to push them open, until the black guard goosed him gently with his nightstick.

"Get going, Tommy boy. Make the most of it. Read up on all them books—while you still can."

The guard's malicious chuckle followed him through the doors.

He sat in his swivel chair behind the scarred counter, automatically filing library cards, checking books in and out, answering questions without thought. Behind his steel-framed glasses he was reliving what had happened to him.

Nine years on the Mall. Starting as a junior engineer, then assistant foreman. And then the tower fire, where his cool-headed heroism had brought him to the personal attention of the governor. The kindnesses that followed, invitations a man in his position didn't rate, the privilege of him and Eleanor and Tommy junior using the swimming pool and tennis courts at Riverhaven on weekends.

He was a young man on the rise, and at twenty-nine he was assistant project engineer on the Mall, the biggest construction job in the nation—at a salary of $32,000 a year.

It wasn't enough. He was the governor's young friend. He needed the money to keep up with his image of himself.

So he made the deal. The arrangement with the head of the Teamster local, which put a hundred thousand dollars in his pocket and closed Tom Christie's eyes to the half million that went to the official.

Everybody knew the stealing that was going on, but in the rush to finish the Mall on time, nobody seemed to care. It was a case of anything goes as long as the work didn't stop.

He hadn't even felt much guilt about it at the time. He knew a dozen people who had taken more of the state's money.

Then an eager beaver from the Office of the State Comptroller stepped in, and Tom Christie was indicted by the grand jury for conspiracy and bribery.

"We can't let you go to trial, Tom," Stewart Gansvoort had said. "There's too much at stake. If you ever got on the stand, God knows what would come out. You couldn't help yourself. They'd drag it out of you. It could stop work on the Mall—and how they'd love that. They've been trying to get at me through the Mall for years. . . .

"This way is better. Believe me. You'll do eight months, a year at most. Then I'll commute your sentence. After that, it's clear sailing. A new identity, background. We'll get you a clean engineering degree so you can work anywhere in the world you want to. And you won't ever have to worry about money. I'll see to that."

The governor held him by both arms and pulled him close. "And, Tom, I understand. Believe me, I do. I only wish you had come to me first. There would have been no need for all this. . . ."

So Tom Christie had pleaded guilty. They gave him eight to ten, and here he was in the ninth month of his sentence. Tom Christie, one of the untouchables at State prison, with a cushy job, his own quarters, and all the privileges available. And only a few more months to serve. . . .

Until today. And what now?

The black guard was standing before his counter, grinning at him.

"How you feel, Tommy boy? Sorta neckid, with all that high-powered protection gone? I'm gon' see you in the shower room."

The grin turned into a leer that chilled him. The guard held his nightstick in front of his crotch and caressed it obscenely.

"I caint hardly wait, Tommy boy."

Tom Christie lowered his head to his hands and began to weep—slow, painful tears that burned his cheeks.

At Homestead Hill on the Maryland shore, one of the several estates that had come to her in the divorce, Olivia Minot Gansvoort heard the news with mixed emotions. First disbelief, then shock, and almost immediately a guilty satisfaction that he was dead—and she was alive.

The thought shamed her.

She began to bring back their years together, the good and the bad, and there had been both, God knew. She was an excellent hostess, completely in command of the social scene. His political life was his own, and she had never allowed it to touch her.

Now, as she sat at her dressing table putting the finishing touches on her makeup, she suddenly stopped and looked at herself. A long patrician face framed by brown-gold hair, the increasing gray expertly rinsed out of it; cool gray eyes with an inner look of pensiveness; a face not without its beauty but, in all, a sad face. She knew when the sadness had started—when she found that she couldn't give him children. It seemed to her that all she had ever truly wanted was to bear his children. She had wanted them then—and she wanted them now. Because loving never went away. It could shrivel with cold or burn with heat, but it was always there. No, it never went away.

She watched the tears form at the corners of her eyes and spill over unchecked.

"Oh, why, Stewart. Why ... ?"

She dabbed at the mascara which smudged her cheek.

"Damn, damn, damn ..." she whispered, beating her clenched fist on the table in time with the words.

3

Time: THE PRESENT
THE COMMISSIONER, GAVIN RIORDAN

Riordan's taxi stopped at the locked gates. The guard came out of the gate house and, when Riordan identified himself, told him he was expected and passed them through. During the mile-long drive to the Big House, Riordan had time to reflect that, in all his visits over the years, nothing good had ever happened to him at Riverhaven.

But whatever was to happen now, he found himself wanting with a familiar intensity to see Ericka, wondering how she would treat him and hoping . . . for what?

He was tired with a weariness that went bone-deep. He hadn't slept in more than thirty hours. The rioting of the night before could have been so easily avoided—if only he could have made the governor listen. God knows he had tried; the years of warnings, surveys, reports to the legislature about what was sure to happen if something weren't done about the intolerable poverty and injustice that choked the City's ghettos. Deaf ears. None so blind as those who would not see.

Well, it had come, just as he had said it would. He wouldn't get a final fatality report on last night's outburst until later, but he knew already that two of his police had died, and at least twelve others were injured. Civilian casualties could be much higher. The lid was back on now. Everything seemed quiet. But for how long? He couldn't hide his conviction that it would happen again. Tonight or tomorrow. Next week or next month. It filled him with a sense of dread and of helplessness.

And now Gansvoort's death. How would the anger in the ghetto respond to that? No way of telling—until it happened. He resented his present errand. He was wasting precious time when he should be at Headquarters, on top of things, ready to jump if things started to come apart again. What the hell was he doing here? It was a stupid question—because he knew the answer. And he couldn't help himself.

The taxi passed the dairy barns, trucks backed up to the loading platform, workers manhandling the galvanized containers. They would know what had happened, but cows still had to be milked. Milk still had to be sold. To the right was the truck farm, row upon even row of vegetables and tall-standing corn. Beyond that were the workers' houses, thirty of them, arranged in pleasing patterns and gleaming with new paint.

Then they were in the pine grove, straight towering conifers that had dropped their needles over the years to form a soft brown carpet. They came out on the winding road to the Big House, lined with rhododendron and azaleas. To the left was the whole lovely sweep of the river. All of this planned magnificence stood as a monument to old Jacob Gansvoort's dictum that the land must produce sustenance as well as beauty.

Now they were surrounded by rising lawns of close-cropped turf, stately oaks and elms placed exactly for maximum effect. Only an occasional sand trap revealed that this was a golf course that disappeared over the hill in the distance.

Closer to the Big House the statuary began with a massive Eastern Island figure. Then the Henry Moore granite abstraction, then the Rodin nudes. A grouping of solid steel girders formed a convoluted shape against the sky. Pieces by Lehmbruck, Lachaise and Nadelman vied with grotesque Aztec deities and a tall Egyptian stele.

Curiously the effect was pleasant rather than overpowering. Everything seemed part of a composite whole. Nothing overwhelmed anything near it. The trees, the slopes, the sculptures, all blended into a harmonious symphony of design.

At the crest of the hill the Big House itself was at first sight unimpressive. Built of gray gneiss quarried on the estate, it appeared small until one realized that it was partially cut into the hill itself and

19

extended a hundred feet or so beyond the front facade. To the right were tennis courts and a swimming pool, both hidden behind an elaborate rose garden and an ivy-covered wall. The stables and garage were just visible beyond the corner of the house.

The graveled driveway made a circle to pass under a porte cochere. In the middle of the impossibly green front lawn was the life-size statue of a nude woman. The figure was from some ancient Greek temple, but to Riordan it looked more and more like Serena Gansvoort, as if her father had somehow known, years before his daughter's birth . . .

He told the taxi to wait and went up the shallow steps to the carved double doors. There was an ornate brass knocker in the shape of a lion's head. He knew that when he lifted it and let it fall it would ring a bell in the servants' quarters.

Serena answered his knock herself. She was dressed in a floor-length white negligee that, with its loose cowl, resembled an acolyte's robe. Her dark hair fell around her shoulders, framing an arresting, square-chinned face, a softer version of her handsome brother's. To Riordan's astonishment she held out her arms to him. When Riordan only inclined his head to her, she came in close and pushed against him. He could feel the hard ridge of her pelvis through the sheer cloth. He shoved her back.

"Jesus, Serena! Have you no . . . ?"

"Respect for the dead?" Her green eyes were bright with mischief. "Your catechism is showing, Gavin. I had none for him alive. Why should dead make any difference? Besides, that isn't what bothered you. You just didn't want us to be seen."

The truth of that upset him.

"Does Ericka know . . . ?"

"Of course. I told her when she got up."

"Damnit! I asked you . . ."

"You wanted me to set up the scene where you could break the news and have the little widow cry on your shoulder? Well, screw that, Gavin. Run your own errands. Besides, I don't think she'd fit the part."

"Where is she?"

"Why don't you ask me where she was last night, like on the cop shows?'' Serena burlesqued it. ''Where was she last night, lady? Out. Where? Out, Officer. She was *o-u-t*.'' She grinned at him. ''We watched the riot until late. Then I heard her go out. She didn't get back till dawn. How does that grab you?''

''Goddamnit, Serena, quit it! Now, where is she?''

''Having breakfast in the studio. Blueberries and cream, scrambled eggs. Four. Canadian bacon, croissants and confiture, a large pot of coffee. And the *Times*. A hearty girl, our Ericka. Nothing interferes with her appetite.''

He tried to brush past her, but she held his arm. Her eyes had lost their mischief.

''I heard Nan was . . . ?'' she began.

''She was there,'' he said cautiously, ''by the reflecting pool. Where they found him.''

''What happened?''

''We don't know . . . yet. She said she didn't do it.''

''You haven't brought out the rubber hoses?''

''Quit it, Serena! She's in shock. Nobody sees her. Now, Goddamnit, get off my back.''

He tried to pull his arm away, but she held him. ''Will she talk, Gavin . . . ?''

''I think so,'' he said reluctantly. ''She'll have to. . . .''

''Jesus, that'll be a bloodbath for the Gansvoort family, won't it? How Stewart would have hated it. I think I'll head for Acapulco.''

She released him then and he strode through the entrance hall toward the studio. Her mocking voice followed him.

''If you haven't eaten, there's more than enough for two. Or four. . . .''

He felt his fists clench. His skin had never been proof against Serena's needling.

The vaulted main hall of Riverhaven always depressed Riordan. Every available inch of wall space was covered with Art, with a capital *A*. There was no attempt at proper hanging; the collection was too huge. Priceless old masters were crowded by pop art from LeRoy Neiman to Andy Warhol. Canvases by Braque, Matisse, Léger and Picasso were side by side with unknown moderns. On little tables, shelves, desks, in shallow niches, were small sculptures, primitive and contemporary.

The whole suggested the owner had bought with no regard for coherence, driven solely by the need of acquisition. And had turned this hall into a madman's warehouse.

Riordan passed through the music room at the center of the house, three stories high and roofed by clear glass, one wall covered by organ pipes. He turned left into the north wing and stopped before the open door of the studio, caught by the contrast of this room with what he had just endured. The stark white of the two walls he could see were broken only by a huge drafting table covered with blueprints, sketches, T-squares and triangles of all sizes, India ink pots, a rack of calligraphers' pens and, incongruously, an exquisite Chinese porcelain figurine of a rearing horse.

The room seemed deserted, but the chink of a spoon told him she was there. He still hesitated, trying to determine what he wanted to say, and then, now knowing what he wanted to say, stepped through the doorway.

She was standing at the glass north wall with her back to him, outlined against the blue of the sky, a coffee cup in her hand. Beyond her he could see the sweep of the river dotted with early-morning sails like tiny puffs of cloud on a sea of glass. And beyond that the City, with the gleaming starkness of the Mall rising beside the skeleton of the unfinished Edifice.

Her blond hair was a gossamer veil in the sunlight, her profile clean and sharp as a cameo. She was dressed in blue jeans and a sheer white shirt tied in a knot at her waist. Her feet were bare.

Without turning she said, "It was nice of you to come yourself, Gavin."

He had a tiny stab of joy that she could feel his presence without actually knowing who was behind her. Yet he wondered why it should surprise her that he had come in person.

Then she turned and, as always, he felt a kind of shock at her beauty, a tangible jolt that tightened his muscles and made him draw in his breath.

"I'm . . . sorry, Ericka."

22

She looked faintly surprised, and he felt as gauche as a schoolboy, as if he had somehow spilled something on the rug.

"I wanted to tell you . . ."

"So I heard . . . from Serena. That was kind, Gavin. But there was no need. It doesn't matter."

"What are you going to do?" He meant about the funeral, eulogies, burial, politicians, friends, the press, all the mumbo jumbo that would descend on her in a few hours. He could help if she let him.

She misunderstood him. She gestured toward the Mall across the river. "Finish it, of course. If they don't burn it down first."

For the first time it occurred to him that she would be one of the richest women in the world. There was no one to stop her. She could do anything she wanted.

"I meant about Stewart. He was a public figure. There'll be a hell of an uproar . . ."

"Nothing," she said firmly. "Charlie Bishop can handle it all. It doesn't concern me."

The Irish Catholic morality in him was shocked. "You've got to make an appearance," he said.

She faced him squarely, eyes steady and direct. "In widow's weeds? With a lace handkerchief for my tears? Look at me. Do I look shocked? Grieving? I'm not. I think what I feel mostly is relief. I don't have to hate him anymore. And I feel an emptiness. Hate is a great sustainer, Gavin. You can feed on it like meat and potatoes." Her voice was calm and emotionless.

He came to stand beside her at the window, wanting to touch her. "If you hated him, why did you marry him?" It was the first time he had dared to ask the question.

She shrugged, just a small lift of the shoulders. "There were . . . reasons. Are you going to arrest me, Gavin?"

The cop in him came instantly alert. "Arrest you? Why should I?"

She turned away from him. He saw her hand clench at her side, and suspicion bit at him.

"What are you saying? Why should I arrest *you*? Nan . . ."

"What did Nan say?" she asked.

23

"She doesn't remember. She says she didn't do it, but she's high as a kite. I haven't questioned her yet. What do you know about this?"

She took him by the hand and led him to a couch. She still held his hand. Her fingers were cold as ice. "Perhaps we'd better wait. For what Nan says. Before I answer that."

He heard himself ask a cop's question. "You were out last night. Where did you go?"

There was a deep sadness in the look she gave him. And what else? Resignation, disillusionment, hurt? He couldn't tell.

"I was at the Mall. I often go there at night."

She wasn't going to say more than that. Her eyes had changed. They were cool and enigmatic now.

He had a sickening sense of having been there before. He questioned her that other time about a death. He saw now the same calm assurance, as though she were not accountable to the laws of God or man. Only to her own.

"That's not enough," he said. "They will want to know why you were there. How long you were there. What you saw there. They won't let you get away with silence. You were the governor's wife. Now you're his widow. It's not the same, you know. The protection is gone. To them you will be just another suspect—the same as anyone else.

"If there is anything... You'd better tell me now, so that I can..."

What could he tell her? Protect her? Why would she need protection—unless...? How could he possibly think that this woman he loved was capable of...? Gavin answered his own question. He knew that she was capable of doing anything she thought was right, regardless of the consequences.

A discreet voice interrupted from the open doorway.

"You're wanted on the phone, Commissioner."

It had started, the whole nightmare of investigation. The questions without answers, questions with answers he wouldn't want to hear. Inevitably there would be agony and pain. Nothing, for any of them, would ever be the same. And in the end, someone would have to pay, because the people and the law demanded it.

24

"Take it in the library, if you'd like." Ericka got up and went to stand by the window once more.

"No, I'll take it in here." He reached for the phone on the end table beside him and heard Macy's voice. Macy was in trouble. The DA had arrived and was giving him a bad time. Would Riordan talk to him?

"No," Riordan said shortly. "My order still stands. If anybody gets in to her, it'll be your ass. Give me half an hour."

"And, Boss," Macy said, "the paraffin test? Negative. The lab guy says no gunpowder particles on her hands. She's clean."

Riordan was silent, puzzling over what Macy had just said. He didn't understand any of it. If she'd fired the weapon, there had to be traces of powder on her hand. . . .

Finally he said, "Gloves?"

Macy was apologetic. "Didn't see any. I'll check her bag and the rest of her stuff. Sorry, Boss."

"Do that," Riordan said. He replaced the phone and looked at the woman by the window.

"Ericka," he said.

She turned slowly and he went to her, arms out. They held each other for a long moment before she pulled back to look at him. Lovely clear green eyes under arched dark brows, faint age lines just beginning to show. Sad eyes that seemed so open and direct, as if she were incapable of concealing what lay behind them. Eyes unmoveably calm, telling nothing.

"You know . . . it won't stop here. It won't go away. Sooner or later . . ." Gavin broke off.

"I have nothing to tell you, Gavin. Why bother?"

He wanted to say, *Because I love you, and I can't bear to see you hurt. Because you mean more to me than anything in my life. And because, God help me, I know I can't trust a word you say. . . .*

But he didn't. He said the only thing left to him.

"Because I'm a cop."

Ericka Gansvoort turned away from him, and he left her there, looking out across the river at the Mall.

*   *   *

Serena stood in the doorway watching her sister-in-law. Riordan had brushed past her without a word as he left.

"Blood in his eye. He's right, you know. They'll be all over you soon. You'll have to answer their questions."

Without turning, Ericka said, "You were listening?"

"Sure. I have an interest." Serena went to stand by Ericka at the window. "Why don't you quit? Let somebody else finish it. The damned Mall has caused nothing but grief since Stewart decided to have it built. It's been a killer from the start."

"Yes," Ericka said softly. "But I must. Everything George Barnstable knows and feels about beauty is in those buildings. I won't let anyone spoil it for him."

"Beauty! It's a monstrosity where it is. It belongs in the middle of Brazil or the Sahara, not in that pigsty across the river."

"It will be there long after the pigsty is gone."

Both women stared in silence at the tall stark shapes of the Mall, lost in their thoughts, each seeing something different. After a moment Serena said musingly, "You know you never should have married him in the first place. It's beyond me why anyone who knew him for more than forty-eight hours would want to marry Stewart. Least of all you. When you had Gavin. Christ, between the two of them . . . Why choose Stewart?"

Ericka's voice seemed drained of all feeling, flat, dead. "It was Stewart's price for keeping George out of jail and letting him finish his work on the Mall. Now . . . he's safe."

Serena was aghast. "You gave up Gavin—and married that bastard for that!"

"George Barnstable is the only family I ever knew. He wasn't my father—but he literally gave me life."

"Family, my ass! No family is worth that. You had it all. And you blew it. Ericka, you're not to be believed. Your head is on backwards. Don't you know it's dangerous to fuck around with people's lives? What the hell! You're not God. . . ."

Ericka turned to look at her. Serena saw the naked anguish in her eyes and impulsively reached out to pull her close. "Oh, Jesus. You poor baby. What a lousy fucked-up mess. . . ."

Ericka let her head rest on Serena's shoulder, her body limp, giving in gratefully to the other's sympathy for just a moment. Then she pulled away.

"You can't carry it all alone, you know," Serena said. "No one can. Somebody's got to take care of you. Because on your own, you're a menace."

But she smiled as she said it.

4

Time: THE PRESENT
THE BOSS,
DESMOND PATRICK DANIHER

He had breakfasted at six A.M. on cambric tea and whole wheat toast—all that he was allowed—then taken his position on the rubbing table. Now he felt his taut muscles begin to loosen under the gently persuasive hands of Donnie Shay. The dribble of warm oil on his back was like a benediction. It seemed to take longer to relax these days. Sleep had ceased to be a healer. Now he woke with cramps and aches—the result, his doctor told him, of the insidious deadly buildup of the fatty deposits in his arteries and vessels, which would some day choke off the supply of blood—and with that, his life. Sometimes he thought he could actually feel the accumulation, like silt in a riverbed, until at last the river could no longer carry its life-giving traffic to the parts of his body. The thought didn't frighten him, nor much displease him. Desmond Patrick Daniher was tired.

Donnie Shay hummed softly as he worked, kneading, stretching, soothing. A labor, Daniher thought wryly, of love. Of a sort. At first it had disturbed him to have his flesh intimately handled by a onetime homosexual. That had soon passed. It was unworthy of him. Considering the circumstances.

Twenty years ago? No. More like twenty-five. Donnie Shay had been apprehended in the public men's room in Rensselaer Park while performing fellatio on a boy of fourteen. In those days Daniher had long since given up active practice in favor of politics. His law firm took the case because Daniher was persuaded that the boy was more than consenting, and more importantly, because Donnie Shay was the nephew of Daniher's housekeeper, Mary Margaret Shay, and the matter threatened to disrupt his household intolerably.

Daniher collected a favor from a compliant judge, got the "contributing" charge dropped, and in thirty days Donnie was out on probation with a stern warning, and Daniher's household resumed its even tenor.

Any apprehension he might have felt about turning Donnie loose on the youth of the city was removed one rainy night in a South Side alley. Along with Donnie's balls. With a sharp knife. By the irate father and older brother of the young boy—Rocco and Patsy DiSalvo.

That changed things. It became a matter of ethnic pride. The Irish against the Italians. Daniher personally saw to it that the DiSalvos got the maximum—fifteen years in the state penitentiary. And Donnie Shay, after he got out of the hospital, became a member of the household, where Mary Margaret could keep an eye on him.

It wasn't necessary. Donnie's homosexuality seemed to have disappeared along with his testicles. The loss left him a gentle, kindly man, prematurely gray and with a tendency to take on weight. He worshipped Desmond Daniher with a devotion Daniher had grown to value and appreciate.

And now the hands of Donnie Shay were massaging life into a body that would soon betray him. Too many years, he thought, too many favors, too many compromises, long hours, hard work, too many years at the beck and call of every lunatic with a vote in his pocket. Fifty years of increasing power, until for a long time now the city had been his—and through it, much of the state. *A century ago we came*, he thought. *The Irish. We wanted in, and we got in. No matter how. And now we're finished. Or soon to be. There's something else just around the corner. The Italians—and the Jews, a brand-new ball game. When they move in, I don't think I want to be around to see it. All the joy, the glory of it, will be gone. Out the window. It's the money will take over. It was the money that bought Gansvoort the governor's seat, not the old loyalties.*

"I'll make this city the most electrifying capital in the world," Gansvoort said. And he would do it, too. Because he had the money and the banks and the voice in Washington. And in the process, the City—Daniher's City—would be destroyed. "A city of marble," the man said, "instead of brick. . . ." The Mall, all two billion dollars of it, was just the beginning. Already the twelfth ward had disappeared, that section filled with the poor and needy and called the Pit—swallowed up by the bulldozers of progress. Nine thousand people dispossessed, some of them gone forever, most of the others still waiting for the public housing they had been promised—and would never get. Three thousand Irish, six thousand blacks, the Irish all solid Democratic votes, gone—as though they had never existed. Only the Cathedral of St. Thomas was still holding out in the Pit, and the cardinal, fighting the march of marble at his very doors. . . .

Was there any stopping the man? Perhaps the cardinal . . .

"We've never exactly seen eye to eye," Daniher murmured aloud. "An alliance with the Devil—and I'm sure the old schemer would call it just that. . . . But still . . ."

"What's that, Des?" Donnie asked in his soft, high voice.

"Just a wicked thought, Donnie," Daniher answered. "But possible all the same. Now let's get these old bones properly decked out. They'll be waiting for me downstairs. The halt, the lame and the blind—and not the least of them, the voice of all God's chillun, bless his black heart. The Reverend Cecil Weems—with blood in his eyes, for sure."

Desmond Daniher, now dressed in blue double-breasted worsted, white shirt, and dark-blue tie, entered his office from the rear door at precisely 6:45. His long thin face was topped by the gray fedora that had become his trademark over the years. His enemies claimed that he slept in it. Before his wife, Sally, died the speculation had been more ribald. Daniher had been bald since his early twenties and was still sensitive about it at seventy-eight. His explanation, when pressed, was that wearing a hat indoors gave whoever was with him the impression that he was on the move, ready to go at any moment. A useful thing for a busy man, who did not suffer fools gladly.

Meg O'Day, his secretary of thirty years, had laid out the file cards neatly at the end of the long table. He counted them automatically. This was the ritual. For years Des Daniher had made himself available to anyone who needed to see him. He held court from 6:46 to 7:45 each morning of the working week, rain or shine, and all who came eventually got to see him. He once said to Meg O'Day, "I'm available to any man or woman in the state who needs my help. All that's necessary is a little perseverance." And he added slyly, "Of course it helps to be a registered Democrat."

Meg O'Day had filled in the file cards with the necessary information requested of each petitioner. Daniher glanced at each of them briefly, absorbing the terse notes like a sponge.

"Only nine? A slow day? Or could it be we're losing our grip?"

"Ten. Including the Reverend Weems. You heard about the rioting?"

"I try not to let the voices of doom intrude on these old ears until I'm forced to. What rioting is that?"

"Looting and burning in the ghetto. Most of the night. It seems to be over now. They say it started . . ."

Daniher waved a hand. "Don't tell me. I'll know soon enough from the Reverend Weems."

"I wouldn't know," Meg O'Day said primly.

He looked up, taking in her small heart-shaped face, her softly curling graying hair, the neat trim figure and still firm breasts, and thought, *You've weathered well, Meg O'Day. A fine figure of a woman altogether. Now, I wonder why you've never married. . . .*

Since after thirty years she still insisted on calling him *Mr. Daniher*, it would never do to ask.

"Is the Reverend Weems to be the first?" she asked.

"And have Mrs. McGrady wait? With her poor heart. And Dooley Evans, whose son is in the slammer—for merely borrowing a stranger's car for an innocent joy ride? In this case the first should be last." He shrugged, a brief lift of his bony shoulders. "But no, you're right. I suppose I owe it to the man not to keep him from his flock. Ask Connie to show him in. And give him ten minutes. No more."

Connie McGurn stuck his head in the door.

"It's a fine morning, Des. And you're looking the very picture of health."

McGurn, a small wizened prune of a man, had attached himself to Daniher years before and over those years had become an unofficial greeter and keeper of the gate, organizer of the petitioners.

"All ready and waitin' for you, Des. Who'll it be, the first? Not many this morning. You'll be done in no time."

"The Reverend Weems, Connie," Meg O'Day said. "Show him in, please."

"The Reverend Weems it is. He'll be with you in a jiff. And, Des, the car will be waitin' when you're ready—with a shine you could shave your face in."

"Fine, Connie, fine."

Daniher saw Meg O'Day's resigned shrug as Connie's head popped out. "What else would he do if it weren't for this? You wouldn't want him drinking up his pension in the bars, would you?"

He watched the sway of her hips as she went through the door.

The Reverend Cecil Weems, pastor of the First Baptist Church of the Ascension, was an impressive figure. His tailored gray suit set off his broad shoulders admirably. Black clerical vest, white clerical collar, black face and snow-white hair made him a study in sharp contrasts.

Daniher held out a hand without getting up and with some apprehension saw it engulfed in a huge black paw. When he got it back unscathed, he waved to a chair.

"Forgive me. Age does creep up. If I rose for every visitor, I'd never make it through the day.

"Now. What can I do for you?"

The Reverend Weems looked at him steadily, his gaze oddly disconcerting, and Daniher realized suddenly that he was in for something more than he had expected. His political antenna, honed to a sharp edge by years of practice, told him to be very careful.

"I'm not sure you can do anything, Mr. Daniher." The deep voice reverberated and made the room seem smaller. Daniher thought fleetingly it deserved a larger forum, a voice to sway his fellow man. "I'm not sure anyone can. It may be too late—for all of us. I think perhaps your years of neglect and oppression of the black community in this city may be about to yield a terrible harvest."

Daniher tried a small smile. "Chickens come home to roost? Eh, Reverend?"

Weems's eyes flashed angrily. "Don't patronize me, Daniher!"

"Forgive me. An unfortunate choice of phrase." He lifted his hands gently. "No offense meant, I assure you. Just what is it you want to talk about?"

"Oppression, neglect, unemployment, the systematic preference for whites over blacks in the job market, segregated schools in the worst school system in the state, the brutal victimizing of blacks by white police . . ." Weems placed his hands flat on the table. The long spatulate fingers seemed about to dig into the polished wood. "Oh, yes, there's a lot to talk about, Mr. Daniher. One-third of the people of this city without adequate housing or proper food—black people, most of them living below subsistence level. You moved thousands of them out of the Pit, which the governor called 'one of the worst ghetto areas in the country!' . . . to build your monument. . . ."

"Not mine, Reverend," objected Daniher. "His. A practical man, our governor. Goes right to the heart of things. I imagine he knew that blacks don't vote. Or if they do, you never know which way. Ergo—*he* moved them out."

Weems's powerful hands curled into fists. "Where do you think they're living now?" he cried, in pulpit tones. "In *tents*, that's where. Or tin shanties on the South Side. Waiting for the housing you and your people promised them. How long do you think they'll wait? Before they explode as they did last night—and blow us all away. We may not be a political force. But we are a *force*. We can fight back if we must."

"I heard," Daniher said. "Just the bare bones. Was it bad? I thought we were over the hump when we didn't get any reaction from your people on the Hopkins conviction."

"I think you got your reaction last night, Mr. Daniher. Just the beginning of it."

"It'll be overturned on appeal, you know," Daniher said placatingly. "Enough reversible errors to fill a law book. Judge was a certifiable idiot."

"*Your* judge, Mr. Daniher. And *your* jury. An all-white jury of his peers." Weems's voice was charged with bitterness. "When a respected leader of the black community can be convicted of murders he couldn't possibly have committed—against all the evidence—then that's the death of justice in our city."

"Now just a damned minute." Daniher allowed himself a mild indignation. "When you get a jury that allows itself to be bamboozled by a smart prosecutor, then that jury has to be composed of people with more than average ignorance. Or worse. Black or white. Of course the verdict was indefensible. And it *will* be overturned by superior court. I think your people know that. And they've been patient and sensible about reacting to it. If you're right about last night—then that should be the end of it."

Weems's shoulders slumped with fatigue. "I didn't come here to argue with you. I came to plead for your help. To try to convince you that you're sitting on a powder keg. Years of neglect and indifference. It's got to be changed, if you don't want this city to go up in flames! You can do it. If you will."

"That's a little heavy, don't you think?" Daniher said defensively. "One man. I don't make the laws, you know. I don't control the legislature."

Weems let the words hang for a moment, and Daniher realized that he'd let himself be trapped into an admission he would rather not have made.

"Don't you?" Weems said softly. "Aren't you Desmond Daniher, the last of the big-city bosses, the King of the Machine? I believe *Time* gave you the title. Or was it *Newsweek*?"

Daniher winced. The article had caused him untold embarrassment. "If you believe that shit, you're naive, Reverend."

"Come off it, Daniher," Weems said bitterly. "For fifty years you've had this city in your pocket. You've called every turn. You know it—and I know it.''

Daniher felt himself growing angry. Not at Weems, but at the true circumstances over which he knew he had little or no control. ''What do you want from me?'' he asked bitterly. ''To wave the magic wand and correct the mistakes of those fifty years? Well, I can't do it. Maybe before . . . Maybe things could have been done differently. . . . But not now. Not since that son of a bitch bought the governor's chair. He owns the Republicans. And he's leased most of the Democrats. He's the one who calls the turns. And you better damn well face it. I have!''

''Maybe not. . . .'' Weems's gleaming white teeth flashed in a chilling grin.

It brought Daniher up short. He could feel the prickling of the skin at the back of his neck. He had a sudden premonition that he didn't want to hear whatever Weems was about to say. *It's odd*, he thought fleetingly, *how clearly we read the silent messages from our fellows.*

''How many people are in the Mall on a given day?'' Weems asked.

The abrupt change of subject confused Daniher.

''Come on, man. Make a guess. It's important.''

To gain time Daniher ticked off on his fingers. ''There's the west wing, the state legislature, the departmental buildings, Justice, the Bell Tower . . .''

Weems broke in impatiently. ''And security, maintenance, the concessionaires—and maybe a thousand sightseers. Make a guess.''

''All right,'' Daniher said reluctantly. ''Ten thousand. On a given day. What about it?''

''And the air conditioning? Biggest plant in the world, all fifteen million dollars of it? You can read about it in the papers every day.''

Something was consuming the man. Fine beads of sweat glistened on the black forehead. Daniher felt again that premonition of dread.

''How much cyanide gas introduced into that air-conditioning system would it take to wipe out ten thousand people? On a given day?''

The words were there in the air like tangible things. They were

34

said and not to be recalled. Daniher's heart gave a flutter, followed by a pain in his chest that he recognized for what it was. He couldn't draw a breath until it subsided. He listened to his heartbeat with a curious detachment, as though he were in another time, another place. He was conscious of Weems towering over him, the black face a study in worry.

"Are you all right . . . ?"

From a distance he heard himself say, "Yes. It will pass. I'm all right." And then, surprisingly, he could breathe again and he thought, *Missed me that time, but you're sure to try again.* He waved Weems back to his seat.

At that moment Connie McGurn shot through the door as though propelled and came to a sliding stop before them, his small face purple with excitement.

"He's dead, Des!" Connie shouted. "It came on the radio! Somebody shot the bastard!"

For an instant they were frozen. Neither man had to ask whom Connie meant, but it took a moment for the shock to pass.

"All right, Connie. Thank you for the news. Leave us now."

"But, Des," Connie protested, "the bastard's dead. . . ."

"Not now, Connie. Just leave us, please."

Connie seemed about to say more, but what he saw in Daniher's eyes changed his mind. His wizened face screwed up as though he were about to cry and he backed through the door.

The two men stared at each other. Weems was the first to break the silence, with a question. "This changes things . . . ?"

"It may," Daniher answered softly. "And it may not. As I remember, you were saying that you and your people had some wildass threat to poison the air conditioning. . . ."

"Don't be a fool, Daniher! It's not *me* and not *my* people. It's desperate men who have been driven beyond endurance. And they are listening to other desperate men. Professionals. Terrorists—who have killed before. . . ."

"Who?" Daniher barked.

Weems looked at him for a long moment. Then his eyes dropped. "I can't tell you that. . . ."

"Then it's your problem, isn't it? For the time being."

At the door Weems turned. "You've been warned."

"That I have, Reverend."

Weems's broad shoulders slumped. "And, as usual, nothing will be done for us."

"It's a fair assumption, given past circumstances. But I wouldn't count on it, Reverend. Things *do* change, you know." He watched Weems walk slowly down the corridor and thought, *And you do know how to shake things up. Oh, yes, you do, Mr. Cecil Blackass Weems. A mover and a shaker for sure.*

But enough of that for now. He needed to take a moment to savor Connie's news. So the man was dead. And good riddance. He felt a savage joy. The blood surged through his veins with its old vigor. He felt like a giant. *God moves in mysterious ways. . . .* he thought. *But there's nothing like the fall of an enemy to put the life back in a man.*

When Meg O'Day came in with more news, he said, "Don't bother, Meggie, dear. I'll get it from the horse's mouth. I think I'd like to talk to the commissioner. Be a good girl and get him for me."

5

Time: THE PRESENT
THE CARDINAL,
MATTHEW PADRAIC MONTEFIORE

His Eminence Matthew Cardinal Montefiore was awakened by the rattle of phlegm obstructing his throat. He reached to turn off the clock radio before its music could begin, and felt a stab of arthritic pain in his shoulder. The digital numbers told him it was 5:15, a quarter of an hour before his usual awakening. He eased himself back on the pillows carefully and lay staring at the shadowed ceiling of his bedroom. He could hear the cooing of the pigeons outside his open window and the chirps of the first sparrows. The cardinal hated pigeons. They were dirty birds and fouled his windowsill with their droppings. They infested the City like a plague and, despite his periodic complaints, defied all efforts of the City's sanitation experts to get rid of them.

The cardinal was a man of habit. Now, as he had for almost sixty years, he set his mind to anticipate the problems and review the agenda of the coming day. But, as had happened all too frequently of late, any hope of serenity was destroyed by his first thoughts.

The Mall.

The cardinal hated the Mall. Had hated it with increasing passion for nine frustrating years as he watched it grow almost stone by stone until its towering buildings dwarfed and made a mockery of the graceful lines of his cathedral. His cathedral, which had dominated the high ground of the Pit for a century, its tall spire visible even from the hills across the river. Yes, mockery was the right word. The House of God demeaned and made small by the massive abomination of the Mall.

And the man whose monstrous egotism had created the Mall . . . The cardinal had asked forgiveness many times, as he did now once again, for this thought about the man—a forgiveness he knew could be found only in the confessional. The governor of the state, whose wealth and influence had so far proven greater than all the powers of the Church; the man who now threatened a final desecration—condemnation of the very ground on which the cathedral stood.

Unless he could be stopped.

The cardinal's thoughts scurried about like mice in a maze. He knew his mind was wandering. It was what he hated most about growing old. The loss of the power to concentrate, to bring to bear the full clarity of his intellect on a problem until it was solved.

His cathedral razed, its hallowed stones beaten into dust. And for what? To satisfy the whim of a man gone mad with arrogance. For the cardinal was convinced that Stewart Stuyvesant Gansvoort was truly mad. In the sense that Nero was mad, or Caligula. A man who sought to buy immortality with monuments to himself, even as any pharaoh of old.

His cathedral gone. To be replaced by a garden. "A hanging garden," the man had said, "like Babylon. Think how beautiful it will be." And then, with that famous grin, "Don't worry about St. Thomas. I'll build you another cathedral. Much bigger. And a new residence, of course, with all the modern conveniences. . . ." That last a gratuitous slur on the erratic plumbing of the present residence, which the governor had had occasion to use at one of the cardinal's receptions.

Talk again to Seamus Tully, the lawyer to the archdiocese?

Perhaps an even stronger letter to the Holy Father in Rome. Surely his outstanding services . . . paying off a debt of more than nine million left by his predecessor; the creation of 30 new parishes, 26 new high schools, 113 new parochial schools; putting the churchly charge entrusted to him on a sound fiscal basis, until now it was the richest archdiocese in the land . . .

But what use was all of that? What use in writing letters when the man could dwarf all his accomplishments with one donation. A donation so huge it closed the mind of Rome to any protests.

But surely his years of friendship with the pope must count for *something*. And it would take the full power of Rome to bring this madman to his senses. . . .

If it could be done at all.

And it *must* be done. To lose his church without a fight—to the death if need be—was intolerable, in man's eyes and, he was sure, in God's. He found himself half wishing for the intervention of his Maker. An illness. Perhaps a fatal accident . . .

He thrust the thought away with a flash of revulsion. But it remained.

He was forced to ask himself just how far he was prepared to go. Here was he, Matthew Montefiore, a prince of the Church and a servant of God, contemplating the . . . elimination of a fellow man. And yet, was it wrong to ask God's help? God worked His wonders through men. He triumphed over evil through the acts of man. Had he, Matthew Montefiore, any option than to use every means to stop what he knew to be a sacrilege?

With an effort that was almost physical he closed his mind to a situation that, at least for the moment, he could not control and turned it to the Byzantine convolutions of running an archdiocese of 2,900,000 people of which he was the spiritual leader.

Spiritual leader? Of what? He had few illusions about his flock. Long ago he had accepted as fact the taint on the human condition. Hardly a virtue in a priest—but then, each of us lives in sin. Even priests.

His most immediate concern was breakfast. He had invited Bishop John Muldoon—his vicar general, his confessor, and his friend of many years—and Monsignor Terrance O'Dowd, his chancellor for the past seven, a young man of thirty-eight whose mind worked with the precision of a racing engine and whose brilliance and attention to detail enabled the cardinal to keep on top of his job.

His job . . . ? More and more he felt like an accountant in a red hat. Real-estate values, interest rates, construction costs, the borrowing and the lending of money, the operation of hospitals, cemeteries and schools. These were the chores that filled his days.

Johnny Muldoon wanted the contract for St. Bardolph's Hospital to go to his friend Gower Demarest, whose contributions to the building fund had been more than generous. His chancellor favored Martin T. Day because, as he put it, "There's likely to be less sand in his cement." And he was undoubtedly right.

His decision was bound to irritate and would certainly do nothing to lessen the rivalry between the two men.

Feeling each of his seventy-eight years, the cardinal got slowly out of bed. Holding the skirts of his voluminous nightgown, he knelt briefly at the prie-dieu for his morning prayer. The prie-dieu was of elaborately carved rosewood and had belonged to his grandfather. He had first seen it as a child at Fiona, the Montefiore estate near Drogheda on the Irish Sea, and it gave him a sense of comfort and of place to have it with him now.

Four hundred years of Montefiores since the first one, that Spanish Jew who had been cast up out of the sea by the disaster of the Armada—the first and last Jew in the long line of Black Irish Montefiore men and women who had followed him. It was a proud line, and the cardinal bore the sin of family pride lightly. He was a sensuous man who enjoyed bodily comfort, good food, good wine and good music, and he regarded these as God's benefits and as such to be accepted. Now, at the prie-dieu, he offered a morsel of prayer to the God whose goodness had created such comforts and given him knowledge and breeding to appreciate them.

In the bathroom he first rinsed away the fetid taste in his mouth with mouthwash, retrieved his false teeth from the glass of Polident and then lowered himself onto the toilet. His bowels had grown sluggish with the years, and his morning stool more complicated by the presence of painful hemorrhoids and what he suspected were polyps on his prostate.

Finished, he plugged in his Braun electric shaver (replaced each year at the duty-free shop in the Rome airport) and began to remove the sparse gray stubble of his beard. The face the mirror showed him was long and ascetic—cheeks hollow; lips thin but still firm; a blade of a nose, thin and patrician; deeply hooded eyes over purple pouches of skin. The bright blue of the eyes was accentuated by the horizontal white hedges of his eyebrows. A broad high forehead topped by a mane of naturally wavy white hair lent him an actor's air—which gave him a certain wry pleasure when he thought about it.

He patted Canöe cologne on his lean cheeks, dropped his nightgown on the floor and considered his naked body in the full-length mirror on the bathroom door. His shoulders were still good, chest deep, but the naked paunch swelled below them, embroidered by meshes of broken blood vessels, split by the evilly incised antique scar of an appendectomy. His wrinkled genitalia dangled uselessly. His thighs were like porridge, calves spindly, traced by swollen rivers of varicose veins, his feet long and bony, toes spatulate and uncomfortably crowded.

He reached for the soap, dropped it and, rather than bend to pick it up, decided against a shower. Instead, he scoured his armpits and between his legs with a warm washcloth, patted more cologne on his chest and left the room.

In his bedroom he selected a pair of silk shorts made for him by Charvet, silk socks, specially padded loafers by Dent of London. He sat on the bed in his underwear and began the laborious business of putting on his socks and shoes, accompanied by a slow panting as he was forced to bend. His black slacks were of the finest English tropical worsted, his silk shirt from Harvie & Hudson of Jermyn Street. Over it all he donned the long soutane of richly soft broadcloth.

The digital clock told him that it was 5:58, and that as always he was exactly on time to say mass in his private chapel—a mass that over the years he personally had come to consider a mortification of the flesh, especially at six o'clock of a troublesome morning.

After a final pat at his theatrically wavy hair, His Eminence Matthew Cardinal Montefiore left his quarters with a firm step, all the ravages of time, disease and good living now hidden beneath the authority of his office.

Still a fine figure of a man.

"Eminence."

Both the bishop and the monsignor knelt to kiss his cardinal's ring and then took their places at the long table over which it was, each morning, his habit to preside. Today John Wong, his Chinese cook and housekeeper, had chosen to serve first melon and then a full complement of bacon, eggs, toast and muffins with several kinds of jam—no doubt in appreciation of the known appetite of Bishop Muldoon, who was approaching 250 pounds. Even at this hour of the morning the vicar general's breath had a sour-sweet smell. He was addicted to sacramental wine.

The cardinal ate only the melon and a piece of toast, watching with faint distaste as John Muldoon stuffed himself. The ascetically lean Monsignor O'Dowd, with unerring instinct, ate sparingly, looking on with his wintry politician's smile, his cool eyes occasionally meeting the cardinal's as though they shared a secret.

"You're looking well, Matthew."

His vicar general was the only priest in his archdiocese who called him by his first name—and usually only when they were alone. It was a familiarity born of long years together, starting when they had both studied in Rome under the man who was now pope. Now Johnny Muldoon was trying to show Monsignor O'Dowd just how close he was to the cardinal. He was also not so subtly reminding the cardinal.

He must know he's on the short end of the stick, the cardinal thought, *and he's trying to get his licks in first. A cheap trick, Johnny—and you know better than to think it will work.* He listened with half his mind to the drone of Johnny Muldoon's recitation of what he was going to do today.

". . . an invocation at the Knights of Columbus. Andy Robustelli of the Giants will be speaking. A fine, fine man . . ."

Terrance O'Dowd glanced surreptitiously at the cardinal. The hooded old eyes were almost closed, as though the morning sun were too much for him. His face looked drawn and pale. He seemed to tire more easily these days. Yet Terrance O'Dowd had no illusions about Matthew Montefiore. When he seemed most vulnerable he could be most dangerous. Those hooded eyes could snap open, the bright blue stare cold and merciless. Strong men quailed. Too often he had seen the cardinal in action. . . .

". . . the Holy Name Society. I'll need to be my best there. They have a legitimate complaint. . . . And then the dedication of the new intensive care unit at St. Thomas Aquinas Hospital . . .''

The cardinal's occasional nod punctuated the vicar general's monolog, although Terrance O'Dowd's practiced antenna told him the old man's thoughts were on something quite different. What? Surely not the contract for St. Bardolph's. . . . There could be no question of that. . . .

The cardinal's heavy lids lifted, and the cold blue stare caught him looking.

Terrance O'Dowd shivered inwardly, and quickly reviewed the bidding. Had he miscalculated somewhere? Those eyes seemed somehow accusing. . . . He could not afford miscalculation. Because he wanted to be a bishop. For seven years he had wanted it with a covetousness that in a priest was a mortal sin. A sin he could never bring himself to confess. And this slowly dying old man who could make him shiver had the sole power to recommend him to the Vatican.

Terrance O'Dowd had no illusions, either, about where he fitted into the cardinal's scheme of things. He was the buffer. Someone to protect the cardinal from the problems and annoyances of the everyday management of the archdiocese. The hatchet man, whose ruthlessness was needed; someone who could talk decimal points with a banker or detect the cushion in a contractor's bottom line. In short, a man to do the dirty work—and, as such, indispensable. For the moment.

If he blundered, the cardinal was perfectly capable of relegating him to the remotest parish he could find.

He realized that Bishop Muldoon was addressing him and reluctantly allowed himself to be drawn into the vicar general's mindless recital. There was only one thing wrong with John Muldoon, he thought viciously. He was a boob.

The cardinal's attention wandered as the two men discussed the various problems and affairs of the archdiocese, which he knew were merely preliminaries to the real business of the building contract that concerned them both. Despite himself, Stewart Stuyvesant Gansvoort once more worried at his thoughts. How to stop him? Who? Perhaps

43

Des Daniher—that noxious man? Daniher was anathema. But still—Daniher had the means. If he chose to use them. Means the cardinal couldn't bring himself to examine closely. And what would be the price Daniher would exact? Always the pound of flesh with Des Daniher. Could he bring himself to ally the church with . . . ? But then again . . . no tool was too mean for God's hand. . . .

There was a knock on the door, and at the Cardinal's summons his secretary, Father Gargan, entered abruptly. The look on his face was alarming. In his agitation he neglected the amenities and blurted, "The governor has been assassinated! It's on the TV. He's been shot. . . ."

It was Monsignor O'Dowd who said, "Calm yourself, Father. Are you sure . . . ?"

Father Gargan was actually wringing his hands. "There can't be any doubt. Every station has it."

In the silence Terrance O'Dowd sought the cardinal's face, searching for a sign to govern his own reaction. He saw that the cardinal's thin bloodless lips were moving, and was enough of a lip reader to realize that the cardinal was saying an act of contrition. What was going on in that complex shrouded mind? Would he ever understand the man?

The cardinal's face showed none of his shock. His thoughts were in chaos. But what surfaced first was an overwhelming stab of elation. And then *I wished him dead*. He quailed at the monstrousness of the thought. And then again *How ignoble to measure my own desires against a man's life*.

The steadiness of his voice surprised him.

"That will be all, Father. Keep me informed if there is anything new. And, Father, cancel my appointments for the morning. . . ."

"Praise be to . . ." Bishop Muldoon began, and stopped, appalled at what he had been about to say.

"Excuse me, if you will," the cardinal said. "I'd like to be alone for a moment."

Monsignor O'Dowd looked at him closely, again with a faint suggestion of that wintry smile. As if he somehow knew. . . .

"Of course, Eminence. . . ."

44

*   *   *

The cardinal was not conscious of their going. His mind was turned inward, filled with fearful speculations that demanded answers.

Did I really pray for this man's destruction? And is this my answer?

His hands were clenched painfully before him, the liver spots standing out starkly. He slowly opened his fists and spread out his fingers on the table.

"God works in mysterious ways. . . . Love the Lord thy God with all thy heart . . . and thy neighbor as thyself."

Surely, he thought, *this is the gravest sin of all—the failure to love.* His mind sought frantically to alleviate the pain and confusion he felt. *And yet . . . am I alone to blame? Surely a God of Vengeance would approve . . . and forgive.*

He walked slowly to his office and sat down at the massive Renaissance desk that had been made for another prince of the Church in 1586. He stared for a moment at the telephone, then picked it up and got through to the switchboard.

"If the vicar general has not left, would you tell him I'd like him to receive my confession later this morning? In the meantime, see if you can get me Mr. Desmond Daniher. He will be at his home, I believe."

Yes, he thought sourly, *it will have to be Daniher. . . . He will have the votes, now—and the power. Between us . . .*

Time: THE PRESENT
THE ADMINISTRATOR,
PUTNAM HERKIMER KENNICOTT

He engaged in tierce, executed a beat, thrust, bind and a full lunge. *Maître* André responded effortlessly with one direct and two spin parries, and Kennicott found himself suddenly open to a stop thrust that would have taken him smoothly over the heart had André followed through. He stepped back, breathing hard.

"Overextended," *Maître* André said. "You must recover more quickly."

Maître André was *not* breathing hard, but then, André had been only defending while Kennicott did the attacking. André was a small, slight man who surely was over fifty, so age wasn't really a factor. Kennicott felt he could match André in speed, agility, strength and coordination. So why couldn't he get past that impenetrable guard? One does not fence so much with the muscles as with the nerves and brain. Fencing is an exercise for the mind, as precise and logical as chess, in its way. So André was outthinking him at every move.

The truth of that depressed him. He suddenly felt all of his years. He removed his mask, saluted formally as custom required and, as the *Maître* followed suit, stepped forward to shake hands.

"Enough for today." And then, "Tell me, *Maître*, have I lost a step or two?"

André considered this judicially, as he did most things.

"No-o-o, it's the concentration, I think. Perhaps too much on your mind."

The truth of *that* followed Kennicott into the shower. If too much meant that his job was now totally out of hand, that neither he nor anyone else could control the runaway cost of the Mall—which seemed to feed on itself like some monstrous cancer—then surely he had more than enough on his mind. And that he could possibly face criminal—certainly civil—charges as a result.

In the beginning he had been almost pathetically grateful for the job offered him by Stewart Gansvoort. It had come at a time in his life he didn't like to think about. And now he faced disaster. It sometimes seemed to him that his life had been one long string of them.

Putnam Herkimer Kennicott had been born to a long line of distinguished ancestors. And little else. "A member of the overly educated and too highly cultured poor," as his mother, with her deprecating smile, was so fond of saying.

The lack of a fortune never bothered Put Kennicott. There always seemed to be enough. Just. To put him through Harvard, following the footprints of so many of his forebears, and to pay for his flying lessons until he could get his commercial license. For early on, the young Kennicott had fallen in love with flight. There was never any doubt that flying was to be his life.

By the time he was thirty-one Put Kennicott seemed to have had it made. He was in the left-hand seat with a growing airline and well up on the seniority list. He was happily married to Mary Mountcastle, whose family equaled his in both lineage and finances.

Then came war. Putnam Kennicott answered the call of duty, just as his ancestors had done, only to find that he was considered too old for combat flying and that he had an inner-ear problem that would make him marginal even for Air Transport Command. Since the Air Force didn't seem to want him, he did the next best thing. He signed up as a contract civilian flight instructor and ended up spending a frustrating four years at Randolph Field in Texas, teaching children half his age the rudiments of flying.

It was there that Kennicott first met young Stewart Gansvoort and had the unpleasant duty of washing him out of the training program, because in an aircraft Stewart couldn't seem to tell his right hand from his left. He just didn't have the kind of coordination it takes to become a flier. Stewart took his failure better than most, and Put Kennicott didn't think of the young man again for years.

Both his parents were dead by the time the war ended, so Kennicott took his meager inheritance and, with three wartime buddies, formed a pool to buy three war surplus Curtis C-46 two-engined transports. This nucleus became TriAir Air Transport, a cargo line willing to carry anything, anytime, anywhere. The business prospered enough so that at the end of six years of back-breaking effort it had eight more planes of various types and was out from under most of the mountain of debt. They were able to borrow enough for a downpayment on five four-engined Douglas DC-6s.

In 1961, after fifteen years, TriAir was a going concern and owned or leased fifty-nine cargo carriers. It seemed that Putnam Kennicott and his partners were well on the way to fame and fortune. From the beginning Kennicott's area had been operations. He had found with the years that he was very good at running a busy freight line and only resented the hard deskwork because it cut his flying time down to an absolute minimum. Put Kennicott was never completely happy on the ground.

Nineteen sixty-one was disaster year. In the space of three months TriAir lost five of its planes, two to weather and pilot error, two in an avoidable hangar fire and one to the partner who handled the financial end of the growing business. The last one carried the partner to Argentina with all the company's cash reserves. Subsequent investigation revealed that Kennicott's good buddy had been systematically looting the till for a number of years.

Insurance didn't cover the losses, and the banks descended like wolves on the fold. When TriAir was finally liquidated, Kennicott and his remaining partner were left with little more than the shirts on their backs.

Put Kennicott had been out of active flying for too long to expect a major airline to take him on. There were far too many good pilots with seniority. So he grabbed the best thing available. He went to work for Air America, the CIA-owned front that delivered supplies, weapons and other things to Southeast Asia. At least they'd let him fly.

While dropping off a load of ammunition to Meo tribesmen on a mountain airstrip in Laos, his DC-3 was ambushed by a Cong patrol. Kennicott was the only one of the crew who survived. It took the Meos three weeks to get him back to safety in Vietnam. He had lost an eye and the rest of the hearing in his bad ear. He was finished with flying.

He had nothing left except his disability pension. In addition he was forced to do the hardest thing he had ever had to do: tell his wife Mary that they would have to move out of Putnam House. The mansion had been in his family for two hundred years. It had been declared a national monument, so it couldn't be sold. It would have to be given to the government—which would at least save him from the back-breaking taxes.

Put Kennicott spent the better part of 1962 and 1963 looking for a job and not finding one. He had been a bold pilot. Now he was an old one, confounding the adage that a flier couldn't be both. There was no place for him. He was too proud to ask for the help he could have gotten from any number of old friends. A gentleman doesn't beg. Nor does he admit that the world has passed him by.

He was almost at the end of his rope when a chance weekend aboard a friend's yacht had brought him and his wife and fifteen-year-old daughter to Stewart Gansvoort's Riverhaven estate. Stewart held no grudge. On the contrary, he was amusingly grateful to Kennicott for washing him out of flying so long ago. It had kept him away from the sound of shots fired in anger and ended him up as air liaison to some general in Berlin after the war.

It was at Riverhaven that his daughter, Nan, had her tragic accident. And it was there that Stewart Gansvoort offered him a job. He never knew whether or not it was out of pity for what had happened to Nan, because Stewart seemed to feel a sort of responsibility for his young guest.

At any rate, he couldn't afford to examine motives at that point. He had no choice. He found himself a trustee of the Jacob Gansvoort Associates, at a salary that allowed him to keep Putnam House—if he lived frugally. The job was undemanding and it lasted for six boring years.

He watched Stewart Gansvoort's rise from state assemblyman to lieutenant governor to governor without envy. He accepted Stewart's interest and friendship because his wife wanted it—and because he found he was only one of a number of "Gansvoort people" in whom Stewart took a personal interest. He came to look on it as the largesse of the king to his subjects—a sort of apology for Stewart's great wealth and good fortune. He allowed Stewart to arrange for Nan's expensive rehabilitation and her education for the same reasons. After all, Stewart owned the hospitals and the doctors and supported the college Nan attended.

When his wife, Mary, died suddenly in 1968, he gave serious if brief consideration on ending a life that no longer seemed to have either purpose or meaning. He found he couldn't do it—for many reasons. Not the least of which was that his upbringing told him it was a mean and shoddy way for a Kennicott to die.

So he took up his life again, content to live it to whatever end. But he knew that Putnam Herkimer Kennicott was a defeated man with no heart left for the battle.

Then came the Mall. And with it new life and purpose. He was named Administrator of the project. It was an act of Providence. Logistics was what he knew best. In his time he had moved tons of material, supplied and equipped small armies. Coordinating and supervising the building of the Mall, with its mere thousands of workers, seemed like a job especially created for his talents. He accepted it with alacrity and joy, and counted his blessings.

But now, after nine years—the job was getting away from him, as it would have from any man. The whole gigantic mess had become a Tower of Babel. Orders given were not carried out. Discipline was a word in the dictionary. There was no such thing as a punishment to fit the crime.

And crime was the problem. Two billion dollars spent on the Mall. How much of it had gone into the pockets of venal state officials, how much to crooked union leaders to keep the work going, how many millions had been lost to actual pilferage?

There was no earthly way to tell. Because his repeated insistence that the project be policed by trained personnel had been just as repeatedly ignored.

At this moment there waited on his desk, hand-delivered the night before, a coldly formal notice from the governor's secretary. It informed him that he was to appear before a grand jury to answer questions on the audit recently completed by the state comptroller.

He hated and feared it. But he understood it. It was Governor Stewart Gansvoort's way of passing the buck, of telling him that he was being left on his own to face whatever the audit would reveal.

He understood it because it was the way he had been brought up. Ultimate responsibility lay with the man on top, not the troops. He accepted it because his whole life was an acceptance of the principle.

He was shocked and dismayed that his friend Stewart Gansvoort would do this to him.

Adjusting his tie before the locker mirror, he studied the man he had become. His years of flying had weathered him like old leather, stretched the skin tautly over his cheekbones, thinned a face already lean. A black patch covered the eye he had lost in Laos. The other eye, a startling blue, peered out of its socket from a thicket of gray brows like that of some watchful Cyclops.

He could see the blood pulsing in the veins of his neck. It both pleased him and daunted him to know that in those veins was the blood of two hundred years of statesmen and warriors. From Revolutionary Generals Isaac Putnam and Nicholas Herkimer down to the man he saw before him.

The last of the line. What a pity that Nan had not been a boy.

The thought of his ancestry cheered him, made him straighten shoulders already square and caused him to smile grimly into the mirror. One more river to cross. One more battle to fight.

When he reached the street he was whistling *The Battle Hymn of the Republic* softly under his breath.

He learned about the death of the governor when he arrived at his office. That seemed unimportant to him when he received the news that his daughter, Nan, was somehow involved and was being held in custody. The office of the police commissioner tried to stall him briefly, but at last told him where she was.

Gansvoort Hospital still throbbed with subdued tension, a pulsing aftermath of the previous night's riot. There were a few reporters left, hoping for a story, and uniformed police in the lobby checking casualties that were still drifting in. People spoke in tones more hushed than usual.

The receptionist parted with information reluctantly, and Kennicott entered an elevator and punched a button for the third floor.

He reached his daughter's room as Gavin Riordan approached from the other end of the corridor. They both stopped before the uniformed policeman who stood impassively at her door.

At Riordan's look of inquiry the man said, "Nobody, Commissioner, except the doctor. He's in there now."

Putnam Kennicott moved toward the door.

"Wait," Riordan said sharply.

Almost simultaneously, as though triggered by some mysterious police grapevine, the elevator doors opened and disgorged Sergeant Macy, an irate assistant DA and a police stenographer, carrying the black box that was his trademark. Macy managed to be first, interposing his big body protectively between the ADA and Riordan.

"I insist on being present. My office has every right . . ."

The ADA had a high, querulous voice. At a discreet gesture from Riordan, Sergeant Macy let him past.

"Name?"

"Kaplan. I . . ."

"Where's your boss?"

"He had to leave. I have been ordered . . ." Already Kaplan sounded defensive.

"No one will be present," Riordan said. "Miss Kennicott has been charged with nothing—as yet. I suggest you find a telephone in the lobby. Tell your boss I'll inform him the moment I determine if his office is involved." They watched the ADA go toward the elevators, muttering to himself.

Macy, close by Riordan's side, whispered, "Gimme a minute before you go in."

Riordan motioned to the steno. The police guard stood aside and

Riordan went to the door. Kennicott moved with him until the two men, who were of equal height, were eye to eye.

"Sorry, Kennicott. I said no one. This is police business."

"It won't do, you know. I am her father. . . ."

Riordan's ingrained dislike of all authority, real or assumed, showed in his face.

"Sorry," he said again, and turned away.

Kennicott's long fingers gripped his arm with a strength that made him wince.

"I am going to see my daughter, sir. Don't try to stop me."

Riordan's immediate reaction to that steely voice was to shake him off. But when he saw the naked anguish in the lone blue eye he couldn't do it.

"No interference?"

Kennicott nodded, one brief jerk of his head. "None. You have your job to do."

Riordan opened the door and let Kennicott precede him. Macy's hand on his arm was insistent.

"Captain Phillips called from Harkavy. Medical Examiner says there were two bullets in the governor. Either one could have done the job." There was a peculiar expression on Macy's face. "Also there was something wrong with his pecker."

At Riodan's raised eyebrows Macy stepped back a pace and lifted his hands, palms upward. "Don't ask me, Boss. Phillips didn't know either."

Sunlight streamed through a tree just outside the window and made a dancing pattern on the stark gray walls. To Kennicott the hospital smell seemed overpowering. The white-coated resident said "Dr. Bourne." It was Kennicott who took his proffered handshake politely, while Riordan motioned the stenographer to plug in his machine and find a chair.

Nan Kennicott looked small in the high hospital bed. Her eyes were closed, her lips the only color in her pale face, her hair spread out like halo on the pillow. To Riordan her beauty had never been more touching.

Kennicott, standing beside the bed, very gently stroked her hand. Her eyes opened slowly, unfocused at first, pupils still dilated.

"Put. What are you doing here?" Her voice seemed wispy with an infinite tiredness.

"She's been sedated," Dr. Bourne said to Riordan.

"Heavily?"

"No."

Riordan took the doctor's arm and moved with him to the window. "I hope you didn't . . ."

"I know an addict when I see one," the doctor said stiffly. "She'll be able to respond, if that's what's worrying you. At least for a while."

Riordan went to the side of the bed away from Kennicott. "Nan . . ."

Her body tensed when she moved her head to see him.

"It's all right, baby," Kennicott continued, with his soothing stroking of her hand. "There's nothing to fear. It's all right. . . ."

Riordan hoped to God he was right. He looked at the steno, who nodded briefly.

Very softly he said, "Nan, I want you to tell me what happened. This is not official. It's just between old friends. But we've got to know . . . to protect you."

It was said. He knew now that he was committed. No longer a cop with this woman—but a friend.

Putnam Kennicott sighed deeply as if he had been holding his breath.

"But I don't know, Gavin. . . ." Her eyes were cloudy with uncertainty. "I'm not sure. I was there by the pool . . . and he was there. He was dead, Gavin. . . . Wasn't he?"

"Yes, honey. He is dead." He was filled with pity for her, knowing all he knew. And a cold anger at what Stewart Gansvoort had done to her.

"Start from the beginning, Nan," he said gently. "It all has to come out now."

"From the beginning . . . ?" Her hand reached for his and clutched it. Slow tears rolled down her cheeks. "But I don't want Put to know. . . ." She spoke as if her father were not in the room. "He would be so ashamed. . . ."

Put Kennicott turned her other hand and held it in both of his.

"Never, my darling. Never. Perhaps we should all go back to the beginning."

The beginning, Gavin Riordan thought. *Where was it for me? It was all so long ago.*

7

Time: 1940
STEWART STUYVESANT GANSVOORT

At seventeen, Stewart Gansvoort wanted nothing more than to be left alone. To be free of the tyranny of his father and his father's name, and all that it implied. To be free of a wealth so enormous that as yet he had no real idea of its extent. To be free most of all of those terrifying words, *responsibility* and *obligation*, which had been drummed into him for as long as he could remember.

Stewart Gansvoort was suffering from a malady found only in the very rich. If he was ever to be loved, he wanted to be loved for himself alone.

From where he lay at the top of the hill, he could see for twenty miles in any direction, up and down the shimmering expanse of the river. He could watch through his high-powered binoculars the endlessly fascinating river traffic—freighters, barges, from all parts of the world—and dream of far places and exotic ports.

It gave him no pleasure today. For before him through the trees lay much of the reason for his depression. Riverhaven—the Estate. In his grandfather's day it had been a thousand acres of rolling hills and woodlands. But the City had moved closer through the years, as inexorably as lava creeping down a mountainside, until now the Estate was surrounded on three sides and was only half its original size.

Immediately below him the Big House sprawled on the hillside. It was built by his grandfather of weather-stained stone quarried on the Estate or taken from some of the old stone walls. Each stone had been carefully selected for form and color and laid out in patterns before being mortared into place. The immense roof was of red slate.

The weather-stained stone gave it the appearance of a home that had withstood time and weather even on the day it was completed. The trees, shrubs, lawns and the contours of the land looked as though nature had placed them perfectly. Only the instructed visitor would know that trees had been moved from one place to another, that thousands of tons of landfill, bolstered in places by retaining walls, had been used to improve on nature, that sixty tons of fertilizer were used every year to make two hundred acres of manicured lawn a lush green.

But that was the way Jacob Gansvoort wanted it. He drew the plans himself. He treated the land as he treated everything else in his life, as something to be subjugated, bent, manipulated until it became the form and shape he desired. His landscaping was so devised that the winding roads caught just the right views at just the right angles, the most impressive outlooks, and at the Big House the whole thing ended in a burst of river, hill, clouds and a magnificent sweep of woodland to crown the whole.

Jacob Gansvoort liked to build things—when he had the time. Things like railroads and shipping lines and oil empires.

Stewart Gansvoort hated him almost as much as he hated his father.

To the left of the Big House was the original carriage house, now a garage, although it still held a polished landau in one remote corner. Beyond that were the stables, built to accommodate thirty horses, of which there remained only half a dozen riding hacks for the family. Just visible through the trees was the dairy barn and the beginning of the truck farm that fed the Estate. Out of sight over a hill were the farmhouse and the cottages that housed the workers.

Altogether too impossibly grand and imposing, from the guards at the entrance to the naked marble woman on the front terrace. Not a place one could bring a friend. He had learned that from bitter experience the few times he had invited some of his fellow students from South Side High. The grandeur of the place had reduced them to embarrassed silence. He was a marked man at South Side, as different from the rest as though his hair were green.

So much better if he had been allowed to go to a prep school where money might not have set him so much apart. But his father, August Gansvoort, was nothing if not democratic. He could still hear the words every time his unhappiness drove him to bring up the subject. "We have the best public education system in the world. It would be improvident not to take advantage of it. Great wealth need not be a barrier to friendship. We have a responsibility to the society in which we live. It is our duty to be a part of it."

Stewart lifted his binoculars and adjusted the lenses to zero in on the servants' quarters at the back of the Big House, focusing first, as always, on the window of the bath and shower room of the women's quarters. He had once seen one of the maids naked from the waist up, toweling herself before the open window, and he lived in constant hope that it would happen again.

Today the window was disappointingly closed. He swept the length of the servants' quarters and found nothing of interest. On the sweep back he discovered his younger brother, Henry, sitting on the kitchen steps, munching on what looked like a piece of cake. Silent, secretive Henry, who seemed to live in a world of his own, far apart from the rest of them. Eating between meals was rigidly forbidden. Stewart filed away this bit of information for future use. At eleven, Henry was easily blackmailed.

His glasses picked up McAllister, the Scottish manager of the Estate, dressed as usual in boots and corduroys. McAllister was tall and lean and bronzed—everything Stewart was not. McAllister still treated him like a child. One more thing to add to his resentment.

As he watched, two riders rounded the end of the stables. One was his sister Serena, laughing over her shoulder at something her companion had said. The other, when Stewart shifted the glasses, gave him a shock. It was Gavin Riordan, the nearest thing to a hero at South Side High. Gavin Riordan, who seemed to float through life on a wave of applause, whether catching an impossible forward pass or gracefully accepting the presidency of his class.

The two were laughing as they dismounted and led the horses through the wide stable doors. They seemed so much at ease with one another. While he . . . The unfairness of it filled him with anger. What could Gavin Riordan possibly see in his fourteen-year-old sister?

He lay there for minutes more, torn between his resentment and the desire to join them, to be a part of their obvious warmth. His loneliness won out. He began to make his way slowly down the hillside. Slowly, because his pride wouldn't allow him to hasten.

It wasn't until he stood outside the stable doors that he realized they should long since have unsaddled and turned their horses over to the stable boy. He was suddenly filled with excitement and a sense of foreboding. He found that he was trembling.

The interior of the barn was dim and shadowy after the brightness of late afternoon. Stewart moved stealthily over the corrugated concrete floor. Whatever sound he might have made was covered by the restless movements of the horses in their stalls. The air was sharp with the acrid smell of urine overlying the milder odors of ancient leather and the sweet scent of new-mown hay.

The barn seemed to be deserted, but Stewart knew it wasn't. He *felt* their presence. He saw everything with an exaggerated clarity; a motionless bluebottle on the rump of the first horse he passed, the gleaming metal bit of the bridle that hung on the post of the next stall, the dust motes dancing in the filtered light. He passed the hay-mow with its pitchfork, handle standing tall, tines buried in the hay. He was so close to where he knew they were.

He stood before the door of the unused tack room at the far end of the barn, and listened, hearing what he knew he would hear—the sound of heavy breathing and a small, half-stifled moan. He heard, too, a rasp of his own breath and was achingly aware of the rigidity in his pants.

With infinite patience he inched open the door.

Gavin Riordan's broad shoulders covered his sister's body; her arms crisscrossed his back. Only her legs were visible, incongruously still clad in her Hessian half-boots. For a moment he watched the rippling muscles of Gavin Riordan's back as he performed his slow ritual. He heard the tick-tock of Serena's boot heels on the floor as the motion lifted her legs and let them fall.

Then, as it had happened before, and would happen again in his lifetime, Stewart Stuyvesant Gansvoort went into a mindless rage.

Without knowing how it happened, he found himself standing before the tack room grasping the long-handled pitchfork, its three steel tines gleaming dully in the half-light. He kicked the door open.

Gavin Riordan rolled off his sister's body. For a brief instant Stewart saw the glistening pink wetness of Serena spread open before him. Then he lunged.

Riordan's instinctive athlete's roll saved his life. Two of the murderous tines went into his body, one into his chest, the other ripping into the muscles of his right arm. The third pinned him firmly to the wooden floor.

Gavin Riordan screamed once and then was silent. He tried to lift himself, and when he found he couldn't he sank back and closed his eyes.

Appalled at what he had done, Stewart backed off. He saw Serena standing pressed against the wall. A shaft of afternoon sunlight came through a dirty window to limn her child-woman's body. His eyes lingered on the soft down at the V of her legs, then on the still-rigid nipples. Serena crossed her arms to cover her breasts.

"What's going on here!"

Ian McAllister stood in the doorway.

No one moved or spoke.

"Goddamnit! What the hell is going on!"

The Estate manager moved farther into the room, saw Serena's nakedness.

"Damnit, girl! Cover yourself!" Then his eyes fell on Gavin Riordan. "Mother of God! What have they done to you!"

"For Christ's sake, pull it out!" Gavin said through gritted teeth.

McAllister put his foot on Gavin's chest and took a firm grip on the shaft of the pitchfork.

"Steady, lad. It will hurt." With a quick jerk of his powerful arms he pulled the pitchfork from Gavin's body. Bright red blood welled

59

up from the holes it left. Gavin gave a long sigh that was half a groan and sat up. McAllister reached for Gavin's shirt and tossed it to him.

"Hold it tight against the wounds—until we can get you to the hospital.

"Now . . ." He turned to the others. "What happened here?"

Serena, now back in her jeans and sweater, wouldn't meet his furious look. He swung his head to Stewart. "You, out with it now!"

Stewart tried, but the words wouldn't come. He lifted his hands and shook his head helplessly.

"It was an accident," Gavin Riordan said softly. They all watched as he got slowly to his feet.

McAllister snorted. "Accident, my arse. With the two of you mother naked."

"Please . . . We were just horsing around. It was an accident . . ."

McAllister saw the naked pleading in the boy's pale face. "So that's the way of it . . . ?" he said slowly.

"That's the way of it. . . ."

After a long moment, McAllister made up his mind.

"All right. Then that's the way it will be."

Stewart felt his eyes fill with tears of gratitude and relief.

Very softly Serena said, "Shit."

McAllister reached for Riordan's pants. "Help me get him clad. Then I'll see he's looked after."

It was Serena who steadied Gavin as McAllister got him dressed. Stewart was still unable to function. There was no way he could bring himself to touch Gavin Riordan. He couldn't take his eyes from the slowly reddening shirt Gavin held pressed to his wounds.

As McAllister got Gavin to the door, Serena said, "I want to go. . . ."

McAllister shook his head. "Best not, I think . . . under the circumstances."

Stewart at last found his voice. "Father . . . ? What about . . . ?"

McAllister glared at him. "You all seem agreed on the how of it.

60

The Mister will hear no different from me. But see you stick to your story. I wouldn't want to be in the middle of this.''

Then they were left alone.

"He'll find out," Stewart said. "I know he will. . . ."

"Not if you keep your mouth shut."

She was standing across the room from him, her arms slightly bent as though she were still trying to cover herself. What flashed before his eyes was the pink wetness of her slit, the whiteness of her belly and the excitement of her nipples. She was looking at him speculatively.

"You want to do what Gavin did to me, don't you?"

He couldn't speak, but they both knew the answer.

"And if I let you, then you'd *have* to keep your mouth shut. Wouldn't you?"

He took a slow step toward her, feeling once more the hard flesh thrusting against his pants.

"Well, fuck you, Stewart," Serena said matter of factly. "You know what? I think you're crazy. That's what."

She brushed past him through the door, careful not to touch him.

It was the first time anyone had ever said that to him.

Stewart Gansvoort was right. His father did find out. Not all, but enough. Add to that the fact that Gavin Riordan was the ward of Desmond Patrick Daniher, the all-powerful political boss of the state—and there were bound to be repercussions. In the crunch Gavin found he couldn't lie to Des Daniher. He loved Des too much. In the hospital Des listened to his ward in silence, and at Gavin's plea that things be left as they were, he shook his head. "Some things, yes. Other things, no. This is a thing that has to be looked after."

It was all handled very quietly. Des Daniher paid one visit to August Gansvoort and was closeted with him for a half hour in the "study" of the Big House. Two days later Stewart was on the train that would take him to Phillips Andover Academy. It wasn't St. Marks, or Groton, or Middlesex, or even Exeter. But it was at the top of the second flight. That's why August Gansvoort had picked it.

It would never do to seem in any way ostentatious. So Stewart got his wish, although not quite in the way he had so hoped for.

It was at Andover, safely away from the rigid rules of Riverhaven and the inflexible discipline of his father, that he smoked his first cigarette, tasted his first drink and got well and truly laid. Three things that were to comfort him the rest of his life.

8

Time: 1946, GERMANY
ERICKA

The I. G. Farben buildings housed the offices of United States Forces European Theater. The huge complex was, oddly, scarcely damaged amid the almost total devastation of Frankfurt.

To the architect's eye of Captain George Barnstable, the few signs of shell damage pitting the walls had small effect on the inexcusable ugliness of the squat Farben buildings. Nor had the barbed-wire concertinas surrounding the buildings.

Barnstable waved a reluctant good-bye to the jeep that had brought him from the airstrip, picked up his bulging Val-A-Pak and his artist's portfolio and presented his identification to the sleepy guard at the gap in the wire. The guard gave him a lackadaisical salute and silently motioned him on. Barnstable awkwardly returned the salute and made his way under the porte cochere and into the reception area.

The lobby seemed to be deserted. There were still relics of Farben opulence—worn leather chairs and couches, frayed carpeting. All covered with the dust that seemed to blanket everything in Frankfurt-Am-Main.

Barnstable dropped his luggage at the empty reception counter and said loudly, "Hey, anybody home?" The silence seemed to shout back at him.

"Nobody here but us chickens."

Barnstable heard the voice echoing oddly in the empty lobby, but saw no speaker. Finally he discerned a figure stretched out on one of the couches. Long legs encased in fatigues almost white from many washings, bloused neatly over scuffed paratroop boots, the hands folded over a faded battle jacket, then the head resting comfortably on what appeared to be a German officer's leather overcoat. The face was covered by a scarred and dented helmet.

The figure sat up and Barnstable saw the single lieutenant's bars on each shoulder, and the engineer castle insigne on one collar point. The helmet, when pushed back, revealed a pleasant young-old face, the lower half of which sported a bristling red beard. The steady gray eyes were surrounded by a network of laugh (or stress?) wrinkles. The mouth was full and generous, curved now in a half-smile. A face Barnstable immediately liked.

"You're a little early, chum. It's only oh-six-thirty. The action won't start for another half hour or so."

"Are you the duty officer?"

"Nope. He's probably sacked out in the back office."

At Barnstable's silent question the lieutenant grinned.

"I'm here every morning. I like to catch the bastards when they come to work. It's the only way I can get to see them. I figure if I bug 'em enough, maybe I can get one son of a bitch to stir his ass long enough to find my service records. Been doing it for four and a half months now. Sons of bitches a-plenty—but no ass-stirrers so far."

Barnstable caught a certain calculation in the lieutenant's eye and hastily shook his head.

"Don't look at me. I just got here."

"Yeah," the lieutenant said morosely. "I can see that."

Barnstable was painfully conscious of his spanking-new custom-made uniform. Against the lieutenant's comfortably casual combat

63

gear he felt like an imposter. The lieutenant stood up. A .45 in a scratched leather holster pulled down the web belt around his lean waist. The lieutenant stooped and reached under the couch to retrieve a folding M-1 carbine, which he slung over his shoulder.

My God, Barnstable thought, *the war's been over for seven months—and this guy is still armed to the teeth.*

The lieutenant saw his look.

"I do some traveling in the boondocks. There's still DP gangs around. Unarmed officer is easy meat.

"What brings you to our fair city?"

"Monuments," Barnstable said. "Historical monuments. Protect and salvage. I'm . . . I'm an architect."

"My, my," the lieutenant said. "I hope you brought your shovel. God, you look new. I can still smell the States on you."

The lieutenant looked him over critically, and Barnstable knew all too well what he was seeing. A stocky middle-age man with graying hair, going to fat around the middle, self-conscious in his unfamiliar uniform.

"No offense," said the lieutenant, "but how long you been in this man's army?"

"Three months and . . . oh, eleven days. They gave me a direct commission. . . ."

"It figures." The lieutenant's tone spoke of a long and resigned familiarity with military caprice. "Incidentally I'm Riordan. Gavin Riordan."

"George Barnstable." George half lifted a hand, but the lieutenant didn't seem to think handshakes were necessary.

"Where you from, George?"

When Barnstable mentioned the City, Riordan's face lit up like a child's at Christmas time, and Barnstable saw that the lieutenant was much younger than he had thought.

"Money from home," Riordan grinned delightedly. "You know Des Daniher?"

"I know of him, of course," Barnstable answered.

"He's my guardian," smiled Riordan. "Lived with him all my life."

Now it seemed handshakes were in order. Barnstable felt his

knuckles crack as the lieutenant pumped his arm and asked, "Why don't we hit the mess hall? At least the coffee's hot."

"I don't know. . . ." Barnstable said uncertainly. "I'm supposed to report in to somebody. I'm not just sure who . . ."

"Take your pick." Riordan pointed to something behind him.

Barnstable turned and saw that on the wall beyond the reception desk was a large chart printed in heavy black letters.

"Tee-oh," said Riordan. "Table of Organization. Find the box where you fit in, and that's the man you got to see. Let's see . . . *Economic, Political* . . . How about *Public Affairs*?"

"It doesn't sound quite right. But I suppose . . ."

"That's my box. The one on the bottom." The lieutenant was suddenly morose again. *US Resident Officers*. Temporary duty. I'm attached to this idiot outfit for rations and quarters—and pay, of course. The rations I wouldn't feed a pig. The quarters would depress a hermit. As for the pay—I haven't seen a dime of it for five months. You got no papers, you get no pay. That's US Army Regulation Number One."

"But with no pay, how do you . . . ?" Barnstable began, and stopped as Riordan's gray eyes, suddenly cool and frosty, fixed his. After a moment the lieutenant seemed to realize that the question had no hidden meaning, and shrugged briefly.

"Oh, I deal a little. Nothing big. This and that. Here and there."

"Deal . . ."

"Yeah, deal. That's black market to you, dad. A man's got to live, you know." Riordan grinned like a conspirator. "Tell you what. There's no sense reporting in before you absolutely have to. Take it from me. I know. We'll go down to my shack. I've got some real honest-to-God java. That, along with a little schnapps, will make this lousy country look a lot better."

The lieutenant took his arm. There was no stopping him. And suddenly there was nothing Barnstable wanted more than some java—with a little schnapps.

With that invitation began a period in George Barnstable's life he would always remember with mingled emotions.

At forty-two he considered himself a reasonably happy and

contented man. His life had known two tragedies—the deaths of his parents and that of his wife. But those had become bearable over the years. He was a wealthy man, eminently successful in his field, and he could look forward to years of building the things he wanted to build. That he would never be the fine artist he had so wanted to be had ceased to trouble him.

He had interrupted his fruitful and well-organized life because of an unaccustomed sense of guilt. When he had been a student in Berlin he had met and married Giselle Ullman, the daughter of a wealthy Jewish publishing family. Now he felt that he owed it to the memory of his dead wife to try to find whatever was left of her family and do what he could for them. It was the principal reason he had accepted his present assignment.

But Barnstable's tour of duty in Germany was to serve another purpose that would drastically alter his life.

Riordan's shack turned out to be a six-room boathouse on the bank of the river, ten miles outside of Frankfurt.

Most of the rooms were stacked with Riordan's stock: gasoline, cigarettes, ten-in-one rations, clothing, soap, Nazi ceremonial daggers, nylons. Anything on which a value could be placed, Riordan either had or knew where to get.

In the beginning Barnstable was appalled and disapproving, but he soon found that there was no point in trying to resist Riordan, who told him, "I takes from the rich and gives to the poor—namely me. If these bastards want to keep me in this man's army, then they'll have to pay for it." Barnstable could only smile at the immense satisfaction Riordan got from doing the military in the eye, a pastime to which he seemed single-mindedly dedicated.

Riordan explained that his 201 file, containing all his service records, was "lost." He was convinced that this was due to an argument he had had with his commanding officer just after VE-Day.

"I knocked him on his ass is what I did," Riordan said. "The bastard had it coming. Not the smartest thing for me to do. If he hadn't been on his way home he'd have stuck me good—with a court-martial. As it is . . ."

"Isn't there anything you can do? Surely . . ."

Riordan showed him a thick folder of correspondence.

"Pen pals. Me and the fucking Army. With a couple million guys to process who have *got* papers, I am strictly down in asshole territory. Still—sooner or later..." Riordan shrugged. "In the meantime a guy has to live."

When Barnstable noticed, hanging on a hook, a dress blouse, the left breast of which seemed covered with ribbons, Riordan laughed morosely.

"Yeah, I got medals comin' out of my ears. Two Silver Stars, three Purple Hearts and a Bronze Star, which is sort of a nothing medal, but it still counts for points. I got enough points to discharge a regiment. But what the hell good are they if I don't have the papers to prove it?"

Riordan's offer of coffee and schnapps turned into something much more. In the middle of the afternoon Riordan produced from a stone crock a dripping piece of gray meat, held it to his nose and inhaled judiciously.

"Been in there almost two weeks. Should be just about ripe."

He put the meat in a pot and covered it with liquid from the crock. He added onions, bay leaves and peppercorns, while Barnstable watched in fascination. The pot he placed on a four-burner US Army–issue bottled-gas stove. After a while a delectable odor began to permeate the kitchen.

By this time they had switched from Steinhager to Geniver gin mixed with GI powdered lemon juice over real ice cubes from a huge refrigerator squeezed into one corner of the kitchen.

"I'm hooked into the Headquarters generator," Riordan explained. "Sooner or later the maintenance crews are going to spot it. Maybe I ought to locate my own generator."

When Barnstable remarked on his expertise, Riordan grinned.

"Uncle Sam runs the biggest trade school in the world. In the Army, when you're not actually shooting at somebody, you're either going to school or teaching. Let's see"—he began to tick off on his fingers—"I been to Bomb Disposal School, Aerial Photography, Radio Communications, Signal Corps, Heavy Ordnance, Vehicle Maintenance—and Cooks and Bakers. Among others I disremember."

At six Riordan served a meal of sauerbraten, kartoffelkloesse and red cabbage, which Barnstable knew couldn't have been bettered at any of the Berlin restaurants he used to frequent. It was accompanied by several bottles of an excellent Moselle labeled PROPERTY OF WEHRMACHT STORES.

At eleven, lying blearily in the big four-poster that was the twin of Riordan's, Barnstable said, "You didn't learn that at Cooks and Bakers School. What did you do before you got in?"

"Well, George," Riordan's voice was soft with remembrance, "I guess I was a lover. A lover of all the sad-eyed women . . ."

Barnstable fell asleep just then.

When Barnstable checked in at Headquarters the next morning he could find no one who had the faintest interest in either him or his assignment. Finally he was permitted to sign on for rations, quarters and pay and told politely to get lost. As for the use of a vehicle—forget it.

Riordan found him in the mess hall over coffee, which was every bit as bad as Riordan had claimed. He listened to Barnstable's complaints with an "I told you so" satisfaction.

"Assholes," Riordan pronounced. "Every one. George, you better hook up with me. We are little lost lambs and we better stick together. I've got a vehicle—and not a damned thing to do. You want monuments, I'll show you monuments. Or what's left of 'em. How about it?"

Four days of touring devastated Frankfurt convinced him that restoration was a job for a wrecking crew—totally beyond the powers of a single man to estimate the damage or even identify what had once stood whole and sturdy and was now rubble piled on rubble.

The stone used to build much of Frankfurt was a dull red Rhenish sandstone. When reduced to heaps of rubble, it had left a coating of red dust that covered everything. It got in the mouth and the nose and the food—if you were lucky enough to find food. Barnstable wondered what percentage of Frankfurt had been destroyed: seventy percent, eighty? The ruined sections all looked depressingly the same. Before the war Frankfurt had not been a handsome town. Now it was ugly. Curiously enough, it still looked old, though. Old and ruined and ugly.

When Barnstable got around to telling Riordan of his hope of helping whatever remained of his wife's family, he found Riordan strangely unsympathetic.

"Jews I can maybe understand. But they are also Germans. I've been killing Germans since D-Day. And I've seen one hell of a lot since. As far as I'm concerned, the only good Germans are dead ones. But if you got to do it, you got to do it. What the hell, I've never seen Berlin.

"One thing. You got to have a permit to get through the Russian Zone. I better find out how we do it."

The process of getting a permit to travel from Frankfurt through the Russian Zone to Berlin proved to be impossibly complex. The request had to be initiated at local Division level, move from there up to Third Army, then to Twentieth Corps, then Allied Headquarters in Germany and finally to SHAEF in Paris. Then, of course, it would have to be bucked back down the chain of command.

"Christ," Riordan said. "We'd be old and gray if we waited for that. Actually, getting there is no problem. I know a guy at the airport who could smuggle us aboard something. But in Berlin, with no orders . . . We couldn't sign up with a mess for food, no transportation, nothing. If we got questioned, we'd end up in Leavenworth quicker than you could say fucking Eisenhower. I think you better give it up, George."

Barnstable was the mildest of men, one who ordinarily wouldn't dream of asking for favors or imposing on friendship, but the mindless military red tape finally succeeded in enraging him. He persuaded the switchboard operator at the I. G. Farben installation to put him through to Allied Military Headquarters in Berlin. While Riordan listened openmouthed, he asked for Colonel Amos Littleton, the deputy commander.

"Amos?" he said, "George Barnstable here. How the hell are you?" And then, "I need some orders to get me and my assistant from Frankfurt to Berlin, through the Zone. Any problem?"

He began to nod, and then to grin, as Riordan hugged him in silent glee.

Within forty-eight hours they had their travel orders, which read "Proceed by first available transport." Riordan said nothing but a car would do, as they could never get hold of one in Berlin for getting around there. First available was a sleek Czech Tatra touring car with an eight-cylinder air-cooled rear engine, which Riordan liberated from an *SS* colonel who, as Riordan pointed out, really had no further use for it. There was room in the Tatra for eight five-gallon cans of gasoline. With a full tank that provided fuel for a thousand miles.

The Autobahn from Frankfurt to Berlin, with its Russian checkpoints, was an adventure in itself. But not even the ruin of Frankfurt had prepared them for the devastation that was Berlin. It was stupefying. Some streets had been cleared of rubble and were passable, but much of the city was choked with huge chunks of granite piled sometimes two stories high. There were craters, caves and mountains of rubble; cables and water pipes projected from the ground like the mangled bowels of antedeluvian monsters. There was neither fuel nor light, every little garden was a graveyard and above all hung, like an immovable cloud, the stink of putrefaction.

In this no-man's-land lived human beings whose lives were a daily struggle for a handful of potatoes, a loaf of bread, a few lumps of coal, some cigarettes. Women were employed at clearing the roads of rubble with their bare hands, stone by stone.

And a new terror had gripped the city: a killing cold. In the streets it attacked the people like a wild beast, driving them indoors, into houses that offered little or no protection. The windows had no panes, but were nailed up with boards and pasteboard. The walls and ceilings were full of cracks and holes covered with paper and rags. People heated their rooms with benches from the public parks, cut down the trees in the Grünewald, even burned up their own furniture. Receding only temporarily, the cold broke into the rooms again with double fierceness, and the wind defiantly whistled through all the cracks and leaks. The old and sick froze to death in their beds by the hundreds.

Within living memory Berlin had not experienced such a winter. More than twenty thousand Berliners died from either cold or starvation in that winter of 1946.

The city was a mountain of ruin, a gigantic monument to its own destruction.

70

At the edge of the Grünewald, the millionaires' suburb of Berlin, Barnstable and Riordan found the house of Barnstable's in-laws miraculously untouched by the war. Behind a high stone wall was a large chalet-style house built of fir and cedar, its interior paneled with still polished oak. Of the house's former owners, the Ullmans, there was no sign. They had vanished.

The occupants now were the former housekeeper, Frau Martz, and her younger twin brothers, both mustered out from the *Wehrmacht*, whom Riordan immediately dubbed the Terrible Twins. Rather than acting as caretakers, the family seemed to have taken permanent possession of the house and barely concealed their resentment at what they clearly considered Barnstable's intrusion. Since there was no question of his identity (Frau Martz recognized him immediately, although she hadn't seen him for thirteen years) and since the Ullman family was absent either permanently or otherwise, there was a certain validity in Barnstable's claim to ownership. Riordan's armament served to prevent any unpleasantness that might have arisen, and the two men moved into the house.

With the family Martz once more in the servants' quarters where they belonged, not without a certain amount of grumbling, Barnstable was free to roam the huge old house.

If nothing else, Frau Martz had been a good caretaker. The rooms were pristinely clean, the massive furniture gleamed with polish, clothes of every description still hung undisturbed in their closets, as though the family was expected home at any moment. It was a miracle that the Ullman home had escaped the Nazi policy of confiscation of Jewish property, a miracle that was explained when he found the uniform of a German general hanging in an upstairs closet. The house had evidently been commandeered by someone who obviously had a certain sympathy for the Ullman possessions.

Sadly he visited the suite where he had lived with his wife before he had taken her with him back to America. All changed in the years since, different furniture, different pictures on the walls, nothing to remind him of those precious times except the pain of memories.

The nursery still held its lonely toys and shelves of children's books. In a much-thumbed illustrated volume of *Till Eulenspiegel* he found the inscription ERICKA ULLMAN, HER BOOK and wondered which of the nieces he had never seen had written it.

In the sitting room which had been his mother-in-law's, he came across a family Bible published in 1888 and listing on its flyleaf all the Ullmans born since that date. There again, at the very last, was ERICKA: BORN TO HEINZ AND BERTHE ULLMAN, DECEMBER 24, 1938.

It was now December eleventh. In two more weeks his unknown niece would be eight years old—if, by some impossible chance, she still lived.

Riordan again proved his genius at foraging. He stocked the house with PX food, some excellent wines from confiscated *Wehrmacht* stores, baskets of black-market coal. His triumph was the acquisition of an Engineer generator truck, which provided the house with electricity for the first time in months. His coup warmed even the glacial face of Frau Martz. The plumbing, however, defeated him. The water mains in the Grünewald had not yet been repaired, so they were forced to carry water from the artesian well in the back garden of the estate.

They spent their first days getting in touch with the innumerable agencies and subagencies that might have any information as to the fate or whereabouts of the Ullman family. The two men combed Berlin, following every possible lead in their effort to find people who had known the Ullmans. Everywhere, on every available surface, were heartbreaking messages, such as "Family Breitz bombed out, moved to such-and-such an address" or "Family Teufels bombed out, moved to . . ." The task grew more hopeless as the days passed, an exercise in futility.

One gray and dreary afternoon they turned a corner and Barnstable grabbed Riordan's arm.

"Hold it. There's something here I want to see. Just go slow. It should be in the next square."

Riordan down-geared until the Tatra was barely creeping.

"There it is," said Barnstable, pointing. "Or was."

Riordan pulled over to the side of the partially cleared roadway, and they sat looking at the scene before them, reluctant to leave the slight warmth provided by the Tatra's heater. They were at one edge of what had been a small square on the outskirts of the city. The surrounding buildings were now heaps of rubble. The only thing standing was the skeleton of a tiny church. Three of the walls remained, windows emptied of glass. The roof was gone, but most of the spire still rose against the leaden sky.

"St. Stephen's Kirche. One of the most remarkable examples of sixteenth-century church architecture in existence. A perfect gem of a church—in miniature. Jesus, what a criminal waste!" Barnstable's voice betrayed his anger.

"Funny thing, blast effect," Riordan said. "You'd think that spire would be the first to go. You never know. One time I saw a farmhouse take a direct hit. Blew the thing all to hell, not a wall standing. Then when the dust settled, there was this old woman sitting in what had been the kitchen. Not a mark on her—except she was deaf as a post."

"We'll have to take a look—to see if there's any remote possibility of restoring it. If there isn't, then it becomes just one more report, one more murder in the cause of Peace on Earth. . . ."

Riordan made a sound in his throat. German architecture had got what was coming to it, in his book.

"We were married here," Barnstable said softly.

Riordan glanced at him.

"You're right," Barnstable said. "It's a Protestant church. Giselle wasn't much for religion. She was only labeled a Jew here in Germany. No, we were married here because it was . . . beautiful. That's all that was important."

"Well, it's a hell of a mess now," Riordan said practically. "Let's get on with it before we freeze our balls off."

Outside the car the cold was like a physical blow, searing the lungs and making the eyes water. Riordan reached in and rummaged in the back seat for his antitheft device consisting of an aircraft wheel chock, a length of chain and a padlock. This he chained to a front wheel so that it was impossible to move the car. Next he carefully locked all the doors.

The wind whipped their coats as they made their way to the gaping doorway of the church. From where the two men stood in the narthex, or entrance hall, the outline of the church as it had been was still discernible in the way the roof had collapsed. They could trace the length of the nave all the way to what had been the chancel, the space around the altar. Above the altar at the far end of the church, the supports of the domed apse were still partially intact, a spidery tracery still holding a few shards of stained glass. At the far end the heavy marble altar stood untouched, glaringly white against the gray stone.

Barnstable was shining his flashlight into the dimness. He let his eyes travel up the juncture to the cornice, where the roof had once rested. "Doesn't seem to be out of true. They really built to last in those days. Foundations are probably solid rock. No problem there."

"What do you think, George? Is it worth restoring?"

"I don't know. It looks like maybe sixty percent of the walls are okay, but it would take an engineer to tell for certain. I'll report it as a possible anyway."

Riordan wandered off toward the rear. After a moment he called. "Hey, George. There's a sort of path through all this shit. Looks like somebody has been using it as a shortcut."

"To where?" Barnstable joined Riordan. There did seem to be a path. The rubble had been pressed down or kicked aside to allow easier passage. The faint trace led toward the altar and beyond. Riordan was the first to see the wisp of smoke rising from the floor in back of the altar.

"What the hell is that?" he asked.

They started cautiously toward the smoke. Barnstable was suddenly aware that Riordan's .45 was in his hand, his big body in a catlike crouch. Behind the altar someone had made an effort to clear the flat stone flooring of some of its burden of dust and broken glass. From around the edges of one of the stones, tendrils of smoke rose a few feet before they were swept away by the bitter winds gusting through the building.

Barnstable reached for Riordan's arm.

"Put it away," he whispered. "A lot of these old churches have a crypt below the altar. It's called a martyrium. Usually the namesake saint is buried there."

"Well, this saint has started a fire. He must be as cold as I am.

74

Come on, George. There's got to be somebody down there. I think maybe we ought to see who it is.''

Barnstable hesitated. "There's probably someone living down there."

"You gonna leave it like that?"

Curiosity got the better of Barnstable. "No . . . I suppose not." He moved toward the corner of the chancel. "There should be some sort of stairway in one corner or the other. . . . Yep, I think this is it.''

Riordan joined him and saw at Barnstable's feet a square of corrugated metal. With his foot Riordan shifted this aside. A flight of worn stone steps led downward, faint light showing on the lowest ones. Riordan went swiftly down the steps, his boots scraping faintly on the grit-covered stone. Barnstable followed more slowly, his heart beating unaccountably fast.

The room they entered was large and noticeably warmer than the church above. The heat was coming from a small potbellied stove set against one wall. Next to it was a crate whose top was crowded with votive candles in their squat glass tubs, interspersed with altar candles of varying lengths. Some of these candles were lit, and their flames caused Riordan's body to cast a monstrous black shadow on wall and ceiling.

One side of the room was jam-packed with black-market goods piled indiscriminately. Barnstable saw a wrecked bicycle, jerry cans of gas, a heap of old clothes topped with worn unmatching shoes, several dun-colored cartons of US Army rations, scraps of wood and crumpled newspapers, a bright blue baby carriage piled high with lumps of bituminous coal, cartons of American cigarettes, matching gold candelabra leaning crazily in one corner.

"Jesus," Riordan breathed. "A million fucking dollars' worth of loot!''

At first Barnstable thought the room was empty, but as his eyes grew accustomed to the flickering light, he saw that there was a man sitting on a mattress. He directed the flashlight beam on the motionless figure. The man was dressed in a filthy *Wehrmacht* overcoat, his head in a Balaclava. The gaunt face was stubbled with weeks-old growth; dirt and soot were embedded in the deep folds of flesh. The flashlight's beam made his sunken eyes gleam, yellowed and bloodshot.

Then there was the smell.

"God," Riordan gasped. "I've seen krauts dead ten days that smelled better than this one.

"We ought to take him in—but not in the car. Maybe we could tie him to the back, and drive slow."

"We don't have any arrest powers. We have no right to take him in. . . ."

"I got arrest powers." Riordan patted the now holstered .45. "What in hell do you want to do? Leave him here—with all this loot?" Riordan waved an arm in exasperation, then, as he took in once more the extent of the supplies, said, "Man, oh, man, could I operate with this stuff."

"We could report it to the MPs. . . ."

"Yeah. And by the time they got off their fat asses to check it out, this bastard will be long gone. And all this beautiful loot . . ."

"One of us could stay, I suppose. . . ."

"Okay, old buddy. You do it. I'm gonna get some air before I blow my lunch. I'll leave you the sidearm—if you know where the safety is."

Barnstable sighed, recognizing the futility of talking about the rights of German citizens.

"Okay, Gavin. We'll take him in."

Riordan drew his .45 once more and gestured to the man. "Okay, Fritz. On your feet."

The man remained motionless.

"*Raus.*" Barnstable tried to make his voice firm and authoritative, and felt that he failed miserably. "*Du kommst mit.* You're coming with us."

The filthy skeleton got slowly to his feet, emaciated hands stretched out in supplication. "*Bitte* . . . please . . ."

At that moment there was a sound and a movement in the pile of old clothing near the foot of the mattress. Barnstable swung the beam of his flashlight. Riordan crouched instantly, .45 extended toward the mound of clothing.

Barnstable saw Riordan's finger tighten on the trigger and quickly called, "*Raus, raus! Macht du schnell aus. Wir werden dir nicht schader.* Come out. Don't be afraid. We won't hurt you."

76

The heap of clothing heaved and out of it rose the naked figure of a child.

Barnstable was first struck by the eyes, huge and luminous, far too large for the dirt-encrusted face. The eyes stared at him directly, unblinking.

Riordan's gaze was riveted on the swollen, inflamed pudenda, its labia crusted with dried blood, which had run down the inside of the pitifully thin thighs. And Riordan felt the rage begin to build within him.

Embarrassed by the girl's nakedness, Barnstable dropped the beam of his flashlight, and at the same time the child took a step forward. The flashlight caught the gleam of metal, and they both heard the clank of chain.

Riordan kicked aside the tumbled clothing. The flashlight showed them the leather collar that encircled the girl's ankle and the length of chain that led to an iron ring embedded in the wall.

"*Bitte, bitte . . .*" the scarecrow figure standing near the mattress croaked again, and moved as though to interpose himself between them and the child.

With one fluid movement Riordan brought the .45 backhanded against the man's head, and Barnstable sickly heard the crunch of bone. The man's body was flung back onto the mattress.

Riordan stooped to examine the padlock with which the chain was attached to the wall.

"He must have a key. . . ." Barnstable said uncertainly.

"Well, *you* look for it. I wouldn't touch the son of a bitch with a ten-foot pole." Riordan moved his body between the girl and the wall. "Stand back, George. There may be some ricochet. . . ."

The crack of the .45 was deafening. The heavy slug blew the padlock to bits. Riordan grabbed clothing indiscriminately from the pile and tossed it to Barnstable.

"Wrap her up and take her up to the car." He held out his keys. "Get the heater started. I'll join you in a minute."

"But what . . ." Barnstable began.

"Goddamnit. Do what I tell you, George!"

Barnstable wrapped the small figure in what seemed to be a

chesterfield. Unsure of her condition, he hesitated, wondering whether she could walk.

"Carry her, damnit! She's barefoot."

The child weighed nothing at all as he carried her up the stairs. He made his careful way through the ruined church, got the car unlocked, the motor started and the heater turned on. When he finally turned to her he found that he didn't know where to begin. The enormity of her situation left him tongue-tied. He could mumble things he thought might reassure her, like "You'll be all right now" and "We'll see that you're taken care of," when he realized that the girl wasn't responding at all. She hadn't said a word since they first saw her.

Finally he asked, "What's your name?" No response. Only those luminous eyes fixed on him.

Riordan appeared, stooped to recover his wheel chock, opened the front door and pushed his big body into the driver's seat. The Tatra took off with a squeal. They had gone no more than a few hundred yards when Barnstable heard the explosion.

"That was the gas," Riordan said tensely. And then, answering Barnstable's shocked silence, "Yeah, scratch one church. And scratch one Kraut bastard."

"My God! You didn't . . . ?"

"Yeah, I damn well did, George. The man was dead. I hit him too hard. If you want to put it that way. So I poured the gas over him and lit the son of a bitch. This way there won't be any questions asked."

I should have stopped it, Barnstable thought miserably, but he knew that Riordan was too strong for him, too tough, too *sure.*

"She tell you anything?" Riordan asked.

"No. She can't seem to talk."

"You better hope so, George. We wouldn't want her talking just now, would we?"

"No, I suppose not. . . . What now? She needs medical attention badly. A hospital."

"I don't think so. Too many questions—and not enough answers. I know a guy . . ."

*   *   *

Riordan's "guy" turned out to be a lieutenant in the 315th Medical Battalion Aid Station in a partially bombed-out hospital on the outskirts of the city. Riordan went in alone and returned with his doctor friend. Barnstable watched Riordan carry the child into the building and was struck by the tenderness with which he handled the frail little body.

Having turned off the motor, and with it the heater, he soon found himself shivering with cold. It was full dusk now, and snow had begun to fall steadily, sometimes whipped by rising gusts of wind that sent swirling clouds of white around the now lighted windows of the building.

When Riordan returned with the girl, now wrapped in brown hospital blankets, Barnstable had reached that stage of misery where he no longer cared about what might happen. All he could think of was the warmth and comfort of the Ullman house.

Riordan, again with that incongruous gentleness, passed the child to him and he held her close in his arms, feeling the shallow rise and fall of her breathing against his chest.

"Nothing wrong with her that time won't cure," Riordan said tersely, and then, the anger showing in his voice, "Except that she's been raped repeatedly—both front and back. My boy Charlie tells me that it wouldn't have hurt too much after the first few times. It seems cunts and assholes stretch with use—even with kids as young as this one. Add to that that she's half starved to death and you got the picture. Pretty, isn't it?

"They wouldn't let me leave her. It seems this facility is strictly for citizens of the good old USA. No Krauts allowed. They gave her some shots and got me in and out like I had the plague. Any ideas, George?"

"Only one. Home. We'll think about what to do in the morning."

"Home it is," Riordan said, and then, "Oh, yes. We'll have to clean her up. They gave me some DDT—it seems the kid is crawling with lice."

Barnstable felt his skin creep in instinctive revulsion and was instantly ashamed.

The good Frau Martz categorically refused to touch the filthy bundle of humanity they brought to her spotless kitchen. The most she would concede was to heat enough water to partially fill the tub in an upstairs bathroom. She begrudged even that because of the precious fuel she was forced to use.

"Tell the old biddy to get her ass in gear and get the Terrible Twins to carry the water upstairs," Riordan said. "The bath can wait. The first thing is to get some food into the kid." With his usual efficiency he got the Coleman two-burner going, opened a can of soup and put it on to heat, then mixed a pitcher of powdered milk.

They had given her a hospital gown at the Aid Station. Now, with the blanket around her shoulders, the child sat unmoving at the kitchen table, her huge eyes watching Riordan's every move. When the bowl was placed before her she grabbed it and began to wolf the food down voraciously.

"Slowly, slowly," Barnstable warned. At the sharpness of his tone the girl stopped gulping instantly and stared at him.

"It's all right," he said more gently. "Don't be afraid. Just eat more slowly."

She made an effort to obey, but the bowl was soon empty.

"My, my," Riordan said. "That is one hungry kid."

"At least she understands what I say."

"Tell her to drink the milk. And then we'll clean her up."

The upstairs bathroom was steamy with warmth. Frau Martz, probably from some feeling of guilt, had laid out heavy towels and a bathrobe and nightgown that must have belonged to some absent Ullman child.

Riordan tested the water with his finger. "Okay, baby. In you go."

Barnstable took the blanket and untied the strings at the back of the hospital gown. The girl dropped it on the floor and, without any embarrassment, stepped into the tub and sat down. Riordan made motions with his hands, indicating that she should lie flat. She slowly let her body slide into the warm water until her head rested on the edge of the tub. Then she closed her eyes.

The men looked at one another, each seeing the question in the other's eyes.

"You ever washed a kid, dads?"

80

"No," Barnstable said uncertainly. "Maybe she can do it herself...?"

Riordan grinned at him. "No way. But there can't be all that much to it." He shucked out of his field jacket and rolled up his shirtsleeves. "Here, hand me the washcloth and the soap. Old mother Riordan is about to go to work."

Barnstable was struck once more by the deftness of Riordan's big hands, the gentleness with which he laved the girl's face. The layered grime took time to remove. The lank hair, which had seemed to be a sooty gray, turned out to be shining blond, the skin, when it was revealed, so white it was almost translucent.

"Tell her to stand up, so I can get at the rest of her."

The hot water had loosened some of the encrusted dirt. Barnstable gasped at what was revealed. All of the emaciated torso was crisscrossed with ugly red welts and dark purple bruises.

"Jesus Christ," Riordan breathed. "The son of a bitch! The son of a bitch..."

He reached out and turned the girl around. Her back and thighs showed the same cruel lacerations. Grim-faced, the muscles jumping in his jaws, Riordan began to clean the wounds with infinite tenderness.

"George, there's a first-aid kit in my room. Go get it. Some of these need sulfa pads—and powder."

Barnstable left on the run, thankful to get away. He had found the first-aid kit and started back with it when he was overcome by nausea. He used Riordan's bathroom to throw up, embarrassed that he couldn't flush the toilet.

Later, with the child asleep in the room next to Barnstable's, they ate a silent meal in the kitchen. With coffee Riordan produced a bottle of schnapps.

"You and your goddamned churches," Riordan said irritably. "If it wasn't for you, I'd be back in Frankfurt, bugging the brass to get me out of this fucking army." And then, voicing what was uppermost in their minds, "What the hell are we going to do about her?"

"Surely there are agencies... Displaced persons..."

"You ever seen a DP camp, George?"

Barnstable shook his head.

"Well, I have. And I wouldn't put a dog in one of 'em. Besides, what did you have in mind? Just leave her on the doorstep like it was a parish church?"

Riordan downed his schnapps in one gulp and poured himself another.

"Face it, George. Sooner or later that kid is going to get her tongue back. She's going to talk—and maybe nothing will happen. And then again, maybe she'll hand it right back to us. If I ever get my ass in a jam like that, I'll never get out of the goddamned army."

"Yes, you might even end up in Leavenworth," Barnstable said waspishly, resentful that Riordan had somehow placed all the blame on him. "*I* didn't kill the man."

Riordan looked at him steadily, and Barnstable found that he couldn't meet his eyes. "And you, George, old buddy, might end up with a fat lip, you give me any more of that kind of shit," Riordan said.

"I'm sorry, Gavin," Barnstable said miserably. "I didn't mean it. Of course, I accept responsibility for my part . . ."

"That's what I'm talking about. Responsibility. Here we got this kid hung around our necks like a live grenade, and all you come up with is cracks about Leavenworth. You got to do better than that, George. You're the guy that picks up the phone and calls big shots at the drop of the hat. You're the guy with the muscle. You're the guy who's lived in this fucking country. Where's all these 'good Germans' you been telling me about? Surely there must be somebody you could lay some of your loot on to take this kid off our hands—and keep a tight asshole. I figure it's up to you, George."

Riordan's sudden abdication of leadership was disconcerting. "I don't know," Barnstable said uncertainly. "Maybe I can think of somebody . . ."

"You do that, George." Riordan got to his feet. "You give it lots of thought—because I'm going to hit the sack now so I can wake up bright and early to hear how you've got our ass out of the sling."

Before going to his own bed, Barnstable looked in on the girl. Her blond hair was spread out on the pillow. Her pale face, which had been so closed and tight, was now relaxed and open with all the

82

innocence of childhood. For the first time his artist's eye took in the planes of her head, the delicate bone structure now too prominent under the skin, the full mouth perfectly placed in the oval face, the small pointed chin with its suggestion of a cleft, and he realized that the child had a rare beauty that cried out to be captured on canvas. In his mind he could see the first rough strokes of charcoal outlining the high forehead, then the prominent cheekbones.

He left her door cracked so that she could see his light if she roused, and went to his room. Lying awake, he tried to resurrect the Germans he had known in what now seemed to him another life that bore no faintest relation to the here and now. The process acted on him like counting sheep, an endless procession of half-remembered faces from a past as remote as the moon. The only reality it held for him was the memory of his wife—and it was of her he dreamed. Of loving her, and being loved—the joy of touching, feeling, being engulfed by her, the remembrance of such sweet warmth.

The orgasm of his dream was so real that it pulled him out of sleep.

He opened his eyes to golden gossamer hair spread across his thighs, a small head bobbing as it received the last of his ejaculation.

The instant of realization brought its instinctive reaction. He struck out blindly, the force of his blow tumbling the child from the bed to the floor. As he leaped to his feet, she curled her body into a tight protective ball, her face a mass of fear and shock, the marks of his fingers already livid against the pale skin.

And then she spoke, her voice a plea for understanding. "I was hungry," she said in German. "He feeds me when I do that."

Barnstable dropped to the floor and gathered the little girl into his arms. He sat there rocking her gently back and forth, crooning to her in German. "I'm sorry! Don't be afraid. Never be afraid again. You'll never have to be afraid. Never again. . . ."

He lay awake for a long time, seriously evaluating George Barnstable. Something he couldn't remember ever having done before. He had grown up in the safety of considerable wealth, in the thoughtful care of loving parents. The things he properly needed or wanted were provided as a matter of course. Even though he had been the gifted one, there had never been the usual sibling rivalry with his older sister. They loved each other deeply, and their relationship had grown even closer with the death of both parents in an automobile accident. That was the first time tragedy had disrupted the even, comfortable tenor of his life.

A lesser disturbance was the early realization that his talent for painting was a minor one and would never provide the fulfillment he needed. Architecture had taken care of that. He had thrown himself into that profession with all the passion and dedication he had first given to art. With the help of family connections and his inheritance, he had become immensely successful with what seemed to him now almost embarrassing ease.

He was not a man who made things happen. He was a man things happened *to*—and most of them had been good. Even his marriage to Giselle Ullman had been without tumult. They had met, they had fallen in love, without doubt or question. Their four short years together had been full of grace and a sublime happiness that he now realized they had both accepted as their due. Her death from cancer had been a numbing shock. As that wore off he found that he had his work to fill the void. And he was very good at what he did. There was an immense satisfaction in creative building, an excitement that was almost sexual.

But here, in this alien atmosphere, he had none of the certainty that had marked his work. He had fallen into a curious lethargy, an inertia, unable or unwilling to relate to the nightmare aftermath of war. He seemed to have lost his identity, become a mere observer, uninvolved, untouched by the life and death that surrounded him. He had come to Germany to try to help the Ullmans. That proving impossible, he had found nothing else to do to assuage his growing sense of detachment, inadequacy and guilt.

Until tonight.

He awoke early and tiptoed to her door. The girl was seated cross-legged on the floor, turning the pages of his portfolio with the rapt absorption of childhood. He watched for a moment as his work unfolded, half-finished renderings of bombed out buildings with his marginal notes, charcoal sketches of people, houses, a wrecked tank

84

on a Berlin street, memory sketches of Riordan in a dozen unposed positions.

"Guten Morgen."

She looked up and returned his greeting gravely, and as gravely went back to his drawings. When he asked her name, she shook her head without looking up.

"I'll see if Frau Martz can find you some clothes. And then come down to breakfast." She was still turning pages as he left her.

Like most Germans, Frau Martz responded best to firm orders, and she was no match for Barnstable's new assurance. By the time Riordan came down she had returned with the girl, who was now dressed in Ullman castoffs, which fitted passably—a plaid skirt, white shirtwaist, stockings and tennis shoes. Barnstable could see from Frau Martz's shocked expression that she had done a complete about-face.

"The beatings . . . !" she said. "How could such a thing happen? Who would do such a thing to a child?"

"I don't know," Barnstable said.

"But such a person should be put in jail. . . ."

"Leave it, Frau Martz," Barnstable said firmly. "There is nothing to be done—except to take care of her now."

That Frau Martz proceeded to do, serving her first and more often than the others, hovering about her solicitously while they ate.

Riordan, who was never at his best in the morning, looked on with an amused eye.

"You come up with anything, George?"

"Later. I think I've got it solved."

Riordan grinned irritatingly. "Somehow I thought you would, George. Nothing like a little thought in the reaches of the night."

If you only knew, Barnstable thought with considerable satisfaction.

After breakfast he took the girl to the nursery. If he had expected childish raptures over the toys left behind by the Ullman children, he was disappointed. She examined each one politely before going to the next, still with that same adult gravity. The picture book of *Till Eulenspiegel* seemed to hold her interest longest. On impulse he left her to go to his room and return with a blank sketch pad and several lengths of charcoal.

She accepted the materials without hesitation and began to make tentative strokes on the paper. When Riordan called she was so absorbed in what she was doing that he felt it safe to leave her.

Riordan had built a small fire in the darkly paneled living room and was drinking an after-breakfast coffee. He looked up expectantly as Barnstable joined him.

Without preamble Barnstable told him, "I'm going to adopt her. We'll send her home to my sister. She'll take care of her until I get back."

Riordan's look of utter incredulity brought him up short.

"What's wrong with that?"

"George, George." Riordan's head was moving back and forth. "You got to be out of your mind."

"Why the hell not?" Barnstable was beginning to be angry and determined not to let Riordan shake his decision. "Why the hell shouldn't I, if I choose to?"

"Listen to me, George," Riordan said patiently. "Just listen a minute. Eisenhower himself couldn't adopt a German national and send her back to the States. There's about three million DPs in this country, and every damn one trying to get to the States—the Land of the Free. And nobody's making it. Because that's the fucking *law*! And here you want to take some nameless kid and . . ."

"I've decided to call her Ericka," Barnstable interrupted irrelevantly, "until she decides to tell us her real name. . . ."

Riordan threw up his hands in disgust.

"Ericka . . ." Barnstable said slowly. "Maybe I've got an idea. Ericka Ullman . . . my niece. Why couldn't we pass this one off as Ericka. Born in 1938. It's in the family Bible. The ages would be about right. The real Ericka is undoubtedly dead. . . . A relative. I'm her uncle. Only living relative. Wouldn't that make a difference?"

"It might. . . . Damned if I know. You sure you want to do this, George?"

"I was never surer of anything in my life."

"Well, now . . ." Riordan began to grin, caught up by one more chance to beat the system. "It's sure as hell worth a try. You'd need papers, of course. . . ."

Both men got up swiftly, moved by the same thought, but their thorough search of the house and an interrogation of Frau Martz produced a meager bag. There was the Bible listing the birth of Ericka Ullman, a thin stack of school report cards and a framed snapshot of a child of about four years who bore little resemblance to the girl upstairs.

Back in the living room Riordan hefted the evidence thoughtfully. "Not much here, is there? Not enough, really. On the other hand, I know a guy who just might . . ."

Barnstable burst into uncontrollable laughter. "I knew you would," he gasped. "Somehow I just knew you would."

This time Riordan's friend was a Catholic chaplain who was in charge of a unit called Collation and Evaluation. Its work was resettling defectors from Eastern Europe in the West.

Riordan said, "He tries to figure out which are the real defectors and which are the ones the Russians are trying to plant on us. Most of these guys want the US, but that's no go, right? So they got the rest of the world to resettle in. So, if my guy guesses wrong, the Reds have spies planted everywhere you can think of. Of course, it can work the other way, too. If my guy can recruit them for the US, then *we* got spies planted all over.

"Part of Parnell's work is to supply *our* guys with the right kind of papers. Man, he has engravers the US Mint would be proud of. They could give Dracula documents to prove he was Winston Churchill—and get away with it."

Chaplain Thomas Parnell proved to be an old friend of Des Daniher and more than willing to oblige Daniher's ward. The documentation required seemed to Barnstable to be staggering. It included a *Kennkarte*, the basic identity card every German had to possess, containing date and place of birth, birth certificate, local police registration, federal government registration, parents' proof of citizenship and, finally, medical history. Each of these papers had to carry a number of stamps, each different from the other.

All this presented no insuperable problem for Tom Parnell's experts. The hitch, as Parnell pointed out, was that the papers weren't worth a damn unless Ericka could learn to play the part created for her. One wrong word in the wrong place and the whole deception would go up in smoke.

Barnstable agreed to take on the job of educating the newborn Ericka Ullman. He had his first doubts when Father Parnell suggested that what George wanted to do came a little close to playing God.

Parnell, his wind-chapped face gravely intent, explained to him, "You are taking responsibility for a living human being. You must realize that the child now has a lifelong claim on you. You must feed, clothe and shelter her. Her claim on you is absolute. You are giving her the right to say to you, 'I am yours forever. And if I am yours—you are mine.' Are you prepared for this?"

"I think I am," Barnstable answered. "I've given it a lot of thought, and it's what I want to do. The main problem, as I see it, is speed. We've got to get her out of here fast. Otherwise too many things might happen. The real Ericka might be alive. The child's parents might surface. Or the Martz twins might turn us in. But once she's out of here I'm sure I can handle anything that comes up."

"So be it," Parnell said soberly. "As long as you know what you're getting into."

What George Barnstable had in mind was to enlist once again the aid of Colonel Amos Littleton. As he explained, Colonel Littleton was more than a friend, he was a first cousin and therefore a relative of sorts to the reborn Ericka Ullman. He could hardly refuse to help.

Riordan had his doubts, and insisted on accompanying Barnstable on his visit to OMGUS, the Office of Military Government of the United States. They found that OMGUS installations were spread out over half of Berlin, for the organization had some ten thousand members. It took them half the morning to find the office of Deputy Commander Littleton.

Their first surprise was to find that Colonel Littleton was now General Littleton. The next came when they were ushered into the anteroom of General Littleton's aide. Barnstable saw a handsome, impeccably uniformed young first lieutenant wearing Air Force insigne who was smiling affably at him. The smile disappeared when the lieutenant's eyes went past him. He heard Riordan's indrawn breath.

"Jesus Christ! Stewart!"

The lieutenant's smile returned. It seemed to Barnstable a little hesitant. Riordan went past him and the two young men faced each other. There was a certain wariness in the lieutenant's face, and Barnstable could sense the tension in Riordan.

Then Riordan said, "Ah, what the hell," and stuck out his hand. The lieutenant took it eagerly.

"What the hell are you doing here, Stewart?" asked Riordan.

"Air Force liaison to General Littleton."

"It figures," Riordan said. "George, meet Stewart Gansvoort, a . . . boyhood chum of mine."

Gansvoort was still pumping Riordan's arm. "Gavin! It's good to see you," he said, and appeared to mean it.

"George Barnstable," said Riordan, retrieving his hand. "He's the general's cousin. *First* cousin."

Gansvoort shook Barnstable's hand with equal enthusiasm. "He's out right now. Back soon, though. Maybe I can help you. Most things go through me anyhow. What's the problem?"

Barnstable started to say it was a personal matter, but too late.

"It's about another relative of George's . . . and the general's, sort of," Riordan said. "We found her over here and he wants to get her back to the States."

Gansvoort was immediately businesslike. He gave the impression that anything could be solved if it had his personal attention. He listened in silent absorption as Barnstable told his story. When he had finished with "So you see how anxious I am to get my niece out of all this," Gansvoort nodded gravely.

"I know Ullman Publishing. I believe my father had some sort of interest in it. We had rather heavy investments in Germany before the war. I suppose there's nothing left?"

"Nothing," Barnstable said, "and no trace of the family."

"Well. You *have* got a problem." Gansvoort smiled charmingly. "We can certainly give it a try. . . ."

Barnstable found he was beginning to like this obliging young man and was surprised when Riordan said, "Stop stalling, Stewart. Can your general do it or not?"

Gansvoort's smile disappeared, replaced by sympathetic understanding, as if they were all in this together.

"That's the thing. He could do it, all right, by bending a lot of rules. The question is, will he? He's pretty gung ho. Plays it mostly by the book. He just got his star a few weeks ago, and he . . ."

He was interrupted by the opening of the office door as Brigadier General Amos Littleton entered. His piercing blue eyes took in the scene and its implications at once. He knew immediately that this was not a purely social visit.

Gansvoort came to attention. Riordan saluted and the general returned it briefly. Despite himself, Barnstable was impressed. Three years older than his cousin, he was used to treating Amos Littleton as a decidedly junior member of the family. He didn't know whether to salute or what. Littleton relieved his uncertainty by holding out his hand and saying, "Hello, George. Nice to see you. Why don't we go into my office."

He strode across the room, Barnstable following meekly, confidence oozing out of him, unsure of how to approach this cousin who now seemed a stranger.

The door closed behind the two men. Gavin Riordan was left alone with Stewart Gansvoort—and an awkward silence.

For lack of something better, Riordan said, "What do you hear from home?"

"If you mean Serena, she's married." And then, "Look, Gavin, I . . ." There seemed to be a kind of pleading in Gansvoort's eyes. Riordan responded to it.

"Forget it, Stewart. I have. All that was in another world. Besides, I guess I had it coming. . . ."

Stewart Gansvoort held out his hand, and Riordan took it. Both men began to grin hugely.

"Serena's a bit of a tramp, you know."

"Yeah. God, how that thing hurt. My first wound. I've had three others since, but that one really scared the shit out of me."

"Three?" Stewart looked at the ribbons on Riordan's uniform

blouse. "What are you doing over here? Surely you've got the points..."

"Well, it's a long story." Riordan sighed. "First the bastards lost my 201 file—sort of accidentally on purpose. Then..." The whole sad story came pouring out of him. When Riordan had laid one last curse on Army red tape, Stewart leaned back in his chair and told him to stop worrying.

"A request from this office has got to get some action. I'll start the ball rolling first thing. Bet we have you straightened out in no time. Should be a hell of a lot easier than Barnstable's niece. That could be a real problem."

At that moment the door to the general's office opened. One look at George Barnstable's face told Riordan the problem was real indeed.

Littleton was saying "—of course, it's thicker than water. But not in the book, and I simply won't do it. You'll have to go through channels. I'll help where I can, but that's all I'll do. It's just too much to ask, George. And you know it."

"I'm damned if I do." Anger had given Barnstable back his confidence. "It seems a simple enough request."

"No," Littleton said. There was no mistaking the finality of the word. "If you want to go through channels, Lieutenant Gansvoort will find out the proper procedure for you."

He held out his hand and Barnstable took it somewhat reluctantly.

"I'm sorry, George." Littleton retired behind his door.

"I was afraid of that." Gansvoort's tone was rueful. Then, with determined cheer, "Maybe it's not so bad, after all. I'll look into the procedure for you right away. Maybe things can be speeded up...."

To Barnstable it sounded like a hollow promise.

Christmas morning of 1946 dawned sharp and bright, the temperature slightly above zero. It was a Christmas Berliners would never forget. There was very little food, and more than half the city lacked heat, water and light. Bands of DPs haunted the streets, murdering and pillaging. The only police protection came from the occupying armies, and that was next to nothing.

In the American zone things were not so bad—for Americans, that is. The supreme commander in Europe had declared that every soldier away from home and mother would have a Christmas dinner. More than a thousand turkeys passed through Tempelhof Airport alone—enough to feed every GI in Germany four times over. Inevitably two of these noble birds ended up in Riordan's hands— plus a No. 10 can of cranberry sauce, six loaves of Army bread, a five-pound bag of potatoes, two bunches of celery and a bag of onions, a can of Planters peanuts and a chocolate cake bearing the legend HAPPY BIRTHDAY TO EDGAR in pink icing. The cake was past its prime but Frau Martz was ecstatic.

Barnstable was determined not to let the official setback spoil Ericka's Christmas. It was decided to wait until after the feast to open gifts so that Father Parnell could be present. Parnell arrived promptly at noon to a house redolent of Frau Martz's kitchen magic.

"Thanks be to God—and General Ike. And I'm not sure which should come first," Parnell exclaimed. "I haven't smelled anything like it since I left my parish." He handed Barnstable four tapered candles. "I brought these to grace the festive board. It's hardly Christmas without candles. And, of course, these," he said, holding out a second offering. "It's all there, everything you'll need."

Barnstable took the fat manila envelope with a feeling close to panic. For the first time he realized fully that, with the acceptance of these papers, he had in effect become a father. With all responsibilities and none of the anticipatory joys of parenthood. The thought was sobering.

"Has she told you anything yet? Her background . . . ? What happened to her?"

"No," he said slowly, "at least, not in words. . . . But come into the living room. There's something I want you to see."

Barnstable had spent considerable time trying to probe the child's mind. His questions had been gentle and ingeniously roundabout, with no results. She had accepted the name Ericka without question, and she had become more open about everyday things and the routine of the household, expressing preferences about food, a dislike for certain clothes and approval of others. In short she had begun acting like any normal child. But about herself—nothing. Just that bland, grave shake of the head, as though his questions had no meaning for her. He had begun to wonder if she were not in fact an amnesiac, if what had happened to her was so traumatic that she had blocked it from her mind.

Then he had picked up the sketch pad he had given her to play with. She had almost filled it with her drawing, and he went through it with rising excitement.

Now he placed the pad in Parnell's hands and watched him carefully as he turned the pages.

At first the child had tried to copy some of the drawings she had seen in Barnstable's portfolio. There was a burnt-out tank, the partially destroyed wall of a building. Then came several pages of faces and figures. The figures were clothed, and the faces always the same, a man and a woman. Next there was what was recognizably a child's room, with a cot, a desk and a hobbyhorse. On one wall hung a crucifix. The last page showed a three-story house with flames coming from every window.

"Well," Barnstable asked eagerly. "What do you see?"

Parnell was thoughtful. Then, "From the crucifix one could presume that she was a Catholic. . . ."

Barnstable almost stuttered. "That's easy. Come on, what else?"

"You want me to say that she has drawn her parents and her burning house? Well, that's possible, of course. But hardly conclusive. . . ."

Impatiently, Barnstable grabbed the sketch pad from Parnell's hands and began to flip through the pages.

"Damnit! You're missing the point. How many times have you seen kids' drawings?" And at Parnell's look of bewilderment, "Kids' drawings are all flat. One-dimensional. Like a primitive. Here, look, can't you see it?" He stabbed his finger at a drawing. "This kid draws in perspective—or at least something approaching it!"

"Yes. I see what you mean. But what . . . ?"

"God doesn't just give you that. It's got to be learned. Somebody had to teach her. An artist . . ."

"You think perhaps one of her parents . . ." Parnell said softly. And then, "Does this change your mind about getting her out? You think her parents could be located using this as a clue?"

Barnstable looked at him, suddenly deflated. His excitement had stemmed from the discovery of a budding talent, nothing else. Now he found that the prospect of losing her was unbearable. All sorts of rationalizations flitted through his mind. She had become a symbol to him, a link to his childless marriage to Giselle, a wish to avoid the emptiness of a childless future, a chance to live for someone other than himself.

"No . . . I made a decision. And I'm going to stick with it. Nothing is going to change my mind."

Parnell's shrewd eyes probed his. "You have your reasons. And you're obviously not asking for advice, so I'm not about to give it. I'll reserve that for my parishioners, if I ever get home. Now—how about meeting your young lady."

They heard the front door slam and Riordan singing *White Christmas* in a pleasant baritone. He was carrying a faded Army barracks bag.

"Tom. How goes the battle? Man, I could smell that turkey clear out in the garage. Why don't we get at it?"

Barnstable walked to the door and called, "Ericka."

"Ericka," Parnell said, smiling. "It does have a nice ring to it."

They waited expectantly as they listened to the child's unhurried footsteps on the stairs.

Frau Martz had resurrected a pink dress with ruffles at its hem, once worn by an Ullman for some long-forgotten party. Her golden hair was held back smoothly with a pink ribbon. She accepted Parnell's hand gravely, and then, surprising them all, she curtsied in a brief bob.

Riordan was the first to speak. "I know presents are supposed to come after dinner, but these can't wait."

He reached into his barracks bag and, with the air of a conjurer, produced one at a time three bottles of Haig & Haig.

"Save us!" Parnell gasped. "In the name of all that's holy, where did you find it?"

"Well, I know a guy." Riordan grinned.

"What are you waiting for?" asked Barnstable. "Get it poured while I put these candles on the table."

When Barnstable had left, Riordan, his back to Parnell, busied himself with the whiskey. "What do you think, Tom? About the kid?"

"I don't know the man, Gavin. But he seems determined. Perhaps it would be best for the child . . ."

Riordan turned to Parnell and passed him his glass. "He's a good man, Tom. In the best Christian sense. He could give her a kind of life she'd never have here, even if her parents showed up. But I'm not sure he knows what he's getting into. He's had a sheltered life."

Parnell turned to where Ericka was sitting primly on the sofa, not understanding, eyes turning to each of them as they spoke.

"She *is* an enchanting child," said Parnell.

"Yes," Riordan said thoughtfully. "You could certainly say that. It's what worries me. . . ."

The long dining room table was set for four, with Barnstable at its head. Father Parnell's candles, now in graceful silver candlesticks, added just the right festive air.

Even Riordan hadn't been able to produce a Christmas tree in this city where every stick of wood was precious. But, over Frau Martz's outraged protests, Barnstable had confiscated one of the Ullmans' linen sheets and on it had painted a lifelike pine tree, complete with tinsel, colored balls and, at the top, an angel whose face was Ericka's.

A meager pile of presents was spread out on the top of the sideboard. The biggest was a cardboard carton, labeled for Frau Martz, whose contents Riordan had stubbornly refused to reveal.

To Barnstable, Parnell had from the first seemed more fellow officer than priest, so he was unprepared when, at table, Parnell placed his palms together, closed his eyes and began to say grace. His voice took on a resonance that gave the occasion a certain solemnity. It was a moving prayer, and Barnstable felt himself caught up by the obvious sincerity. He said his own amen in heartfelt agreement.

"And now," Parnell finished, "having done my Christian duty—in heaven's name, let's eat."

The meal was a complete success, a tribute to gluttony. They ate until they could eat no more, washing down the food with the last bottles from the Ullmans' wine cellar. The men had relaxed with lighted cigars when Barnstable noticed Ericka's eyes straying toward the presents and was immediately ashamed of his thoughtlessness. He called Frau Martz from the kitchen and they set about opening gifts, with Barnstable acting as Santa.

Ericka's first gift was from Frau Martz, a set of colored ribbons for her hair that Frau Martz had carefully hand-sewn from remnants of fabric. Ericka thanked her properly, and Barnstable thought, not for the first time, that her unknown parents must have been people of refinement. Her huge eyes sparkled when Riordan handed her a full box of Hershey chocolate bars.

Riordan's present to Frau Martz proved to be the hit of the show. When he broke open the carton for her, he revealed a portable sewing machine to replace the one she had so regretfully parted with long since in exchange for black-market food and fuel. The candle-light flickered on the black enamel and gleaming chrome of the compact little marvel and on the tears in Frau Martz's eyes. Not content with her grateful kiss on his cheek, Riordan gave her a robust buss and a firm pat on the bottom, which turned the tears to giggles.

For Father Parnell, Riordan produced a box of Havana cigars, and for Barnstable a German officer's leather coat lined with sleek dark fur that Barnstable was certain was sable.

"My God. Sable is worth a fortune!"

"Then the guy I got it from didn't know it. He seemed happy enough with two cartons of Luckies."

Barnstable's gift to Riordan was a watercolor of Riordan leaning against a burnt-out Tiger tank. He had captured Riordan in a contemplative mood, eyes squinted, smoke curling upward from a cigarette jutting through his bristling red beard, battered helmet pushed back on his head, carbine slung from one shoulder.

Riordan was speechless. His awed appreciation warmed Barnstable's artist's soul.

"That's damned good," Parnell offered.

"Yes. Isn't it," Barnstable agreed objectively.

"George . . ." For once Riordan fumbled for words. "What can I say? There's nothing I would rather have had. . . ."

At that moment came a firm knocking at the front door. They looked at one another. A knock at the door in devastated Berlin seldom heralded good news. Riordan started to get up, but Frau Martz waved him away. Looking apprehensive, she went to answer the summons. Presently they heard voices. After a few moments Frau Martz ushered in Stewart Gansvoort. Surprise kept them silent. Gansvoort took in the remains of the feast, the crumpled gift wrappings.

"I'm sorry. I didn't mean to interrupt . . ."

Belatedly Barnstable jumped up. "Of course not. Come in. You're just in time for a drink."

"No, really." Gansvoort seemed embarrassed. "I just came by to leave this. . . ."

He held out a manila envelope, which Barnstable accepted without looking at it, at the same time taking Gansvoort's arm insistently.

"Of course you'll stay. It's Christmas, man."

Gansvoort looked briefly at Riordan, who said, "Relax, Stewart. Share the wealth." He held up his bottle of Scotch.

"Stewart Gansvoort, Father Tom Parnell," Barnstable said. "And this is . . . Ericka."

They were all looking at the child except Riordan, who happened to be watching Stewart Gansvoort. He saw on Gansvoort's face the immediate appreciation of the girl's beauty—and something else. Just a vague reminder of something he had seen before in the dimness of a tack room long ago. It was gone before he could be certain, as Stewart smilingly took the little girl's hand.

Frau Martz took Gansvoort's cap and greatcoat. Father Parnell poured generous drinks and raised his in a toast.

"To Christmas past, and Christmas present, and let's hope future ones will be happier."

Barnstable still held the envelope Gansvoort had brought, and Stewart said, "You'd better open it."

Barnstable raised it, and they could all see the legend, boldly black: OFFICE OF MILITARY GOVERNMENT OF THE UNITED STATES FOR GERMANY. Barnstable briefly looked at the papers inside and silently handed them to Riordan. They all watched as Riordan read.

"Stewart . . ." Riordan was unbelieving. "What the hell . . . ?"

"It's official, Gavin. Signed and sealed. You're on a MATS flight at 8:30 A.M. on New Year's Day. Destination: Fort Dix, New Jersey.

"And you're taking the young lady with you."

A slow grin broke over Riordan's face. "I'll be a double-dyed son of a bitch. Stewart, you're a *genius*. How the hell did you get the old bastard to okay it?"

"Military secret," Stewart said, his grin matching Riordan's. "It's sort of a Christmas present."

Barnstable was pumping Gansvoort's hand. "Wonderful! Wonderful! I'll have to see Amos and thank him."

Stewart lost his grin. "I don't think I'd do that, sir. . . ."

Barnstable looked bewildered.

"Stewart," Riordan said very softly. "Did you cut these orders yourself?"

Stewart shifted his weight uneasily. "Not exactly. . . ."

Riordan examined the signature on the travel order.

"He signed them, all right," Stewart said defensively. "He just didn't know what he was signing. They'll stand up, if that's what's worrying you."

Riordan shook his head from side to side. "You dumb bastard. Don't you know if he finds out, it's your ass in the sling for sure?"

"No reason he ever should." Stewart tried a brief smile. "Besides, what could he do—fire me?"

Riordan realized that what he really meant was *You don't fire Gansvoorts*.

George Barnstable said, "I can't let you do it, of course. Although I appreciate . . ."

"Oh, yes, you can," Riordan interrupted, "because it's already done. Stewart can take care of himself."

His eyes held Gansvoort's. "And, Stewart . . . many, many thanks." He saw that Stewart understood his meaning, that things were evened-up—as of now.

For the first time since he had arrived, Gansvoort appeared completely at ease. He smiled his charming smile at all of them.

"Think nothing of it, Gavin. And now duty calls. I've got to run. Thanks for the drink." And as Frau Martz got him into his coat, "The best of luck, and Merry Christmas to all."

Then he was gone. Barnstable, remembering the tension he had sensed between the two men, couldn't contain his curiosity. "Why the devil did he do it, Gavin?"

"To bury a bad case of the guilts, I think." Riordan shook his shoulders as if to rid himself of an unpleasant thought. "I hope it works for him. Stewart's got more problems than a man really needs."

Riordan began to grin and then to laugh. He pounded Barnstable on the back. "Hey, George! I'll be home for Christmas. Or almost. What do you think of that? French fries and Mom's apple pie in the good ol' USA!"

Barnstable had a momentary pang of envy. Then, over Riordan's shoulder, he saw Ericka watching them, her face alive with curiosity. "I almost forgot," he said to her. "There's one more present for you." He handed her an oblong box from the sideboard.

It was a set of artist's colored chalks. He watched her face as she opened it. For a moment she stared at the bright sticks, one hand coming out tentatively to touch them. Then she looked up and smiled at him.

It was the first time he had ever seen her smile, and his heart turned over.

For Barnstable that smile made all Christmases worthwhile.

9

Time: 1947
GAVIN RIORDAN

Riordan played poker the whole flight home and won more than six hundred dollars in Occupation scrip. The big loser, a finance captain from I Corps, assured him he could cash it in at the Paymaster's Office at Dix. While he played, two Navy nurses, one of whom spoke a little German, happily took charge of Ericka.

The MATS plane landed at McGuire Air Force Base and Riordan cadged a ride for himself and Ericka with a mail truck returning to Fort Dix. Barnstable's sister was waiting for them in the visitors' lounge at the main gate.

Melinda Price was a striking woman who seemed considerably younger than the thirty-nine years Barnstable had claimed for her. She was dressed in a wrinkled skirt and a cashmere cardigan and carried over her arm a fur coat that Riordan's practiced "dealer's" eye identified as mink. She looked terribly tired.

Since the language barrier made introductions difficult, he merely said, "Ericka, Melinda. Melinda, Ericka," enunciating very clearly, and watched the older woman vacillate between opening her arms and holding out her hand. Ericka settled it by curtsying gravely.

"Been waiting long?"

"Six hours. Nobody seemed to know when the plane was due."

"Well," Riordan said awkwardly, "you must be tired. Maybe you should . . ."

She seemed relieved. "You're right. We should be off. Has she had anything to eat?"

Riordan grinned. "Everything she could get her hands on. She is some little eater, that girl."

"Well, then . . ." Her tired face managed a smile. "I'm sorry. I haven't thanked you for bringing her. George has told me so much about you. He's very fond of you. Thanks for that, too."

"Nothing. The kid was my ticket home." He looked at his watch, suddenly consumed with the desire to begin the process of getting his freedom.

This time her smile was warm. "You'll come to call, I hope. You have the address?"

"Sure. I've got sort of an interest."

She took the little girl's hand and he watched them go, wondering if he'd ever see either of them again.

It took Riordan two weeks and three days to get his freedom. Not knowing whether or not the Army would ever pay off, he devoted his time to serious poker. He accumulated another $2,400.

Then the Army, with predictable unpredictability, came through in spades. The Eagle flew, and when it landed Riordan found himself with five and a half months' back pay and six months' terminal-leave pay, which amounted to something over eleven thousand dollars. He left Fort Dix with close to fifteen thousand dollars in his pocket and considered himself a rich man.

Des Daniher spread himself for Gavin's return. After a good night's sleep the warrior awoke to a second Christmas. There were visitors all morning to welcome him home. Des, in his gray fedora, held court like an Irish king, as was his right, glowing with pride and affection for the returning warrior. There were friends of Daniher's, friends of Gavin's from high school and Boston College, people he had grown up with, people who had known his dead parents. Somehow they all seemed unreal because none of them had seen what he had seen. None had cowered in terror under mortar fire, or trembled at the chatter of a burp gun, or dug at the earth with fingernails to bury himself from searching 88's. None had watched

101

men die, friend and foe alike. There was no way he could tell them what it was like.

They kept at him with their questions, each new visitor, and he felt as alien as a Martian. He finally took refuge in monosyllables or smiling silence, until his lips felt stiff with tension.

Birdie Connors rescued him. She took him by the hand and asked if he would help churn the ice cream for dinner. He let her lead him through the kitchen, where Mary Margaret Shay bustled about her magic, and into the enclosed back porch, where the big freezer was kept.

"Jesus! I couldn't take much more of that." Despite the January cold, he found that he was sweating.

"I know. I could see," she said.

"You don't suppose there'd be a drink around here, would there?"

"Uncle Des still keeps it in the study, locked in the cabinet...." And then, doubtfully, "I'll see what I can do."

He watched her as she left, the long slim legs, the sway of her hips, and was faintly surprised at how much she had changed from the gawky fifteen-year-old she had been.

Birdie Connors had come into their lives when she was ten and Gavin was going on sixteen. Another of Desmond Daniher's waifs, an unexplained orphaned distant cousin come to live with them. She was as quiet and shy as her name, accepting them all with equal gratitude.

Gavin was at high school, and Birdie was immediately enrolled at St. Agatha's. Gavin's weekends were devoted to earning varsity letters in five different sports, so they saw little of each other. He hardly remembered her, except that she was *there*, silent at meals, unobtrusive about the house, her great sad eyes following him wherever he moved.

She returned with a half-full bottle of Cutty Sark and a jelly glass, and he saw that her eyes were hooded now by delicate, almost transparent lids. Her nose was long and thin, her mouth too wide and full, her jaw too narrow, her chin too sharp. She would never be pretty but she had an interesting face. There was nothing whatever wrong with her figure.

She saw him looking at her breasts and colored deeply.

102

* * *

Mary Margaret had outdone herself on the Christmas spread. There was a roast beef with Yorkshire pudding, and a Virginia ham, in addition to the obligatory bird. Des Daniher removed his hat for the occasion and his bald head gleamed like a beacon. Des had opted for just family, with the exception of Father Martin Touhy, the local parish priest who had known Gavin since childhood. Father Touhy gave a moving thankful grace, which he then topped off with lines from Robert Louis Stevenson's "Requiem": *Home is the sailor, home from the sea, and the hunter home from the hill,* as his old voice broke with emotion.

While Father Touhy blew his nose, Daniher went about the ritual of carving. He heaped Gavin's plate extravagantly, and Mary Margaret placed it before him like an offering to a king, her bright little eyes gleaming in anticipation. Gavin gave her his best smile and thought, *Pearls before swine. They all expect so much from me. What the hell am I supposed to do?*

He caught Birdie looking at him and was reminded of another girl and another Christmas. For an instant he wished he were back there, where he seemed to belong. Any place but here, where he was suddenly a stranger at this feast.

It killed his appetite. For the rest of the meal he picked at the food, trying his best to do it justice, conscious all the while of their disappointment, so politely disguised. His head was filled with confusion, not helped by the drinks he had had.

The uncomfortable meal finally came to an end. Father Touhy embraced him and left to go about his parish duties. Birdie and Mary Margaret busied themselves with cleaning up. Des Daniher indicated the study with a nod.

"Shall we?"

There was no getting out of it. Gavin followed him reluctantly.

His head again covered by the gray fedora, Daniher settled himself in his big reading chair. Gavin perched on the window seat, as he had since he could remember, for one of their "talks."

"Something troubling you, boy?"

Knowing he couldn't explain without hurting this kindly man who had been father and mother to him all his life, Gavin said, "It's just that it's all so strange, coming home. Everything is ... different, after ..."

"Takes a bit of getting used to, I shouldn't wonder." Daniher lit a cigarette with brown-stained fingers. He seemed not quite comfortable and shifted in his chair. "Look, Gavin, I've read all the crap about the returning veteran. Adjustment problems and all. I hope there'll be none of that for you. . . ." Then, seeing Gavin's disturbed look, "How about a drop of the creature before we get too serious?"

Gavin nodded in relief. Daniher took the key ring from his pocket, went to the massive oak cabinet and came up with a bottle of Bushmill's. He poured drinks into the heavy shot glasses that were always in a tray atop the cabinet.

"Hard to get, this stuff. During the war. Stuck you with a case of rum before they'd give you a half-dozen of the whiskey. The rum went to Father Touhy, who has a fondness for it." Back in his chair with the bottle beside him, he raised his glass.

Gavin drank quickly, feeling the welcome burn of the liquor in his throat.

"Another?"

"Why not?"

As he returned to the window seat, Gavin began to realize that his Uncle Des had something on his mind besides a casual talk. Daniher's eyes fixed his thoughtfully.

"Have you given a thought to what you want to do with yourself?"

"Not really. Just being out is enough for a while."

"You'll finish college?"

There it was. The inevitable Irish conviction that an education was the first necessary step toward solving all of life's problems. The prospect of books and classes and spending his days on campus held no appeal whatsoever. Or the nights, for that matter.

Yet he said, "I suppose so."

"And after? Have you given no thought to that?"

"It's a little too soon, Uncle Des."

"Is it, now. Too soon is never too late. What would you say to the law? It's a grand profession. And the money's there—for a smart lad like yourself."

"You're pushing me," Gavin flared. "Why not the cops, so I can get my head shot off like my old man? Or medicine? Or driving a milk truck? I'm just not ready yet. . . ."

Daniher seemed to pay no attention to his outburst. "Not a bad idea. Combine the two, cops and the law. A lawyer cop could go right to the top."

Gavin knew that "right to the top" meant with the help and backing of Boss Desmond Daniher, and he wanted no part of it. He wanted . . . The trouble was that he didn't know what he wanted.

"And marriage, too. It's the time a young lad should be thinking of marriage, and kids of his own. Along with a sound career. It's a time for planning ahead."

The switch bewildered Gavin.

"Things were handled better in the Old Country. A father picked a wife for his son, or a husband for his daughter. The fathers had a good chat and settled things. And everybody lived happily ever after. Not such a bad system when all's said and done." He smiled benevolently at Gavin. "I had it in mind that you and Birdie . . . would be good for each other."

"Yeah . . ." He couldn't believe what Daniher was saying. "Well, marriage is a long way off. . . ."

"There'd be the dowry, of course," Daniher went on obliviously. "A big one. Very big. I'd see to that."

Gavin took a deep breath and let it out slowly. "Let me get this straight. I want to be sure I know what you're talking about. I think what you're saying is that you want Birdie and me to get married. Not sometime, but now."

"In a nutshell," Daniher said calmly.

Gavin exploded. "Jesus Christ! I hardly *know* her! I've got a lot of fucking years before I get fucking married. . . ."

"*She* hasn't."

Something in Daniher's voice stopped him. Daniher's eyes bored into his. "She's pregnant," Daniher said.

"That kid . . . ?" The warning bells went off all over in his head, cutting through his shocked disbelief. Then, "Why me? Why for Christ's sake me! *I* didn't . . ."

"The man is dead. He had an . . . accident."

105

An accident. Gavin stared into Daniher's eyes. They glittered like a cobra's. Whoever the man was would never make a mistake like that again. You don't knock up a pure Catholic girl under that protection.

Of course she couldn't have an abortion. Of course she had to marry someone.

So, in his wisdom, Daniher was prepared to put things right by sacrificing Gavin Riordan on the altar of his belief. And Birdie. Riordan had an instant of compassion for her, caught with him in the same trap.

But then, it wasn't a sacrifice of two lives to Des Daniher. It was a business proposition. Or a bribe, as cold as the price of ice. The bait was an assured career, safety and comfort as long as they lived. And the dowry. Don't forget the dowry. What was he to Des Daniher? He didn't know. What was Des Daniher to him? Everything. For he loved Des Daniher and knew he always would. And he owed him. God knew he owed him. All it needed was a simple yes, and part of his debt would be paid.

He stood up. "No way," he said, and was surprised at the steadiness of his voice. "I'm sorry. I can't do it. You'll have to find another boy."

Behind him, as he walked out, he heard his Uncle Des say, "Think it over, Gavin. There's not a hell of a lot of time."

There was no suggestion of defeat or dismay, just a calm confidence in the rightness of what he asked. It shook Gavin, but not enough to stop his going.

He moved into a small hotel, ordered a bottle of whiskey and proceeded to get blind drunk, Black Irish drunk. He stayed drunk for two days and, when he came out of it, was driven from the stinking room by an overwhelming craving for a rare hamburger. He couldn't wait to shower or shave, but stumbled out onto the street the way he was, possessed like a pregnant woman with the one thought.

He wolfed three hamburgers, washing them down with cup after cup of scalding coffee, and started back to the hotel. He had reached the marquee when dizziness and nausea caught up to him. He hung onto the marquee's metal support while everything he had eaten splashed into the gutter, and an outraged doorman tried to move him along.

A woman's voice reached him through his haze.

"Gavin! Gavin Riordan. Are you ill?"

The silliness of that question occupied his mind until he stopped throwing up. When he could speak, he looked up and saw Serena Gansvoort. He gestured to the persistent doorman and said, "Tell him I live here."

Serena took charge. She helped him maneuver the revolving doors, brushed aside the bellboy and the room clerk with an imperiousness that cowed them and got him into the elevator.

In his room she took in the empty bottles, the stained sheets, clothes strewn on the floor.

"What a pigsty. How in hell did you get so drunk?"

"Drinking," Gavin said, and headed for the bathroom.

He was stripped to the waist, trying to shave with an impossibly unsteady hand, when she came in and turned on the hot water in the tub. She plunked herself down on the john seat and watched him critically.

"Jesus, what a mess. Careful you don't cut your throat. I couldn't bear that. Not until after you tell me what caused the binge."

He wasn't about to confide in Serena. She'd be too apt to laugh. He couldn't take that at the moment.

"Stewart told me you were married."

"*Were* is the word. You're not telling me that. . . . No, that couldn't be it. You're trying to change the subject. What happened?"

"Put it down to battle fatigue. Too many punches to the head."

She kicked him lightly on the shin. In his supersensitive state it startled him into cutting himself.

"Jesus, Serena . . . !"

"Serves you right." She leaned forward to turn off the tub water, testing the temperature with her hand.

"Okay, in you go." And when he hesitated, "Don't be a prude, Gavin. I never got a really good look at you. Now's my chance."

He wasn't up to fighting for his privacy. He shucked out of his clothes and slipped into the tub. The hot water made him gasp, but it

107

acted like balm on his jangled nerves. He slid down until his head rested on the edge of the tub and closed his eyes.

Serena was quiet for so long that he thought she had left. He opened his eyes to find that she was kneeling by the tub, looking at his body through the clear water and crying silently. He sat up in alarm.

"Hey, Serena . . . ?"

Her eyes were on the mangled biceps of his left arm. He saw her look travel down to the deep pit of the bullet wound in his thigh, then to the puckered welt across his belly. Her hand reached out slowly to touch the round white scar just under his right breast.

"That one was the pitchfork?"

"Yeah . . ." He was embarrassed for her memories.

"Oh, God, Gavin. They hurt you so. . . ."

She leaned over to kiss the scar. Her lips moved up to circle his nipple. He felt the nipple grow rigid as her tongue caressed him. After a moment she sat back on her heels.

"Turns you on, too, I can see. Just like me."

Gavin tried to cover himself.

"Okay, okay. I'll leave." She got up abruptly, not looking back as she closed the door behind her.

Jesus, he thought, *I don't really need this.* . . .

He took his time drying himself, combing his red hair carefully, patting on after-shave, not letting himself think about just why. As he wrapped a towel around his waist, he wondered if she'd still be there when he opened the door, and what he would say if she was.

She was sitting by a table, which held a quart of milk, a large coffee pot and a mound of toast. She licked her fingers as she finished a piece of toast. The empties were gone, the rumpled bed smoothed, his scattered clothing out of sight.

He made for the milk like a homing pigeon and drank gratefully from the carton, feeling the cold elixir damp the fire in his stomach.

She was examining him like a side of beef she planned to buy, no trace of tears now.

"My, you're a big one. I didn't remember you as so big. You've grown, Gavin."

He didn't answer because his mouth was full of toast. He poured the hot black coffee and this time took it in small swallows.

"I have, too."

He looked for the double meaning and decided there wasn't any. Her eyes were cool and remote, as if she were thinking of something quite apart. She was right. She had grown. She was dressed in a camel's-hair skirt and a soft silk blouse that hugged her breasts. Her long legs were in sheer nylons, the first he'd seen since he had hit the States. The heels of her alligator pumps were impossibly high, her feet long and narrow. Her face had thinned out, the square Gansvoort jaw more prominent. The gleaming dark pageboy hair softened features that alone might have been too masculine. She held her head high, almost regally, indomitably. Background and breeding were unmistakable. So was the money—as much a part of her as her skin.

"A penny, Gavin."

He swallowed the last of the toast and shrugged, not wanting to meet her look.

"Black Irish blues, I guess."

"Nothing more?"

"Nothing I can't handle."

Suddenly she grinned raffishly, like the naughty schoolgirl he remembered. "Let's go to bed, Gavin." Then, seeing his indecision, "Please. For old times' sake."

He watched as she stood up, dropped her skirt, stepped out of its circle, unbuttoned her shirt and let it slide off her shoulders. She continued slowly for prurient effect until clad only in nylons and garter belt. She posed for a moment, one hand in her hair, her smile full of mischief. Then she sat on the bed to pull off her stockings and lay back, one leg slightly raised, her hands clasped behind her head.

Gavin shook off his towel and went to sit beside her. He began to stroke her elegant breasts, fascinated by how her nipples grew under his hands until they looked like round ripe cherries. He moved one hand down to her crotch and leaned to kiss her lips.

"You've a breath like a goat."

She moved away from him to the far side of the bed.

"Lie down. You'd better let me take care of this."

When he was on his back, she got to her knees and took his member in both hands. She began a slow indolent exploration with lips and tongue. Finally she took him in her mouth, the movement of her head lazy, without urgency. He could see the ripple of the muscles in her long, supple back.

She made love to him in her own time. Gradually her breathing deepened, became ragged. When she was ready she got astride him, lowered herself, inserted him and gave a small gasp as he entered her fully.

She began to rock, gently at first, then with gradually increasing speed. Her eyes were closed, her lips parted, her hair a cloud about her head. She moved to some silent music only she could hear, curiously removed from him, as though his only corporeal presence was what was inside her body.

He reached out to fondle her jutting nipples and she shuddered under his touch, but it didn't disturb the unheard complicated rhythm of her private melody. Her thighs opened and closed on his sides like wings.

He came suddenly, without warning. If she knew, she gave no sign of it. She kept at her pumping, using his disembodied phallus to reach her own orgasm. Her mouth was wide now, she breathed in short groans, lost in her own sensation. He wondered if she knew he existed.

When she opened her eyes he was looking at a stranger. He watched her eyes widen in what could only be recognition, and then widen still farther, filled with what he could read as pain and remorse.

"Oh, my darling . . ." she said hoarsely. "Gavin. It's *you*! How could I . . ."

He slipped out of her as she fell forward on him, her face buried in his shoulder. He could hear her broken murmur, "I'm sorry . . . I'm so sorry," and feel her hot tears on his skin.

She made him dress and take her to lunch. He couldn't face a cocktail, but the wine with his steak helped a lot. She didn't talk while he ate, just watched until he had finished. Over coffee she asked, "Is it so bad, Gavin?"

110

"Bad enough. I don't seem to be adjusting properly to civilian life."

"Okay," she said, "I'll drop it." And then, "What are you going to do, now that . . . ?"

"Haven't the faintest. And I'm getting a little tired of the question. Just want to relax. Look around at all the beautiful unscarred, untouched, unaware people—happy as clams now that rationing is gone and everybody can get back to Sunday driving."

"Don't be bitter. It's not like you."

"What the hell do you know about what I'm like?"

"I know," Serena said softly.

He let it go, having no way to explain to her the changes in himself and not much wanting to. "I'm sorry. The hell with it. So I'm bitter. I'll get over it in time. What about you?"

"Me?"

"Yeah. Marriage and all that?"

"I was bored," she said.

"Is *that* all."

"I thought I could get away from Gansvoort-land—particularly the name. So I took another one. Damiani sounded nice."

"It didn't work?"

"No." Serena obviously didn't want to talk about her problems any more than he wanted to talk about his. She toyed with her wine glass. Her eyes had a sad, brooding look, and he wondered briefly what it must be like to be a Gansvoort with all that the name implied, never to have to *want* anything you couldn't just go out and buy.

Abruptly she was smiling at him with that wicked schoolgirl mischief. "You said no plans?" she asked. "None at all?"

"None."

"Well, I do."

The rapidity of her changing moods made him cautious. "Hmm. What?"

"We have a place off Georgia. An island. I'm going there tomorrow. How would you like to come along?"

* * *

The plane was a twelve-passenger Beechcraft belonging to Gansvoort Associates. Serena was pale, preoccupied and noncommittal. She explained that she had a monster hangover and promptly went to sleep. Gavin spent the trip talking to the pilot.

The island looked, as they circled over the small airport for a landing, to be several miles long and a half-mile wide. At the north end was a large plantation house surrounded by broad lawns on which sheep were grazing. The land sloped to a white beach on the landward side. A stretch of woodland separated the estate from a golf course, impossibly green in the midafternoon sunlight. The airstrip was in the middle of the island. At the southerly end stood another much smaller building half hidden by a stand of tall Georgia pines in a deep cove.

Serena drove the Jeep when they disembarked. She turned south instead of north toward the big house. The rutted sandy road wound through the woods that followed the shoreline. Serena drove with authority and in silence, and Gavin was content to let it remain that way, already regretting his decision to come along.

The last part of the road was on the beach itself and ended before a charming glass-fronted single-story house. "You're on the left. I'm going to shower. Make yourself a drink if you want."

Serena was across the wide veranda and into the house before he could get his case out of the Jeep. There was no sign of her when he came in. Directly in front of him was an open kitchen separated from the main room by a long counter, part of which was a well-stocked bar. On the left was a fireplace with a log fire ready for lighting. The furniture was rattan, chairs and couches done in tropical shades of greens and blues. Tan hemp rugs were spotted over the white tile floor.

Gavin went through a door next to the fireplace into a room dominated by a king-size bed with a bright orange spread. Here the rugs were deep sculptured pile, springy under his feet like new-mown grass. There were mirrors everywhere. The beach, the dock, the moored boats and the broad expanse of the sea reflected a constantly changing pattern. The wide windows to the porch were closed, but the room was pleasantly cool. He could hear the low hum of air-conditioning machinery somewhere in the back of the house.

He put his case on the bed and unpacked. Not really believing Serena's crack about sunglasses only, he had brought white duck slacks, a number of sport shirts, white socks and underwear, tennis shoes and shorts and a blue terrycloth robe. He put it all away, with barrack-room neatness, in a chest of drawers, got into swim trunks and opened the glass doors to the veranda. He selected a beach lounger, manipulated its joints to suit and stretched out to wait for Serena. The sun was warm and soothing on his skin.

When Serena didn't appear after fifteen minutes he went inside and made himself a drink and wandered down to the dock. The water was a startling turquoise blue, clear enough for him to see the schools of brightly colored fish as though it were his own personal aquarium. When he finished his drink he dove off the end of the dock.

It was a shock, colder than he expected. It set him gasping, his blood atingle. He swam toward the white sea floor and found the water much deeper than it looked. When he surfaced, Serena was running naked down the dock. She hit the water with hardly a splash and disappeared. He waited for her to come up and the next thing he felt was her hands yanking his trunks down to his knees, then over his feet, and they were gone forever. Her arms went around him tightly, her body seemed to burn against his in the cold water, her lips were salty and urgent. Then she broke away and went at a fast crawl toward the shore. She waited for him in the shallows, knee deep, wet dark hair tangled about her face.

Gavin picked her up, carried her up the beach and into his bedroom. Her body made a wet imprint on the bedcover, droplets of water glistened on her white skin. She looked small and defenseless on the huge orange bed. Serena defenseless? He laughed aloud at the thought, and she laughed with him. This time there wasn't any question that she knew who he was.

Hunger drove them from the bed as the sun went down behind the Georgia coastline.

In the main room Serena said, "Light the fire, darling. It gets cold here at night. I'm going to get a robe." She started across the floor, stopped suddenly, ran back to him and threw her arms around him and kissed him hard.

"Darling. Oh, my darling. How I love that word."

They dined sitting on pillows in front of the roaring fire, on cold langouste heaped with mountains of mayonnaise, and drank bottle after bottle of icy Mexican beer. Serena ate with the greedy concentration of a child. Twice he wiped away the grease that glistened on her chin.

Later, she pulled aside his robe and kissed the jagged scar on his belly.

"Tell me now," she said. And suddenly he found he could.

"Funny. That one. Only man I ever heard of who got wounded by a dead German. We were on this sunken road, hedgerows on either side, when a heavy machine gun cut loose ahead of us, right down the road. Hell of a racket. Everybody scrambled up the banks and busted through the hedgerows to get out of the line of fire. Except me.

"There was this dead German. He had fallen on his rifle when he got hit, and he had his bayonet fixed. Funny. Only time I ever saw a bayonet on a rifle in the whole damn war. You used bayonets for a lot things—but hardly ever on your rifle.

"Anyway, I busted up the bank and there's this guy with his bayonet sticking through the hedgerow. I jabbed the thing right into my gut. Never even saw it. It wasn't much. Went in sort of sideways, just under the skin. But I didn't know that at the time.

"My sergeant kept yelling at me to get my ass down. But I couldn't. There I was, pinned up there in plain sight like a stuck pig, .50 calibers cutting up the dirt all around me.

"Funny . . ." Gavin stopped, as the memories came flooding back. He could hear the shells snicking through the hedgerow, the screams of Sergeant Bo Evans to get down, feel the blood hot on his groin, the mindless, paralyzing helpless terror . . .

Serena bit him.

"Damnit! What happened?"

"I ripped it out and got the hell out of there. . . ." He could hear Evans, furious in his relief, "You stupid son of a bitch! What the fuck you think you were doin' up there!" And himself, "Goddamnit!

114

Get me a sulfa pad. My guts are leakin' into my pants. . . ."
Evans . . . dead now from a mortar shell landing right on top of his
helmet.

Serena ran her finger over the puckered scar.

"You mean you ripped it right through the skin?"

"It wasn't much. It sort of slipped in between the skin and the
muscles."

"Didn't it hurt?" Her voice had a little girl's curiosity.

"Hell, yes, it hurt. But not until later."

"Go on," Serena said. "I want to hear it all. Every bit of it. Not
just about the war. About you, Gavin—so I'll know."

It amazed him that he not only could but wanted to talk to this
girl, who was child at one moment and age-old wisdom the next—
and totally unpredictable in between.

He told her about his war. Not war yarns, but how he felt and
thought and changed, about so many friends cut off in the midst of
life, so many friends dead that friendship became an unbearable
burden, closeness to another human being to be avoided at all costs.
He described to her the realities of combat, the sights and sounds
and smells, and found that, miraculously, she seemed to understand.
He told her of numbing fear and she trembled. He told her crazy
soldier stories, and she laughed with him.

It all came spilling out over the lazy days and nights. His cop
father, blown away in a dark alley by person or persons unknown;
his mother, who died a year later; and Des Daniher—the only family
he had known since the age of five. Des Daniher, who had advised
and counseled, bound his wounds in childhood, eased the hurts of
boyhood and, now that he was a man, expected a sort of payment in
return. She was outraged when he told her of the dilemma of Birdie.

"But he *can't* ask that. It's not fair!"

"Fair has nothing to do with it. To him it's a deal. Politics is his
life. And that's what politics is—one deal after another. You scratch
mine, I'll scratch yours. To him, he made me a good offer, and
believe me, he'd pay off in return. You can't really fault him for it.
That's the way he thinks."

"But to marry some slut who got herself knocked up. . . . How
can he . . . ?"

"Hey, now," Gavin protested, "Birdie's not a slut. Last person in the world I would have thought to get herself pregnant. I don't know how it happened. I didn't stay around long enough to find out. But Birdie's a good kid. Happen to anybody, I guess."

Serena grew thoughtful.

"Mmmm, I suppose it could. . . ."

Their days were spent on or in the water. They went fishing and Serena cooked what they caught. Serena taught Gavin how to sail. Gavin taught Serena how to shoot the .22 rifle kept in the house, until one day she brought down a gull on the wing and wept uncontrollably when he fetched the dead bird for her. They made love when the notion took them. Their lovemaking ran the gamut from playful tenderness to exotic abandonment, depending on Serena's moods, all of which he found entrancing.

By the end of the week, Gavin Riordan, age twenty-five, was in love—for the first time in his life.

On the tenth evening, once more stretched out before the fire, he asked her to marry him.

Serena stared into the fire without answering, for so long that it began to irritate him.

"What the hell is it?" he demanded. "The money?"

"It's not money. It's wealth. There's a difference."

"Not to me. I don't give a shit either way. It's you I want to marry, not your fucking money."

"You don't know. There's so much of it you can't even count it. It's all over the world. It's power, and it corrupts absolutely." She was still looking into the fire, and he saw her shudder. "It stinks, Gavin. It's . . . evil. And dirty."

Not really understanding, he reached out to comfort her, his irritation gone. "Hey, you were the one who wanted out of Gansvoortland. Now's your chance."

"I said that," Serena said slowly. "I tried—and it didn't work. Because all the rest of it comes with me. There's no getting rid of it. They bought him off. Cheap. That's what hurt."

He felt a stab of resentment. "You don't think I . . ."

"Oh, Christ, no! Not you, Gavin. Never you." She rolled over on top of him, her mouth hungry on his, her hands pulling his robe apart. After a moment she lifted her head to look at him. "Not now, darling. We'll talk about it in the morning. Tonight I just want to be loved until I die of it."

There was a new urgency in her lovemaking, a wild insatiability that left them both exhausted.

Something woke him in the middle of the night. He reached for her and found the bed empty. After a moment he heard her sobbing in the next room.

She was crouched before the dead embers of the fire, shivering uncontrollably with cold. He took her in his arms and carried her back to bed. She clung to him like a child. He turned on the night light and rocked her gently back and forth until her breathing became easier and her sobs stopped.

"What's wrong, darling?"

"Nothing. It's my period, I guess. Sometimes ladies get like this. . . ." And then, "Oh, God, Gavin, I do love you so. . . ."

In the dim light her eyes were like owls, and they held a sadness he couldn't fathom. She went to sleep lying half on top of him, her head nestled in the crook of his neck, her breath soft against his skin.

In the morning she was gone.

When the Beechcraft landed him at LaGuardia he called her from the nearest booth. A servant told him that she had gone to California and wasn't expected back for several months.

Gavin Riordan went home to the house that belonged to Des Daniher. Aside from greetings, there were no words spoken between them and none needed.

On January 29, 1947, Gavin Riordan and Birdie Connors were married in the Chapel of St. Teresa by Father Martin Touhy. Attendance was small because Des Daniher wanted it that way. Mary Margaret Shay, in an ancient flowered hat, wept noisily. A few family friends, several chums of Birdie's from St. Agatha's School and a police captain who had known Gavin's father made up the gathering.

Des Daniher, suitably solemn, gave the bride away. Mary Margaret's gentle nephew Donnie was Gavin's best man.

When Gavin lifted the veil to kiss his bride, her nose was red from weeping, her eyes held the mournful adoration of a spaniel. Her lips trembled as she tried to smile, and Gavin thought, *Oh, God. All the sad-eyed women. . . .* Was his life to hold nothing else?

They spent their honeymoon at the Frontenac Hotel in Quebec, only three days because Gavin was enrolled for his last term at Boston College under the GI Bill. They set up housekeeping in an apartment near campus, which a friend of Daniher's provided.

Gavin was graduated with honors in June, and a week later was accepted by the police academy.

In July, Birdie was delivered of a stillborn baby boy, and two weeks later went into a serious postpartum depression.

10

Time: 1947
ERICKA

Melinda Barnstable Price's mother was of the Buells of Richmond, one of the first families of Virginia. Her father, Clinton Mather Barnstable of Marblehead, Massachusetts, was descended from the Clintons and the Livingstons of New York on one side, and half the old New England families on the other. Privately she was a convinced Democrat who rarely talked politics with her friends, a liberated woman before the term became popular.

Her early marriage to Porter Price was a sort of backsliding because of the proximity, the still-powerful forces of her heritage, and because everyone, including herself, expected her to marry someone in her own circle. She soon found out that her husband was opposed to almost everything she believed. Not from conviction but from inertia. His opinions were inherited. It hardly mattered that Porter Price was bisexual. She would have divorced him if he had been as masculine as Clark Gable.

She chose to be an interior decorator; it let her employ her good taste, judgment and sense of fitness. She admired her brother's talents; decorating was *her* way of being creative.

Melinda read her brother's letter about Ericka Ullman with dismay. What he asked was an imposition. But she was close enough to George to know that he would have considered this, and if it was important enough to him to override her feelings, then it had to be important to her as well.

But what on earth would she do with a nine-year-old girl who spoke no English? The prospect appalled her. When she got over her initial panic she called Mrs. Whitcomb's Service, which had supplied her with servants for years. She wanted a governess who spoke German and was well supplied with the proper references. No luck. Several other calls produced nothing. Her panic had started to return when she thought of Walter Richter of the Richter Galleries, where she bought objets d'art at a decorator's discount.

As he had so many times, Richter came through. He produced Frau Irma Gertner, a recent refugee, widow of a Jewish film producer.

Irma Gertner was a trim, lively little woman of fifty-two. Initially Melinda was a trifle put off by her assurance until she recognized it for the confidence of a mature and capable woman. Soon she was absurdly grateful for the smooth efficiency with which Irma took charge not only of Ericka but of running the household as well.

The household occupied a tall brownstone on Gramercy Park. The top floor was rented to Tobin Wright, an artist friend of George's, and Melinda's lover for several years. The floor below Wright's was George's when he was home. Melinda had converted the first three floors into a charming apartment. The top one served her as office and workspace.

That was the first dislocation. Office and workspace became two apartments, one for Irma Gertner, the other for Ericka. The second was that Melinda's fairly frequent trips by elevator to see Tobin Wright became a source of embarrassment to her. She sensed Irma's disapproval.

The basement of the building housed an elaborate kitchen and living space for Mrs. Dancy Jones, who had been her mother's cook when Melinda was born. Dancy disapproved of Irma Gertner on sight. By the end of the first month Dancy's disapproval had ripened into open enmity.

"If that woman come into my kitchen again without tellin' me, I'm liable to bus' her haid. An' you better tell her so."

Melinda did, with some trepidation. Irma took it like the lady she was. "I understand perfectly," she said in her soft English accent. "It's her domain. I shall be careful to respect it in future."

The result was that Melinda was driven to install a wall kitchenette in Irma's sitting room to keep peace.

Ericka, on the other hand, was welcomed by Dancy with open affection. The two of them evolved some method of communication that Melinda couldn't fathom. Occasionally she would hear them laugh. It puzzled and intrigued her, because at first Ericka rarely laughed with anyone else.

There began in her house a cold war of which Melinda was unaware for too long a time. Melinda's business kept her on the run, and her time with Ericka was confined to breakfast, dinner and the few evenings her social life allowed her. What Melinda saw on these occasions delighted her. As the months went by, Ericka began to blossom. With Dancy's cooking, her thin body began to fill out and her cheeks took on color.

Irma Gertner had a way with children, as she did with everyone except Dancy. She set herself to capture the child, and she succeeded. She was witty and gay and full of fun, and shared herself unstintingly. Ericka learned to laugh. At first most of their private amusements were in German, but remarkably soon Ericka's English improved to such an extent that Irma laid down the dictum that no German was to be spoken except in dire emergencies. Ericka's new language had an English lilt that Melinda found charming.

Melinda watched Ericka become a model child, polite, attentive, well behaved, dressed impeccably in clothes selected by Irma, who also bought games and toys and books, which they shared delightedly. With German method Irma kept accounts of every penny spent.

Under Irma's tutelage Ericka was learning to sew, as all young ladies should, and above all to read English with remarkable fluency. She took to simple math as if born to it. Irma showered her with praise in front of Melinda.

It was the shopping that brought about a major clash with Dancy. Irma casually suggested that, since she and Ericka went for walks every day, they could so easily attend to the household needs as well. And of course there was Dancy's age, which must make it difficult. Thoughtlessly Melinda agreed.

Dancy hit the roof. Dancy loved her marketing jaunts. She had been dealing with the same purveyors for years. They gave her special treatment—and special prices. They were the only friends she had. She wasn't about to give that up for anything. When she had allowed Melinda to calm her down, she said, "That woman is a mean-hearted woman. No good for that sweet chile. That chile live in fear an' tremblin'. I know."

"Nonsense," Melinda said too sharply. "They're very fond of each other."

Dancy's look was dark with foreboding.

"You jes' wait. You'll see."

Dancy fought her war with the only real weapon she had: food. Ericka's appetite was prodigious, and Dancy wooed her with every delight she could devise. The only extended hours they had together were on the weekends, when Irma took her days off to visit a cousin. Dancy made chess tarts, pecan pies, pineapple upside-down cakes and every sort of wickedness.

As she grew in accomplishments, the child grew in girth on Dancy's meals and between-meals treats. When George Barnstable was mustered out the following Christmas, Ericka weighed close to a hundred pounds, and Barnstable saw little resemblance to his Berlin waif. He remarked on this to his sister.

"Let's face it," Melinda said worriedly. "It's fat. She eats like a horse. But you can't just deny food to a child. . . ."

"Well, she spent a lot of years thin—and hungry. You can't blame her for trying to make up for it."

"Were the Ullmans fat? Giselle certainly wasn't."

"No . . . Not exactly." In fear of military censorship his letters had kept up the fiction that Ericka was an Ullman. Now he was reluctant to tell Melinda the real truth.

The changes in the child didn't affect George's tenderness and affection. She accepted him as if they had never been apart. In very short order they developed a relationship that was quite special. On Ericka's part it showed itself in a need to touch, to be held and cuddled. Since she was now, by dead reckoning, over ten years old and had topped a hundred pounds, it made for some awkwardness. In George it became an inability to deny her anything. He spoiled her rotten.

George was immensely excited at the progress in drawing she had made under Irma Gertner, so he was disposed to like Irma from the start. Irma presented him with her most charming self. Privately she resented his closeness to the child. Irma had come to feel that Ericka was hers by right.

Melinda, who had a feeling for people, became, when her busy life allowed, more and more concerned. It started when she became aware that Ericka's splendid progress was the price Ericka had to pay for Irma's approval, something Ericka desired with desperate intensity. Irma's punishment for less than perfect conduct was a pursed-lipped silent withdrawal, which could bring Ericka to the point of tears and induce a nervous tension that caused her to spill food, knock over glasses or make any number of mistakes. These small disasters only made the punishment last longer.

With the awareness of children Ericka was conscious of the undercurrents around her. It made her increasingly unsure of herself.

The second thing Melinda noticed was more puzzling but equally worrisome. She happened to be in the bathroom when Ericka started to get into the tub, wearing her panties. When Melinda protested, Ericka flatly refused to take them off.

Melinda let it go. She asked Irma how long this curious behavior had been going on.

"From the first." Irma didn't seem to find it unusual. "She prefers it that way. She is very modest."

The third thing happened late one afternoon. Melinda, watching from her window—which looked out over Gramercy Park surrounded by its high iron fence—was enjoying the active play of the dozens of children who had park privileges. She looked for Ericka and found her sitting quietly on a bench while Irma read to her. She saw the child's head turn to watch the others romping. Irma spoke to her and Ericka became rigidly attentive.

That made up her mind. Melinda decided that Ericka's education had reached the point where Ericka could be entered in school. By pulling all the strings of a lifetime she got Ericka accepted at Briarstone, where she herself had gone.

In all the world there is perhaps no worse cruelty and snobbishness than that at an exclusive girls' school. It is more than the thoughtless cruelty of children. It is honed and pointed by the wealth, position and attitudes of parents—translated without understanding to their offspring.

The pecking order is inviolable. Class distinctions unbreakable. And each class has its misfits, known at Briarstone as "monsters." Not being completely at home with the language, with none of the assurance needed to make friends easily, and carrying one hundred and eleven pounds on a four-foot-four-inch frame. Ericka qualified immediately.

The life of a monster is proscribed. She is allowed friendship only with other monsters. She is the butt of casual jokes and slurs and is teased unmercifully by the more favored. Here is a loneliness that is like no other.

Strangely, despite her acute unhappiness, Ericka did well in class. She genuinely enjoyed learning and had a desperate need to please. The combination gained her the only two friends she was to find at Briarstone, both teachers: Miss Terhune, who taught both French and German, and Mrs. Rosati, who taught art and art appreciation and who was something of a monster herself. Mrs. Rosati was tall and angular and inclined to peasant blouses and Indian jewelry. She was overjoyed to find one student who had a real feeling for her subjects, plus a burgeoning talent. Ericka was a find. In Mrs.

123

Rosati's judgment she had the "eye," which meant the God-given ability to transfer what she saw to paper. Crude perhaps, but the gift was undeniably there. Mrs. Rosati smelled an artist with a capital *A*. With the proper training . . . If the child was willing to work.

Miss Terhune was not so dedicated as Mrs. Rosati, but she was equally pleased to find a student with a natural ear for languages. German Ericka already had. French came to her with gratifying ease, and Miss Terhune's grades were extravagantly generous. The rest of her teachers found Ericka bright and intelligent and hard-working, if not gifted, and their grades, too, showed their approval.

At home, her excellent marks brought lavish praise from everyone. It was a help, but it wasn't enough.

Ericka took refuge in food.

In her first two years at Briarstone she grew six inches and gained thirty-nine pounds. She also began to suffer from migraine headaches and acquired a speech hesitation that was not quite a stutter. Inevitably the headmistress wrote a letter to Melinda warning that Ericka might have a medical problem.

Even the indulgent George Barnstable realized that they had a serious problem on their hands. Melinda had long since given up trying to control Ericka's eating. Irma had never tried because Ericka's weakness in that area strengthened her dominance. Dancy, who weighed a comfortable one hundred and seventy pounds herself, refused to be persuaded that there *was* any problem and continued to fatten her lamb whenever possible.

Melinda pointed out the disadvantages a fat girl would face in later life—popularity, dating, clothes. Since Ericka's experiences so far had convinced her that there wasn't going to be any popularity or dating or pretty clothes, Melinda's talk made little impression. The talk did something for Melinda, though. She realized that it was time to introduce Ericka to the facts of life. So she bought her a book and told her they would have a long talk after she had read it.

At that time Ericka was in the middle of a long series of visits to doctors and nutritionists and tests of every description, none of which came up with a certain solution to whatever ailed her. Melinda lost sight of the talk they were to have. It wasn't until Dancy found the mutilated textbook in the trash can that Melinda realized something was wrong. The book had been slashed and torn with a knife of some sort, so violently that it frightened her.

"Where she get books like that?" Dancy demanded indignantly. "No wonder she tore it up."

"I gave it to her. I thought she needed to know."

"She just a *chile*." Dancy looked at her darkly. "Hope you knows what you're doin'."

Hoping she did, too, Melinda sat Ericka down and faced her with the damaged book.

At first Ericka refused to talk at all, but Melinda stuck at it and Ericka finally came out with "I'm *not* a woman. I never want to be a woman!"

"Honey, all of us become women eventually. Some earlier than others. Menstruation is part of growing up. It happens with all women. It's perfectly natural, nothing to be afraid of. It's part of the cycle that allows us to have babies."

"It's horrible! I won't let it happen to me. I'd rather die!"

It wasn't the extravagant exaggeration of what Ericka was saying; it was the look on her face that stopped Melinda. She recognized fear—bald, stark fear—when she saw it. She didn't know what to do about it.

Ericka locked herself in her room and refused to come out until hunger drove her. She went straight to Dancy's kitchen and wouldn't join the others for lunch. Melinda reluctantly told Irma what had happened, to keep her from insisting that Ericka be present, and saw by Irma's face that Ericka was in for some more of Irma's special brand of punishment.

"You are not to talk to her about this," Melinda said rather sharply. "I forbid it. Do you understand me?" And realized it was what she had been wanting to say for a long time.

"But surely . . . *something* must be done. I am perfectly capable of explaining . . ."

"I'll handle this myself. I don't wish to have Ericka even suspect that I've told you. I'm depending on you to see that she doesn't."

"I don't agree. It's my duty to . . ."

"Not a word," Melinda interrupted, knowing that it was important to win this clash. "Not one word. I mean it."

She held Irma's eyes firmly until Irma dropped her head. "If you think that's best, Melinda."

Melinda called the headmistress for advice and was referred to an old Briarstone girl who was now a respected child psychiatrist. She was mildly surprised to find that Dr. Emily Murray insisted on interviewing the parents first.

"But I'm not a parent," Melinda said, and had an instant's intuition that that could well be one source of the trouble.

George refused to go with her to Dr. Murray's. He knew little about psychiatry and had never had the need to know more. Obscurely he believed that sharing one's intimate thoughts with a stranger was not compatible with good breeding. He felt the same way about Ericka's past.

Melinda knew somewhat more, but only from what she had read in passing. Her several preliminary sessions with Dr. Murray were a revelation. She expected the doctor to listen to Ericka's symptoms, diagnose what was wrong and prescribe a cure. After all, Ericka was the patient, not Melinda. She learned that psychiatrists didn't diagnose, didn't prescribe and asked very few questions.

Under Emily Murray's gentle urging, Melinda talked herself hoarse. She discovered the real depths of her animosity toward Irma Gertner. She was forced to examine the relationship between Irma and Ericka, to recognize the needs of each. Childless Irma wanting to love and possess and to be loved, which had resulted in the unconscious wish to keep the child grossly fat. If Ericka was unattractive to the others, then it followed that Ericka's needs would drive her closer to Irma, who, far from rejecting her, would love her all the more.

On the other hand, there was Ericka's need for love, affection and approval, so strong that she would go to any lengths, obey any commands, to get them—and could be so desperately wounded when those things were withheld. The opposite face of that coin was resentment, anger, rebellion, attention-getting behavior—and a profound unhappiness—all of which showed itself largely in compulsive eating.

None of these insights came as revelations to Melinda. She had to apply deduction, intuition, logic and some soul searching to hammer them out. They were by no means crystal clear to her, but they seemed to have a pattern that fit the situation.

Of the immediate problem Dr. Murray said, "It's not uncommon for young girls approaching puberty to have an unreasoning fear of it. It can be traumatic at times. However, we won't know about that until she starts treatment, will we?"

On her last visit, as she was leaving, Melinda asked, "Should I fire Irma?"

"Don't you think that decision is up to you?"

So Melinda as usual was forced by Dr. Murray's technique to seek the answer within herself. Dreading it, she put it off by consulting George first.

George Barnstable found Melinda's Murray-induced assessment of Irma hard to understand and harder to believe. He was comfortable with Irma Gertner and found her subtle attentions to him pleasant. He dreaded the disruption her dismissal would create.

Melinda had a long talk with Irma about her attitudes and her handling of Ericka. Irma was at first hurt and tearful, but Melinda was patient, and in the end Irma seemed to understand. The silent, disapproving punishments stopped, at least as far as Melinda could see. Melinda had her misgivings, but Irma stayed on.

Ericka began a series of biweekly visits to Dr. Emily Murray, which lasted for a year. At the end of that time Ericka had grown another three inches and was almost fourteen. She had also put on fifteen more pounds.

Dr. Murray called Melinda to her office. "I think you should consider another therapist," Dr. Murray said. "I don't seem to be getting through to Ericka. There's some deep underlying problem I don't seem to be able to crack. I can get so far and no further. She keeps herself closed to me. She refuses to talk about anything that happened before the ages of eight or nine. It's possible that she really doesn't remember. In any case something is blocking off that period in her life. Tell me, did she suffer any significant trauma in her early years? Of course, it needn't have been significant. Sometimes something that may seem trivial to the layman . . ."

Melinda, who didn't know, could only say so.

"Well, another therapist . . . perhaps hypnosis . . . it's a tool many doctors have used with good results."

"No," Melinda said. "That's a hell of a thing to do to a child. It isn't fair."

"I'm sorry." Dr. Murray's words had a disturbing finality. "I wish I could have helped more. . . ."

"But what do I do now?"

"I'd suggest you try loving her." It was the only direct advice Emily Murray had ever offered.

The night of December 18, 1951, was one to remember. At four A.M. Melinda was in the apartment of Tobin Wright, her lodger-cum-lover. She had just experienced the last of a series of satisfying orgasms and was thinking about the cold trip back to her own bed when Ericka began to scream. The scream went on and on.

"What the hell is that?" said Tobin with real alarm.

Melinda grabbed her robe and tried to get herself into it as she ran for the door. She didn't bother with the elevator, but took the stairs downward, two at a time. As she passed George's landing she heard him call out. Before she reached the floor below another scream started, hoarse and full of terror. Scream followed scream.

The light was on in Ericka's bathroom. Irma was framed in the doorway. Melinda grabbed her shoulder, spun her around and slapped her hard enough to knock her down. Irma stopped screaming. But Ericka didn't.

Ericka was naked, her pitifully fat body rigid. She was holding her left wrist with her other hand. From the wrist a steady stream of blood pulsed, to drip down and form an ugly pool on the white tile floor. Melinda snatched a bath towel and tried to wrap it around Ericka's arm.

By that time George Barnstable had reached the room. Ericka's slashed wrist was hidden from him by the towel, so what George saw first was the thin rivulet of blood running down her inner thigh. He had an instant vision of this same child, very different then, standing in a filthy Berlin vault, with blood encrusted on her legs. Gavin Riordan's voice saying "Jesus Christ!" was as real as if Gavin were in the room.

Then he realized what the real problem was and took charge. Ericka was still screaming, drawing in great gulps of air. This time it was George who did the slapping. The sound stopped, the sudden silence a blessed relief. Ericka still breathed in painful shuddering gasps. There was no intelligence in her eyes. She didn't seem to recognize either of them.

When George wiped away the blood he saw that the slash was clean and deep enough to have nicked the large vessel. He put his thumb several inches above the wound and pressed hard. The bleeding slowed and then stopped.

"Get something for a tourniquet. . . ."

From the doorway Tobin Wright said, "I'll do it."

"Right. Necktie or something." And to Melinda, "Put your arms around her and hold her tight."

Melinda pressed the taut unyielding body against her and felt the muscles quivering with tension. Suddenly Ericka collapsed like a sack of flour on the toilet seat, pulling Melinda to her knees beside her. George lost his pressure point and had to find it again. Melinda felt a hot spurt of blood on her bare breast and realized that she had lost her belt somewhere in her rush down the stairs and that her robe gaped open. She was too busy trying to hold Ericka upright to cover herself.

Tobin Wright returned with a necktie and one of Ericka's rulers. While George substituted a piece of hard soap for his thumb and applied and tightened the tourniquet, she saw that Tobin, with his unshakeable sense of propriety, was dressed in pajamas, robe and slippers. There was a paisley scarf tied at his neck.

"I called an ambulance," Tobin said.

"How long?"

"They said within fifteen minutes."

"This thing has to be loosened every few minutes and then tightened again. We better get her back to bed." George picked up Ericka with a grunt of effort and carried her into the still, dark bedroom.

Clutching her robe together, Melinda snapped on the light. There was a deep groan. Irma Gertner was still on the floor. They had all forgotten her. Irma tried to sit up, and they saw there was blood there too. In falling, Irma had hit her head on the bedside table. The blood had run down into one eye. Irma put a hand to her cut and drew in her breath to scream again.

"Don't do that!" Melinda said fiercely. "Just stop it!"

"For Christ's sake, get her out of here." George laid Ericka down on her bed and sat beside her.

"I'll do it." Tobin helped Irma to her feet and led her to her own room.

Melinda went to the other side of the bed, tried to pull up the rumpled bedclothes. Ericka lay still, trancelike, her eyes empty. Melinda caught the tracery of red on her inner thigh, glistening in reflection from the light, and followed it to its source.

"She's started to menstruate. Maybe that . . . . Dr. Murray said it was traumatic for some kids. . . ."

She didn't know whether to be relieved or burst into tears. Ericka's naked chubby body, scant pubic hair almost hidden in the creases of fat, looked so defenseless, so desperately vulnerable. Melinda covered her and reached to take her free hand. She was touched almost unbearably when Ericka clutched her hand so tightly that it hurt. Her eyes were now focused on Melinda's face. There was an expression in them that Melinda read as pleading, entreaty. For what?

Ericka sighed deeply. Her eyes closed. Her grip on Melinda's hand relaxed and she began to breathe evenly and normally.

"No. There's more to it than that."

There was a certainty in George's voice that puzzled her. She watched as he loosened the tourniquet, waited for the blood to flow and tightened it again.

"Melinda, there's something I should have told you. . . ."

The arrival of the white-coated intern and his helpers interrupted whatever he had been about to say. The ambulance was from Doctor's Hospital, a private institution that catered mostly to the rich or famous. Typically it was the only hospital Tobin Wright had been able to think of.

The intern advised that Irma Gertner be hospitalized as well, in case there were a possible concussion. They watched from the front windows as Irma insisted on getting into the ambulance under her own power, and Ericka, still unconscious, was wheeled in on a stretcher.

Later, after Tobin Wright had returned to bed, Melinda, now in slacks and sweater, was trying to clean up the mess in the bathroom. She wasn't up to waking Dancy and the fresh hysterics Dancy was sure to bring. She was on her hands and knees when George appeared with Scotch and glasses.

"Drink?"

"God, yes." It was impossible with the towel she was using to get at the blood in the cracks between the tiles. She made one last ineffectual swipe and gave up. When she left the bathroom George called to her from Irma's room. When she joined him he was crouched in front of the open door of the small refrigerator Melinda had installed along with the wall kitchenette.

"I was getting some ice. Take a look at this."

Melinda stared unbelievingly at the array of cakes, cookies and pastries that crowded the shelves. Irma never ate desserts, so . . .

"That stupid, wicked woman. How could she!"

"Don't ask me. You're the psychiatry expert."

They took their drinks back to Ericka's room, George once again on the bed, Melinda slumped in an easy chair. George didn't know how to begin what he knew he had to say. He began clumsily but with growing determination launched into his recital of things he had never told Melinda about Berlin and Ericka. Melinda listened in rapt fascination.

"Oh, God, George," Melinda said at last. "If you'd only told me in the beginning. That's probably what Dr. Murray was trying to get at. Something buried deep. If she had only known, maybe she could have helped . . . Why the hell didn't you, George?"

George shrugged helplessly.

"Afraid of offending my delicate sensibilities?"

"Partly that, I suppose. . . . And it didn't seem fair to her. . . ."

"Good God," Melinda said. And then, after a considerable pause, "Question is, what are we going to do about her?"

"You tell me." George looked around the room. "You don't suppose there are any more surprises in here, do you?"

"Let's find out."

In the bottom drawer of Ericka's desk George unearthed a sketch-book, opened it and gave a sibilant whistle.

"My God, look at this!"

They sat side by side, turning page after page. The pad was filled with drawings, all variations on the same theme, the obscene grotesque figure of a woman, impossibly fat, immensely gross. Some showed gaping wounds; on one a pendulous breast had been excised graphically. The heads of all of them were unmistakable faithful portraits of Irma Gertner.

"How she must have hated the woman. It's hard to believe . . ."

"Or herself," Melinda said thoughtfully.

"But look at the drawing. It's superb. It's frightening—but it's beautiful." His voice showed awe.

"Oh, George. That's not important now. . . ."

"But it is," he interrupted. "Even more important. You can't let a talent like that go to waste." He stared at the drawings before him a long time. "What's it to be?" he asked at last. "Back to Dr. Murray?"

"I'm not sure. Something she said sticks with me. She said, 'Why don't you try loving her?' I *do* love her, George. I have from the very start. I don't know how I'd feel about children of my own, but I don't think I could love them any more than I do Ericka. Maybe the problem is that she doesn't know it. You feel you ducked your responsibility. But so did I. You left it up to me and I passed it on to Irma. We're both guilty. I am damned well going to try to make up for it. How about you?"

George looked at her for a thoughtful moment. "Okay, hon. If you think it will work."

"It's *got* to work."

Melinda began to grin. "What?"

"I was just remembering how good it felt when I hit that woman. It was a long time coming."

Despite her exhaustion, Melinda reached the hospital by eight in the morning and was told that Ericka was still under sedation. George arrived shortly after nine and they both sat by her bed, waiting for her to come out of it.

It was ten o'clock before Ericka opened her eyes. Her head was toward Melinda. She immediately twisted to look away and found George. George reached for her bandaged hand, took it in both of his and leaned to kiss it gently.

"It's all right, honey. Don't be afraid. You'll never have to be afraid again." He felt tears come to his eyes as they had once before, in Berlin, when he had said the same words to her.

Melinda took her hand and Ericka turned toward her. Intuitively Melinda found the right thing to say. "She'll be gone when you get home. You'll never have to see her again." And then, "We love you, darling. More than you can possibly know."

Ericka began to smile, but before it could grow, her eyes closed again and she was asleep.

In the corridor, as they were leaving, the resident therapist stopped them and suggested that Ericka stay for at least ten days for psychiatric observation and possibly therapy.

"No," George said firmly. "No more fooling with her head. We want her home as soon as she's able."

"As you wish," the resident said. "However . . . about the obvious obesity problem. It would be best, of course, if she had some desire to lose weight on her own. Failing that, I suggest a careful watch of calorie intake. A pity, under all that fat there may be a pretty girl, as they say."

Irma Gertner was released from the hospital the same afternoon. Melinda had a twinge of guilt when she saw the neat white bandage on Irma's forehead, but she fired her anyway. She had paid two weeks' rent for Irma at the Gramercy Park Hotel, and by six o'clock Irma, assisted happily by Dancy, was packed and gone, her resentment silenced by a fat check.

The house seemed twice as big, and Melinda felt light on her feet. On impulse she decided to redo the whole third floor as a studio apartment for Ericka. She called the movers to have the furniture removed and stored. Her head was busy with decorating plans until it struck her that Ericka should have a say in the end result. It occurred to her that Ericka could share her queen-size bed until the apartment was finished. The prospect delighted her.

When Ericka returned two days later, the three of them had a conversation. Melinda and George pointed out to Ericka the real lesson to be learned from her near-tragedy: that none of them had the right to deprive the others of herself or himself. It would be too hurtful because of the love they felt for each other.

"I won't do it again," Ericka said, "if that's what you're worried about."

George and Melinda had to be content with that. Again, it was a beginning.

There followed two years of plotting. Melinda and George set out to woo Ericka as assiduously and subtly as any lovers. Melinda cut her workload to the bone, and George spent all the time he could at home. He worked with Ericka on her drawing, the techniques she had already studied with Mrs. Rosati—watercolor, wash, graphite pencil, gouache—and finally introduced her to brush and oil and the endless color variations these provided. They took long sketching walks about the city on weekends and covered the museums again and again.

The day came when George sat back, critically admiring a still life she had done of a corner of Gramercy Park, and said, "Honey, one day you're going to be a very fine artist." He said it with a touch of envy.

"But I don't want to be an artist."

It was such a throwaway line that he wasn't sure he had heard it.

"Oh, it's fun. And I love it. But it's not what I want to be."

Unbelieving, he protested. "But you've got a hell of a talent."

"I'm going to be an architect. I thought you knew. Painting is just something I like to do."

"No," George said slowly, "I didn't know. You're sure it's not just because I . . . ?"

"That's part of it, I guess. But it's really what I've always wanted to be. I want to design things where people can live. Things you can see."

When he got over his astonishment he was overjoyed. Thereafter Erica spent as much time as she could at Barnstable & Company, watching, learning and making a nuisance of herself as George's young tigers worked on the firm's various projects.

134

There wasn't all that much free time, for Melinda was tireless in her attention and fierce in her determination to gain Ericka's friendship. Friendship came first; after that, she could only hope for something deeper. She wanted to be fair, to avoid the mistake of overwhelming the girl with too much kindness, too much sympathy, too much attention. She was firm when she had to be. She talked over a gradual reducing program with Ericka, and when Ericka reluctantly agreed to give it a try, she bearded Dancy in her basement lair.

"What I know about them calories?" Dancy complained. "When that chile hungry, she ought to eat. Jes' baby fat anyhow. Come right off when she's growed."

Melinda handed her a calorie counter. "You better learn about them calories. If I catch you feeding her anything that's not on the list, it's back to Lynchburg—and you better believe it."

Dancy cheated anyway. Ericka was not totally committed to the plan, so the pounds came off with agonizing slowness.

When Melinda found out the true situation at Briarstone, she was outraged. She stormed into the office of the headmistress, determined that things would change or Ericka would be removed from the school.

The headmistress smiled her frosty smile. "Think, Melinda, wasn't there a girl in your class called 'Cow-Cow' by everyone?"

It stopped her. She was forced to remember that she herself had coined the nickname for a girl with huge breasts. "Well, it fit," Melinda said weakly. "She was obscene."

"Things do come back to haunt us, don't they? I hope you'll reconsider. The child seems to be doing well here. She is an exceptional student."

Still furious, Melinda wanted to go through with her plan. Ericka vetoed it almost tearfully. So Ericka stayed at Briarstone.

In truth Ericka was less miserable there than before. She showed no signs of missing the companionship of her peers. Melinda and George seemed enough for her. There were vacations on Cape Cod, and twice a cruise to Bermuda. Given the the chance to mingle with other youngsters, Ericka preferred to go her own way, unapproachably aloof.

Melinda longed to take her in her arms, but Ericka had long since abandoned or repressed her early need to touch and be cuddled. Now though Ericka would accept a caress politely, Melinda had the feeling she considered any such gesture an imposition.

All that changed one afternoon in May when the headmistress called to tell Melinda that Ericka was to be allowed to graduate a year ahead of her class.

"No thanks are required, Melinda," the headmistress said drily. "I had nothing to do with it, except to give my approval of the recommendation of the staff. She's a rather remarkable girl. Pity you don't make her lose more weight."

Melinda hung up feeling reprimanded and somehow blamed for letting down the side, something the headmistress could do to her without fail.

She had poured herself a drink and was sitting in the living room, alternating between resentment and pride, when Teresa Rosati brought Ericka home from school. That was unusual in itself, but the look at their faces told her that she was in for another surprise. Ericka gravely laid an envelope in her lap. She saw that it was addressed to Mrs. Teresa Rosati. As Melinda opened it, Teresa said, "She wouldn't let me tell you for fear she wouldn't make it. But she did, by God! She did!"

Melinda read slowly:

Your pupil Ericka Ullman has won first prize for composition and drawing in the Annual Junior Competition, for her work entitled *Mother*. (Exhibit No. 804)

Enclosed find our check for $250.00 (two hundred and fifty dollars).

First Prize entitles Miss Ullman to a scholarship for one year at the American School for Arts and Design. Registration must be completed by June 1, 1953.

"We'll have to take it back because they want it for the exhibit. But I thought you should see it first."

Teresa was stripping the brown paper wrapping from a flat package. Melinda held her breath.

The picture was a three-quarter head-and-shoulders pastel study of Melinda against a window, with the tops of Gramercy Park trees as background. It had captured Melinda at her best, head up, chin out, eyes alive with animation. But what got to her was the obvious love and devotion that had gone into the rendering of it. Melinda burst into tears.

Ericka's arms were around her, Ericka's hand stroking her shoulder, and suddenly it was Ericka providing the comfort and support Melinda had so longed to give. Then Ericka was crying too as they clutched each other tightly.

"My God," Melinda said, "we'll drown if we don't stop."

But she knew that she had won. Ericka was hers and she was Ericka's, and she thought her heart would break.

Once they found they could show their love for each other, Ericka began to learn to value herself. Almost overnight, to Dancy's despair and Melinda's delight, food became her enemy. She fought fat with all the single-minded dedication of a fasting Hindu guru. She exercised each day, and as the pounds began relentlessly to come off, she discovered clothes and makeup. Her hair regained the silvery sleekness George remembered from her childhood, her skin the same translucent milkiness. It wasn't easy. It had its periods of deep despair. But now there was Melinda to lean on. George was no help. He could only grin with idiot pleasure as the transformation progressed.

The day she cracked one hundred and thirty, Melinda took her to Hicks to celebrate. They each had banana splits with all the trimmings. Convinced that celebration called for a more permanent memorial, Melinda took her across the street to Saks and bought her a wickedly expensive raccoon coat.

Midway through Ericka's scholarship year, George Barnstable was offered a commission to design and build a boys' school just outside of Paris. It meant two years abroad at the least. At first he didn't want to take it, but then he had an idea he considered brilliant.

That evening, over lean grilled lamb chops and watercress salad dressed with lemon juice, he said, deadpan, "How would you two like to live in Paris for a while?"

Melinda looked at him as though she thought he was crazy, Ericka with the serious attention she always gave him.

"École des Beaux Arts." George started to grin. "It's where I went, and it's the best architectural school in the world." And then to Melinda, "We could get her launched for a couple of years—and then come back here. They want me to build a school over there."

"But my business . . ." Melinda began, and stopped. "What the hell," she said. "Why not. How about you, honey?"

There was no need to ask. Ericka's eyes were bright with delight.

When they boarded the *Ile de France* for Paris, Ericka was five feet six inches tall and weighed one hundred and eighteen pounds. With immense satisfaction Melinda watched the heads turn as they made their way along the crowded deck.

11

Time: 1951
STEWART GANSVOORT

In the four years of his marriage Gavin Riordan had heard a lot about postpartum depression. It was easy to diagnose, sometimes hard to cure. It could last for weeks—or years. It affected some women suicidally, some by paranoia, both mild and acute, some catatonically. Birdie ran the gamut.

In the first year Birdie was hospitalized for three months. She came home apparently cured. Des Daniher had provided them with a comfortable house a few blocks from his own, and Birdie became a compulsive housekeeper. The house was never clean enough. She couldn't bear dirt or disorder. Gavin, who was naturally neat and organized but not overly concerned about it, soon found the house oppressive.

Birdie from the start was pitifully grateful for Gavin's name and protection, although the reason for it was only mentioned once. Gavin, studying police manuals, had filled an ashtray with cigarette butts. He was startled when Birdie's thin arm came over his shoulder to empty it. He hadn't heard her approach.

"For Christ's sake, Birdie, leave it!"

The words were sharper than he intended.

The arm was withdrawn. She was still standing motionless behind him. He felt her hand briefly touch his hair. He turned to her to say he was sorry and found that she was crying.

"You don't need to stay, Gavin. There's no reason, since the baby . . . I could go back to Uncle Des."

He was overcome with pity. His arms around her, he said, "Don't talk like that, Birdie. We're doing just fine. Everything will be all right." And he thought, *It's not her fault. I'm the one who made the bargain.*

As it often did, his holding her close seemed to arouse her. He felt her body curve into his, her pelvis urgent against his leg. He took her upstairs and made gentle love to her.

Their sex life puzzled him. At times she strictly observed the prescribed rhythm method. At others she seemed deliberately to violate it. During those periods she was intense and abandoned in her lovemaking, crying out for his sperm as though she wanted to become pregnant. The idea of a child rather intrigued him, but nothing came of it.

When she had been out of the hospital for five months, Gavin came home to find her locked in the bathroom. He had to break down the door. Birdie was crouched over the open toilet bowl holding something under the water. She had made a rag doll out of scraps of cloth and was trying to drown it.

For three weeks she wouldn't leave the bedroom. The house was neglected, no meals prepared. Gavin brought dinners from the Italian restaurant on the corner. At the end of that time Mary Margaret Shay appeared with her suitcase and commandeered the spare room. A week later Birdie was back in the hospital.

Mary Margaret left as abruptly as she had arrived. A day later Annie Brian, another of Mary Margaret's endless cousins, moved in. Her salary was paid by Des Daniher, although it was never mentioned.

In another three months Birdie was out again, seemingly herself. That remission lasted exactly six months and Gavin began to wonder if that was to be the pattern. When he asked, the doctor was patient.

"It's possible. Of course in these cases one never knows. She could be perfectly normal the rest of her life. On the other hand..."

In the next three years Birdie was home for a total of eleven months. Annie Brian became a permanent fixture, and Gavin got used to being a bachelor. It wasn't hard. His days were full as a cop, his nights occupied by law school with two more years to go for a degree. He settled into a mindless routine largely governed by the clock. He had little time or inclination to think about himself.

Patrolman Gavin Riordan was attached to the Third Precinct in the Twelfth Ward, Des Daniher's particular stronghold in the city. The Twelfth Ward was a curious racial mix. Originally, when Daniher had first started his career, it had been predominantly Irish, Old Country Irish, its storefronts and taverns sporting names like O'Garrity, Mooney, Fitzgerald and Carney. The ward started with the riverfront warehouses and factories and crept up to the top of the hill, which was then called Schuyler Heights, until it all but surrounded the State Capitol Building at the crest. It was a mile wide and something over three miles long. A hundred years ago, before the Irish started coming, it had been an area of graceful colonial brick houses with families like the Livingstones, the Blauvelts, the Grosvenors, the Stuyvesants and the Van Rensselaers. As the city grew over the years, the old families moved or died out; their lovely bowfront mansions were subdivided into flats.

The Irish immigrants first settled on the riverfront, which became a teeming, bustling slum full of crime and poverty, noisy with

140

traffic, dark and dirty, a place of wharves and ships, factories, churches and graveyards. As the Irish came up in the world, they moved farther up Schuyler Heights, and with them came cheap housing, until the old homes were crowded by ugly brownstones and wooden three-deckers.

The Italians took their place on the waterfront. The storefront names became Gagliardi, Ricci, Mangione and Testa, but the character of the slums changed very little otherwise.

The blacks came last, filling in the gaps as the Irish moved up the hill and spread out on its other side.

The Twelfth Ward had been ripe for young Desmond Patrick Daniher, five years out of County Cork, a fresh law degree in his pocket and the brogue still on his lips. He molded the Irish into a cohesive political entity, made a mutually beneficial peace with the new Italians. Between them they kept the blacks in line. Des Daniher, with his solid block of voters, elected his councilmen, his assemblymen, his mayors and finally, as his power spread through the state, his governor. But his heart still stayed with the Twelfth Ward. The needy got coal for their stoves in winter, their streets were cleared of heavy snows, there were free turkeys at Christmas. Any mother's son of them could call on Des Daniher for help with anything at all. And get it, too. Provided they were Democrats of voting age.

The Third Precinct was at the heart of the ward, and the heart of the Third was Deacy Street. There the ethnic stewpot bubbled like a witches' brew. Over the years Deacy Street had become a place of dance halls, sleazy nighclubs, horse parlors and whorehouses, all of it surrounded by decent hardworking people in walkup flats and what was left of the old buildings. At one end of Deacy Street was the Teamsters Hall, at the other St. Thomas Cathedral, started in 1847 and finished in 1891. Between the two flourished all the ancient sins of men, with some new ones as well. Over it all brooded the State Capitol Building, built in 1853. A red sandstone monstrosity, squatting like a laying hen in some dirty barnyard.

The Third Precinct was now known as the Pit, and it was the job of the men of the Third to keep order in this volatile area. Not so much order to seriously interfere with the normal conduct of business, of course. For all of these were Daniher's people, from the self-respecting to the thieves, including the ones in the State House. An occasional raid was allowed when the cries of the reform movement got too raucous. The police commission got headlines and took the credit for cleaning out the vice, and Deacy Street went back to what it did best.

On Saturday afternoon, on his day off, Gavin had returned Birdie once more to St. Malachy's Sanatorium, this time at her own request, before he had seen any disturbing symptoms. She said she felt safer there, which struck him as curious, although he wasn't prepared to argue about it. He ate from the refrigerator and settled down to study for a law exam scheduled for Monday night.

It was one A.M. before he realized it. He wasn't tired, just vaguely depressed. Because he didn't want to think about Birdie, much less about himself, he decided on a walk before bed. By force of habit he made for Deacy Street, his daytime beat.

In daylight Deacy Street was quiet, closed, its few markets and delicatessens doing a desultory business. At night it hummed with a sound peculiar to itself from behind the neon-lighted fronts of bars and clubs; the night-people sound. A disturbing sound, always on the edge of violence, ready to explode.

Gavin approached from the back, along silent streets past darkened houses. Occasionally a dog barked. The June night was pleasantly cool after an unseasonably hot day. Above the gabled roofs the sky was clear. The moon cast grotesque shadows of gabled roofs on the deserted roadway. In the near distance the music from the Roseland Palace seemed muted and sad to Gavin's sober ear.

Gavin entered a back alley that was a shortcut to the rear of the buildings on Deacy Street. He was headed for another alley that would take him along the side of Annie Gorman's expensive bordello and into Deacy Street. He was crossing the dingy rubbish-filled backyards that separated vice from respectability, dodging clotheslines draped with damp laundry, when he heard the shot. Then came the sound of a policeman's nightstick rapping frantically against a stone curbing, the signal of a cop in trouble.

All hell broke loose. There was a fusillade of shots, the flat familiar sound of a Police Positive .38. Sirens started, one nearby, others in the distance. Gavin began to run, then slowed down when he realized he wasn't armed and that he could break his neck on invisible litter.

The back door of Annie Gorman's opened and spilled a path of light. Gavin saw the naked figure of a man clutching a bundle to his chest in the brief moment before the light was cut off. He heard the man stumble and quietly curse. The man came toward him, and Gavin tackled him hard. His driving shoulder caught the other's midsection. He heard a satisfying whoosh of breath as they both slammed to the ground.

"Police!" Gavin gasped. "Just hold it. Right where you are."

He was lying on the man's body, pinning him, their faces inches apart. He could smell the sour whiskey odor.

"Jesus Christ!" the man said, "Gavin. Gavin Riordan."

Gavin saw he was holding Stewart Gansvoort.

He took this in swiftly, like a smart cop and the son of a cop. "What the hell happened?"

"Crazy guy stabbed a girl. In the next room. Somebody called the cops. I just ran." It was a simple statement. It needed no explanation or excuse, Stewart being who he was, and Gavin believed him.

"Did you see it?"

"No. Just . . . afterward. I told you, I ran."

Again Gavin believed him and made his decision.

"Okay. Get up." On his feet, Gavin said, "What the hell is that you're carrying?"

"My clothes. I just grabbed everything."

"For Christ's sake, put 'em on and let's get out of here."

Stewart got up painfully.

"I think you broke my leg."

Gavin steadied him as he struggled into his pants, thinking briefly of another time when the situation had been reversed. He had got no help from Stewart then. It had been Serena who helped him into his clothes. . . .

The police siren growled to a halt. They could hear car doors slam, the sound of loud voices from Deacy Street. The back exit from Annie Gorman's opened, someone looked out briefly and the door creaked shut. Stewart was trying to get into his shirt. Gavin knew there was no way he could answer the questions that would be asked if they were found here. He shoved Stewart ahead of him.

"Goddamnit. Run!"

When they reached the next street Stewart slowed to a limping walk.

"My car. I'm parked on Deacy. . . ."

"Worry about it tomorrow. Maybe they won't check out parked cars. If they do, say you were in a bar. Or the Democratic Club. Lotta people in there."

"Democratic Club. That's a laugh. Where we going? I can't get far on this leg."

Gavin considered for a moment and then said, "My house."

In Gavin's kitchen Stewart pulled up his pant leg to reveal a nasty gash just below the knee. Blood was still welling from it.

"Jesus, that hurts. . . . I could use a drink."

Gavin brought disinfectant and gauze pads and a bottle of Bushmill's. Stewart winced and sucked in his breath as Gavin cleaned the cut with peroxide and fixed a bandage with adhesive.

"Nothing to worry about. You'll live. What the hell were you doing at Annie's, anyway!"

Stewart looked at him quizzically and Gavin realized what a silly question it was. "I mean, with all the free stuff around, I wouldn't think *you'd* have to pay for it."

"You wouldn't think so, would you?" Stewart seemed somehow aggrieved. He reached for the bottle, poured himself a hefty drink and downed it. His eyes were round and owlish, watering from the bite of the whiskey. Gavin saw that he was more than a little drunk.

"We better get you home, old buddy. Before you fall on your face."

"Home is where the heart is. Last place I want to be. Don't think they like me much there." Stewart reached again for the bottle and this time poured them both drinks.

"Stay here if you want," Gavin said reluctantly. "There's a spare bedroom."

"Only one? Thought you'd do better by this time. Thought you'd

144

really be something. Serena told me you're a cop. Why would you want to be a cop?"

"It's something," Gavin said. "How's she?"

"You know, I used to think the sun rose and set on your ass, Gavin. You were everything I wanted to be and wasn't. And then, Serena . . ."

"Forget it," Gavin said. "How is she?"

"Serena? She's fine. Married again, to some asshole named Summerlin. . . ." Stewart considered this briefly. "No, he's not an asshole. He's just . . . Oh, to hell with it. Serena is not lucky with her men." And then quickly, "No offense. Present company and all that."

Stewart downed his drink. Gavin sipped at his, wondering how to get him to bed. He didn't look forward to wet-nursing a drunk for what was left of the night.

"I'm a little drunk," Stewart said, seeming to read his thoughts. "Nuisance. I haven't thanked you for tonight, Gavin. Always thank people. Thank you, Gavin." He closed his eyes and seemed to sleep, then abruptly opened them to look intently at Gavin. "In Berlin you said we were even. Now I'm in your debt. Deeply in your debt. How can I repay you? It's something we should think about."

"Forget it. Tell me, how did it go in Berlin? You ever get caught?"

"I always get caught," Stewart said sadly. "Littleton reamed my ass. Boy, did that son of a bitch ream my ass! But what could he do? Fire me? Father got me transferred to the embassy in London, where he could keep an eye on me. Three months and, zip, I was out of there and into Harvard Law." He began to doze again.

"Me, too," Gavin said forcefully.

"What?"

"Law school. Boston College. One more year to go."

"Nobody goes to B.C." Stewart seemed to find this ludicrous. "That's what I was doing tonight. Celebrating my graduation. And drowning my sorrows."

"Both?"

"Both. You know what that old bastard said to me?"

Wanting to keep it going, Gavin asked "Who?"

"My father. I'll tell you what he said to me. There I was, graduating from the best law school in the world. In the yard next to Langdell Hall. Cap and gown. Hundreds of people waiting to congratulate their offspring. And who was there for me? Nobody. That's who. Fucking nobody."

Stewart poured himself another drink. Gavin refilled his own, resigned to staying up. Stewart seemed to be drinking himself sober.

"The best . . . no, the toughest law school in the world. And I beat it. They elected me editor of the *Law Review*. The top. The very top. I graduated second in my class. And you know what he said? I'll tell you what he said. He said, 'I expected a son of mine to be first.' That's what the old bastard said." Stewart seemed overwhelmed by it. "'A son of mine to be first.' What the fuck does he want from me, anyhow?" He stared at Gavin, demanding a reply.

"What the hell," Gavin said. "Everyone has a father. Mine was a mick cop, got shot in an alley. Yours owns half the world. Nobody's perfect."

This had the desired effect of dissolving Stewart's self-pity. He laughed. "Half the world. Hey, Gavin. Remember in my office in Berlin? When I said the Gansvoorts were into Germany pretty heavy?" Stewart was looking at him slyly. "You know, I could see what you were thinking."

"No, you couldn't. I was thinking your old man probably financed the whole fucking war."

"He could have," Stewart said morosely. "And I wouldn't be surprised. You got an idea how much he's got?"

"No." Gavin didn't really want to know.

"You can't even count it."

"I know." Gavin was hearing Serena say the same thing in front of a dying fire and felt a sudden sharp loss.

"I mean it. You can't even count it. Not just oil companies. Airlines. Shipping lines. Gold mines. Hotels. Factories. Banks. Lots of banks. You name it, he's got it. I don't think he even knows all he's got. And more all the time. You know there's two hundred and fifty people just trying to keep track of it?"

"Must be hell to be so rich."

"You're fucking-A right!" Suddenly angry, Stewart's eyes blazed

146

into his. "What do you know, you stupid sumbitch? What do you know how it's like?"

"So tell me," said Gavin, trying to keep it light.

"I'm only talking to you because you don't want anything. You don't *need* anything. You never did. You always had it all."

"I need," Gavin said softly. "Believe me."

"Not from me, you don't. Everybody wants something. Do you know, every friend I ever had, every girl, everybody . . . wanted something from me. Because they knew I had it. The goddamned fucking money. It's in their eyes. I can see what they think. They think, 'This guy's got all that lovely money. Why can't he rub some on me? Couple of million or so. He'd never even miss it.' And they end up hating me when I won't. They'd end up hating me anyway, if I did. What the hell. It's a no-win deal."

Then his private sun must have come from behind another cloud. Stewart began to grin again. "What the hell. I keep 'em all guessing. They think I got all this fucking money—when I don't. The old man's got all the fucking money. I ain't got a pot to piss in. Well, maybe a few pots. But nothing, really. Until he dies."

"What would you do with it if you had it?"

"Burn it!" The thought seemed to give him immense pleasure. "In Rensselaer Square. The biggest fucking bonfire since Nero lit Rome. Have everybody come from miles around to see the sight."

"Seriously," said Gavin. "It'll all be yours someday. What will you do?"

"Seriously? There's too much of it to be serious about. It's a fucking joke. But if you want to be serious . . ." There was a faraway longing in Stewart's eyes, and Gavin knew he was seeing something Stewart wouldn't ordinarily reveal. "I'd like to build something. A big something. Like a city. Maybe this city. Tear down all the ugliness and put something beautiful in its place. Big and beautiful. Where people wouldn't want anything, because they wouldn't *need* anything. Have it all right here." Stewart shook himself, his mood again changed. "Shit. I'd like to rebuild the whole fucking world, for that matter. Turn it into one big dance hall, with Benny Goodman leading the band. Or maybe just pave it, like

Patton wanted to do to Germany. Not a bad idea, considering what's happening."

Stewart poured drinks and lifted his glass solemnly. "To General George Patton, bless his practical soul."

Gavin, beginning to feel pleasantly drunk and genuinely sorry for Stewart, followed suit. "To General Douglas MacArthur, who won't return anymore."

"And to Harry S-for-nothing Truman, who fired his insubordinate ass out of Korea." Their glasses were empty. Stewart filled them again. "They after you for Korea yet? All those medals and all?"

"No way," said Gavin. "The fucking Army would have more trouble getting me back than they got with the Chinese. I've had it with combat. What about you?"

"My father called a congressman. Or maybe the President. I don't know. Anyway, I'm exempt." Stewart lifted his glass again. "Don't walk down those stairs, Father dear." Stewart spoke with exaggerated concern. "You'll-slip-on-your-ass-an'-break-your-fucking-neck-you-clubfooted-old-son-of-a-bitch."

This time Gavin could laugh without restraint. He suddenly felt very friendly to Stewart.

In the silence after laughter, Stewart chuckled. "Tell 'em I was in the Democratic Club, you said. The old man would love that. He thinks Democrats all eat garlic and don't take baths, and in this town they all say *begorra* and *bejabbers*."

"That's with a long *A*. Be-*jay*-bers."

"What about you, Gavin," asked Stewart. "Why a cop?"

"My father was a cop," Gavin said.

"Mine's a prick. It doesn't necessarily follow . . . "

"It's not a bad life. . . . "

"But for you, Gavin? For you?"

Gavin looked at Stewart's earnest face, slightly flushed now, a lock of dark hair falling forward. A handsome face, long and patrician, with a curved mobile mouth that saved it from austerity. Stewart's eyes seemed to hold a sort of entreaty, as though he wanted Gavin to tell him that being a cop wasn't true. That it was a bad joke, an ugly masquerade that Gavin could dispel with a laugh.

And then the real Gavin Riordan would run out on the field to the roar of the crowd.

As though Stewart had actually said all this, Gavin answered him. "I'm no fucking hero," he said roughly.

Stewart seemed to follow him. "But you are. You're the only hero I know."

"Get off my back, Stewart. I'm a cop. And I'm going to be a good cop. I'm going to be a good lawyer, too. That's all there is. Don't ask for any more."

"Who's asking?" Stewart's face had the volatility of an actor. He was smiling his charming smile again, eyes sharp with mischief. "Can I see your badge? And your gun? Oh, boy! You want to be a cop—be a cop."

"Fuck you, Stewart." He wanted to strike out. "What are you gonna do with your goddamn life? Cut coupons?"

"Well," Stewart said reasonably, "I always wanted to be a fireman. Never a cop. Ride on one of those big red engines and ring the bell. Or maybe be a race driver. Good way to fill my urge for self-destruction, wouldn't you say?"

"Fuck you, you patronizing son of a bitch."

"I am, aren't I," said Stewart reasonably. "It's a failing of the rich. Makes us hard to get along with. I'm sorry, Gavin. Let's talk about something else."

Gavin allowed himself to be mollified. "Okay. So talk."

"What'll it be? Religion? Politics? I don't know shit about either one of them. That leaves—what? Sex? No, I've had enough of that for tonight."

"I suppose you'll vote for that asshole Henry Cabot Lodge, the Great Brahmin," Gavin said morosely. "It figures."

"Who else? I think he's a cousin, or something. If I vote at all."

"James Delaney Conroy. That's who."

"Another mick politician. Except he's rich. Not *rich* rich, but rich enough."

"Went to Harvard, too. That ought to clean him up a little for you. But he's a lot more than that. He's one hell of a guy. He stuck it up their ass as a representative. He'll stick it up their ass when he

149

gets to be a senator. He's for all the right things. I worked for him in the last campaign. You ought to hear him talk. He could make a believer even out of you."

Stewart surprised him by saying, "Okay. Why not?"

"You serious?"

"Sure. Wouldn't that fry my old man's ass. Maybe he'd cut me off without a sou. That'd be a gas."

"Okay." Gavin was intrigued.

"You want to meet him? I'll introduce you."

"You know him?"

"Yeah. He wrote a letter to every veteran in the state. He found out I won the Distinguished Service Medal and asked me to lunch. I was sold in five minutes. He's the best thing that ever happened to this fucking state."

"I didn't know that," Stewart said.

"Didn't know what?"

"The medal." Stewart was gravely impressed.

"Didn't know it myself. It only caught up to me when I got back."

"But that's a hell of a thing, Gavin. Next to the Medal of Honor. How'd you get that?"

"It's shit. All medals are shit. Stewart, you got to remember, you only get medals when you are in the wrong place at the wrong time. I spent the whole war trying to avoid that."

"If you say so . . . ol' buddy."

Stewart gave a long sigh. His eyes dropped shut and he slid off the chair. His face was as peaceful as a child's.

"No head for the stuff," Gavin heard himself mumble. "No head at all—at all."

He thought about getting Stewart up and then said to hell with it and left him as he lay.

Stewart evidently came to sometime in the night, because in the morning the guest-room bed had been slept in. There was a note and a check for a thousand dollars on the bureau. Stewart had borrowed one of his shirts, and the note was written on the shirt cardboard. "Don't know any other way to say thanks," Stewart had written.

"Another failing of the rich. Buy yourself a new shirt. Call you about Conroy, if I ever recover."

Gavin tore up the check with shaking hands.

12

Time: 1951
DESMOND PATRICK DANIHER

"No," Des Daniher said. "I'll wait."

"You'll be left holding your hat, you know." Gavin was impatient with his uncle's stubbornness. "He's going to win. He's proved it twice."

Hat on head, Daniher made a small sound that meant no..

"How much wooing do you want. I know his father has been after you."

Like Gavin himself but on a grander, plutocratic scale, Jim Conroy came of old Irish power. And, like Gavin, Conroy was moving on into a new age of broader ideas. A Catholic breaking barriers, moving to the very top.

"Ed Conroy is not James Conroy. I'll go to no man who is unwilling to come to me."

"He *isn't* unwilling. It's just that he's fought shy of his father's political friends from the beginning. He's always said the old line politicians can bring you their friends, but they saddle you with their enemies as well. I think he's right. His people are all young, mostly vets. And they've put him in the House twice. You can't knock that."

"Never. A fine bunch of lads. And smart. But this time it's for the Senate. It's statewide, a very different barrel of mackerel."

"That's my point," Gavin said earnestly. "You both need each other. He needs all the support he can get. And God knows you need a winner. Otherwise, Ike and the Republicans will sweep every office in the state."

"It's happened before, though not often, thank the good Lord. It may even happen again before they put me away, though I doubt it. No, thank you. I'll sit this one out."

"Jesus, Des. It doesn't have to be like that. Neutral ground. Just a casual meeting. I can arrange it."

"I don't need an introduction, you know. I've known the boy since he wet his drawers."

They were in Daniher's den, seated before the TV set. The volume was turned down. Daniher's eyes were fixed on the silent picture as an announcer mouthed words. He was waiting for a documentary to begin on the recently concluded hearings of Senator Kefauver's crime committee.

Gavin watched his guardian, searching for a way to reach him. Daniher sat straight in his easy chair, as if it were impossible to lounge. At fifty-one Daniher was a vigorous man, tall and slim, with none of the sag of middle age. His eyes had lost none of their penetrating blueness. They could sparkle with humor or turn cold as Arctic ice, though the bristling brows were shot with gray.

"You think he can't win without you?" asked Gavin.

"Gavin, me dear. You've a lot to learn. I'll wait. And that's the way of it. Now turn up the thing an' we'll listen to the voice of doom."

For the next half hour they watched the parade of witnesses. It was old stuff to both of them. The hearings had been on TV since the first of the year, but the show still held its fascination. Senators, lawyers, hoodlums, played out a drama of good against evil, the white hats versus the black hats. Kefauver, with his long horse face and his Appalachian drawl, his presidential ambitions showing clearly. Rudolph Halley, the committee's chief counsel, relentlessly probing, trying to break through the protection of the Fifth Amend-

152

ment, painting an incredible picture of national crime and corruption. The telltale hands of Frank Costello, twisting in his lap.

"It's all shit," Gavin said. "And you know it. Nothing will ever be done about it."

"Don't be too sure. Publicity is something the boys can't stand. See how the camera makes them nervous."

"Twenty billion dollars," Gavin scoffed, "the take in illegal gambling alone. I could stand being nervous for twenty billion a year."

"They'll never stop the gambling," said Des.

"Then they'll never stop any of it. Because twenty billion buys a lot of protection for the rest of the rackets—loan sharking, prostitution, dope. You name it. There's a dozen judges in this town getting rich off the Mob. With the right judge, anything goes. Even murder. The pad in the Third alone runs to fifty thousand a year."

The program came to an end. Gavin switched off the set and leaned back to find Daniher looking at him speculatively. That bit about the judges had got to him, since most of the judges were Daniher's.

"You on it, Gavin?"

"The pad? You know I'm not."

"Do I, now. Now how would I be knowin' that?"

The brogue had thickened, a warning signal.

"Because you know everything that goes on. Particularly in the Twelfth Ward. You could probably tell me how the take is split."

"Does it bother you, the pad?"

"Among a lot of things. Enough so I'm thinking of another line of work."

"A better one? Gavin, lad. The world is a dirty place, and man a pretty bad piece of work, all in all. It's the nature of the beast. Can you change that?"

"Maybe it's worth a try," Gavin said morosely, feeling in his heart that it wasn't. That Daniher was probably right, that all the promise of a Jim Conroy, or men like him—if there were any—was merely a lonely whistling in the wind. At least, he thought, if I got out, I wouldn't have my nose rubbed in it every day. Or be suspected

153

because I won't take a few lousy dollars in graft, sent out on the street when payoff day comes in the station house.

"How's Birdie?" asked Daniher.

Gavin recognized it as a preliminary to dismissal.

"She's better. They say she can come out again in a month or so." *Birdie*, he thought, *I can't even remember the color of her eyes, the sound of her voice, the feel of her body.*

"A grand girl," Daniher said, "when she's herself. The doctors will have her well in no time. You'll see." He still kept up the fiction that Birdie's trouble was temporary. "Well, now. A drop against the night before you go?"

"No," Gavin said. "I'm on duty at midnight. Thanks just the same, Uncle Des. I'll take a raincheck."

Des Daniher waited until he heard the door close before he poured himself a drink. He held his glass up against the light in a silent toast. He was thinking, *I seem to have raised myself an honest man. And a cop fighter, to boot. Is it the war that did it, or just the Irish rebel in him?*

Des Daniher seldom looked back at what had been. But tonight he felt the Black Irish sadness. He poured another drink, warmed it in his hands, his mind, despite himself, roaming backward over the years.

Desmond Patrick Daniher had hung out his shingle on the edge of the no-man's-land separating the new Italians at the bottom of the hill from the Irish moving up. Two storefront rooms, the front for working, the back for living. He could afford nothing grander.

It was a bad location because the Irish didn't want to come back down the hill to find a lawyer. The Italians had no such compunctions. But they had no money, either, so many of his fees were paid in kind in the beginning. At least he ate well and learned the delights of Italian cooking.

And there was excitement in the City. The air was filled with the screech of streetcars, the cries of Italian vendors, the whine of winches as freighters from all the world over unloaded their goods. Young Daniher was never lonely, for he felt the breath of the City, as hot and bloody as a jungle animal. An animal waiting to be stalked.

He absorbed the wild energy of the City through his pores, feasted on it and grew strong.

In a search for clients of his own race he joined the Hibernian Athletic Club—the real beginning for Daniher. The Hibernian boxing team was City champion that year, and at one-seventy Daniher was a natural light-heavy. Tall and broad, he made up in ferocity what he lacked in skill. With his shocking hair against the pale white skin he was spectacular in the Friday-night bouts.

His single-minded destroyer's instinct both repelled and thrilled Sally Anne Kinkaid. Then she found that, once the battle was won, the mild-mannered young man in neat blue serge could be both tender and gentle. He quite won her heart. She was the daughter of Martin Kinkaid, District Leader of the Twelfth Ward. That fact allowed her to break all the rules of the all-male club and cheer with the best of them from a ringside seat; Martin Kinkaid had donated the building to the Hibernians.

It was Kinkaid himself who introduced his daughter to Desmond Daniher. There were few times when he regretted it. One of them was about to come up.

Daniher was beginning to prosper. His reputation as a fighter was translated into clients. Small cases at first, more important ones as this quietly confident young man began to prove himself. Under Martin Kinkaid's sponsorship he joined the Twelfth Ward Democratic Club. At that time the Republican machine, which had controlled the City for decades, was showing signs of coming apart. The machine controlled the mayor's office, judges, legislature and police. Over the years the machine people had become fat and careless, their plundering of the City too blatant. The Democrats sensed that their time had come, and battle was joined.

Desmond Daniher was fascinated by it all. He smelled the power that was there and learned something of its uses. He fell in love with it.

He made a move up the hill to Blauvelt Street. Four rooms now, with proper living space and a front office he needn't have been ashamed of. It was about this time that Daniher received a summons to appear before Angelo Pavane. Angelo Pavane was the boss of the waterfront. He was president of the longshoremen's union and controlled bootlegging, gambling, loan sharking and whatever else he could lay his hands on. Pavane wanted Daniher to defend his brother Domenic on a murder charge. The victim was a cop named Eddie Mulvey.

"Why me?" Daniher asked. "Surely one of your own . . . "

"You kiddin'? Irish judge, Irish DA an' a fuckin' Irish jury," Pavane pointed out. "What chance would a wop lawyer have?"

Pavane had a point, but Daniher felt it was a no-win proposition. If he took the case, his own people would resent it. If he won he'd be tagged as the lawyer who got off the wop who murdered a fine Irish boy. If he lost, as was likely, it would do his reputation no good at all.

Suddenly Pavane lost his toughness. Daniher was surprised to see tears in his eyes. "I love my brother, Mr. Daniher. You been a good friend to people down here. Everybody says so. I'm beggin' you to be my friend now. Without you Dom don't stand a whore's chance. They'll burn him for sure. An' he didn't kill that cop. I swear it on my mother."

It was the first mention of innocence. Daniher had assumed that Domenic Pavane *had* killed the cop. "I'll listen," he said. "I won't promise anything."

Domenic Pavane owned a restaurant. Behind it was a blind pig where known customers could do their illicit drinking in peace and security—provided the owner kept up his payoffs to the cops. On the night in question, the way Angelo Pavane told it, Patrolman Eddie Mulvey and an unidentified male companion dropped in for the usual weekly protection money. The two men, in plain clothes, stayed on to sample Domenic's hospitality. Too much of it, it would seem. At closing time Mulvey decided that the small sum he had collected wasn't enough. So he relieved Domenic Pavane of the night's take—some thirty-five hundred dollars.

Domenic promptly called his brother Angelo, who in turn called Captain Spelvy of the Third Precinct. Spelvy told him not to worry, that he would take care of it. By this time it was ten A.M. and the body of Patrolman Mulvey had been found in the alley beside the restaurant, stabbed to death with what subsequently turned out to be one of the restaurant's excellent steak knives.

Angelo Pavane called Captain Spelvy again and was told to send his brother into the Precinct and things would be straightened out. Domenic did as he was instructed, only to find himself charged with Murder One. On his last phone call Angelo was informed that the police had a witness and that all bets were off. Angelo Pavane lost his temper with Captain Spelvy and made some injudicious remarks about what could happen to lying witnesses—and even to fink precinct captains. There the matter stood.

To Daniher it seemed fairly obvious. Either Domenic Pavane had killed the cop and lied to his brother—and if so, the police and their witness had him dead to rights—or Domenic was innocent and the police were using him as the patsy to cover up for someone else. "Who," he said, "was the guy who was with Mulvey that night? The witness?"

"Jesus! If I knew that, why would I need you? I'd burn the son of a bitch so fast..."

Daniher stopped him. "There'll be none of that! Or I walk right now!"

Pavane was instantly contrite. "Okay. I swear. I will do nothing. But, Mr. Daniher, I know what you're thinkin'. I want to say one thing to you. Dom don't lie. My brother don't lie to me. If he done it, he would tell me, so I know how to move. If he done it, you think he'd leave the guy layin' in an alley all night? That guy would'a been up to his ears in cement in an hour. You can believe me...."

And suddenly Daniher did. Put that way, it made sense. "I'll ask around," he said. "But no promises. Understood?" He took Pavane's proffered hand reluctantly.

In Captain Thomas Spelvy's office at the Third Precinct, he listened to quite a different story. Spelvy was exuberant; he had an airtight case. The official story was that Patrolman Mulvey and his friend had gone to dine at Domenic's Restaurant. There had been an argument with Domenic Pavane over the check, which had moved outside into the alley. The friend waited on the street while Mulvey went into the alley, "to take it out of the bastard's hide." The friend heard loud voices and then Mulvey's cry. He ran because he was scared and didn't come forward until the body was discovered.

157

Daniher listened without comment. When he decided he wasn't going to hear anything more, he asked, "Wonder why Pavane didn't try to get rid of the corpse? Seems sort of stupid, wouldn't you say?"

Spelvy shrugged. "Who knows what a crazy wop will do?"

"What about your witness?"

"Him? Oh, we got him buried. So deep they'll never find him."

"How so?"

"Threats to his life. We got phone calls. Other wops and all . . . "

"You don't say?" Daniher said mildly. "What is the world coming to?"

It was a touch too broad. Spelvy's little eyes narrowed in suspicion. "You got an interest in the case, Counselor?"

"No. Just a friend," said Daniher. "I eat in his restaurant. Hell of a cook, you know. I'll miss him."

"Cook? Well, that's one cook is gonna fry."

Daniher left without shaking hands, knowing that if the powers that be wanted to railroad Domenic Pavane there was nothing he or any other lawyer could do about it. With unaccustomed cynicism he wondered if, given cops like Mulvey and Captain Spelvy, Angelo Pavane didn't have the right idea after all. Eliminate the witnesses. Out of sheer perversity he decided to ask a few more questions about the chickenhearted witness the police now had under protection. It was the least he could do—in fact, all he was prepared to do—for Angelo Pavane.

What he learned was odd, but it didn't change his mind. It merely confirmed a hopeless situation. The name of the witness was Carol Zabriski. Carlie, for short. The present Republican mayor was Michael Zabriski. Carlie was his nephew. Carlie was at present in the Marymount Asylum, a curious place to stash a police witness. Unless you were willing to assume that everyone was crazy.

While he was still debating the morality of passing on his information to Pavane, he got a phone call from Martin Kinkaid. The message was that if he was thinking of taking on the case, to forget it. It was against the best interests of all concerned—particularly himself. When Kinkaid finished, Daniher asked, "Why you, Martin? I should think you'd want to do the Republicans in the eye. If the case could be won."

Kinkaid laughed, "It can't. Besides, Republicans aren't all bad. We scratch backs from time to time. Never know when you'll need a favor."

"Would it make any difference if the man was innocent?"

"You kidding, Des? No Pavane's innocent. They're gangsters. If he doesn't burn for this killing, they'll get him for the next one. Matter of time."

That was certainly one way of looking at it. Shortly afterward Daniher had a visitor. A plainclothes detective from the Homicide Squad who said he represented an Irish police club of vast power. The detective explained that the society felt strongly about the brutal murder of one of its own, as did the whole police force. His message ended with "Anybody who tries to get that wop off is in for trouble from us. We just thought you ought to know how it is, Counselor."

"Every man is entitled to representation," Daniher said mildly. "It's in the Constitution."

"So let him get a wop. Those people should stick with their own."

"You know, they're Catholics, too. Attend the same churches. Pray to the same God."

"Yeah," the detective said dismissively. "Just wanted to be sure you knew how people feel about it, Mr. Daniher."

He weighed the possible consequences against his anger that they should so blatantly expect him to knuckle under. In the afternoon he walked down the hill and told Angelo Pavane that he would take the case. That was a Wednesday.

On Thursday, Daniher obtained from a reluctant judge a subpoena that would allow him to question Carlie Zabriski at a pretrial hearing. When he tried to serve it, a Marymount doctor informed him that Carol Zabriski was under treatment and could not be interviewed.

The Hibernians had scheduled for Friday night a boxing-team elimination meet with the East Side AC. Daniher's light-heavyweight bout was to be next to last. Seated in his corner, waiting for his opponent, it should have alerted him when Martin Kinkaid sat silent at ringside and wouldn't meet his eyes. He dismissed it as pique over his accepting the Pavane case. Sally Anne was her usual uninhibited, cheering self.

When the crowd grew silent as his opponent came down the aisle, he thought it curious but nothing more. The rival light-heavy was introduced as Young Terry, and during the referee's instructions Daniher saw that he had done considerable fighting. His nose was off-center; his brows already showed beginning scar tissue.

The echo of the timer's bell was still in his ears when Daniher realized that he was up against a seasoned pro, a ringer. And that the crowd knew it, too, because Sally Anne's voice was the only one he could hear in the ominous quiet.

The bout went the full six rounds, largely because the referee had obviously been told not to stop it short of murder and because Daniher refused to stay on the canvas.

Toward the end the mood of the crowd shifted. There were cries of "Stop it!" Daniher's worried second tried to throw in the towel. Daniher wouldn't let him. He took a methodical merciless beating from a man who knew his business. He was carried to the locker room. The Hibernian coach, who doubled as cut man, patched him up as best he could. "Why the hell didn't you quit?"

"Couldn't figure out how," Daniher mumbled through his mangled lips.

The coach smuggled him out the back entrance and Daniher staggered toward home. His eyes were swollen almost shut and his head rang like a church bell. He had difficulty negotiating curbstones. He made it to his door before he collapsed. He woke up in Good Samaritan Hospital. They kept him there a week. When he got out he was as bald as an egg. Some sort of nerve damage, they told him; his hair would grow back in time. It never did.

Domenic Pavane vs. *the People* was a sensation. It turned out that there was good reason for stashing Carlie Zabriski in Marymount Asylum. It was where he belonged. He was a very disturbed young man. There was no way the prosecution could avoid putting Carlie on the stand, since he was the only witness they had. The DA took him through his story, and his identification of Domenic Pavane as the killer, in twenty minutes flat. Carlie was letter perfect. At the end of the second day the prosecution had completed its case.

Daniher spent two days trying to establish Carlie's history of emotional disturbance and violent acts. He was only partially successful. The signs of Daniher's fearful beating were still on his face. In the newspapers he looked like a punch-drunk pug, and the Republican press played that for all it was worth.

Domenic Pavane was a good witness, cool and matter-of-fact. The DA was unable to shake him, but the jury seemed unimpressed. The judge ruled that Pavane's accusations about police payoffs were not germane. None of the witnesses Daniher had planned to call were allowed to take the stand. The press, however, reported Pavane's story in banner headlines.

Finally Daniher got Carlie Zabriski on the stand and kept him there for six hours. At the end of that time, despite 123 objections, most of which were sustained, he had completely demolished the witness. Carlie Zabriski was reduced to gibbering hysteria, and Daniher had pulled off that most spectacular of legal dramas, a courtroom confession. Carlie Zabriski had admitted that he himself had stabbed his friend Mulvey—for the $3,500 Mulvey had stolen from Domenic Pavane.

Daniher emerged a hero. They called him the "Bald Legal Eagle" in the headlines. The Democrats belatedly realized they had a magnificent political handle in the case and embraced both it and Desmond Daniher with equal enthusiasm. It was the beginning of the end of the Republican grip on the City.

The Democrats wanted to run Daniher for district attorney or the state assembly. He refused both because the sensational publicity of the trial had appalled him. He had found that he didn't like being a prominent lawyer. He preferred the anonymity of a job as assistant district leader to Martin Kinkaid, who became his father-in-law six weeks after the trial. He set himself to learn how to build an unbeatable machine.

Machine politics is a relatively simple business whose sole purpose is to ensure that the populace will give its votes to the party's choice. Every citizen is subject to its wiles.

Des Daniher didn't wait for people in trouble to come to him. He began to walk the streets—with a pocket full of goodies. He could help with tax forms, get you off jury duty, arrange for favorable building or sanitary inspections, take care of your legal problems, fix tickets, on occasion get you out of jail or into City Hall to see the right official. Best of all, he could get you a job on the City payroll.

Daniher saw to it that the Democratic Club provided food and coal for the needy, Christmas and Thanksgiving turkeys. The Club organized picnics and river excursions with free beer and hot dogs. It sponsored baseball and bowling teams, gave scholarship prizes to bright students.

When Martin Kinkaid was chosen to run for mayor, Des Daniher asked for and got a place on the ticket as City tax assessor. He had given it a lot of thought, and it seemed to him the job provided more raw power than any other position in government. He was elected, and thus young Desmond Daniher became the sole judge of the amount of taxes to be paid by every business and property owner in the City. It was a position of almost unlimited power, and Daniher kept it for six profitable years. It led eventually to his behind-the-scenes control of the Democratic party throughout the whole state. But only political insiders knew this. Des Daniher became an excessively private man.

Now, as he sat in his den, Daniher felt the weight of the years. The Lord giveth and the Lord taketh away—though hardly in the same proportion. Could anything balance the taking of Sally Anne? No, not even the giving of Gavin, who had become the son Sally Anne had died trying to birth.

And then there was Birdie. It had seemed an ideal solution. Two good people so suited one to the other. . . . How could he have known? All his expertise in manipulating men and events hadn't equipped him to deal with Gavin's problems. Because Gavin was his own man and would work out his destiny by himself. Daniher knew his only role must be to wait, to be there to pick up the pieces—if pieces there were to be. The thought depressed him. The stairs to his bedroom seemed longer than ever before.

*   *   *

Gavin hadn't expected Stewart Gansvoort to remember their drunken conversation. He was surprised when Stewart reached him at the precinct as he was going off shift. "I hear your man is speaking at the Forum tonight. How about taking me along?"

Sober, Gavin couldn't see much point in it. Gansvoort seemed a most unlikely Conroy convert. "You really want to go?"

"Sure I do. Pick you up at your house about eight." He hung up before Gavin could beg off.

The Forum was in the Ninth District, the heart of Republican territory. Conroy would be facing a hostile audience, solid backers of Henry Cabot Lodge. But that was Conroy's style. He'd take on an audience wherever he found it.

Gavin and Stewart arrived a few minutes early. It was a warm evening for June, and people were milling about outside the Forum to catch a last breath of air. Stewart greeted a number of people, nodded casually to others.

"Hello, Gavin."

He didn't need to turn to know who it was. For a moment he wanted to run away from a familiar pain. He caught Stewart looking at him, watching for a reaction, and realized that this was Stewart's real reason for coming. He said, "Serena. You're looking well. It's been a long time." It came out smoothly, easily. And she *was* looking well. At twenty-four Serena had gained poise and maturity. She seemed thinner and taller than he remembered.

"Four years," Serena said. "This is my husband, John Summerlin. Gavin Riordan, an old friend."

"Delighted, I'm sure."

Gavin found himself shaking the limp hand of a tall willowy Englishman with a luxuriant guard's mustache and protuberant eyes.

"Rather different over here," Summerlin said. "Your politics. All very confusing."

"Never thought you'd be interested, Serena," said Gavin. "You come to cheer or to jeer?"

"Oh, definitely to cheer," Stewart interjected. "She's a Conroy freak. Drives Father up the wall. So I thought I'd try it, too."

163

"I've worked for him from the beginning," she said. "Early convert."

Gavin was surprised. "Why haven't I seen you before this?"

"We worked different districts, I suppose."

The crowd began to move into the auditorium and they followed. They found seats together, Gavin next to Serena; Stewart had deftly maneuvered it. The seats were narrow and he could feel her thigh warm against his. He was furious with himself at the strength of his reaction. She had dumped him, and after four years he ought to be over it.

There were six speakers on the program, three Republicans and three Democrats. Conroy was scheduled to be next to last. Not the best position, but better than first. The chairman of the meeting, the president of a local chamber of commerce chapter, felt it necessary, in introducing each speaker, to use the phrase, "a fellow who came up the hard way" so many times that when Conroy's turn to speak finally came, he drew a laugh with "I must be the only fellow here tonight who *didn't* come up the hard way."

The first part of Conroy's speech was dull, uncertain, full of vague generalities. He seemed ill at ease, uncomfortable, and Gavin suddenly realized that he was in pain. He stood awkwardly, favoring his back. Serena whispered, "Oh, dear, it's not going well."

From somewhere in the rear came a loud razzberry. Conroy smiled then for the first time. A quick boyish smile. "The sound of music," he said. "I should be getting used to it in this district. You're Republicans. I'm a Democrat. Put it down to an accident of birth. Most of us here tonight follow the beliefs of our immediate forebears. It's a matter of habit. When it should be a matter of intelligent choice. Let's compare the two. . . ."

Conroy seemed to come alive, no longer hesitant, caught up in the force of his own beliefs. He went on to outline the doctrines and history of the two parties, sometimes amusingly, sometimes with deadly seriousness. If the crowd wasn't exactly cheering, he had them listening attentively. There was occasional applause as he spoke. When he finished, the applause was more enthusiastic than Gavin had expected. Conroy had made an impression, even in this conservative bastion. The last speaker was a dreadful anticlimax.

The audience began to trickle away. Gavin's party went with them to wait outside, so that Stewart could meet Conroy when he came out.

Outside, Gavin was surprised to see the size of the crowd that still remained. Very few were leaving. There was a hushed expectancy. They, too, were waiting for Conroy.

"Hi, Serena." Bill Conroy gave Serena a casual kiss. Serena started to introduce the others. Bill jerked a thumb at Stewart. "Him I know—from college. What the hell are you doing here, Stewart?" Without waiting for an answer he turned to Gavin. "Who's this?"

"Gavin Riordan. And my husband, John Summerlin."

Bill shook hands perfunctorily with Summerlin, his eyes still on Gavin. He held Gavin's hand longer.

"Riordan, Gavin. DSC, Purple Heart, Silver Star. Twelfth Precinct. You did canvassing for Jim. Right?"

Gavin was amazed at Bill's memory and pleased to be recognized. Also a little put off by his brusqueness.

James Conroy was coming toward them through the crowd now, shaking outstretched hands. A young girl kissed him, pulling him down to her, as he suppressed a grimace of pain. An older woman clung to his arm. "I know your mother. . . ." "Mrs. Raylor? I'll tell her you were here. Thank you, thank you. . . ."

He was near them now. Bill went toward him protectively. They heard Conroy say, "Jesus, get me out of here before I bust in half." Then he saw Gavin and the smile returned. "Gavin. Glad you could make it. I wanted to see you." Then to the others, "You'll forgive me if I borrow him? Hi, Serena. Sorry for the rush."

Gavin could see that Bill wasn't going to do it, so he pulled Stewart forward. "Stewart Gansvoort, Jim."

Conroy's smile slipped for just a moment. "Glad to meet you. I know your father. . . ." The smile returned. "Though not as well as I'd like to. . . ."

In the face of Conroy's obvious hurry, and because it was no secret that August Gansvoort was one of Lodge's principal backers, Stewart said stiffly, "I'm sure you do. Don't let us keep you."

Conroy took Gavin's arm. To the others, "I really do need him. I know you'll forgive me. Don't see enough of you, Serena. . . ."

Gavin had only time to give Stewart an apologetic look before he

165

found himself propelled toward the Conroy car. He hadn't the faintest notion of what was happening, but was powerless to object.

Bill Conroy drove. In front with him was another man Gavin didn't know. Gavin rode with Conroy in back. As the car pulled away Conroy groaned.

"Hand me that pillow, will you?" He leaned forward and Gavin slipped the small pillow between the seat and Conroy's back.

"Are you all right?"

"It only hurts when I laugh." Conroy relaxed with a heavy sigh. "And there's a lot of laughs in this campaigning business."

Gavin felt Conroy's hand on his arm. "Gavin, I need your help. I want a meeting with Des Daniher."

Gavin tried to see Conroy's face, but it was concealed in shadows.

"On the quiet," Conroy said. "Can you arrange it?"

"I don't know. He wants you to come to him. He won't go to you. He's a stubborn man."

"So am I. Can you do it?"

"I can try," Gavin said slowly. "Where? And when?"

"What's wrong with right now?"

The house was dark when they pulled up. Bill Conroy and the stranger stayed in the car. Conroy stood beside Gavin as he rang the bell. They waited. And waited. Gavin rang the bell again. Finally they heard footsteps, and Mary Margaret Shay, her hair in curlers, opened the door.

"Gavin?" she said. "Save us! What's wrong . . . ?"

Gavin was feeling sure they'd made a mistake when Daniher's deep voice came from the inside stairs.

"All right, Mary Margaret. I'll take care of it. Off to bed with you."

Mary Margaret retreated with her worry and Daniher took her place. He was dressed in a figured Charvet robe over pale pajamas. On his head was his gray fedora. Conroy gave the hat the briefest glance and said, "How do you do, Mr. Daniher. I'm Jim Conroy."

Daniher stared at Conroy, his face showing nothing. "Your idea, Gavin?"

"No. Mine," Conroy said. "Will you ask us in?" No apology, nothing said about waking a man in the middle of the night.

For a moment Gavin thought Daniher might refuse. What price Irish hospitality? Then Daniher stepped back. His gesture had all the courtesy of a lord of the manor. No words were needed. He led them to the darkened study, snapped on the light and indicated chairs. "Coffee? Or perhaps a drink?"

Conroy sank back gratefully in his chair, looking suddenly tired and drawn, deep lines etched in his cheeks. "I could use a brandy."

"Only Bushmill's, I'm afraid."

"Bushmill's it is."

While Daniher got the whiskey, Conroy looked around the room and Gavin could see the quickening interest in his eyes. Thirty years of Desmond Daniher hung on the paneled walls. There were pictures of Daniher with every president since Herbert Hoover, every governor of his home state since 1923. Daniher with senators, Supreme Court justices, with the king of Sweden and Edward, Prince of Wales. Daniher, complete with green and white band across his chest, grand marshal of the Saint Patrick's Day parade.

"You've seen it all, Mr. Daniher. I envy you."

"Most of it. Some of it good. Some of it bad."

Daniher served them their drinks and went to sit behind his desk. He said nothing, asked no questions, merely waited. Gavin felt the power of his waiting and a quick admiration.

Conroy wasted no time. "I need your support, Mr. Daniher. All the way. What will it take to get it?"

"I can't believe you're running scared."

"No. Just playing it safe. I wouldn't want to see it go the other way."

"To a Republican? Granted, it's a Republican year. Eisenhower will bury Stevenson, poor man. But you've no worries, Mr. Conroy."

"Then I take it you're with me?"

Gavin wanted to warn him that he was pushing too hard. Or was it just another ploy in the game waged by two players whose expertise was over his head?

Daniher waved a deprecating hand. "A few questions, perhaps. Only if you care to answer."

Conroy's face broke into a knowing smile. The sparring was over. "Fire away," he said.

Daniher seemed to search his mind for something important enough to ask. "The Kefauver hearings. What did you think of them?"

"Three-ring circus. Dramatic as hell. It got Kefauver what he wanted, though, a shot at the top spot. I wish I'd had that kind of exposure."

Despite his easy answer, Conroy seemed wary.

"Do you, now?" Daniher leaned back, his eyes on the ceiling as though trying to recall something that eluded him.

"Let's see . . . as I remember, there were twenty-seven pieces of legislation proposed by the committee—all of 'em designed to stop organized crime. You voted no on seven, abstained on eleven and were absent from the House on the rest of them. Now, why was that, I wonder?"

Yes, Gavin thought. *Why?* It didn't seem consistent with his image of Jim Conroy.

"Bad legislation," Conroy said easily. "Of course, their ideas were right, but the bills were badly conceived. Pork-barrel stuff."

"Nothing to do with your father's, ah . . . business connections, I suppose?"

The words hung in the air. Gavin was stiff with shock. Gavin knew about old Ed Conroy's old-time closeness to gangland, of course. But why was Des doing it?

Briefly Conroy's eyes flicked from Daniher to Gavin and back again. "Nobody tells me how to vote. Not even my father."

"Of course not," Daniher said blandly. "Merely an old man's curiosity." Casually Daniher changed the subject. "Tell me, how do you feel about the federal insurance bill?"

Conroy studied him, as though willing Daniher to reveal how *he* felt about it. At last Conroy seemed to make up his mind.

"I'm for it."

"Strongly?"

"I'll lobby for it. If that's what you want."

Daniher's lips lifted a little at the corners. "A great benefit for the state. A grand bill, all in all. I'll see that you get the information you'll need."

"You do that, Mr. Daniher," Conroy said shortly. And Gavin

knew that the deal had been made. He hadn't an idea what the federal insurance bill was about, but he knew it was the price Conroy was willing to pay for the votes Daniher could deliver.

As he was leaving, Conroy said, "Thanks for your help, Gavin," and held out his hand. Gavin hesitated, then took it. Conroy smiled briefly. "Don't take it so hard, Gavin. It's all politics, you know. Name of the game."

Gavin didn't go back to the study to say good night to his Uncle Des. He waited until Conroy's car had left and then walked home.

The next day, when he reported for duty at the precinct, Patrolman Gavin Riordan declared himself in on the pad. If Des Daniher knew about it, he never mentioned it.

13

Time: 1955
GAVIN RIORDAN

Detective Sergeant Gavin Riordan was catching a ride home in Johnnie Murphy's No. 102 when they heard the "robbery in progress" squeal. The liquor store being robbed was less than a block away. They could see its blue and white neon sign. Murphy reached for the siren switch and Riordan caught his hand.

"Sneak up," Riordan said. "They may be in there."

Murphy responded to the dispatcher's message, eased the squad car to the curb and cut the lights.

"I'm not carrying," Riordan said. He never did off duty. "You got a throwaway?"

"No. Take the riot gun."

Riordan removed the stubby weapon from its roof clip and checked the load. They got out of the car quietly.

Murphy whispered, "There's an alley this side. Courtyard in back."

"Okay." Riordan checked his watch. "I'll take the front. Give you sixty seconds. Right? Then I'll go in."

He watched Murphy disappear in the alley and moved toward the store, checking the street as he went. On the corner a drugstore was still open. Between that and the liquor store there were only dark buildings. Opposite him was the discreetly lit entrance of Bob's Club. As he watched, two women and a man emerged and stood talking under the marquee. Riordan, as he edged to the corner of the liquor store window, willed them not to move in his direction. The sudden laughter of one of the women grated on his nerves. Since the street was otherwise deserted, he wondered briefly who had phoned in the squeal.

He inched his head forward until he could see into the store. An outsized black man, dressed in a tan Windbreaker, was half turned away from him, holding a double-barreled over-and-under sawed-off shotgun on two people behind the counter. No one else.

The proprietor, a tall bald man, was taking bills from the cash register and stuffing them into a paper bag. The small gray-haired woman beside him pressed her hands tightly to her mouth. The black man said something and gestured with the shotgun. Riordan figured his best chance would be when the black man reached for the money. That would leave him with only one hand for the gun. He crouched beneath the lighted window and waddled to the entrance.

When he straightened, the moment had passed. The black man now had the bag tucked under his arm. It would be suicidal to go through the door now; the shotgun would cut him in half. Gavin couldn't fire first without getting the store owner and his wife. He would have to wait for Murphy to come through the back door.

When it happened Riordan knew the robber had neither seen nor heard either Murphy or himself. With no reason for doing it the black man took two steps back and fired both barrels, one after the other. The man and woman slammed against the shelves of splintering bottles and slid from sight behind the counter. Riordan jammed the barrel of his riot gun through the glass door and pulled the trigger. The black man jerked as the pellets hit him, then turned and ran toward the back of the store. The riot gun didn't have much stopping power.

"Murphy!" Riordan screamed, and fumbled frantically to get the door open. By the time he had the man had disappeared. Riordan pounded after him.

He heard the sound of a single shot. Another scream.

In the courtyard the black man was on the ground, curled into a tight ball. Two paces beyond, Murphy crouched, holding his Police Positive straight out with both hands.

"I got him." Murphy straightened and let out his breath in a long sigh. He looked a question at Riordan.

"Both of 'em. The son of a bitch blasted both of 'em. For no fuckin' reason!"

The black man moaned. Riordan kicked him in the spine to straighten him out. The man rolled over on his back. Money from the paper bag spilled out onto the concrete. There was a spreading stain high up on the shoulder of the tan Windbreaker. He clutched his shoulder with his good hand.

"I'm hurt bad, man. I need a doctor. You gotta get me a doctor."

Riordan stooped and frisked him for another weapon, came up empty and straightened. "Gimme that," he said to Murphy. "The gun. The fucking gun. You got to report in, dummy."

"Oh. . . . Yeah."

Murphy handed his .38 to Riordan and started up the alley. Riordan waited until the sound of his footsteps faded, flipped the black man over on his face. He held the revolver behind the man's knee and fired. The man screamed and wouldn't stop. Riordan hit him sharply with the barrel of his gun and the sound was abruptly cut off. He moved the leg; the slug was flattened to the size of a silver dollar. Ballistics would never know what gun it came from. He left it where it was.

Murphy came pounding back down the alley. He was breathless when he arrived. "What the hell happened?"

"Tried to get away," Riordan said calmly.

Johnnie Murphy looked at Riordan unbelievingly. "Jesus," he said. "Why'd you do that?"

"He was trying to get away, I told you. You expect me to *talk* him out of it?"

Murphy's face was pale, his hands shaking. Riordan reached forward and put the revolver back in Murphy's holster.

"Jesus," Murphy said hoarsely. "I can't believe it."

"Look at it this way. It keeps him off the street. He won't gun down anybody else just for the hell of it."

The men from the precinct arrived first. Then the meat wagon and the police doctor with his attendants. When they saw what had happened, no one looked directly at Riordan. They spoke to him only to get the information they needed. No one questioned his statement.

In the squad car, as Johnnie Murphy drove him home, Riordan looked at the young man's set face, the smooth pink skin now stretched tight over his cheekbones.

"Look, kid," Riordan said. "You better start getting used to it. You got to figure it's the animals or you. That's one more asshole who won't be shooting at you."

Murphy stared straight ahead.

"Ah, fuck it," Riordan said. "Just remember. You saw nothing. In case you were thinking you did. There was nothing to see. Because you weren't there."

In the morning, as he expected, there was a message to report to Captain Onderdonk. Onderdonk was a tall spare man with a lined leathery face. His eyes were a cold, clear gray. He kept Riordan standing. "Once I could accept," Onderdonk said. "Some kind of fluke. Twice I could barely stomach. But three times is too much. What the hell did you think you were doing?"

"Look at it this way, Captain," Riordan said. "The man was a mad dog. You bring him to trial and maybe they nail him. And maybe they don't. Even if they do, he's out again in a few years—with a gun. The way it happened, he's off the streets for good. All it cost the taxpayer was thirty-five cents—the price of a bullet."

"You really think that's your decision to make." Onderdonk's disgust was deadly. It made Gavin cringe in his guts. "You're a rogue, Riordan. You make me want to puke."

"Then why the hell won't you let me transfer out?" Riordan flared.

"I kept you here because I thought maybe I could make a cop out of you—as a favor to an old friend."

"What the hell are you talking about?"

"This is what I'm talking about," said Onderdonk. "You want out? You got out. I'm bringing you up on charges. There'll be a departmental hearing as soon as I can arrange it. And this time your Uncle Des won't save your ass. I know because I checked it out with him first."

Riordan was coldly angry. "Listen, you son of a bitch, I never asked a favor from Des Daniher in my life!"

Onderdonk's eyes widened in disbelief. "How the hell do you think you been getting away with acting like a one-man gang around here for years? I'd have had your balls in six months if it wasn't for him."

"I don't believe it. . . ." Riordan said slowly.

Onderdonk stared at him in silence. Then he shrugged tiredly. "I don't give a shit whether you believe it or not. Because it's over now. You're suspended from duty. Put your gun and badge on the desk. And then get out of my sight. You'll be notified about the hearing."

The detectives in the squad room seemed preoccupied with desk work. No one looked up as Riordan walked through. He didn't go to his locker to clean it out because he hadn't decided yet whether or not to let them get away with railroading him. Because he, Gavin Riordan, had the power to destroy much of their way of life. If he chose to use it.

It was when he was a rookie cop that Gavin Riordan was introduced by Sergeant Otto Bassett to that police phenomenon known as the pad. At the end of his first month of duty, Sergeant Bassett handed him a plain brown envelope. In it was ninety-two dollars in rumpled bills.

"Don't spend it all in one place."

"Okay," Gavin said. "But what is it?" He had never heard of the pad.

Bassett feigned shock. "You dumb kids. It's your share of the take."

"What take?"

Sergeant Bassett smiled at him. "You're tellin' me you don't know what take? Is it my ears I can't believe?" Bassett studied him for a moment. "Well, aren't I the lucky one. Do I get to keep all this pretty money for myself?"

He waited for Gavin's reaction, and when he found only genuine puzzlement, his voice hardened. "Take it, you dumb mick. Put it in your pocket and we'll say no more about it. That's an order." Suddenly he roared out across the squad room.

"Massey. Take this dummy out for a beer an' explain him the facts of life."

In the bar Massey ordered up. Staring sideways at Gavin over his boilermaker. Massey seemed uncomfortable. "You really don't know, do you?"

Over the course of the next hour Gavin learned.

The next morning Gavin returned the envelope intact to Sergeant Bassett with a polite "Thanks, but no thanks."

He hadn't reckoned on the consequences. He was summoned to the office of Lieutenant Brian Casey and told that he either went on the pad or else. The "or else" proved to be every shit detail the lieutenant or Sergeant Bassett could drum up. When at the end of a month Gavin still declined to accept his envelope, he met with the lieutenant again.

"Look, Riordan, I don't give a shit whether you take the money or not. I won't try to justify the system—if you haven't got the sense to see it for yourself.

"Personally I don't think you belong on the force. But you're here and there's something you ought to know. You gotta work with the people here. It calls for confidence in each other. And trust. That's it, trust. You gotta know where your partner stands. All the way.

"Now, you wanna buck the system, you go right ahead. But don't expect any cheers. You won't get 'em. I don't think the guys are gonna trust a guy like you. A guy like you makes me very uneasy.

174

"One more thing. If that big conscience of yours gives you any ideas about blowing the whistle . . . forget it. And that's the best advice you'll ever get as long as you live. I'll be watching you. And so will the rest of 'em."

Gavin took the lieutenant's advice to heart. Not knowing how far Casey's enmity would go, Gavin began to keep a record against the day when he might need it. He logged everything he could observe—payoffs, ripoffs, petty thievery. Amounts, times, dates, places and witnesses. At the end of his first year on the force, he estimated that the pad for the precinct came close to fifty thousand dollars. He asked Des Daniher for the name of a good lawyer and deposited with him each notebook as he filled it.

Gavin Riordan had been on the force four years before he gave in and decided to go on the pad himself. It had been four years of increasing isolation from his fellow policemen. Riordan was a good cop. He had led in arrests on every squad he had been assigned to. He had the best crime connections on the force because of a lifelong friendship with Patsy Pavane. Patsy was the son of Angelo Pavane, the crime czar of the City. He had played halfback on the teams on which Gavin had starred as quarterback. Patsy had become a respected lawyer, a *consiglione* in his father's Mafia family, and was willing, when it suited him, to supply Gavin with helpful information. Through Patsy, Gavin developed his own network of informants, without which a policeman cannot function successfully. Gavin's rise was spectacular. In four years he had reached detective second-grade, and was preparing to take the sergeant's exam.

Gavin Riordan went on the pad because of an increasing disillusionment. As a cop he dealt each day with thieves, murderers, child molesters, drug addicts, rapists and every sort of pervert. He saw these people arrested, tried and all too often come away free or with ridiculously lenient sentences. All the result of a system of corrupt judges, prosecutors, bailbondsmen, criminal lawyers and influence peddlers that made police work very near to futile. Was it any wonder that cops went on the pad?

The pad was a way of life to the men he worked with. There was the catch for Riordan, because increasingly the men he worked with became all the life he had. Cops are a breed apart. They are forced to hang together because there is no way they can communicate to the general public what they see and hear and do. Their daily grind is too brutal, dirty and degrading to lend itself to casual conversation with outsiders. So they talk together, drink together, live apart in their own society. They neither trust nor understand a maverick.

So, to make life easier for himself, Gavin went on the pad. But he kept up his precautions. He gave the money that was passed to him to his lawyer to be put into an escrow account, along with a record of how and under what circumstances it was obtained. He was getting close to finishing law school, so he took all the legal avenues he had learned about to protect himself. For he was convinced that sooner or later the pad would be blown sky high.

As for getting closer to brother cops, he found his decision had come too late. Four years of being a sanctimonious weirdo in the eyes of his peers wouldn't go away. They respected his ability, admired his courage, would trust him with their lives—but not with their secrets. They were wary of him. Moral superiority creates its own resentment.

So Gavin Riordan became a loner. He also became a total cop. When he got his law degree he briefly thought of quitting, but by that time he was hooked. He liked being a cop and all it entailed. Since his nights were no longer devoted to study and law school, and Birdie was more often in the hospital than not, he took to roaming the City. He became a hunter, a one-man scourge for criminals of all kinds. He haunted sleazy bars, back alleys. He made a survey of his territory, pinpointing all the places most likely to be hit. He became an expert on safety devices—and how to disarm them. He learned the banking habits of the merchants, the weaknesses of their banks. He refined and perfected his informer net until he knew within hours the arrival and departure times of known criminals and narcotics dealers.

The first time he permanently disabled a perpetrator was a fluke. During one of his night stalks, the naked body of an eight-year-old girl was thrown directly in his path from a tenement rooftop. Gavin met the killer coming down the rickety stairway, and shouted "Hold it! Police!'' The man turned to run, and in turning both his legs were in line. Gavin's single shot shattered both of his kneecaps.

Gavin watched a young black intern strip away the man's trousers and was appalled to see the damage he had done.

"That's the way, baby. Cut 'em off at the knees." The intern laughed, a flash of white teeth. "Sure is one way to keep 'em off the streets."

The second time it was a fifteen-year-old youth Gavin knew to be a five-time rape offender. This time the victim was a seventy-year-old woman living alone. She knew the boy and identified him by name to Gavin.

The kid ran when Gavin located him in a bowling alley on James Street. He caught up to him in the alley behind the place. When he tried to handcuff him he got a six-inch switchblade just under the ribs on the right side. Gavin knocked the boy senseless with his handcuffs.

He stood there, blood streaming down his side into his crotch, not knowing how bad the wound was, thinking that this was a cruddy way to die. The rapist lay on his back, arms outstretched, and Gavin thought, *Six months in juvenile detention. Then he'll be out on the street again*. Gavin fired two shots into the boy's knees before he passed out himself.

The switchblade had penetrated an intestine, and it was touch-and-go for twenty-four hours. Gavin was back on the street in a month. But he was a very different man.

For the first time in his life he was truly afraid. In combat in Europe he had never felt that enemy fire was aimed at him personally by some satanic force.

Now he did. He became convinced that they were out to get him. Every man became his enemy, fellow cops as well as the criminals. In Gavin fear took the form of suicidal recklessness, the compulsion to prove to himself by acts of bravery that fear didn't exist. To the men around him Gavin was not only an enigma, he was now a certifiable nut, dangerous to work with. Without knowing it, Gavin Riordan was dangerously close to paranoia. His confrontation with Onderdonk and his subsequent suspension were all that saved him.

* * *

Now he stood on the station house steps, still seething from the meeting with Onderdonk. He knew in his heart that Onderdonk was right about the protection Des Daniher had provided for him, couldn't understand how he could have been so insensitive as not to see it. He'd have to take it up with Daniher. But not now.

Right now he had something more immediate to deal with. For the first time in eight years he had nothing to do. No duties, no routine, nothing. No revolver on his hip, no badge. Suddenly he felt himself defenseless, a sitting duck for anyone, without the familiar protection of his profession. He was out in the open where any of them could reach him. He had to get under cover, somewhere where he could put his back against a wall.

Although the day was cool, Gavin Riordan began to sweat. He hailed a cab and gave the driver his home address.

Father Touhy's Ford was parked in front of the house. There was a bicycle leaning against the curb just behind it. Since he wasn't up to Father Touhy's rambling chitchat, Gavin made for the garage, meaning to get his own car and drive somewhere.

When he was seated behind the wheel he realized that the keys were where they always were, in the glass bowl on the small table in the front hallway, just in case Birdie wanted to use the car. It wasn't like Gavin to forget like that, but it was an unusual day.

He had resigned himself to facing Birdie and Father Touhy when he felt the cold pressure behind his ear. He knew instantly what it was. The voice from the backseat cracked with tension. "Knew you had to come sometime. You or your wife. Don't matter which. Either one will do."

The sweat had soaked through Gavin's shirt. Now it was cold as a shroud. He could feel the prickling of the hairs on the back of his neck where the gun barrel rested. There was nothing he could do but talk. In an ordinary voice he said, "If you were going to shoot, you would have done it by now. I'm going to turn around. Slowly. Maybe you'd like to tell me what's bugging you."

The gun barrel dug into his neck but Gavin stayed slack. Then the pressure lessened. He turned his head and shifted his body so that he could see into the back seat.

The light from the open garage doors showed him first a crude zip gun held in a hand that trembled, then the glint of tears on a black face that couldn't have been more than fifteen years old.

"Now," Gavin said. "What's it all about? Why the hell do you want to kill *me*? I don't even know you."

The voice was sullen now, but the zip gun stayed pointed at Gavin's head. "Don't want to kill you. Jes' do you like you done Jodie. Show you how it's like. Want you to *live*, man. Without no leg to walk on."

So that was it. If he could keep the kid talking . . . "Who the hell is Jodie?"

"Jodie Biggs. My brother. Hospital say might as well cut that leg off. Ain't gonna be no use to him. Now I'm gonna do the same to you. My name's Leroy. Jes' so's you know who's doin' it to you."

"You know they'll get you for it," Gavin said slowly. "You'll do hard time—shooting a cop."

"What I care. He my *brother*, man!"

Gavin thought of lunging for the gun, but it was too close. The black hole of the pipe barrel stared him in the eye.

"You know what your brother did, Leroy? He gunned down two innocent people. Old people. Just for kicks. No reason. Just to get his rocks off. He's a fucking animal, Leroy! Not worth the powder to blow him away. They'll send him up for life. One leg or two. Makes no difference. You think he's worth doing time for?"

"Not jes' Jodie," Leroy Biggs said doggedly. "Jodie do what he has to do. It's you. You got to find out what it's like." His voice once again changed pitch. He gestured with the gun. "Now you get out. Nice an' easy. 'Cause I swear fo' God I'm goin' do you. Don't you reach for nothing. Real slow, now."

Gavin did as he was told: depressed the door handle, opened the door and stepped out onto the concrete floor. He waited tensely as Leroy opened his own door and started to get out.

The zip gun showed first. As soon as the weapon was clear of the jamb, Gavin threw his body against the door panel. The heavy door caught the skinny black arm midway between wrist and elbow, and the weapon bounced onto the floor. Gavin kept his full weight on the door, trapping the boy while he scrambled for the gun with his foot.

When he had pulled it close enough he stepped back, bent and picked it up.

"All right, now," Gavin said. "Come on out."

There was no movement inside the car. Gavin opened the door cautiously. Leroy sat huddled over his arm in the corner of the backseat, the tears streaming down his face. Gavin reached in and pulled him out.

"Let's take a look at that arm." The skin wasn't broken but there were signs of swelling. "Move your fingers," Gavin said, "and then rotate your arm."

Nothing seemed to be broken.

Gavin looked at the zip gun still in his hand. It was a crude piece of pipe bound with copper wire. Its trigger mechanism was activated by a piece of rubber inner tube. The rubber would have had to be stretched to its limit to impart sufficient force to fire whatever was in the barrel. The weapon wasn't even cocked.

"You make this?"

The boy shook his head. "Borrowed it."

"You were really going to use this?"

"Had it in mind." Leroy had stopped crying. There was no defiance in him now, just a look of hopeless resignation.

"You got anybody else? Besides Jodie?"

"Jes' my mother. She works nights in the state house. You goin' to take me in?"

Gavin thought about it. Would this one grow up to be another animal to stalk the streets like his brother? Was there any chance at all this kid could make it in a world that was stacked against him from the start? Very long odds.

"That your bike out front?"

Leroy nodded.

"Well, get your black ass on it. And don't come back. You hear?"

The boy turned as he reached the garage doors. For a long moment they held each other's eyes. Leroy Biggs nodded once as though he had come to some decision. Then he was gone.

Gavin took a hammer from the workbench and pounded the zip gun flat.

* * *

Birdie was giving tea to Father Touhy in the living room. He tried to go past to the kitchen, because he wanted a drink, but Birdie called out to him.

"How are you, Gavin?" Father Touhy said. "We haven't seen much of you lately." A reprimand. Gavin had long ago given up attending mass.

Gavin sat down while Birdie poured him a cup of tea and handed it to him. Birdie did it gracefully, as she did most things, with a remote efficiency. Her mind was somewhere else, with the holy saints. In the periods when she was allowed to come home she spent much of her time in St. Ann's, on her knees, her lips moving in a never-ending prayer. It was the same around the house. There was always a constant whisper, too soft for the words to be distinguished.

"And how are the boys at the Third, a grand group of men, all of them?" asked Father Touhy, who was the unofficial chaplain of the Third and knew more than Gavin did about its men, since he heard their confessions.

"They're grand as ever, Father," Gavin said. Father Touhy turned back to Birdie. Gavin was sweating more now. He was wondering what Daniher would say when he told him that he could blow the Twelfth Ward right out of the water.

Father Touhy's soft voice intruded on his thoughts. "It's grand," Father Touhy said, his little eyes showing his pleasure. "You should come to see them, Birdie, with their little faces all scrubbed and clean, waiting to receive the Blessed Sacrament. And the Sisters like mothers to them, who have no mothers of their own."

Warning bells went off in Gavin's mind. Father Touhy shouldn't be talking about children to Birdie. He wondered how to stop him and listened in growing alarm as Father Touhy went blindly on.

"Ah, Birdie. You should have children about. Such a great comfort to a woman. There is one little boy with hair as red as Gavin's. A grand, sturdy little fellow. You'd love him on sight. . . ."

Gavin saw Birdie's hands begin to flutter in her lap. Her eyes moved from side to side, her lips trembling. He stood up abruptly, his forgotten teacup crashing to the floor.

"Father." His voice was louder than he intended. "I think Birdie

181

should rest now." Father Touhy looked at him in bewilderment. Gavin took him by the arm and propelled him to his feet.

"What . . . ?" Father Touhy's cherubic face was the picture of concern. "Of course. I . . ."

Gavin got him to the door, handed him his black hat and hissed, "Never talk to her about kids! You want to set her off again?"

"Oh, dear. I didn't realize . . . Of course, her poor dead little one . . . Perhaps I should . . ." Father Touhy made a move to return to the living room, but Gavin opened the door and pushed him through it.

"Not now, Father. Not now." Gavin shut the door on Father Touhy's worried face.

The broken teacup crunched under his feet as he returned. Birdie was sitting exactly as he had left her. She was looking straight ahead, her eyes as vacant as a summer sky, slow tears rolling down her cheeks. Gavin thought it was time to call St. Malachy's to come and get her. But first he had to get her upstairs and into bed.

Her nightgown was on the back of a chair in the bedroom, her mules beneath it. There was a crucifix over the bed, a picture of Mary on the wall opposite. Her sewing basket was on the bedside table, overflowing with brightly colored cloth, a pair of shears stuck upright in a ball of wool.

Birdie let him lead her as though she were a sleepwalker. She stood motionless and unknowing as he got her out of her skirt and blouse. Her unhooked brassiere revealed breasts that had begun to sag just a little. He noticed the faint stretch marks on her belly as he bent close to remove her panties. She stood as though she were posed, her naked body as impersonal as an artist's model, raised her arms obediently as he slipped the nightgown over her head. He turned down the bed, led her to it and pulled up the covers. Sunlight streamed through the window, highlighted her hair with glints of gold. He crossed the room to lower the shade, throwing the room into sudden dimness. He heard a rustling behind him, and when he turned, she had thrown off the covers and pulled up her gown. She lay back, legs spread apart. "Gavin . . ." she whispered. Her arms went out to him.

He wasn't at all sure he could oblige her, but he wanted to try. As

182

he took off his clothes she lay with eyes closed, hand between her legs, rubbing. He had never seen her do that before, and it both shocked and aroused him.

When he came to her she pulled him into her with both hands, arching to him powerfully. Her body writhed under him with a violence that shook him. She made mindless mewling sounds in his ear. She screamed as she came to her climax and redoubled her movements, reaching for yet another. She was using him as she had her fingers, with a frantic urgency. He felt her go rigid under him and for a moment thought she had climaxed again. She was growling deep in her throat, an animal sound that had nothing in it of passion. It frightened him, and he raised his head to look at her. Her mouth was stretched in a rictus, her eyes pools of stark madness.

"No!" she screamed. And again, "No!"

It was then he felt the shears from her sewing basket go into his back. Once, twice and a third time. He could hear the blades grate on his ribs. She continued screaming as he rolled off her, a sound that tore at her throat.

In his dreams Gavin Riordan reconciled himself to death. For a long time he thought he *was* dead. In death he saw Serena, and machines, and white-coated figures urging him to come back. Even the man who looked like Jesus, with his full brown beard and mournful eyes, ordered him to go back. Gavin resisted, and for a while he thought he had won, because the dreams had faded and he was left with nothing but a profound sense of peace.

Now he knew he had lost, because he heard the sound of soft music and felt the whisper of a breeze across his face. Someone said, "I think he's coming around," and he felt the gentle pressure of a hand on his. Against his will he opened leaden eyes and saw Des Daniher bending toward him. Wonderingly he saw the tears on Daniher's cheeks.

"Welcome home, lad," Daniher said huskily.

Behind Daniher's shoulder was the man with the Jesus face, and as Gavin gazed at him he smiled. Gavin tried to smile back and felt himself drifting once more into sleep.

Serena was waiting in the corridor as Daniher and Dr. Blakeney came out. "He'll make it now," Blakeney said. "The human body is a miraculous thing. Give it a fair chance and it will heal itself come hell or high water. Of course, he has the constitution of an ox."

Serena took a deep breath, eyes bright. She looked away.

Des Daniher visited Gavin each day. From Daniher he learned that the whole episode had been quietly hushed up. Birdie was back in St. Malachy's.

"She remembers nothing, poor child. She's happy with her saints and her prayers, they tell me. It'll be a long time before they'll let her out again. Everyone thinks you've been laid up with a bad bout of the pneumonia."

"There's a limit to what a man should have to bear," Gavin said slowly. "I've given it some thought. I don't think I could go through all this again."

Daniher was uncomfortable. "The truth of it is, I don't think she'll ever be coming out again. You're not to worry, lad."

Talking tired him, but Gavin had to ask. "I dreamed—or I think I dreamed—that Serena . . ."

"No dream, Gavin. She was here. Every day."

Now, why? Gavin wondered. "Why would she do that?"

"A question you'll have to answer yourself. Or ask it of her."

It puzzled Gavin. Serena? What was she to him or he to her? Except a memory, an empty room in the heart?

"By the by," Daniher said, "who's Leroy?"

As day followed day, Gavin waited, hoping that Serena would come. But she didn't. He felt a vague resentment.

Instead there was a visit from Captain Gus Onderdonk. The captain sat awkwardly straight in the visitors' chair, his hat balanced carefully on his knees. "There'll be no hearing, Riordan. The charges are dropped. I wanted to tell you myself."

"Uncle Des?"

"We had a word." Onderdonk was uncomfortable.

"All is forgiven? I'm to have another chance? Well, thanks for nothing. I'm not sure I want it. This policeman's lot is not a happy one at the moment."

"Quit it, Riordan," Onderdonk said sharply. "This visit is my own idea. Des told me what you had. Notebooks you left with a lawyer. Money in escrow. Des found out when they thought you were dying. I want the notebooks. I think you're still a cop—and I need your help."

"Des found out about that? And told you?" Onderdonk was silent. Presently Gavin said, "When will you two stop fucking with my life?"

The day he left the hospital, Gavin phoned Riverhaven and asked for Serena. He was told that she was in Nice. Shortly afterward he went to see Desmond Daniher and told him that he had decided to take Onderdonk's offer.

"I think you know I won't pull any punches."

"I know," Daniher told him. "Like they used to tell me, protect yourself in the clinches. I wouldn't expect anything else of you, and that's the truth."

Daniher didn't seem surprised or reluctant when Gavin asked to borrow enough money to get him to Europe. Gavin told him that he had to see Serena.

"Well, then, it still applies," Daniher said. "Watch yourself in the clinches. I think maybe you're out of your class. Give her my best when you see her."

14

Time: 1955
ERICKA

In the beginning Paris, for George Barnstable, was total frustration. He had arranged for office space with Jacquard et Cie, a medium-size architectural firm with which his own firm had established reciprocity some years before. The building was on avenue de Friedland, and he had a superb view of the Arc de Triomphe, which was nice, but from there on it was all downhill.

To Jacquard et Cie reciprocity meant something quite different from what George expected, if it meant anything at all. George's friend from his student days, Henri Jacquard, had unfortunately died and left the firm to his sons. The brothers Jacquard were extremely busy with their own projects and had little time and less inclination to help George with his problems.

George's employers, the Societé des Humanities, had a laudable purpose: to build a school for underpriviledged boys, to provide them with opportunities and an atmosphere otherwise unavailable to the poor. George had been selected for the commission because a similar project of his in the States had won considerable acclaim.

The Societé had plenty of money and clear title to six acres of beautiful land just off the avenue de Neuilly, opposite the Bois de Boulogne. Beyond that there was nothing—except the best of intentions. No construction company had been selected. None of the thousand and one permissions and permits had been arranged. The availability of material and machinery was murky, to say the least. The Societé's directors had neither the knowledge nor the expertise to cope, so George was left with portfolios stuffed with plans and blueprints—and little else. These had all been enthusiastically approved by the Societé—but not by the bureaucracy. The Societé was long on humanity, woefully short on practicality. The small team of tigers George had brought with him from New York were reduced to pussycats before the mountains of French regulations and the barriers of an unfamiliar language.

Then there was the house.

Living arrangements had been left to Melinda. A friend of a friend in New York had a cousin named Yvonne de Villiers who owned a house on the Rue de Babylone. The house was long and low, three stories propped one on the other as though each one were the builder's afterthought. The Villiers family lived on the first floor. The rest of the place was a warren of corridors, salons, closets, sewing rooms, alcoves, all of which seemed slightly askew. The plumbing was antedeluvian, the heating both noisy and chancy, the kitchen a disaster.

"At least there are working fireplaces in practically every room," Melinda said, trying to persuade herself. "And there's got to be plenty of coal to burn. The whole damned city is covered with soot. And God knows, there's plenty of room. But that kitchen . . . !"

Melinda was glad now about Dancy's refusal to leave Gramercy Park, considering that kitchen.

Then there was the way the place looked. After a week of shuffling someone else's furniture, rugs, pictures and knickknacks, Melinda's decorator's soul gave up. "Short of throwing it all out and starting from scratch, there's nothing I can do about it. So the hell with it." Melinda settled in, reserving the right to complain if she wanted to.

Ericka had no complaints at all. She staked out her turf on the top floor, bedroom, study and studio. In the studio she had north light and gorgeous floor-to-ceiling windows hung with delicately traced embroidery sheers.

The building stood back from the street in a cobblestoned court enclosed by a high stone wall. The street entrance was a heavy green gate that matched the louvered window shutters of the otherwise austerely drab facade. The courtyard was bare except for two horse chestnuts and a tall plane tree with a lovely satin-smooth gray-brown trunk whose branches almost touched the window of her bedroom. The courtyard was kept impeccably swept by a busty concierge of indeterminate age who lived in a little cage off the entrance hall and was given to incongruously fluffy wrappers, which she pottered around in all morning, talking endlessly to an asthmatic white Pomeranian that lolled on a faded plush cushion.

If Ericka was entranced and Melinda merely tolerant of their new home, George Barnstable hardly had time to notice it at all. For him it was a place to eat, bathe (when there was hot water), change clothes and try to sleep away the frustrations he faced during the day.

It was awhile before Melinda realized there was something seriously bothering her brother. When she sat him down and heard his tale of woe, she was appalled.

"But I thought they were supposed to take care of all that."

"The Societé? The Societé is a bunch of very rich, very old parties who wouldn't know a building permit from a dog license. The land was donated by a member, since deceased. The title is clear, the lawyers tell me. The conditions of the will require that a boys' school be built on the property. And that's it. After that, nothing. I talk to the president, who is a charming old gentleman who has white piping on his vest and wears a Legion of Honor rosette. I tell him what has to be done. He smiles at me and says, 'Of course. I shall speak to the minister. It will be arranged.'"

George was pale with agitation. Melinda went to the sideboard and poured them both a drink.

"I don't even know what minister he's talking about," George fumed on. "I'm not allowed to see the man in person. It's not done that way. It's my own goddamned fault. I should have checked it out first before coming over here. But there just wasn't time."

"Drink your drink, George." Melinda waited while he took a deep swallow. "What about Jacquard? Can't they help? Surely they know the ropes . . . ?"

"Those bastards!" George exploded. "They've got me by the balls. They're just too busy right now. 'Perhaps next month things will be easier. . . .' Bullshit! What they want is for me to hire them as consultants. Then all the problems will be solved. Like clockwork. I would have done it, too. It's what I had in mind—if they hadn't been such shits in the beginning. This way it's plain blackmail. And I'm damned if I'll sit still for it!''

"Why not move out? Find another firm who'll work with you."

"Start all over again? Where?" George said morosely, and then, "You're right, of course. There's no other solution. Trick is to find the right outfit. I just don't know anybody over here anymore. Everybody is either gone or dead."

"Let me give it some thought," Melinda said. She had that look that George knew from past experience meant that she was about to go into action.

That same day Melinda called an old Briarstone schoolmate who, in the intervening years, had first become Mrs. Spiro Naxos and more recently the Marquise Maxine de la Tour d'Azur, whose present husband was a prominent member of the National Assembly.

The conversation was long and interesting. Melinda hung up smiling to herself and reflecting how nice it was that Maxine Bullard of Greenwich, Connecticut, had come up so far in the world and, further, that Maxine had been a bit pushy even as a girl.

Ericka had been even less aware of George's troubles than Melinda. Her first days in Paris were one long exploration. She walked the banks of the Seine at dawn as the sun rose from behind the Cathedral of Notre-Dame, watched the barges from the north drift down the yellow-brown stream, in which huge fluffy clouds were mirrored upside down. She listened to the cheerful banter of the early workers as they clustered around the counters of cafés drinking coffee spiked with rum or cognac. She discovered the little miracle of St. Severin with its Gothic carvings, its gargoyles more gentle than grotesque.

And museums. The museums of Paris! She liked best the small out-of-the-way ones, and especially the Musée Rodin. She learned that Auguste Rodin was a lover, and not platonic, either. She saw study after study of sex, fusing together half-emerged male and female in the smooth cool oneness of a single block of stone. Rodin moved her deeply and at the same time disturbed her. . . .

She liked the Jeu de Paume, too, though it was harshly lighted and full of dutiful tourists. Except, that is, on early Sunday mornings when everybody was sleeping off Paris by night. Then she could go past the Douanier Rousseau's storybook lion, peering tawnily from behind plastic palms, to Monet's gallery and see cathedrals and lily pads slowly disintegrate and reassemble in a kaleidoscopic morning mist.

Then there were the little brown men. The problem was that she was too obvious. No matter where she was, little brown men would sidle up and leer at her with inner knowledge. "Doo yoo spick Eengleesh?" How could they tell? It must be her clothes, or hair, or maybe the lipstick.

Getting to know her way around Paris on the bus was really worth the ride. You boarded at the back of the vehicle and then had to file past a sort of miniature ticket station cropping out of the wall and all glass-enclosed. There was no such thing as a transfer, but you did have to hold on to the flimsy little tickets with serrated edges that the ticketman would dispense, one if you went two stops, two if you went four, and if you were going far you ended up with a whole handful. The tickets looked like recycled toilet paper and would automatically self-destruct in a sweaty palm or in the bottom of a pocket, so she took to folding them lengthwise and slipping them under a ring along the back of her hand as the French did.

There didn't seem to be any particular logic in plotting out the bus routes; it was as if the drivers were free to meander around in the neighborhoods they liked best.

During one of the frequent work slowdowns, only one bus out of every four would be running, which meant being squeezed and jammed stomach to stomach or shoulder under armpit. A sticky plight for girls since stray hands and other insinuating members were sure to take advantage of the situation. She'd found that if she shielded her breasts, kept her back to the wall and jabbed a vicious elbow or two she was pretty safe.

Ericka loved every minute of it. But it wasn't until Hughette Martin came to cook for them that her real Paris education began. Ericka's habitual dieting gained her immediate access to Hughette's parsimonious soul. Hughette could pinch a centime until it screamed

190

for mercy, and her daily shopping expeditions were like military forays against a determined enemy—the vendors and shopkeepers of the local markets.

At first Ericka's Briarstone French was hopelessly inadequate. But, wonder of wonders, Miss Terhune had managed to pass on to her an impeccable accent. Hughette delivered the accolade.

"Ma petite," Hughette told her, "I think you have the ear. Without the ear you could live in France a lifetime—and always be a foreigner. Now you must learn the argot. And, of course, marry a Frenchman."

By the time of the cocktail party of the marquise de la Tour d'Azur, Ericka was still unsure of her spoken French, but she *had* learned to listen and was acutely conscious of the nuances of the conversations around her. It gave her a wraithlike, disembodied feeling, as though she herself were invisible yet privy to all sorts of delicious secrets.

The D'Azurs had a place near St.-Cloud just outside Paris proper; it was a stone manor house dominating two sides of a huge cobbled courtyard. The third side was devoted to stables evidently in active use from the pungent smell of horses, leather and new-mown hay. In the field beyond was an exercise track, and beyond that the southern edge of the Bois de Boulogne. An attendant relieved them of their rented Citröen and a butler ushered them through the wide front doors into a vaulted hallway. The sounds of the party came from the right.

The room they entered was dominated by a fireplace surely big enough to roast a boar. The decor was hunting-lodge-cum-racing-buff and would have made a perfect retreat for Henry IV and his merry intimates.

The marquise was a small bouncy woman with a flaming red mouth and an inquisitive expression who kissed and hugged Melinda with real affection. Her husband had commanding height, a long, aquiline nose, a wide, generous mouth, and sparkling gray eyes that showed an instant appreciation of both Melinda and Ericka. With George Barnstable he was warmly friendly and took him off immediately to a group of men in the far corner of the enormous room.

191

Melinda and Maxine were engrossed in bringing each other up to date, so Ericka drifted through the crowd, acquiring a glass of champagne on the way and listening to snippets of the animated chatter of the guests.

She heard: "What Philippe didn't know was that her mother had binoculars. . . ."

While she puzzled over that she saw a slightly swaying young man drain his glass and say in accented English to a willowy model, "I feel the need to drain this incomparable instrument that is my body. Then perhaps more champagne. . . ."

A woman who waved a real believe-it-or-not lorgnette said in a voice as ripe as a melon, "They must either invite a more suitable class of guests, or lose my patronage. . . ."

In a nook between the fireplace and adjacent wall a young girl, partially hidden by the figure of a man in a tweed hacking jacket, seemed to be weeping, tears trickling silently down pale cheeks. In a voice of cold rage the man said, "Control yourself. A tragic ingenue with the sniffles is too ludicrous. As far as I'm concerned, this conversation is over . . ."

Melinda had taken Ericka to Coco Chanel's to outfit her for this party where George's cause was to be forwarded. With unerring judgment Salon Chanel had clothed her in an A-line ecru lace with a V neck just deep enough to stay within the bounds of good taste. The soft skirt swirled about her excellent legs as she moved. There was nothing *jeune fille* about it. She wore a single strand of Melinda's pearls. The only touch of color was the lavender chiffon kerchief tied around her wrist to hide the faint scar she would always carry. Her huge green eyes were startling against the pale silvery sheen of her hair.

Melinda, watching the stir of interest that followed Ericka as she passed, felt a fragmentary irritation that Chanel had done better for Ericka than for herself in her own elegant black silk sheath. And then she felt an overwhelming pride. The girl moved with the controlled grace of a forest animal, head held high and even by the long neck, shoulders softly rounded, no trace of awkwardness in the arms or hands. And the eyes . . . those incredible green eyes, so steady and direct. She had more than beauty. She had quality.

192

Ericka paused behind a languid young man standing close to a striking dark girl in a bright red sweater.

"My bed," the young man murmured, "is usually crowded on weekends—but I could make room for you. I would like, as they say, to get into your pants."

With no change of expression, the girl considered him. "Don't think I don't appreciate the offer. But . . . one asshole in these pants is quite enough."

Ericka was still laughing when a voice behind her said in accented English, "I'm Even." Or that's what it sounded like. She couldn't resist answering, "And I'm Odd."

The man behind her was scarcely taller than she was.

"No, no, I think you misunderstand me," he said. "Eevon, I-V-A-N. Eevon ven der Veen. It's Dutch. And you are American."

"How do you tell?" she asked.

He stared at her seriously from behind thick-lensed horn-rimmed glasses. "You are so healthy. Only Americans are so healthy. Except possibly Swedes. You are to study for the Beaux Arts."

"Yes. How did you know *that*?"

"Maxine is my aunt. She has asked me to speak to you. My father is Piet ven der Veen, the architect."

"But . . . I thought he was dead," she blurted. Her gaucherie made her blush violently. "I mean . . . I'm terribly sorry. But he has built so many things." The gravity of that owlish stare embarrassed her further. She felt almost *fat* again. "He must be terribly old. . . ." she heard herself say, and blushed more deeply.

Surprisingly Ivan grinned at her. The grin changed his whole personality, transforming the solemn face into something immensely likeable. She saw that he couldn't be more than a few years older than she. She drew a deep breath and managed to smile back at him.

"Could we start all over again, if I promise just to listen?"

"Certainly." He took first her glass, and then her arm and led her to a window seat.

"I'm used to it. His work is so . . . prodigious. Buildings, stadiums, museums, sculptures. So many, many sculptures all over the world. Not surprising people should think he is dead. But he isn't. He is merely . . . resting. No, not *resting*. How do you say . . . ?"

"Retired?"

"Of course, retired. But only in part. His firm is still very active. He devotes himself now to the Atelier ven der Veen—for students of the Beaux Arts."

The possibilities ran through Ericka's head like caged mice let loose. The Atelier ven der Veen. Being accepted by the right atelier . . . the right patron, was desperately important. Half the battle, if one were to graduate from the Beaux Arts with impressive marks. To be the pupil of Piet ven der Veen!

"Are you at . . . ?"

"Oh, no," he said quickly. "*Sciences po*. Political sciences. I am studying to be a diplomat."

Ericka had an instant vision of him in frock coat and silk hat. Instinct stifled her giggles. Instinct also told her that she had her work cut out for her. First she widened her remarkable eyes, then blinked several times—slowly. Next she put her hand on his arm and wriggled just a little closer. "A diplomat . . ." she said with exactly the right catch of her breath. "That's fascinating. I want to hear all about it. . . ."

Melinda would have been proud of her.

Melinda, at the moment, was having her own breath problems. Maxine had just introduced her to a man named Paul Geroux who was still holding her hand and looking at her as though she were money from home. She felt a weakness in her knees and longed for a place to sit down.

"Maxine tells me you are quite unattached."

"Quite."

"Ah," the man said.

"Yes," Melinda breathed. "Ah."

"Then perhaps I . . ."

"Yes," Melinda said again. "Definitely perhaps." And had a fleeting twinge of guilt as she thought of Tobin Wright. But Tobin was 3,000 miles away. And getting farther by the moment.

George Barnstable was also feeling a little weak in the knees. *His* weakness was a mixture of joy and relief. He was in the billiard room, standing between François Letts, who was the *ministre des travaux*, and Étienne Gilbert, who was the *ministre des affaires culturales*. The introduction of the Marquis de la Tour d'Azur had been more explanation than introduction. The marquis had been well briefed by his wife and laid out George's problems to the two men in a few forceful phrases ending with "It's unthinkable that a man of such worldwide reputation should have so many difficulties in France. I know I can count on you two to see that matters march forward smoothly."

The marquis had then stepped back and presented the stage gracefully to George. For the next fifteen minutes the three men had listened attentively and sympathetically to George's tale of woe.

"So you see," George concluded, "I'm over a barrel. Henri Jacquard was a close friend from student days. But the sons . . ."

"Unconscionable," said the minister of works.

"Terminate," said the minister of cultural affairs.

"But . . ." said George.

"An association with another firm," said the minister of works.

"But who . . . ?" said George.

"Ven der Veen et Cie, of course," said the marquis. "Piet is my brother-in-law."

"My God . . ." said George.

"I will arrange it," said the marquis.

"Come to my office on Monday," said the minister of cultural affairs.

"And to mine," said the minister of works.

George said nothing. He began to grin like the Cheshire cat. *Arranger,* to arrange. It was a verb George was to come to know and love. There is nothing in France that cannot be arranged if one has the right connections.

"Of course," the marquis said, "you understand that very little can truly be accomplished until the middle of September."

"But," George said, "that's two months away."

"In July and August," said the cultural minister, "there is *no one* in Paris. Except the tourists."

"No one," said the works minister.

"You are to spend the time with us," said the marquis. "Maxine and your sister have arranged it."

"I . . . I didn't know. . . ." said George, feeling outrageously manipulated, but too relieved to care. "You are too kind, Marquis."

"Call me Bobbie," the marquis said. "Everyone does."

"And I, François," the works minister said.

"Étienne," said the cultural minister, and held out his hand.

So it was arranged.

That was how George, Melinda and Ericka found themselves in a huge pink villa in the village of Menton on the French Riviera.

For George Barnstable it was a time of frustration, only made bearable because his two ladies were having themselves such a ball. Their delight was irresistible and he did his best to join in.

For Melinda it was a rebirth. Paul Geroux had the guest house, just 128 steps away from the main villa through a pine forest. Melinda knew because she counted them each night. Melinda was in love, helplessly, girlishly, breathlessly in love. At forty-seven she was going through something she hadn't felt since fifteen, when she had a hopeless crush on her history teacher. Now—with a man ten years her junior. She trembled at an inadvertent touch. She couldn't bear to look at him when others were present for fear that . . . And yet, she did, stealing surreptitious glances—and feeling as naked and exposed as the day she was born. She counted hours—and hated herself for it—until she could steal through the dark forest to be with him.

Paul Geroux was the perfect lover. And she knew with absolute conviction that it couldn't last. She cried a lot. Whether from sorrow or happiness, she didn't know.

George, with amiable brotherly cruelty, said, "Go to it, old girl. You only live once. 'Gather ye roses while ye may.' You're a long time dead, and all that sort of stuff. Incidentally, seems like a hell of a nice fella. . . ."

She was unbearably aware of Maxine's knowing worried looks. But what was she to do? Goddamnit. Ten years wasn't all that much. Or was it?

For Ericka it was a summer of awakening. The blood seemed to stretch her veins. Her body was constantly atingle with a strange excitement. The villa was never empty. There was a constant flow of people, both young and old. College students, skinny bare-chested youths with corkscrew bellybuttons and knife-sharp ribs. Tawny girls with freckles and friendly smiles, butterscotch thighs and jutting, nubile breasts.

It was a summer of scary car rides on winding roads above the sea; of winning (some) and losing (more) at Monte Carlo, Nice and Cannes; long hours of tennis and swimming; nights of dancing till dawn in the *caves*, which throbbed to *le Jazz Hot*, the guitar of Django Reinhart, the violin of Stephane Grappell. Her favorite song was "Petite Fleur" by Sidney Bechet. She ate sausages from street corner vendors and washed them down with an orange drink called Psshit and had to explain why she laughed. She dined on pressed duck at three-star restaurants and dug out the succulent meat of langoustes in waterfront bistros.

Toward the end of their stay Maxine took the three of them for lunch at the Colombe d'Or, near La Colle sur Loup, just outside of Nice. Ericka was entranced by the friendliness of the white doves that settled on their table and picked unconcernedly at the crumbs. They walked the white halls of the inn and admired the priceless artwork on the walls.

None of them knew that, behind one of the doors they passed, two people were making love. Serena Gansvoort Damiani Summerlin and a policeman named Gavin Riordan.

15

Time: 1955
SERENA

Gavin Riordan sipped gin and tonic from a paper cup that was rapidly becoming too soggy to handle and tried to concentrate on the match unfolding on the court. He was acutely conscious of Serena's empty chair beside him, of her perfunctory welcoming kiss when the attendant had led him to his seat and then the quick "Gavin, darling. How nice. I've got to run. Back in a mo." After pressing the drink in his hand, she was gone, leaving him bewildered, increasingly irritated and acutely conscious of the speculative sidelong looks of some of the people near him. That had been all of twenty minutes ago. He resisted looking around for her because he didn't know which of the people were in Serena's party and was determined not to show his impatience.

"Advantage Summerlin." The referee's voice came tinnily over the microphone.

Serena's husband, whom he had met just once and recognized now only because of the spectacular guard's mustache, seemed to have the match in hand. The Englishman was leading two sets to one, three games to two and serving in the fourth set. His opponent, a short, agile Spaniard, seemed to be tiring.

Gavin watched John Summerlin's service, which seemed to be his big weapon, and heard a linesman call "Out." Then, moments later, another "Out" and the referee's magnified tones, "Double fault.

Deuce." Summerlin walked to the net beneath the referee's high chair and pointed with his racquet. There was a low-voiced protest that the referee obviously overruled. The tall Englishman was pale with anger as he stalked back to the baseline.

The Stad Menton in Monte Carlo was jammed with people for the Tournament de Monaco. Beautiful people, as Gavin looked about him. There seemed to be no extremes, no one very fat, no one very old, and surely no one markedly ugly. Slim, tawny-haired women in all sizes and colors. Tall, muscular men glowing with health. All strangely anonymous behind the inevitable shades.

The sides of the stadium were lined with boxes and large stone bowls filled with jasmine and roses of every shade, ranging from white through pale pinks and yellows to huge bloodred blooms. The scent of the flowers was languorous, overpowering.

Gavin found the rhythmic *spat* of the balls hypnotic. The warm Mediterranean sun was making him sleepy. It had been a tiring flight. The Paris–Nice connection had been delayed. He had arrived at Nice Airport in midmorning an hour late, only to hear himself being paged over the PA system. He was met at the airline desk by a uniformed chauffeur who said, "Mrs. Summerlin is expecting you."

Stewart Gansvoort, who had told him Serena's whereabouts in the first place with some reluctance, had undoubtedly wired ahead, whatever his reasons. Gavin had wanted his arrival to be something of a surprise for Serena, feeling it would give him a small advantage. Obviously Stewart had his own ideas.

Gavin hesitated, wanting only to find a hotel room, take a shower and get some sleep. And, above all, not to be dependent on Serena's largesse.

"This way, please," the chauffeur said. "Your bags will be in the car."

Reluctantly Gavin followed him through the lobby, out into burning sunshine, and was helped into a gleaming Rolls-Royce. Enclosed in plush gray comfort, he decided that American summerwear was not exactly the thing for Mediterranean outings. He took off his jacket, loosened his tie and leaned back to enjoy his first look at the fabled French Riviera. Instead he fell into a doze that lasted until the speaker at his ear said, "Eden Roc, sir. You will be in Cabin 12."

The Rolls-Royce slid silently into a grove of trees that was the parking lot. Ancient *platanes*, gnarled and twisted by siroccos and mistrals, looking like survivors of some volcanic age. To the left, at the top of a long sloping lawn was the Hôtel du Cap, gimcrackery and steep gables lending an air of Victorian elegance, its long dining veranda open to the sun.

The chauffeur turned Gavin over to a porter, who lifted his battered Val-A-Pak and started off at a fast pace. Gavin took his time. To his right, at the end of the promontory that gave it its name, was Eden Roc proper—a few houses and a small hotel and bar. In between were tennis courts and a pool built into a rocky terrace. There were flowers everywhere, yellow mimosa, wisteria, jasmine, clumps of palms, spreading fig and cherry trees. To the left, at the edge of a steep cliff, were the cabins in pastel blues and pinks, each surrounded by its own small garden bursting with hot Mediterranean colors. Beyond was the deep blue of the sea, dotted with white sails and the trails of water-skiers.

Cabin 12 was decorated with quiet elegance: deep chairs; soft, roomy sofa; rattan tables; bright prints on the walls. The porter, with the theatricality of a magician, whipped open the door of a small refrigerator, displaying splits of wine, Haig & Haig Pinch, squat bottles of Perrier. Another dramatic gesture indicated a basket piled high with fruit on one of the tables. A third sweep of the arm, with a simultaneous lift of the shoulders and eyebrows, took in the adjacent bedroom, the shoddy Val-A-Pak at Gavin's feet, and asked silently if monsieur wished him to unpack?

Monsieur didn't. Gavin handed him a dollar bill, watched it disappear by magic, and got his first smile. The porter bowed and left.

A luggage stand in the bedroom held an expensive kangaroo hide bag that bore the initials M.H-B over a small crest of a lion rampant on a shield. On one of the identical dressing tables was a matched set of silver-backed brushes with the same crest and initials and a quart bottle of Canöe cologne. There were twin closets faced with full-length mirrors. One closet held several expensive summer jackets, slacks and a cream-colored dinner jacket with a shawl collar. The contents of the other closet almost duplicated the first, except for two tennis racquets in their presses, which leaned in one corner, and a pair of soiled white sox stuffed into the tennis shoes. The jackets in the second closet all bore club patches on the left breast.

He obviously had a roommate, possibly two, one of whom was a tennis player who liked to smell sweet. There were only two beds, which puzzled him until he saw laid out neatly on one of them pale yellow slacks, a beige wide-necked Basque shirt and a pair of espadrilles. On top of the pile was a note.

> Colors should go with your hair. Hope they fit. No socks. Not the done thing here. Michael will bring you to the matches.
>
> Love, S.

Wondering who and where "Michael" was and what matches, Gavin stripped to his shorts, opened a bottle of wine and sat down next to the fruit bowl. Fifteen minutes, two pears, one apple and a bunch of grapes later—and still no Michael—he polished off the wine and headed for a shower and shave.

When he emerged, toweling himself and feeling much better, he found a short, muscular young man in tennis clothes eating the last of the pears.

"Shouldn't eat before a match," the young man said. He waved the dripping pear. "Can't resist fruit." He held out his hand and Gavin took it. The grip was strong and firm and Gavin saw that the right arm was considerably more developed than the left. Powerful muscles rippled under the tanned flesh.

"You're Riordan," the fellow said. "Hicks-Beach here. Serena says we're to share these digs. Welcome aboard. Hope you'll be comfortable."

"I sort of had a hotel in mind. Wouldn't want to put you out."

"Hotel room? In season?" Hicks-Beach appeared slightly puzzled at Gavin's innocence. "Doesn't exist, old boy. Not in season. Afraid it's make do here—or sleep on the beach. Why don't you deck the bod and we'll be off. Like to catch John's match before my own doubles."

While Michael Hicks-Beach munched grapes, Gavin put on the clothes laid out for him and found that they fitted perfectly. He started to thank Hicks-Beach for lending them when he realized from the difference in their sizes that the outfit couldn't have belonged to the Englishman. He had an instant suspicion that the clothes hanging in the closet would fit him equally well. It added to his irritation at Serena's high-handedness, her automatic assumption that a mick cop wouldn't know what to bring to the French Riviera. Well, she was right. He hadn't brought a dinner jacket because he hadn't planned to wear one. He'd pictured his meeting with Serena quite differently. A time and a place of *his* choosing—not hers. He should have known better. Never anticipate Serena. What had Des Daniher said? "Watch yourself in the clinches. I think you're out of your class...."

Serena slipped into the seat beside him.

"Sorry. Couldn't help it. What's happening?"

Gavin was conscious that the crowded stands were now alive with excitement. The scoreboard told him that the match was even, the Spaniard leading five-two in the deciding set.

"Shit," Serena said. "The poor boy just doesn't have the killer instinct. He's blown it and he'll pout all evening. Then it's back to the practice courts until the next one."

"Is this what he does?"

"What?"

"Play tennis?"

"Yup. He's what you call a tennis bum. Not exactly Wimbledon class, but what the hell, he can afford it."

"Or you can?"

"You could say that," Serena said slowly. "If it's any of your goddamn business."

"Jesus, Serena. I didn't come over here to argue with you."

"I didn't ask you to come over here at all. Why did you, Gavin?"

Gavin was burning with frustration, knowing he was in the wrong and resenting it. "I wanted some answers—from you."

Serena's smile was wickedly sweet. "Is that all? Be my guest."

"I seem to be. I hadn't planned it that way."

"Well, the best laid plans ... Or is *laid* the wrong word? Just what *did* you have in mind, Gavin?"

"Not this. Come on, Serena. Can't we cut this out?"

"You started it. You and your cracks."

202

Gavin was willing to make almost any concession to get things back on the right track. "Okay, I'm sorry. Truly I am. I take it back. Play like I never said it. Let's start all over. Okay?"

"Now, that's better," Serena said complacently. "More like the Gavin we know and love." Then she turned to him, and he saw that her eyes were misty with tears. "Dear Gavin. I *am* so glad to see you. I'm such a bitch. . . ."

He ached to reach out and hold her.

"Let's get out of here," Serena said huskily, "before I make an ass of myself and cry all over you. . . ."

Conversation in Serena's open Mercedes 300 SL was impossible. Traffic was light on the Moyenne Corniche, and Serena took it like a Grand Prix driver. It was dark when they reached the tiny town of St.-Paul-de-Vence and the inn called Colombe d'Or perched on top of a hill above Nice.

There was no concierge, no reception desk, no porter, but Serena moved confidently through the crowded bar, waved to the bartender and led Gavin down a long white corridor to a room at its end. The door was open. Serena pulled him inside, shot the iron bolt, turned on a dim bedside lamp, crossed the room to close the curtains at the single window and turned to face him.

Gavin moved toward her, overwhelmed by the need to touch her. She met him with a finger against his lips.

"No questions."

With crossed arms she pulled the sweater over her head, her shorts dropped to the floor and she was naked.

"Now," Serena breathed.

Sometime before morning Serena slipped from the bed, careful not to wake Gavin. She got a long white silk robe from the closet, opened the curtains and let the moonlight stream into the room. The shaft of light fell across Gavin's naked body. Serena sat watching the rise and fall of his breathing. He lay on his back and the moon rays highlighted the raised welt of scar tissue across his stomach, made a darker pit of the bullet hole in his thigh. She couldn't see the puckered wound in his arm or the more recent wounds in his back.

Toward dawn she began to weep. Outside, the soft restless cooing of the white doves of Colombe d'Or seemed a fitting accompaniment to her slow silent tears.

As the day came awake, Serena padded down the hallway into the deserted barroom. From the telephone there she called the Hôtel du Cap and told a sleepy desk clerk to inform her husband that she would be spending the next few days with some friends. To this she added certain other instructions. Next she made her way to the kitchen to be greeted as an old friend by the proprietor's pretty wife, Lisette. Serena supervised the preparation of a tray: slices of *jambon d'Ardennes* topped by four fried eggs, mounds of toast *avec confiture,* a crock of sweet butter, a huge thermos of steaming coffee, a jug of thick local cream. Lisette added two ripe pears and a vase with three yellow roses.

Serena pushed open the door with her tray to find Gavin standing before her open closet, looking at the clothes hanging there. She was struck by the beauty of the wide shoulders tapering to a trim waist; long smooth muscles rippling under the pale skin; tight, firm buttocks with their twin indentations. Her breath caught in her throat and there was a weakness in her knees. She felt vulnerable as a girl.

"Home away from home," she said, answering the question in Gavin's eyes. "A hideaway from the Riviera rat race." Then, as he looked again at the closet, "No. No male bathrobes. And no shaving gear. You'll have to use the one I shave my legs with. But eat first. You must be starved."

Serena confined herself to toast and coffee and watched while Gavin polished off the rest. When he had finished and lighted a cigarette over the last of the coffee, she saw by his serious expression that his questions were about to begin. She wasn't ready for them. Not just yet.

"Why don't you shave? Then we'll swim. There's a pool just outside our window."

They had the pool to themselves. Gavin was glad, as the trunks Lisette had lent him were impossibly small. They swam quietly for a while until the arrival of two exquisitely blond children with a nurse told them that the inn was ready for the day. Then they stretched out in beach loungers close to one another. The early sun bathed them in warm Mediterranean comfort.

"You owe me, Serena," Gavin said, and she knew the time had come. "Why dump me seven years ago and then pull a Florence Nightingale when I was in the hospital? Des told me you practically saved my life."

"They said you were going to die . . ."

"Why dump me in the first place? Was the thought of marriage to me that awful?"

"Was it . . . so bad?" She tried not to look at him.

"You know it was." His eyes wouldn't release her.

"Because I love you." She reached out to take his hand, willing him to understand. He turned her hand over, his thumb into her palm with a gentle insistent pressure.

"I know you do, my darling. And I love you. Then and now. For a time I wasn't sure. I am now. That's why you aren't making a hell of a lot of sense."

"The only kind of sense. You don't know me, Gavin. Not really. You don't know me at all."

He looked at her, gravely intent. "I know myself."

"Are you so sure?" Wishing it were so and knowing in her heart that the pressures of great wealth would be too much for him. For any man who wasn't born to it, as she had been. She'd seen it all too often, and each time it had sickened her.

"Never surer. I wish I were as sure of you. . . ."

"I'll make a bargain with you," she said slowly, seeing for the first time a possible way to make him see things as they truly were. "One month. Together. We'll talk, morning, noon and night. Everything we think and feel. No holding back. Then, if . . . Well, we'll see."

Gavin began to grin. "One whole month? I can't afford it."

"I can. As you so kindly pointed out. Will you do it? And no holding back. You promise?"

"Sure," Gavin said, "why not? I might as well get used to your money."

That, Serena thought sadly, *is the point. You'll never make it.*

205

In their room Gavin's battered Val-A-Pak was on the floor of the open closet. Above it, next to Serena's, hung the clothes she had bought him, all delivered from the Eden Roc while they swam. She watched his mouth tighten briefly and then break ruefully into a smile.

"How'd you know my size?"

"I know every gorgeous inch of you, my darling. Besides, you're changing the subject. Enough of this lovemaking. Let's go to bed."

They had a late lunch after most of the midday diners had left. In daylight Gavin had a chance to admire the loveliness of the Colombe d'Or. Set on a hillside with a charming bucolic view, the inn gave the impression of being centuries old. Serena told him it wasn't. It had been put together piecemeal by the original owner in the 1920's, each door, each windowpane the result of careful selection. The whitewashed walls and corridors were waxed to give the impression of great age.

After lunch Serena led him through corridors and passageways that were hung with one of the finest collections of modern art, Picasso, Modigliani, Miró, Renoir, Bonnard, Dufy, Buffet, Léger, Matisse, Chagall, Braque.

"Remind you of home?" Gavin needled. "Surely not as impressive as Riverhaven."

Serena answered him seriously. "It takes more than money to collect. It takes a very special eye. I don't think the Gansvoorts have it."

"Except you?"

"Yup. Except me."

The racetrack at Cannes is one of the most beautiful in the world. It is on the sea between Cannes and Nice, just north of Antibes. From their privileged window table in the clubhouse, Gavin and Serena could look out over the oval track to the deep blue of the Mediterranean.

The trotters and pacers seemed smaller than the ones Gavin had seen in the States. Clean-limbed, prancing, compact little horses with smooth gaits, pulling their sulkies with effortless grace. The

206

program was more than half over when they arrived, only three races left.

Gavin followed her to the betting cages, looking for the equivalent of the two-dollar window back home. Serena made for the booth that accommodated only high-stakes betters and placed 150,000 francs on a horse called Éminence Grise, at seven to two odds.

"Why him? You know what you're doing?"

"No. I just like his name."

Serena reacted to the race as though she owned the horse herself, jumping up from the table, upsetting her drink and adding her yells to the roar of the crowd in the grandstands. Éminence Grise broke first and, by the three-quarter pole, had two lengths on the next horse. He increased his lead to three in the backstretch. Then the flying gray horse broke his gait, an automatic disqualification, and finished a poor fourth.

Serena sat down, scowling. "Did you see that! The son of a bitch pulled him up on purpose. I told you trotters were fixed!" She seemed as down now as she had been up a few moments before.

"Come on, Serena. Any horse can break gait. Happens all the time."

"Not to me it doesn't."

"What the hell, it's only money."

"It's not the money," Serena said angrily.

"Then, what?"

"I hate to lose is all. Especially like that."

"Jesus, honey. You never even *heard* of the horse until ten minutes ago." Gavin was having difficulty keeping up with her moods.

"What difference does that make? I still think it was fixed. Come on, let's get the hell out of here."

Gavin followed without a word, because he couldn't think of a single thing to say that would make any difference.

There were a number of cars in the courtyard when they returned. Serena eased the Mercedes into one of the few spaces available. The poignant beat of a Piaf song came through the open doorway of the inn along with the babble of voices, English accents clearly distinguishable from the staccato French.

"Anyone you know?"

Serena hadn't spoken on the trip home. Now she shrugged and said, "It doesn't matter. If we go through the bar quickly no one will notice."

It didn't happen that way. The first person they saw was Michael Hicks-Beach, who looked surprised and a little disconcerted. There was a party of eight or ten people at the far end of the room.

"Mike," Serena said brightly. "What are you doing here?"

"Ah . . . bit of a victory bash. I won my match." He held out his hand. "Riordan. Wondered where you'd got to. That is . . ." He stopped in confusion, then low-voiced to Serena, "John's here. He's had a bit, I'm afraid. Feeling sorry for himself. . . ."

If it was a warning, it came too late.

"Serena." John Summerlin was approaching them, walking in a straight line with just slightly exaggerated care. "This is the 'friends' you're spending a few days with?"

"You remember Gavin Riordan."

"Oh, yes. Childhood chums. You show me yours, and I'll show you mine, and all that."

Wanting to save her the embarrassment of an ugly scene, Gavin said, "Perhaps I'd better wait in the car."

"Why not Serena's room? I'm told it's quite comfortable—if you don't mind the flow of traffic."

"You're offensive." Serena was stony-faced. "And you're drunk."

"A man gets a little tired of being made to look a fool."

"Mother Nature took care of that. Don't make it any worse. Go somewhere and sleep it off. I'm warning you, John." Serena's voice was ominous.

"And what will you do, my dear? Cut off my allowance."

"Yes," Serena said furiously, "exactly."

Michael Hicks-Beach put a restraining hand on Summerlin's arm.

"Look, old chap. No place for all this. Why don't we . . ."

Summerlin threw him off. Suddenly his eyes were wet with self-pity. "Mike, you don't know what it is—to be married to a tramp. A damned tramp!"

208

Gavin hit him. All his frustrations of the past forty-eight hours were in the blow. Summerlin's head cracked sharply against the edge of the bar as he went down.

"Jesus," Serena said. "What did you have to do that for?" She dropped to her knees and cradled Summerlin's head in her lap. Gavin was paralyzed by Serena's reaction and could only stand there rubbing his bruised hand.

"He'll live," Hicks-Beach said. "Frightful headache, though I shouldn't wonder." He looked a question at Serena.

"Put him in my room. He can sleep it off there. Gavin, get a towel. You and Mike carry him."

As the two men carried Summerlin down the corridor a babble of voices broke out behind them. They heard Serena say, "Don't worry, folks. He ran into a fist. You'll have to excuse him for now. He'll be all right in the morning."

Gavin and Hicks-Beach laid Summerlin on the bed with a towel under his head, although the bleeding seemed to have stopped. His breathing was even enough. He began to snore gently.

"Not like old John," Hicks-Beach said with a faint note of apology. "Usually meek as a lamb. Kind to flies and all that."

Gavin leaned over the limp body and wiggled Summerlin's slack jaw experimentally.

"Nothing broken, I take it?" asked Hicks-Beach.

"Seems okay."

"I wonder. Frightful bash you gave him."

From the doorway Serena said, "*Macho* gives me a pain in the ass. Did you have to hit him so hard?"

"Come on, old girl. He *was* rather asking for it."

"I suppose he was," Serena said doubtfully. "He'll be all right, won't he?"

"Right as rain in the morning," Hicks-Beach assured her. "I'll bunk here tonight. Hold his head when he wakes. And, Serena..." He seemed acutely embarrassed. "Won't be using my digs for a while. Off to London tomorrow. All yours if you like."

"I like," Serena said. "Mike, you *are* a dear. I won't forget it." And then, "Come on, Gavin. Let's go."

* * *

Michael Hicks-Beach's "digs" turned out to be a sizeable house in the hills above Cannes. There were lights on the ground floor, and at Serena's knock the door was opened by a grizzled man in dark trousers and a white shirt, complete with black bow tie.

"Good evening, Harris."

"Good evening, Miss Serena. You're expected. Lord Saint Aldwyn rang up a few moments ago. He suggested you might be wanting something to eat."

"We're starved," Serena said. "Could we have it on the upstairs terrace?"

"Of course, Miss Serena."

As they followed him up the broad staircase, Gavin whispered, "Lord Saint Aldwyn? Mike?"

"The blood of kings run in those veins. Sky blue."

"Somehow he doesn't seem . . ."

"No, he doesn't."

Unspoken between them was the thought that Gavin wouldn't know a lord if it bit him—and Serena would.

Harris ushered them into a long low room that was both bedroom and sitting room dotted with low chairs and sofas, a king-sized bed at the far end. The wall facing the sea was entirely of glass.

Harris opened sliding doors and led them out onto a balcony with more chairs and sofas, this time of rattan. The view was spectacular, the twinkle of Cannes below them. Farther out the lights of the American fleet at anchor flashed and glittered.

Harris brought them mounds of thick roast beef sandwiches and a tall carafe of the sharp wine of Provence, then discreetly disappeared. They both ate ravenously and, when they were finished, settled back in silence over cigarettes.

After a while Gavin asked, "Why *did* you marry him, Serena?"

"Does it matter?"

"No. Just curious."

"He was attractive. And charming. . . . No. The truth. We promised. I was lonely, I guess. And he was there. I get lonely a lot. . . ."

"Not anymore, my darling. Not now."

"No," Serena said softly, "not now . . ." and held out her arms.

* * *

Gavin woke first, to the sound of cocks crowing somewhere nearby. He was conscious of her warmth on his back and turned to take her in his arms. Sleepily Serena mumbled something and fought him off, curling herself into a tight ball. Reluctantly Gavin left her alone. In the blue-tiled bathroom he showered and shaved with a gold-handled Rolls razor.

"Gavin," Serena called, "come back."

She had thrown back the covers and was lying stretched out straight on her back, arms behind her head, which made her breasts jut out. There was no sun line around her breasts, but the white area around her hips was startling against her body tan.

"Where were you when I needed you?"

"Damn it, I'm awake now," Serena said crossly. "Come back to bed." She spread her legs slightly and lifted her hips toward him.

"You had your chance. Besides, I'm starved."

"Master's voice?"

"Something like that."

Serena grinned wickedly. "Two can play that game."

"I wouldn't. Punch like a mule. Remember?"

He picked up his underwear gingerly. "I could use a change. Somehow I don't seem to be able to keep up with my clothes."

"We'll go into town and buy you some more. Dozens of 'em. In the meantime, wear some of Mike's."

"Don't think they're big enough."

"Quit bragging. They're in the dresser. Second drawer."

At Gavin's silent question she said, "Yes, I've been here before, if that's what you're asking." And then, relenting. "I've known Mike almost as long as I've known you. He's one of the best friends I've got."

"He in love with you?"

"He thought he was. A long time ago. Now, get out of here and let me get dressed."

Downstairs an arcade opened off the main hall. The smell of cooking bacon led him through it and into a sunken kitchen. The walls gleamed with burnished copper kettles, ladles, sieves. There was a medieval farm table with a soft lustrous patina. Garlands of dried peppers and garlic hung from heavy oak beams, along with

211

cured hams and sausages. At the far side of the room was a modern electric stove presided over by Harris, now in an apron of bed ticking.

"Good morning, sir," Harris said. "How would you like your eggs?"

"Doesn't matter. As long as they're plentiful."

"Miss Serena prefers them coddled."

"Fine with me," Gavin said, wondering how you coddled an egg. He wandered back into the hallway and out the front door. The air was soft and lazy. A glimmering haze of morning sun veiled the curving coast in a gauzy mist of lemon yellow and green and beige and white. Jagged outcroppings of copper-red rock jutted up from the sea where the city ran down to the waterfront. Gleaming yachts crowded the harbor, like toy boats in an azure bath. Farther out the sea was already dotted with sails.

Behind him the house was a sturdy, two-storied block of creamy rough-grained stucco with a peakless, lean-to roof of tiles faded to a mosaic of rose and salmon and ocher. The wide terrace ran all around the second floor, guarded by curved wrought-iron railings set in stucco pillars. On the ground floor broad French windows, rounded at the top into Roman arches, opened onto stone steps to the lower garden or directly out to graveled paths, where the incline was greater. There was no lawn, nor were there any flower beds. Orange trees were set out in heavy wooden tubs and a many-tiered rock garden overgrown with tiny succulents and crawling tendrils banked up steeply in a sunny corner. Bougainvillea and plumbago twined up the rainpipes as high as the roof, lush and glossy. On each side of the iron grillwork gate, cut into the thick stone wall that rose along the hill and wound round the whole garden, stood two towering eucalyptus trees drooping long skeins of aromatic leaves. Here and there a dwarf palm or a cactus cropped up out of the gravel.

Gavin found the scene entrancing. And somewhat overwhelming.

"Come and get it," Serena called from the balcony above him.

She was leaning over the railing, dressed in a white terrycloth robe sizes too big for her. And she looked like a million dollars.

He was breathless when he came out on the terrace behind her and put his arms around her.

*   *   *

Serena delighted in buying him things. She bought him handkerchiefs and ties at Charvet; a leather toilet kit and silver-backed brushes at Hermès; loafers and espadrilles (no socks) at Gucci; shirts, jackets and slacks at Polombo; a gold lighter and pearl shirt studs at Cartier; a thin wafer of a wrist watch at Piaget.

It embarrassed Gavin at first. But Serena's pure pleasure kept him quiet. He finally drew the line at a magnificent star sapphire ring set in platinum when he saw the price in francs and worked it out in his head at just over twelve thousand American dollars.

"It's only money," Serena protested. "You said it, remember? Money is only to buy you what you want."

"But this is ridiculous. I don't wear rings."

"Get in the way when you hit people?"

"Jesus, Serena, I don't even know where to put the stuff I've already got."

That only got him a matched set of alligator luggage delivered to the house.

Dressed in his new cream-colored silk dinner jacket and his black pearl studs (Serena in something pale green and diaphanous), Gavin won seven hundred dollars in his first twenty minutes of play at the Winter Casino in Cannes. Serena lost seven thousand. Serena went to the cashier for more. Losing only made her mad. Gavin quit while he was ahead. The implied criticism made her madder.

Gavin refused to watch her lose any more and went to stand at another roulette table with several other kibitzers. The attention there was focused on a swarthy gentleman whose lips were curled around an unlighted cigar. In half an hour the man lost ten million francs, which Gavin calculated at thirty thousand dollars.

Serena rejoined him in a foul mood. At Gavin's unspoken question she snapped at him, "Okay. I lost it all. It's no fun playing alone."

"I told you money doesn't mean a hell of a lot to me. But I do have a certain respect for it. I hate to see it pissed away. By you or anybody else." He nodded toward the swarthy man across the green baize table. "Like that joker, for instance."

213

"That joker," Serena said, "is named Paterno, and he owns half the tin mines in the world—among a lot of other things."

They stayed for another half hour during which Signor Paterno lost forty thousand more.

"Seventy thousand bucks in no more than an hour. Feed a lot of starving Armenians on that." Gavin shook his head. "Know what? I think it's obscene. That's what."

"Well, look at it this way," Serene said sweetly. "In that hour you're talking about, the money he already has has earned him maybe five times what he lost. That's the thing about money. It reproduces itself. Makes rabbits look like pikers."

"I don't believe it." Gavin was aghast.

"Well, think about it. Because the Gansvoort money earns maybe ten times more than that."

"Jesus! Nobody can *force* you to keep it, you know."

"No? It multiplies a lot faster than you can give it away. Take my word for it."

Serena's legerdemain produced a local driver's license for him and she insisted he drive her Mercedes. At first he was cautious, too respectful of the great machine. The car had the guts of a burglar and handled as though it were an extension of himself. Gavin fell in love with its smooth perfection.

They drove the old route Napoleon through the Grande Canyon du Verdon, the narrow road winding dangerously through magnificent gorges high about the rushing river, sudden green valleys occasionally interrupting the stark gray stone of the mountains. They made a two-day excursion down the coast to the ancient city of Arles, with its Roman fortifications still intact, and dined at the Hôtel du Poste under a centuries-old *platane* tree whose branches covered almost all of the central square. On the way back, in Marseille, Gavin, having been raised on Friday fish, found the famous bouillabaisse something less than it was cracked up to be.

On the fast waterfront highways and the new mountain route between Fréjus and Nice, Gavin learned about the other drivers. Serena taught him to recognize the different nationalities by their license plates.

"The worst," Serena said, "are the Belgians. They have a thing about not letting you pass them. Strictly *macho*. Germans are the same, except they are just plain mean and aggressive by nature. Scandinavians are okay. But Italians—Italians play chicken. With *your* life. And you can't win.

"But if you see a license plate ending in *06*, pull over and stop. Zero-sixes are local inhabitants, and they never got past the horse. They've never learned to drive, but they do it anyway. So watch your ass."

They cavorted like children in the Coney Island town of Juan-les-Pins. Cotton candy, Dodgem cars, the Love Canal, strip-tease, jazz festival, hot dogs and hamburgers American-style. Gavin had his hair cut at two in the morning, and they listened to the songs of a transvestite singer named Coccinelle until dawn.

Gavin was agog at the bare breasts of the golden girls of St.-Tropez. He learned the rudiments of *petangue* from fishermen in the village square. He met Brigitte Bardot; her former husband, Roger Vadim; Sacha Distel; Claude Chabral; Françoise Sagan; René Clair; Prince Victor Emmanuel; the young Aga Khan; Elena von Furstenburg; Patrice Rockefeller; Stauros Niarchos; Oliver Rae, and Geoffrey Bocca. Although the season was nearing the end, more than forty yachts were tied up in the small harbor; they party hopped from boat to boat, because Serena knew all their owners. They made love on the beach as the sun was coming up.

Gavin, uncomfortable at first, began to accustom himself to famous people and famous names, and then to feel more and more at home. Serena watched the change with a sinking heart, convinced that it was the first step in the erosion of the man she loved. She had seen it all before and she knew the signs.

Because she seemed to be enjoying herself, Gavin broke the promise they had made to tell the truth to each other, and refrained from telling her that he found most of her friends vapid, uninformed, uninteresting and generally a pain in the ass. He was immensely relieved when they left Saint-Trop.

So was Serena. But she neglected to tell Gavin.

They got lost in the limestone caves of the Valley of the Moon, and Gavin learned something about himself he had never known. He was claustrophobic, terrified of confinement underground, certain of imminent cave-ins, trembling with fear. Serena saw his naked vulnerability and provided an instinctive remedy. She slipped out of her dress and spread it on the rocky floor. She was gentle and reassuring as she guided him into her. She arched herself under him and began to come almost immediately. She was wet with perspiration from his sweating body. She forced him out of himself and took away his fear with his semen.

They found the way out around the very next corner.

It was a time made for lovers.

It was also the end of summer.

16

Time: 1955
GAVIN RIORDAN

They returned from an afternoon at the beach to find a message for either of them to call Michael Hicks-Beach at the Hôtel du Cap. Serena did while Gavin was showering. When he came out, toweling himself and smelling of Canöe, to which he had become addicted, Serena told him that she had insisted that Michael reclaim his home.

"He wants us to stay on here with him. There's plenty of room. I told him we would." Serena was naked, seated before the dressing table, doing something to her face. Her eyes were on Gavin and she saw the slight tightening of his mouth. "That is, if you don't object." She knew that Gavin was still troubled by the openness of their behavior. At times it amused her to shock him, at others it irritated her that he couldn't seem to rise above it. "We could go somewhere else if you'd like. There's a little hotel up the coast. . . . "

"Why not stay here?" he said, plainly making an effort to cast off Catholic discomfort. "Nice of Mike to ask us. I've taken a liking to the place." He moved behind her, reached down to run his hands over her breasts. In the mirror his grin was wide. "I'll miss not being able to go naked half the day. But what the hell, there's plenty of time. . . . "

Serena felt an instant chill. It was getting too close to decision-making time. She wanted to put it off forever. She gave her shoulders a little shake and he took his hands away.

"Oh, yes. I almost forget. There's a man named Onderdonk who's been trying to reach you at the Cap."

She saw his face change in the mirror, all the loving softness gone, eyes clear and electric, the tightened muscles along his jaw. "What time is it?" Gavin reached for his new watch on the dresser. "Twelve noon back home. Maybe I can get him before he goes to lunch."

His call to the States went through without a hitch. Gus Onderdonk's voice answered on the second ring. "Where the hell you been?" he demanded, but instead of listening to the answer, Onderdonk went on at machine-gun rate. "Just as well. If I couldn't find you, then nobody else could. Gavin, the ball is rolling, just like I said it would. Special crime commission under Judge Marcus Belding. And he's the best there is. Special investigative unit under him. Forty-eight men. You're now a lieutenant. Full pay and allowances started the first of the month. We're preparing one hundred and nine cases. Top priority on eighteen of 'em. Now, listen close. We won't be ready to put you on the stand for another three months. I don't want you around until we are. We're after the big ones—and you're our surprise. I don't want anything to happen to you. So get a pencil and take this down."

The excellent Hicks-Beach had left writing things by every phone. "Got it," said Gavin.

"Okay. You're to report to Captain Étienne Tabard at the Police Judiciare. Number 36 quai des Orfèvres in Paris." Onderdonk's

French was less than rudimentary. He had to spell the address out slowly. "Got that?"

"Got it. What am I supposed to be doing?"

"You're on detached duty. You're to observe and report on French police riot procedure. And, Gavin, give it your best shot. Learn all you can. Way things are around here, I think we're going to need top riot training."

"When?"

"Get up there as soon as you can. I'll let you know what's going on through Tabard. Incidentally he's one hell of a good cop, so don't fuck him around. Now, you got all that?"

"Yep, I got it."

There was a long pause while Gavin waited for more. Then Onderdonk said, "Your Uncle Des sends his best."

Gavin caught the subtle change in Onderdonk's voice. "Is Des...all right?"

"He's clean. So far. But we're workin' on it. You ought to know that. Nobody's immune."

"I guess so," Gavin said. "Well, say hello for me, will you."

"Take care, kid. I'll be in touch."

Gavin hung up thoughtfully, his mind far away.

Serena, watching his face, was stung that she could so quickly be cut out of his thoughts as though she didn't exist.

"Well, damn it. Tell me. What was that all about?"

"What?" Gavin came back slowly. "I'm assigned to Paris Riot Control...for the next three months or so."

"I hate Paris. It's a shitty town. Full of shitty people."

"What...?" Gavin said again. "Yeah...well, I've never been there." His eyes were still remote. "I better call this guy Tabard. Find out when I'm supposed to report."

"You do that," Serena said too sharply. "Let me know when you find out."

"Sure. Right...." He was hardly aware that she had left the room.

Serena wandered out the back of the house and sat on the hillside, looking out to sea. She was desperately unhappy. More than that,

218

she was unsure of herself. Which wasn't like her. Part of her wanted a life with Gavin Riordan, any kind of life—even on his terms. But she knew she wasn't capable of giving him what he needed. A supportive wife, loyal, home and children. Even if there weren't any Gansvoort millions, she couldn't provide that. But there *were* Gansvoort millions— and they would corrupt him as they had everyone else.

It was during the lonesome year of her mother's death that Gavin had penetrated Serena for the first time. The time they were interrupted by her brother Stewart. The incomplete episode had left Serena unsatisfied but knowing she wanted more.

Because Gavin wouldn't return to Riverhaven, where they could have been alone in dozens of places in its secluded acres, they made love only three more times in the school year. Once in the deserted school boiler room, where Serena trapped him after football practice, and twice in the backseat of Des Daniher's black Oldsmobile. Serena was doing the pursuing. It was Gavin's senior year and he had a number of distractions, including some older girls. Thus Serena got her first and only taste of unrequited love.

When Gavin went away to college, Serena decided she must stay true to him. She was convinced that sooner or later he would return to her for keeps. So she contented herself with lonely orgasms in which Gavin was always the sex object. This lasted until midway of her senior year, when she was aroused enough by three shots of rye whiskey and the caresses of a boy named Curtis Boggs to give in to her very powerful desires. It wasn't at all the same. But it did get her pregnant.

Since Curtis Boggs was unwilling to help her out, Serena was forced to run into her money face to face.

"With all your dough, you ought to be able to handle it yourself," Curtis Boggs said. "Besides, how do you know I'm the one?"

Serena found that her allowance was inadequate for an abortion. She wasn't about to put herself in Stewart's power by trying to borrow from him. Her younger brother Henry couldn't possibly help, although he would have wanted to. Some transparent inquiries to F. James Skidde, one of the executors of the trusts her mother had left her, brought the information that she couldn't touch any of her money without the consent in writing of himself and two other trustees—and then, only when she reached eighteen.

Serena's only other out was the family doctor, a local man who had never attended the Gansvoorts for anything more serious than the common cold. His examination was gingerly, unpleasant and decidedly painful, but it left no doubt as to her condition.

What price privileged communication? The frightened doctor, a dutiful slave to Gansvoort money and power, waited only until Serena was safely out of his office before he called her father.

That same afternoon Serena found herself in a private room at Gansvoort Hospital. The pain, this time, was indescribable. Six hours later she was back at Riverhaven in her own bed, white-faced with shock, trembling and tearful, but with her body free of a three-month-old fetus. She listened to August Gansvoort's footsteps coming down the hallway, and the only thing she felt was rage that they had done this without consulting her. It wasn't that she wanted to keep her baby. But it was *her* choice. Not theirs.

The "they" in her mind changed to "he" after she had listened to her father for ten minutes. It was the first time she fully realized the absolute power of the Gansvoort money. Abortion had been August Gansvoort's decision. He had other options. He had considered placing her in a home—founded and owned by Gansvoort Associates—where she would remain under supervision until such time as he felt she was ready to assume the duties and obligations made mandatory by the Gansvoort name. One of the options *never* considered was that she be allowed to have her baby and legitimize it by marriage to Curtis Boggs. She learned much later that Curtis Boggs's father had been fired from his job and that the family had moved to another city.

August Gansvoort made it crystal clear to her that her behavior was not to be condoned and that any repetition of it on her part would be followed by drastic action on his.

Six months later Serena learned what drastic action meant when she ran away with a local band leader twelve years her senior. They were married in Elkton, Maryland, by a justice of the peace. The marriage was never consummated because, in the motel where they

220

planned to spend the night, the band leader excused himself to make a phone call to August Gansvoort, to tell him where they were. Fifteen minutes later Maryland state troopers were hammering on their door.

"Sorry, kid," the band leader said. "But what your father will cough up to get you out of this will set me up for the rest of my life."

Serena, out of her disillusionment, asked, "How can you be sure he'll pay? I'm not exactly his favorite offspring."

"He gives me trouble, I go to the newspapers. Simple as that. I think he'll buy it."

Evidently he did. The state troopers took the band leader away and that was the last she saw of him. Serena didn't resist when she was taken to the Bidwell Sanatorium in Lakeville, New Jersey. She stayed there for six weeks.

For the rest of her life it was a remembered horror. She was kept under sedation most of the time, so the things they did to her were a nightmare medley of ice baths, canvas restraint jackets, shock treatment, a constant probing and prodding of her body and the all-pervading hospital smells of disinfectant and raw alcohol. In her few lucid moments she knew she was mad. Then, for no apparent reason, the treatments and the sedation stopped, and she knew she wasn't. *They* were mad. She was sane. The world was upside down.

During her last ten days at Bidwell she rested and got used to being Serena Gansvoort again, testing her mind and her body to make sure that everything worked. She knew that she was beaten— at least for now; that her father could keep her at Bidwell forever, if he so chose. She also knew that there was nothing, absolutely nothing, she wouldn't do to get out. She spent a lot of time plotting how to do just that. Then she asked to see Dr. Hartman, who ran the sanatorium, and requested permission to call her father.

August Gansvoort listened in silence to her carefully prepared speech of repentance, her promises to do anything he required of her, and at the end asked only to speak to the doctor.

Dr. Hartman, after a few preliminaries that seemed to Serena a sort of groveling-in-place, gave his opinion that Serena had improved sufficiently to be allowed to come home. *If,* of course, Mr.

Gansvoort wished it. Serena had to remind herself to breathe as she waited.

That same afternoon she found herself in the chauffeur-driven Cadillac limousine on her way home, surprised and profoundly suspicious at how easy it had been.

At Riverhaven she was told that her brother Henry was still away at camp and that Stewart was taking summer courses at Harvard. So she was to have dinner alone with her father at 7:15. She spent some time going through her wardrobe, trying to find something that would fit. After six weeks at Bidwell she was alarmingly skinny.

They dined by candlelight, in silence, after Serena's first dutiful greeting and August Gansvoort's nod of acceptance. She forced herself to overcome her nervousness and ate everything that was put before her. Throughout the tense meal August Gansvoort kept his eyes firmly on his plate. It wasn't until coffee was served and he had lighted the one cigar he permitted himself that he looked at her. A long, cold, emotionless stare that seemed to her to hold both accusation and judgment. Then his gaze lifted to the space above her head.

"Your . . . marriage has been annulled on the grounds that it was never consummated. At considerable expense, I may add.

"You have told me that you are now ready to face up to your responsibilities. For reasons of my own I choose to believe that you are sincere." August Gansvoort's tones were impersonal, as if he spoke to one of his employees. "However, that can change. Bear it in mind. This is what I will require of you. . . . "

Serena strove for an expression that would convince him that she was in truth sincere, a difficult effort to keep up since he did not look at her at any time. She learned that she would be attending Mount Holyoke in the fall. Any outside contacts she might have with members of the opposite sex—in other words, dates—were to be first checked with F. James Skidde for approval.

"I realize that it would be inappropriate to isolate you. There would be talk. And speculation. But at least I can be sure that you will see only those men who are . . . acceptable to me. You will spend your weekends and vacations here at Riverhaven—unless I allow otherwise. I will expect you to apply yourself diligently and to

222

graduate with honors. I know you have a good mind. It could not be otherwise. I have chosen your curriculum so that you will finish with a knowledge of money and its uses. Eventually it will be important to you."

In one last unbidden stirring of rebellion Serena heard herself say, "Why won't you look at me? Do you hate me? I *am* your daughter." The words came out more plea than question.

He did look at her then. "Because you remind me too much of your mother."

She stared at her father, stunned, uncomprehending. The candle-light flickering slightly gave him a look of madness. "Your mother betrayed me in every way a woman can betray a man."

Everything in the room seemed to become still, the curtains no longer stirred in the last-of-summer breeze, even the candle flames ceased to waver. Serena was frozen in shock, her eyes forever fixed on his.

Then August Gansvoort lifted his hand to cover his eyes and bowed his head for a long moment. When he lowered his hand he was once again himself, the familiar stranger she had known all her life.

"Yes, you are my daughter. My blood in you . . . as well as hers. That is why I can still hope that breeding . . ." He stopped and made a small futile gesture with his hand. "Enough. Is it clear what I wish of you?"

Serena, incapable of speech, could only nod.

"Then we won't speak of it again," he said.

Serena found her voice. "Thank you, father. I'm glad you told me. It explains so many things. I'll go to bed now." She got up and left the table, hoping that she could make it to the hallway and out of his sight.

Several things happened to Serena when she reached eighteen. She was asked to a Harvard weekend by a friend of Stewart's named Peter Damiani (vetted by F. James Skidde and found adequate), who fell madly and hopelessly in love with her. That first weekend led to several others, and on the fourth one Peter Damiani asked her to marry him.

Serena thought he was sweet. It was nice and warm and comforting to be loved. Something which had been singularly lacking in her life. She still thought of Gavin Riordan. But Gavin had gone off to war, and might never come back. Peter Damiani, on the other hand, was 4-F because of congenitally weak eyes. Peter's father was a highly respected scholar who held a chair in anthropology at a Midwestern university. His mother was remotely connected to the Lovells of Massachusetts (which was what got him past F. James Skidde). There was no money in the family, but that didn't matter since Serena was due to come into the first of her trust funds at any moment. Two hundred thousand dollars seemed more than enough to support a marriage until Peter could finish law school and start a career.

Serena began to give Peter's proposal serious thought. Its main attraction was that it would get her out of Riverhaven and everything it meant, at last give her a life she could call her own.

To be on the safe side she checked with her brother Stewart. She didn't trust Stewart, but she didn't know anywhere else to go. After all, he was in prelaw and should be able to give her some legal answers. She asked Stewart to find out whether there was any way August Gansvoort could keep her from getting the money from her about-to-be-matured trust fund—just in case he disapproved of her plan to marry.

Stewart had no need to look it up. He already had, in the interest of his own similar trust, which had matured the year before. "In my case, no," Stewart told her. "In yours, I'm not so sure."

"What's so different?"

There seemed to be concern for her in Stewart's eyes, something she had rarely seen before. "Well . . . " Stewart hesitated. "He could have you declared legally insane. Incompetent to handle your own money."

"What the hell do you mean?" Serena was stunned.

"Don't yell at me," Stewart said defensively. "*I* didn't put you away in Bidwell. *He* did. He could do it again, you know. Not that he would. But he *could*. Why the hell do you want to marry that guy, anyway? He's a born loser. You'll have to support him for the rest of your life."

Serena, from the depths of her fear, had a thought. "But if I marry Peter . . . then he couldn't do anything. I'd be somebody's *wife*. He couldn't, could he?"

"I don't know. Probably not. You'd have *some* legal status then. . . . But don't forget, you're still a minor in the eyes of the law—and as far as the rest of your trusts go. He could maybe hold up this one . . . if he really wanted to. But who the hell knows what he could do. He'll never let you marry Peter, anyway. He doesn't exactly fit the Gansvoort image. He's a fucking *wop*."

"Maybe you're right," Serena said slowly. "We'll just have to see. . . ."

Serena obtained control of her trust without incident. Three weeks later she and Peter Damiani were secretly married by a justice of the peace over the state line, in Connecticut. Serena hastened to consummate her nuptials in a nearby motel. There would be no annulment this time. Whether it was from tension at the thought of the certain confrontation with her father or some other reason, she failed to reach orgasm. What should have worried her at the time was that neither did Peter.

Facing her father took considerable courage for an eighteen-year-old. At the same time she looked forward to it with immense satisfaction. At last she would be out from under.

August Gansvoort's reaction was expressed in two brief sentences. "It's not a suitable marriage for a Gansvoort."

And when she told him, "There's nothing you can do about it now," his cold eyes held hers, and he said, "We'll see." Then he turned and left her.

Serena forgot about those ominous last words in the excitement of moving her things out of Riverhaven and into the apartment she had taken near the Harvard Law School. She set about getting pregnant as soon as possible, since that somehow seemed a further protection against anything her father might do. That had its problems, because Peter Damiani was intensely shy and a sexual innocent. Serena's determined tutelage both embarrassed and angered him. But Serena was adamant. Her demands on him were relentless. She coaxed him to orgasm again and again, and when after six months she remained unimpregnated, she insisted that they get some medical advice. When Peter called a friend at the Harvard Clinic and found that he would be expected to produce samples of his sperm—hand-delivered, so to speak, and in a doctor's office—he rebelled. He flatly refused to submit to what he considered an unbearable humiliation and threatened to move out of the apartment if Serena persisted. So Serena went on her own.

The pelvic examination was painful and unpleasant, as was the dye injection for the uterine X-rays. Still, the unspoken concern the gynecologist showed during his slow and thorough examination did not prepare her for what he had to say at its conclusion.

"How can you expect to become pregnant when you obviously have had your Fallopian tubes tied off?"

"What are you telling me?"

The doctor looked appalled at her ignorance. "You *can't* have had such a surgical procedure without knowing it. It's impossible."

"Oh, yes, you can." Serena knew instantly what had happened. Her father had done this to her. She remembered the nightmare of her stay at Bidwell, and she thought of the small scar on her abdomen and the emergency "appendectomy" that had caused it. A cold smile formed itself on her lips, and quickly vanished.

Serena arrived at Riverhaven in her recently purchased car at four in the afternoon. She had two hours to wait for her father's return. She spent them sitting at August Gansvoort's huge bare desk in the sacrosanct study with its view of the river. Her outrage over what had been done to her became a cold implacable anger, which crystallized into a determination to protect herself in the future. For the first time in her life she was facing facts squarely and trying to come to some logical decisions that weren't based on unhappiness or rebellion.

By the time her father arrived, Serena had worked out a plan much more far-reaching than she had at first intended. It was a plan that excited her. It gave her a purpose, a goal—and the determination to reach it.

August Gansvoort paused in the doorway, coldly disapproving, as he saw her at his desk. Serena took her time getting up. She moved deliberately to stand in front of the desk and waited until he had seated himself.

"I've been to a doctor." Serena wanted the first word—and the last, if she could manage it. She kept her voice low and as emotionless as his own. "You had me spayed. Like a bitch in heat. You had no right!"

August Gansvoort merely lifted his eyebrows.

"It seemed appropriate. You . . ."

"You had no right to tamper with my body. No right at all."

"A temporary expedient," he interrupted. "The process can be reversed. When you are ready to have children . . ."

"That's not exactly what my doctor said. But it doesn't really matter because I'm going to make you a proposal I think you'll accept. Because you don't have much choice."

She seemed to have gotten through to him. He appeared surprised. His pale blue eyes widened a fraction.

"You wanted me to learn about money? Well, that's what I plan to do. Everything there is to know—about the Gansvoort millions . . . or is it billions? I want to find out what it's like to have the kind of power you have. The power of life and death.

"I'm not going back to Holyoke. I'm going to work at the source—Gansvoort Associates. Where the action is. And I expect all the help you can give me."

"Laudable." He looked speculative. "But what makes you think . . . ?"

"Because you haven't any choice," Serena said coldly. "First my doctor said that the chances of putting me back together again were poor to none. If he's right, I'll never be able to have children. And that's a criminal act. *Your* criminal act. And my doctor is willing to testify about the operation. The *illegal* operation . . . without my consent."

"Preposterous. The word of a disturbed young girl . . ."

"Think about it. Think about how disturbing the story of that young girl will appear in the newspapers. I'm positive you can't control them all. Just picture the headlines—and what they will do for the Gansvoort name. I don't think you could bear that."

She saw her father's hand on the desk, long slim fingers slowly closing in on themselves until they made a white-knuckled fist, and she knew she had won. She felt a joy so fierce that she closed her eyes. When she opened them, August Gansvoort was looking at her enigmatically, weighing, calculating. She could almost hear the wheels turn.

"I've left a deposition with my doctor," she said. "And another with . . . a friend. If they don't hear from me . . ." She let it stop there, feeling that it was a magnificent throwaway line.

August Gansvoort began to smile his small frosty smile, in which for the first time in her life Serena detected a glint of admiration. Serena went for broke. "By the way, you were right. Peter is not . . . suitable as a husband. Perhaps you can get me out of it. As you did before. And, Father, I'm glad we understand each other . . . finally."

Serena made it out of sight of the Big House before she was forced to pull over. It was a good ten minutes before she could stop her trembling.

She spent the next ten minutes savoring her victory. She intended to do exactly as she had told August Gansvoort. Only her real purpose was something quite different. She planned to acquire knowledge and power, all right—and use it to destroy his fortune or give it away. It was what would hurt him most.

It took her a little less than six months to realize how childishly, pitifully naive was her plan to hurt her father through what he cared about most—his money. She discovered that money, the stuff you keep in your wallet for taxi fares, was merely a convenience, an accommodation. Money with a capital M was something quite different. Big Money had a life of its own. If left alone, it grew like crabgrass, just as tenacious, just as impossible to get rid of. If you took too much of it from one thing to give to something else, you could cause disastrous dislocations in the first area. Her thought that it could all be given away was ridiculous. In all the world there weren't enough places to put it. If you gave it to a nonprofit organization, it suddenly began to proliferate—to make more money and so cause more problems.

Gansvoort Associates employed 258 executives, expert in various fields. Of these, ninety-one devoted their time and energy to giving money away. The rest of them were concerned with making more money. Serena was forever puzzled to find that it didn't seem strange to any of them that this was so.

Serena learned that her father was right. She had an excellent and inquiring mind and a real gift for financial analysis. She applied herself to absorbing the intricacies of the Gansvoort empire with a single-minded absorption that eventually earned her father's grudging approval. Surprisingly she found this gratifying. Praise from the master was praise indeed.

As she began more and more to see the big picture, it was the political and moral uses of great wealth that appalled her. She watched Gansvoort money suborn a South American country, finance a minor revolution and cost the lives of hundreds of people. On the other hand, a Gansvoort company built a whole city in a Middle Eastern state, bringing a new and better life to thousands (in return for a number of oil concessions, of course).

Serena learned that even the biggest governments could be bought. She found that this was true of her own country as well as of banana republics. If put to the test, Gansvoort could count on influencing thirty-two senators, more than one hundred representatives, any number of key committee chairmen. The Gansvoort enterprises employed forty-one lobbyists on the national level. On state levels there were too many to count.

Since she now had an apartment of her own in the City, her social life burgeoned. Because she was who she was, invitations poured in and men swarmed on her. She soon became convinced that her numerous dates, without exception, had a nose for her money. She knew she was attractive, but that certainly didn't account for the ardor with which she was pursued.

In the process she learned the reasons for the various trusts her mother, who must have been a very rich woman, had set up for her. They were to protect her from both strangers and friends, who were equally importunate. There were charming adventurers, plausible swindlers, impecunious young men looking for the better life, all with a firm eye on her wealth.

In short, everybody in the world seemed to have a price.

The knowledge sickened and revolted her.

At the end of three years she quit. She found the business of money degrading, disillusioning and corrupting. She wanted no part of it. A visit to a world-renowned gynecologist revealed that the damage that had been done to her body was not reparable by surgery, given the current state of the art. That, along with everything else, sufficiently disturbed her to make her think seriously of suicide.

Visits to a psychiatrist on a daily basis convinced her of the futility of that and also that the *fact* of her money had a certain inevitability that must be faced. By the time Gavin Riordan returned from the war, she had almost learned to live with it.

But not quite. Not enough to subject Gavin to the pressures she herself could barely handle. That was why she had left him on the Georgia island the morning after his proposal of marriage.

Now there was Gavin again. And John Summerlin. And others. She had changed and Gavin had changed. But the situation was basically the same—and what the hell was she going to do about it all? Serena was startled out of her reverie by Gavin's yelling from the house that she was wanted on the phone.

"Somebody named Guido," Gavin told her.

She took the call on the downstairs phone, intensely aware of Gavin standing near, waiting for her to finish. Feeling guilty because Guido Tesca was one of the "others." In fact, the most recent "other" before Gavin's abrupt appearance on the Riviera scene. It was difficult to be noncommittal in the face of Guido's Italian effervescence, but she did her best.

Gavin, wrapped up in what he wanted to tell her, heard only, "We'd love it. . . . Yes, I'll be bringing a friend. . . . See you at nine tonight. . . ." And then, "Of course, Guido. *Ciao*."

"Hey, did you have to do that? We've got a lot of talking to do. I was sort of planning."

"You'll love it, darling. He's got this huge yacht full of gold-plated bathrooms, and when a lady sits down on the john there's this disembodied recording that says, 'Jesus Christ, lady. There's men working down here.' How's that for vulgarity?"

"Can't you get out of it? I . . ."

"No," Serena said shortly, "I can't. Besides, there's plenty of time for talking."

"No, there isn't. I have to be in Paris in one week. We've got to make some plans. A lot of things to straighten out before we go."

"I told you, I hate Paris."

"It's only for a few months. Then home . . ."

"But I don't want to go to Paris."

With a sinking sensation Gavin recognized the stubbornness in her voice. "Don't you ever do anything you don't want to?"

"As seldom as possible. As long as you're asking."

"Jesus, Serena, what are you doing? I'm trying to make plans for both of us, and you . . ."

"And I'm trying to tell you that you're taking one hell of a lot for granted. *You* go to Paris. Not me."

Gavin was tight-lipped. "What's that supposed to mean?"

"That I'm not going to Paris, that's all."

"Christ, Serena. It's my job."

"Well, it's not mine."

"I guess you're saying a lot more than just that," Gavin said slowly.

"Yes, I am." Serena had been using her self-induced anger as protection. She wanted to stop it, to get things on some reasonable basis. But it was going too fast for her, and she found she couldn't control it. "You're damn right I am. You come crashing into my life, and expect me to . . . I didn't ask you, you know. . . . I'm supposed to jump when you decide to go to Paris. Where you go, I go. Is that it? We're not . . ."

"Married?" Gavin's voice was dangerously soft. "But we are. To two other people. That's one of the things I wanted to discuss with you. I've got plenty of grounds for divorce. I checked it out before I left. . . ."

"You? A Catholic?"

"Not that Catholic. I can handle my problem. I figured you could handle your end. You've had the experience."

"You're damned right I have," Serena snapped. "Too much. And I'm not sure I want any more of the same. I don't think the Policeman's Ball is exactly my style."

Gavin slapped her, not hard.

Serena hit him with a left, much harder, and was drawing back for another shot when he grabbed her arm.

"You two need a referee? Or can anyone play?"

Michael Hicks-Beach stood in the doorway, laden with luggage and tennis racquets.

Serena, struggling to free her arm, changed tactics and drove a knee at Gavin's crotch. He twisted easily and took it on his thigh.

"Not exactly Queensbury rules," Michael said.

Gavin let her go. She rubbed at her arm and said, "You hurt me," in a little-girl voice. "And then you laughed . . ."

And then they both laughed, and she came into his arms.

"I'm sorry, hon," he said. "It was a stupid thing to do."

"I'm sorry, too, Gavin."

Gavin grinned down at her. "You know, you might like the Policeman's Ball at that. It's a hell of a brawl."

"Calls for a drink, don't you think?" said Michael. "I'll find Harris."

When Michael had gone off, they were both serious. The air had been cleared temporarily. But nothing was settled.

"I really *am* sorry, Gavin. It's just that things are happening too fast. I get to feeling sort of harried. And I'm not sure we could make it together. Our lives are so different. *We're* so different. . . ."

Gavin turned her to face him, hands on her shoulders. "You're right. I was taking too much for granted. I'm a cop, a guy with a job to do. I can't change that to live the kind of life you live. No way. I thought you knew that. I thought that was what you wanted too. . . ."

Looking at his serious face, the searching blue eyes, Serena thought, *If I could only believe that. That nothing could change him.*

The party on the yacht started badly. Michael had insisted on taking them to dinner at a place far up a dirt track near St.-Paul. Michael and the pretty proprietress seemed to have something going. They all drank too much and stayed too late. It was well after ten when they trooped, a little unsteadily, down the gangplank and onto the teakwood deck of the *Annabelle*.

The *Annabelle* was huge, gleaming white, festooned with lights, sparkling with brass. There were women dressed in everything from

232

long evening gowns to the skimpiest of bikinis. All of them were young and all were beautiful. The men tended to be a little older on average but were enjoying the party with equal abandon.

"Serena," someone yelled.

To Gavin, Michael muttered, "Our host, the Speed King."

Guido Tesca was a tall, beautiful young man. He greeted Serena with both arms, placed his hands firmly on her buttocks and pulled her pelvis to him, hard. "*Cara mia,* I thought you had deserted me."

Serena wriggled free and, as Gavin stepped forward, put a hand on his arm and introduced him smoothly.

Tesca allowed Gavin only the briefest of handshakes, waved familiarly to Michael and led Serena away with an arm about her waist. Gavin had started after them when Michael's voice stopped him. "I wouldn't, old man. Guest in the house and all that."

"Son of a bitch acted like he owned her."

"Serena can take care of herself. Come on, I could do with a drink."

In the crowded salon were the devastated remains of an elaborate buffet. Attendants in blue flared jeans and *matelot* blouses carried drinks on Moroccan brass trays. There was a four-piece band at one end of the salon, although the room was too full for dancing. The odor of powder and perfume, combined with spilled food, was overpowering. Michael captured two drinks from a passing sailor and pointed toward a dart board on the far wall.

"My game. Care to try it?"

"Why not." As they pushed through the crowd side by side, Gavin said, "What's with this guy Guido?"

Michael had to raise his voice over the crowd noise. "I never mix with international affairs."

"What's that supposed to mean?"

"Nothing that needs an explanation." Michael removed six darts from the board and handed three to Gavin. "Care to wager? I warn you, old boy, I'm an expert." Then, at the shake of Gavin's head, "No? Then perhaps I can show you some of the finer points of the game." In rapid succession he placed all three of his darts in the small bull's-eye.

Gavin, a natural competitor, did fairly well at first. But after forty minutes and several more drinks his concentration was gone, and on his last throw he missed the board altogether and buried the dart in Guido Tesca's rosewood paneling.

"Think I'll go look for her."

The words were a little fuzzy, and Michael raised his eyebrows. "I'll come along."

"Damn it," Gavin protested, this time distinctly. "I'm not drunk."

"Perish the thought. But you Irish are an unpredictable lot. Need very careful handling. Steady hand on the tiller never hurts."

"Ah, fuck it." Gavin pushed his way through the crowd.

On the deck the balmy Mediterranean air was a blessed relief. Gavin breathed great gulps too fast and then had to concentrate on the lights of the Cannes waterfront until they steadied up. The yacht was moored broadside to the dock. The brilliant illumination that had festooned its superstructure was now dark, the deck lights dim. From the far side of the vessel at the stern came low laughter and an occasional splash. Gavin headed toward the sound.

There seemed to be a number of naked people on the fantail. As Gavin and Michael approached, a woman climbed up on the taffrail, posed there a moment and dove overboard. There was no mistaking that it was Serena. At his shoulder Michael said, "Think nothing of it. Everybody on the Riviera takes his clothes off—or hers, as the case may be. Mark of a free spirit. Innocent as babes."

As Gavin approached, Serena came up the ladder and over the taffrail, laughing. "God, that was cold."

Guido Tesca, naked as Serena, wrapped his arms around her and pulled her close, molding her body to his. "You need warming, *carissima*."

Serena deftly wriggled away. "I'll warm myself, thank you."

Gavin stumbled over a towel, bent to pick it up and also to get his head together. He was determined not to make a scene. Tesca started after Serena, reached for her arm and pulled her to him again.

"Cut it out, Guido," Serena said sharply. "I mean it."

Gavin spun him away harder than he meant. Tesca tripped and hit the deck heavily. Gavin tossed the towel to Serena.

234

"Get dressed. Time we went home." He turned back toward Tesca.

"Forget it, Gavin." Serena began to dry herself, seemingly as oblivious of her nakedness as if she were in her own bathroom. "No harm done. As you can probably see, we're not exactly strangers."

"Yeah. It occurred to me." Gavin was watching Tesca struggle to his feet, ready for any move the man might make.

"Where did you find this American pig?" Tesca spat.

Gavin knew enough street Italian to get the gist of it. He started forward. Behind him, Serena giggled.

"In a shanty in old Shanty Town," Serena sang, and then, "Quit it, Gavin. Can't I take you to a party without you wanting to bang somebody? I told you he's harmless."

Gavin took another step. Tesca backed up, raising his hands defensively. "Keep him away," Tesca snarled. "I'll kill him!"

Just for the hell of it, Gavin took another step, and again Tesca backed up. He was about to turn away when he felt himself gripped from the back by both arms. Two of the sailor-waiters held him immobile. Tesca reached out and slapped him hard across the face. Tesca drew back his arm for another blow. Gavin was powerless to avoid it.

Serena, now wrapped in her towel, stepped between them.

"Stop it!" Her voice was a command. "You're acting like children. I won't have it!"

Over her shoulder Tesca shouted, "Throw the pig off!"

Serena spun around, eyes blazing. "Let him go!"

Reluctantly the two men released him.

"Wait for me on the dock, Gavin. I won't be long."

Gavin's two escorts stayed close as he and Michael walked down the deck and over the gangway. On the dock they were obviously alert to any attempt to return to the ship.

"Silly bugger, Tesca. You'd have taken him apart."

Gavin was relieved that it hadn't happened. With the release from tension he was feeling more than a little drunk. He began to grin. "Sumbitch *slapped* me. When he coulda' busted me good. What kinda asshole would do that? What kinda asshole?"

At that moment one of the sailors rabbit-punched him and dropped him to his knees. He heard Michael's surprised "I say!" and the sharp *splat* of a fist. Then the other sailor kicked him in the stomach. He felt the sour bile rise in his throat and swallowed painfully to keep it down. The sailor kicked him again, and something happened to Gavin's head.

He came up wild-eyed and swinging and decked his man with a roundhouse right. Michael and the other man were rolling together on the dock. Beyond them more sailors pounded over the gangplank to the rescue of their fellows. Gavin gave a tremendous bellow and piled into them.

He was Finn McCool with the strength of ten. He was Cu Chulainn, who battled the twelve tribes of Ulster. He was Brian ap Mor, the giant of Emain Mocha. The blood of Irish heroes raged through his veins. His rush carried the sailors back over the gangplank and onto the deck. Women screamed, men cursed. Gavin proceeded to do his level best to take apart a seventy-five-foot yacht.

He woke up bruised and bloody in a cell at the headquarters of the Cannes Gendarmerie Regionale. Since he had no wallet, no money and no watch, he asked the black American sailor who was his cellmate for the time. When he found it was past noon, he closed his eyes and groaned.

The sailor, hardly out of his teens, was sympathetic. "Man, you a mess. They gon' have you up fo' life, way you fightin' and screamin'. Took four a' them frog fuzz put you in here. Then one little tap an' you sleep like a lamb. Never moved once."

Gavin, who could feel the lump on his head without touching it, never wanted to move again. He had the kind of hangover known as "shame-is-my-middle-name." He couldn't bear to think about what he had done.

"Yes, suh," the sailor sighed. "They goin' throw away the key. You be old an' gray."

Michael Hicks-Beach arrived shortly after one, and after some delay Gavin was released in his custody after listening to a stern lecture from the sergeant in charge, not one word of which he understood.

"No bail in this country," said Michael. "Chap can get lost for

life in the French penal system. Had to lie like hell to get you out."
Michael looked at him speculatively. "By the way, in case you
missed what that bobby was trying to tell you, you're to be on the
first plane out tomorrow. Out of this earthly paradise—never to
return. Otherwise it's back in the nick."

"Can they do that?"

"Oh, yes, my boy. They can, and will. Quick as wink at you."
Michael had a lovely shiner.

"I do that . . . ?" asked Gavin.

"Oh, my, no. I was on your side. Remember?"

"Not much. Why didn't they bust you?"

"Simply bolted when the flics arrived." Michael sounded faintly
defensive. "Seemed a bloody good idea. Fight again another day
and all that."

Gavin groaned. "Jesus! What a fucking idiot thing to do. Why
didn't somebody stop me?"

"They tried, old boy. They tried. My," Michael said admiringly,
"you were spectacular. Truly rousing dust-up."

On the road in Michael's Jensen Interceptor, Gavin tested his
muscles.

"Oh, God, even my aches have aches."

"Fix you up as soon as we get home. Hair of the dog."

"If it's animals, horse's ass would fit better."

He wanted desperately to ask about Serena and found he couldn't.
He'd know soon enough. He made the rest of the trip slumped in
miserable silence.

Back in their bedroom, he had a momentary relief. Everything
seemed the same. The dressing table still held Serena's lotions and
makeup. Then he looked out the window at the harbor of Cannes.

The gleaming white yacht was gone. He knew with utter conviction that Serena was on it.

He stood on the terrace for a brief moment, head tilted back,
feeling the warm cleansing sunlight on his bruised face, trying to
puzzle out what it was in him that sent her away each time.

Shaving was something of an ordeal. There was a bruise on his
left jaw and a small cut over one eye. His whole face seemed puffy

237

and swollen. When he came out of the shower, Michael was waiting for him with a tall glass full of a pale-green frothy liquid. He eyed it dubiously.

"Drink it," Michael said.

"What is it?"

"The cure. Just let it slide right down."

Feeling sure that nothing could make him feel worse, Gavin did as he was told. The result astonished him. Partly sweet, faintly tart, tasting of sunlight, white grapes and honey, with just a suggestion of something stronger, the drink was an elixir, the stuff of magic. His nerve ends began to tingle, tired muscles relaxing as the smooth liquid flowed through him. After a moment he felt well enough to joke.

"What sort of hivven's delight is this you've invented for all the souls in glory?"

"It's the stuff," Michael said gravely, "that made the gods of the old Romans feel sure that they *were* gods." Then, as he watched the color come back to Gavin's face, "It does jolly up the blood, doesn't it?"

"You'd make a fortune if you bottled it."

"I already have a fortune."

"You, too?"

"I've been rich and I've been poor," said Michael. "Believe me, rich is better."

"Serena seems to think so."

Michael lifted a quizzical eyebrow. "Do you blame her?"

"Maybe I wouldn't—if I could understand her. She makes no fucking sense to me."

Gavin saw the sudden change in Michael's face, the hardening of the jawline, the glint of anger in his eyes. "What the hell do you expect of her? Give up everything and accept the policeman's lot? Live in a two-room flat, supper on the table and wash your socks? The world well lost for love and all that shit? Isn't that asking rather a lot? What in Christ's name makes you think you're worth it?"

"You've got it all wrong," said Gavin, surprised and defensive at the unfairness of the outburst. "I don't expect her to give up anything. I've got nothing against money. I wouldn't mind spending Serena's—up to a point. . . ."

"Money!" Michael snapped. "You don't know the meaning of the word. Not a clue."

Gavin's irritation began to surface. "You people make such a fucking big deal of it. *That's* what I don't understand. You let it control your lives. Everything you do and think is colored by it. That's a hell of a lousy way to live."

Michael looked at him strangely for a moment, then began to shake his head slowly.

"Do you have the remotest idea why she won't marry you?"

"I wish to hell I did. All I know is that it's the goddamned money that seems to bother her. If *you* know, I wish to hell you'd tell me!"

Michael's voice was very soft. "Because she thinks you'd end up like John Summerlin. And you know something, laddie? So do I. You couldn't survive it."

"How the hell do you know?" Gavin demanded furiously. "Either of you. You don't know me. How the hell do you know how I'd act?"

In the same soft voice Michael said, "Have you ever done anything to make her think any different? Look at you."

Gavin saw Michael's eyes were on his hands and realized that his fists were clenched, the muscles in his arms jumping. Michael's eyes moved up to his face, and suddenly Gavin felt his bruises. It brought him up short.

"You're a bruiser. You think with your fists. Why the hell don't you get out of her life? You'd only bring her misery. She's had enough of that." Michael was looking at him with something like pity. "Nothing personal, old man. Don't like the Dutch uncle role. None of my business, really. But a few things needed to be said. No offense, I hope."

"No," Gavin said slowly. "No offense."

"Well, then, how about a last night on the town before I tuck you up on the plane tomorrow morning?"

"Sure," Gavin said. "Why not?"

17

Time: 1955
ERICKA

Ericka set out to register at the Sorbonne on a sparkling fall day, buoyant as a balloon in the crisp air. Clutched in her hand she held a businesslike folder containing *carte de séjour,* transcripts, birth certificate and all the other official impedimenta the Byzantine administration might require.

To her horror the queue of applicants (all foreigners like herself, including Hindus and tall Germanic blondes and a large number of little brown men and, surprisingly, a few little brown women, whose existence she hadn't suspected) stretched all the way down the Galerie Richelieu, past the murals of Joan of Arc and halfway into the central courtyard. After two hours of inching progress toward the registration office, she finally squeezed into the office, where a harried secretary grabbed her folder, fingered it rapidly and tossed it back at her with a volley of words of which she grasped only the horrendous *"Incomplet."* She politely tried to inquire what was missing, but the woman had already turned to the next in line.

As she turned away, trying to hold back tears of pure rage, a deep male voice said, "You forgot a stamped self-addressed envelope. You don't expect the French to pay for sending you your acceptance notice, do you? It would wring their parsimonious souls. Anyway, it's nothing to cry about. Here, take this."

Ericka found herself clutching a huge handkerchief and dabbing at her eyes. Through her tears she saw dimly a tall blond man who seemed all shoulders and no waist. When her vision cleared she was treated to a wonderfully kind smile under brilliant blue eyes.

At that moment the chapel bell rang noon and everything suddenly closed down instantly. In seconds the lines melted away, secretaries disappeared and a hush settled over the rooms.

"No more action until two o'clock," said the man. "We better get you an envelope and a stamp." He calmly walked to the desk just vacated by the secretary who had been so rude to her, pulled open several drawers and triumphantly held up a blank stamped envelope.

"But you can't do that," she stammered.

"Anything to beat the system," he said, pushing a pen at her. His English had an accent—not French. "Here, fill it out."

When she had finished, he said, "Let's get something to eat," and strode away without waiting for her. There was nothing to do but follow him. He was wearing jeans and a black V-necked pullover under an ancient tweed jacket. She had to trot to keep up with him.

He took her to the Escholin, which could hardly be dignified by the name of restaurant. The noise of feeding students could be heard before he pushed through the doors. Inside was bedlam, a shouting, laughing madhouse. Many of the tables, covered with dirty paper tablecloths, were empty; the students seemed to prefer to take their nourishment standing up or wandering through the aisles. Tired waiters in dingy jackets dodged through the crowd.

They made their way to a table in a sudden hush. Then someone started a chant of *"Chapeau! Chapeau!"* accompanied by the banging of glasses on tabletops and spoons against heavy white plates.

"It's your hat," the tall man said.

Ericka was wearing a little red Tam o'Shanter, which she now saw was the only hat visible. She snatched it off and stuffed it into her bag, and the chanting subsided.

"Conformity. You must adjust. Be like the others. It's the message printed on every school blackboard. The bland leading the bland. You must learn to become invisible." He looked at her appreciatively. "Although in your case it might be difficult. Well, what will you have?"

Ericka, seeing no menus, decided to play it safe. "A sandwich, maybe?"

"The French have never mastered the sandwich. Better stick to *kek*, which is what they call fruitcake. And tea. Or wine, if you prefer?"

"Tea," Ericka said meekly. "Are you an American?"

"No. Canadian. *French* Canadian. There's a difference." He frowned, as if to warn her to pay attention to the difference. "Jean-Bapiste Moreau, Montreal. You?"

"Ericka Ullman . . . from New York."

"New York." His frown deepened, this time in disapproval. "You're rich, then. Otherwise you wouldn't be here."

"I don't really know," Ericka said honestly. "I'm going to be an architect."

The frown dissolved into his wide smile. "Ah, that's better. '*Going* to be'? Not 'want to be' or 'hope to be'? But 'going to be'?"

His smile nettled her. "I have been accepted at the Atelier Ven der Veen."

His eyes widened and he became grave. "Ven der Veen!"

"Of course, I've got to pass the entrance exams for Beaux Arts. That's why . . . the Sorbonne. It's required."

He considered her. "Do you know that there are more than five hundred applicants for Beaux Arts each year? Only about fifty are accepted. And of these, only . . ." He made a shaking gesture with his fingers. "Damned few are foreigners. Very long odds."

"I'll make it."

Moreau widened his eyes and nodded a little in respectful wonder. He caught the jacket of a passing waiter and gave their order. By the time Ericka had finished her *kek*, which seemed to be sawdust pressed around rock-hard raisins, and he his bowl of grayish soup, she had told him about George and Melinda, Hughette, the house on Babylone, her stay on the Riviera and that she had once been very fat. On his part Jean-Baptiste had revealed nothing. He seemed a little old for a student.

242

"Is it always like this?" Her gesture took in the press of deafening students in the dismal room.

"Yes. This is a Restau U, Restaurant Universitaire. Just for students—and very cheap. You might as well get used to it. You'll be eating in dumps like this for years to come." He looked at his watch. "Now, you'd better get back to the registration line or you'll be all day."

Back on the street she wanted to ask if she would see him again and got as far as "Will I . . . ?" when he interrupted, saying, "Oh, yes, I'll be around. Never fear." He grinned at her and closed one eye in a slow wink, then turned and left. She watched him swing down the street. He didn't look back.

This meeting with an obviously experienced man, on her own in this marvelous new life in Paris, led Ericka to reflect on her own readiness to live as a grownup, to meet with men like Moreau as an equal. Was she really up for it? It was this train of thought that brought on the first of Ericka's two most memorable experiences with Ivan ven der Veen.

It was at one of those gatherings of young Parisians where one discovered that America was only a place that Charlie Chaplin and all the jazz musicians had to run away from; everyone drinking orange juice and warm Coke, the American ice cube not having got this far as yet. Across the room Ivan was surrounded by four girls who seemed to be hanging on his every word. She was piqued and wished she could be alone with him to find out what was so fascinating. The thought was father to an idea. In her studio on the top floor was an automatic record player and stacks of records by Josephine Baker, Piaf, Aznavour, along with some fine jazz numbers she had brought with her from America. How nice it would be to escape this intolerable boredom and relax to some music. Alone? Or with Ivan ven der Veen? Decidedly with Ivan. Besides, she couldn't very well leave without him. But how to get him to cooperate?

As if reading her mind, Ivan disengaged himself from his gaggle of admirers and motioned her to join him in the middle of the room, the only open space.

"If I hear another giggle I may strike someone," Ivan whispered. "Is there any way we can leave without embarrassing you?"

"What did you have in mind?" The innocence of her look belied the sudden excitement in her blood.

"Anything to get out of this menagerie."

"We could play records... in my studio." She dropped her eyes to avoid the speculation in his.

"How...?"

"Leave it to me."

She was surprised at how easy it was to carry out her deception. They found their hostess, Madame de Villiers, in the next room and Ericka glibly explained that her uncle was ill and that she really must leave to take care of him. Madame accepted this with a certain amount of skepticism, but there wasn't much she could do about it. The rest of the good-byes were soon over, and they were on their way laughing like conspirators.

George, lying on his bed reading, was acutely conscious of their surreptitious entrance. His first reaction was to let them know he was there, but when he heard the stealthy creak of the stairs he knew his opportunity had passed. It would only be embarrassing if he called out now. Obviously they thought he was out of the house. He lay there for a long time, listening to the faint music from above. He was thinking that in the end Piet ven der Veen was right—and wise. Perhaps it was the time for an end of innocence. And if this was the man she chose... why, so be it.

After a while the music stopped.

Upstairs, Ericka was just getting over her surprise that a stiff penis bore no relation to what she had been led to expect.

Ericka's knowledge of sex came almost entirely from "intelligent" books and was in black-and-white graphics. At Briarstone she had learned that the clitoris was spoken of by Briarstone sophisticates as the "little man in the boat" and was the source of some mysterious pleasure. That same night she tried locating the little man with a finger and discovered that she had a strong reluctance about touching herself.

She discovered the pleasures of masturbation inadvertently in the bathtub with the aid of the hot water faucet. She experimented and soon found that if she lay on her back in the tub and pushed her bottom right up against the end of the tub, legs wide apart, feet upon the edges of the tub, the warm gushing water could play directly on her parts. Particularly pleasurable if she held herself open to it.

Her fantasies were usually of bondage, herself tied spread-eagled on a bed, someone faceless but decidedly male approaching her. The terror was delicious but all anticipation. The act she feared never took place. The lovely warm water playing on her clitoris always spasmed her muscles and brought on a delightful feeling before anything could happen to her. The most notable result was that she slept like a top when she got into her bed.

What was happening to her now was something quite different. Ivan had undressed first, leaving the night lamp on. She didn't take her own clothes off because she was lost in wonder at the size of his erection. He pulled back his foreskin to reveal the glistening bright-red helmet with a hole in the middle. She couldn't take her fascinated eyes away. She was hardly aware when he lifted her dress over her head, slipped off her panties and pushed her gently onto the bed. He placed her hand on his penis, and instinct made her move it up and down. She had never imagined anything remotely resembling its velvety smoothness.

His lips and tongue on her breast was electrifying but mild compared to his hand between her legs. His gentle sucking was in rhythm with the knowing finger that rubbed her clitoris.

She came almost immediately in a flood of wetness and convulsing muscles. Her first orgasm was like nothing she had ever experienced before, and it brought her to the edge of fainting. Ivan rolled on top of her and she felt his hardness at the mouth of her vagina.

Then something happened.

He wasn't actually inside her, and yet she felt pain, a raging ripping pain, as if he were tearing her apart. She pushed him from her so violently that he rolled onto the floor. She sat cross-legged on the bed and began to scream. Not loudly, but a low, agonized sound that went on and on.

George heard it only because his ears were reluctantly tuned to whatever was going on above him. He came out of bed in a rush and headed for the stairs, the blood of anger pounding in his head. The few seconds it took him to get to Ericka's room gave him just time enough to think. Anger wouldn't help. Calm and reason might. Instead of bursting through, he forced himself to open it naturally and to reach for the light switch after he had entered.

Ericka sat naked in the middle of the bed with Ivan ven der Veen, equally naked, on his knees, obviously trying to calm her. The sound coming out of Ericka was intolerably painful. There was no intelligence in her eyes. He brushed past Ven der Veen and slapped her sharply across the face. She stopped screaming, and her silence was a blessed relief. She looked at him as though seeing him for the first time and then lifted her arms to him as she had as a child. He sat down on the bed and cradled her, rocking her gently.

Ericka stirred in his arms and then pulled away. "I'm all right now. I don't know what happened. . . ." She was suddenly conscious of her nudity and crossed her arms over her breasts in the age-old pose. Her eyes clouded with shame. "Oh, God. I'm so sorry. . . ."

"No need," George said gently. "And don't be afraid. Nothing's going to happen." And then, as an afterthought, "Did he hurt you?"

They both said "No" together. Then Ven der Veen, who had been industriously pulling clothes on and was now getting into his shirt, said "No" again. "Everything was all right. I didn't . . . Nothing really happened. . . . All of a sudden she . . ."

"All right, Ivan, wait for me downstairs." Then, at Ven der Veen's look of alarm, "Don't worry. I'm not going to play the outraged parent. But I do want to talk to you. Both of you. Ericka . . . if you feel up to it?"

She nodded wordlessly, and he saw that tears were now filling her eyes. She looked so forlorn and childlike. . . . Why was growing up so painfully difficult? But there was nothing childish about those reddened nipples, still hard and distended.

"Oh, Christ." George's voice was infinitely gentle. "It's nothing to cry about. Come on, honey, put something on and join us downstairs."

Ven der Veen carried his shoes and socks, and George politely carried his jacket and tie, as they left the room.

When they were both seated in the living room, George waited while Ven der Veen put on his shoes and socks. Things somehow seemed easier with those naked feet out of sight.

"Now, tell me exactly what happened."

"Well . . . nothing really happened. She is still . . . virginal. If that's what you mean. . . ."

No, she isn't, George thought. He was suddenly impatient with Ven der Veen's embarrassment. "Now, cut the bullshit," he said. "I want to know *exactly* what happened. Everything you did. Everything she did. I'm not looking for a cheap thrill, Goddamnit. It's important! So no bullshit!"

Ven der Veen saw that he meant what he said and for the first time met his eyes. George was impressed by the steadiness of his look in a situation that was certainly sticky for him.

"Who started it?" George asked.

"We both did. No, she . . . But I would have if she hadn't. We both knew . . ."

"Go on."

"We undressed. That is . . . I undressed her, and we got on the bed." It was coming out with great difficulty. "I . . . I kissed her breasts . . . and put my hand between her legs. Everything was all right. I think, no, I'm sure she had an orgasm. She seemed to enjoy . . ."

"Then what? I want to know exactly."

"Well . . . I got on top of her. That's when it started. She threw me on the floor. And began to scream. I couldn't stop her. I . . . I didn't know what to do. Everything was all right, and all of a sudden . . . I don't know what happened."

"Were you actually inside her?"

"No . . . just barely touching her with my . . ."

They both heard Ericka coming down the stairs. She was now in a long flannel robe. Her hair was neatly combed and she looked freshly scrubbed, and George's heart turned over at the sheer beauty of her.

"I'm so sorry." The words were addressed to both of them. "I feel so ashamed. I don't know what happened to me." Her eyes found George's and he saw there a desperate appeal for help, for reassurance, and knew that he must be very careful of what he said.

"Sit down, honey," and when she moved to the couch, "I'm not angry, not disapproving, not condemning. I want you both to understand that right off. You are not to feel guilty. What happened was—and is—perfectly natural—and would have happened sooner or later anyway. But there's more to it than that."

George took a deep breath to give himself time to formulate what he had to say.

"Normally a young girl doesn't go into hysterics over her first sexual experience. She either enjoys it or she doesn't. Depending on the circumstances—and her partner. I think there is a reason why you didn't. Above all, I don't want you to be frightened by what happened. I think there's an explanation for it. But first I want to ask you some questions. I want you to think carefully about your answers."

Ericka stared at him with bewildered attention.

"First, how much do you remember about Berlin? I mean before we found you. It may be painful, but it's important."

"Dr. Murray wanted me to remember," she said slowly, "and I couldn't. . . ." There was a frown of concentration as she looked into herself. Her hands were clenched tightly in her lap. "I tried. But I didn't want to. Something . . . something bad. I don't want to remember it. . . ."

Her face was very pale. George got up, went to sit beside her and took her hand in both of his. "You don't have to. It's just as well you don't. But I can tell you what happened. And once you know, then there's nothing to fear anymore. You were raped by a man when you were eight years old. Yes, I know it's bad. But not all that bad. It's happened to thousands of women, and most of them recovered from it without any permanent scars—that is, the strong ones. And you're a strong one, Ericka. I know you are."

He felt her hand contract between his palms.

"I'm glad you don't remember. But you must know that you can go ahead and have a perfectly pleasant sex life as a grown woman—with nothing to fear. It's all in the past. Over and done with."

"But . . . but why can't I remember?"

"Because you've blocked it out, as people often do with painful things. I wouldn't even try if I were you. There's no point now."

George saw her troubled eyes begin to clear and felt an immense relief. In his ignorance he began to congratulate himself on how well he had handled the situation. What price the Dr. Murrays of this world, with their professional mumbo-jumbo. All it took was a little common sense, along with a lot of love and understanding.

"That brings up another point." George was a little light-headed in his euphoria. "I wanted Ivan to hear this because the chances are you'll try again. But, for God's sake, can you manage it without being caught? It could become embarrassing, you know."

He was rewarded by a small tentative smile from Ericka and an audible sigh from Ivan ven der Veen.

That night Ericka had the first of many similar dreams she was to have for the rest of her life. It wasn't about sex or rape, although there was an aura of sex mixed up in it. In the dream she was chained to a wall in a burning house. The flames crept closer and closer to her until she could feel them licking at her flesh. She awoke briefly in a cold and clammy sweat and almost immediately fell asleep again.

The Atelier Van der Veen was one of about twenty ateliers accredited at the Beaux Arts, but it was by far the most prestigious, having turned out more Grand Prix de Rome winners than any of the others. The atelier system gave architectural students their training under certain established architects rather than in a central school of architecture. The importance of being a member of the right atelier was inestimable. The *patron* had three principal functions, the first being to teach. The *patrons* had the knowledge and the desire, but not the all-important ability to pass on their expertise. Some only bothered to turn up for weekly critiques and confined themselves to acid criticism and general denigration.

The second was to analyze and advise students on their "projects," of which there was a new one each month. Each project was judged by a jury selected by Beaux Arts members. Failure to pass the Beaux Arts jury meant loss of time and, in some cases, dismissal.

The third and most important function of the *patron* was that of a sort of combination defense attorney and high-powered salesman for the projects of his own students before the jury.

The Atelier Ven der Veen was like nothing she had ever imagined. It was one huge, impossibly high room, one side of which was wholly of glass, so dirty it admitted only a pale and misty light. The chief furniture seemed to be scarred planks propped on sawhorses, rickety stools and a dilapidated piano in one corner. Along the walls were nooks and crannies partitioned off by rusty file cabinets or ancient steel lockers to create "corners" for scale models, drawing materials, odds and ends of lumber. Along the three wooden walls, and extending out into the room, were complicated mezzanines roughly constructed of planks and metal scaffolding. It was worth your life to walk under them for fear of falling objects. The whole room was a hive of activity, with students rushing everywhere, all of it made more bewildering by unintelliglble shouting, laughing, talking in several languages.

Timidly Ericka asked a hurrying student where she should report. "The *massier*," the young man answered, pointing to a far corner of the cluttered room. Then, at her look of incomprehension, "The boss—after the *patron*. All things go through him. That's his office."

Ericka made her way through the chaotic madness to where the student had directed her. The "office" consisted of packing cases stacked one on the other to a height of seven or eight feet. The door was merely a narrow gap between stacks. In this space she saw a man standing on his head in one corner of the tiny area. Since there was barely enough room for a small table and a stool, she didn't see how he was going to maneuver himself upright—if he meant to do so at all. In fact he did it with ease, jackknifing his body and coming to his feet with fluid grace. Upright, he turned into her friend from registration day, Jean-Baptiste Moreau.

"Why didn't you tell me you were..."

He gave her his grin briefly. "I did. I told you I'd be around."

She stared at him.

"Why," he said, "did I not reveal to you my august position at Ven der Veen? You'd have been speechless with awe. Why spoil a pleasant luncheon?"

"I don't even know what a *massier* is. . . ."

His face became grave, even stern. "I am the master of your fate." He waved an expansive hand at the bedlam outside. "The master of their fates. I am father, advisor, confessor, and wet-nurse. All communications between students, teachers and officials of Beaux Arts must come through me. It is my duty to impart the history, traditions and rules of the institution. I handle all financial matters of this atelier. I am both judge and executioner. In short *I* am the law. First, within these hallowed walls, you will address me only as Monsieur le Massier. Is that clear?"

Ericka nodded wordlessly, unable to think of any other response.

"Ven der Veen you will call Patron. Never anything else. I mention this because you must be at least an acquaintance, since you were enrolled as apprentice without consulting me."

He began to smile, just a suggestion of a smile that barely reached his eyes. "Now, since you are only an apprentice—not yet even a student, it is permitted that you lunch with me after the morning session. It is a great privilege." At last the faint smile widened into a grin. "If you are sufficiently impressed, I will take you to a bistro I know where the food is somewhat more civilized than the last time. Okay?"

Again she could only nod. She *was* impressed and, as he had said, a little awed. He slithered around the desk and took her arm.

"It's time to meet your sponsor. He is a very gifted student of the second class. You will obey his every command without question. From him, with any luck, you will begin to learn to be an architect, so pay attention to every word he says. After that you newcomers will be welcomed by the *patron*."

Her sponsor, who would guide her work from now on, was introduced only as Anton. He turned out to be an immensely tall, gangling man, thin to the point of emaciation, totally preoccupied, indifferent to the clamor around him. He lifted his head from a drawing spread out on the boards in front of him, gave her a brief nod, held out a thick china mug and said, "Coffee."

Ericka took the mug and shuddered at the mess of soggy cigarettes nestled in the dregs.

"The *necessaire* is down the hall to the left," Jean-Baptiste said. "Coffee maker just past that. See you later."

The *necessaire*—and there was just the one—held only what was necessary, a rust-stained toilet bowl with a cracked seat, and a chipped enamel sink. No mirror, no shelves, no toilet paper—and no way to lock the door. When she pushed it open a student in underwear shorts was washing several pair of socks in the basin. From the looks of the dirty gray water they were long past the need.

The student gave her a quick look. "*Uriner? Attendez un moment.*"

Ericka said "No" and held out her cup. She had used the English *no* and the student smiled and said in purest Alabama, "Be done in a jiff an' it's all yours. *Admissioniste?*"

"No. I'm an apprentice."

"Sho' 'nuff? Well, honey bun, it's a mighty hard life."

When he had left, Ericka dumped the brown mess in the toilet and rinsed out the cup as best she could. At the coffee urn down the corridor it almost turned her stomach to think that anyone would drink from this, but if that's what he wanted, that's what he'd get.

When she returned, the *patron*, Piet ven der Veen, was already in the room. Tables and stools had been pushed away to provide an open space in one corner. Ven der Veen was surrounded by a small cluster of students. Ericka delivered the coffee to Anton, with not the slightest acknowledgment from him, and went to join the others.

There were fourteen newcomers in the group. Four second-class students attending the Ven der Veen atelier for the first time, eight *admissionistes* and only two apprentices, of whom Ericka was one. The other was a tiny, frightened-looking girl with long tangled black hair whose face was so pale it was alarming.

Piet ven der Veen afforded Ericka no recognition, launching immediately into what she supposed was meant to be a welcoming speech. "You are here to learn the rudiments, the basic principles, of a great art. It is based on beauty and utility—although they are not necessarily compatible. You will learn first from the past. The methods, the practical applications of those methods, the reasons

252

why the past masters built as they did. You will learn to adapt the beauty of the past, such as it is, to the necessities of the present. Only then, when you are thoroughly grounded in what has gone before, will you be allowed to experiment."

The old man's eyes shone with an inner fire that seemed to come out to them like sparks. "Only then will you know that each new project has its own life, its own special challenge. Each new building is a living, breathing entity, a single theme. It must follow its own truth. The site, the material, the *purpose*, determine the result. And the result is the beauty of total integrity."

Ven der Veen paused, and the light seemed to go out of his eyes as he looked around the room. "If I can open your minds to *ideas*—teach you that there is no compromise with integrity, then..." The old man sighed and gave a brief shrug. He seemed suddenly weary.

"Those of you who are gifted, or lucky, may then be able to add something to what you have learned. To bring something new to your art, to innovate, to reach out for far horizons—to live in beauty—in short, to *create*. The unfortunate among you may become rich and famous and successful, but if you do not learn to think and to *feel*, you will never be architects in the true meaning of the word—merely builders."

His words sent a thrill down Ericka's spine. This little man, with his ridiculous mop of untidy white hair, suddenly became a mystic giant, a prophet of the future, his ideas and ideals shining through to her.

The next weeks were a feverish nightmare of activity for Ericka: at the Sorbonne from nine to five, running to classes in different buildings, trying to get used to the awful food she had to grab as she ran, finding toilets in odd places to take care of the tourist's diarrhea the food gave her. Five o'clock until eight at the atelier, then busing home for dinner, again wolfed in haste because she had to study until total exhaustion forced her to bed. Up again at dawn for more hasty studying. Then rushing to catch the bus, praying there wouldn't be a strike, because at that time in the morning all the cabs were busy. It took awhile, but against all reason she finally got used to it and organized her day like clockwork.

The three hours at the atelier were the worst—and the best. The excitement and the madness were contagious. The atelier was heated—and impossibly overheated by ancient potbellied stoves that made the already stuffy air almost unbreathable. Because of the heat, most students worked in as little clothing as possible, exuding a heavy aroma of stale sweat. Dust was everywhere. The apprentices were supposed to sweep and tidy up, but there was never time. She and her tiny co-worker were kept unceasingly busy running out for ink, or beer, or anything else the older students shouted for.

There were never enough tables or work space, so sometimes projects had to be spread out on the bare floor, with people constantly coming and going, stepping on the materials, spilling wine, throwing bread and food, putting greasy delicatessen papers of pâté or blood sausage all over, not to mention smoked fish, a favorite Beaux Arts delicacy. Raw leeks were also highly prized as brain food. The chewed-up remains were simply tossed over a shoulder into the nearest corner.

There was only the one lunch with Jean-Baptiste, at a charming little restaurant where the food was like ambrosia. The rest of the time at the atelier he was cool and remote, the master of all he surveyed. She saw him only when she had a question no one else had the time to answer. She did learn that he had been graduated from Beaux Arts with honors the year before and was now employed by Ven der Veen et Cie. All his spare time was spent at their offices on boulevard Hausmann. She was piqued by his lack of attention and determined to ask George about him. When she had the time.

The traditional initiation ceremonies took her completely by surprise. Her only warning was a scream from Angenette, her fellow apprentice. She turned around to see two strapping students holding Angenette while a third was stripping off her clothing. She had time to notice that the tiny girl had no breasts at all, that her pubic hair was as black as the hair on her head and almost as long. The dark beard between her legs hung halfway to her knees. There was a roar of amazement and approval from the crowd.

Then Ericka herself was seized and subjected to the same treatment. She fought hard until Anton, her sponsor, who was one of the men holding her arms, whispered urgently in her ear.

"Don't struggle. It will only be worse. Everyone goes through initiation. Be a good sport and you won't get hurt. Otherwise . . ."

Overcoming her outrage, Ericka made herself submit. The hands pawing at her filled her with a nameless terror. In seconds she was naked and shivering in the overheated room. It wasn't being naked that frightened her, it was being *forced* to be naked.

There were ten initiates, eight male *admissionistes* and the two girl apprentices. One of the boys was putting up a fight, which was a break for the two girls. It took some of the attention away from them. The recalcitrant student was stripped, stretched out on a beam and his ass painted green. Then someone painted a grotesque face on Angenette's belly, complete with pirate's mustache and the beard between her legs. Ericka got one yellow breast with black aureole and one blue one with red nipple, matching bull's-eyes in red, white and blue on her buttocks and an excellent replica of a chocolate ice-cream cone on her stomach. Somehow the crowning indignity was painting red stripes in her lovely blond hair.

The fun climaxed with all ten besmeared initiates being sent out in the streets half-dressed to beg whatever they could from passersby, proceeds to go to food and drink for the whole atelier. Ericka drowned her indignation in good red wine until she no longer cared. It was a dandy party.

During this period Ivan ven der Veen dined at rue Babylone several times, at George's invitation. Ivan and George seemed to have formed a liking for each other, and Ericka looked on Ivan as a youthful ally. When she learned of a huge demonstration that was to take place on a coming Saturday, she asked Ivan to take her to see it.

"You are a fool," Ivan protested. "Such things can be dangerous. What do you know about French politics? And why should you care? Don't get mixed up in things you don't understand."

"I only want to watch. It's exciting. I want to see what happens, that's all."

When he was convinced that she would go without him, Ivan gave in and agreed to accompany her.

At eight o'clock on the night of the rally, Ivan and Ericka took up a strategic position on the corner of boulevard Saint-Michel and the rue Racine. The march was to form in Maubert Mutualité at eight, so they were in plenty of time. Ivan had chosen a dark blue suit of impeccable cut, a white shirt and dark maroon tie. His black shoes gleamed with recent shining. Not for him to run the risk of being mistaken for student riffraff.

Through there was some time before the demonstration would reach their position, all the shopkeepers had turned off their window displays and lowered iron shutters or grills. The streetlights were just beginning to flicker on as dusk slowly settled on the normally brisk and lively boul' Mich', in a silent and ominous haze. Their breath was misty in the frosty air. From far down Saint-Germain, muffled by distance, they could hear the noise of the crowd at the rally as some speaker made a popular point.

Ericka shivered and drew her cloth coat more closely about her. She was beginning to feel that the expedition was a mistake and was about to suggest that they head for some friendly bistro when Ivan said, "This is madness. If we could watch from some upstairs window . . . then all right. But out here in the open is stupid. Besides, it's getting damned cold. Why don't we get the hell out of here?"

Ericka was about to agree when it was suddenly too late. The night had suddenly burst into sound and motion. Across the boulevard, on the rue des Écoles, a whole fleet of gray armored troop carriers had moved into place and parked with motors idling. As they watched, police spilled out and formed into orderly squads. Behind the cars several Black Marias disgorged more gendarmes. The helmeted men moved to take up positions on each of the four corners. Voices were kept low, responding to the tinny distorted sounds of walkie-talkies from some invisible command post. The men looked more elegant than menacing in their graceful capes. Squads of motorcycle cops in black leather uniforms pulled up beside the cars, the staccato sound of their big BMW 950 motors drowning out the low exhausts of the troop carriers. Ericka couldn't understand how a bunch of harmless students could trigger such overreaction from the authorities.

256

"For God's sake, let's get out of here!" Ivan's hand was pulling urgently at her arm. "Before it explodes. This is no student protest. Those flics are expecting something a lot bigger than that. Look at the guns. Jésus!"

Ericka saw that many of the police were carrying riot guns. Canisters of tear gas hung from their belts. Plastic body shields were being passed out to each man. Groups of men were placing barricades at strategic points, wooden sawhorses linked together by chains. She decided that Ivan was right. It was time to get out. She yielded to his pressure and they started down the boul' Mich' away from the four corners.

They had cut things a little too fine. Ahead of them the side streets were already blocked off by squads of men whose purpose was to contain the marchers and confine them to the main artery. If they tried to run the gauntlet they would surely be stopped or even shot at by some trigger-happy cop.

Toward the Seine, from down Saint-Germain, came a sullen roar pierced by an occasional yell more strident than the rest. For the first time Ericka was hearing the sound of a mob, the angry, terrifying, mindless *thing* that was converging on the four corners. From all around them came the snick of weapons being cocked. Men crouched low finding whatever shelter was available.

The hoarse gutteral clamor of the crowd suddenly swelled as the vanguard turned the corner into the boul' Mich'. Without warning the sky burst open in a torrent of rain, almost obscuring the marchers. Ericka and Ivan ran for the nearest recessed doorway and were soaked before they could reach it. They huddled together, but the water was hitting the sidewalks with such force that shelter from it was impossible.

The rain seemed to enrage the demonstrators. The ordered front ranks suddenly dissolved and became individuals. Isolated figures broke away, spewing out of the heaving mass of bodies, to dig up cobblestones and pry up the articulated iron grills protecting the tall chestnut trees that lined the boulevard. Others came out swinging bicycle chains and metal signboards ripped from buses, hacking at shuttered café windows, destroying mailboxes.

A solid wedge of motorcycle cops gunned their heavy machines directly into the front ranks of the mob, toppling and scattering bodies as it cut a ragged swath. The momentum stopped momentarily. Then came the plop-plop of tear gas guns from the police at the corner of rue des Écoles.

The pause lasted only seconds before the marchers broke through the haze of gas and poured down the boul' Mich'. Ericka and Ivan saw they would soon be engulfed. They had two choices, neither of them good. If they became part of the mob they would suffer the same consequences, broken heads or arms or legs. The best chance seemed to be to try to keep ahead of the demonstrators and throw themselves on the mercy of the lines of police farther down the boul'. They couldn't stay where they were. The drifting clouds of tear gas would soon drive them out.

"Come on!" Ivan shouted. "Better the flics than these madmen." He grabbed her arm and they began to run toward the solid phalanx of police that blocked the street from wall to wall.

The escape route was up the boul' Mich' toward the Luxembourg Gardens, where rue Soufflot and rue Monsieur le Prince ran into the boulevard. That made two blocks along the blind facade of the lycée Saint-Louis with no cross streets, but they would be moving faster than the milling chaos of marchers. They hadn't gone fifty yards, however, when the lines of policemen split to allow a mounted charge of troopers to pound toward them. The crash of hoofbeats on the cobbled street was deafening. Wide-eyed and pale in the green light of the street lamps, they galloped past without a sideways glance.

Ericka felt a numbing jar as the flank of the last horse hit her a glancing blow, enough to knock her to the pavement gasping for breath. They lost precious seconds while Ivan jerked her to her feet and pulled her stumbling after him. He was shouting *"Américaine! Américaine!"* as they reached the line of blue-clad men. A hard-eyed beefy cop lifted his flexible rubber nightstick and brought it down hard on Ivan's shoulder. Ivan yelped with pain, but kept on screaming, *"Américaine!"* The cop drew back to strike again, when an officer grabbed his arm. Then they were through the line and momentarily safe.

But the delay had been too much. At that moment all hell broke loose as the front line of charging demonstrators crashed into the police. In a fraction of time they were in the midst of chaos, swirling, struggling bodies, shouts and screams, as the cops mercilessly beat at the agitators.

From then on everything seemed to move in slow motion for Ericka. Ivan was gone. Even the sounds seemed to come to her with an echo-chamber remoteness. Just in front of her, three cops were kicking a large blond man who was lying on his back while a fourth policeman pounded him rhythmically about the head with his truncheon. The man had his fingers locked across his face, rivulets of blood seeping through. One of the cops kicked the man between the legs. It brought his hands down with a scream of agony, and Ericka was looking at the bloody contorted face of Jean-Baptist Moreau.

Ericka heard herself yelling, "Stop! Stop it! Stop it!" It was at that moment the first shots were fired, a single rifle first, then the staccato chatter of a machine pistol.

Everything stopped, trapped silent and motionless in a frozen tableau for just an instant. Then Ericka, released from paralysis, threw herself on the body of Jean-Baptiste. She saw the lifted truncheon, actually heard the whistling sound it made as it descended. Then everything came to an end in a burst of red light and searing pain.

18

TIME: 1955
MELINDA BARNSTABLE PRICE

Melinda awoke languidly from her nap. The bedside clock told her that it was seven o'clock, so she had two hours before she was to dine with Paul Geroux. There were faint domestic noises from the kitchen, but the rest of the house was quiet. She was alone except for Hughette. She stretched luxuriously, savoring the anticipation of what was to come, dinner—and then Paul's apartment. Soft music, soft lights and then the slow undressing and the rediscovery of each other's bodies, which seemed forever new to her.

She got up and went to the window. The sky was gray and leaden with the promise of rain. Dusk was just beginning. Streetlights cast a pale greenish glow on the cobblestones. There were lighted windows in the houses across the way.

In the bathroom Melinda started the water in the sit-down tub, hoping the ancient storage tank held its quota of warm water. While she waited for the tub to fill, she slipped off her robe and stood before the full-length mirror examining herself, wondering if her lover saw her with the same critical eye.

The body is a calendar, and on hers the years rested lightly. Her breasts were remarkably firm and full, the aureoles and nipples still freshly pink. Her stomach was flat, with firm musculature, hips gently rounded, buttocks beginning to show just the tiniest sag—hardly noticeable as yet. She was blessed with excellent health and an exquisitely fair coloring. All in all she was pleased with what she saw.

After her bath, which she took quickly and efficiently, once again before the mirror, she covered her entire body with a lanolin cream, massaging it in until it disappeared, paying particular attention to elbows, knees and the backs of her heels. Next she dabbed perfume behind her ears, between her breasts and to each thigh just beside the silken triangle. Now she was ready to do her face, with as little artifice as possible because heavy makeup on a bed partner put a man off.

She was dressed and ready by eight-thirty and took a cab to Le Grand Vefours, where Paul Geroux waited for her. In the closed cab she heard the shots fired by the police on the boulevard Saint-Michel. To her they sounded like cars backfiring in the distance, and she paid no attention to them.

Melinda lay in the wide bed, fine perspiration drying on her nakedness, sleek and contented as a purring cat. Paul, just touching along the length of her thigh, was smoking a cigarette, hands behind his head.

"Stay," Paul said softly. "It's so lonely when you leave."

It was a tiny disturbance in her happiness. Her sense of propriety dictated that she wake up in her own bed, show her presence to George and Ericka, no matter what they might speculate about her evenings. She had never spent a whole night with Paul Geroux, never shared the joy of a new day in his arms. She resented this—but only when she was away from him. Nevertheless, she couldn't resist saying, "How I wish we could. . . ."

It was a gentle rebuke, only a suggestion that the fault was not hers alone. But it was there. It hung in the air between them. Paul stubbed out his cigarette abruptly and sat up.

"I know. I have been thinking about it."

She felt a sudden stab of excitement. "What do you mean?"

He grinned down at her. "Not now. Now I have to get you home. So that you can observe the conventions."

"I know. I just can't help it. It's the way I was brought up."

"I wouldn't have you any other way."

It was all she could get him to say. In the cab on the way home he told her only that he had asked certain questions of certain people and that she would have to be patient until he got some answers. Then perhaps . . .

They were still in the cab, lingering over a good-night kiss while the cabbie slouched resignedly behind the wheel, when Hughette jerked open the passenger door. Her face was pale with alarm. "You must go to the hospital," she said without preamble. "Ericka has been injured in the riot. They are at the American Hospital. Monsieur Barnstable says to come at once!"

Geroux slammed the door and called out to the sleepy driver to get them to the hospital as quickly as possible. As the cab careened through deserted streets, she clung to Paul's hand as though it were her only anchor, her mind blank with fear.

George Barnstable was waiting for her at the hospital, a worried and disheveled Ivan ven der Veen standing next to him. There was a tall red-haired man with them who looked vaguely familiar. George put his arms around her. "She's all right, honey. She got caught in the riot and some goddamned cop hit her. But she's all right now. They'll release her as soon as she's patched up. Please don't worry. You're shaking."

Melinda pulled herself away. "I am not shaking. I am perfectly all right. Now, will someone tell me what happened?"

"I'm afraid . . ." Ivan was covered with guilt. "She wanted to see a demonstration. We didn't realize . . ."

"And you took her? What an unforgivably stupid thing to do!"

"Come on, honey," said George. "It wasn't his fault. . . . Although if it weren't for Gavin here . . ."

"Don't 'honey' me," Melinda said furiously, ignoring the reference to the tall man. "I'm absolutely furious. What do you mean, 'patched up'?"

Embarrassed, George said, "You remember Gavin Riordan. He brought Ericka to the States, remember?"

Only then did Melinda realize who Gavin was. "What in God's name are you doing *here*?" she asked.

Gavin Riordan smiled at her, his startlingly blue eyes gentle and rueful. "Well," he said slowly. "It's a long story."

The day after his arrival in Paris, Gavin Riordan had reported to the office of Captain Étienne Tabard promptly at nine o'clock. In the anteroom two shirt-sleeved cops were already creating a steady clack-clack from battered Olivetti typewriters. On each cluttered desk were half-filled coffee cups and the crumpled wrappings of whatever the two had been eating. On the walls were the inevitable wanted posters, most of them yellow with age. All available space was crowded with file cabinets. The bare wood of the floors smelled from years of mopping up with Javelle water. That, and the odor of stale sweat, established a certain familiarity that made Riordan feel at home. The habitat of policemen was much the same the world over.

Captain Tabard breezed in at nine-thirty and ushered his visitor to a straight-backed chair in the inner office, which boasted a stained washbowl under a fly-specked mirror and a vase of wilted flowers on the desk. Tabard dumped the flowers, with an expression of distaste, into a metal wastebasket, then sat down in a creaking swivel chair and regarded Riordan with an appraising eye. He seemed satisfied with what he saw, for he began to smile.

Étienne Tabard was a compact man of medium height and medium age. Shiny dark blue suit, dark tie, neatly combed hair. A heavy graying mustache bisected his long face. The smile lifted the mustache comically to reveal small even white teeth. "And how is my friend Gus?" Tabard spoke with an excellent broad-*A* English.

"Still the same, I guess. I haven't seen him in a while."

"He spoke highly of you. He has a certain fondness . . . ?"

The question seemed to require a reaction. Riordan said, "I'm not so sure. But he *is* one hell of a good cop."

Tabard's eyes held a faint amusement. "We attended the FBI school together in Washington, DC. A long time ago. Those were great days. I remember . . . But enough of that." Tabard leaned forward and put his elbows on the desk. "Reminiscence is a bore to the young. You will want to know what we have planned for you. Gus seems to think you will have need of riot control in your city?"

Gavin shrugged. "I suppose it's always a possibility. We're heavy on blacks. Poor blacks. And we don't do a hell of a lot for them."

"Ah, yes. With us it's Communists on the left, *Poujardistes* on the right, students, both left and right. And of course, the troubles in Algeria. Both sides of that business. To the Frenchman politics is a very serious thing. Not like America?"

"No. With us it's more like a joke."

Tabard raised his eyebrows. "You can read the history of Paris from the record of its riots. We have learned that the only solution is to apply force, instantly and with great vigor. It has been a costly lesson over the years. A lot of men have died, both theirs and ours. So we have had to become very proficient at it. I've arranged for you to join the officer class presently training at the École Technique de Police. These are the men who will eventually command both intervention and support companies. These are the units directly responsible for riot control, and without doubt they are the best in the world at what they do. I think Gus Onderdonk will be pleased with you."

Tabard stood up. "Have you a place to stay?"

"I'm at the Georges Cinq at the moment. But it could get pretty expensive. . . ."

"Good. We'll put you up in the barracks at the Institut de Police on rue du Faubourg Saint-Honoré, a very pleasant place." Again Tabard raised his expressive eyebrows. "Unless you want to make other arranements . . . ?"

"No," Gavin said. "Sounds fine."

"One more thing. Since you don't speak French, I have assigned an interpreter to you. Sergeant Guyot will be at your disposal at all times."

Gavin caught a glint of amusement in Tabard's eyes.

"Get Guyot," Tabard suddenly roared.

There was an unintelligible answer from the outer room, and Gavin and Tabard waited in silence for the arrival of Guyot.

The young woman who came through the doorway didn't walk, she floated in, cool and clean and so darkly beautiful it hurt. She was wearing a simple beige suit with a light brown blouse casually unbuttoned to show just the right cleavage. Around the alabaster column of her throat was a thin gold chain. She wore no other jewelry.

"Sergeant Narcisse Guyot," said Tabard. "Lieutenant Gavin Riordan." His voice contained a hint of laughter as Tabard looked at Gavin's face. Gavin realized that his mouth was slightly open. He closed it.

"Sergeant Guyot is a graduate of the Sorbonne and the École Pratique des Gardiens de la Paix. She will be taking the course at École Tech right along with you—in preparation for the lieutenant's exam. She, too, is one hell of a good cop."

Narcisse Guyot took his hand, her face serious and intent, and said, "A pleasure to meet you, Lieutenant Riordan," in purest American English.

"Where did you . . . ?"

"My father was with our embassy in Washington for many years. My English is better than my French."

"It should suffice," Tabard said dryly. "Now, Sergeant, why don't you give him the Cook's tour. Then perhaps you both will join me for lunch?"

Gavin nodded wordlessly and followed Narcisse Guyot out of the room. They walked down the corridor together, shoulder to shoulder.

"I have a feeling," Gavin said, "this is some kind of new-boy joke. It would be simpler if you let me in on it. What is . . . ?"

"A nice girl like me doing in a place like this? I assure you it is no joke. Or if it is, it's meant to be on me—not you. My male associates think it's funny to throw me at any attractive man who enters the place, hoping that one of them will succeed in getting me into bed . . . which all of *them* have tried—and failed."

"What have you got against going to bed? It seems a fairly universal pastime."

"Nothing. Except that *all* Frenchmen expect it of *all* women. I am serious about my career. I expect them to be serious, too."

They had stopped before the elevators, and Gavin saw that she was indeed serious. Her heart-shaped face was composed, eyes cool and remote, devoid of any interest in him as a man. He found it unsettling, like talking to a piece of sculpture.

"But why a cop? Surely . . ."

It provoked an unexpected reaction. Those cool eyes were suddenly blazing with intensity. The change was so abrupt that he had to resist the impulse to step back.

"Because I *want* to be a cop. My father—and my mother—were killed by terrorists. In Hanoi. The police did nothing. They were incompetent. But worse, they didn't *care*. 'Don't rock the boat. We Frenchmen have trouble enough in Vietnam.' Not much consolation for a kid of seventeen."

Gavin knew her anger for what it was. "So you want to take it out on *all* criminals," he said slowly. "That's the worst kind of emotional involvement a cop can have. Judge, jury—and executioner. Believe me, I know. . . ."

"Do you, Lieutenant? Do you indeed." The elevator arrived. "We'll see the museum first," she said. "A little history and background on the police of Paris." They rode to the top floor in silence.

The museum was small but impressive. Narcisse Guyot was an excellent guide, with a compelling sense of history, and there were centuries of it represented on the museum walls. There were portraits of every prefect of police who had ever served the people of France, LaReynie, Dubois, Count of Empire. There were lifelike wax figures of both criminals and police, including the famous *Sergent de Ville* by Debelleyme. In all available spaces were hung prints of the *ordonnances* proclaimed by various prefects, traffic regulations dating from the time of Napoleon and Louis-Philippe. It seemed that Paris had always had a traffic problem.

From Narcisse Guyot, who seemed to have a particular fondness for the man, Gavin learned about Joseph Fouché, Duc d'Otrante, who had more political lives than any cat. Fouché had been minister of police three times, first under the Revolutionary Tribunal, then under Napoleon, finally as head of the government that established Louis XVIII as king. Fouché had bloodily put down revolts in Brittany, the Vendée and Lyons, and had kept rigid order in the city of Paris.

"He was the man who formulated the principle for riot control," Narcisse Guyot said. "Force. Applied with speed and vigor." Gavin recognized Tabard's phrase. "Paris has had more than its share of violent mobs and riots," she said. "For centuries, the Parisians' expression of discontent has been to take to the streets. It's still a major problem with us."

The rest of the tour took them through the forensic lab, photo ident, criminal investigation and all the other departments of the Police Judiciaire, most of them common to any well-run police organization, old hat to Gavin. Until they got to the interrogation rooms in the basement. Through a small glass panel in a door they watched, but could not hear, the action inside.

Three seemingly bored plainclothes detectives sat around the sides of a scarred, stained wooden table. In the fourth chair was a shirt-sleeved prisoner whose feet were bare. There was a sizeable lump on his forehead. Suddenly one of the detectives slapped the prisoner, hard enough to knock him from his chair and onto the floor. A second cop picked the man up and sat him in his chair again. The third cop duplicated the blow of the first one. Once more the prisoner was jerked to his feet and propped in the chair. This time his lower lip was split and a trickle of blood ran down his chin.

The cops' mouths moved in turn in silent questioning. Again the man was slammed to the floor.

The soundless drama began to get to Gavin. "How the hell do they get away with that stuff?"

"What?" Her voice was impersonal, faintly puzzled.

"Beatings. Police brutality. In the States the guy's lawyer would have him out on a habeas writ in twenty minutes, taking pictures of his injuries. You'd hear the screams from here to San Francisco."

"We don't have habeas corpus in France. What they're doing is called *passage à tabac,* which means literally to sit down at a table for a smoke. In practice the purpose of the table is for the criminal to sign his confession on. Article 10 of the Criminal Code states, in part, 'If there is urgency, the police may perform all acts necessary to uncover the truth of crimes or offenses against internal or external security of the State...' Those men are merely performing their duty under the law."

"You must get a lot of confessions." Gavin's indignation was showing. "You beat on a man long enough and he'll sign anything. Give me the land of the free every time."

"Freedom? A former prefect of police summed it up rather well. 'The French citizen is free to do whatever he likes—but always under police supervision.'" She turned away with a shrug of dismissal. "It's time we rejoined Captain Tabard. He lunches promptly at noon."

At lunch Étienne Tabard was genially expansive, while Narcisse Guyot said almost nothing, addressing herself to her food with silent absorption, taking only small, delicate sips of her wine.

Tabard appreciated his wine and kept Gavin's glass always topped up. "Enjoy your tour?" he asked. "*Esprit.* Second to none."

Gavin, still appalled, mumbled something diplomatic.

"He doesn't approve of our interrogation methods," said Sergeant Guyot.

"Oh, that." Tabard shrugged. "Police work is too often boring. A little excitement never hurts. When we get a suspect who doesn't want to cooperate, we beat the shit out of him until he changes his mind. The sight of blood, particularly one's own, is a great persuader. Does him no permanent harm—and does us good. Great for morale. I recommend it to you."

"If you say so, Captain," Gavin said shortly.

Tabard's good humor was hard to dampen. "Call me 'Ten.' Short for Étienne. We French are great ones for nicknames. Our gangsters especially: *Grosse-Tête*, Big Head; *Giudicelli*; *Gros Roger Sennanedfi*; *Lolo l'Accordioniste*; *Moo-Moo la Vache*, because he bellows like a cow when we question him. Many others. Most of them Corsicans." He grinned hugely. "But so are the cops—the best of them, that is. Half the time we are hunting our own cousins. Incestuous business."

"I didn't know that," Gavin said politely. And then, in an effort to keep up his end of a conversation he was finding slightly difficult because of the determined silence of Narcisse Guyot, "You hear mostly about the Sûreté when you read about the French police."

"Those glamour boys!" Tabard was contemptuous. *"We* are the real elite. Intervention and Support. Four thousand of us, each man personally approved by the prefect himself. What would the force be without us? Eh, Narcisse?"

"What indeed?" She had stopped eating and was looking at Tabard with an expression Gavin couldn't interpret. "Or the *barbouses*? Why don't you tell him about the *barbouses*?"

Tabard's frown was formidable, and Gavin thought that if he were a sergeant serving under Captain Tabard, he would pay strict attention to that frown and watch his step.

"None of my business, that," Tabard said shortly. "Or yours."

Perversely, wanting to see just how far she would go, Gavin asked, "What is a *barbouse*?"

Deliberately ignoring Tabard's stormy glance, Narcisse took a sip of her wine. *"Barbou* means bearded. The bearded ones. You have the same expression, I think. A beard is a person used to conceal, to cover up for another. With us, the *barbouses* bury our dead. To save us the embarrassment of admitting we have dead to bury. By dead I mean anyone who becomes a . . . nuisance to the government. Or to the secret service. The *barbouses* cause such people to . . . disappear."

"Merde!" Tabard snapped. "You don't know what you're talking about!"

"Don't I? It was the *barbouses* who . . . eliminated my parents in

Hanoi." She was speaking to Gavin, her voice as matter-of-fact as though she were giving instruction to a student. "They began to form in 1940, after the fall of France, when they joined de Gaulle. The hardcore were French Jews, Algerian criminals. And..." with a nod of her head toward Tabard, "Corsicans. After the Indo-China War they were reinforced by Vietnamese of the Black Hand Society. *Our* kind of Vietnamese—professional torturers. Now, with the troubles in Algeria, they recruit *pied noires,* army deserters, anyone who qualifies.

"They are a branch of the secret service, although you won't find them on any official budget. They are truly 'beards.' One seldom sees a *barbouse*—unless one is about to die."

"Sergeant, you are out of order." Tabard's voice was steely with anger, his fist clenched on the table. "Lieutenant Riordan is our guest. It is inexcusable to wash dirty linen in front of him."

Unexpectedly Narcisse Guyot smiled. "You're right, Captain. It *was* inexcusable. I apologize...to both of you."

"Well." Gavin pushed back his chair, hoping to relieve the awkward situation. "Shouldn't I be getting settled in the barracks? Move my stuff over? I haven't unpacked yet."

He reached for his wallet, but Tabard stopped him.

"No. I insist."

"Expense account," Gavin said. "Just think of it as Gus Onderdonk's treat."

"Well, in that case..."

In the cab, headed for the Georges Cinq, Narcisse Guyot moved to the farthest corner of the seat and stared out of the window. Gavin studied her: long, graceful legs, full breasts, the perfect face framed by silken dark hair. It was impossible to look at her without wondering what she'd be like in bed.

"Why'd you step so hard on your boss's tail? You like to live dangerously?"

"Because he pinches mine when he thinks nobody is looking."

"Why is he so upset about the *barbouses*?"

She considered her answer briefly. "Because he thinks there's just one chance in a million that I'll come across the people who killed my parents. I saw them, you know. Very awkward for everybody if I

269

do. They may be Corsican cousins of his. It's safe enough to bait him. He can't fire me. He can only try to grind me down.''

The Institut de Police was housed in the former Hôpital Beaujon, several large airy buildings set around a courtyard with adjacent green fields for sports and physical training. Since Gavin was determined to be a participant rather than observer, he signed up for the full course. That consisted of four hours of classwork, which included French law and the Code Napoleon, police science, routine and procedure. The rest of the day was spent in weapons training (small arms, machine carbines, gas guns), equipment use and tactics (radios, transport tenders, motorcycles, mobile commissariat command post for riot control) and last, but far from least, physical training (boxing, judo, hand-to-hand combat).

In the beginning the routine left him quivering with fatigue at the end of each day, but after a week his muscles began to accommodate the rigors of the course. Narcisse Guyot was truly one hell of a good cop. That magnificent body housed muscles that could match his in every phase of the training. He learned the hard way that she held a black belt in karate. And she was a tremendous help in the classroom work. There would have been no point to it without her.

When at the end of the second week he realized that it had been days since he had thought more than fleetingly of Serena, he came to the wry conclusion that it is not love which triumphs over all, but responsibility—and hard back-breaking work. Even the memory of pain begins to fade. That same day he asked Narcisse Guyot to dinner.

She considered him gravely and with some hesitation before she said yes. They dined in an excellent small restaurant on the rue de Douai, near where she lived. Gavin found her a good dinner companion, with a dry sense of humor that he hadn't expected and an insatiable interest in all things American. He was again surprised when he found that she was twenty-six. She looked barely twenty. When he questioned her briefly about her parents, her face lost its animation and she looked her years.

''He spoke out strongly against the war. Atrocities—senseless killing. . . . He was an embarrassment to the military—and the government. They couldn't shut him up. So he suffered . . . an accident. Caught in the middle of a terrorist battle. Unfortunately my mother was with him in the car.''

"You saw them?"

"I saw some of them. . . ." she said slowly. "Not all."

"Are you really looking for those people?"

"No. It's been too long. I'm not even sure I'd know them." She began to smile, her lips curving gently. "But *they* think I am. It makes them very nervous. Which is a good thing."

"But risky. You're bucking City Hall. They could just dump you."

"My uncle *is* City Hall. He's the prefect of police."

"Oh," Gavin said. It explained a lot.

He walked her home in the clear chilly night. At her doorway he held out his hand. She looked first at his hand and then at his face, a long, searching inspection. Then she said, "I think you'd better come up."

Her apartment was Spartan, the only touch of femininity a flowered robe tossed at the foot of a wide double bed. She undressed quickly and lay supine, waiting for him to get out of his clothes. In the dim light her her nakedness gleamed like pearls, her young breasts pink-nippled and erect, the dark triangle between her legs in stark contrast to the pale translucent skin. She gasped, and her body gave a convulsive shudder as his finger found her clitoris. That was the last aggressive move Gavin made.

For Narcisse Guyot the love couch was a battlefield. She was as expert and competitive as she was in karate, and Gavin thought, when he had the time, that in this too she deserved a black belt. She screamed each time she came, in a sort of triumph, as though she had won the match. He found it both exciting and exhausting.

When it was over, and they lay side by side smoking, Gavin said, "Why me?"

Her voice was cool and still just a little breathless.

"Because I love to fuck. And because you're not one of *them*. You'll be gone in a little while. In the meantime . . ."

Gavin moved in the next day.

*　　*　　*

At the end of six weeks Gavin had fallen into a comfortable routine, days packed with hard demanding work, nights full of surprises from Narcisse. It occurred to him more than once to ask where and how she had gained her experience in the art of lovemaking. But he never did. He knew that she would consider it an invasion of her privacy, a very important thing to her. Since there was no way that he could in his mind couple the loving of Serena with Narcisse Guyot, his thoughts of Serena were more and more of the things she had said or felt—a fleeting expression, a wink, a touch of her hand in crowded places, the sound of her laughter, a fragment of Edna St. Vincent Millay she had once quoted: ". . . she tossed her brown delightful head, among the long remembered dead . . ."

He also found that the old adage was true—that the best way to learn a language was two heads on a pillow. His French progressed remarkably.

During the second month Gavin's Provisional Training Company got its first face-to-face look at what their training was all about. A Communist deputy named Degas was arrested (Gavin never found out what the offense was) and the event called for the usual strong protest from the leftists. Gavin's unit was to act in support of the regular forces. Gavin's special status earned him an invitation from Captain Tabard to join him in the mobile commissariat command post. It was an ideal place from which to follow the action.

Gavin learned later that there were only fifteen hundred demonstrators in the place de la Nation, a rather piddling turnout as Paris demonstrations go. At the time it had seemed more like fifteen thousand. The riot squads were kept under strict control through a hail of bottles, stones, furniture, pieces of broken barricades and anything else that could be thrown. The discipline was excellent until the mob started overturning the *pissoires,* the public urinals that dot Paris squares. For some reason this infuriated both the uniformed rank-and-file and their commanders. The order was given to break it up, and battle was joined. It could be called nothing else. Full-scale war. Gavin was left with several indelible impressions: the willingness of Paris citizens to risk serious bodily harm as long as they could get a crack at anything in uniform; the terrible effectiveness of the capes worn by some of the gendarmes, capes with lead bars in their hems, which could break bones and heads; the utter abandon, the sheer deliberate brutality, with which the police crushed the rioters. Gavin read in the next day's papers that there had been one hundred and fifty injured, of which thirty-five were cops, and over three hundred rioters arrested. Only two men had been killed. It seemed an impossibly low figure.

The big lesson he learned was to fear and respect the power of the mob. Could it happen in the States? And if it did, could American police handle it? Not a prayer, without proper training. Could American cops ever be brought to believe (as the Paris police obviously did) that the citizen, in sufficient numbers, was the *enemy*—and had to be destroyed? Gavin strongly doubted it.

Gavin's second riot call came weeks later. He was in Ten Tabard's office, picking up his mail. Tabard was on the phone, and because of the mail Gavin wasn't paying much attention to Tabard's conversation. There was a letter from Des Daniher, which was full of local gossip and little else. It read like a duty letter and it worried him a little. It wasn't like Des to write unless he had something specific to say. Only one item was of any particular interest. *It looks like your friend Stewart Gansvoort is developing an interest in politics*, Daniher wrote. *He gave a speech at the 20th Ward Republican dinner, along with, I'm told, a generous contribution to the cause. You don't suppose he wants to run for something, do you? If so, I can't think what.*

Gavin's other letter was from Gus Onderdonk. Onderdonk gave him a detailed report on the progress of the Belding commission. *So far,* Onderdonk related, *we're developing 112 cases. Everything from petty police corruption, through some much bigger stuff in the narco squads, to one assistant DA and a Criminal Courts judge. There's plenty more where those came from. Before we're through, we'll shake up this old town like a dog with a rag. We've issued three hundred and forty subpoenas up to now, with maybe a couple hundred more to come. We'll be needing you on the stand very soon, so don't get too fond of Gay Paree. You're still our big surprise.*

The letter was obviously the result of Onderdonk's two-finger

273

typing. It was the postscript, hastily handwritten, that gave Gavin a cold chill.

By the way, so you won't be surprised, one of those subpoenas is for your Uncle Des. Judge Belding wants to go after Angelo Pavane. Nothing small about Belding. Thinks maybe Des can help him.

No other comment from Gus Onderdonk. Just the bare facts, a warning of what Gavin had feared all along. Des Daniher went back a long way with Angelo Pavane, and Gavin thought he knew where Daniher's loyalties would lie.

For some time he had been vaguely aware of the rising tempo of Ten Tabard's voice. Now he jumped as Tabard slammed down the telephone receiver.

"Oh, the bastards!" Tabard grated. "Oh, those fucking stupid pigs! They think we don't know what they're up to."

"What's up?"

"The real thing this time. Thank God for informers. Started out as a nonviolent student rally. Routine. Nothing to worry about. Then the Commies decided to make it an occasion. They're taking it over. Thousands of them. What the stupid jerks don't know is that *Jeune Nation*, those homicidal bastards, are setting up a counter demonstration."

Underneath his anger, Ten Tabard's worry was showing. It was contagious and Gavin began to feel an apprehension of his own.

"What the hell is *Jeune Nation*?"

"The leather jacket bunch. Far rightist. Crash helmets and bicycle chains, to begin with. Now it's guns and grenades. And plenty of money too, and Mafia strong-arms. All in the interest of keeping Algeria French. If Algeria ever goes Commie, all the juicy *fric-frac* between Marseilles and North Africa goes out the window. What a fucking country I live in! What a fucking world!"

"Is it that serious?"

"You can bet your ass it is. Those vicious bastards will try to bust up the Commies. And the poor dumb students will be caught in the middle. Unless we can break up the mobs one at a time. If not, it could be a very unpleasant situation."

Tabard was looking at him indecisively.

"Maybe you should sit this one out. . . ."

"It *is* that serious, then."

Tabard nodded wordlessly.

"You're probably right," Gavin said, already regretting his decision, "but I think I'll go along anyway. If it's all right with you."

Tabard shrugged. "Provided you stay in the mobile command unit. Gus would never forgive me."

In the command vehicle, stationed just behind the first line of police, Gavin could hear through the bulletproof glass windows the noise of the Communist march coming toward them from St. Germain. The silence behind them down the boul' Mich, where the *Jeune Nation* toughs were forming, was ominous. All around him voices crackled from the special wavelength communications system that was keeping track of each group.

"They're massing in the Luxembourg Gardens." Tabard had removed his white helmet and had earphones clamped over his head. "And along rue Soufflot and le Prince, across the Boul' . . ." He was listening intently. In the subdued light of the command post his face was pale with tension. He lifted his microphone and spoke hoarsely into it. "Are the fire brigade in place? Well, then what the hell *are* they doing? . . . As soon as you have a solid target, hit 'em with the hoses. . . . What do you mean? How can there be no pressure? . . . *What*!" His voice rose to a shout, shockingly loud in the crowded truck. Tabard lowered his mike and looked at Gavin unbelievingly.

"There is no fucking *water*! Because the fucking waterworks is on strike! Would you believe it? Nobody will have water until tomorrow morning. In the whole of fucking Paris. Oh, what a fucking country!" Then, at something that came over his earphones, he was shouting again into the mike. "No! There will be no firing! Use gas on the bastards. . . . Unless they fire first. Only then. . . ."

At that moment the rain struck. Through the streaming windows Gavin saw the front ranks of the Communists turn the corner of St. Germain and surge toward the police cordon blocking the boul' Mich. The motorcycles hit them first, riders helmeted and masked to protect against the clouds of tear gas, looking like aliens from outer space. Then the police ranks parted to let the mounted troopers

275

through. The charge looked orderly and disciplined until it hit the mob. Then it seemed to disintegrate like sand thrown against a wall.

In the small clear space between the police cordon and the battling demonstrators, Gavin saw two people running toward them. First the long-legged figure of a girl in skin-tight pants, blond hair streaming out behind her, then a man pounding along after her. In the brief seconds before the rioters surged against the police line, Gavin thought the man was chasing the girl. Then he heard the faint cry, *"Américaine! Américaine!"*

Without thinking, Gavin pulled open the side door of the command van and leaped to the street. He heard Tabard shout, "Stay here, damn you!" and paid no attention. He went forward at a run. The man and the girl reached the solid line of police just steps before the vanguard of the Communists. In moments there was chaos. Gavin was fighting to break through the cordon from behind while the rioters hit it from the front. He saw the girl throw herself on the body of a man and heard the sickening crunch as a cop's truncheon met her head.

From behind, toward the Luxembourg Gardens, firing broke out. In the momentary pause Gavin forced his way through the struggling mass and reached the girl. The cop had his nightstick raised again and Gavin shouldered him aside.

"She's American," he yelled, and the cop seemed to understand. Beside him the man who had been with the girl was tugging at his arm.

"Please! Please, will you help us. . . ."

The police searchlights suddenly came on, flooding the scene like a movie set. Gavin found himself looking at a small, owl-eyed young man with a smear of blood on one cheek.

The girl was spread-eagled over a huge blond man who was moaning, his head moving mindlessly from side to side. She was weightless and as limp as a sack when Gavin picked her up. "Command car . . ." Gavin gasped. "You get him," with a jerk of his head indicating the unconscious man.

The owl-eyed young man looked at him uncomprehendingly, and Gavin saw that he was half the size of the man on the ground.

"Drag him, Goddamnit!"

Ten Tabard was at his side, yelling over the sound of the mob. "What the hell you think you're doing!"

"They're Americans! For Christ's sake, help me get 'em out of this!"

"As if I don't have enough. . . . !"

Gavin left him, pushing his way through the police with the girl, who wasn't weightless anymore, but all too solid flesh.

In the lee of the command car there was comparative peace. The cops now had the Communists on the run, and the battle was moving away back toward the Seine. There was no room in the van, so Gavin put the girl down on the wet cobblestones. The raindrops fell on her pale face like tears, but her eyes were open.

Ten Tabard and the owl-eyed young man arrived, dragging the unconscious giant between them, and plopped him down beside the girl. From down the boul' Mich there was more sporadic gunfire, punctuated by the mournful *ping-pong* of arriving ambulances.

"There'll be hell to pay if I don't stop that." Tabard was out of breath, his voice shaking with tension. He disappeared into the command truck.

An ambulance pulled up beside them, and Gavin commandeered it. Inside there were already three bloody flics seated on the hard wooden benches. The attendants helped them get the girl and the huge blond into the vehicle. At the last moment Gavin decided to go along. He'd had enough of riots for the time being.

Gavin and the owl-eyed young man had the groggy girl propped between them on a bench. The other man was stretched out on the wooden floor.

"I'm Ivan ven der Veen," the young man said. "I don't know how to thank you. She . . . she wanted to see a demonstration. . . ."

"Well, she saw one," Gavin said shortly. "Lucky it wasn't her last. And him?" He indicated the man at their feet.

"One of her teachers at Beaux Arts, I think. She is Ericka Ullman. Her uncle is George Barnstable—the architect. I must let him know . . ."

"Son of a bitch," Riordan said.

* * *

When a worried George Barnstable arrived at the hospital, Gavin was able to assure him that Ericka was intact and had suffered no permanent damage.

"You have a way of showing up in her life," said George. After a long moment during which the two men looked at one another, remembering events from the past, George impulsively threw his arms around Riordan, then stepped away to examine him better.

"I miss the beard," George said.

"Hardly appropriate on a police lieutenant."

"My, my," George said. And then, "Jesus Christ, it's good to see you!"

"Likewise. You haven't changed much."

They stood there, smiling delightedly at each other, until George had a thought. "By the way, she doesn't seem to remember a damned thing about those days."

"She won't learn it from me," said Gavin.

George studied him critically, now with a small worried frown.

"She'd never recognize you without the beard anyway."

"Probably not."

For the first time George seemed to realize that there were a lot of questions to be asked and answered.

"My God, Gav, what are you doing here? How in the devil . . ."

It was at that moment that Melinda hurried in with Paul Geroux close behind her.

They waited for fifteen more minutes before Ericka appeared in a wheelchair pushed by a perspiring orderly. She looked spectacularly dramatic, her pale face framed by the long silken blonde hair spilling from the strip of bandage around her head. Melinda rushed to the girl to put her arms around her and then refrained for fear of hurting her.

"Poor baby. Does it hurt? Are you in pain?"

Ericka shook her head and couldn't suppress a wince.

"I'm still a bit dizzy." She got out of the wheelchair a little unsteadily. "It's just hospital rules. They have to wheel you to the door when you leave. I'm really okay. Honest."

To George's relief she showed no sign of recognition when

278

introduced to Riordan, merely a pretty gratitude for her rescue. Then her face clouded as she asked hesitantly, "Is Jean-Baptiste . . . ? They hurt him terribly, you know."

It was Gavin who answered. "He'll have a few scars. Nothing he won't get over. He'll be here for a few days. After that . . . I think the police will want to question him." He didn't say what that might mean. Scars on top of scars, if the man had anything to tell.

"Well," Melinda said, and then, always practical, asked him where he was staying. Seeing Gavin's momentary embarrassment, she rode right over it. "Wherever it is, you're to come and stay with us. We have loads of room, and George would never forgive me if I didn't insist." Her look was tender and appealing. "He's missed you, you know. I believe he thinks the times you two had were the best in his life."

Gavin was on the point of making some excuse when he saw the delighted expectation on George Barnstable's face. At the same time he had the thought that life with Narcisse Guyot had become a touch wearing. Why not spend his last few days in Paris with his old friend? He also had a lively curiosity about Ericka Ullman. "I'd like that," he said, "if it won't put you out. I'll have to make some . . . arrangements. Would tomorrow be too soon?"

After they had exchanged telephone numbers, Gavin left.

He didn't expect any trouble from Narcisse, and he didn't get any. After all, it was she who suggested their arrangement, and it had been on her terms from the beginning. After they had made love for the last time, he was surprised to see the glint of tears in her eyes.

"Jesus, honey, don't cry."

She shook her head angrily. "I'm not crying. I *never* cry. After all, you'll be leaving in a few days anyway."

"I won't go if you don't want."

"Fuck off. We owe each other nothing. It's been good, I think, for both of us. And no good-byes."

She was gone when he awoke. He packed his things hurriedly and after one last look at the apartment—which *had* been good for both of them—grabbed a taxi in order to drop his bags at rue de Babylone before going off to school.

As he entered the École the desk attendant motioned to him and handed him a message to report to Captain Tabard on the double. In Tabard's office there was a cable from the States. Tabard watched him silently as he read it and interpreted his smile correctly.

"You're leaving us?"

Gavin tossed him the flimsy. Tabard read it slowly aloud.

"Snowball is rolling. You have one week. Cable arrival time to me personally. Gus."

"Snowball? What's that?"

"It means his investigation is picking up speed, like a snowball rolling downhill. The 'personally' bit means he's trying to sneak me into town. I wonder why."

"Well, you've got a week. No sense busting your balls at the École. See something of Paris. You haven't had much time to look around. Place Pigalle. Montmartre. Lots of action there. You shouldn't miss it."

Gavin thanked Tabard for everything.

"I think I've had about all the action I can handle," Gavin said ruefully.

Tabard's incongruous mustache began to twitch. His eyes were amused. "Strange girl, that one."

"Not so strange. She just doesn't like her ass pinched—by over-the-hill cops."

Tabard shook his hand extra firmly. "I'm going to miss you, Yank. Tell Gus hello for me. And keep in touch. I'd like to know what happens when you get back."

On his first morning at the Barnstable apartment, Gavin awoke early, reached for a cigarette, lay back and luxuriated in not having to face another strenuous day. He suddenly realized that for the first time in years he felt alive and whole, full of strength and well-being—and at peace with himself. There was impatient anticipation at the thought of going home to a job he knew he could handle with the best of them.

He slid out of bed and went through the routine of French army calisthenics, which had become a habit. His body tingled with good health, muscles loose and responsive. It came to him that what he was feeling was like a rebirth. A whole segment of his life had ended. Something new and exciting was about to begin.

The hurt of Serena was still there, but, he was surprised to find, it was buried now, just one of the sad parts of living.

The house was silent. Gavin shaved and sponged himself down as quietly as possible in the inadequate bathroom down the hall from his room. By the time he was dressed he could hear kitchen sounds. He followed them down the creaky stairway. The smell of coffee made his mouth water as he approached the back of the house. Hughette gave him her best smile, showing off the dimples in her fat cheeks. "And what do heroes eat for breakfast?" Then at Gavin's look of surprise, "Oh, yes, I heard. The little one owes her life to you."

"Hardly that," he said. "How about some coffee? It smells like heaven. Just black, if you will."

Hughette hastened to pour him a steaming breakfast mug. He sipped gratefully as he watched her prepare a tray. On the tray were a vase with a single rose, a silver coffee carafe, napkin-covered croissants and a jar of dark red jam.

"The little one," Hughette told him. "She must stay in bed for a few days until her head is better."

On impulse Gavin said, "Let me take it up to her. I'd like to see how she is."

Hughette gave him a look at first suspicious and then conspiratorial. "Good. What could be nicer than to be greeted by a handsome man. She is on the top. Take the back stairs."

There were three doors on the top floor. One of them was partially open, and through it Gavin could see a chintz-covered chair and part of a dressing table. He pushed it open with the edge of the tray and stepped into the room. He had assumed that she would be awake, since breakfast had been made for her.

For once the ancient radiators were working and the room was far too hot. The girl had thrown off the covers, and it was all too obvious that she slept in the nude. She lay on her back, long blond hair spread like foam on the rumpled pillow. Her face in repose had the open innocence of childhood, and for a fraction of time Gavin captured his first image of her as she stood in the Ullmans' tub when he and Barnstable had washed the caked dirt from her face. The rest of her was quite different. Now those childish breasts were full and firm, the nipples rosy as cherries. Her flat belly sloped down to a prominent mound covered with hair as pale as that on her head. Gavin thought he had never seen anything so heartbreakingly lovely. He started to back out of the room, trying to maneuver the tray so that he could close the door and knock to awaken her. He backed into Melinda.

"Here, I'll take it," Melinda said matter-of-factly. She took the tray from him as he tried to get past her into the hallway.

"I thought she was awake. I'm sorry. . . ."

"Don't be. George has told me how you found her."

There was certainly no embarrassment in Melinda's face, just tenderness as she looked past him at the naked girl. "My God, she is lovely, isn't she?" Melinda sighed. "And so goddamned *young*."

"Certainly different from the last time I saw her like that," said Gavin. "You could count every rib."

"It must have been terrible," Melinda said softly. "Well, we'd better wake her now."

"You better do it," Gavin said.

Melinda watched him go, his broad shoulders almost filling the narrow passageway, moving with his athlete's grace until his red head disappeared down the stairs. She put the tray on the bedside table and stood looking down at Ericka's enchanting nakedness, a very thoughtful expression on her face. Happily in love with *being* in love, Melinda wanted everyone else to be happy, too. Gavin Riordan was such a beautiful man. . . .

Despite Melinda's protests and Hughette's outrage that such a thing should be allowed, Ericka came downstairs for dinner the next evening. She was determined to make an event of it. Not too reluctantly Melinda gave in and invited both Ivan ven der Veen and Paul Geroux for dinner. The two days she hadn't seen Paul seemed a lifetime to Melinda.

To Gavin it was touchingly obvious how it was between Melinda and Paul. Their love for each other was so transparent it was almost embarrassing. He felt a mild envy at their happiness.

Hughette had outdone herself with roast ducks and a chestnut puree, light as a feather. Ericka tucked into hers like a longshoreman. At first everyone at the table stole anxious glances at her, treating her as though she had some terminal disease that could take her off at any moment. Gavin was amused at how she handled it.

"Quit it," Ericka said to all of them. "There's nothing wrong with me except a lump on my head. I'm not going to fall on my face, as you seem to expect. So just quit looking at me like that. As a matter of fact, I'm going back to school tomorrow."

It was said with such finality that no one protested. Ericka smiled at them in turn and said, "There, that's better. And I'll have some more duck, if you please." And then to Gavin, "Could you tell me what happened at the riot, Mr. Riordan? I seem to have missed most of the action."

Ericka was looking at him with an expression that belied the lightness of her question. Gavin had spent part of that morning on the phone, arguing with Ten Tabard about a certain Jean-Baptiste Moreau, and he thought he knew what was on her mind. He hadn't been able to forget the image of her throwing herself on the man to protect him.

"Well," he said, "it turned out to be a beaut, even for Paris. Official figures say more than ten thousand people were involved eventually. The thing lasted about four hours before the police finally damped it down. The box score is scary. Four *Jeune Nation*, or *Poujardistes*, or whatever they're called, were killed. Three Algerian nationalists and a labor union secretary also got it. There were two hundred and thirty injured—eighty-two of them cops. Six hundred and nine arrests. Your friend Moreau was one of them, by the way. He's all right, though. I had a word with Captain Tabard, and he'll be released tomorrow."

"Thank you," she said calmly. "That was thoughtful of you."

He didn't tell her that by the time he got to quai des Orfèvres, Moreau had already undergone Ten Tabard's brand of interrogation and was now in the police hospital, recovering from it. Tabard had only agreed to release him because all his "persuasion" had failed to make Moreau confess to anything that could be held against him. Moreau wouldn't be a pretty sight for days to come.

By the time Hughette served coffee in the living room, it became obvious to Gavin, if not to the others, that Melinda and Paul Geroux could hardly wait to get away. Melinda was doing everything but biting her nails, while Geroux lit one cigarette after another and stubbed them out half-smoked. Gavin decided to lend a helping hand.

"Why don't you two show me a little Paris nightlife? I haven't had much chance—so far. I was told not to miss the Grand Guignol in Montmartre."

"Why don't we, Paul?" Melinda said eagerly. "I've never seen it, either."

George, who had never cared for the show when he was a student, said he thought he'd stay home with the young people.

On the sidewalk outside the house, Gavin said, "Look, all I really wanted was a walk and a little fresh air. I'm sure you two have something better to do. So why don't you take off?"

Melinda squeezed his hand. "You don't miss much, do you?" She reached up and gave him a quick kiss on the cheek. "Gavin, you're a dear. And thanks." Paul Geroux shook his hand, started to say something and then merely smiled. Gavin left them trying to flag down a taxi.

From Here to Eternity was playing at the Pagoda Cinéma, and on impulse he bought a ticket and went in. When he got back to the house on rue Babylone he slipped in quietly and was headed for the stairs when Ericka called from the living room. She was curled up with a book in a deep easy chair. She had changed into a white terrycloth robe, her hair now in a ponytail tied with a pink ribbon. The embers of a dying fire flecked her huge green eyes with pinpoints of gold.

"I waited up to thank you for helping Jean-Baptiste. He'll really be all right?"

"Sure," Gavin said. "Slightly bloody, but still unbowed."

"Why did you do it? I mean, how did you . . . ?"

Gavin began to grin. "I saw your heroics, remember? I figured he must mean *something* to you." Then suddenly serious, "Are you in love with him?"

She took her time, her face grave and thoughtful. Then she gave

284

an impatient shake of her head. "I don't really know. I've never been in love, so I don't know what it feels like. I do feel *something* for him. But I don't know. . . ."

Gavin's grin came back. "Believe me, you'll know when it happens. No mistake about it."

"I wonder if I'll ever . . . ?" Her voice held a sadness, as though she knew something she was withholding from him, saw something in herself he couldn't see. She got up and walked past him to the stairway. On the second step she paused and looked back at him. "Well, thanks anyway. It was . . . kind of you."

"Good night, Ericka. And sleep tight."

Her look was enigmatic. "I wasn't asleep, you know."

For a moment he didn't know what she meant.

Two days before Gavin was to leave for the States, Melinda announced at breakfast that all plans for that evening were to be canceled. She was giving a surprise dinner—"just for the family"— because she had something she wanted them all to hear. She refused to say more. Ericka had to leave for classes and hadn't time for questions. George Barnstable looked at his sister affectionately.

"You've got that look in your eye. I know you're up to something."

Melinda blew him a kiss. "You'll just have to wait."

To Gavin, George said, "She's done this to me all my life. She would never tell me what she was going to give me for Christmas. But she'd tease me for days by making me guess."

"Christmas is seven days away," Melinda said. "So you'll have a whole week to speculate. But tonight is something different. Tonight is just for me."

When George had left for his building site, Gavin poured a last cup of coffee for the two of them, and they sat in comfortable silence smoking after-breakfast cigarettes. Gavin, who had heard Melinda sneak in close to four o'clock, was struck by her dewy freshness just four hours later. Gavin would never lose his policeman's habit of watching other people's body language or trying to read the thoughts behind the masks we show to each other. Now Melinda had a sort of radiance about her. Whatever her surprise turned out to be, she was obviously delighted with it.

"Look," he said, "if this is only 'family,' why don't I go out to dinner? I don't want to intrude. . . ."

Melinda came back from wherever she had been and reached across the table to take his hand.

"No, you don't." Her eyes were serious, but there was a small smile on her lips. "I want you here. Somehow it seems right for you to be here. You are a part of all our lives, Gavin. Without you there wouldn't *be* a family. We owe you a lot, dear Gavin."

Gavin felt a sudden smarting in his eyes. What she said had taken him completely by surprise. He was appalled at the thought that he might cry. He cleared his throat before he could speak.

"You know," he said. "That may be the nicest thing anyone ever said to me."

The first surprise of the evening was the presence of Paul Geroux. For the first time their love for each other was out in the open. Melinda flaunted it as if it were no longer important to hide behind the proprieties. Over cocktails in the living room she perched on the arm of his chair and couldn't keep from touching him.

Gavin caught the amusement in Ericka's eyes and George's faint surprise. But even George's innate conventionality wasn't proof against their shining happiness, and soon they were all infected by it. The air of anticipation was almost tangible. Gavin knew something had to happen, but he couldn't for the life of him imagine what.

Melinda, enjoying every moment, let it go on as long as possible. She and Paul, sharing the secret, kept smiling foolishly at each other like naughty children.

Geroux, a slim, compact man whose hair had started to go gray at the temples, was what the French would call *distingué*. He had an air, a manner, that commanded attention. Now he seemed to alternate between blushing and going pale, like a schoolboy asked an impossibly embarrassing question.

Ericka finally broke it up. "Melinda, lick the feathers off your chin and tell us what it is before I bust."

"We-e-ell," Melinda drew it out, "with the help of God, the pope, the Vatican secretary and the Catholic Church—in that order. . . I think Paul and I can get married. Paul's wife has agreed with him to petition the Vatican to annul their marriage. I don't know just how it works, but Paul says it can."

Paul Geroux was smiling and holding Melinda's hand. "I assure you, it *can* be done. I have spoken to my uncle, the Cardinal of Lyons. And he has spoken to His Holiness in Rome. The answer is favorable. Provided certain procedures are followed. There are donations involved, quite sizeable ones. I will be a poor man, I think, before it's over."

"As if that mattered," Melinda scoffed.

"By God, I love this country!" George said. "*Si tout s'arrange,* if that's the proper phrase. Everything can be arranged—if you have the right uncles."

Ericka dropped to her knees beside Melinda and hugged her tightly. The tableau brought home to Gavin once more the enviable closeness of this family. He felt an overwhelming happiness for them all, grateful that he had been asked to share it with them.

"Of course," Geroux said, "we must be very careful until everything is settled. The Church is most firm about that. There must be no hint of scandal."

"So we're going to Japan." Melinda was breathless. "As far away as we can get. Where nobody will know us."

"How long? How long will it take, do you think?"

"A few months, my uncle tells me. No more."

Hughette announced dinner. Either Melinda had briefed her or she had felt in her Gallic bones the importance of the occasion. There was a rack of lamb done exactly to the proper pinkness, firm tender flageolet beans and small white potatoes glazed with a hint of brown sugar. George unearthed a magnificent Bordeaux, which even Gavin's amateur palate could appreciate.

Gavin could never remember exactly what was said at that festive meal. The talk was in half-sentences. Few words were needed—they seemed able to divine each other's meanings, understand unspoken thoughts. Toward the end of the third bottle of wine, George got to his feet and lifted his glass.

"A toast."

"Only if I can drink it, too," Melinda said laughingly. There was

287

a fine sheen of perspiration on her upper lip. Her face was delicately flushed, her eyes sparkling in the candlelight.

"Of course, hon," George agreed. "A toast—to all of us. May we all be as happy as you two are now."

George drained his glass. Paul Geroux took a proper swallow of his wine, Ericka a sip of hers. Gavin raised his goblet. His toast was privately to Melinda. He thought he had never seen anything more appealing than her shining radiance.

Melinda took one last bite of lamb before she raised her glass. Her toast was to her lover. Her eyes were suddenly misty with tenderness.

And then she choked.

Her eyes widened alarmingly as she tried to take a breath. And couldn't.

Gavin, who realized instantly what had happened, was around the table in two long strides, while the others sat frozen. He began to pound Melinda on the back, the only thing he could think to do. He could hear the awful sound in her throat and feel the convulsion of her muscles as she fought for air.

"For Christ's sake, call a doctor! She's choking!"

It broke the paralysis. Paul Geroux went on the run toward the phone in the living room. Ericka and George watched helplessly as Gavin pried open Melinda's locked jaws and probed her throat with his finger, trying to dislodge whatever was there. With some detached part of his mind he listened to Paul Geroux struggling with the abominable French telephone system and knew suddenly that it was too late. Melinda's body went limp. She slid off the chair onto the floor.

She was dead before he could pick her up again.

Paul, Gavin and George accompanied the body to the States. Ericka had made no protest when George insisted that she stay at school. She was detached and remote, but in her eyes was the same question that was agonizingly in them all: *Why, dear God, why?*

Melinda Barnstable Price was buried in the family plot in Marblehead, Massachusetts, among her distinguished ancestors. It was a gray, comfortless day. A misty cold rain fell as an Episcopal minister read the service for the dead. George Barnstable and Paul Geroux were dry-eyed and silent. It was only Riordan, with his Irish emotion, who wept.

19

Time: 1956
DESMOND PATRICK DANIHER

The years had not been kind to Angelo Pavane. Daniher reckoned that Pavane couldn't be much more than sixty. His glossy black hair was now reduced to a few strands carefully combed from one side of his head to the other. His little eyes disappeared in folds of fat. His heavy belly pushed against the table. There was a fine beading of sweat on Pavane's sallow skin, although air in the restaurant was cold. To Des Daniher's acute senses the sweat had the smell of fear. These two old allies were meeting out of state, where neither of them would be recognized.

The napkin tucked into Pavane's collar was streaked with sauce from the rapidly diminishing mound of spaghetti Pavane shoveled into his mouth. Fear didn't spoil his appetite, apparently. But if Pavane was running scared, Daniher had best find out what was bothering him. "I hope your books are clean, Angelo. Because these people are pushing pretty hard. You get a subpoena yet?"

Pavane nodded, swallowed and stopped eating long enough to say "You?"

"Oh, yes. Fishing expedition only, I think. The Republicans need some headlines to reelect their idiot in the statehouse."

Pavane wiped his mouth on the stained napkin, dropped it on the floor and pushed his empty plate away. "What you gonna tell 'em?"

"Depends on what they ask."

Pavane belched softly. "How long you and me been partners, Des?"

Daniher allowed his eyebrows to rise, kept his face bland. "Partners, Angelo? We've never been that. I've merely advised you. As a lawyer. From time to time."

"Hey, Des, come on." Pavane's eyes opened a little wider. "You got stock in the coal company, the breweries, the cement company" —he began to tick off the items on his stubby fingers—"the construction company, the State Street Maintenance, Acme Vending, Capital Bus Lines . . . and International Hotels. Don't forget them hotels. What do you call that if it ain't partners? You set the whole *schmeer* up."

"I'm not the attorney of record in any of those," Daniher said gently. "Your son Patsy is. As for the stocks, a lot of people own stock. I have nothing to hide there." What Daniher neglected to say was that there wasn't a single share of stock on which the name Desmond Patrick Daniher appeared.

Angelo Pavane's hands were now on the table. Daniher watched those bloated fingers writhe together like so many pale sausages, waiting for what he knew was coming.

"What are you trying to tell me, Des? That you ain't in with me up to your eyeballs?"

"Exactly that, Angelo. All I've ever done was advise. Lawyer-client relationship. I suggested—*suggested*, mind you—that there were ways to clean up dirty money. If a man had a lot of dirty money to clean up." Daniher smiled his soft Irish smile. "Why, it never occurred to me that *you* would ever have such a need. Perish the thought."

"And that's what you'll tell the fuckin' commissioner?"

"If they ever get around to asking me, which I doubt."

Pavane was looking at him. His eyes were cold and bleak. "Des," he said. "You don't see it. You're a problem to me, Des. We go back a lotta years. I don't like you to be a problem."

The room became suddenly stuffy and hot. "What's that supposed to mean?" Daniher asked.

"Your boy Lieutenant Gavin Riordan. He *is* the investigation. He

290

is getting too close. And I want him stopped. It's what I been payin' you for."

Pavane's hands were still now.

Daniher felt a rage building in him and knew he must conceal it, damp it down. His mind went back around a lifetime of corners, through a thousand dark rooms filled with silent faces. He knew that Angelo Pavane could and would do exactly what he had to do. Des Daniher knew all this because over the years, in his careful lawyer's way, he had documented most of it. He knew where all the bodies were buried—or enough of them to fill a graveyard. Angelo Pavane's graveyard, if need be. Pavane didn't hold all the cards yet. "I can't do that," Daniher said softly.

Pavane took out a silk handkerchief and wiped the perspiration from his face. "You got no choice." Pavane sounded oddly reasonable. "I go, you go. Think about it."

Daniher smiled grimly. "A chance I'll have to take, Angelo." He folded his napkin, placed it carefully on the table by his half-empty plate and got to his feet. "Thanks for the lunch. I'll be going now."

Pavane raised his right forefinger and waved it slowly before Daniher's face. The star sapphire held Daniher's eyes like a magnet. "Control your boy. I ask you for both our sakes."

"I can but try." He gave Pavane a formal nod and left. Pavane turned his big body to watch him go.

When the door had closed, Pavane motioned to a young man who had been sitting quietly at the rear of the restaurant. When the young man stood beside him he gestured toward the door. There was no need for words. The young man nodded and slipped silently from the room.

Daniher was one of the first to board the small feeder plane that would take him back to the city. He took a window seat near the rear of the plane and, as was his habit, watched the other passengers as they went past. Daniher was interested in people. They were a constant source of enjoyment and speculation to him. The young man hesitated and glanced down at Daniher before he made his way up the aisle. Daniher wondered briefly at his interest but, because he couldn't fit him into any instant category, dismissed him from his mind and settled back to do some thinking.

Desmond Daniher reflected on the years he had known Angelo Pavane. To Daniher the acquisition of wealth for wealth's sake was a foolish vanity. A fatal flaw in a man like Pavane. Money as such meant little to Daniher. He still lived in the frame house he had bought when he married. His needs were simple, his desires modest. The considerable income he derived from his law practice went where it would do the most good. To people. To people he either needed or who needed him.

Money had its uses, but it couldn't buy what Daniher wanted. It couldn't buy power. Only knowledge could provide power. Knowledge was the real key to the control of men and events. With the knowledge and information he had about Pavane he could put the man behind bars any time he decided to. And it might come to that. Without repercussions. His skirts were clean. He had made no personal profit out of Pavane's operations. Except legitimate legal fees. All of which were justified. Every man had a right to legal representation. His advice to Pavane had been personal—and private. No witnesses.

No, Pavane couldn't hurt him. Unless Pavane knew something he, Daniher, didn't. So why the threat? *I go, you go.*

Angelo Pavane was a worried man. Worried men were unpredictable. And therefore dangerous. Daniher had meant it when he told Pavane that his son Patsy was a good lawyer. He was careful, cautious—and ambitious. Daniher found it hard to believe that Patsy Pavane would leave either his father or himself vulnerable to the kind of snooping the Belding commission was doing. Patsy Pavane's books and records would be impeccable. Besides, Belding's staff wasn't equipped for that kind of investigation. Uncovering Pavane's hidden empire would take batteries of highly expert accountants, Internal Revenue people, Treasury—in short, the federal government. Belding's area was strictly the City and possibly the state.

In that area the Belding commission was doing well. Both Onderdonk and Gavin were good cops, and Judge Marcus Belding was incorruptible. Thirty-one indictments in the police department, eight convictions so far. Twelve voluntary retirements. Mostly on

Gavin's evidence. Young Gavin was getting to be something of a hero. Glamour cop. The newspapers loved him. And more to come. But the commission was getting nowhere near the Pavane empire.

So what was making Angelo Pavane sweat? And why Gavin? What was Gavin on to that was putting the fear of God into Pavane? He couldn't ask Gavin. Maybe Gus Onderdonk? Pavane didn't make idle threats. Was he worried enough to put out a contract on Gavin? Did Patsy Pavane know what was eating on his old man? Patsy wouldn't stand for the old rough stuff. Patsy was legit. He had too much going for him to risk. . . . Perhaps Patsy should be told about this meeting.

Daniher had parked his car at the airport. He reclaimed it and drove to his home. He left his coat and hat in the hall and went into the living room. Something drew his glance to the window. The young man who had noticed him on the plane was paying off a cab. Through the lace curtains he watched the young man walk to the corner newsstand, buy a paper, move to a recessed doorway across the street and become absorbed in reading.

Belding commission snoop? Surely not. No real reason. Unless they were trying to connect him with Pavane. Then Pavane? More likely. And, if so, very, very interesting. Yes, it was time to get through to Patsy Pavane. . . .

He left the window, went through to the den and poured himself a generous glass of Bushmill's. He sipped at it thoughtfully before he picked up the phone.

What Patsy Pavane told him was a shock, but it didn't solve his problem. He learned that the old man had terminal cancer, complicated, if that was the word, by advanced syphilis, which had begun to affect his brain. As for what was on his mind now, Patsy had no idea. He promised to look into it.

The next morning Daniher found out himself without Patsy's help. At the early morning audience he held each day for the people of his ward, his secretary Meg O'Day handed him the briefing card of a woman named Maria Mangione. He went back a long way with Maria Mangione. All the way back to his days as a young lawyer in

Little Italy. He had defended her husband successfully on a homicide charge that turned out to be a bum rap. When her nineteen-year-old son Vito had suffered brain damage in a construction accident, it had been Daniher who had made both the union and the construction company pony up for the best brain surgeon in the state. When it had turned out that the boy would be partially disabled permanently, Daniher had arranged for top dollar from workmen's compensation and a hefty settlement from the insurance company. He also had gotten Vito a job with the parks department, a job he still held. Daniher looked at the card Meg O'Day had given him.

> Maria Mangione: widow
> Age: 68
> Occupation: housekeeper
> Employer: Angelo Pavane, 142 River Street
> Registered Democrat
> Church of Our Lady (Father Logiodice)

The woman Meg O'Day ushered in looked closer to fifty than the sixty-eight years the card indicated. She hadn't changed a hell of a lot over the years, Daniher thought. Strong, sturdy body, black hair just tinged with gray, eyes full of peasant shrewdness, her olive-skinned face just now creased with worry.

She looked at Meg O'Day and said, "Please, Mr. Daniher. Just you alone. No offense, but . . ."

Daniher nodded and Meg O'Day slipped silently from the room. Daniher pretended to study the card in his hand, wondering what in God's name Angelo Pavane's housekeeper had to tell him for his ears alone. When she continued to stare at him wordlessly, he said, "How is Vito? All right, I hope."

The question seemed to confuse her. "What? Oh . . . Vito is fine. Mr. Daniher, he's writing it all down. Everything he does, from the very beginning . . ."

The woman's anxiety was very real. Alarm bells began to ring in Daniher's head. "Who," he asked carefully, "is writing what down?"

"Mr. Pavane. I read part. When he left it out on the table. He

294

done terrible things. I never knew. . . . I am afraid. But I had to tell you . . . because you are in it, too."

Daniher went to the door and opened it. When he was sure that no one was in the corridor, he closed it carefully and came back to his chair. "Now, Mrs. Mangione. There's no reason to be afraid. Nothing you say will ever leave this room. Now, tell me exactly what you saw. . . ."

Half an hour later he had it all, and it appalled him.

"Tell me, Mrs. Mangione. Have you relatives in Italy?"

The woman looked at him in bewilderment and then nodded.

"I think perhaps you should pay them a visit. In the meantime . . ." He raised his voice, "Miss O'Day," and when she appeared, "Take Mrs. Mangione to Mary Margaret Shay. She'll be spending a few days with us. After that, it's off to the Old Country." He patted the distraught woman gently on the shoulder. "It's better this way, believe me. I'll take care of everything. You'll have a nice visit with your relatives. You and Vito together. And then later I'll send for you. And don't worry about money. This one is on the house." He turned to Meg O'Day. "Get the information you need from her. Adresses, names, tickets, the works. And, Miss O'Day, there's no real need for anyone but us to know about these arrangements. Am I clear?"

"Yes, Mr. Daniher." Meg O'Day looked him in the eye, her face enigmatic.

He reached Patsy Pavane at home on his private line.

"Guess what," Daniher said. "Your old man is writing a book."

It was two days before Patsy Pavane called him. "It's worse than you thought. There's over two hundred pages of it. The works. The doctors told me the paresis was getting to his brain. But I didn't know he was *that* crazy. Jesus, God, he could have got us all hung. We'd better have a meet."

Daniher smiled. "Your place or mine?"

Patsy Pavane paused briefly, then said, "How about the Public Library. Nine sharp. When it opens."

"As long as there's an easy chair to read in, I'll be there."

Daniher was still smiling as he hung up. Sometimes he covered up even when alone. He still didn't know what Gavin was on to that was spooking Angelo so badly. It couldn't be the notebook. So what the hell was it?

The quiet hush of the reading room was broken only by the rustle of pages turned by the few people who sat at the long tables at this hour of the morning and the hushed voices of the clerks at the inquiry desk. Daniher chose a deserted table in a far corner of the huge vaulted room and sat down to wait.

Patsy Pavane was five minutes late. Daniher watched as he made his way down the aisle and pulled out the chair next to him. Pavane put his briefcase on the table, flipped the catches and handed Daniher a bulging looseleaf notebook. Daniher opened it and began to read. Pavane clasped his hands on the table, leaned back in his chair and closed his eyes.

In the hour it took Daniher to absorb what was in the notebook, Pavane didn't move. From time to time Daniher glanced at him and noted the deep circles under his eyes, the faint lines of fatigue.

"Well," Daniher said at last.

Pavane opened his eyes and smiled tiredly. "Something, isn't it?"

It was hard for Daniher to believe that Patsy Pavane was the result of any union his father could possibly have consummated. What Daniher saw was a tall, compact young man dressed in Brooks Brothers gray flannel. Unlike his father's, Patsy's fingers were long and lean. Daniher could recall from the old days those hands catching the passes Gavin wafted to him on the green turf of South Side High. Patsy had a pleasant open face and a genuine smile and large brown eyes, both a heritage from a mother Daniher could barely remember.

Daniher closed the covers of Angelo Pavane's diary and took a deep breath. "No style. But I'll grant that he has a flair for the dramatic. What got into him?"

Patsy gazed at him, immobile. Then he said, "You should see the rest of what was in that safe." He let that sink in. After a while he went on. "He couldn't change, you know. He was like one of the old dons. He had to run his own show. He trusted nobody. Not even me. So he got an outside guy to do his records. There was enough in that safe for the IRS to put him away for life. Just his personal operation. Nothing that could blow the rest of the organization."

Pavane gestured to the thick looseleaf folder Daniher still held. "Except that. Dynamite."

Daniher noted that Patsy was talking of Angelo Pavane in the past tense.

"What now?" he asked.

A look of intense pain crossed Pavane's face and was gone.

"Why not leave it to God?" Daniher asked. "You say he is a very sick man."

Patsy shook his head slowly. "No. Too risky. With the stuff that's eating away his brain, who knows . . ."

"Have you talked to your . . . friends about it?"

"No. It's my problem. Not theirs."

"They may not like that," Daniher said.

"He's *my* father," Pavane grated. "Goddamnit! *My* family. I will take care of it." He would not meet Daniher's eyes.

Daniher considered him thoughtfully. "There may be another way," he said softly. "If you're willing to sacrifice a few heads. You would be in the clear—or as near as may be. No connection. All it would take is some judicious editing of what you found in that safe. Leave a few bones for the law. Enough to make it look good. . . ."

"I'm listening."

As Daniher talked he saw the hope begin to dawn in Patsy's face. When he finished, Patsty asked, "You're willing to take the risk?"

"That I am," Daniher said, and waved a hand. "Besides, the risk is small. They'll have no reason to doubt me. Merely a good citizen doing his duty."

Patsy Pavane held out his hand. Daniher took it. "You have my deepest thanks, Mr. Daniher. If ever . . ."

"And this," Daniher tapped the notebook in front of him. "I'll feel the better for it if I'm the one to dispose of it."

Pavane nodded soberly. "You have the right."

"Of course," Daniher said slowly, "once he's in custody the problem is back in your lap."

"He'll never come to trial." Pavane's face was expressionless. "His health wouldn't permit it. I assure you."

297

As they left the library Daniher brought up what had been bothering him for several days.

"He was worried about Gavin when we talked. Something about Gavin getting too close. Any idea?"

"None. I'll look into it."

What Gavin Riordan had was a man named Leon Schwartz, known in the trade as a figure nut, a man who could cook a set of books faster than you could boil an egg. Gavin had him stashed in a ramshackle motel in a small town just north of the City. Two members of the Belding commission task force were baby-sitting Leon night and day, along with a tape recorder that was never turned off.

Leon Schwartz was happy to be where he was, because his alternatives were unthinkable. He was cooperating—but very slowly. Just enough to maintain the status quo. Gavin visited him every other day and was getting very impatient with Leon's coyness.

Leon Schwartz had an unimpressive record, a mere two-year stretch in Dannemora for embezzlement. It was easy time because embezzlers, bank robbers and narcotics big shots are at the top of the heap in any prison, very respected people. Even so, Leon barely made it with all his marbles. He couldn't take prison. Another six months would have put him in the psychiatric ward.

The next stretch would be quite different, because Gavin had him for impairing the morals of a minor, child molestation and sodomy rape. Enough to put him away for ten to twenty. Unlike embezzlers, child molesters are the lowest form of life in the prison pecking order, contemptible, subject to every harassment and indignity the inmates can dream up—including gang rape. It would be very hard time, and Schwartz knew with utter certainty that he couldn't take it.

There was an added complication. When Schwartz had been released from prison he went to work for Carmine Buglione, who owned the Empire Race Track and was the son-in-law of Angelo Pavane. Carmine couldn't resist taking advantage of Schwartz's undoubted genius at manipulating figures. Under Schwartz's guidance he began to skim off the top of the track's daily seven-million-dollar take. Since the track was under the supervision of the state racing commission, this was a dangerous thing to do. However, the scam seemed foolproof. It could only be discovered from the inside. Which, of course, it was.

When Patsy Pavane got the information he immediately blew the whistle. As a legitimate operation the track was an endless gold mine. It seemed outrageous to Patsy that anyone would be stupid enough or greedy enough to jeopardize it. He proposed that a first-priority contract be put out on Carmine Buglione. It was only through the determined intervention of Angelo Pavane that his son-in-law didn't end up in cement. The upshot was that Carmine was allowed to keep his job, but only under close supervision.

Leon Schwartz was fired. And immediately rehired. By Angelo Pavane, as his personal accountant. Angelo knew a good man when he saw one. The relationship lasted for six years, and at the end of that time Schwartz knew everything there was to know about the operation of Angelo Pavane's end of the family business.

It was then that Leon Schwartz had been picked up on a morals charge. The victim was a twelve-year-old girl, and the identification was solid. No way out. Gavin heard about it almost immediately through a friend, and used his Belding commission authority to obtain custody and spirit Schwartz away from the local police.

Leon Schwartz had now been missing from his usual haunts for eight days. Which was what had caused Angelo Pavane to demand a secret meeting with Desmond Daniher.

Gavin couldn't believe his luck. He knew all about Leon Schwartz and he knew that he had him by the balls. Sooner or later Schwartz would sing. It was only a matter of time. But time was precious, for sooner or later Angelo Pavane would find out where Schwartz was stashed. And the shit would hit the fan. Gavin had no illusions about what Angelo Pavane would do to shut Schwartz's mouth.

Schwartz refused to do any serious talking to anyone but Gavin Riordan. He treated the two task force men as his personal nursemaids. He knew his own importance and he never let them forget it. They soon grew to hate the sight of him. In the meantime Leon Schwartz enjoyed rare steaks and bourbon.

Des Daniher's name came up on the day of interrogation. And

again on the sixth. Gavin didn't push it because he dreaded to hear that Daniher was criminally involved. In passing he learned that Daniher had been given stock in a number of Pavane's companies. Legitimate companies. At least on the surface. What Daniher had done in return for the stock was another matter. Gavin let it lie. For the moment. He was after Angelo Pavane.

And he was getting what he wanted. Among his other talents Leon Schwartz had a photographic memory. He quoted names, dates, places and amounts of payoffs to various public officials, law officers, criminal-courts judges and, in one instance, to a state supreme court justice. He linked Angelo Pavane personally with two unsolved gang murders. He described the various ways the Pavane interests laundered the dirty money from loan sharking, prostitution, numbers and narcotics.

And on the eighth day of the interrogation, without being aware of Gavin's relationship, he casually let drop that Desmond Daniher had set it all up.

Gavin thought for a moment of erasing what he had just heard from the tape recorder. He watched the slowly spinning reels with a sick fascination—and found he couldn't do it. *Protect yourself in the clinches, Des. You're the one who said it.* He was filled with unreasoning rage that this little toad in front of him would be the means to bring Des Daniher down.

What Leon Schwartz was giving them was great stuff. No doubt of it. But without corroboration there was every chance that it wouldn't stand up in a court of law. They needed books, records, something in black and white, figures that wouldn't lie. Such things existed, for Schwartz had told them so. The question was where. And that's what Schwartz was holding out on. He wanted a deal.

Gavin could feel it coming. Something in Schwartz's mean little eyes told him that the moment had arrived. The other two cops felt it, too. "Look," Schwartz said finally, "I give you what you want. I tell you where to find everything you need. But I gotta walk out clean. My life ain't worth a nickel if I don't. No rape charge. No nothing. An' you gotta bury me a mile until you put him away for good. Otherwise . . ." Schwartz smiled nervously and held out his hands in appeal. "Jesus, you guys know how it is. I gotta have protection. Or I'm deader than Kelsey's nuts."

Now was the time for promises. Assurances of safety. Anything to get the information. Gavin could see the wet patches where sweat had soaked through Schwartz's shirt, the fine beads of perspiration on his forehead. But in his eyes there was triumph. Suddenly Gavin couldn't bear the thought that Schwartz would walk away clean from everything, a free man—to do it all over again.

"No deal," he said through his teeth, "you fucking little creep. No fucking deal! You're going up for everything we can throw at you. You'll do hard time. Very hard time. I'll see to it personally!"

Schwartz looked at him unbelievingly, his pale face mirroring his outrage. Then he turned to the two task force cops. "What's with him? You guys know you gotta deal. You'll never find the stuff without I tell you."

The two cops were as puzzled as Schwartz. This wasn't how things were supposed to go. There was nothing to do but play along. Schwartz saw that they would be no help to him. He looked back to Gavin's implacable face and realized that Gavin meant everything he had said. Suddenly anger took over.

"Fuck you guys! Without me you got nothin'. I just turned into a clam. You can stuff it up your ass!"

Gavin hit him. Not once but again and again and again. By the time the two task force men pulled him off, Schwartz's face was a sickening pulp. But he had begun to talk, although it was hard to understand what came out of the bloody gap where his front teeth had been. It was then that Gavin learned about Angelo Pavane's diary. That, and all the evidence required to put him away for life, was in the wall safe at Pavane's house in the City.

An hour later Gavin parked his car in the police lot. From the backseat he took the suitcase full of tapes that could break the back of organized crime in the City. Tapes that might ruin Des Daniher, if not worse. As he headed for Gus Onderdonk's office he reflected that the worst he had feared had come to pass; his professional triumph was gall in his mouth. Well, he had got the job done. Now it was up to Belding and Onderdonk.

Onderdonk was on the phone. Gavin waited impatiently, not really listening to what was being said. Until a phrase caught at him. "Will he be all right?" Onderdonk listened and then said, "Keep me informed. I want the best there is for him."

Onderdonk hung up and stared at Gavin. "You," Onderdonk said softly, "are one lucky bastard. You must have just missed it."

"Missed what?"

"A bomb. At the motel. They got Charlie Evans. And Schwartz. Bradock was in the can, so they tell me he's okay. But he may lose a leg. They won't know for a while."

Gavin was still holding the suitcase. He hefted it onto Onderdonk's desk.

"This time the son of a bitch won't get away with it. It's all in there on tape. Enough to throw away the key. He'll never see the outside again. All I need is a search warrant for Pavane's house. The corroboration is in his safe."

Onderdonk was looking at him strangely, his bristly eyebrows raised.

"Forget it, kid. We picked him up less than an hour ago. And we got what was in the safe. He's in the detention cage now, screaming his head off for a lawyer. Who no doubt will have him sprung by nightfall. But we've got all we need to hang him."

"Who?" asked Gavin.

"The tip came from your Uncle Des," Onderdonk said slowly. "I thought you knew. . . ." Then, seeing that Gavin didn't, "It seems Pavane's housekeeper. . . ."

Gavin turned and ran.

Desmond Daniher was lunching at the Capital Grille with an upstate senator. Testing the waters, he would have called it—an endless process for Daniher.

"We'll keep what we've got in the senate. And this time I think we'll have the assembly as well. The governor is another matter. The son of a bitch is getting too many headlines." The senator dipped the end of his expensive cigar into his Three Star Hennessey, both of which Daniher had provided, and searched his pockets for a match. It was then that the news of the bombing came over the radio behind the bar. Through the senator's pompous chatter Daniher heard only that two members of the Belding commission task force had been killed, along with a third man. None of the victims were identified by name.

Daniher had one of the few instants of sheer panic he had ever experienced. For a moment the restaurant became dim and wavering. He had the curious sensation that his body was slowly floating from the chair to the floor. When he recovered he was still in his chair, seeing the concerned face of the senator and hearing the man say, "You all right? You looked like a ghost there. . . ."

"It's nothing," Daniher said. "A little indigestion." He excused himself and went to the men's room. From the wall phone he called Gus Onderdonk. As he listened to the ringing of the phone he knew with utter certainty that the bonbing was the result of whatever Gavin had been working on. *If Gavin . . . ?* He couldn't face the thought.

When Onderdonk came on the line, Daniher could say only, "Gavin?" His voice sounded strange in his own ears, and he was surprised that Onderdonk identified him immediately.

"He's okay," Onderdonk said. "They missed him. But it was close. He . . ."

Onderdonk wanted to tell him what had happened, but Daniher cut him off by hanging up the receiver because the bile was rising in his throat. He barely made it to the toilet booth.

When he came out he was shaking with exhaustion. He hadn't wanted to hear the details from Onderdonk. He wanted to hear them from Patsy Pavane, because he had the strong suspicion that Pavane had crossed him. That Patsy had decided to kill all the birds with one bang. He could hear himself giving Patsy the information that Gavin was onto something. What was more logical than for Patsy to . . . ? It was another thought he couldn't face.

He put another coin in the wall phone. He dialed very slowly because his hand was still trembling. When Pavane answered, Daniher said only, "I want the truth. Level with me."

Pavane's voice was calm and unhurried. "I know what you're thinking. Don't jump, Mr. Daniher. It was the outside accountant I mentioned to you. Gavin had him. The old man's people were out looking for days. I learned about it only this morning. By then it was too late. They already found him."

"This morning?" Daniher said slowly. "You didn't bust your ass to let me know what was going down."

"No, I didn't, Mr. Daniher." Pavane let the words hang.

Slowly Daniher replaced the receiver.

When Daniher got home, Mary Margaret told him that Gavin was waiting for him. He took his time hanging up his coat. In the hall mirror he set his gray fedora more firmly on his head.

Gavin was on the window seat, staring out into the backyard. Daniher put a hand on his shoulder and squeezed gently, feeling the ridge of muscle beneath the fabric. "Thank God you're all right. Gus told me it was close. The luck of the Irish. May it ever be with you."

Gavin's eyes bored into his. His voice was hoarse with anger. "Luck! Two men died in that lousy motel. And you talk about luck!"

"Oh . . . ?" Daniher removed his hand, rounded the corner of his desk and sat down in his ancient swivel chair. "I thought it was three. The radio said it was three."

"Ed Bradock is alive. He may lose a leg."

"Infinite mercy," Daniher said. "Thank God it was no worse for the poor lad."

"Don't give me that pious shit, Des. Not now."

"I'm feeling pious," Daniher said mildly. "At the moment. What would you have me say? I regret what happened. But right now I'm just thankful that you're alive."

"Regret!" Gavin grated. "Is that how it is? You have *regrets*?"

"I do," Daniher admitted, "and I don't. I can't be responsible for every gangster whose brains are scrambled with syphilis."

"But you were *in* it, Goddamnit! I spent eight days with that creep Schwartz, and he spilled his guts. You were in it all the way. It's all on tape. Every dirty word of it."

Daniher's palm hit the desk like a pistol shot. "*Words!* And what the hell are words? You listen to me, boy. And listen good. I never took a dollar from Angelo Pavane that I didn't earn honestly. You better believe it—because you'll never prove otherwise."

Gavin lost his anger as he stared at his uncle. "But why, Des? Why...? I'm not talking about getting the goods on you. I mean *why*?"

Daniher considered him soberly. The swivel chair creaked as Daniher leaned back and clasped his hands behind his head, his eyes remote, fixed on the past. "You could put it down to being Irish, I suppose," Daniher began. "Did you know there was a time—and not so long ago—when the help-wanted ads in the paper used to say 'No Irish need apply'? Oh, it was all right to be a hod carrier, a cart driver or maybe muck out sewers. But nothing better. We came in by the thousands from a land that could no longer support us. Looking for the streets paved with gold. The Land of the Free."

Remembering, Daniher had a brooding look that pulled his bushy eyebrows down. "And what did we find? We found we were at the bottom of the ladder. With never a hand to help us up. But plenty of boots to kick us down. So we adapted to it as best we could. Mainly the corruption. If that was the way it was, who were we to buck the system? When in Rome... It made for an easy conscience. A man had to live."

Daniher cleared his throat noisily and straightened in his chair. "Jaysus. I've done more talking today than since I ran for office on old Martin Kinkaid's ticket. The only public office I ever held, by the by. Do you think you could pour me a drink, Gavin lad?"

As he handed Daniher the shot glass it struck Gavin how drained Daniher looked. "I won't be keeping you too long," his uncle said. "Tax assessor. I suppose it started with that. The first exposure to the big graft. There seemed little harm in it then. Since most of the money I took for the favors I did went to Sally Anne. Ah, she was the one for the big causes. Wayward girls, indigent mothers, orphans. The sick, the halt and the blind. There was no end to her goodness. She even tried to save the whores on the street." Daniher smiled bleakly. "As if old Martin Kinkaid would have let her put a stop to that.

"At least the money was spent to good purpose. It seemed fitting to take from the rich and give to the poor. She never asked where it all came from. And I never told her. Although, come to think of it, she must have known. She wasn't Martin Kinkaid's daughter for nothing." Daniher gave a tired sigh.

He took a sip of his whiskey and shrugged. "So we come to Angelo Pavane. The man who provided the City with all the vice it wanted. I did him a big favor once. I saved his brother from the chair when the power boys tried to railroad him. After that it seemed easy to do him others. I suggested—suggested, mind you—how to make his dirty money clean. It was sound legal advice, if I do say so. I got well paid for that legal advice, and I closed my eyes to where the money came from. Never a thought to where it came from, at least none I couldn't persuade my conscience to accept. You see, *I* wasn't the crook."

Daniher had so far spoken without emotion, but now Gavin was conscious for one brief moment of his desperate need for understanding. It was a look in the eyes that was gone almost before it came. "I told myself that if it wasn't Pavane, it would be someone else. Vice is with us always. The nature of the beast. The way of the world. Well, I was wrong. It's brought me to this, where the only man I ever loved, the son I never had, is almost bombed to hell and gone. It's that I can't forgive myself. It's a heavy burden on a conscience that was never too strong at best."

They were the only words of love Daniher had ever spoken to him, and they tore him apart. He knew how it was because he had never been able to tell Daniher of his own love. He wanted to now. To tell this man, who had been father and mother to him, how much he loved him. He wanted Daniher to know that he understood, that he could forgive Daniher anything. But he couldn't say the words because the cop in him had still another question. "The stocks, Des . . . ? Schwartz told me . . ."

"Ah, yes, the stocks." Daniher got up and went to the big safe in the corner of the room. Gavin watched as he bent to twist the dial, thinking that the chance to tell him how he felt might never come again. Daniher took a strongbox from the safe and opened it on the desk. There was a sizeable sheaf of stock certificates held together by a red ribbon neatly tied in a bow. Daniher undid the ribbon and pushed the stack toward Gavin.

306

Gavin looked at the embossed highly decorated certificate that read EMPIRE RACE TRACK. FIVE HUNDRED SHARES. He let his eyes drop to the bottom line.

The owner of record was Gavin Francis Riordan. It was the same on the rest of the shares, forty-one in all. In Angelo Pavane's various companies.

"About six hundred thousand, give or take," Daniher said softly. "If the market don't drop all to hell. In lieu of legal fees."

Through his shocked astonishment Gavin was aware of the implications. If the stock deals ever came to light, out in the open, then it wouldn't be Desmond Daniher holding the bag. It would be Gavin Riordan, hero cop. Chief investigator for the Belding commission. In it up to his eyeballs. And who would believe otherwise?

"Jesus Christ, Des," he breathed. "You had it going and coming. You've the balls of a brass monkey. 'I did it all for you.' Is that the way of it?"

"You might say that." Daniher's face was blandly innocent. "Of course, I had the thought that you might take care of a tired old man. In his declining years. A poor devil of a mick who couldn't make do for himself. . . ."

"Jesus Christ," Gavin said again. He began to grin and then went around the desk to put his arms around Des Daniher. He felt Daniher's hug in return.

Oh, Des, Des . . . You had to love a man like that.

Two days after his release on bail, Angelo Pavane died in Gansvoort Hospital. The death certificate listed cardiac arrest as the cause of death, although Daniher was never convinced.

Weeks later, out of a policeman's curiosity, Gavin Riordan checked the information on Leon Schwartz's tapes against the documents recovered from Angelo Pavane's safe. There were a number of discrepancies. Pavane's safe had yielded only enough to convict him of monumental tax fraud. If he had ever come to trial. Nothing else. Since Pavane's demise had ostensibly closed the case, Gavin destroyed the Schwartz tapes.

When Governor Everett Harrison lost the election by an embarrassing landslide, the Belding commission died a natural death following an age-old political pattern. It had done its work well, as such things do. Three criminal-court judges convicted of malfeasance; one state supreme court justice committed suicide rather than face criminal proceedings; three assistants and one district attorney nailed for accepting bribes. The police department was rocked from top to bottom. Thirty-one rank-and-file convictions on various charges, forced resignations by nine senior officers.

And, of course, Angelo Pavane.

It was a respectable bag, all in all, although, as Gus Onderdonk raved, six months more of funding for the investigation would have doubled the take.

The police commissioner appointed by the new governor sent Captain Gus Onderdonk back to the boondocks, his old job in the Twelfth Ward. Onderdonk resigned in disgust. He didn't have much choice. He knew his career was a shambles. He and Gavin and the Belding commission had stepped on too many toes. There was nothing else for him to do.

So Gavin got the Twelfth instead. As a sop, there was talk of a captaincy for his work in the investigation, but nothing came of it. Gavin was tempted to follow Gus Onderdonk's example, but Des Daniher talked him out of it.

"Death and taxes," Daniher said with a wink. "Two things that are certain. You can add to that—political change. You have my word on it."

So Gavin waited. Though he was not a patient man.

20

Time: 1960
STEWART GANSVOORT

Stewart Gansvoort was an excellent lawyer. He had an incisive mind and the energy to use it both logically and imaginatively. In nine years at Gansvoort Associates he had risen to become head of the legal staff entirely on merit. His father would have it no other way.

At thirty-seven Stewart was on the board of the Law Institute, a member of the Metropolitan Club, the Racquet Club, the New York Athletic Club and several others. He was considered one of the most eligible bachelors in the City and was so named yearly by the periodicals that chronicle such things. He was a bachelor by choice, as many men would be in his position, one to which agreeable young ladies felt drawn. The younger the better for Stewart, who found the conversation of women closer to his own age an unwelcome addition to the only thing he really wanted from the opposite sex—their cooperation in bed. He asked nothing more and expected nothing less. He was seldom disappointed.

His preferences took nothing away from his charm, but rather lent him an elusiveness that intrigued most women, including matrons with marriageable daughters and the daughters themselves.

Stewart Gansvoort was also well liked by most men. He skied (mostly for the social amenities that surrounded the sport). He sailed (for the privacy his yacht afforded). He played an excellent game of tennis (mixed doubles whenever possible). He used his money intelligently, rarely flaunting it to the discomfort of others less fortunate, striking just the right note of generosity without ostentation. He spent his leisure time between the various Gansvoort establishments: Bar Harbor, Maine (rambling mansion built in 1899 by his grandfather); Princess Bay (a private island off the coast of Georgia, complete with golf course and landing field); Bel Repos at Chamonix in the Swiss Alps (a chalet which could house twenty guests in opulent comfort). And, of course, there was always Riverhaven, which Stewart avoided whenever possible because it was his father's permanent residence.

Stewart's relationship with his father was ambiguous, to say the least. They saw each other from time to time in the normal course of each business day. In his nine years there, Stewart had never been able to get over his childish sense of gratification whenever his father approved of the way he handled the endless legal problems that plagued the Gansvoort Foundation.

During the day their relationship was strictly business. Even at their lunches together Stewart had the conviction that his father was using him only to satisfy a need for continuity.

It was different on Sundays. Attendance at dinner at Riverhaven was mandatory for all of the Gansvoort children who were available. No excuses were acceptable. These family occasions seemed to give him little pleasure. Conversation at the formal dinners consisted largely of reports on where each had been and what each had done since the last meeting. Serena took pleasure in trying to shock and often made up things that had never happened. Stewart kept his version of his activities as pure as the driven snow, despite the skepticism that he often caught in his father's pale blue eyes. Only Henry took the gatherings seriously and tried to give a fair and true account of himself.

The three of them often puzzled among themselves over the reasons behind the command performance, Stewart and Serena with resentment and plans of rebellion that were never carried out. Henry, who still lived at home at Riverhaven, surprised them both by saying, "Did it ever occur to either of you that he might be lonely?"

"That would be giving him credit for an emotion," Serena said. Stewart gave it some thought and decided that Henry might just

310

possibly be right. He could think of no other reason for August Gansvoort's insistence on their presence.

Stewart knew something about his father that the others didn't. It was a knowledge that had been terrifying him all his life.

Perhaps *knowledge* is not the right word, because Stewart was not quite sure that it had actually happened. The nightmare quality of the episode had taken it almost out of reality.

At thirteen Stewart came down with a bad case of the flu, with a temperature of 102 degrees, enough to cause his mother some concern. He remembered her coming in to say good night. She was dressed to go to a ball in something gossamer and light that swept the floor. She was as lovely as the Faerie Queen, her eyes alight with animation, which turned to worry as she felt his head. He remembered the cool comfort of her hand.

His father was out of town, and her escort for the evening stood in the doorway just behind her, in white tie and white shirtfront, a tall young man whose dark hair came down in a widow's peak. His mother took his temperature and squinted frowningly at the thermometer.

"Oh, dear," his mother said. "A hundred and two." She turned from him to the young man. "Perhaps I shouldn't go. Would you mind terribly, Evan?"

The young man moved his shoulders impatiently. "Come on, Emily. Kids can go up to a hundred and four or five. Nothing extraordinary. Hundred and two is nothing to worry about." He smiled at Stewart. "You wouldn't want her to miss the ball, would you, sport?"

Stewart wanted her to stay, because he was feeling miserable. His head was fuzzy, his eyes smarted and his nose was painfully raw from blowing it. But he only shook his head.

She looked from him to the young man and then back to him again. "Sure you'll be all right, darling?"

This time he nodded, fighting back tears. She leaned to kiss him, her lips soft as eiderdown as they brushed his cheek. At the door she paused.

"Go to sleep now. I won't be late, darling, I promise you."

But she was.

He never knew just how late. He awoke in the dark to the sound of whispers outside his open door. His head was splitting, his nose now stopped up altogether. He listened to stealthy footsteps go down the hallway toward his mother's room.

He got out of bed. In his feverish state he had some idea of going to her and croaking to her just how terribly sick he felt. When he reached the corridor he saw them in the soft light of a bedside lamp, clutched in each other's arms, and heard his mother say, "This is madness. . . . I shouldn't let you stay. . . ."

"Who's to know . . . ?" the young man's voice was husky, with a sound Stewart had never heard before. "If we're quiet . . ."

"Oh, God . . ." his mother groaned. She reached behind her and closed the door ever so softly.

Stewart crept back to bed, his mind a confusing jumble of unbearable hurt and sick despair. He knew about sex. He was acutely conscious of the girls at school, their burgeoning breasts and the mysterious power they held between their legs.

But not his mother.

His fevered head whirled with images of the act itself, contorted bodies, humped backs.

Not his mother.

Sometime during the next few hours he learned that hate could be a part of love, at one and the same time. His sense of betrayal was absolute. And devastating.

Much later, in the half-life between dreams and waking, he was conscious of another presence in the house, of footsteps on a creaking stair, and knew, without knowing how he knew, that it was his father. He had one consuming instinct—that his father must not find out. As though sleepwalking through thick molasses, he got out of bed and went down the corridor to stand before the closed door of his mother's room.

Against the faint light from below he saw his father coming up the great stairs. First his head, then his shoulders, and finally his whole long body. Stewart heard no sound from the room behind him. Only the small sounds of his father coming toward him over thick carpet. There was a faint glint of light from something his father carried in his hand, and Stewart knew it was a gun.

Father and son faced each other in a silence, broken only by August Gansvoort's harsh uneven breathing. His father took one more step, the gun held out before him. Stewart backed up until he felt the door against his shoulders. He spread his arms as if to ward off the catastrophe he knew was coming. He smelled the strong, acrid odor of his father's sweat.

For endless agonizing seconds, when time seemed to be suspended, they confronted one another in the dark. Then August Gansvoort's shoulders slumped. Stewart could almost feel the charged atmosphere lose its electricity as the gun was slowly lowered.

"It's all right, son," August Gansvoort said very quietly. "Go back to bed now."

Stewart waited until his father disappeared down the stairs again before, light-headed and weak-kneed, he got back to his bed.

By morning Stewart's flu had turned into a raging case of bronchial pneumonia and he was delirious with fever. He learned later that it was McAllister, the estate manager, who bundled him into a station wagon and took him to Gansvoort Hospital.

During the ten days Stewart spent at the hospital, his father visited him only twice, his mother not at all. On the first visit his father told him that his mother was ill in another hospital. The second was to take him home. The drive was made in silence.

Stewart was safely home in his own bed, feeling very much the invalid, when his father told him that his mother had died of her illness. Something in his father's voice told Stewart not to ask *what* illness. He thought he knew. His mother had caught his own pneumonia and succumbed to it. For a long time he blamed himself for his mother's death, torn between a terrible remorse and the thought that possibly it was a sort of retribution for her betrayal of his love.

It wasn't until years later, in the office of the state registrar, that he learned there was no record of the death of Emily Stamford Gansvoort.

Stewart's thirty-seventh year brought two events that were to change his life drastically. The first began unpleasantly, to say the least. At lunch in the Bankers Club, August Gansvoort slid a letter across the table to him.

"In view of this," he told Stewart, "I think it's time you were married."

Stewart dropped his eyes from his father's expressionless face with a foreknowledge of impending trouble. The heading read CANTOR AND GLANTZ over an address in the Bronx.

Dear Sir:
My client, Mr. William Burns, wishes me to discuss with you the paternity of a male child born to his daughter, Mary, aged seventeen, on Nov. 10 of this year. It would be best if you were to consult your son, Stewart Gansvoort, in this matter before arranging a meeting at your earliest convenience.

Sincerely,
Reuben Cantor

"Careful, isn't he? No direct accusation," August Gansvoort said. "I take it you know the girl?"

Stewart nodded briefly, still looking at the letter.

"And you are the father of the child?"

"Hard to tell. And harder to prove."

August Gansvoort reached across and retrieved the paper. "It won't come to that." He waved the letter gently. "Mary Burns, aged seventeen. Of the *Bronx*? How do you meet such people?"

"I get around," Stewart said shortly. "She was a hatcheck girl."

"You do indeed." August Gansvoort's voice was dryly brittle. "Which brings me to the meat of the matter. First, it will never happen again. Secondly, your marriage. Since you seem to be unwilling or incapable of making a suitable choice for yourself, I have done it for you. I have discussed the matter with the young woman's father. We agreed that such a match will be mutually advantageous. I wish it to take place early in the year—say, sometime in January, at Riverhaven. I have cabled your sister to that effect. She will act as hostess, since she has had considerable experience with weddings."

It was a long speech for August Gansvoort. Stewart listened to it, appalled, unwilling to believe what he was hearing. Finally he met his father's gaze and was shocked at the calm finality in those frosty eyes. August Gansvoort meant every word he said. There was no escape.

Faced with the steel of his father's will, Stewart felt all the anger and resentment drain out of him, the inevitability of defeat close in. "Who's the lucky bride?" Stewart asked. "If it's permitted to ask." Sarcasm was the last tiny indication of the rebellion he felt. His father stared him down.

"She is Olivia Minot, of Easton, Maryland. An old Tidewater family. Impeccable background. A quite remarkable young lady. Or so I'm told. Your cousin Agatha has known her since childhood."

"I'll bet she's remarkable," Stewart muttered.

"Come, now, Stewart. It's time you married. A bachelor of thirty-seven is not quite . . . respectable. You should have children. Perpetuate the name." There seemed to Stewart to be an undertone of flinty amusement in his father's voice. "Perhaps you'll be more fortunate in yours . . . than I in mine."

Stewart looked up. There was a thin and totally unexpected smile on his father's lips.

The second and far more important change in Stewart's life came about by accident. As a contributing member of the American Management Association, Gansvoort Associates was asked to provide a speaker for a symposium at Ardsley House, a huge mansion in the Ramapo Mountains. Stewart was selected to represent his company. His subject was to be Government and the Law, and his audience was composed of fifty or so executives from various AMA member companies.

Stewart was not a forceful speaker. He had never had the need to be. But he *was* logical and well organized, and he knew his subject cold. Also he was an extremely personable and engaging man, with the indefinable confidence and assurance of the very rich. Altogether he gave an impressive performance.

It was particularly impressive to Mark Hanna Barrett, who was monitoring the symposium because it was his business to keep an eye on rising young men. At fifty-eight Mark Barrett was the head of a prestigious law firm whose principal business concerned both federal and state governments. Mark Barrett would never call either himself or his numerous associates lobbyists. But thirty years of behind-the-scenes maneuvering in the jungle of politics had given

Mark Barrett's law firm an enviable reputation for getting things done for a great many people.

Barrett was also one of the principal fund raisers for the Democratic party in Stewart's home state. Both Stewart's name and his wealth, combined with the pleasing surprise of his appearance, personality and obvious ability, intrigued Barrett.

Mark Barrett unobtrusively arranged to be seated beside Stewart at lunch and was pleased to find that, despite the long tradition of Gansvoort Republicanism, Stewart himself had no firm political convictions. It was interesting that Stewart was a mild fan of Senator James D. Conroy, the Democrat for whom the word *charisma* seemed to have been coined.

The casual luncheon acquaintanceship turned into a further invitation to lunch at Barrett's club. There was a veiled implication that Barrett's interest in Stewart was as a lawyer and a possible addition to Barrett's firm.

Stewart was flattered at the attention paid him by the well-known lawyer, attention Stewart felt was based on his abilities and not his name. He was also excited by the possibility, however remote, of getting out from under his father's thumb. He was fed up to the teeth with Gansvoort Associates and all it represented.

The job offer never came up during a series of luncheons with Barrett. But something else came up.

At the time, the Democrats held the governorship and maintained a tenuous hold on the state legislature. It was the Democrats' fervent desire to reapportion legislative representation in such a manner as to produce more Democratic seats in the assembly. The Republicans quite naturally opposed this—with considerable heat and acrimony. They contended that a convention was necessary to change the state constitution before such a thing could come to pass.

In the face of all the uproar, the governor felt that he wasn't sure of the necessary votes to ramrod the plan through the state legislature. To cool the heat, he trotted out a familiar political ploy. He created a bipartisan commission to study the matter, the Temporary Commission on Reapportionment. It was composed of five Republicans and five Democrats, plus a chairman who would be accepted by the public as nonpartisan.

Mark Hanna Barrett had a quiet word with Des Daniher, who was the motivator of the reapportionment plan in the first place. Daniher was wryly amused. "You'll be pushin' Machiavelli next. Who'd ever question the integrity of a Gansvoort? Do you think the lad could be . . . talked to—if the need arose?"

"No . . ." Barrett said thoughtfully, "at least, not yet. He'll do the job he's supposed to do. Without fear or favor. The young man wants to prove something to himself. And to me."

"Fair enough. I've no doubt an honest survey will show the voters in favor of reapportion. 'One man, one vote' is catching on."

"And, Des," Barrett went on. "Keep an eye on him. I've an idea he could be a vote getter. For us. He's virgin soil politically. Also, I detect a strong desire to do the old man in the eye. What better way?"

Daniher chuckled. "A Gansvoort Democrat. What a whirling of dead men in their graves."

Barrett was cautious. "I may have read him wrong. . . . He'll need the right staff, of course."

"I think not. I'll have a word with the governor. As for the staff, I've a young man in mind. . . ."

Daniher's word to the governor got a favorable response, as he expected it would. The governor saw Stewart Gansvoort as an excellent figurehead whose name would provide good publicity for the commission.

When Stewart braced his father for a leave of absence, August Gansvoort merely nodded. "Public service is admirable for any man. Bear in mind that a responsibility goes with it."

Not quite sure of what his father meant, Stewart got out of the office as quickly as possible. He felt an elation that made him want to jump and click his heels, a sense of freedom he wouldn't have believed possible. His gratitude to Mark Hanna Barrett was unlimited. So was his determination to do an outstanding job.

In the suite of offices provided for the commission in the state office building, Charlie Bishop was waiting for him.

Charlie Bishop was five years younger than Stewart—and a thousand years older as a political animal. At thirty-two Charlie Bishop had managed successful campaigns for more than a dozen state lawmakers. He was a genius at political infighting, with an unerring instinct for an opponent's jugular. He had an extraordinary knowledge of the real workings of government, as well as a hard-nosed cynicism about the end results. As Des Daniher had once remarked, Charlie would break his grandmother's arm if it meant an extra vote.

Not knowing what Des Daniher had in mind when Daniher assigned him to this project, Charlie Bishop was surprised when Stewart vetoed three of Charlie's selections to fill out the staff. In a phone call to Daniher, Charlie said, "What do I do with this guy? He don't know the rules."

"Just stick in there, Charlie. Build up the lad," Daniher told him. "If he gets too far out of line, let me know. Otherwise just let him go."

"Suppose he fires *me*?"

Daniher laughed. "No chance. You were recommended by Mark Hanna Barrett, in case you didn't know. Your boy thinks he owes him. So you're safe as a sow in the mud."

Charlie Bishop had to be content with that. He knew Des Daniher too well to question his motives. He just wished to hell he knew what the motives were. Charlie Bishop settled down to what he felt would be the long process of teaching Stewart Gansvoort the facts of political life.

Stewart fooled him.

When Stewart found that, in the wisdom of the state, the TCR budget was strictly limited, and that he could get no agreement from his fellow commissioners on just what experts should be used, he dipped into his own pocket and hired a team of top-notch people. Since he had no party axe to grind, he was determined to get facts, not opinion, and to arrive at an honest conclusion.

Charlie Bishop was first appalled at Stewart's innocence, then secretly delighted at Stewart's boldness. It wasn't often that Charlie got a chance to buck the system.

When he reported to Des Daniher, Daniher told him, "Let him have his head. More power to him if he can bring it off. Just be sure you keep him in the headlines. Stir things up so there'll be no chance to bury the final report, whichever way it goes." Daniher paused and added, "Incidentally the lad is about to be married. That should give you a little fodder for the press."

318

When Stewart read the final version of the statement of goals that had been hammered out at great length by the commission, with all its political ambiguities, he placed it carefully in the bottom drawer of his desk and closed the drawer. "That's the last of that," he told Charlie Bishop. "As I see it, the problem is simple. One: Is reapportion needed or desired? Two: If so, does it require a change in the state constitution to bring it about? Three: Would such a change require convening a state constitutional convention to amend the constitution? The last two points are purely legal questions. It's the first one that matters. What do the people of the state want?"

"Now, *that's* a new approach," Bishop said. "Who ever heard of asking the people?"

Stewart grinned at him. "Right. So let's find out."

Stewart went about the job in the straightforward way of the hugely rich. If you want to know what people think, he figured, the simplest way is to ask them.

Stewart did a personal canvass of the state. He hit cities, towns and hamlets, always accompanied by appropriate news coverage provided by Charlie Bishop, the best advance man in the business. He talked to local and county political leaders of both parties, lower-echelon party workers, farmers, merchants and businesswomen, lawyers and college professors, members of chambers of commerce and women's clubs. Including one charming lady he interviewed in the privacy of his hotel bedroom, courtesy of Charlie Bishop, who early on had spotted Stewart's particular weakness.

He accumulated a staggering mass of information on the pros and cons of reapportionment and constitutional reform. More important, under the careful guidance of Charlie Bishop, he learned the devious ins and outs of state politics. At the suggestion of Des Daniher, Charlie gave him what amounted to a cram course in the mechanics of state government.

Stewart was an apt pupil and graduated with honors. What's more, he found that he loved every minute of it.

Despite his father's insistence on a democratic education, at both Andover and Harvard, Stewart had been surrounded by his own circle of friends; in the Army the rarefied atmosphere of an aide-de-camp called for little or no mingling with ordinary dogface GIs. Later the prestige of his position at Gansvoort Associates, plus his wealth, limited Stewart's friends and acquaintances to his own general stratum. As a consequence Stewart had reached his thirty-seventh year with hardly a clue as to how the other half lived.

His conducted tour of the state was a revelation to Stewart. For the first time in his life he was exposed to People, with a capital *P*—and found that he liked them. They were easy to like. What was more astonishing was the realization that they liked *him*. It was immensely flattering and a surefire ego builder.

Charlie Bishop watched his protégé develop an easy grace and manner with all sorts of people, watched him use his new confidence to draw people to him, manipulate them—just for the enjoyment of it. And there was no doubt that Stewart was enjoying himself hugely. He was getting out from under the Gansvoort name.

There came a night when Stewart addressed a meeting of the League of Women Voters (speech provided by Charlie Bishop), finished to wild applause and was mobbed by thrilled ladies as he left the podium. Charlie observed the clamoring women surrounding Stewart, eager to touch him, their shining eyes, rapt expressions. It was a reaction Charlie had seen before, and it spelled out that illusive thing called charisma. At the time, Jim Conroy owned most of the charisma in the world, but Stewart had a big piece of the rest.

Charlie Bishop looked on his creation and found it good. He felt like Pygmalion.

Later Bishop found Stewart having a nightcap in the hotel bar. Stewart was reading the local paper of the previous day, on the front page of which his picture was prominently displayed, a studio portrait provided by the advance team that preceded him to each town on his itinerary.

Bishop took the adjacent bar stool. "You certainly wowed 'em tonight, Stewart; I thought they'd tear off your pants."

Stewart smiled. "I did, didn't I. They seemed to eat it up." Then Stewart's eyes clouded. He extended his finger toward his picture in the paper. "Jesus, Charlie, can't we provide them with better photos than that?"

And Charlie Bishop knew he was hooked. Bitten by the bug that never dies. Stewart Gansvoort was at last a political animal.

It pleased Charlie, because by now he thought he had a pretty good idea of what Des Daniher had in mind for Stewart.

Stewart passed Charlie's final test in the little upstate town of Amity. Charlie introduced him to a young Jaycee who planned to run for mayor of the traditionally Republican community. The young man was earnest, personable and dedicated. Stewart spent a pleasant half hour listening to local problems, problems that two months ago would have bored him stiff but now held a considerable interest due to his recent discovery of the common man.

"Nice kid," Stewart said when the young man had left, wondering briefly just why Charlie Bishop had arranged the meeting.

"He's a comer. In a few years he'll be running for state assembly," Charlie told him. "*If* he makes it this time."

Stewart looked his question.

"Underfinanced. Hard to raise money. In a town like this they keep their hands in their pockets. He'll have to ring a lot of doorbells to raise thirty thou."

"That much?" Stewart asked curiously.

"Give or take a buck or two. Lot of expenses to campaigning. Printing bills, telephone, headquarters, secretaries, campaign workers, advertising—maybe a spot or two on local radio. It mounts up." Bishop's gaze was blandly innocent. "Care to make a contribution?"

Stewart's instinctive reaction was negative, because the years had conditioned him to turn a tin ear to such requests. "But he's a Democrat," he dissembled.

"He's a politician," Charlie Bishop said gently. "Every little bit helps. You may need him some day. When the time comes."

The words hung between them like feathers in the air while Stewart played with their implication. "You really think I could . . . ?"

Charlie Bishop grinned. "Like the old joke. We settled that long ago. Now we're talking price."

He watched Stewart sniff around the bait like a wary trout, nudge it a few times, then gobble it up, hook, line and sinker. He could see the images form in Stewart's head and wondered what Stewart saw.

What was behind that handsome open face? The governor's chair? Senator? The catbird seat at the very top?

For the first time Charlie Bishop had the thought that this one just might go all the way. It was a little like discovering a future heavyweight champ in a tank town gym. With the right manager to bring him along—slow and easy . . .

It was very heady stuff, and Charlie put it out of his mind. For the time being.

The Temporary Commission on Reapportionment completed its hearing and, true to the nature of such bodies, divided along strict party lines. Five Republicans against, five Democrats for.

Stewart Gansvoort submitted his own report to all the members of the commission. It was balanced and well reasoned, based on careful research. It had all the answers, and the findings showed a clear and present need for voting reform. It also expressed the opinion that there was no legal basis for calling a constitutional convention and that reapportionment was strictly a matter for legislative action.

It pleased none of his fellow commissioners. The Democrats wanted a constitutional convention for a number of purposes other than reapportionment. They didn't want reapportionment to be left to the legislative body because they weren't at all sure they could muster the votes to swing it. The Republicans wanted neither a vote on reapportionment nor a constitutional convention.

So, since Gansvoort, as chairman, had no vote, the commission deadlocked. It was finally agreed to put out one of those blandly ambiguous, on-the-one-hand-and-on-the-other reports so typical of supposed fact-finding legislative bodies.

Stewart Gansvoort was enraged, disgusted, frustrated and completely powerless. He demanded that Charlie Bishop go to the press with Stewart's report, along with a searing condemnation of the members of the commission.

"No way," Charlie told him. "Boy Scout stuff. You'd be strictly sour grapes. Worse, you'd make a lot of unnecessary enemies. Pols have longer memories than elephants."

"Enemies!" Stewart raged. "What the hell do I care what those party hacks think? How can we get them get away with this? It's a fucking fraud on the public."

"Relax, Stewart. Wait and see what happens. Maybe it's not so bad."

One newspaper put the commission's report on page four. The rest of them buried it. Which was exactly what the commissioners wanted. It doesn't do for the body politic to look too closely at the workings of government.

The next day Stewart's report made headlines across the state. Accusations and denials flew back and forth. At a press conference arranged by Charlie Bishop, Stewart flatly denied any knowledge of how the report was made available. His fellow commissioners used words like *amateur busybody, publicity hound, millionaire playboy* and the like. Even the governor was forced to admit that it was possible that his choice of a Gansvoort as chairman had been ill-advised.

"I was persuaded," said the governor, "that Mr. Gansvoort, since he has no firm political affiliation, would be firmly unbiased. . . ." Completely ignoring the fact that Stewart's report could hardly be less biased.

On the third day of the battle of the headlines, it came out that a young secretary to the commission named Maeve O'Hare (hired by one of the Republican members) had been responsible for the leak.

COMMISSION BURIED GANSVOORT FINDINGS, SAYS O'HARE
. . . "It didn't seem fair," said Maeve O'Hare, "after all the work Mr. Gansvoort had done. . ."

GANSVOORT: EXCESS OF LOYALTY FORGIVEABLE
Unauthorized release of Gansvoort report was unfortunate, said a Gansvoort spokesman, but the public should have the facts. . . .

The forgiveable Miss O'Hare was publicly reprimanded and subsequently fired. She spent the following two weeks at a resort hotel in Bermuda. When she returned, tanned and rested, she accepted a position in Desmond Danhiher's insurance agency.

"Do you have the votes?" Charlie Bishop asked Daniher.

323

"Never doubt it, Charlie boy. When the roll is called up yonder, we'll be there. Fat and sassy as a sow. The people want reapportionment. Didn't you just prove it?"

"That we did. What happens to our boy?"

"I think we let him stew for the now. Work up an appetite for the table. When he gets hungry enough, we'll see. In the meantime, keep up the good work. Concentrate on the wedding, maybe. Should be a splendid affair, what with his newfound friends and all. And, Charlie"—Daniher paused—"talk to his sister. I think it might amuse her to lend a hamd. Very heady lady, that one. So watch yourself in the clinches."

Olivia Ravenal Minot was a product of Mary Baldwin School for Girls, Sweet Briar College for Young Women (both in Virginia) and the stables at Oak Tree Farms near Easton, Maryland. Those three places had been home to her for most of her life, since her mother had died when Olivia was nine.

Her father was Raoul Duclos Minot, principal stockholder of I. R. Minot Industries of Wilmington, Delaware (chemicals, petrochemicals, textiles, banks and shipping), an empire whose tentacles stretched around the world.

As far back as she could remember, Olivia's relationship with her father had been one of "Hello, how are you?" a quick kiss and then, "See you soon" and "Good-bye." All her father's time and energy had been devoted to that mysterious thing called business, about which there was little information to be gleaned at Oak Tree Farms. The only supervision Olivia got was from Mrs. Parsons, an exceedingly busy housekeeper. Her father's distance didn't seem strange to Olivia, since she had no basis for comparison. Besides, Olivia got all the companionship a girl could want, as far as she knew. Like lots of girls, she loved horses most of all.

Olivia was eleven when she first fell in love with a horse. Marigold was a small chestnut mare as gentle and affectionate as a dog. She had a coat that shone like burnished copper and huge liquid brown eyes that were pools of intelligence. She came when she was called and showed her love with a delicate lipping of Olivia's shoulder.

324

At the time it was near-tragedy, because the stable manager sold her loved one. Marigold went to a leathery lady who was looking for a hack for her son. There was no recourse, because that was the business of Oak Tree. And nothing could be allowed to interfere with business.

Olivia was inconsolable. Until she fell in love again. This time with a stallion who went sixteen hands, had a rolling, wicked eye and a devil of a temper with everyone but Olivia. The stallion was the first of many. There began for Olivia that curious relationship between women and horses that has puzzled men for ages. To her, horses were beautiful, magical creatures whose mysterious instincts and responses were like a foreign language, half learned, that spoke of love given and returned. The sight and smell of them filled her with a sensual excitement. And she was content.

Just past her twelfth birthday three things happened. Her father got divorced from a second wife. A month later he had a heart attack and came to Oak Tree to recuperate. And Olivia began to menstruate, an unpleasant surprise to everyone.

The six weeks of enforced idleness Duke Minot spent at Oak Tree were something of a trial. He was allowed the telephone only one hour a day. At first there was a constant stream of Minot executives, until the doctor limited that, too, to one hour. Which left only the ticker tape, with its stock-exchange quotes, the television, which bored him stiff, and a succession of nurses, most of whom lasted no more than a week. The days became one long series of demands, which became a strain to everyone in the household.

Olivia kept out of the way as much as possible, but she did learn a few things of great interest to her. Waiting outside the bedroom door during one of the doctor's visits, she heard him say, "Sex can be beneficial for most heart patients—in careful moderation. But for a man who seems to have spent the past year trying to fuck himself to death, I'd recommend caution."

"I think that's what she had in mind," her father said. "When do I start being cautious? For instance, how about today?"

"You needn't cut off sexual activity completely—but for Christ's sake, be moderate. And easy does it. Nothing very exciting. It's the excitement that's bad for the heart."

Olivia retreated down the hallway before the doctor came out.

So a man could be fucked to death. That was something to file away. It must take an awful lot of fucking. It didn't seem to bother horses, as far as she could see.

Her father seemed a lot less demanding when Mrs. Parsons began to spend at least part of her nights in his bedroom.

At fourteen Olivia entered Mary Baldwin in Staunton, Virginia, at the urging of her friend Agatha Gansvoort Terhune, one of the rare young guests at the farm, with whom she had corresponded regularly over the years. Three years later both girls were accepted at Sweet Briar College and became roommates.

Olivia kept her own horses and rode every day at school and college. Olivia had partially converted Agatha to the horse cult. Both girls rode in local horse shows and once as far away as the Keswick Hunt Club in Charlottesville. Their room was filled with trophies and ribbons, mostly blues for Olivia, lesser prizes for Agatha. Both girls were looked upon as freaks—and possibly worse. As one cuddly blonde from Alabama put it, "You s'pose they play ugly together? They gotta do somethin'. Ridin' those horses all the time, rubbin' up an' down."

Her love of horses had its sexual side, all right, and Olivia knew it. But it was far more than that. The incredible thrill of being in command of something five times bigger than she was, the feel of great muscles responding to her touch as her horse gathered for the jump, the soaring leap, the moment when horse and rider, perfectly in tune, were no longer earthbound, but something free as the air. There was nothing to compare with it.

Gossip crystallized when, in her nineteenth year, Olivia ceased to menstruate. After three months of freedom from the curse, Olivia told Agatha her problem. Agatha couldn't keep her mouth shut, and soon their dormitory began to buzz. Inevitably the news reached a member of the faculty, and Olivia, who was inclined to ignore the whole phenomenon, found herself in an unfamiliar pair of stirrups, riding the examination table of the matronly school doctor.

"Amenorrhea," the doctor said comfortably. "It's not uncommon in young women. I shouldn't worry. No doubt you'll resume your normal courses before long."

326

Olivia asked her roommate, "What am I supposed to do now? Wear a big *V* around my neck to prove I haven't been laid yet?"

Agatha, who was feeling very guilty about the tempest, said, "It'll die down as soon as they find something else to snipe about. And, Olivia . . . I'm terribly sorry."

"Next time," Olivia said grimly, "maybe you'll keep your big mouth shut."

In the normal course of events a letter describing her problem went from the school doctor to her father. It stayed on his desk at Oak Tree until he found it weeks later. Not wanting to take on any new worry in his condition, Duke Minot turned the problem over to Agnes Parsons, who first consulted the family doctor to find a suitable gynecologist. What the family doctor told her sent her back to Duke Minot.

"I think you'd better talk to him yourself," she said. "He has a very odd idea, and you'd better hear it."

Dr. Mark Longworth was Tidewater born and bred, a lifelong member of the Maryland Hunt Club. He had known Duke Minot for thirty years, and Olivia since birth. He was extremely fond of Olivia, due only in part to their shared passion for prime horseflesh. The rest of his affection grew out of pity for the lonely life she had been compelled to lead. The one time Longworth had protested that it was no way to bring up a child, Minot had snapped at him, "What the hell am I supposed to do? Take her with me wherever I go?"

"No," Longworth had said. "But a little affection wouldn't hurt."

Now, facing Duke Minot over a battered desk in the tack room at the stables, Longworth was determined to make Minot listen to him. Longworth, in cords and an old tweed hacking jacket, looked more at home in the cluttered room than Minot did. He played with a broken jumping bat with a chewed-off wrist strap, wondering just how to get through to the willful man in front of him.

"Of course, I haven't examined her. It may well be some physical dysfunction. Need a good G.Y.N. man for that. But I have an idea that's not the problem."

"Then what the hell is ?"

"I think it's horses."

Minot's long aristocratic face was a study in puzzlement. "You lost me somewhere in there. What's horses?"

Longworth saw that it was to be hard going. "It's a curious thing about young girls and horses. Some girls, that is. They seem to form a very strong emotional attachment to horses. Possibly as a substitute for something else."

Minot's expression was very skeptical.

"I'm not talking through my hat, you know," Longworth said. "This is horse country. I've been practicing here for better than thirty years, and I've seen it happen before. It's not surprising for a young girl who hasn't got a normal love object, like a parent—or a boyfriend—to turn to something else."

Duke Minot was smiling broadly now. "Are you trying to tell me that my daughter is in love with a *horse*?"

"Not *a* horse. Horses," Longworth flared. "And you're damn right. . . I'm telling you. I had one horse woman who stopped menstruating at thirteen and didn't start again until she was twenty-eight."

Minot was swayed by Longworth's vehemence. "You mean women get some sort of sexual bang out of riding horses?"

"Not necessarily sexual as you think of sexual. It's something much more subtle than that. Dogs, cats, whatever, can also become substitute love objects. But horses seem to have a much more powerful pull. Size, beauty, maleness, power, a combination of all those. But whatever it is, it's there, all right."

"Well, how'd you cure her? For instance."

"I didn't. She fell in love with a man and got married."

"And that's the cure?"

"How the hell do I know," Longworth said in exasperation. "It's my own personal opinion that she gave up trying to be a centaur when she became a woman. But you'd have to have a qualified shrink to prove it. Christ knows, we tried every *medical* approach we could think of."

"Marriage," Minot said slowly. "She's not exactly the world's greatest beauty, you know. . . ."

Longworth threw up his hands in disgust. "I didn't say marriage was a *cure*, you numbskull. What I was trying to get through your thick head was that a little love and affection *might* help. And that it's about goddamned time you took some responsibility for your own child. If it's not too late altogether.'' Longworth stood up and threw the broken jumping bat on the table. "But I guess that's too much to ask. You are about the most selfish bastard I ever knew—and there's no cure for that.''

Duke Minot wouldn't look at him. As he went through the door he heard Minot mumble, ''All right. All right. I'll give it some thought.''

Since Duke Minot had no recurrence of his heart problem and appeared to be in excellent health, he was allowed to return to his own love, the business of Business—with the warning that he must reduce his work schedule. That proved to be impossible. He was soon going at full speed with the same drive and energy he had always had. Left on her own, Olivia Minot, at the age of twenty-five, found herself running a sizeable racing stable with responsibility for producing enough winners to keep her father satisfied. It was an arrangement that suited them both. Olivia could safely leave stakes racing to her extremely competent trainer while she herself concentrated on jumpers. By this time Olivia was a member of the US Equestrian Team.

On a pleasant weekend in June, Duke Minot was in Washington, at the invitation of President Eisenhower, to be a member of a panel of businessmen to advise the president on the nation's economy. The invitation included Sunday golf at the Burning Tree Club, and Duke Minot found himself in a foursome with August Gansvoort, a member of the same advisory body.

The two men had been business rivals for years and had no particular liking for one another. However, in the club bar, after the round, they shared a table. Duke Minot was relaxed and on his second bourbon and branch. Gansvoort, who never relaxed and rarely drank, sipped at Apollinaris water.

At that time Stewart Gansvoort was also in Washington defending a particularly difficult antitrust case against the Justice Department. Stewart's name had figured in some business page stories in the Washington papers, so it was natural that conversation between the two men should turn to their offspring. Gansvoort took Minot's polite congratulations on the way Stewart was conducting his current case with noticeable calm and listened with equally polite interest to Minot's bragging about his stables and the efficient way his daughter was running them.

Minot, expanding even further on his third bourbon, confided that he had always wanted a boy. "Grandsons, too," Minot said. "Carry on the name. Be nice to have someone to take over after I'm gone. Seems sort of pointless otherwise. But no luck, so far. She's . . ."

He left the sentence unfinished, and there was a silence, each man momentarily lost in contemplation of absent children.

"It's time Stewart married," Gansvoort said slowly. "Someone suitable."

They stared at each other, Minot with quick speculation, Gansvoort enigmatically. Gansvoort smiled his wintry smile. "You don't suppose . . . ?"

Minot began to grin. "I do indeed. No merger, though. Have to be separate holdings. Or else the Justice Department would kill us both. Hell of an idea." His grin faded into a look of doubt. "Not sure she'd go for it, though. Damned stubborn kid. How about yours?"

Gansvoort too turned serious. "There would be no problem there, I assure you." Gansvoort had utter confidence that Stewart would do as he was told if pressure was applied.

Duke Minot was studying the politely expressionless face of the other. He thought he could read Gansvoort's mind. The old bastard was weighing all the possibilities of their accommodating each other to their mutual benefit. Gansvoort was thinking that he was smarter than Duke Minot, so he was bound to come out on top. Well, that was a highly debatable point and, like a high-stakes poker game, depended on how the cards fell. But what could he do if Olivia balked—threaten to sell the stables out from under her? She'd marry a coal-black nigger before she'd let that happen.

"The stables at Riverhaven are quite adequate," August Gansvoort said softly. "Why not spend a weekend with us? Soon. I'm sure we could make you both quite comfortable."

Duke Minot was grinning again. "Sounds fine. I'll be in touch."

Book Two

21

Time: 1960, PARIS
ERICKA

Ten Tabard wrote Gavin:

> Narcisse Guyot and I were married one month ago today. Knowing your suspicious nature, I assure you it was not a marriage of convenience. We have a real affection. Although there was the other as well. As her uncle, the Prefect, put it, "It is not fitting that Narcisse marry a mere Captain of Police." So now I am a Deputy Chief Inspector. The Tabard family should go far, if the Communists don't win the next elections.
>
> We speak of you often. There is no jealousy on my part. What a woman has enjoyed before marriage is no business of the husband's. However, a famous courtesan of ours, Ninon de Lenclos, once said: "Women detest a jealous man whom they do not love, but it angers them when a man they do love is not jealous." A dilemma?
>
> By the way, there was a curious business with your young friend Ericka Ullman. For a time it looked very serious for her—but in the end there was no proof. Although I have my own ideas. You remember the agitator you persuaded me to release? Well, you could have saved yourself the trouble. . . .

Gavin read on to the end and wondered if he should call George Barnstable. Then, because Ericka seemed to be in the clear, decided against it. No point, unless he could offer help. Which didn't seem to be needed. Unbidden, the picture of Ericka Ullman sprawled naked on her bed came to his mind. That girl capable of what Tabard suspected? He put it out of his head.

Melinda's fatal accident had a profound effect on Ericka. She was forced to recognize just how important Melinda had been to her. In a sense she *was* Melinda, a crucible into which Melinda had poured her attitudes, her beliefs, her faith, her goodness, her kindness and her deep love. Melinda was both steady anchor and driving wind. Melinda's belief in her was rock solid. Therefore, so was her belief in herself.

Now all that was gone. It left a vacuum that had to be filled with many things, among others a deep cynicism linked to the notion that if one didn't allow oneself to love, one couldn't be hurt. And Ericka saw plainly that there was no *reason* for Melinda's death. Therefore life itself had no reason, no pattern. Merely a series of events whose outcome depended largely on oneself. Ericka felt desolately alone. Of course, there was George, but George had his own life. She could clearly see it diverging from hers, no matter how much he cared for her.

There was no wavering in her mind about what she wanted: to be the best architect it was in her power to become. And that depended on one person. Ericka Ullman.

Melinda's death affected George Barnstable quite differently. He, too, was at first overwhelmed by the unfairness of life in general, but he had suffered tragedy before and accepted its inevitability. The principal effect was to make Paris anathema to him. The city he had loved was suddenly hateful and oppressive. He wanted out as soon as it could be arranged, as though a change of scene could erase what had happened. He accepted a commission in Canada and speeded up work on the Paris school.

As he had known she would, Ericka refused to go with him. And there was no real reason why she should. He recognized her dedication and, with some reservations, her ability to take care of herself. He had a talk with both Ven der Veens and with Étienne Gilbert, the minister of cultural affairs, who had become a good friend. Each promised to keep an eye on Ericka and to help in whatever way he could. Thus reassured, he deposited twenty-five thousand dollars to Ericka's account in the Paris branch of the Morgan bank and took off for Vancouver, feeling guilty at the relief he felt at being once more footloose and fancy-free.

Ericka herself was relieved that there would be no more demands on her time or her emotions; she could now concentrate entirely on herself. She gave up the house on rue Babylone and said a reluctant and tearful good-bye to Hughette. Hughette's last piece of advice was typical: "Watch out for the weather and keep your legs together."

Thus forewarned, she moved temporarily into a hotel and began her search for an apartment. She needed something near the heart of the Latin Quarter, boulevard Saint-Germain or boulevard Saint-Michel. The want ad sections of *Figaro, France-Soir* or the *Parisien Libere* were useless. Someone always beat her to it. She read the notices tacked up on bulletin boards at the Beaux Arts and followed countless concierges up enough stairs to reach the moon, learning how broad marble stairs carpeted in thick red changed to waxed wood and jute runners after the first three opulent floors, which changed again in the upper regions, where scuffed bare planks led to maids' rooms. Dark, dank, cold garrets with a communal WC on the landing and a cast-iron pump from which all water was drawn.

After she gave up on the garrets, she inched her way into cramped wart-shaped flats obviously partitioned off from larger apartments. Wallpaper peeled off in successive layers, sometimes ten thick. Rusty sinks stood in jerry-built kitchens with plastic-curtained showers tacked on in a corner and still no WC, which meant trotting out to the landing or, worse still, to the clapboard dunnies in the courtyard downstairs. The floors were worn into ruts in which you could follow generations of drudgery. What depressed her most were the vestiges of shabby, anonymous, caged-in lives, a chain she could not bear to enter. It might be catching.

Finally she had a stroke of blind luck. She must have passed it a dozen times on her way down the rue de Seine, but one morning the timbers that shored up the walls, the canvas tarpaulins and the sheets of corrugated tin had been removed, and there it stood. Behind all the scaffolding and paraphernalia that she had passed without really seeing was her building. A freshly renovated structure, flush with its neighbors like all the houses in the old quarters of Paris, but standing out from the others because it was built to fit a bend in the street. There was something cozy about the narrow facade, only broad enough for four windows on each floor. The exterior had been smoothed and the shutters repainted, but stayed true to the strict rules set down by Les Monuments Historiques, which ensured the harmony of old Paris. On a level with the first floor hung a sign advertising studios to let.

The entrance hall had been redone in polished sandstone and dark brown wall-to-wall carpeting, but the antiquated elevator, dating from some past splendor, had been spared. In a cage like the ornate grillwork of the *métro* signs, hung what looked like a mahogany telephone booth with swinging doors and glass all around, through which you could see an enormous spring and sagging cables. Once she and the concierge had negotiated the openwork gate and the two wooden doors, for which at least six arms were needed, and had squeezed into the leather-fitted interior, it jerked and heaved and cranked itself rheumatically up to the fifth floor.

The studio itself was below the level of the landing. Three broad oak steps descended gradually into the high-ceilinged main room. It wasn't a monotonous rectangle or your run-of-the-mill square, but a lovely eccentric polygon that followed the unusual design of the building. Not a bee's cell, but almost—with warm terra-cotta tiles and sturdy oak beams standing out against the bright whitewashed ceiling and rough-grained white walls. The outside was ultra-Parisian, but the inside was pure Mediterranean.

There was a small efficiency kitchen with a waist-high refrigerator and stainless-steel sink and a two-burner electric stove. No windows but bright nonetheless, thanks to pale pine cabinets and sunny yellow walls with a decorative panel of white and yellow and brown ceramic. Flanking the kitchen (or "keetchnet," as the concierge called it) was an even tinier but well-appointed bathroom that opened off the top step. That might prove acrobatic, but it was

336

definitely interesting. It was fitted with a pale ochre lavatory and WC and a sit-down bathtub, short but deep, with a ledge to lounge on so that you were at just the right height to relax with a good book without getting a crick in your neck.

From the living-room windows directly overlooking the rue de Seine, she could just see the top of Viollet-le-Duc's spire on Notre-Dame above the blue-gray slate roofs and chimney pots. Beneath the windows she would set out plants, creeping ones and crawling ones and climbing ones that would wind up to the beams in the ceiling. Two narrow beds end-to-end could double as a sofa against the wall, with Tunisian blankets in earth colors and perhaps a touch of orange and tons of throw pillows to relax on. A Berber rug or two of shaggy wool would soften the tiled floor, and there would be posters everywhere—Toulouse Lautrec and maybe a litho of Leonore Fini's dreamy catwomen.

The bedroom was perfect for a studio: a slanted skylight, room for a long drafting table and enough bare wall space to display her projects-in-progress.

It was a clean slate of a place, in a framework of history but without history's oppressive weight. The cobwebs and stains of someone else's life had all been varnished and enameled and whitewashed away. She would live the next three and a half years here, and she thought of it as her first step toward total independence.

As a final exam, second-class students were required to do a construction project, known in BA slang as a *construc*, and by far the most difficult task so far allotted. The assigned subject was a small museum. The emphasis was on the quality of drafting, bird's-eye views of linear floor plans, the more complex and detailed the better. But this time there was a little more leeway for talent. Sections, facades and a simple background were permitted. The project called for two plates instead of the usual one.

The format was rigid. It had to be submitted on Big Eagle paper, thirty by forty inches, in pen and ink and color. Students had to purchase their own paper, but local art dealers lent out at no cost the wooden frames on which the projects must be mounted. The Big Eagle paper first had to be wetted down and then carefully stretched on the frames to dry. If improperly mounted, the paper had a tendency to crinkle, something severely frowned upon by the judges.

Two days before her *construc* was due, Ericka had finished a frugal supper and was dawdling, putting off as long as possible the chore she hated. Despite two years of mounting Big Eagle paper on its framework at least once a month, she was still not sure of exactly how good the end result would be. The knock on her door was a relief. One more reason for delay, although she couldn't imagine who it could be.

For two years the intense pressure of her work had confined Ericka to occasional dinners *en famille* at the Ven der Veens', an infrequent outing with Ivan, who was equally busy with his studies, and a few home-cooked meals shared with Angenette, the only other girl in her class. A number of hurried lunches with Jean-Baptiste could hardly be counted as social occasions, since conversation was exclusively and impersonally about her work. But now she opened the door on Jean-Baptiste. He was holding a bottle of wine in one hand and a jar of colorless liquid in the other. He looked past her at the apartment she had worked so hard to make charming and gave a silent whistle.

"A palace. Fit for a queen. The other half lives well."

He handed her the bottle of wine and moved past her, seemingly lost in admiration.

"I have come to mount your plates for you, since you don't seem to be able to do it properly yourself." He nodded at the bottle in her hand. "If you'll open that. A little wine would make the work more pleasant."

She started to say something, but he held up his hand. "Please. First the wine. Then you may thank me."

In the kitchen Ericka was aware that her pulse was unaccountably faster. In the past two years her original attraction to Jean-Baptiste had changed to something more comfortable, a combination of friendship and gratitude for his help with her work. His own gratitude to her, after the affair of the riot, had been a brief thanks for her intercession with the police—and very little more. He had

338

seemed reluctant to talk about it any further. She had accepted that he must have reasons for his reticence. Probably something to do with communism, which was only a vague concept in her mind, since she was totally apolitical.

Now, as she poured wine, she could hear him in the studio as he put the wooden frames on her drawing table. He was clear in her mind's eye. The only outward sign of his police interrogation was a broken nose, which had healed slightly askew. It gave him a raffish air that lent maturity to his face. It was a strong face, lean, all planes and angles, with a wide mouth that turned up at the corners.

Suddenly she wanted to paint him and wondered what the rest of his body would look like.

In the studio Jean-Baptiste stopped what he was doing long enough to down his wine and gesture for more. She sipped her own as she watched him work. He had flattened the Big Eagle paper on the drawing table and with a two-inch brush was wetting it down with liquid from the jar he had brought.

"Something like varnish," he said, absorbed with what he was doing. "Although it isn't. It doesn't affect the absorbency of the paper, but it does make it stiff. Won't wrinkle. My own formula. Perhaps it will make me rich some day."

He tested the paper with his finger and began to apply a second coat. When that was finished, he began the tricky business of stretching it on one of the wooden frames and tacking it down.

By the time both plates were prepared and stacked side by side against the wall, the wine was finished and Ericka went to the kitchen to get another bottle. On the way back she had to detour to her tiny bathroom. In the mirror over the washbasin her face was more flushed than usual and her eyes sparkled from the wine. On impulse she released her hair from its ponytail and let it fall around her shoulders. She debated fresh lipstick and decided against it. She wasn't at all sure why she did these things, but she did them nonetheless. Her body felt tinglingly alive, but curiously her mind refused to think.

When she returned, Jean-Baptiste was sprawled on her bed-couch, propped against the wall. She was excitedly aware of his appraising

339

look, but she couldn't quite meet his eyes. She sat beside him and concentrated on filling their glasses.

"They'll take all night to dry," he said, referring to the plates. "We shouldn't open any windows."

She forced herself to look at him. He was gazing at her, holding her eyes, with a wholly serious expression. Its meaning was unavoidable but not welcome—not just yet.

"You are about to be promoted to first class," said Jean-Baptiste. "Only a few more days. Don't you think it's time for us, Ericka?"

Suddenly she knew it was. More than time. She helped him undo the buttons of her blouse.

Ericka's initiation to lovemaking was surprisingly uncomplicated. She felt only a small discomfort, none of the pain she had been expecting. After all, her hymen was a thing of the past. There was little foreplay, although Jean-Baptiste was both tender and gentle. If there was no pain, there was no ecstasy, either. Nothing like the powerful orgasm she had experienced with Ivan ven der Veen. But at least this time she felt no fear. It was disappointing, but Jean-Baptiste assured her that time would make it better.

He proved to be right. For the week after she was admitted to first class, Jean-Baptiste moved in with her. Sex did get better, but it confirmed her conviction that each human being was essentially alone. She found that she was using Jean-Baptiste to manipulate herself to orgasm. The orgasms were marvelous, but they were *hers*, not shared. She found nothing disturbing about that.

Living with Jean-Baptiste had other compensations that more than made up for what she didn't even know that she was missing. For one, a shared companionship full of laughter and gaiety. Experiences she might never have had without him.

In the next year and a half she found that she was essentially uneducated, except in her chosen sphere. She learned to read books that informed rather than entertained. She discovered Sartre and Camus, Karl Marx and John Maynard Keynes, Simone de Beauvoir and Descartes. Her tastes were eclectic and opened her eyes to the world around her.

She fell in love with ballet; thrilled to the play of Raymond Kopa, France's greatest soccer player; became an avid fan of Edith Piaf; acquired a working acquaintance with vintage wines and a much deeper appreciation of classical music. She never saw beauty without wishing Jean-Baptiste were there to share it.

Jean-Baptiste Moreau was so many things to her, companion, teacher, lover—and sometimes like a father in his concern for her—that she was shocked to find that she was also in love with him.

It happened gradually, and when the realization finally dawned, she backed away from it, filled as she was with the conviction that such love could only bring eventual pain. She tried to bury it deep inside her. But it was there, and she had a dreadful foreknowledge that it would lead to disaster.

He attended a lot of political meetings and sometimes had small groups of people come to the apartment. Ericka never joined them, preferring to work or study in the studio. Politics bored her, especially French politics, which seemed to makc little sense. There were so many factions, each passionately devoted to separate causes. Some for Algerian freedom, more against it. There were royalists, the Secret Army (OAS), *Poujardistes* (who sounded like McCarthyites), *Jeune Nation* (so far right they resembled Fascists). There was UNEF, the student union, CGT and CFDT, Communist workers' unions. There was SNESUP, not quite but almost Communist, and finally PCF, the Communist party itself. To say nothing of just plain everyday citizens. And always, of course, the Gaullists. It was all far too confusing for anyone who hadn't been brought up in it.

To add to the confusion, Jean-Baptiste had his own pet cause, the Quebec Separatist Movement in Canada. She knew that Jean-Baptiste was a Communist, but in France there seemed to be so many different brands of leftists that she wasn't sure just what *kind* of Communist he was. She knew there were bombings—of government offices, banks and businesses—that were blamed on the Communists, but there were other bombings where the OAS was named the

341

culprit, or *Jeune Nation*, or any other of the jumble of letters designating political factions.

Ericka was vaguely alarmed that Jean-Baptiste would get mixed up in something *serious*, something that might disrupt their life together. She couldn't bear that, for her love for him had become frighteningly possessive and important to her; often she confided her fears to him.

"Politics is a part of life," he told her. "For the whole world. Except Americans. For them it is some kind of game they play every four years. I don't understand Americans."

The famous riotousness of the Beaux Arts students centered around certain annual frolics. As February fifteenth approached, the day the subject for the Rougevin Prize was to be given out, the ateliers began to boil and bubble like some witches' cauldron. For most students the Rougevin competition was solely an excuse for the Rougevin parade. Each atelier built its own float on the banks of the Seine, mounted it on a truck or wagon scrounged from a local vendor.

From time immemorial the basic theme had been the same: the phallus as a many-splendored thing. No one seemed to know the origin, but to the students it represented a sort of "up yours" attitude toward the staid academicians of the Beaux Arts. The penises were made of wire and papier mâché, and ingenuity was the order of the day. Some were enormous, reaching as high as three stories. Some were garlanded with flowers, some swathed in priestly robes, all grotesquely lifelike.

On the eve of the fifteenth all the ateliers gathered at the BA to wait for the assigned subject. The idea was to make last-minute alterations on the floats to conform with the chosen subject. If a door, then the tip of the phallus should open and close. If a bridge, then the member should be raised and lowered like a drawbridge. The designers and builders had only twenty-four hours to make their changes, so the work verged on the frantic.

The assignment turned out to be a double gate for a horticultural park.

The route and customs of the Rougevin parade were traditional.

On the day the serious students completed their entries and handed over to the authorities, the floats would form at the Seine, each attended by twenty to thirty students from the ateliers represented. They would proceed with music, shouting and dancing in the streets, to the huge central courtyard of the BA, there to line up around the yard to be judged by a mock jury in a parody of Judgment Day. A prize of a barrel of wine would be awarded to the float most ingeniously obscene. Enormous firecrackers would be thrown from the floats and the surrounding windows. Broken panes, flying glass and wounded onlookers would be inevitable.

As night was about to fall, the parade would reform and wend its now thoroughly drunken way to the boulevard Saint-Germain, turn right on the boul' Mich', then left on rue Soufflot to the hallowed walls of the Parthenon.

In the broad paved area in front of the Parthenon the floats would be set on fire, surrounded by screaming, chanting students, most of them stark naked. With any luck the fire brigades would refrain from hitting the revelers with hoses, and the police wouldn't use their lethal lead-lined capes. But since the whole affair took place right under the noses of the police commissariat across the street, you couldn't count on it.

Ericka wanted no part of it. She preferred to do her drinking in comparative privacy and spent most of the night getting quietly soused with Jean-Baptiste, in agonized anticipation of what would happen on the morrow, when the judges' decision on the real competition would be announced. Ericka was of course a competitor of the most serious type.

The next day the bulletin board at the BA told her that she had won the coveted Rougevin Prize and thus accumulated more credits and cut a few more months off her stay at the school of architecture. By that time she was almost too exhausted to care. She went home in a daze and collapsed in tears on Jean-Baptiste's shoulder.

That night, for the first time, their lovemaking had the quality of sharing. She *gave* herself to Jean-Baptiste, and he to her, in an ecstasy of passion that left her shaken.

It was a new experience for Ericka. The next morning, thinking about it, she knew that such bliss was dangerous, too good to last.

Loving Jean-Baptiste, as she now knew she did, was asking for trouble, laying herself open to hurt and pain. She was convinced that nothing good could come of it.

Six weeks later, in the impersonal clinic of the American Hospital, she learned that she was pregnant, and all her forebodings came true.

Her first reaction was an unreasoning rage at Jean-Baptiste for getting her in this predicament. The unfairness of that made her instantly ashamed. Obviously her diaphragm had failed. But the resentment persisted despite its unreasonableness. She put off telling Jean-Baptiste because she wasn't sure how he would take the news.

A talk with Angenette and several of Angenette's friends at the Beaux Arts persuaded her that abortion was hard to come by in Catholic France. Denmark or Sweden? Ah, another matter entirely. But she couldn't afford the time. The Prix de Rome competition was just around the corner. She'd be up against aspirants from all over the world. Pregnancy was a complication she just couldn't afford.

Jean-Baptiste caught her helplessly bent over the pale ochre toilet bowl and immediately guessed what was wrong. He reacted just as she had suspected he would. Jean-Baptiste was a lapsed Catholic, but abortion was still a sin to him. He wouldn't hear of it.

"What right have you to decide? It's my body. I can do what I want with it. And I *don't* want a baby. I won't *have* a baby!"

"You didn't do it by yourself, you know," Jean-Baptiste said. "Surely I should be consulted...."

"Well, I'm by myself now. And you *have* been consulted. For all the good it's done. You've already made your contribution. From here on it's my show."

"Look." Jean-Baptiste was trying hard to be reasonable, his blue eyes intent and concerned. "I don't have anything against marriage. Not really. If that's what's bothering you, we could...."

Ericka exploded. "What the hell has marriage got to do with it! You don't seem to understand. I'm *not* going to have a baby! If you won't help, then just stay the hell out of my way! I'll take care of it myself."

Jean-Baptiste's face hardened with his own anger. "Have it your own way. I can't stop you. And I *won't* help you. So the hell with it." He left the apartment without looking back.

Ericka watched him go with something close to murder in her heart. She felt doubly betrayed, first by the unwelcome fetus in her womb, now by the man she loved.

That afternoon she bought a ticket to Copenhagen for the following weekend and later wheedled the name of a doctor out of one of Angenette's friends. She left the airline folder in plain sight on the living room table.

For two days there wasn't much said in the small apartment, although neither of them could avoid the telltale envelope in the middle of the table. For Ericka they were two days of confusing ups and downs. When she was sick each morning she came close to hating Jean-Baptiste. In the evening, each silently absorbed in books or studies, she longed for his arms around her. Suddenly she noticed things she had never really seen before. The way the fine blond hairs on his forearms curled and shimmered in the light from the end-table lamp when he moved. His fingers, with their square-cut nails, inordinately long as they cradled a book. His habit of pulling at an eyebrow as he read. A hundred other things that now were unbearably endearing to her. She couldn't bear the thought that it all might end if she went through with what she intended.

On the third evening he picked up the airline ticket folder and juggled it in his hand. "I give in," he said slowly. "I hope you can afford another of these, because I can't. I'm going with you. I can't let you go alone."

All her pent-up tensions came boiling out in a flood of weeping that verged on hysteria. He took her to bed and made love to her with a violence he had never shown before, almost as if, with his rigid member, he was trying to destroy the life he had placed there. When it was over she lay panting and exhausted, grateful for his warmth beside her. It was then she felt the movement inside her. Her body went rigid with shock. He turned to her in alarm.

345

"I felt it!" she gasped. "It moved!"

Jean-Baptiste burst out laughing.

"It's impossible. Too soon. You must have gas, or something."

"Damn it, I tell you it *moved*!"

"Honey." He was patience itself. "You couldn't possibly have felt anything. Babies don't move for months. Right now it's about as big as a peanut. Ask anybody. Or look it up."

The next day the encyclopedia told her that he was right—with pictures and text. She didn't believe it. She knew her baby had moved. She wasn't about to be swayed by another's opinion, no matter how expert.

It added a new dimension to her thinking. Try as she would, she couldn't control the pictures in her head. Or the questions. Babies. Boy or girl. Do boys look more like the father? And girls, the mother? Blue-eyed like Jean-Baptiste? Or green like hers? There was some law that governed that. She must look it up. . . .

But she never did. She would stop there, or at some similar point in the unbidden images that flooded her mind. Because there wasn't going to be any baby. She was still determined on that.

They were sitting in the airport lounge, waiting for the Copenhagen plane to be announced, when she realized that she wasn't going through with it. Come what may, she was going to have Jean-Baptiste's baby.

Jean-Baptiste was overjoyed. Practical as always, he insisted on turning in the tickets before they left. He returned with his hands full of francs and a grin that stretched his face.

"Time to celebrate, little mother." He waved the money at her.

She didn't feel like celebrating. She felt that her life was over, that everything she had longed for was down the drain, beyond recall. "Oh, Jean-Baptiste. What am I going to do?" she wailed. She, who rarely cried, was once again close to tears.

"You're going to win the Prix de Rome, my darling. The first pregnant woman in history." He assumed a comical sobriety. "At least as far as we know. . . . Perhaps a little research on the subject . . . ? Who can predict what women will do to get attention?"

She rubbed her flat stomach. "How can I . . . like this?"

He sat down beside her and hugged her close.

"It will be months before you have our baby. Long after you get your diploma. There's nothing for you to worry about. I've already started to put together your team. I think perhaps fifteen people. The very best people in first and second class. Along with a few *admissionistes* as go-fers. You will need all the help you can get. And it will be monumentally expensive. Food and drink alone . . ." He threw up his hands. "Thank God for your fortune in the Morgan Bank. A most excellent institution."

He lifted her chin to look at her, eyes twinkling in amusement. "Then, of course, there will be the expense of the wedding. I think just after you have won the Prix. By that time my claim on you should be apparent. . . ." He made a circle of his arms suggesting a huge belly and puffed out his cheeks. Then, once more comically serious, "I trust your uncle is familiar with the custom of the dowry. For a man with my prospects it should be substantial, perhaps even enormous."

Against her will she was forced to laugh at him.

The next few months were hectic. Along with the rest of her worries, she found that she was consumed with unreasoning fears. No longer could she run to jump on the back of a bus. She might miss the step. The sliding doors of the *métro* seemed diabolically determined to crush her. Crossing streets through French traffic became a terrifying hazard, leaving her short of breath, heart pounding erratically. She awoke sobbing in the middle of the night, her flesh clammy with sweat, with no idea of what had frightened her, pathetically grateful for Jean-Baptiste's arms and his gentle reassurances.

She knew she was being a nuisance and a bore to everyone. But there wasn't much she could do about it. Through it all there was still that sense of foreboding, the conviction that something bad was sure to happen.

Like Murphy's Law, it did, although nowhere nearly as bad as her imaginings. Jean-Baptiste was away at one of his frequent political meetings, and she was standing idly looking out of the window at the rue de Seine, watching for his return. At ten in the evening the street was quiet except for the occasional late passerby. The bar across the way was still open and she could hear faint music.

A group of men passed under the streetlight just below her. She recognized Jean-Baptiste's blond head. At first she thought he was drunk, because two of the men seemed to be supporting him. Then she saw the light glisten on the dreadful stains on his face and shirt. Her knees gave way and everything went black.

She came to seeing the worried face of a stranger bending over her. She was lying on the cold tiles just under the window, and the man was mopping her face with a wet towel even colder than the tiles. "It's all right," the man said. "Nothing to worry about. Just a few cuts and bruises."

At first she thought he was talking about her and wondered how she could have gotten cut and bruised merely from falling on the floor. Then she remembered and sat up abruptly.

There were three other men in the room, none of whom she recognized. All wore the same concerned expressions, as though attending a deathbed watch.

As she got shakily to her feet, assisted by the first man, who treated her as if she might break if not handled with care, Jean-Baptiste came in from the bathroom, holding a towel to his forehead. His shirt was torn and streaked with his blood.

"It's all right," he soothed her. "It's nothing. A scratch. See for yourself."

"What happened?" Ericka asked. "How did you . . . ?"

Jean-Baptiste seemed oddly embarrassed, avoided meeting her eyes. "*Jeune Nation,*" he said. "We heard they were storing arms in the basements of the law school. I went to take a look. They were, too. The place is a regular arsenal."

"But why . . . ?"

"We must know what they are planning," the stranger answered her. "To protect ourselves."

"From what?" Ericka asked stupidly. "Surely the police . . ."

"The police already know about it," Jean-Baptiste said defensively. "They will do nothing. We will have to defend ourselves against those *salauds*. No one else will."

Ericka sank weakly onto the daybed. "You all must be crazy. Or I am. . . ." She gestured to the stained towel Jean-Baptiste held. "For this you get yourself hit on the head. And frighten me half to death. What the hell difference does it make if Algeria is free? What's it to you? You're not even a Frenchman."

Jean-Baptiste had the look his face always seemed to assume when he talked politics. "Freedom is the business of all right-thinking people. To be free is everything."

Any thought of politics became unimportant, subordinate to the intense period of preparation for the two competitions designed to reduce the number of aspirants for the Prix de Rome to a final ten. The first project lasted for twelve hours with contestants locked up in the "lodges"—the prisonlike cells in the old Beaux Arts building. The second project called for twenty-four hours of this sadistic treatment. Both were grueling ordeals. Ericka made the final group of ten by the skin of her teeth, the last student to be chosen.

Both Jean-Baptiste and, more importantly, Piet ven der Veen were disappointed in her. Ven der Veen expressed himself in one terse comment: "You are not *thinking* architecture. You must *think*."

Since there was now not the slightest doubt that her baby was moving most alarmingly, Ericka found it difficult to concentrate when her insides were being kicked about at odd moments. Jean-Baptiste told her that she was making too much of the whole process of gestation. "Nothing new about it. So let's get back to work." Work consisted of training like a prizefighter for the Prix de Rome.

The Prix de Rome. Top of the pyramid. Only one person could win it each year. All the great names of architectural history, from Charles Percier, through Henri Lobrouste and Charles Garnier, to the great moderns like Max Abramovitz.

An impossible dream, as Jean-Baptiste insisted on pointing out to her.

"All very well to joke about, but you mustn't get your hopes up. Women just don't win the Prix. Never happen. The *best* you can hope for in all practicality is Second Premier Prize—or even Honorable Mention. That in itself would be something no woman has ever done."

It went in one ear and out the other, because Ericka couldn't imagine *not* winning. It was simply something beyond conscious comprehension.

The subject for the Prix de Rome competition was finally announced, and Jean-Baptiste was sunk in gloom.

"A cathedral in the style of the Second Empire! It couldn't be worse for you. Lush, eclectic, meticulous detail. No innovation, no imagination, no room to show your stuff. You simply don't have the temperament for it. It's merely a matter of copying past masters—no relation whatever to the present."

"I can do it," Ericka insisted.

"No, you can't. Don't you realize that you will be judged by *old* men, members of the academy, director of the Beaux Arts, members of the Institute of Fine Arts, the minister of cultural affairs . . ."

"Him I know. Étienne Gilbert. He's a friend of George's."

Jean-Baptiste paid no attention. "Old, old men who haven't had an original idea since 1920. Men who refused to recognize Le Corbusier and quiver at the mention of Bauhaus. A Second Empire church, with all its gingerbread and gimcracks! What a stupid, useless project."

"I don't care," Ericka said. "I can do what I have to do."

Jean-Baptiste looked at her speculatively, as if he were trying to guess her weight. "You have one thing going for you. You are an artist. You can draw better than any of them. That's important to those old men—because light and shadow and the use of color is practically a lost art to the architects of today. That just might get you through."

The scale of the project was enormous, and required six plates, ten by six feet in dimension. Since the atelier was far too crowded, Jean-Baptiste insisted that Ericka rent a nearby empty loft big enough to let her team spread out. He reduced the team from twenty to ten of the most talented members of Atelier Ven der Veen with three *admissionistes* to assist. Everybody was happy to get the work along with the free meals, despite the biting criticism and slave-driver tactics of Jean-Baptiste, who kept them working every moment they could spare from their own studies. Their task, working from Ericka's original concept and sketches, was to take the bits and pieces of the elaborate cathedral and turn them into finished work, tracing shadows on facades, repeating patterns of ornament, inking plans. It was then up to Ericka, under the critical eyes of first Jean-Baptiste and, in the later stages, Piet ven der Veen, to assemble the whole for presentation to the judges.

Ven der Veen seemed pleased by what he saw and delivered another of his many homilies. "Architecture is of the soul as well as the eye. When the architect has deeply probed his heart, when he is aware of his reactions, caught by surprise under a clear luminous sky or a dark and sad horizon, then his spirit takes fire, his imagination yields a kind of ecstasy, a vision, and he can recognize and create a temple for the Deity."

Jean-Baptiste had more practical advice. "Planning. Planning is the key. The requirements of a particular structure, with attention paid to proportion and symmetry—and the elevations follow as natural consequents. The principle of all design is that every building should have its own character, according to what it is to be used for. You've got a place of worship. Therefore, make it divine. And pay strict attention to the ornaments. It's something the old fogies will be looking for."

The final few days were frantic, with people working round the clock until at last everything had been done that could be done and the project was ready for submission. On the final night the whole team got falling-down drunk, and Angenette, stretched out on a cluttered drawing table, finally lost her virginity. At least that was her recollection the next morning.

On Judgment Day the whole team shepherded the horse-drawn cart that took the six huge plates to the Salle Mepomene, where the prestigious panel would sit in judgment of the competitors—this time in secret session.

There was nothing left but to wait.

Nothing, that is, except that Quat-Z-Arts ball.

Ericka had refused Ivan ven der Veen's suggestion that she accompany him and his father to the Beaux Arts ball held each year at the school, the high point of the academic spring season. The ball was a very formal and prestigious affair. She was sure her condition was beginning to show and wasn't about to display herself in a slinky evening dress. The Beaux Arts was mostly for alumni, *patrons,* government officals and the like, a time to see and be seen. Many students didn't attend, either because of a lack of formal wear or because of the exceedingly steep entrance fee.

The Quat-Z-Arts ball, also held in the spring, was quite a different matter, an affair no student able to walk unassisted would think of missing. It was a costume ball held in the huge ballroom at Salle Wagram, near the Arc de Triomphe. Each year a theme was chosen, such as Babylonian, Byzantine or Imperial Chinese, and for the month preceding, each atelier was busy constructing its booth along the sides of the ballroom, true to the period chosen and stocked with food and drink for the revelers.

The night of the Quat-Z was a time for all of Paris along the route march to shutter its windows and lock its doors, a night of dangerous pranks and wanton destruction. Traditionally the students, all in costume, gathered in the courtyard of the BA and marched on foot from there all the way to the Champs Élysées and then to avenue de Wagram, more than two miles, laying waste to everything along their path. Most of the more cautious shopkeepers had long since buttoned up. Any restaurant left open was promptly invaded by the mob, grabbing anything that came to hand, including the food from the diners' plates. The night was alive with the sounds of smashing furniture, breaking china and glassware and the howls of outraged customers. True, a number of restaurants along the way, rather than have their establishments wrecked, played along with the madness by preparing a ransom of food and wine, which they trotted out on trays as soon as the uproar approached. It didn't always appease the riotous students.

The Quat-Z had a history of tragedy. One year five students piled into a friend's apartment to sleep it off and were asphyxiated by a faulty gas heater. Another time a group went skinny-dipping in the fountain at place de la Concorde and were electrocuted when one young man dove in and broke an underwater spotlight.

After having despoiled a sizeable part of Paris, the marchers, bearing their trophies, finally made it to the Salle Wagram for an all-night orgy of drinking, dancing, eating and indiscriminate sex. Girl students weren't safe from mass rape unless staunchly protected by husky members of their own ateliers, although there were always costumed hookers, tramps and camp followers ready to take on all comers.

The only semblance of order was kept by the praetorian guard hired for the event by the students, forty or fifty of the biggest, toughest, meanest BA students, who could not always be counted on not to organize the disorder.

The theme of the ball this year was to be Egyptian, the period of King Tutankhamen, which featured long skirts and bare breasts for both sexes, along with diadems and serpent amulets. The praetorian guard were to be dressed as Nubian warriors carrying short swords and shields, wearing feathered helmets and painted black from head to foot.

In her years at BA, Ericka had so far avoided this mass idiocy, but this time was different, since Jean-Baptiste, because of his size and reputation, had been elected captain of the praetorian guard.

"Nothing will happen," Jean-Baptiste told her. "You'll be perfectly safe. The guard will protect you. Besides, it's part of your education. No one should graduate from BA without attending at least one Quat-Z."

Reluctantly Ericka allowed herself to be persuaded. "I'm damned if I'll let my boobs hang out. They've gotten too big. I'd look like a cow."

On the night of the ball the march of chanting, shouting, ravaging students went along about as expected, winding its way from the BA up the quai Malaquais to quais Voltaire and France, to the Pont de la Concorde, and then from the place de la Concorde up the Champs Élysées (with some sneaky zigzags to various side streets) toward the Étoile and avenue de Wagram. Nothing truly outrageous occurred, except on one of the side streets off the Champs, where there was a small nightclub below pavement level. The proprietor had barred both doors and windows, but had left the windows open a few inches at the top to let in a bit of necessary night air. Several dozen students, feeling deprived of their fun, promptly quit the parade to piss through the windows on the hapless customers. All good, clean fun.

Ericka, safely guarded by several large and beefy praetorians and Jean-Baptiste, who looked truly fearsome in his gleaming coat of black paint and feathered helmet, was beginning to enter into the spirit of things by the time they reached the Salle Wagram. She had imbibed enough confiscated wine to feel light-headed and carefree. The wild excitement of the march was contagious and at the same time nostalgic. It saddened her to realize that this was the last time she would ever be a part of such shenanigans. The close-knit camaraderie of students, all with the same interests, working toward the same goals, would soon be over forever. She knew she would miss the Beaux Arts.

The huge ballroom was dimly lit, murky with smoke, redolent with odors from every imaginable kind of food and crowded to the rafters with dancers and revelers. The half-naked crowd truly resembled some bacchanalian orgy from out of the past. In the shadows at the far end of the great hall, bodies both single and coupled sprawled against the wall.

Jean-Baptiste delivered Ericka to the booth of the Atelier Ven der Veen and went off to marshal his troops in case of trouble. Tiny Angenette had been put in charge and was dressed for the period. As she saw Ericka eyeing her minuscule bare breasts, Angenette shrugged. "What difference? I haven't got anything there, anyway. Even when I pinch the nipples, I still look like a boy." Angenette's eyes were slightly glassy as she offered Ericka a paper cup of wine. "Take it. It's good. A contribution from the *patron* himself."

"Is he here?" Ericka didn't relish the thought of a conversation with Piet ven der Veen in her present state of mild intoxication.

"Fat chance," Angenette scoffed. "With this *canaille*? He wouldn't be caught dead here."

A black praetorian caught at Ericka's shoulder.

"Where's Jean-Baptiste? I think there's trouble."

Jean-Baptiste pushed his way through the dancers. "What's up?"

"There's a rumor that *Jeune Nation* is going to try to break us up!"

"Where'd you get that?"

The tension in them sobered Ericka instantly.

"The doorman at Théâtre de l'Étoile, next door. He is one of us. He heard it in the lobby after the show."

Jean-Baptiste gripped his shoulder. "Find a phone and call the union headquarters. If it's true, we're going to need all the help we can get. Then pass the word to the rest of the guard. But quietly. We don't want a panic. See that all the entrances are covered. Use their swords if they have to. There's nothing else."

The praetorian nodded shortly. "You? Where will you be?"

Jean-Baptiste jerked his head to Ericka. "I've got to get her out of here. She's pregnant."

Again the praetorian nodded, this time doubtfully.

"Come on, man, get going. You're in charge until I get back. I won't be long. Just long enough to find a cab."

Jean-Baptiste hustled a subdued and frightened Ericka toward the rear of the ballroom, past sleeping drunks and copulating bodies, to a small door that led to a courtyard and then an alley. The alley terminated on rue de Wagram. At this hour there were no cabs in the huge plaza surrounding the Arc de Triomphe, so they turned right toward the busier place de Ternes, four blocks away. They were crossing the rue de l'Étoile and could see the neon lights of place de Ternes when they ran into what seemed to be a group of five black-painted praetorian guards. Jean-Baptiste had already hailed them before he realized his mistake. Though they looked like guardsmen, the streetlights glinted on the bicycle chains and metal-studded belts they carried.

Jean-Baptiste pushed her and shouted "Run!" before he charged into the five men.

Ericka ran as she had never run before, although her progress seemed to be a slow crawl. She heard pounding footsteps behing her, and someone yelled, "It's Moreau! Get the bastard!"

A hand clutched her flying hair, and she was jerked to a stop so hard that she landed on her back, all the wind knocked out of her. She lost her sandals as she was dragged over the pavement back toward the melee. The pain in her scalp was unbearable. She was aware of scuffling feet, panting breath and sickening sound of metal chains meeting solid flesh, the aftermath a deep agonized groan.

A hoarse voice said, "Out of the light! Get 'em into the alley!"

She was pulled, bumping and twisting, over cobblestones, felt the rough stones lacerating her bare feet. The light from the street lamps barely penetrated the alley. Dimly she could see Jean-Baptiste, back against the wall, lashing out with the short blunted sword the praetorians carried. She watched as if in slow motion a bicycle chain raised high, which seemed to take forever before it descended on Jean-Baptiste's head with a sound like the cracking of a ripe melon. She saw him go down, the chain rise and descend again. And again. He tried to roll away and his assailant dropped to his knees beside him. The light flashed on a switchblade in his hand as it too rose and swiftly fell. Jean-Baptiste gave a sound that was more a sigh than a groan and ceased to move.

The man with the knife was panting harshly as he rose, his knife now dulled with blood.

Ericka's captor twisted her hair brutally. "What about this one?"

The man with the knife laughed sharply and leaned down to wipe his blade clean on Jean-Baptiste's still body.

"Fuck her. What else?" He began to move toward her.

From the darkness another voice said, "Better get out before the flics come."

The knifeman laughed again. "Plenty of time. Let's see what we've got."

He dropped his knife on the stones, bent over her and with both hands ripped off her skirt and then her panties. She was too shocked to resist as he pried her legs apart and knelt between them. She realized that it wasn't black paint that covered him but shiny black leather, smooth and clammy on her bare skin. As though all this were happening to someone else, she saw him open his pants. His erection was monstrous, as if his violence had acted as an aphrodisiac. It all became real as he pushed himself hurtfully into her dry flesh. She began to struggle frantically.

"Hold her, Goddamnit!"

The man clutching her hair released it and shifted to pin her shoulders to the stones. She twisted her head, trying to reach him with her teeth, and saw the switchblade lying beside her. The knife was cold and firm in her hand. She buried it in the back of the man on top of her. For a moment his piston drive went on, and then he shuddered, as though the plunging blade had triggered his orgasm. His body became a dead weight.

The man holding her shoulders was leaning over her, unsure in the darkness of what had happened. She pulled the knife out of the dead man and drew it swiftly across the throat above her head. There was a wet strangled gasp and a rush of blood blinded her and filled her open mouth.

Suddenly the weight of both bodies was gone. She never saw the looped chain that whipped her head. Only blackness.

She awoke in the hospital at La Santé prison. Deputy Chief Inspector Étienne Tabard was sitting in a straight-backed wooden chair beside her bed.

"You're awake."

She tried to nod and winced with pain. There was a constriction about her scalp. She lifted her hand and felt the wide bandage.

"We seem to meet only when your head gets in the way of something," Tabard said. "Mind telling me what happened?"

"Jean-Baptiste . . . ?" The words came out a whisper, and he leaned forward to make sure he heard.

"The agitator? Moreau?" His eyes were very clear and sharp above the comical mustache. "He was dead when we arrived. And the others. Two of them."

The pain of that was so intense that it wasn't to be borne. Tabard's face seemed to float before her, unattached, wavering. For an instant she could taste again the salty tang of the river of blood choking her. Then she retreated from all reality.

Ten Tabard got up from his chair and leaned close. He lifted her eyelid to see if she was faking. When he saw she wasn't, he sighed. He got a Gauloises from a battered pack, lit it and inhaled deeply. While he smoked, he stood looking down at the pale, angelic face. The white bandage lent her the look of some old master's Madonna. He watched the slow rise and fall of her breathing.

When his cigarette was finished, there was no place to stub it. He went out into the corridor, dropped the butt on the linoleum and stepped on it. The plainclothes detective waiting there asked "Anything?"

"Nothing," Tabard said slowly. "Not a damned thing." He came out of whatever he had been thinking and was his usual energetic self. He gripped his assistant's arm so hard that the man winced.

"The weapon!" he snarled. "Find the fucking weapon! Without that, what the hell have we got."

The detective rubbed at his arm when Tabard released it and jerked his head toward the closed door.

"You think *she* did it?"

Tabard looked his irritation. "Who the hell knows? Anything could have happened. If she did, it's ten to one she'll say she doesn't remember a thing. And the fucking doctors will back her up—faking or not. Let's get out of here. I want that fucking weapon!"

An hour and ten minutes after Tabard left, Ericka awoke, aware of a burning pain between her legs. Her hand told her that she was padded there. She thought first of the rape, which she could remember in all its detail like a clicking reel of film running through her head. Then she knew that she had lost her baby.

A blue-clad nurse came in, took one look at her and gave her a sedative. She slept again.

By the time Ten Tabard returned the next morning, Ericka had reached the same conclusion he had come to. She had already erased from her mind things that had happened in her childhood. Now she was going to forget what happened in the alley. They would have to believe her. The pain of Jean-Baptiste's death had retreated deep into her mind. The baby was something she had never quite believed in, anyhow. Her pregnancy, and its end, seemed like something that had happened to another girl another time, in another place.

Time. She must hang on to time. Because time kept getting away from her. She had no real idea of how long she had been in the hospital, for instance. A few seconds could turn into an hour, or what seemed like an hour could be only a few seconds. Time was very slippery.

And connections. She was having problems with connections, too. At first she had a real doubt that any of this had actually happened. Perhaps it was all something she had read in a novel. If

358

that was true, then how far back did fantasy go? Was there ever a baby? Or someone named Jean-Baptiste Moreau?

There *was* a Jean-Baptiste. And he was dead. She had to treat that as fact, too, because the policeman had told her so.

Gradually it became clear to her that there was no fantasy. That it was all true. Finally she was able to accept what had happened and still maintain her sanity, because it seemed to fit the philosophy she had evolved after Melinda's death. Life really *was* fair. It broke everybody's heart—without exception. One makes one's plans, but it is accidents that control them.

There was no order, no cosmic plan, no rhyme or reason. Things just happened. Each good thing had its opposite. Which right now was very bad. It was up to Ericka alone to protect herself from the bad things. No one could do it for her.

Tabard was her enemy because she had killed two men. For whatever reason, Tabard would try to make her pay for that because that was his business. It wouldn't matter to Tabard that French courts would probably find her act justified. It was the process that concerned Tabard, the orderly administration of the law. If that was satisfied, then Tabard would be satisfied.

But why should she be forced to have her life disrupted, her purpose blunted, go through the whole dreary business of courts and guilt or innocence, when she herself felt no remorse, no guilt, no sorrow? She had done what she had to do to protect perhaps her life, but surely to defend the thing inside her, the firm inner core that was truly Ericka. Which refused to be violated without retaliation.

She would say that she couldn't remember. That she had been dragged into the alley and hit on the head. What could they prove?

And that was all Tabard could get out of her. She was sweet, she was reasonable, she was trying to help. She was a young woman who had gone through a shocking experience and, because of it, had lost her baby. Her story was unshakeable. And, as deputy chief inspector, Tabard didn't believe a word of it.

Ten Tabard, the husband of Narcisse, the friend of her friend Gavin Riordan, wanted to take off his hat and cheer. She was getting away with murder, not matter what the justification. And she was doing it with considerable panache. He found he didn't give a damn.

Ericka saw it in his face. Her contracted muscles relaxed. She tried to smile. The corners of her mouth felt peculiar, as though she had no control, as if her mouth, her whole face, might dissolve and melt away.

But she managed it, and Ten Tabard smiled back at her. "Do you have any plans?" he asked.

"I'm going to be an architect."

It took a moment for him to make the connection. She could understand that. She had her own problems with connections.

"I see," he said at last. "And a very good one, I suspect. Well . . . you're free to go. Your friends are waiting to take you home."

The Ven der Veens had brought clean clothes from her apartment, and the nurse helped her dress. The business of her release took some time. After she had signed all the documents, Ivan and his father met her in the lobby. The old man put his arms around her, and she stifled the desire to pull away. She had a reluctance to touch. Or be touched. Ever again.

She didn't win the Prix de Rome. She did get third prize and a chance for further study in Rome. She turned it down. She had an overwhelming need for the comfort of Gramercy Park, where she had grown up with people who cherished her. Her own personal retreat to the womb. Life at the moment was just too tough to face.

Ivan ven der Veen took her to the airport, shepherded her through ticketing, took care of her baggage and, at the departure gate, planted a swift kiss on her cheek. "I'll miss you, Ericka. You know that."

"Yes, I know." She wanted to say that she would miss him, too. But she couldn't. Ivan, his father, Paris and all that had happened there were now wiped out of her life. As though none of it had ever existed. She hoped that she would never have to think of any of it again.

The flight home was uneventful. Until she was standing outside

360

the TWA terminal at Kennedy, waiting for a cab to take her to the city. There a man took her arm, rather more firmly than he needed.

"Give you a lift, baby. If you'd like."

She jerked away violently and heard herself say, "Don't touch me, you son of a bitch!" She watched the suggestive smile on his lips turn to outrage as he backed off. Ericka felt great satisfaction in his discomfort, because men had become her enemies.

22

Time: 1961
SERENA GANSVOORT DAMIANI
SUMMERLIN PERCIVAL

"What do you make of that?" Riordan slid the cream-colored envelope across the table.

Knowing that it contained an invitation to the Gansvoort-Pinchot wedding, Des Daniher let it lie and raised an innocent eyebrow. "It should be a grand affair. All the gentry from round about. I look forward to seeing you there."

"You, too?" Gavin's face mirrored his suspicion. "What the hell is going on?"

Charlie Bishop laughed.

The three men were lunching at Tiernsy's Clam Bar near the statehouse. The restaurant was crowded with politicians, lobbyists and bureaucrats. The loud buzz of important conversations would have made it difficult to hear had not Daniher been given his usual secluded corner table.

"Miss Serena's idea of fun, inviting us." Daniher's eyes crinkled in sly amusement. "Auld acquaintance, childhood chums."

"What's Serena got to do with it?"

"She's running the show," Bishop answered. "The other team turned the whole thing over to her. The great Duke Minot couldn't be bothered. Five hundred and nine invitations, so far. Including the reception. Every important pol from here to Canada. Plus Washington, D C. Jim Conroy will come if he can."

Gavin was aghast. "Conroy at Riverhaven? The old man will never stand for it, even if he is the President."

"Besides," Charlie Bishop cut in, "old man Gansvoort don't know about it. He's in London and won't be back until the week before the wedding. By that time it'll be too late. He can't very well call the whole thing off."

"I wouldn't count on it. Jesus!" Gavin looked at Daniher's benignly innocent face. "Your idea, Des? Making it a political shindig?"

Daniher nodded toward Bishop. "Charlie did the talking."

"How in God's name . . . ?" Gavin still couldn't quite believe that Serena would . . .

The expression on Bishop's face showed that he, too, couldn't quite figure it out. "You know," he said wonderingly, "it wasn't as hard as I thought it would be. You forget about her money and talk to her like your kid sister. . . . Explain to her that Stewart's got a real chance of making it big—if he can convince the people that a Gansvoort is just plain home folks, like anybody else. . . . By God, she was like a puppy you tickled on the stomach. Miles ahead of me. Took over like the whole thing was her idea. Let me tell you, that is one hell of a girl."

Gavin could see all too well how it was. Of course, Serena would delight in such a monumentally offensive joke on her father. Full speed ahead.

"There's no stopping her," Bishop went on. "She's loving every minute of it. Caviar by the barrel. Flown in from Iran, no less. Spare no expense. What the hell, the bride's family gets the bills, if I got my Emily Post right." Bishop began to grin. "Of course, Stewart is shitting in his pants. But at the same time, he's kind of enjoying it, too. The guy has a big hate for his old man. Big, big hate. I wonder what the hell the old bastard did to 'em. They both got a real hard on for him."

Serena was indeed enjoying herself. As her father had pointed out to Stewart, Serena knew a lot about weddings (three public and elaborate, one clandestine by a justice of the peace in Elkton, Maryland). The present incumbent was Tom Percival, a yacht broker and designer of excellent family, whose only ambition was to win the America's Cup and whose only duties were to be in attendance when Serena required him. It was an arrangement that suited them both.

When Stewart introduced Serena to Charlie Bishop, she pegged him immediately for exactly what he was, a diamond in the not-so-rough, interested in only one thing: power and its uses.

Which was why Serena was inclined to believe him when he told her that Stewart could make it big in the world of politics. Provided he followed the rules. Rules laid down by Charlie Bishop. It was also the reason she reacted so enthusiastically to Charlie Bishop's plot to make Stewart's wedding a political event of the first magnitude. If Bishop said it was the first step in a promising career for Stewart, it was probably true. And the idea of opening the halls of Riverhaven to *politicians* would certainly be anathema to her father. The fun of it!

Because she liked Charlie Bishop and believed she understood him, Serena felt a word of warning was in order about the danger of launching Stewart as a power seeker. "Be very careful how you motivate him. Because if Stewart ever wants something—really *wants* something—he's capable of killing for it."

At Bishop's doubting smile she said sharply, "Don't underestimate him. It's the arrogance of the very, very rich. That kind of money makes all things possible. It's shocking. It's amoral. And you better believe it because it's true. Don't try to understand it. You can't, unless you're one yourself. Just take my word for it."

Listening to her own words, Serena was suddenly appalled at the thought of what Stewart might be capable of if he ever got real power of his very own. There was absolutely nothing in Stewart's character to hold him back. Except his father. And how long would that last?

Serena threw herself wholeheartedly into planning the wedding. Aside from several phone conversations with Duke Minot, who was grateful to be relieved of all but financial responsibility, her only contact with the bride's side was with a Mrs. Agnes Parsons, who proved to be a model of efficient helpfulness. Mrs. Parsons provided the bride's guest list, which seemed to be pitifully small compared to her own—a mere sixty-two people, most of whom seemed to be friends of the bride's father rather than the bride. It was arranged that Mrs. Parsons and Olivia Minot arrive at Riverhaven two weeks before the wedding to assist in final preparations.

Olivia Minot was a puzzle to Serena. She couldn't imagine a less likely object for Stewart's affections. Olivia was a tall girl, just under six feet. She was painfully shy, dressed in clothes that were uninspired at best. She had the look of a poor country cousin.

Curiosity mixed with pity led Serena to help with the unpacking. She found that Olivia's idea of a trousseau ran to tailored suits and low-heeled "practical" shoes. There seemed to be an overabundance of jodhpurs and turtlenecks.

Serena took Olivia on a whirlwind tour of couturier shopping, using her money like a club. Threats and promises got her fittings, alterations and the guarantee of timely delivery. Serena rolled over oppostion like Patton's tanks.

Olivia proved to be both docile and almost pathetically grateful. She reacted to all the pretty clothes like a child in a toy shop. Serena began to feel like a doting mother.

She really began to feel her age in the fitting room of a famous lingerie house when Olivia had to strip to the buff for try-ons. Once out of her tweeds Olivia had a lovely figure: long, white neck; high, firm breasts; narrow-muscled waist curving gracefully into perfectly proportioned hips, and long, slim legs. Her skin positively glowed with youthful health. Serena's resentful envy was somewhat leavened by her obvious superiority to Olivia from the neck up. Olivia's brownish hair was too straight (something a stylist could fix), her nose was too short, her mouth too full and her chin too firm (things even God couldn't fix). Only her eyes were good, a deep, dark brown. Her brows were heavy as a man's.

It was when Serena first saw the girl on a horse that her opinion of Olivia began to revise itself. Along with Olivia, a string of four hunters arrived from Oak Tree Farms, to be housed with the only two hacks still stabled at Riverhaven.

From a shy, reticent, insecure girl who seemed ten years younger than the twenty-eight that showed on the form books, Olivia Minot astride a horse became something truly magnificent. She rode like a centaur, she and the animal all of a piece, a meld of muscle, bone and sinew flowing dramatically together.

Serena, having been around horses all her life, considered herself several cuts above a journeyman rider. Compared to Olivia, she felt like the rankest sort of hacker. Olivia had chosen a gray mare, a deep, rich hue dappled with dark rosettes, head slim and delicate, huge intelligent black eyes. Her legs were long and sinewy, sloping shoulders melting into a short topline and superbly muscled hindquarters.

Serena had the choice of a black gelding with a nervous disposition, a chestnut who stood all of seventeen hands, and a dun-colored mare with gentle eyes. Putting discretion well ahead of valor, Serena chose the dun and learned that her name was Bluebell.

Olivia's gray danced and curvetted crabwise, pulling hard against the bit. "She's a little rank," Olivia said. "Needs a good run."

"I'm not sure how the bridle paths are," Serena warned. "There may be some growth. They haven't been used much lately."

She should have known better. Everything at Riverhaven was kept in shipshape order, whether used or not. The paths were neatly trimmed and clear. They breasted a hill and came out of the woods at the head of a long meadow. They paused there, Olivia studying the contour of the land, picking out a route through patches of week-old snow.

"Ready to go?"

Serena nodded, not knowing quite what to expect.

"This one's got the legs on Bluebell, so I'll take it first. That is, if you don't mind." For just a moment Olivia reverted to her old apologetic role.

"What the hell," Serena said. "Take it away."

Olivia gave the gray a tiny bit of slack and the mare exploded. One moment the horse was standing still. The next it was in full stride, the dark body stretching out impossibly over the hay stubble. Bluebell caught Serena by surprise, flinging herself into a reaching canter, willing to make a race of it. Serena pulled back on the reins, which only served to make Bluebell lengthen her stride. The gray was far ahead as Serena found herself caught up in a rushing gallop across the sun-dappled field. She could only crouch over Bluebell's neck and give the horse its head.

At the end of the field was a stone boundary fence, put there years before there was a Riverhaven. Serena had known that fence all her life. She judged it to be at least six feet high and four feet deep. To the best of her knowledge it had never occurred to anyone to try to jump it.

Despite her own problems, Serena watched in stricken disbelief as the gray mare approached the fence without shortening stride or gathering itself to take the impossible obstacle. The horse seemed to soar in one beautiful fluid motion, airborne, detached from all relation to the earth. One heart-stopping moment and the gray had cleared the fence with room to spare.

Bluebell seemed to take it for granted that the thing to do was to follow the leader. There was nothing Serena could do about it except to clamp her knees as tightly as she could. She saw the stone barrier approaching at frightening speed until she could pick out the blue-green patterns of the lichen on its surface. Bluebell had the sense to slow down and set herself for the leap. Serena could feel the great muscles gathering under her as the dun horse lifted. There was the momentary sensation of flight and she was over.

Serena was so surprised that she had made it at all that she promptly fell off. The jarring impact on the winter-hard earth knocked her breath out, and she saw stars through a veil of blackness. The next thing she knew she was cradled in Olivia Minot's arms, Olivia's head outlined against the blue of the sky.

"Oh, God. Are you all right? I'm so sorry, Serena. I didn't know you'd follow. . . ."

Olivia's anxiety was genuine and her concern touching. Serena felt vaguely like a babe in arms and began to resent it. She struggled to sit up. Olivia lifted her to her feet. The strength of her arms was formidable.

"You sure you're all right?"

"I haven't fallen off a horse since I was ten," Serena said indignantly. "What the hell were you trying to do? Commit suicide?"

It took Olivia a moment to make the connection. Then, looking toward the stone fence, "Oh, that. Sort of a challenge, I guess. I knew Mousey could take it."

Stewart's return from Washington in time for dinner that night provided his sister with another surprise, for it became obvious that Olivia Minot was hopelessly, madly, embarrassingly in love with her husband-to-be. Serena gave up trying to put it all together and watched Olivia turn into helpless mush every time Stewart looked at her. Stewart treated her to the easy charm he used with most women, but had the grace to look embarrassed when he caught Serena's eye.

Later Serena, lying in bed just before turning out the light, puzzled over why Olivia hadn't given any indication of her feelings for Stewart long before this. Surely the eve of her wedding was a time for girlish secrets. Serena was reaching for the light when Olivia knocked once again and came in. The bedroom was dark except for the bedside lamp, so Serena saw only a shadowy form in a long nightgown until Olivia sat down on the side of the bed, bent over and clutching her stomach. Her face was alarmingly pale and there were deep circles under her eyes.

"Do you have anything for cramps?"

Cramps? Well, Serena reflected, *there goes the honeymoon. Hadn't the girl checked her calendar before setting the wedding date?*

Serena rarely had cramps herself. She said, "No. Except some

367

gin. It's in the little fridge in the dressing-room closet. If that'll help."

"No." And then Olivia said something curious. "Is it always this bad?"

Serena speculated on that for a moment. "Haven't you ever . . . ?"

"Not since I was nineteen. The doctor said . . ."

The time for girlish secrets had arrived with a bang.

There was room in Riverhaven's small chapel for no more than forty witnesses to the ceremony, performed by the Episcopal bishop of the diocese. The words *obey in all things* were omitted, at Serena's insistence, as a blow for women's independence. The bride couldn't have cared less. It was obvious from her dewy-eyed adoration of the bridegroom that she would have gone through the ceremony stark naked and standing on her head if Stewart had so commanded. Serena wept at a wedding for the first time in her life. Even August Gansvoort seemed momentarily affected, while Duke Minot beamed inanely throughout the proceedings.

Holding her hand in the reception line, Des Daniher was hugely entertained.

"How'd I do?" Serena whispered anxiously. And then, "Where's your hat?"

"Safely in the hands of the high priest who guards your door. It wouldn't do to desecrate the temple. And you did fine as any queen, considering your humble origins. As for you—you'd grace the very Halls of Tara." And then in a whisper, "How is your father taking it?"

"Bloody but unbowed. The second shoe is yet to drop." She squeezed his hand and passed him on to her father, next in line.

When Daniher reached August Gansvoort, his face was composed and solemn. "A grand occasion. How happy you must be. And proud."

He felt the faint twitch of Gansvoort's fingers in his and had a certain grim satisfaction.

"Yes. Indeed. Mr. Daniher . . ." August Gansvoort cleared his throat. "I wonder if you'd join me in the library? When this . . ." He inclined his head briefly toward the crowded room. "Say, in half an hour?"

"A pleasure." Daniher allowed himself to smile. "I look forward to it." *And that,* he thought, *is the God's truth.*

August Gansvoort's cold eyes followed him as he made his way toward the long bar and saw him greeted by high and low alike. Some with fawning deference, some with real friendliness. A United States senator, a woman in an outrageous flowered hat, a red-faced man totally out of place in a loud "mod" suit, and finally the governor of the state, who placed a familiar arm around Daniher's shoulders. What they all had in common was a noticeable respect, which Daniher accepted with easy grace as his due.

August Gansvoort, too, began to look forward to the coming interview.

Gavin Riordan was late for the reception. There were only a few people ahead of him in the line. He, too, had persuaded himself that he had accepted the invitation only out of curiosity. Why he had chosen to wear his departmental dress blues—complete with rows of decorations, both military and police, including the Distinguished Service Cross, with its red, white and blue ribbon—was something he preferred not to examine too closely, skirting what he suspected was the real reason—the sort of juvenile bragging he deplored.

He knew she had married again. Why had she asked him? For the fun of twisting the knife? It would be like her. And then again, it wouldn't. Six years had persuaded Gavin that Serena no longer had the power to hurt him. He had long since forgiven her desertion. He felt that Serena's part of his life was rather like a bad appendix. Once excised, it shouldn't be missed, since it performed no useful function.

Still, he was curious. He wondered what she would say.

What Serena said, as he took her hand in the reception line, was, "Good thing you're not a welterweight. Your chest wouldn't be big enough for the fruit salad. All you need is mayonnaise."

And Gavin cursed the silly pride that had caused him to wear his uniform.

"Still with the needle, Serena? I should have known."

"What'd you expect. You haven't called me in six years."

The sheer gall of it left Gavin speechless.

Since August Gansvoort was waiting, he passed on down the line, feeling his face redden with indignation. Behind him he heard Serena giggle.

He saw Des Daniher at the bar among a crowd of people and recognized the new attorney general, Bill Conroy.

"Gavin, dear boy," Daniher greeted him. "What an impressive array." He turned to Conroy. "You know each other, I believe."

Bill Conroy held on to Gavin's hand while he checked out the rows of ribbons. "Impressive indeed. You get that law degree?"

"I did," said Gavin.

"Ever practice?"

"Thought about it. But no. By the way, congratulations to you and the President on your win. Now that *was* impressive."

"Hardly," Conroy said. "Too close for comfort. One hundred and eighteen thousand votes, give or take, is not exactly impressive, but we did the job. Do you ever get to Washington?"

"Tourist only."

"Justice could use guys like you. You've got the background for it. We're going to be doing some exciting things."

"Am I to take that as an offer?" Gavin asked.

Conroy smiled his extraordinary smile. "Invitation only. For a talk. Give it some thought."

"I will," Gavin said. "I will. And thanks for your interest."

The insistent beat of Peter Duchin's music drifted to them from the ballroom. "Duty dances," Conroy said. "Then I've got to run."

"Glad you could make it." Daniher held out his hand. "I'll say good-bye now, then." And Gavin was struck once more by the extraordinary power of his Uncle Des. Conroy was here only as a favor to Des Daniher.

August Gansvoort was seated behind his desk as Daniher remembered him. Twenty years had left their mark, in hair and eyebrows now snow white, hollowed cheeks, a jawline more sharply defined, a further thinning of the lips, a gauntness of the neck muscles. The eyes, however, held the same remote chilliness.

Daniher sat in a leather chair facing the desk. The sounds of the reception came faintly through the library doors.

Gansvoort gestured briefly. "Your doing, I take it?"

"Partly," Daniher conceded, "although by no means entirely."

"May I ask why?"

Daniher considered this, thinking of all he had to gain if Stewart lived up to his expectations, thinking, too, of what this cool inflexible man could do to stop what Daniher had in mind. If he chose to.

"My business is politics, Mr. Gansvoort. In politics you need winners. I think your son could be just that. He has more qualifications than most. Intelligence, ability, charm—and money."

"*My* money," August Gansvoort said dryly. "Stewart's personal income might not be adequate to support a life in politics."

"True"—Daniher nodded—"there's that. But there's a thing that's more important. Call it ambition. Or desire. Or whatever it is that drives a man. I think the lad has found something he truly wants— perhaps for the first time in his life. He'd be hard to stop." He paused and then added, "With the proper counsel."

He was treated to August Gansvoort's wintry smile. "Yours, of course?"

"Mine." Daniher let the word lie between them while August Gansvoort considered it.

"You think my son would defy me, Mr. Daniher? If I chose to fight his decision?"

"I think he would—if I showed him how. But then, it would be my fight, too. The Irish are a curious breed, Mr. Gansvoort. They have a lust for battle. A glory in it. It's a thing in the blood. Someone said, 'All our wars are merry and all our songs are sad,' and it's true, Mr. Gansvoort, it's true. A dangerous heritage."

Daniher took the time to run his hand over the shiny baldness of his head.

"I'll run him for assembly for a start. If he gives the word. And I think he will. From your own district, too, the Ninth. The party will find the money. Never doubt it, Mr. Gansvoort. And I'll win with him as well. After that, we'll see."

"How do you propose to do that? The Ninth hasn't elected a Democrat in forty years."

It was Daniher's turn to smile. "By adding a sizeable part of the Twenty-seventh District to the Ninth. Stewart's report on reapportionment gave us that chance. Gerrymandering, Mr. Gansvoort. It will give the new Ninth a two-to-one Democratic majority."

August Gansvoort put his elbows on the desk and steepled his hands.

"You really believe my son can be successful . . . in politics?" He pronounced the word as though it had the taste of gall.

"The lad was born to it," Daniher said confidently. "All he needs is guidance."

"So you have said." Gansvoort slowly lowered his hands and placed them palm down on the polished wood. Fascinated, Daniher watched the long, slim fingers press gently on the surface of the desk, press and release, press and release. "Then," August Gansvoort said slowly, "you have my blessing. And my backing."

By an effort of will Daniher kept his mouth from dropping open. The most he had hoped for was Gansvoort's neutrality in the face of defeat. But this . . . It opened up endless possibilities. With the Gansvoort millions—or was it trillions . . . He saw the faint satisfaction on Gansvoort's face as Gansvoort watched his reaction. He couldn't for the life of him keep his speculations from showing.

"On two conditions," August Gansvoort said gently.

Daniher recovered quickly. He let his eyebrows rise slightly.

"First. Stewart must agree to accept *your* . . . guidance, in all things. All Gansvoort . . . 'contributions' will be administered by you alone."

August Gansvoort began to smile in earnest now, and Daniher found the curling lips somehow ominous.

"In short, Mr. Daniher, I am abdicating whatever responsibilities I may feel toward my son's . . . career. It is now in your hands. A sort of proxy father. So to speak."

The implications flooded Daniher's mind. He had a dreadful sense of foreboding. If he accepted, he laid himself open to all sorts of disaster. Monies could be traced. Stewart's unpredictability . . . the impossibility of divining what was in August Gansvoort's Machiavellian brain. In too many ways he would put himself in Gansvoort's power. "And the second thing?"

"I want your word, Mr. Daniher, that you will do your best to take my son to the top. The very top, Mr. Daniher."

The sound of Daniher's indrawn breath broke the silence.

"No man could promise a thing like that. If you mean . . ."

"I do indeed. The presidency. 'Best efforts,' Mr. Daniher, if you're familiar with the phrase. I ask no guarantees."

"You're mad, man, you don't know what you're saying. You can't just . . ." Daniher found that he was breathing shallowly. He could feel a rivulet of perspiration run down his side.

"Perhaps. Perhaps not. I seem naive to you?" The beautifully kept hands lifted, palms upward. "But then, I have the utmost confidence in your ability to produce a . . . winner—in your chosen field. If any man can do it . . . with unlimited resources at your disposal . . ."

Again Daniher's brain was seething with the possibilities. Unlimited resources? It was barely conceivable that it could be done. Very slowly. Very carefully. First the state assembly, the meticulous buildup, the right speeches in the right forums . . . Then national office? Or perhaps governor? Light-years away . . . but . . .

He heard himself speak his thought. "It would take years. And millions . . ."

"You have both, Mr. Daniher. I impose no limits—on either time or funds."

"Why?" Daniher asked. "Why are you doing this? What's in it for you?"

Gansvoort studied him, the pale blue eyes hooded now. "If you must have a reason, consider this. My son is an unprincipled man who has an infinite capacity for evil, with very little knowledge of the verities most men live by. An interesting combination fraught with possibilities—for the observer. Believe me, Mr. Daniher, in view of the recent elections, I am convinced that my country and my son deserve each other. A certain sense of the fitness of things, I

373

think. Come, now." August Gansvoort held out his hand. "Do we have a deal?"

Serena seemed to have no substance in Gavin's arms, floating weightless as a cloud. Duchin's velvet instruments were caressing "Where or When" and the lyrics came unbidden to Gavin's mind. At the right place Gavin found that he was whispering the last couplet under his breath.

"I do," Serena said. "Like yesterday."

"You do what?"

"Remember where and when," she said.

She pulled away from him slightly to look around the crowded room. There were drink stains on priceless tables, plates with half-eaten remains. A waiter went past them, carrying the shards of a broken Lalique vase. "Animals," Serena said with distaste. "I need some air. Let's get out of here."

Outside, the air was clear and cold, their breaths misty. Far out on the river a single sailboat with a striped red and white sail suddenly heeled over as a gust of wind took it. Immediately below them was the boathouse and its dock at the end of a long flight of steps. Gavin thought she'd head for that, but Serena turned left along the graveled path toward the stables. They walked in silence until they reached the cobbled courtyard.

"She brought her horses. Sort of a contribution. She's really something on a horse. Want to see?"

"Sure. Why not."

Serena pushed open the stable doors. Gavin followed her, his breath coming a little faster, remembering.

Serena made straight for the tack room at the far end of the long building, paying no attention to the restless horses in their stalls, except to gesture toward the sleek rump of a dun and say, "I fell off that one."

The tack room was no longer used. Its former dusty emptiness was now swept clean. There were calico curtains on the one window. A well-worn leather armchair with a standing lamp beside it stood next to a neatly made cot. Over the cot was a shelf that held a row of paperbacks and a pair of gleaming spurs.

374

Serena turned and stood facing him. The green dress clung to every curve of her body.

"Remember?"

Gavin stayed where he was, determined not to make a move, fighting the urge. Serena grinned wickedly, took a pace forward and put her arms around him. In an instinctive and familiar reaction he cupped her buttocks with both hands and pulled her close.

Serena winced. "Easy, darling. I've got a bruise on my ass as big as your hat."

Serena stepped back, lifted her skirt to her waist and turned her bare bottom to him. "Take a look. . . ."

Gavin looked.

And was lost.

23

Time: 1963, RIVERHAVEN
Nan Kennicott

At fifteen Nan Kennicott had the nubile beauty of emerging womanhood. Her body's lines verged on lushness. They were a constant source of surprise and excitement.

Because of the heat she had left her bunk and come on deck. A seat cushion from the cockpit was now her bed. She lay on it, comfortably drowsy, under a blanket of a million stars. Lulled by the gentle motion of the yacht against the Riverhaven dock, her head was on a trip she had recently taken more and more frequently.

She was on a desert island, the sound of waves in her ears, the smell of exotic flowers in the air. Paul Newman, in ragged shorts and nothing else, was coming toward her. He loomed above her, blocking out the stars. Slowly he dropped his shorts. With infinite tenderness he pulled down the sheet that covered her and bent to kiss her breast. She could feel his warm breath on her rigid nipple. His hand was between her legs. He lowered himself on her body and murmured, "Nan, my darling . . ."

At that point fantasy stopped—because she wasn't quite sure what should happen next—and sleep took over.

She was awakened just before dawn by low voices coming from the open porthole under which she had arranged her nest. She recognized her father's voice first and then her mother's. She was instantly alert and lay almost without breathing, her first thought that she might hear them doing what *they* did when *they* slept together.

The scene unfolded like a movie in her head, dialog by Gregory Peck and Bette Davis.

Bette: You haven't slept . . . (rustling and creaking . . . silence)

Gregory: I'm sorry, darling. I just can't get it up. Chalk up one more failure.

Bette: Don't, Put. (soothing) Things will work out. They always have.

Gregory: I'm not so sure, this time. . . . I'm fifty-four years old, and maybe I've had it. Nobody seems to want an old birdman with one eye and one ear. There just aren't any jobs. God knows I've tried.

Bette: You'll find something. I know you will. (silence)

Gregory: Honey, there's something I have to tell you. And I think I'd rather cut off an arm. We'll have to get out of Putnam House. Not enough money to swing it.

Bette: (shocked) Oh, no . . . !

Gregory: There's just nothing for taxes. Or upkeep. Nothing left but my pension. I've borrowed ahead on that. . . . (silence)

Bette: (very low, hard to hear) Nan's school . . . ?

Gregory: I'm not sure. . . . (pause) I don't suppose public school will hurt her. (pause) It'll mean cutting to the bone.

	Small apartment somewhere until . . . (pause) Jesus! There's *got* to be a job!
Bette:	It's not like you to give up, Put. You've always . . .
Gregory:	Let's face it, hon. I don't know where the hell to turn next. (pause)
Bette:	Couldn't you talk to Stewart . . . ?
Gregory:	(roughly) You know I can't.
Bette:	But why not? Stewart must have a thousand jobs . . .
Gregory:	I can't presume on friendship—especially from a man I busted out of flying school. And I damned well won't ask for charity. That's how he'd see it. And that's how I'd see it.
Bette:	Maybe I could drop a . . .
Gregory:	(angrily) You'll do no such thing! I won't have it. And that's an order. You hear me? (silence)
Bette:	(very softly, tenderly) Wonderful what getting mad will do for a man. (pause) There, darling. Right there . . . (a sound Nan had never heard before)
Gregory:	(hoarsely) Oh, God, I love you so. . . . (creaking of the bunk)

Nan left her seat cushion where it was and crept, on silent tiptoes, back to her cabin. She had no concrete understanding of what she had just heard really meant to her or her parents. But she knew the sounds of anguish and despair and she was terrified.

Putnam Kennicott, his wife Mary and his daughter Nan were guests of old family friends named Palliser aboard their sixty-five-foot power cruiser, which accommodated fourteen passengers in the luxury to which all but the Kennicotts were accustomed. The Kennicotts had background and breeding but no money. The other passengers all had money, and a few of them had all three.

The occasion for this visit to Riverhaven was the seventieth birthday of August Gansvoort. Since the Big House was full of guests, the Palliser party slept aboard the *Bellerêve*, and from there went up a flight of steps to the boathouse-cum-summerhouse, then up the winding flagstone path to the Big House to attend the weekend festivities.

Despite her mother's urging, Nan stayed aboard Saturday morning when the others went up to the tennis courts. She wanted to be alone with her new and confusing knowledge. What she had heard appalled her. It wasn't having to leave Miss Finch's, although she adored it there, nor was it moving from Putnam House. It was the fact that her parents were suddenly not parents anymore. They were *people*. No longer the familiar loving and loved Mother and Dad, dependable, wise, comforting—but strangers now, living their own lives, with their own pains and agonies, in which she had no part.

And yet, she knew that she was bound to them, and they to her, by a love whose strength had grown overnight and that had suddenly become the most important thing in her life. The Nan Kennicott of just hours ago was a memory. The new Nan was daughter, mother, father and protector to them both. And her heart was breaking for them at their despair.

By the time the others returned to shower and change for lunch at the Big House, Nan was composed. She had a little difficulty in meeting her mother's eyes, for fear her thoughts would be read. Her mother and father showed nothing beyond a mild concern for her, and when she reassured them, they both seemed as cheerful and normal as ever. Knowing what she did, she wondered how people could so successfully conceal their private tragedies from the world.

The Kennicotts, and a few others, had been invited by Stewart Gansvoort for cocktails before lunch at the boathouse, because liquor was never served at the Big House, only wine on special occasions. Nan dutifully followed her parents up the steps from the dock to the wooden sundeck that ran along the side of the boathouse, which faced the river. She was dressed in white shorts and a figured bandana halter in red and white. The August sun was uncomfortably warm and she felt a faint beading of sweat on her upper lip. Her mood had lightened sufficiently for her to wonder if she'd be allowed a cocktail with the rest. Also she was ravenously hungry, and her stomach was growling. The thought of canapés and hors d'oeuvres set her mouth to watering.

The boathouse was really a dwelling. The glass front of its long main room overlooked the river and the City beyond. The room was filled with couches, lounge chairs, deck chairs and pillows of every description, all covered in brilliant striped canvas. At the north end of the house was an apartment, two bedrooms and two baths, with an open kitchen between the suites.

Nan met first Serena Percival and her husband, a tall weatherbeaten man in a blazer with a club insigne. Then Serena's brother, Henry Gansvoort, much younger, with sad, gentle eyes, who took her hand as if it were a privilege. Serena led her to a man in a wheelchair who was dressed in a fuzzy terrycloth robe, opened to show his tanned hairless chest. He looked like Cary Grant (except for his mustache), clear smiling eyes with just a hint of mischief, dark curling hair with the barest graying at the temples, a smiling mouth that told her that she was appreciated.

Serena was saying, "And this is my brother Stewart. Nan Kennicott."

Nan made the connection with a shock. This was the Stewart who could give her father a job, the Stewart her mother was ordered not to speak to. He held her hand longer than he needed, looking into her eyes with a certain speculation, as though he knew what she was thinking.

What she was thinking was that, unlike her mother, she was under no such orders. *She* could talk to this Cary Grant, persuade him with her eloquence, sway him with her charm, bend him to her will, bring all their problems to a happy ending.

She gave him her most provocative smile and then lowered her eyes demurely.

"Well, Nan Kennicott," Stewart Gansvoort said, "would you do a poor cripple a favor and get me a drink? Over there." He gestured toward the open kitchen and its bar, where a man was making drinks. "Vodka and orange juice. Charlie will fix it for you."

The man at the bar said, "Hi, Princess. I'm Charlie Bishop. Chief bottle washer around here. What'll it be?"

"He wants vodka and orange juice. I'm Nan. Nan Kennicott."

"Sounds like Stewart. And what'll it be for you, Nan?"

The open friendly face didn't seem to expect her to ask for Coke. Recklessly she said, "I'll have the same."

Charlie Bishop poured vodka over ice already in tall glasses. She noticed that he measured the same amount for each and was pleased that there was no pandering to tender years. He topped off each glass from a sweating pitcher of orange juice.

Her mother and father and Serena Percival made a tight group around Stewart Gansvoort's wheelchair. She handed Stewart his glass with the guilty hope that her parents would think that hers was pure orange juice and not make a thing of it.

Stewart was saying, "It's not that serious. I can get around if I have to. But the doctor says stay in this contraption as long as possible. That's why I'm bunking down here. Can't manage all the stairs in the Big House yet. And it's a damned nuisance for Olivia to have to take care of me."

"The price you pay for eternal youth," Serena said dryly. "Whatever made you think you could play touch football with the Conroy boys? You were out of your league. Football is not exactly your kind of touch."

There was something a little forced about Stewart's grin.

"The price I paid for the President's endorsement, you mean." He patted the arm of his wheelchair. "Worth all the aches and pains. I've got a tough reelection campaign coming up. I should be out there now. Less than three months to Election Day. Not much time."

Nan's mother made familiar sympathetic sounds while Nan thrilled to the thought that this man was actually a friend of the President of the United States.

"Why not do it on your wheels?" Serena said acidly. "Create lots of sympathy. Like FDR."

Stewart grinned at his sister.

"My biggest booster. You know, I don't think she's ever voted."

"What's the point?" Serena shrugged, tired of the subject. "How do you plan to get up to the house for the birthday party tomorrow? You better not try to duck it."

"Henry said he'd take me up in Father's golf cart. Crutches once I get there."

Hearing his name, Henry Gansvoort detached himself from a nearby group and came to stand by the wheelchair. To Nan, there was something appealing in the way he placed his hand on his brother's shoulder.

"How goes the battle, Stew?"

"No sweat. No pain. I'll be all right."

The words were brave. Looking at the faint wrinkles at the corners of his eyes, Nan thought he really *was* in pain and was gallantly trying to reassure his friends. Her heart went out to him. Forgetting what her drink held, she downed the rest of it in gulps because her empty stomach needed the sustenance of orange juice. The generous dollop of vodka made her eyes water and spread a delicious warmth through her tummy.

At that moment a bell chimed discreetly.

"Drink up, everybody," Serena called. "That's lunch."

There was an emptying of glasses and a general movement toward the French doors at the back of the room. Her father's hand was a gentle pressure on her arm.

"Coming, Nan?"

Henry Gansvoort leaned over his brother's chair.

"I'll have something sent down, Stewart. Anything you'd like?"

"Why bother?" Nan heard herself say, knowing it was an opportunity she couldn't afford to miss. "The refrigerator is full of stuff. I can make us sandwiches. It would be fun. Besides, I'd like to hear about the election . . . the campaign, I mean. For social studies . . . and all." She hadn't meant to babble, but her tongue seemed to run away with her.

Henry Gansvoort said, "That's very kind of you, Nan," and the words had a genuine meaning.

Serena Percival, already on her way to the doorway, turned and gave her a deliberate look of appraisal, as if seeing her for the first time.

"Great idea." Stewart was smiling at her. "I accept with pleasure."

"You sure you won't mind, Nan?" Her father was asking if her offer was merely politeness.

"Course not. It'll be a lot more fun than *lunch*." Her emphasis showed how she felt about snowy napery and crystal stemware.

"I suppose you're right," Put Kennicott said, and winked at her.

They were alone, the sounds of the guests receding toward the Big House. Nan's head was whirling in her search for a way to bring up what she was going to say, disjointed phrases, parts of sentences, none of which seemed right.

"Come on. Let's raid the box." Stewart took off with surprising speed, maneuvering his wheelchair through the jumbled furniture like a race driver.

Before the display in the open refrigerator, Nan's hunger took precedence over everything else.

"I'll make a drink," Stewart said, "while you prepare the feast."

"What would you like?"

"Surprise me." He removed the pitcher of orange juice and maneuvered himself to the bar.

There was a bowl of fresh grapes, frosty with droplets of moisture. Plates of Virginia ham, sliced chicken, part of a duck's carcass, a half-lobster, were surrounded by packets of various cheeses in their silvery wrappers. Unable to make up her mind, Nan pulled out everything that caught her eye and loaded it on a nearby table. Stewart told her where to find cutlery, napkins, condiments and two wine glasses while Nan munched grapes as she worked. Stewart brought a tall green bottle of wine.

When she was seated, Stewart lifted his drink. "A toast. To the prettiest cook in town. Come on, you can drink to that."

She found that he had made a drink for her as well as himself. She clinked glasses with him and, eager to get at the food, again swallowed too much too fast.

They ate in silence, Stewart sparingly, Nan ravenously, while Stewart watched her in amusement. "I haven't seen a spread like this since I was a . . . kid. But you're not a kid, are you . . ." His eyes were briefly on her snug halter. "More like a growing girl, I'd say."

Unable to speak around a mouthful of chicken, Nan could only nod. Stewart filled her wine glass. She would have preferred milk, but she had to have something to wash down the food she was gulping.

At last she was finished and could bring her mind back to her problem. It seemed much easier now. She felt reckless and sure of success. "I wanted to ask you for something. . . ."

Stewart watched her speculatively. "So it wasn't social studies? Or the pleasure of my company? I wondered about that. . . ."

His prescience confused her.

"No. I mean yes . . . partly. I'd rather be here with you than . . ."

"Than having to eat like a lady with the old folks? Should I be flattered?"

"No. Please. . . ." Nan went ahead determinedly. "It's about my father. . . ."

Stewart's eyes widened in surprise. "Put? What about him?"

The words came rushing now, tripping over one another. "He can't find a job. And . . . and there's no money anymore. They'll have to give up Putnam House . . . and live in a little apartment. And public school . . . Mother said you had a thousand jobs you could give him. He wouldn't let her ask you. So I . . ."

She stopped because she saw that he was frowning. "He was right," Stewart said shortly. "You shouldn't have. Tell him to see Charlie Bishop. He takes care of things like that."

Nan was aghast, her newfound confidence dissolved in apprehension. Not so much at Stewart's blunt refusal but at the thought that she, or anyone, would tell her father that she had even asked.

"Oh, no! Please. . . . No one must tell him. If he ever found out . . ."

"He'd what? Spank your pretty bottom? Surely not."

"Please. . . . I only meant . . ." Her eyes began to fill with tears.

"Now, cut it out." He was sorry for his abruptness, uncomfortable with her tears. "Look, Nan, if Put had wanted to ask, he could have. It was his decision. You shouldn't fool around with things that are none of your business. And I promise that I won't tell him.

Come on, now. No more tears.'' And then, hoping to distract her, ''Look, how about putting on some music?'' He wheeled himself to a hi-fi system set into the wall nearby. ''Help me pick something out. What do you like?''

Nan followed him as if in a dream, crushed that all her plans had ended in disaster, her head woozy, the food a leaden weight in her stomach, sick with embarrassment and shame. Listlessly she picked her favorite Beatles album from those he spread out before her, put it on and stood by his chair, not knowing what else to do or say.

Thoughts tumbled about in her mind like clothes in a washing machine. How could she have been so wrong about this man? When her instinct told her he was attracted to her?

After a while the music set Stewart's fingers to drumming on the arm of his chair. She felt herself begin to move, almost unconsciously, to the insistent beat, as she had done so often before to this same music. She knew he was watching her, and something told her not to stop. She swayed her hips in small concentric circles, shifting her weight from one leg to the other. Her breasts bounced just a little under the tight halter.

Almost without volition Stewart's hand moved toward her. She waited as it hovered just over the taut fabric and thought, *Maybe it's not too late*. . . .

Suddenly her brain did a somersault, and she was Marilyn Monroe in *Bus Stop*. She was Lauren Bacall in *To Have and Have Not*. As his hand was about to touch her she jumped back.

''Catch me!'' she called, and whirled away toward the other end of the room.

Stewart Gansvoort hesitiated—and then decided to play.

For it was a game. At first.

The room was an obstacle course. She twisted and turned like a broken-field runner, laughing over her shoulder, keeping just ahead of him, for he was amazingly fast and adept with his wheelchair.

It was one of the big pillows scattered on the floor that brought her down. Stewart loomed over her, blotting out the light, like Paul Newman in her fantasies. His robe had come open in the wild chase. This time she saw what was there and was astounded at its size.

She lay, panting, as he stood up and dropped his robe. He kneeled beside her and then fell partly on top of her. His hand pulled down her halter and cupped her breast. His head seemed huge as he groped for her lips. She clutched his wrist and twisted her head away.

"Don't . . ."

It slowed him for a moment.

"Stewart . . ." She was breathless, her heart pounding violently. "Stewart. My father . . ."

That stopped him short. His hand released her breast and he pulled back, not knowing whether she meant her father might return or . . .?

"Do you want me, Stewart?" She was Elizabeth Taylor in *Cat on a Hot Tin Roof.* She was Natalie Wood in *Splendor in the Grass.* She was Audrey Hepburn in *Breakfast at Tiffany's.*

Stewart was leaning on his elbow, grinning down at her. "You're a calculating little bitch, aren't you?" And then, "Does it mean that much to you?"

She was Jean Simmons in *Elmer Gantry.* "Everything," she breathed. "Everything. . . . Will you promise?"

"Sure," Stewart said. "Why not."

She was sweet Melanie Wilkes in the rerelease of *Gone With the Wind.* She dropped her head back, closed her eyes and murmured, "Be gentle, my darling."

It was closing her eyes that did it. That and the exertion of the chase. The vodka and the wine caught up to her. She was adrift on a sea of nausea. Her head was swimming, her scalp felt as though it were crushing her skull.

He undid her halter, her shorts slithered down over her calves. She was naked, her skin clammy and cold as a frog's. His hand was between her legs, fingers sliding over her wetness. Then he was on top of her, forcing his thing into her.

Suddenly she wasn't anybody—except Nan Kennicott, and he was hurting her dreadfully.

She vomited all over his chest and shoulders.

"Jesus Christ!" Stewart rolled away from her.

She couldn't breathe. She knew she was going to vomit again, and her one idea was to get somewhere where it wouldn't ruin the rugs. She got up and weaved groggily toward the sliding glass doors that led to the sundeck. She didn't quite make it. She began to vomit again before she could reach the outside railing. Once there, she bent over, the wooden bar harsh against her stomach, her body wracked with convulsive heaves that wouldn't stop.

Stewart's first thought was to clean himself of the foulness. He grabbed a kitchen towel that hung from the refrigerator door and scrubbed furiously. Then he heard the ugly sound of her vomiting and it hit him that she was out in the open, bare-assed, where anyone on the dock could see her. Hurriedly he got into his robe, picked up her shorts and halter and hobbled after her, conscious for the first time of the pain in his back.

What he saw when he reached the porch was her bare bottom staring at him like an accusation. Her legs were spread and there was a thickening thread of blood inside one thigh.

"Jesus Christ," Stewart said again, "a virgin. . . ." And then, "You stupid little bitch . . ."

The enormousness of the consequences he faced swept over him. His whole life could go up in flames. He had to get her covered and back inside. He forced himself faster. As he reached her he slipped in her vomit, lost his balance and caromed into her.

It was enough to send her over the railing.

Stewart saw her land on her back on the rocks fifteen feet below. Her body bounced once, rolled inland, out of sight under the porch overhang.

The stairs were agony, but he made it to the bottom. The dock was deserted.

Her body was spread out, limp as a child's doll. Her face had the paleness of death, but her breathing was steady. His hand underneath her breast felt the strong beat of her heart.

"Nan! Nan . . ."

She didn't answer. Her eyes remained closed.

Crouched there beside her, he was acutely conscious of her nakedness, the young jutting breasts, the sparse silky down between her spread legs. It seemed to him an obscenity, like surreptitiously

386

watching a child in her bath. He still had the kitchen towel, and he wiped hurriedly at the blood on her thighs and then at the traces of vomit on her lips.

Her defenselessness cried out to be covered. He lifted her upper body and got her halter in place. He put her limp legs together, struggled with her shorts and finally got the zipper pulled up. And all the time, like a litany in his head, were the words, *Oh, God. Be all right, Nan. Be all right. Oh, God, be all right. . . .*

She opened dazed eyes, and he thought his prayer, if it was a prayer, was surely answered.

"Are you all right, Nan?"

"I . . . think so. . . ." Her voice was like a child's. "What happened, Stewart . . . ?"

He had an instant guilty hope that she didn't remember, that somehow the fall . . .

"You got sick, Nan. You went to throw up all that food. And you fell over. . . ."

She looked up to the porch roof so far above them.

"From there?"

"From there. Over the railing. But you're all right, Nan. Everything will be all right now."

He held his breath while he watched her effort to piece together what had happened. Her hand crept down to her crotch and lingered there. He saw by the sudden awareness in her eyes that she did remember—something.

"You promised, Stewart. . . ."

"Yes. I did. . . ."

His brain began to function lucidly. He had been treating her like a child. She wasn't. If deliberate loss of virginity meant the gain of womanhood, then she was a woman. A woman who wanted something. "Listen to me, Nan. Your father will be all right. He'll never need a job again. He'll keep Putnam House. I promise. And you'll be all right. No public school. You'll have anything you want. But you've got to help me. . . ."

She tried to sit up and fell back with a grimace of pain. "My back hurts. . . ."

He was instantly fearful, remembering the sickening force with which she had landed on the rocks. "Lie still! It's important that you lie still. Don't try to move. I'm going back up to call a doctor." Then, seeing her alarm, "Don't worry. It's just in case you might have injured something. I'll get your parents, too."

He took her hand in both of his and looked steadily, deeply into her eyes, trying by intensity to fix in her mind what he was about to say. "I want you to listen very carefully. Nothing happened up there. Nothing at all. You had too much food and wine. You started to vomit, ran out to the porch—and fell over. I haven't been down here at all. I couldn't, because of my back. The wheelchair. It's important to remember that. I wasn't here at all. If you can do that, Nan, for me . . . for your father, then everything will be all right. You have my promise. Do you understand me, Nan?"

Her eyes searched his questioningly.

"I promise," he said again. At last she nodded, and he could let out his breath.

"I'm going up to telephone now. Your parents will be here soon. And the doctor. I want you to lie here very quietly until they come. And you're not to worry. Everything will be all right."

He stood up to leave and looked down at her. Some of her color had returned, but there were blue circles under her eyes.

"Are you all right?"

She tried to smile and couldn't quite make it. "I don't hurt anymore. I don't feel much of anything. . . ."

Back in his wheelchair, Stewart first called the Big House for Charlie Bishop. He explained the accident and asked Bishop to bring Nan's parents as soon and as quietly as possible. He hung up on Bishop's questions, dialed the Jacob Gansvoort Hospital and got the chief resident on the line.

"This is Stewart Gansvoort," he said. "I'm calling for my father. There's been an accident at Riverhaven"

When he had supplied all the information the doctor requested, he added a warning. "This is a private call. Mr. Gansvoort wants no press, no publicity, no reports and no records to be kept—for the time being. The family will be in touch later if there are any further

388

instructions. And, Doctor, you will come yourself with the ambulance as quickly as possible."

The room was heavy with the odor of vomit. Carefully avoiding the mess on the floor, Stewart wheeled himself to a bathroom and doused his chest and shoulders with *Royall Lyme* cologne.

It was only then that he remembered the soiled kitchen towel he had left lying by Nan's body.

At the Gansvoort Hospital, the chief resident, Dr. Mohandas Moomjii, had taken Stewart's call in the emergency room, where he had been checking an intern's diagnosis of a suspected case of typhus. The charge nurse had listened to Dr. Moomjii repeat Stewart's instructions about press and publicity, and as soon as he had left, went out in the corridor.

Donnie Davelin, the patrolman assigned to Emergency, was sitting on his usual bench, reading a comic book. The charge nurse had a certain fondness for Donnie, who was six feet three, with a face like a cherub's. She told him what she had heard, and Patrolman Davelin, knowing that anything concerning the Gansvoorts was important, called the Third Precinct. On the same premise the desk sergeant rang through to the office of Lieutenant Gavin Riordan, who was acting captain of the Third, and relayed the news.

All of this took less than five minutes. So Riordan was on his way in a squad car almost as soon as the ambulance left Gansvoort Hospital. His first thought was that something had happened to Serena, so he didn't spare the horses. He arrived at Riverhaven just as the ambulance was going through the gates. Since he didn't yet know what the squeal involved, he let it lead him.

He had a touch of reassurance when the van stopped at the path leading to the boathouse. Serena wasn't much of a water person. But with Serena you never could tell. He stopped the procession of three white-coated men at the top of the path, showed his credentials and inquired what was wrong. A worried Dr. Moomjii introduced himself and explained that a young girl had fallen from the sundeck. Riordan followed him to the boathouse, then down the steps and over the railing to the gravelly depression where a small group of people waited.

He saw first Putnam Kennicott, whom he didn't know, then a woman kneeling by the side of a girl and, last, Charlie Bishop, whom he knew very well indeed. Bishop seemed surprised to see him, then looked in irritation at Dr. Moomjii, and Riordan deduced that the doctor had been told to keep the lid on—and had failed.

He nodded briefly to Kennicott, noting that he appeared dazed and distracted, and said, "Hi, Charlie. What happened?"

Bishop took his arm and led him a little aside, almost as though Bishop wanted to isolate him. The doctor brushed past them and joined the woman by the girl's side. Over Bishop's shoulder Riordan could see that the injured girl was indeed young—very young—and that she was conscious and able to answer the doctor's low-voiced questions, which he couldn't quite hear.

"Kennicott's daughter," Bishop whispered. "Kid fell off the porch."

"Now, how would she do that, Charlie?"

Bishop looked uncomfortable. "I wasn't here. I didn't see it. Seems she got sick, went to the rail to vomit—and fell over."

"Who did see it?"

"Just Stewart. They were having lunch. The rest of us were at the Big House."

"Hmm," Riordan said. "I see. And where is Stewart?"

Something in the way he said it triggered Charlie Bishop's anger. "Goddamnit, Gavin. Quit being a cop. Stewart's upstairs. In a wheelchair. With a bad back. It was an accident. Nothing he could do about it. He can hardly get around. The kid was nice enough to fix lunch for him, and that's damn well all there is, so come off it, will you?"

"Slow down, Charlie," Riordan said mildly, and then, "Is she bad?"

"How the hell would I know?"

They both looked upward at the overhanging deck above them.

"Hell of a fall." Riordan measured the distance and estimated the angle. "Must have landed on the rocks." He moved past Bishop, and Bishop let him go.

390

There was nothing to show where the girl had fallen. His eye followed the line her body must have taken when she rolled down the slope of the granite outcrop to where she now lay. Halfway he saw the pool of vomit and again estimated the angle from the deck. He joined the group surrounding her.

The intern and the attendant had unrolled a stretcher beside her. She was pale, but she seemed completely aware of what was happening around her. He was struck by the symmetry of her body, the clean lines of her face with its last hint of baby fat, the clear blue eyes so like her father's. He could see no signs of injury, no cuts, no bruises. She appeared to be merely resting.

He watched as the doctor took a sharp probe from his bag and pressed it firmly into the flesh of her left thigh. At the doctor's unspoken question she shook her head. The doctor repeated the test on her right thigh, and again she shook her head. But now her eyes were wide with fear.

"Why don't I feel anything?" she said wonderingly.

For just a moment those frightened eyes caught Riordan's. He smiled at her and nodded, as if such a simple gesture could ease her. But somehow it seemed to. He saw her lips try to form an answering smile and fail. Unaccountably, and against all his training, something cut through his tough cop's shell of noninvolvement and touched him deeply. It surprised him and disturbed him.

Dr. Moomjii stood up.

"I'm afraid, sir and madam," he said in his soft apologetic Indian English, "your daughter has suffered injury to the back. Perhaps slight. We cannot know until . . ."

"Oh, no . . . !" Mrs. Kennicott was fighting hard not to weep. The knuckles of her clasped hands were white.

"What the hell does *that* mean?" Putnam Kennicott's voice was rough with emotion.

"Please, sir, there is paralysis. Possibly only temporary. We must get her to hospital. There we have X rays and many tests to determine how serious. Until then it is pointless to agitate yourself." He motioned to the intern and the attendant, who began to ease the girl's body onto the stretcher.

As they moved first one leg and then the other, Riordan saw what

391

seemed to be a bloodstain between her thighs. To him it was glaring against the white shorts, but none of the others seemed to notice. It was the first outward sign of injury he had seen. Why just there? Something to ask about later?

"Most carefully, please." Dr. Moomjii's eyes traced the path they would have to negotiate, to the railing, over it and up the stairway. "We will need assistance, I think."

All of them except Riordan followed the stretcher.

"Charlie," he called. "Tell Stewart I'll be up to see him." He watched their careful awkwardness as they maneuvered the girl over the stairway railing and out of his sight.

There was a crumpled rag where the girl had lain. He picked it up—gingerly, when he caught the acrid odor of vomit—and moved from the shadow of the porch overhang to see better what he held.

From his wheelchair, leaning over the sundeck rail, Stewart Gansvoort saw Riordan appear, the sunlight bright on his red hair. He watched Riordan examine the dish towel. He heard the others coming up the stairway and knew he had to be there when they reached the level of the boathouse.

Below, Riordan's head came up at the faint creak of the floorboards as Stewart wheeled himself away. The habit of suspicion ingrained in all good policemen told him that these people weren't giving him the whole truth. He could smell it, as plain as the stench from the rag he held in his hand. The stains of regurgitated food and bile were easily recognizable, but there seemed to be others not so simple to account for, a deeper, darker brown.

Perhaps Stewart could tell him.

Stewart in his wheelchair was alone when Riordan entered the boathouse, carrying the rag. Stewart's eyes went to it immediately, but his "Gavin, what are *you* doing here?" seemed genuinely surprised.

"Routine," Riordan said easily. "The precinct got the squeal. Thought I'd come myself, rather than . . ."

"Glad you did. But how . . . ?"

"Part of the system. Hospitals report all accidents."

"Oh, shit," Stewart said. "Not the press, too?"

"Not part of the routine, at any rate. Nothing to worry about. They couldn't make much of this. Accidents *do* happen."

"The bastards write what they want to write. This close to election. If you trip over a curb, they have you falling down drunk."

"So sue 'em," Riordan said mildly. "Besides, Uncle Des tells me you're a shoo-in."

"I hope he's right. But Des is only one vote, you know."

Riordan raised a cynical eyebrow. "You don't say." He took in the soiled rug, the intermittent trail toward the porch, the larger puddle there now drying in the sun.

Stewart followed his eyes. "She started to get sick in here and headed for the deck. She was going too fast when she hit the rail. . . . Jesus! I saw her go over. Nothing I could do. . . ." He indicated his wheelchair by a helpless gesture with both hands.

Riordan considered Stewart's anguish, which was certainly warranted by the circumstances. It could have happened just as Stewart said. Except . . .

"I think she sneaked a couple of drinks. There were a lot of people . . . Maybe Charlie would know—he was bartending. . . . And then all that food . . ." He pointed to the cluttered table near the kitchen, and Riordan noticed the wine bottle and the two empty goblets. "I never saw a kid eat like that. Like she'd been starved half to death."

Unbidden, another picture came to Riordan, another half-starved kid in a German kitchen, and then instantly the same girl in a murky basement, her thighs encrusted with dried blood. . . . He held out the stained rag.

"What's this, Stewart?"

"I don't know. What?"

Riordan moved closer. Stewart leaned forward and wrinkled his nostrils in repugnance.

"Looks like a dish towel. She must have grabbed the first thing handy when she started to . . . Why? Is it important?"

"No," Riordan said slowly. "I guess not. . . ."

At that moment Serena came through the French doors at the back of the room, moving fast, as she always did, and talking as she entered. "For Christ's sake, Stewart, what happened . . . ?"

She stopped short as she saw Riordan.

"Gavin? I didn't know you . . ."

"It's all right. Nothing to worry about. I was just leaving."

"Nice to see you, Gavin. We don't see enough of you."

She had assumed the friendly formality she always used when they weren't alone, but he caught the faint emphasis on the royal *we*. He realized guiltily that he hadn't called her in more than a week.

After Riordan left, Serena and Stewart listened as his footsteps faded up the flagstone path.

Very softly Stewart said, "The son of a bitch took it with him. . . ."

"What . . . ?"

"The towel! The goddamned towel."

Knowing her brother, Serena barely breathed, "Sweet Jesus, Stewart, what have you done . . . ?"

He wouldn't look at her.

In the patrol car Riordan handed the towel to his driver.

"I want this analyzed. Take it to Forensic. And I want an answer as soon as possible. Not next week. To me personally. Tell 'em it's not official . . . yet."

The rest of the weekend was a troubled one for the Third Precinct, so it wasn't until Monday morning that Riordan got the chance to answer the several messages from Forensic on his pad. The lab technician told him that the towel showed traces of type "O" blood in several places.

"And roast beef, pickles, mayonnaise, chicken, dairy products and several other things," the technician went on. "Along with enough alcohol to flunk the balloon test. I don't wonder the guy popped his cookies. He was a walking delicatessen. You want a report on this?"

"No," Riordan told him. "Don't write it up yet. Mark it with my name and hold it. For the time being."

He called Dr. Moomjii at Gansvoort Hospital and confirmed that Nan Kennicott's blood was type "O."

"Tell me," Gavin said casually, "I thought I saw some blood on her shorts. Was she cut or something?"

"There was some laceration of the back. Superficial."

"Between her legs?"

"Nooo . . ." Moomjii seemed to hesitate and then said quickly, "Ah, yes. The young lady was in her menstrual cycle, my dear sir. Perhaps that . . ."

"How's she doing, by the way?"

Moomjii seemed glad to change the subject. "There is certainly damage to the spine. A massive morbid enlargement of surrounding tissue makes it impossible to learn further until such swelling has been reduced. Then we will find the full extent of the injury."

"In other words she's still paralyzed?"

"Unfortunately, my dear sir, that is true."

Riordan thanked him and hung up, again feeling that disturbing sense of personal involvement. Why was he pushing it on such vague suspicions? The girl's accident seemed straightforward enough on the surface. There could be any number of explanations for the blood on the towel. If there was more, Nan Kennicott had been perfectly capable of saying so. She hadn't. So that should be that. Yet somehow it wasn't. It nagged him most of the morning. Finally he called Forensic again.

"Can you tell the difference between menstrual blood and the standard brand of gore?"

"Sure," the lab technician told him. "Lots of ways. In the first place it has sloughed-off vaginal tissue in it. Then there's . . ."

Riordan cut him off. "The blood on that towel? Menstrual?"

"No way. Perfectly normal type 'O,' like I told you."

Riordan hung up thoughtfully, wondering whether to take it any further. He decided to let it rest. For the time being.

Later he called Serena and arranged to meet her that evening at their usual place.

*   *   *

He was at home, changing for his date with Serena, when his Uncle Des telephoned him. "Gavin, me boy, we don't see enough of you these days."

"Been busy, Uncle Des. A policeman's lot and all that. How you been?"

"Hmm, yes," Daniher said absently. Which told him that his Uncle Des had something more on his mind than a social call. "The Kennicott girl . . ."

He was instantly alert. He knew what was coming. So he had been right after all. "What about her?"

"There have been no charges?"

"Not yet."

"I'm told there won't be. An unfortunate accident, the poor wee thing. . . . Everything will be done for her. The best. Spare no expense."

When his uncle put on the Irish, Riordan knew he was being conned, and it made him mad. "It stinks, Des. And you know it."

"Do I now? But it's not *our* stink, lad. Let the others wear it . . . like the grand people they are."

"Shit," Riordan said.

"As a personal favor, Gavin?"

For a moment he was tempted to refuse, and then he knew he wouldn't. "There's really nothing concrete to go on. . . ." He knew he was making a justification to himself as well as to his uncle.

"Thank you, Gavin." Des Daniher had no more need for the brogue. "Why don't you come for dinner next Sunday. It would be a pleasure."

Later, as they lay side by side, not touching, Serena remote as always after their lovemaking, he lit cigarettes for both of them.

"Somebody . . . Stewart or somebody . . . got the word to my Uncle Des. He got the word to me. The Kennicott thing is closed. I thought you'd like to know."

"What's to close? Surely you don't suspect Stewart of lying, do you?" And then, before he could answer, she went on, in her perfect imitation of Desmond Daniher, "Why, Stewart is just a boy at heart. No harm in the lad at all, at all."

Three weeks later Lieutenant Gavin Riordan got his captaincy. He was at last out of the Third Precinct, and he devoutly hoped it was forever. He was assigned to Internal Affairs and instructed to report to Inspector Kevin O'Boyle, the most feared officer on the force. He was cynical enough not to question either the captaincy or the assignment.

Sufficient unto the day is the evil thereof.

They had given her something in the ambulance, so she felt no real pain. The white-coated doctors treated her with the impersonality of a specimen on a lab table. Nobody seeemed to realize that it was she, Nan Kennicott, they were prodding and poking at. She responded to their questions with nods or shakes of her head. She had a strong conviction that she mustn't say anything out loud, mustn't talk to anyone.

As the drug began to take over, her mind retreated somewhere else. She couldn't quite remember why she was here. She had fallen . . . and hurt her back. Stewart Gansvoort's anxious face. He had promised her something. And she had promised him. What was it about Stewart Gansvoort? Something bad. She couldn't quite remember what. But something good also. That, too, eluded her.

She could hear them talking over her body, but it was in a language as foreign as Chinese. All she knew was that, try as she would, she couldn't make her legs move. When the full realization of that finally hit her, she passed out completely.

She slept the night through. When she awoke she was lying on her side, facing the window. Outside was the first faint graying of dawn. There were pigeons cooing softly somewhere out of sight. She started to turn over and stopped when the sharp pain in her back caught at her. After a moment she was conscious of another pain, between her legs. Not exactly a pain, more like an ache. Exploring with her fingers, she found she was wearing a sanitary napkin. Which was odd, because she wasn't due for weeks. Maybe the fall had brought on her period . . . ?

The fall! In sudden alarm, despite the pain, she turned on her back and found she could move her torso—but not her legs. Her legs were independent. They didn't belong to her anymore. She threw back the covers. Her legs looked the same, long and tanned and pulsing with life. But when she pinched herself there was no feeling.

She fought back her terror by telling herself that nothing was really wrong, that they could fix anything nowadays. They could give her back her legs. Just as soon as her back got well.

"You're awake. Time for your bath, honey."

The young nurse was pushing a cart laden with basins and pitchers, washcloths and soap. A toothbrush stuck up from a plastic glass beside a tube of toothpaste. With smooth efficiency the nurse removed her hospital gown, soaked a washrag in warm soapy water and began to bathe her.

"How are we feeling today?"

Nan couldn't respond to the cheery young voice. She could only say, "Am I menstruating?"

The nurse looked quickly at the white napkin between her legs. "Why . . . uh, no."

Which was curious. But not alarming.

Then suddenly it was. She remembered the game.

Nan let the nurse carefully manipulate her body, rub her with alcohol, dust her with powder. She brushed her teeth as she was told. At last she was dressed in a clean cotton gown, propped with pillows on either side to relieve any pressure on her back, the head of the bed very slightly raised.

"You're not supposed to move around until the doctor tells you, you know. You'll remember to lie still, won't you?"

The nurse maneuvered her cart to the door, opened it and disappeared. Her impersonal parting smile seemed to hang in the air after she had gone. In a few minutes the door opened again and a doctor came in, followed by another nurse. The nurse pulled a chain and a screen cut them off from the rest of the room.

"Morning." The doctor picked up the chart that hung from the end of the bed and both he and the nurse studied it. Not looking at her, the doctor asked, "How's the back feel?"

"Sore," Nan said. "It hurts."

"It would. You had quite a fall, they tell me. Let's have a look at it."

They turned her on her stomach. She winced as the doctor probed her.

"There's still a lot of swelling. And bruising. But that will soon go away. Now . . . tell me if you feel anything."

Nan couldn't see what he was doing, but she imagined that he was prodding at her legs as the others had done. She felt nothing.

"X ray shows you have a hairline fracture of the spine, young lady. Just a tiny crack. But that's not what's causing the paralysis. It's the swelling and bruising. A lot of blood seeps into the tissues. And that causes pressure on the nerves that make your legs function. Soon as we can reduce that, the feeling should come back. After that it's just a matter of the spine healing—and you'll be good as new."

They turned her gently on her back again and replaced the supporting pillows.

The doctor had a charming smile. Nothing impersonal about it. He took her hand in both of his. "So, honey, you're not to worry. I want you flat on your back for the next eight or ten days. No moving around more than you have to. Then you can sit up and we'll begin to get you back on your feet again. Now," he was suddenly serious, "I want you to do something for me. I want you to try and urinate. It's important, so try hard."

The nurse disappeared around the screen and came back with a bedpan and a flat packet of toilet paper. She lifted up Nan's hips and placed the bedpan under her. Nan shivered as the cold metal touched her bottom. At first she thought she wouldn't be able to do it, whether from embarrassment or . . . She saw from the look on their faces that it *was* important and concentrated. There was a moment of apprehensive silence before she succeeded. First just a trickle, then they all listened to the gush of her urine as it splashed into the pan.

The doctor grinned hugely, as though she had produced a minor miracle. The nurse was smiling, too.

"Atta girl. That's just fine."

The doctor moved to the foot of the bed and began to write something on her chart with a fat gold pen.

"Sometimes paralysis affects the bladder—and the bowels. Feel like a bowel movement?"

That seemed too much to Nan. Peeing was one thing, but defecation before an audience, no matter how appreciative, was something else altogether.

"Not right now."

"Check it out," the doctor said to his nurse. "Let me know if she does." And then to Nan, "About time for your breakfast. I'll see you later." He seemed immensely pleased as he left.

The nurse removed the bedpan and let Nan cleanse herself.

"What was that all about?"

"It was a very good sign. Sometimes paralysis like yours affects the body functions. That could mean catheters all the time, daily enemas. All sorts of unpleasantness. You're a very lucky girl. I'll bring your breakfast in a minute."

Suddenly Nan was feeling much better and unbearably hungry. The nurse pulled the chain again and the curtains rustled back into place, so that she could see the room once more.

Stewart Gansvoort was standing by the window, his arms full of long-stemmed red roses.

"What are you doing here," the nurse said sharply. "Visiting hours are not until . . ."

"I'm Stewart Gansvoort." He held out the roses. "Can you find something for these?"

"Oh . . . yes, of course." She took the flowers and left the room.

Stewart stayed by the window, contemplating her gravely, looking more than ever like Cary Grant. He was taller than she remembered, now gracefully elegant in a soft summer suit. There was a look of sadness on his face, deep circles under his eyes. She was aware of the rapid beating of her heart and the rise and fall of her breasts under the coarse hospital gown.

"Do you hate me, Nan?" His voice was heavy with emotion. "I don't think I could bear that. Thank God the doctors say you'll be all right." He moved slowly and awkwardly to pull a chair close to her bed and lowered himself gingerly. After a moment he reached for her hand with both of his and held it briefly before she jerked it away. Suddenly she couldn't bear his touch. Remembered pain

400

clouded her mind. She saw her own pain mirrored in his face, the gathering of tears in his eyes. He bowed his head until it rested on the bed. She was conscious of the neat part in his dark hair, the pinkness of his scalp, the touch of gray at his temples.

She watched her hand move without volition until it rested on his head.

She was (who was it? Bette Davis?) in *Magnificent Obsession*. Doomed forever to a bed of pain by this man beside her who had struck her down in his motor car. Then she knew that she mustn't do that. She mustn't fantasize ever again. She wasn't anybody but Nan Kennicott. And she was hurt and bewildered and not quite sure of what had happened to her. Except that Stewart Gansvoort had . . . She took her hand away.

Stewart lifted his head and brushed at his eyes. "You mustn't blame yourself, Nan. It was all my fault."

That confused her. Was there some question about whose fault it was? Surely she hadn't *jumped* off the porch.

"Can you forgive me, Nan?" There was a touching appeal in his eyes. Since she couldn't remember *exactly*, it wasn't all that hard to nod. Stewart reached for her hand again, and this time she let him keep it.

"Will I . . ." She had been about to ask for his reassurance that she would be all right. But Stewart's mind leaped to something else.

"No. There's no need to worry about getting pregnant. You can put that out of your mind."

So it *had* happened. They had done *it*. And if they had, why *shouldn't* she worry about getting pregnant? It was all very confusing, but at least it accounted for the Kotex between her legs. Something of what she was thinking must have shown on her face, for Stewart was looking at her strangely.

"Are you sure, Nan, that you want to keep your promise?"

What promise? Something told her that it was a good time to keep her mouth shut, because Stewart obviously had more to say.

"I want to be sure you know precisely what's involved. Then you can decide." He was very serious now.

"You can tell them I . . . raped you." He seemed to have some

401

difficulty with the word. "Although it wasn't exactly rape. I didn't . . . You seemed . . ."

Nan's idea of rape was something gangs of soldiers did to helpless conquered women, something bestial and horrible. Surely Stewart hadn't . . . All she knew was that whatever happened had hurt her. And still did when she thought about it.

"Still, you're not of age. And it could ruin my life. Yours, too. It would be a horrible ordeal. For both of us. But . . . if that's what you decide . . . I'd understand. I couldn't blame you. . . ."

There was a gentle pressure of his fingers on hers, and she felt he *would* understand. Whatever it was.

"On the other hand . . ." His voice deepened and became compelling, willing her to accept what he was saying. "I'll keep my promise to you, Nan, if you keep yours to me. Your father will have a job for the rest of his life. Neither you nor your family will ever have to want again. You'll have your school and the house. Anything you want, just ask me and you'll have it. From now on. I'll be grateful to you. Always. Think about it, Nan. Anything you ever want."

She did. Fast and hard. So that was how it was. Her mind was clicking over like a machine, wild new vistas opening up like film through a projector. In living color. Stewart Gansvoort forever at her feet. Her slave and her protector. All it took was her silence.

"I will," she said, "I'll think about it." She was lost in the sense of her own power. She had no real idea of how cruel her words were to him. But she did see his distress, and instinct told her not to push her luck. At least not just yet. She decided to relent. "All right, I'll do it. I'll keep my promise, Stewart."

He raised her hand to his lips and kissed it. "Thank you, Nan. You'll never regret it." His immense relief gave her a delicious pleasure.

"No," she said softly, "I don't think I ever will . . . Stewart."

The name tasted sweet on her lips.

Outside her room he limped toward Dr. Mohandas Moomjii, who was waiting for him. "You can let her parents see her now," Stewart said. "And, Doctor, I want you in there with them. Don't leave them alone with her."

"But, my dear sir . . ." Moomjii began to protest.

"Goddamnit! Do it!" Stewart's voice was a snarl, the pain of his wrenched back horrendous. "Every word. I want to know every word that's said. Do you understand me? Every word."

Moomjii's eloquent lifting of his hands expressed his distress. And also his acquiescence. "If you wish it," he said. "If you wish it, my dear Mr. Gansvoort."

The nurse came bringing Stewart's flowers in a vase. She was followed almost immediately by Nan's parents and Dr. Moomjii. Nan greeted them all with a bright smile. She was filled with a sense of well-being. Everything was going to be all right. They were her parents—but she was no longer their child. She was a woman now, in every sense of the word, secure and reveling in her woman's power. She could take care of herself—and of her parents as well. The knowledge was heady as wine.

She accepted her mother's kisses and her father's hug as regally as a queen. She answered her mother's first worried question with calm innocence. "It was the vodka, I think. And all that food. I got sick and ran out on the porch. After that—I just don't remember."

She noted their reactions with care. First her father, his one bright blue eye alive with sympathy, then her mother, whose eyes were slightly narrowed, not quite believing. (She'd have to watch her step there.) And last, Dr. Moomjii. *His* large beautiful deep-brown eyes were awash with pity. And something else. The certain knowledge that she was lying. Dr. Moomjii smiled his gentle smile, and she knew her secret was safe with him.

24

Time: 1967
STEWART GANSVOORT

Ericka Ullman stood at the window of Lieutenant Governor Stewart Gansvoort's oak-paneled office, looking out over the drab expanse of the Pit below. The previous week's heavy snow had turned to dirty gray except on a few isolated rooftops. Two sanitation department snow trucks were still working at clearing the streets, since the Pit was low priority and always last on the department's schedule. Snow pushed from the roadways was piled high at curbside, leaving only narrow pathways on the icy sidewalks. Like humpbacked whales, cars were marooned by mounds of snow until their owners got around to digging them out. A thin January sun cast enough radiance to expose the Pit in all its ugliness.

Stewart came around the ornate mahogany desk, which gleamed with a century of polishing, and went to stand beside her at the window. "It's an eyesore, isn't it. You get used to it, I guess, so you don't really notice it."

"It should be burned. Like Rome. And built again so it's fit for people to live there."

The words struck a chord of memory that eluded him. He moved closer to her and casually put an arm around her waist.

"You're right, Princess. We'll burn it. And you can build me a palace that'll put Nero to shame."

Just as casually she slipped away from his encircling arm.

"Not palace. Housing. For people. A decent place to live and bring up families. You've got urban renewal. Why not use it on your own doorstep?"

Just as simply as that, the idea was born in him. Not housing as she saw it, but a seat of government, huge, imposing, the most beautiful state capitol in the world. A magnificent monument of marble to take the place of the slough that was the Pit. He didn't know how, but he knew that he would do it.

And she would help him build it. No architect could refuse a prize like that. She would sell her soul for the chance. And Stewart Gansvoort would be there to buy it. Excitement began to build in him, because he knew that after a year of futile pursuit he had the key to her at last. A way to melt the Ice Maiden. It would take time ... if he could bring it off.

He must, because he had known from the first day he saw her that he wanted this woman above all others. The prize was worth the waiting. "Let's go to lunch," Stewart said. His voice showed absolutely nothing of what he was feeling.

Ericka and George Barnstable had been facing an angry mob of pickets in front of the almost completed Front Street Office Building in the black ghetto along the riverfront when Stewart and Charlie Bishop drove up in a government limo.

Stewart greeted George Barnstable, whom he had last seen more than twenty years before in war-torn Berlin, and waited to be introduced to the woman beside him. Barnstable seemed unaccountably reluctant. Stewart was struck by the extraordinay beauty of Barnstable's companion and had an instant's speculation. Daughter? Surely not wife. Then memory jogged itself, and he knew before Barnstable spoke that this was ... Lisa? Gretel?

"My niece, Ericka Ullman," Barnstable said. "Lieutenant Governor Gansvoort."

"Ericka! My God, I'd never have believed it." He took her hand with his special charm and held it in both of his. "How you've grown."

"It happens." She looked at him with her remarkable green eyes, her expression cool and remotely questioning, no more impressed by his important title than she was by his charm.

"Berlin. Of course, you wouldn't remember . . ."

"No." She removed her hand from his.

The crowd noise swelled just then, and Charlie Bishop said nervously, "Let's get on with it before the animals eat us for breakfast."

Stewart was representing the governor, who had an understandable reluctance to face an aroused citizenry if it could be avoided. These citizens were certainly aroused, because the Front Street building was a typical bureaucratic mistake. In a community whose crying need was for more and better housing and the space to put it in, a thoughtless government had condemned two whole blocks to put up a twenty-story office building—on the theory that its full occupancy would be beneficial to the entire blighted area. The community leaders wouldn't buy it and had managed to inflame enough irate blacks to picket the site.

The occasion was the traditional topping-off ceremony, the raising of the last piece of steel, complete with its American flag, which signaled that the skeleton of the building was finished. The schedule called for speeches by the architect, George Barnstable, the president of the construction firm, the head of the ironworkers' union, the Reverend Cecil Weems of the First Baptist Church of the Ascension and Stewart Gansvoort for the state. All to take place on the flag-draped platform at the edge of the site.

The unscheduled speaker was a militant black man with frizzy hair, wild eyes and impassioned rhetoric who called himself Ackmet Mohammed and claimed to represent the Black Muslims, the Black Panthers and the black community at large. No one seemed to know how he got onto the podium, but he was there, complete with brilliant *dashiki*.

The ironworkers on the job were largely blacks and Italians, and there seemed to be some high feeling about just who was to perform the actual ritual of attaching the flag to the last girder, which would then be hauled to the top of the building. The principal contestants were a large black man and a squat Italian whose breadth made up for his lack of height. Their low-voiced argument, coupled with the shouts of the picketers behind the chain-link fence that surrounded the project, formed a continuous accompaniment to all the speakers. The crowd of onlookers had grown to such proportions that their weight pushing against the fence was causing it to bulge alarmingly.

By the time Stewart's turn came, things had progressed to the point where Charlie Bishop had plucked at Stewart's sleeve and whispered, "Forget the politics. For Christ's sake, make it short and let's get the hell out of here."

Stewart said only what was absolutely necessary, and when he had finished, everyone on the platform turned to watch the ceremony. The two rival ironworkers both had a grip on the flag, which neither seemed prepared to give up.

At that moment the wild-eyed black man with the frizzy hair leapt from the podium and clutched at the flag. The two men holding it were surprised into letting go. The militant threw the flag to the ground, stomped on it with sandaled feet and finished the desecration by spitting on it repeatedly.

The onlookers were momentarily shocked into silence.

Stewart, who was frankly looking for the nearest exit, saw Ericka Ullman jump to the ground and run lithely toward the angry man. Her two outstretched hands caught him on the chest and sat him squarely on his *dashiki* in the dirt. Ericka picked up the flag, calmly attached it to the girder and called to the crane operator, "Take it away!"

The cables squealed and clanked as the heavy girder swung free and started its journey to the top.

The Reverend Cecil Weems cheered and began to clap his hands.

It was the right thing to do at the right time. The Reverend Weems was a tall impressive man with a shock of prematurely white hair. His lips were now split in a wide grin showing impossibly white teeth. And such is the nature of crowds and leaders that most of the onlookers joined him in laughter. True, the militant black man's pratfall did have its elements of humor. It disarmed what could have been a nasty situation.

Stewart asked George Barnstable and his niece to have lunch with him and was accepted. He asked the Reverend Weems, too, which was only politic, but the Reverend Weems declined politely. Charlie Bishop made a mental note to check up on Cecil Weems. He seemed like a good man to have around.

Since the Reverend Weems's color was no longer a factor, Stewart took his guests to the Ticonderoga Club, a select and strictly segregated bastion on the hill beyond the statehouse. The Ticonderoga Club was one of the old federal mansions, and Stewart's great-grandfather had been a founding father. Over the years the club had relaxed its standards to admit certain members whose background and lineage would not have been acceptable to the original patroons, relaxed to the point where August Gansvoort no longer cared to lunch there.

So Stewart had a faint stab of irritation when his group ran into Des Daniher and Chief Inspector Gavin Riordan on the club steps. Stewart was not a noticeable snob, but couldn't avoid a brief "Is nothing sacred?" feeling as he shook Daniher's hand and greeted Gavin.

His resentment sharpened when Ericka put her arms around Gavin Riordan and gave him a kiss. Barnstable's obvious pleasure over meeting Riordan led to an invitation from Daniher to combine forces for lunch. There was no denying him, and the party turned into a sort of old-home week of shared experiences that left Stewart decidedly an outsider and wasn't what he had planned at all.

When Riordan unknowingly repeated Stewart's earlier "My, how you've grown. I can't believe it's thirteen years," Ericka's reaction was quite different. He was puzzled to see her blush and drop her eyes. There was something too intimate in Gavin's grin. A shared secret? Stewart was astonished to find, on such brief acquaintance with Ericka Ullman, that what he was feeling was very close to jealousy. It was something new to Stewart and increased his irritation even more.

Gavin, by just being the kind of person he was, had always been able to make Stewart feel his own inadequacies. Added to that was Stewart's conviction that over the years Gavin knew far too much about him, which had made Stewart cast Gavin as a sort of imp of conscience perched unwanted on Stewart's shoulder, forever observing, forever judging. Des Daniher, because he held the purse strings and called the turns on Stewart's career, had been a source of deep resentment from the beginning. One more mark to chalk up against his father. All in all, Stewart felt decidedly put upon. He set himself to using his undoubted charm to focus Ericka's attention where he felt it belonged.

Charlie Bishop, whose ear was attuned to Stewart's psyche with the sharpness of an illegal wire tap, began to realize that there seemed to be some sort of antagonism going on between Stewart and Gavin Riordan. Charlie mistakenly put it down purely to bull-moose rivalry syndrome over the blond girl. Because the blond was really something to see. Charlie, for all his acuity, hadn't yet fully realized the strength of Stewart's feelings about Des Daniher—or Gavin.

Knowing what he did about Stewart's approach to women in general and unsure of Ericka's vulnerability, Gavin was at first merely feeling protective, thinking of Ericka as the burgeoning teen-ager he had last seen thirteen years before. A quick mental count showed him the silliness of that. The cool, composed beauty who sat opposite him bore only a physical resemblance to the naked young girl feigning sleep on a rumpled bed in Paris. She had to be all of twenty-eight now and, from the look of her, more than capable of taking care of herself. Still, he found himself competing enough to keep the cattle prod firmly on Stewart's ass. Baiting Stewart's ego came under the heading of child's play. It was such a tender target.

George Barnstable's affection for Gavin and his joy at seeing him again made him oblivious to any overtones. To George, Stewart's attentions to Ericka were only her due. Over the years he had become used to panting males around his niece.

Desmond Daniher watched it all with wry amusement—mixed with a sharp sense of disappointment that Stewart seemed unable to change his spots. The fatal flaw remained just that. The man's erect penis had no conscience. And no discretion. And never would.

Daniher was about ready to give up on Stewart Gansvoort. Only his bargain with August Gansvoort held him back.

* * *

In the beginning Stewart had readily agreed to his father's designation of Daniher as all-powerful political guardian, but had soon found that he might have been better off with the devil he knew. Stewart was a stranger to self-discipline. He had never felt the need to say anything other than exactly what he wished to say—to anyone but his father. He had no need to please, no need to say what others wanted to hear—except in his own interests.

Under Des Daniher discipline was absolute. No public utterance was to be made without checking first with Daniher or Charlie Bishop. No ideas expressed, no positions taken, no opinions casually voiced. Stewart found himself in a training program as rigorous in its way as that of a professional athlete. Charlie Bishop, tireless student of the political sales technique, had learned a lesson from the Kennedy-Nixon TV debates and insisted on weekly sessions with a well-known drama coach. Charlie was an early convert to the personality cult for candidates for public office. It was Charlie who persuaded Des Daniher to purchase, through a dummy corporation, a controlling interest in the smallest of the three local television stations.

Daniher had thought it wise to consult August Gansvoort before making this move. It was his first chance to test the real strength of Gansvoort's financial commitment.

"You'll find, Mr. Daniher," August Gansvoort had said dryly, "that I meant what I said. No strings. In future . . ." He let the sentence hang, its inference all too clear. The less "in future" the better, as far as August Gansvoort was concerned.

The old man steepled his hands in what Daniher now recognized as a characteristic gesture. "However, in this case I suggest that the purchase be made by a loan to your company from one of the Gansvoort banks. A Mr. F. James Skidde should be able to arrange it for you."

So it was arranged.

Daniher's dummy company was the buyer-of-record of fifty-one percent of the TV station. In reality Daniher's front owned just under five percent of that controlling interest. The rest of it was owned by anonymous clients of the Gansvoort banking affiliates.

410

It was better than nothing. But surely, Daniher had thought bitterly, a laborer is worthy of his hire.

Stewart's first campaign for the state assembly had gone as predicted. Daniher had been right. Stewart was a natural. He had found his niche and gloried in every exciting minute of the battle.

In his freshman term Charlie Bishop had seen to it that Stewart came out for all the right causes and protested all the wrong ones. Stewart was for education financing, minority-housing projects (which employed lots of union construction workers), veterans' tax exemptions and hospitals (where Stewart's military service could be shown to good advantage), a statewide campaign to eliminate the gypsy moth, highway safety and new construction, tax reduction, mental-health programs and any number of equally innocuous causes that could get him the highest possible public exposure. He was strongly against welfare cheats, deficit financing, crime in the streets and drunk driving.

Through Des Daniher's good offices Stewart accompanied James D. Conroy on the famous visit to the Berlin Wall and got himself photographed several times standing next to the President. He was also appointed to the President's Committee on Medical Care for the Aged.

It was this last that had helped to provide Charlie Bishop with the ammunition he needed for Stewart's second run at the assembly. Through a fluke Charlie latched on to what the media called "a disgruntled employee" in the nursing-home industry. Daniher persuaded the governor to form a Temporary Committee on Senior Citizens Rights and appoint Stewart as chairman. Charlie Bishop's information triggered a major scandal, and Stewart sailed in on the strength of it. It also got Stewart national print coverage in everything from *Time* and *Newsweek* to the *Armed Forces Journal*. The TV networks had a brief but intense field day.

Daniher felt that it should have been the turning point in Stewart's political career. Onward and upward. But it wasn't. The headlines lasted only long enough to get Stewart his second term. Daniher had to take Charlie Bishop's word that Bishop had gotten all the mileage

411

he could out of it. It was the first time Daniher had ever had cause to fault Charlie Bishop.

Daniher had no fault to find with Stewart's ability or his application of it. Stewart was used to hard demanding work. He was careful in his research. He did his homework or hired top experts to do it for him. By the end of his second term he had the largest staff in the assembly, and by far the best paid—out of his own funds.

It was the *business* of government that seemed to bother Stewart, the endless persuasion, the bargaining, the trading of favors for favors needed. Petty, time-consuming and, for Stewart, somehow degrading because the people he was forced to deal with were infinitely inferior. His impatience with the slow grinding of bureaucracy was monumental.

Daniher understood and sympathized with that. After all, he did have Charlie Bishop riding Stewart with a tight rein. It was what invariably happened between sessions of the legislature that had soured Daniher. Even Charlie Bishop couldn't fill all the time with speaking tours, and there would always come the slack periods when Stewart had nothing pressing him and would head straight for trouble. The kind of trouble no politician could afford.

The first was the bare avoidance of being involved in an exceedingly lurid divorce case. Only the media's gentlemen's agreement about the private lives of public figures saved Stewart from that one. Then the business of the Kennicott girl, which could have been ruinous. There had been other incidents as well. Of that Daniher was sure. And now there was a current bit of nastiness with the teen-aged daughter of an Italian dockworker who was threatening to go to Patsy Pavane with his problem. Charlie Bishop had told him that it would take fifty thousand to square it, with no real assurance that it would stay squared. Patsy Pavane was too close to home, and Daniher had not the faintest intention of becoming involved in that one.

In the nature of things, Stewart's third step up the ladder should have been a run for the state senate, since he was by no means ready for national office, except that the incumbent from Stewart's district was on his third term, a tried-and-true party campaigner. It was neither politic nor possible to oust him.

That left only the prospect of a third try for the assembly. But this time Stewart's opposition would be a young crime-busting Republican DA, and Daniher's nose told him that Stewart would have a hard time winning. Rather than risk what could turn into a disastrous setback, Daniher applied his considerable pressure to get the governor to accept Stewart on the ticket as lieutenant governor. Since it was a thankless job few ambitious Democratic pols wanted, the governor agreed, and Stewart had ridden into the statehouse on the coattails of the popular chief executive.

So now, after two years as lieutenant governor, Stewart had no place to go as far as Daniher could see. The thought of running Stewart for governor—the next logical move—filled Daniher with apprehension. The man was uncontrollable. National office was possible but remote. The incumbents were firmly entrenched. Besides, even if he could win, in Washington Stewart would be once-removed from the state and even more difficult to keep in line. It wasn't worth the risk. The leopard and the spots. Daniher couldn't afford to be tarred with the brush, as he inevitably would be if Stewart landed in the soup. He hated to admit mistakes. But he couldn't avoid this one. It was time to fold the hand. Cut the losses and run.

The problem was how to convince August Gansvoort. The man had every right to hold him to his bargain. The prospect that he would depressed Daniher immeasurably.

Now, as Daniher listened to Charlie Bishop's subtle plugging of Stewart's cause with Ericka Ullman, Stewart's glowing praise of Ericka Ullman's display of courage at the morning's ceremonies, Gavin's effort to monopolize Ericka by cutting up some old touches—all in that order—he was struck by the suspicion that none of them was making that much of an impression on the cool, remote, ethereally beautiful young woman sitting opposite him. In Gavin's case it was just as well, since Daniher had long ago decided that stunningly lovely women seldom lived up to expectations between the sheets. As for Stewart, he hoped she'd break his balls, if it came to that. And he had no doubt it would.

He couldn't have known at the time how right he was.

*   *   *

For a solid year Stewart Gansvoort used every ploy he could devise to get into Ericka's pants. That's how he thought of it at first. But as weeks of failure lengthened into months, it became something quite different.

Stewart was capable of an admirable single-mindedness of purpose when something he wanted was involved. It was what kept Charlie Bishop's hopes for him alive and flourishing. Charlie Bishop kept close track of Stewart's sexual adventures—for everybody's protection. He steered Stewart toward the safe ones and tried his best to block out the ones who spelled trouble. Charlie had a sneaking admiration for Stewart's prowess but a sure nose for danger. He got a vicarious kick out of keeping Stewart endlessly supplied with the warm bodies Stewart so obviously couldn't do without. Not that Stewart had much trouble on his own. Even the most unlikely women seemed to find him irresistible.

Charlie believed that all attractive women had a price, some high-ticket, some low. They were trained from birth to put a value on what they had between their legs, and sooner or later they peddled it—in one way or another. The smart ones learned early just how important the eternal quest was to most men and held out until the price was right.

But this one was beyond Charlie's experience. She took everything Stewart threw at her, from dinners to diamonds, with the same calm friendliness, as though Stewart were some sort of indulgent rich uncle. Her thanks placed no more importance on the diamonds than the dinners. She didn't seem to *need* anything. It was as if she had placed herself out of the market because she had no desire to compete.

Charlie Bishop didn't believe it. And that's what worried him. Stewart could take just so much opposition before it came to a point where unpleasant things were liable to happen. And Stewart was rapidly reaching some sort of crisis level. For Stewart's need for Ericka Ullman, and his determination to get her, bordered on obsession. Charlie had never seen Stewart so involved before. What was worse was that by now Charlie knew the lengths to which frustration could drive Stewart. Serena's long-ago warning about Stewart's capabilities for violent action had proved to be all too true.

414

Charlie had a vivid memory of a weekend in Acapulco when Stewart's drunken attentions to a nightclub dancer had been resented by her partner, a man half Stewart's size. In the resultant fight in the parking lot Stewart's mindless, insensate brutality had been a terrifying thing. Charlie was convinced that Stewart would have killed the smaller man if Charlie's nicely timed tire iron hadn't caught Stewart behind the ear. The next morning Stewart remembered nothing of the incident. Or said he didn't. He seemed almost as appalled as Charlie had been when Charlie told him what had happened. Yet, somehow Charlie had the feeling that it wasn't the first time. The wafer-thin Patek Philippe watch Charlie now wore was the result of Stewart's gratitude.

What bothered Charlie Bishop most was that Stewart's infatuation with Ericka was interfering with the business of politics. Charlie was well aware of Stewart's drawbacks, but, unlike Des Daniher, he was convinced that he, Charlie Bishop, could keep the lid on. Instead of being a dead end for Stewart, the office of lieutenant governor, for Charlie's purposes, was an opportunity made of pure gold.

In any given week the governor's staff received and processed hundreds of requests for personal appearances, thousands of letters full of grievances, wrongs unredressed, complaints of every conceivable nature. All except the most important of these were shunted by some faceless bureaucrat to the lieutenant governor's office, stamped with recommendations such as "No Comment" or "Appropriate Action Requested."

These were the grist for Charlie Bishop's mill, and Charlie's mill did in truth grind exceeding fine. No letter was left unanswered, no request ignored, no speaker's engagement unfulfilled. The way Charlie handled things gave Stewart an unparalled opportunity to practice his craft and allowed him to travel the state extensively. No town meeting was too insignificant. Stewart appeared before audiences of twenty (the Garden Club of Wahaxie, population 1,280) and gatherings as large as eighteen hundred (the State Volunteer Fireman's Organization). He offered advice and encouragement to endless graduating classes, charmed women's clubs from one end of the state to the other. And always Stewart was understanding, sympathetic and honestly helpful wherever possible.

415

Through all of this Charlie Bishop was planting his seeds: an attentive ear, promises—and money. Charlie was meticulously building that base so necessary to all successful politicians, a grass-roots organization that could get out the votes. When the time came.

And the time was getting very close. Charlie had a major decision to make. For Charlie had an ace in the hole even Des Daniher didn't know about. Charlie had a small file so full of dynamite that it could blow the state Democratic organization out of the water. He knew that Daniher would never let him use it.

If Daniher ever found out about it.

That was Charlie's problem. And it scared the shit out of him.

August Gansvoort had returned the day before from an extended stay in Europe to find that, through F. James Skidde, Desmond Daniher had requested a meeting. He stood now looking out the rear window of his study, his back to the door, waiting for Daniher to be shown in. What he saw caused his lips to thin with anger, his heavy white brows lowered against the morning sun.

Behind him a log in the big fireplace cracked like a pistol shot, and Gansvoort's hands clenched in irritation. He had no objection to fires as such. What he resented was having fires become a necessity. The heating system in the old house was no longer adequate to warm him in the winter months. He was faced with having it torn out and replaced. Which meant workmen, disruption—and change. Above all, August Gansvoort hated change.

What he was looking at on the hill that sloped upward from the Big House represented a change so repugnant to him that it aggravated his heartburn and brought on a sour belch. The landscaping and grading so carefully and expensively created by his father was a thing of the past. A muddy jerry-built track now cut from the main road straight up the hill to accommodate the equipment that had been needed to build a house. Or what he had been told was a house. To August Gansvoort it was a desecration.

When Stewart had asked his permission to build a house and stables for his wife, he hadn't objected. He rather liked Olivia and approved of her because he respected expertise in any chosen field. It had never occurred to him that Stewart would not employ the prestigious architectural firm that had handled all Gansvoort building projects for years. He had taken it for granted that the result would be made to fit harmoniously into the planned beauty of the estate.

But this woman Stewart had hired had created a monstrosity. He was silently estimating the cost of having it torn down and the land restored to its original harmony when Desmond Daniher came through the door.

He shook hands with Daniher and motioned him to a chair while he himself moved to stand before the fire to warm a body that, increasingly with age, felt the need of warmth.

Daniher seemed uncomfortable, although he wasted no time coming to the point of his visit. "I've come to tell you that I've taken your son as far as he should go, Mr. Gansvoort. I won't take him any further."

"Won't? Or can't?"

Daniher shrugged. "It's of little matter. It's no longer . . . practical. And it could become dangerous. For both of us."

Daniher was thinking of what he had learned some months before. A chance remark of Stewart's about the Italian dockworker father of the girl he had gotten into trouble. The man who had threatened to take his grievance to Patsy Pavane. What Stewart had casually said was "Somebody ought to do something about that guy." The man who heard him say it happened to be a strong-arm bodyguard, part of the entourage that accompanied Stewart on his travels. What Stewart didn't seem to realize (or did he?) was that the bodyguard was perfectly capable of acting on Stewart's suggestion and causing something terminal to happen to the dockworker. As Henry II had said of Thomas à Becket: "Who will rid me of this pestilent priest?" Stewart's words could have had the same results Henry's had. Death, at the hands of an overzealous employee. Luckily Charlie Bishop had been there to put a stop to the action.

That's what Daniher had meant when he used the word *dangerous*, although he wasn't about to explain it to August Gansvoort.

Gansvoort was looking coldly at him. "We had a contract, Mr. Daniher. I see no reason to abrogate it."

"You don't understand. I can't control the man. Unfortunately your son can't keep his pecker in his pants. Sooner or later it will catch up to him. Not so bad for a private citizen, maybe. But for a public figure . . . it could be . . . embarrassing. For everybody. I can't afford that kind of publicity. I don't think you'd like it much, either. It's best we let it stop now, where it is."

"As I recall, you were warned about my son's capabilities." August Gansvoort's voice was dryly brittle. "You chose to accept the risks involved." Gansvoort began to rock gently back and forth on his heels in front of the fire. "No, Mr. Daniher. I think I shall hold you to our bargain. Best efforts. Remember? I shall expect no less of you. I'm impressed with your success so far. And hopeful of the future."

"And what if I won't?" Daniher flared.

Gansvoort's eyes opened wide in feigned surprise.

"I hardly need tell you there is a record of all our . . . transactions. It should be of considerable interest to the attorney general. Perhaps even to Internal Revenue."

Daniher felt helpless in the face of Gansvoort's inflexibility. His Irish demons were at him with a will. He silently cursed the day he had allowed himself to be trapped by his own greed. The fates had a way of calling in all the markers, of making a man pay for his follies—through the nose.

"I'm trying to tell you the man is a menace to us all. You won't listen. So be it. You leave me no choice. But take it from me, Gansvoort, you don't know what the hell you're doing!"

August Gansvoort's smile chilled Daniher to the bone. "Oh, but I do, Mr. Daniher. Believe me, I do."

When Daniher had left, Gansvoort rang for a servant. "Find out if Miss Ullman is . . ."—he gestured toward the desecrated hillside, not wanting to put a name to what was there—"and bring her to me."

Serena and Olivia reined in at the top of the rise to look back at the field behind them. Olivia's horse cavorted nervously, impatient at the stop. Olivia calmed the animal with sure, gentle hands. "It's lovely."

418

"Ummm." Olivia's voice was noncommittal. "It may be the most efficient small horse farm in the country."

At the bottom of the slope the old stone wall that had caused Serena's painful fall was now dismantled, some of its mossy stones forming one wall of a building that looked as though it had been there from the beginning, as ancient as the stones themselves. To its left the flat floor of the valley held two long oval tracks, one within the other. The inner was turf, the outer dirt, both encircled by clean lines of white fencing. To the right a long low rough-hewn structure housed the stable, with its row of individual stalls. From there a blacktop road bisected the valley until it disappeared in the trees at the valley's southern end, eventually to connect with State Highway 9 and afford access to the farm without using the Riverhaven road out.

"It's what you wanted, isn't it?"

"Let's say it's what Stewart wanted *for* me. I'm not quite sure of his reasons—yet." Olivia pointed ahead of them down the long grade to the river and the Big House. "You should see the house. It's just beyond those trees. Not quite liveable yet."

The tall dense stand of Norway pines hid whatever was behind them, although Serena could see the raw earth of a road that began just south of the Big House and came straight up the slope to disappear beyond the pines. The quiet symmetry of the land as she had always known it seemed brutally disturbed.

Knowing what the answer had to be, Serena still asked, "How's Father taking it?"

"No comment. As yet."

"How is he?"

Serena had spent the last six months traveling and had returned only a week before. She had had no burning desire to see either Stewart or Olivia. And certainly not her father. She had much preferred spending the past week making up for lost time with Gavin Riordan. It had been an active week. They couldn't seem to get enough of each other. Serena had brought it to a reluctant and temporary close by saying, "If I spend any more time on my back, I'll be getting bedsores." Gavin had reacted to this with barely concealed relief, so Olivia's invitation for the weekend had come at the right time. Besides, Olivia's phone call had sounded something more than casual. Serena was curious.

Serena had used Stewart's marriage as an excuse to make a permanent break from the Big House. For the past six years, when she wasn't traveling, she had maintained a duplex in one of the new anonymous highrises north of the City on the bluffs above the river. As Stewart had become more and more politicized, Riverhaven had become an important base for him, which in turn had resulted in August Gansvoort's prolonged absences from the estate. He was willing to bankroll Stewart's career, but not to entertain Stewart's constituents. Serena could hardly blame him for that.

She had been careful to arrange both her time and her trips so that she saw as little as possible of her family, and she wasn't exactly up-to-date on the current status of Olivia's marriage. She had followed it with some interest, up until Olivia had her third or fourth miscarriage and been told by her doctors that any more pregnancies would be unwise if not dangerous. It was disappointing because Serena had rather looked forward to seeing what kind of offspring Stewart and Olivia would produce. By Gansvoort out of Minot, as in the *Racing Form* books.

She realized that Olivia had taken a long time answering and glanced at her sharply. Olivia had changed considerably in six years. There was little left of the open, ingenuous girl Stewart had married. She still had the bloom of superb health, but now could be seen a certain sadness in her eyes and tiny telltale lines at their corners. She had acquired a cool protective poise that Serena found a little disconcerting, as if an old acquaintance had suddenly slipped on a disguise. Her long, angular face had softened with maturity and become infinitely more attractive.

Catching her eye, Olivia said, "I'm not sure. He's...aged. I don't think he's really well."

Serena felt a sudden chill. She couldn't imagine her father ill. He defied time. He was so firmly alive, so relentlessly himself, that she expected him to outlive them all.

"You'll see for yourself," Olivia said. "He'll be at lunch." And then, loosening her reins, "Let's go. You've got a treat coming."

They rounded the stand of pines at a trot. At first Serena was

420

hardly aware of the house. It was so much at one with the land and the trees that it seemed to have been there forever. Only the signs and sounds of the workmen disturbed its peace.

What Serena did see was a figure in the foreground, dressed in faded jeans and a worn leather jacket, measuring with a carpenter's rule a board suspended between two sawhorses. The winter sun glinting on pale golden hair told her it was a woman.

Olivia pulled up abruptly. "It's best from here."

A male voice called from somewhere invisible and the woman straightened. Serena was struck first by the indomitable look of her as she stood, arms akimbo, head thrown back, and then by the clear beauty of her face with its clean perfect lines. She watched the woman fold her rule and start up the slight incline. She walked with a long swinging stride that seemed to exude both confidence and competence.

"Who the hell is that?"

"Ericka. She built the house."

Something in Olivia's voice made Serena turn. The cool poise was gone. What Serena saw was so naked and revealing that she caught her breath.

"Yes, I love her," Olivia said simply. And then, at Serena's raised eyebrows, "Love. Not 'in love.' Although there's that, too, I suppose. If she'd have it. But I'm not a lesbian, Serena. I prefer men. I learned that from Stewart. Women do have their excitement for me. I learned that from Stewart, too. He likes to watch."

Olivia, all her self-possession back again, smiled tightly at Serena's expression. "Shocked?"

"Not since I was fourteen, honey," Serena said. "Well, it's better than horses. My, you do liven up a conversation."

"It doesn't matter, really. It's the house I wanted you to see."

Serena looked. And was overwhelmed.

She thought she knew every inch of Riverhaven. She couldn't have counted the times she had been in this pine grove, walked the soft cushion of brown needles that was its floor. There had been a massive outcropping of granitelike gneiss stone on the riverside. She remembered the times as a child she had sat on its cool roughness,

421

watching the freighters navigate the river, listening to wind in the pines and the far mournful whistles of the ships below.

The gneiss shelf was still there, but it seemed to have reproduced itself, grown angles and new levels of clear glass and dark wood that welded the land and the stone and the towering pines together as nature surely would have wished, if nature had had the builder's gift. The house flowed over the terrain, followed the lines of the ancient metamorphic rock, lifted itself to merge with, and almost disappear in, the green symmetry of the trees.

Serena thought she had never seen anything more right, more beautiful.

"I knew *you'd* like it," Olivia said softly. "Now, come and meet her."

They tethered the horses to a low pine bough, and Serena followed Olivia over a natural terrace, through sliding glass doors and into the house itself. Obscurely she was reluctant to meet its maker, because human frailty made it certain that the builder could never possess the perfection of the concept. Nor would she want it so. The dreamer of this dream house should speak with a Brooklyn accent, have a harelip or unsightly wens. Anything less would be sacrilege, not to be borne.

"The grain is all wrong, Tom. Find a better length."

The voice was low and throaty, with an actress quality, and came from a room on their right. They waited as a man maneuvered a twelve-foot plank through the aperture, grinned at them, shook his head at something he was thinking and disappeared outside.

The room was a marvel of glass and wood integrated by a huge stone fireplace on the opposite wall. The flooring, of random widths of planking, was not quite complete and showed bare stringers through a three-foot gap. There were sawhorses, kegs of nails, rolls of electricians' wire and sawdust everywhere. A half-empty case of bottled beer was next to the fireplace.

Ericka Ullman had taken off her leather jacket and dropped it at her feet. The carpenter's rule protruded from the back pocket of her tight jeans and drew attention to the rounded buttocks. The faded blue workman's shirt moded itself to the gentle curve of her breasts. Her head, with its wreath of gold hair, sat regally on her long elegant neck. The heart-shaped face needed no coloring. The huge green eyes were enough, the luminous green of ancient jade.

It isn't fair, Serena thought as she was shaking hands and being treated to a dazzling smile.

"How nice," Ericka Ullman said. "Gavin has told me about you."

Serena's mind was jumbled. What the hell did Gavin have to do with . . . ? He damned well *didn't* tell me about *you*—and why the hell didn't he? What came out aloud was "Gavin?" And she hoped that what she was thinking didn't show.

"Oh, yes. I've known him practically all my life."

"Is that so? Funny he never mentioned it."

There was an instant's faint amusement in those remarkable green eyes, quickly gone as Ericka turned to Olivia.

"It's getting there," Ericka said. "You'll be able to move in before long. Still some landscaping to be done."

"I thought the setting itself did that. It's perfect the way it is." There was a breathless quality in Olivia's voice that told its own story.

"It needs some color here and there—for spring and summer. Not much. Just enough to soften the starkness of the pines."

Ericka straddled a sawhorse, long legs stretched out before her. She gestured to the case of beer and took an opener from the pocket of her jeans.

"Have one?"

Ericka let Olivia open the bottles and hand one to each of them. Serena couldn't tell whether it was from a nice sense of who the householder was or whether she just expected to be waited on.

Serena took hers to the front of the room with the vague notion of giving the two of them some degree of privacy. Through the glass wall to her left was a sizeable sparkling pool formed from the native rocks and woods plants. The pool was fed by a low waterfall and the sound of the rippling water came faintly to her. The way the glass had been joined with natural wood created the impression of living in the open in the grove of pines. The setting was so pastorally right that she wouldn't have been surprised to see a deer come down to drink.

"How . . . ?"

Olivia joined her and answered her unfinished question. "It's a deep well. The water is filtered and recirculated. Since it's always moving it will never freeze. The same well cools the house in summer."

They were both looking down toward the Big House, and for the first time in her life Serena thought that from this sylvan aerie its familiar lines looked somehow out of place. As they watched, a white-aproned maid came out of the back door and started up the slope toward them.

"It *could* be a telephone call," Serena said.

"No such luck. I've been waiting for the summons. I think this is it."

Serena turned to Ericka. "Do you know my father?"

Ericka took the time to light a cigarette before saying noncommittally, "We've met. Briefly."

"Have you any idea how he's going to react"—she made a sweeping gesture with her arm—"to this . . . ?"

Ericka blew out a long streamer of smoke. "My commission came from Stewart. Surely . . ."

Serena laughed harshly. "At Riverhaven nothing comes from Stewart. I'm amazed he had the guts. Stewart doesn't usually fiddle with fire."

"You seem so sure your father won't like it. Perhaps he will. He seemed a . . . civilized man."

"Oh, he's civilized, all right," Serena said dryly. "About as civilized as Attila the Hun. And just as ruthless when he wants to be."

"In any case it's a little late for objections, isn't it? This house is a point of view. It was built for the person who's going to live in it." Ericka's eyes swung briefly to Olivia. "I think she'll be happy in it. It's a point of view that can be defended."

Ericka's unruffled serenity was beginning to get to Serena. A lamb to the wolves. The voice of sweet reason. August Gansvoort would eat her alive.

424

"Oh, baby. You've got a lot to learn about my father. You can't just bat those lovely green eyes at him. He's impervious. Skin like a rhino."

Those lovely green eyes looked back at her, calm, undisturbed, filled with an unshakeable confidence. Serena suddenly knew why Stewart had been driven to risk his father's anger and felt an instant stab of pity for Olivia, caught in the middle by the two of them.

"We'll see," Ericka said softly.

In the doorway the Riverhaven maid stood for a moment looking curiously about her.

"Miss Ullman? Mr. Gansvoort wants you in his study." Her tone had something of the command August Gansvoort must have used when he gave the order.

"I knew it." Olivia put both hands to her mouth in a curiously childlike gesture.

Ericka didn't move. She took another drag on her cigarette, still straddling the sawhorse. "Tell him I'll be there presently."

"He said now, Miss Ullman," the maid said stubbornly.

"That will do," Serena said to the maid. She turned to Ericka. "Might as well get it over with. I think I'll come along. You'll need all the help you can get. Coming, Olivia?"

"Nooo . . . I think I'll sit this one out." Olivia was speaking directly to Serena as if Ericka were not there. "I don't want to see her . . . hurt. I couldn't bear it."

Serena left her horse for Olivia to tend to and walked with Ericka down the slope. As they approached the rear of the Big House they saw Stewart's official limousine come down the driveway.

"Good timing," Serena said. "Maybe there'll be some safety in numbers."

Ericka said nothing.

Not one for chitchat, Serena thought.

As they reached the long hallway, Stewart and Charlie Bishop were just coming through the front door. Stewart nodded to his sister, made straight for Ericka and took her hand in both of his.

"You'll join us for lunch, I hope?"

425

Ericka removed her hand and looked down at her stained jeans. "I think not."

Charlie Bishop, who was a fan of Serena's, grinned fondly at her. "Long time no see, Princess. How goes the battle?"

"Tell you later. After we've seen Father. The summons just came." And then to Stewart, "He's waiting in the study."

"Uh-oh," Charlie Bishop said. "The house?"

"The house."

Stewart looked uncomfortable. "I'll just wash up. Won't be a minute." He had started toward the stairs when Serena put a firm clamp on his arm.

"Oh, no, you don't. You got her into this. You can damn well help to get her out."

"Don't be a bitch, Serena. Of course I will." He disengaged his arm and once more made for the stairs.

Watching his retreating back, Serena said bitterly, "His famous imitation of the broken reed. Only it isn't imitation."

"I don't need his help." Ericka's voice was sharp. "Or anyone's. The house speaks for itself. If it needs defense, I'll defend it."

Head high, she held them both with her look. Then she turned away and walked toward August Gansvoort's study.

Serena was struck once again by the word *indomitable*. This woman wore it like a cloak. It was in the squared shoulders, the unforgiving back, the easy grace of her movements.

"That's what *she* thinks," Serena said. And then to Charlie, "Go get that bastard, Charlie. This is one time he's not going to dog it. Tell him I said so."

"Don't worry, Princess. I'll have him down here in jig time."

Bishop skipped toward the stairs, and Serena went purposefully toward her father's study.

When she entered, August Gansvoort was in his all-too-familiar place behind the big desk. Ericka Ullman was standing by the window, looking up toward the house on the hill. Obviously something had already been said. *The command post*, Serena thought. *How many times have I played this scene?*

426

"Serena." Her father greeted her without surprise. "I'm told I missed you in Paris. I didn't know you were there."

"Just long enough for the divorce," Serena said shortly. "I was pretty busy."

"It went well, I trust?" August Gansvoort's cultured voice was deceptively mild.

"Lose one, win one."

"I'm not sure I follow. Are you planning to marry again?"

"No. Just a figure of speech." Serena was wondering how to stop this inane conversation and get to the point. Ericka saved her the trouble.

"Why do you hate it so?" The question was calm and uninflected, a request for information, for an answer to a puzzle.

August Gansvoort steepled his hands and turned his head toward her. "Not hate, Miss Ullman. It merely offends me. It has no place on my land."

"I don't think you understand. It's the land that made the house so right. That house has its own integrity. Every plane, every joint is there because the land cried out for it. It's a place to be lived in, and loved in and cherished. Look at it, Mr. Gansvoort."

She lifted her hand in a wide gesture. Their eyes followed her pointing finger. Pale sunlight seeped through the tall pines and dappled the clean straight planes of glass. At that moment a breeze swayed the branches and the house seemed to shimmer with gold and silver ripples, suspended in air and space.

"Open your eyes. And your mind. Really *look* at it. Then tell me, Mr. Gansvoort, that you can destroy it."

"Oh, no!" Serena breathed. "You can't . . ."

At that moment Stewart pushed open the door, took two paces and stopped, frozen by the tension in the room. August Gansvoort swiveled slowly to face his son. "Ah. Stewart. Come in. I've just asked Miss Ullman to give me an estimate on tearing down what you allowed her to construct—on my property. Without consulting me. And to restore the land to what it was."

Stewart's mouth dropped open. "You *can't* do that!" His voice was hoarse and strangled.

"Oh, but I can," August Gansvoort said mildly. "And so intend. A little forethought might have told you that."

"That's it, then." Ericka's tones were lifeless in defeat. "There's nothing more to say."

"No. You'll be paid, of course. It seems logical to use those contractors you have already employed. I should like the work started immediately."

"No need. A few sticks of dynamite should do the job. I won't have it murdered bit by bit. Do what you like with what's left of it." Ericka moved to the door and went through it without looking back.

August Gansvoort motioned to Serena. "I won't put up with that. See that she is stopped."

Serena, already on her way after Ericka, paused long enough to say, "If she wanted to blow up the Big House, I don't think I'd stop her. You'd have it coming." She slammed the door behind her.

Stewart was left alone with his father.

August Gansvoort gave an involuntary shiver and moved again before the fire, lifting his coattails to its warmth in an old-fashioned gesture.

Stewart dropped slowly into an armchair and considered this man who was his parent. He was thinking of all the years, and all the fear that had colored his whole life, until he wore it like a second skin. Until this moment. *Flesh of my flesh, blood of my blood. Honor thy father.* For what? For the hatred that filled him. For that's what it was. What Serena had long ago divined about their father was now clear to Stewart for the first time.

He now saw his father with different eyes. The tall, supple figure was now spare with the wasting of age. The skin now stretched like parchment over the bones of the face, the long, graceful hands now gnarled and liver-spotted.

"You know," Stewart said with the satisfaction of certain knowledge, "you're going to die soon. And when you do, I'll have her build it all over again."

August Gansvoort raised his eyebrows. "I think not. I'll make it a part of my will if necessary."

Stewart's short laugh grated. "An old man's foolishness. You know as well as I that there never was a will that couldn't be broken. Control beyond the grave? It's a nice legal point."

August Gansvoort dropped his coattails and clasped his hands in front of him. Stewart caught the tremor of his fingers.

"Tell me, old man, because I don't think you have much time... why have you hated us all these years? Serena and me. Why not Henry? You never seemed to use the whip on him. I'm curious."

"Because I'm not his father. That dubious honor belonged to some other man. I hadn't the right. She told me before she died...." The words seemed torn out of him against his will.

"So it was Mother...." Stewart said slowly. "And you took it out on us. All those years. What a stupid waste of time and energy— when you could have had our love. You know, you should have killed her that night when I was a kid. It would have been better than what you've done to all of us. You know, old man, I think you're nutty as a fucking fruitcake—and have been all along. I wonder why it never occurred to me before."

"She was evil... a foulness...."

The whispered words were slurred, almost unintelligible.

Stewart watched his father with a strange detachment. Something curious was happening to August Gansvoort. The left side of his face seemed to droop like molten wax, the eyelid almost covering the eye, a trickle of spittle forming at the corner of the thin mouth. Suddenly the old man's body crumpled like a puppet whose strings had been released, and he fell backward into the fire.

The head was propped against a burning log, and the flames took first the white hair, then the heavy brows. The old good eye stayed fixed on Stewart. If the eyes were windows to the soul, what could he read in that?

Stewart began to retch helplessly as his nostrils filled with the sudden stench of burning flesh. From somewhere came the sound of knocking, as of someone knocking cautiously on a door. Then he heard Charlie Bishop's troubled voice.

25

Time: 1968–1969
CHARLIE BISHOP

Daniher had expected Stewart to begin kicking up his heels after his father's death, but requests for funds still came to him as usual from Charlie Bishop and were passed on to F. James Skidde at Gansvoort Associates. Stewart seemed strangely docile. He was preoccupied with something called the Temporary Committee on the Future of the State Capitol, which he had nagged the governor to create.

It was when Charlie Bishop came to Daniher with the news that some upstate people had put together enough names to qualify Stewart for a place on the ballot to oppose Governor Haskell in the primaries that Daniher got his first whiff of rat. "It's not the first time that a lieutenant governor has split," Charlie told him. "He smells the roses and he wants to make the run."

"Not a snowball's chance."

"Sure. I know and you know. But Stewart doesn't. He's got the idea he can buy it, and I can't talk him out of it. It's hard to argue with all that money. Why not let him do it?"

Des Daniher looked at Charlie Bishop's blandly innocent face and thought, *Just what is it you've got up your sleeve, boyo, that the butter won't melt in your mouth?*

"Look, Mr. Daniher," Charlie said deferentially, "I've known for a while—even before the old man died—that you'd gone sour on Stewart. If he was hard to control before, think what he'll be like when he gets all the loot. Point is, there's no need to dump him outright. With that kind of clout, who wants him for an enemy? I'll bust my stones for him—just like he had the chance. All you got to do is sit on your hands for the primaries. Let him run and get his ass kicked. Then he's off the ticket and out of politics to all intents. And everybody is still friends."

Charlie had the look of a bright schoolboy who had just come up with the right answer.

"Sounds okay," Daniher said. "I'll give it some thought. By the by, how the hell did they collect enough names for the ballot—without anybody hearing about it?"

"Beats me. Who the hell knows what those upstate yokels will do?"

You do, Daniher thought.

Daniher thought it only prudent to call on F. James Skidde in person. He found that austere gentleman completely in agreement with his own opinion.

"After all," F. James told him, "I have known Stewart almost all his life. I am well aware of his . . . character. You have every reason to be concerned. But let me assure you, Mr. Daniher, it would take a battery of federal accountants half a lifetime to establish any financial connection between Mr. August Gansvoort and yourself. Mr. Gansvoort saw to it that upon his death certain of his instructions went immediately into effect. He, too, knew his son's . . . failings. It would have been folly to put Stewart in a positon, vis-à-vis yourself, to . . ."

"Then I'm well out of it," Daniher said. "You'll deal with Stewart direct?"

"I will, Mr. Daniher. And you are. As completely as though you never existed."

The thought has its comforts, Daniher reflected. *If what Charlie Bishop and Stewart had in mind was a spot of blackmail.*

The nursing-home scandal that got Stewart elected to the state assembly for his second term provided Charlie Bishop with a weapon beyond his wildest dreams. The very thought of the power

431

he possessed made him giddy. For five years he had plotted just how best to use what he had. And now he knew the time had come.

The nursing-home investigations had uncovered a shocking tale of secret ownership by interlocking corporations and individuals, millions of dollars collected from the federal and state governments through false claims and fraudulent tax returns. In the end nobody was hurt—except a few nursing-home figures who made the slammer. The scandal subsided almost as quickly as it had begun, and the relieved legislators settled back to devote themselves briefly to passing laws to assure that nothing like it could happen again.

The reason the spectacular exposé had died with such unusual speed was not, as some of the media speculated, a massive cover-up. In reality the fires had been damped by Charlie Bishop and the "disgruntled employee" Charlie had unearthed. The employee received immunity for his testimony and a substantial sum from Charlie Bishop to be very selective in what he revealed.

Charlie, in turn, got the goods on a number of important people. Names, dates, places and amounts—and in some cases canceled checks—of sums paid over, sums that under no circumstances could be called campaign contributions. The brains of the nursing-home syndicate had kept very careful and precise records, and Charlie was appalled at the stupidity—and the cupidity—of the men involved.

On the copier in Stewart's office suite, Charlie ran off a dupe of all the lovely pieces of paper and sent them to his mother, who lived in Des Moines, Iowa, with instructions to put them in her safe-deposit box. The originals he placed in his own safety depository in a folder marked, appropriately enough, Insurance Policies.

Charlie Bishop needed now to nudge a number of elbows, remind certain people of past favors, even twist a few arms, and he would be ready for the dramatic announcement that Lieutenant Governor Gansvoort, in the interest of good government, had decided to break with his administration and run for governor himself.

Charlie Bishop had no intention of using his secret ammunition unless he absolutely had to. All he wanted for the moment was to organize enough support, and create enough noise, to keep Stewart's move from looking foolish. He had two things going for him. First, Stewart *was* owed a lot of favors, for Charlie had spent August

Gansvoort's money wisely and well. And, second, most of the people Charlie approached believed, as Des Daniher did, that while Stewart could get a lot of headlines, he had no real chance of winning.

In truth Stewart Gansvoort wasn't all that interested in Bishop's plans—for the moment. He was devoting himself to the Temporary Committee on the Future of the State Capitol. The task of the committee was to recommend a site for a huge complex of buildings to house the state government all in one place, something that no one could deny was badly needed. The statehouse had long been crowded beyond its capacity, and the runaway mushrooming of legislative staff, new departments and the personnel to run them had forced the state to find more and more office space until now the various parts of the government were spread out over half the City.

With his usual thoroughness Stewart had instructed his experts to comb the City for the best possible site. The choices boiled down to two. One was the valley separating the hill that now held the statehouse from Hickory Knob, the next hill to the north. Construction logic favored this location. The valley could be filled in— always cheaper than excavation; there was an existing road net that could be easily expanded; comparatively little demolition would be required.

Compared, that is, to the Pit, which was the site Stewart had in mind all along. It was there that he planned for Ericka Ullman to build the most spectacular state capitol in the world.

He had his experts prepare two reports, one favoring the valley site, the other, the Pit. He arranged for the findings on the valley to be judiciously leaked to a few carefully attentive ears. The Pit report he kept locked in his safe. He next bought the services of a clerk in the county clerk's office, Department of Deeds and Records, to keep him appraised of all real-estate transactions in the valley site, and sat back to wait.

Stewart had learned his lessons well from Charlie Bishop.

Sure enough, the key legislators in the senate and house, to whom Stewart had leaked his information, one by one acquired cheap property both on Hickory Knob and in the valley itself, thus insuring

433

that they would be in no position to oppose him when Stewart's tame committee submitted a report unanimously favoring the Pit.

It was time to call on Charlie Bishop's expertise.

"Charlie," Stewart said, "I want to introduce a bill that will allow the state to start condemnation proceedings against the whole area of the Pit—and also appropriate the money to implement. And I don't want any foul-ups. Can you write it?"

Charlie Bishop, seated in the red leather chair next to Stewart's antique desk, looked at him as if he were out of his mind.

"I could write a bill making Joe Stalin an honorary citizen. Getting it passed would be a little harder. What the hell for?"

"Because that's where I'm going to build the new state capitol complex. Right outside this window."

"Jesus, Stewart. They play a lot of good jazz on Deacey Street. Duke Ellington, Charlie Mingus, Sidney Bechet and the like. And what'll you do with all the hookers? Where would the boys go to get their rocks off? To say nothing of the jigaboos. Where you gonna put 'em?"

"Just answer me," Stewart said, and Charlie saw by his expression that this was not something that could be passed off lightly. Stewart had latched on to an idea of his own, and the stubborn set of his mouth told Charlie he wasn't about to let it go. That was a worry, because Charlie wanted Stewart's attention firmly fixed on the main chance for the next months. No diversions whatever.

"Supposing I could," Charlie said slowly. "What then? You got any idea what the thing would cost? Millions. Maybe a billion. You willing to pay for that with your own money? Because that's the only way you could do it."

"No, I'm not."

"Then it would have to be a bond issue. And the law says you got to have a statewide referendum for that."

"So we'll have a referendum. Sell it to the public. Hard sell, Charlie. TV. Big ad campaign. Whatever it takes."

Charlie Bishop was trying his best to keep calm, to think of something, anything, to break through Stewart's determination. He was acutely aware of the danger to all his plans, because if he ever

434

got Stewart in a position to run for governor, such a referendum was likely to kill whatever chance Stewart might have.

Suddenly the bulb lit in Charlie Bishop's head. He knew what was driving Stewart. He wanted something grand and imposing for Ericka Ullman to build. The outrageous irresponsibility of it. The man was willing to corrupt a whole state legislature—bilk millions of people—to get into one broad's pants.

In that instant—or a fraction of it—Charlie Bishop wanted out. Daniher was right. This maniac was just too crazy to fuck around with. And then his own ambitions took hold once more.

"Stewart," Charlie said reasonably, "you've got to realize that there is no way the voters are going to okay spending their money to put up a fucking state capitol complex. No fucking way. Even if you could sell the idea, you'd never get it past the Crows. That's what they call the Bond Counsel, because they all wear black. You can't sell a single bond in this state unless you got the negative on their sister Kate in the sack with the milkman."

Stewart, who was by no means insensitive, had caught the telltale knowledge in Bishop's eyes. Now that Bishop had guessed, there was no sense in pulling punches. It didn't really matter what Bishop thought—as long as he performed. Stewart smiled thinly. "I've got a pretty good idea what you have in mind for me, Charlie. . . ."

"It hasn't all jelled yet," Charlie interrupted quickly.

Stewart went on as though he hadn't spoken. "And I'll go along—provided you understand this thing has first priority. I don't want any mistakes, Charlie. Otherwise . . ."

Charlie Bishop, thinking that of all the mistakes that could be made, this one might be the biggest, gave it one more try. "Yeah, I understand. But listen to me, just for one damn minute. A referendum would never pass. State money is out. Because the law says money appropriated in one year has to be spent by the following September. So you can't hire contractors on a long-term job. The money just won't be there. You got to be able to say, 'Look, Big Chico, we got the loot all in a bundle, so you can start pouring cement.' Otherwise you got to go back to the legislature each year and you got to have something to trade to each and every one of them—or you don't get your appropriation. You're talkin' millions.

Maybe billions. So just how the hell do you finance this thing? You tell me that and it's all go."

Stewart's smile had the same chilling quality. "No, you tell me, Charlie. It's what you get paid for. You better get going, because I'm hiring Ericka Ullman to draw up plans—for the most magnificent edifice you'll ever see. That's something I *will* pay for—personally."

It took Charlie Bishop three weeks to find and cultivate an obscure lawyer named Mark Epstein in the comptroller's office who told him that there *was* a way to solve the money problem. Even Epstein said it was improbable and would require total control of the legislature and both City and county officials, but legally it could be done. Charlie put Epstein on the lieutenant governor's staff at $45,000 a year and told him to get it all on paper—and report to him personally.

Charlie knew that in politics anything is possible, but Epstein's plan had a drawback Epstein wasn't aware of. It needed the complete cooperation of Desmond Daniher for any chance of success. The City and the county were Daniher's home turf, the hardcore of his power.

So Charlie set himself to find the carrot for Daniher's stick. One more surprise among the many Daniher had coming to him.

Stewart Gansvoort got his own surprise.

Ericka Ullman turned him down. She saw his motives with utter clarity. Her faint amusement was devastating.

"Nice try, Stewart. But it won't work. Why don't you give it up? There's no percentage. Besides, I don't think you'd like what I would turn out. Try some other architect."

He saw in her eyes that there was no changing her decision. It infuriated him. He had been so sure that his price was right. It had never once occurred to him that what he had to offer had no real meaning for her.

In the next few days his passion for her turned temporarily into something close to hate. If he couldn't have her, he wanted only to destroy her, to make her suffer as he was suffering. He spent a number of sleepless nights, but in the end his determination had hardened into something that even Stewart recognized as ugly. Her last words stuck in his head. "Some other architect . . ." Which was why he was now sitting in the offices of Barnstable & Ullman in Manhattan.

George Barnstable came out to greet him personally and usher him into a spacious corner office. Barnstable was cordial enough as he gestured Stewart to a chair and seated himself behind the large drafting table he used for a desk.

Stewart opened with "I need your advice," a surefire attention-getter. He drew a deep breath and set himself to use all his charm, all his powers of persuasion, to paint a picture George Barnstable couldn't resist.

It was easier than he had hoped.

And at the end of three hours Barnstable's drafting table and the floor surrounding it were covered with sketches, great slashes of buildings reaching to the sky with a grandeur Stewart hadn't believed possible. They had worked straight through with no thought of lunch, because Barnstable's enthusiasm was irresistible.

Somewhere in those three hours they switched roles. Barnstable became the persuader, Stewart the convert. He was caught up in Barnstable's excitement as he watched Barnstable's pencil rip across virgin paper in raw black lines, adding, tearing away, breathing life and beauty into something so magnificent that it took his breath away and caused his heart to pound.

At some point, and he was never sure just when, all his scheming reasons came tumbling down around his head. Ericka or no Ericka, he knew he must build this miracle for its own sake. A Gansvoort monument, a last great pyramid that would live forever. It was an emotional upheaval he had never experienced. It had the mystery of religious awakening, as though he had somehow been invested with the power to create. At that precise moment the Gansvoort inheritance caught up with Stewart Stuyvesant Gansvoort. He lost his touch with all reality. Except the reality of power.

26

Time: 1969–1970
DESMOND DANIHER

"Charlie," Daniher said mildly, "you are as full of shit as a Christmas turkey."

"Come on, Des. It worked out just like I . . . just like you predicted. He got his ass kicked like you said. And that should be the end of it. Where's he gonna go from here?"

"Where indeed. That's a question I've been giving some thought to. Come to think of it, how'd he get all those primary votes in the first place? Out of the woodwork? Forty-six percent is hardly an ass-kicking. You must have put in a lot of overtime, Charlie me boy."

Bishop looked at him quickly, his face a study in innocence.

"Yeah, who coulda figured it? I gave it my best shot, like I said. You know we been traveling the state. Talking to a lot of town chairmen, county chairmen and the like. Bound to make some friends. But forty-six percent? Jesus. I didn't think I did *that* good a job. Had me scared there for a while. Looked like Stewart was really picking up steam. . . ."

"You had a lot of people scared, Charlie."

Bishop laughed.

"By God, we did, didn't we. I never woulda believed it. It just seemed to snowball once his name was up. Surprised the shit out of me. You know, if we'd had some *real* issues, Stewart might have made it at that. Governor Haskell ain't all that strong. He's gonna have a problem in November. Bi-i-ig problem.''

Daniher looked at Charlie Bishop's round interested face, at those eyes fixed steadily on his, radiating sincerity—and had a moment's regret at what he was about to do.

The two men sat at a table in the preferred corner near the bar of Lober's Restaurant. Near them the open dumbwaiter, mounted on gleaming brass rails, creaked and rattled as it carried drinks to the upper dining rooms. In the center of the polished mahogany bar, soft gaslight shone on the fabulous silver free-lunch dishes, whose covers were suspended from the ceiling by an elaborate system of counter-weights. Lober's had come into being in the 1890's and had changed little since. Daniher found its ornate electroliers, floriated mahogany decor, its ceiling of cherubs and angels now dark with the smoke of years, infinitely soothing.

He had asked Charlie Bishop for drinks only, because he didn't want the interview to spoil the excellent lunch he was anticipating. Daniher valued loyalty. He himself gave it unstintingly and expected it in return. When he found it was misplaced, he blamed himself rather than others. Charlie Bishop's suspected defection was doubly hurtful because Daniher had trusted Charlie more than he did most men. Now he sighed deeply and decided he might as well get the unpleasantness over with.

"How long you been on the party payroll, Charlie?''

"Jesus, I don't know." Bishop looked puzzled. "Why?''

"Because you're fired.''

Charlie's puzzlement turned to hurt surprise. "Jesus, Des. Why would you say a thing like that?''

"Because I can't trust you anymore. Did you really think you could steal it right out from under my nose?''

"Honest, Des . . . I swear to God . . .''

"You know, I think what offends me the most is you thinking you could treat me like some bog trotter fresh off the boat. Expecting me to swallow all this innocent shit you been handing me." Daniher considered him sadly. "Charlie, Charlie, you got a lot to learn. What the hell you promise those guys? A free hand at the mint?''

439

"Goddamnit, Des. I didn't. I swear. The thing just got out of hand. . . ."

There was such frantic sincerity in Bishop's voice that Daniher had his brief moment of doubt. Which well he might. For Charlie Bishop was telling the literal truth. It *had* gotten out of hand. Once Stewart's name was before the delegates, some unaccountable perversity seemed to take over. People Charlie hadn't even approached came out for Stewart. Put it down to disillusionment with the incumbent, Governor Haskell. Resentment of the heavy hand of the Democratic machine. Whatever it was, the delegates had almost played a huge joke on the bosses. Almost kicked the Establishment's ass instead of Stewart's.

Which wasn't what Charlie had had in mind at all. All Charlie had wanted was for Stewart to make a respectable showing, just enough to keep Stewart's name in the media as a viable alternative. If by some wild chance Stewart had actually defeated the governor in the primary, he would automatically have become the head of the party in the state. And at the same time its slave. For in the general election Stewart would have had to depend on the Democratic organization to get out the vote if he was to win. Which meant he would have had to make a lot of deals, a lot of promises, go in debt to a lot of people, and all those favors would have to be repaid. Charlie Bishop had had a quite different scenario for Stewart Gansvoort.

"I didn't rig that thing, Des. No matter what you think. I swear to you on my mother's honor."

"I don't know your mother," Daniher said mildly. "But you're still fired. I feel safer that way. I'm too old for shenanigans."

For a moment Charlie Bishop looked as though he might cry. His eyes mirrored his hurt.

"I didn't try to cross you, Des. You got to believe that."

"Don't take it so hard, Charlie. Stewart looks after his friends. You shouldn't have to worry."

Daniher watched the emotions chase each other across Bishop's face, the pleading look change to resignation.

440

"You've made up your mind. I guess there's nothing I can do about it. I hope there's no hard feelings."

"Should there be?"

"No, Des. I swear it."

"Then that's that. See you around, Charlie."

Daniher held out his hand and Bishop took it reluctantly. It was interesting that Bishop's hand was clammy with nervous sweat.

"Yeah," Bishop got up. "See you around."

Two days later Des Daniher learned from the six o'clock news exactly how badly Charlie Bishop had outmaneuvered him. He sat at his desk, cursing his own stupidity as he listened to the press conference Stewart Gansvoort had called to announce that he would run for governor on an Independent-Conservative ticket. He watched Stewart's handsome intense face mouthing old familiar phrases, which rattled around in Daniher's head like the trump of doom.

"... corruption and tyranny. The machine patronage system, filling the state's payroll with thousands of superfluous workers ... manipulation of tax assessments ... vote bribery, intimidation and fraud ..."

Daniher had heard it all before. The battle cries of all reform tickets. Much of it was true and always would be.

"My party is the People," Stewart said in ringing tones. "I will crush the bosses who run this great state and return the power to all of you who have suffered under years of mismanagement and corruption. I want a better life for all of us. A vote for me is a vote for all of you. . . ."

The scenario played itself out for Daniher as though he had written it himself. Stewart would get the disaffected Democrats, as he had proven in the primary. The Gansvoort name would pull in Big Business and the American Manufacturers Association. The Republicans, whose candidate was a weak sister, would smell a winner in Stewart and cross over to the Conservative line. Labor? Well, labor alone couldn't beat him. What had seemed like a shoo-in for the Democrats and Governor Haskell was now a toss-up. It would be one hell of a fight. And in the end, Daniher could sense, it might all be slipping away. If he won, Stewart would owe nothing to anyone. All the favoritism, all the patronage, all the jobs, all the *power*—out the window. The machine Daniher had built so carefully would be fighting for its very life. And it could lose.

By the time the commentator had finished with the newborn candidate and switched to another topic, Daniher was shaking with rage and self-disgust at his own blind complacency. He should have seen it coming. All the signs were there in hindsight. All the ifs and what-might-have-beens went racing through Daniher's mind, to finally focus on the one defense he had left. Now was the time for dirty tricks. Now was the time to trot out the *real* Stewart Gansvoort. Reveal nasty scandal that had been so smoothly covered up. Show the public the kind of man they were being asked to vote for. The possibilities were there. Maybe the Kennicott girl would talk—for enough money? Paternity suit by the Italian dockworker's daugher? There should be enough mileage in that alone....

Daniher reached out for the phone to call Patsy Pavane. He would need Patsy's help with the dockworker. And maybe other things.

His hand never reached the receiver. He felt again the stabbing pain in his chest, this time unbearably intense. He slumped sidewise in his chair as though in slow motion, every nerve in his body screaming in the effort to draw another breath. *Just one more breath, dear God. One more ...*

On the second day in his private room they let him see Gavin for ten minutes. Gavin smuggled in a forbidden newspaper, but when Daniher demanded that a television set be installed, Gavin protested. "Jesus, Des, they don't want you excited. The doctor said ..."

"You tell the man I'll be a damn sight more excited if I don't get it," Daniher said grimly. "I want to see what the bastards are doing to me. How the hell can I fight 'em if I don't know what's going on?"

Des Daniher didn't *look* sick. His face was ruddy, his eyes disconcertingly bright. His short-sleeved hospital gown was open and the muscles of his arms and chest still held their firm resiliency. But Gavin had had his half-hour with the doctor and knew better.

"The man has had a serious coronary infarction." The doctor had shown an understandable irritation. "Luckily there was no brain damage. But it's a *heart attack*—not a goddamned sprained ankle! And the phone has been ringing off the wall from every half-assed hack politician in the state. I won't have it! He is not to be disturbed. No phone calls. No visitors except family. And that kept to a minimum. I hope I'm getting through to you, because if he tries to take up where he left off, I won't be responsible. He's got a long, hard road to recovery. No shortcuts."

Looking at his uncle, Gavin thought the doctor was in for a hard time.

A nurse reminded Gavin that his ten minutes were up and he left reluctantly, feeling deeply worried about what the future held for his Uncle Des.

The next day Mary Margaret and Donnie Shay were allowed their ten minutes, along with Meg O'Day. Meg O'Day refused to talk about what was happening to Daniher's daily petitioners, except to say that everything was being taken care of, just as he would have wanted. All of them spoke in hushed tones, as if he were something so precious that a raised voice could shatter him like a wine glass. Ten minutes of that was more than enough.

Not so with Serena, who showed up outside of the prescribed visiting hours, the Gansvoort name as usual serving to bypass all the rules. She was dressed in summer silk, something blue and clinging, and to Daniher she was like the promise of springtime, so full of life he could feel it touch him, sweep over him like a freshening breeze.

Within thirty seconds Serena knew that talk about the weather wasn't what Daniher wanted to hear. "They shafted you, didn't they, Des?"

Daniher looked for pity in her eyes and found nothing but a lively interest. He began to grin.

"That they did, darlin'. They put it to me with both feet. An' me a poor sick spalpeen without the strength to fight back."

Serena grinned back at him. "That'll be the day. Can they pull it off?"

"They can." Daniher turned serious. "Just possibly. If I don't get out of this rat's hole to organize things."

Serena showed her concern. "You sure it's worth it, Des? You've had a pretty good run. Why not let it go for now?"

"And let the bastards take all the marbles? Stewart as governor? And maybe more? That's what your father had in mind, you know. As I remember, he said Stewart and the country deserved each other—and seemed to take considerable pleasure from the thought. He had no high opinion of either. And that's a fact."

"A nasty thought," Serena conceded. "Maybe they won't elect him."

"If they do, I've no one to blame but myself. I should have seen it coming a mile away. I gave Charlie a free hand because I trusted him. A damn stupid thing to do in politics.

"Serena . . ."—Daniher looked at her searchingly—"I may have to do something you won't like. Dirty tricks. If he's to be stopped. Perhaps you'd better get out of town . . . avoid the unpleasantness."

"I know," Serena said calmly. "You'll trot out everything you know about Stewart. And it *will* be unpleasant. In fact, it will be one hell of a stink. And I'll hate every minute of it. But no, I think I'll stick around. Maybe I can help."

Daniher's eyes widened abruptly.

"You mean that?"

Serena grinned. "Don't I owe it to the voters? What do I do?"

"I need to know what they're up to." Daniher was now all business, taking Serena at her word. "Charlie knows everything I know about Stewart. Maybe more. He knows I can spill it all. So he must think he's got a way to stop me. And maybe he has. It's what I've got to find out."

"I don't see a lot of my brother these days." Serena was dubious. "For one thing, he seems to be obsessed with his plans for building a new state complex. Up to his ass in blueprints. And the lady who's doing it for him. I don't think he's bedded her yet, but it's almost obscene to watch how hard he's trying. Quite a girl, our Ericka." She paused, caught up in what she was thinking. "It's very tough on Olivia. I think he would divorce her, except the voters will never stand for it. Maybe she can be talked into suing *him*. Now, how's that for an idea? I don't think it would take much. She's certainly got plenty of grounds."

What Serena was saying began to ring faint bells in Daniher's mind. So Stewart was using his ridiculous scheme to build a government complex as bait to get the girl. Strictly a pipe dream. Even if he got the governorship, Stewart would never be able to swing it. Unless Stewart used Gansvoort money, and even Stewart wouldn't be that foolish. Surely, even if the girl was a political ignoramus, she would know it couldn't be done. The simplest questions to her uncle, George Barnstable, would tell her that. Yet, according to Serena, plans were going ahead. So Stewart must have convinced them both that it *could* be done.

How? What the hell did they know that he, Daniher, didn't?

"Well, how about it?" Serena asked. "I could talk to her at least."

Daniher came out of his reverie. "What?" And then, "Sure, it's worth a try. A nice messy divorce action wouldn't do him a bit of good. Couple that with a paternity suit, and Stewart can kiss it all good-bye."

Daniher looked at Serena's earnest face and felt a qualm at what he might be forced to do. "You sure you want to do this? You know what you could be getting yourself into?"

"No, I'm not at all sure," Serena said slowly. "It's a dreadful can of worms. I hate it. But the alternative scares the hell out of me. You see, I know Stewart far better than the rest of you. I haven't my father's cynicism. Odd as it may seem, I find I *do* have some sort of obligation to people, to my country—whatever you want to label it. Real power, unlimited power, in Stewart's hands . . . it's something so dangerous it doesn't bear thinking about. So I'll do whatever has to be done."

Back at home Daniher was allowed five visitors and ten phone calls each day, no more, on pain of total isolation. His whole household conspired like prison guards to see that he didn't break the rules. He used his downstairs office (now a bedroom, too, for he was forbidden the climb to the floor above) like a war room, his visitors like corps commanders, Daniher sending them out to shore up defenses, twist arms, call in old debts, to threaten and cajole—

above all, to breathe some life into an organization that had grown slothful, wallowing in its own complacency.

The day came when Meg O'Day informed him that Charlie Bishop was waiting to see him. Since, for all Meg O'Day knew, Charlie was still almost a member of the family, she considered Charlie an exception to the five-visitor rule; that is, if Daniher felt up to seeing him.

Daniher did indeed. He could hardly wait until Charlie Bishop was ushered in and assigned to a chair.

"You're looking great, Des."

Daniher said nothing. Charlie fidgeted, not quite sure of his welcome, and Daniher wasn't about to help him out.

"Sorry it had to be like this, Des. Believe me."

"You're not in yet," Daniher said grimly. "It's a long ways till November."

"As good as, Des. As good as." Charlie seemed to be gaining confidence. "That's not what I'm here about. Thing is, Des, we need your help."

Daniher, for an instant, had the wild hope that Charlie had miscalculated somewhere and needed bailing out. He let a sour grin be his answer.

"It's not much. Just something Stewart has got his heart set on. The world won't stop if he doesn't get what he wants. But it's little enough, and there'd be a thing or two in it for you."

"Charlie, you have the balls of a burglar. What makes you think I'd deal with you?"

"Aw, Des." Charlie was aggrieved. "It was just politics, what happened. Nothing personal and no hard feelings. You of all people ought to know that."

"Okay," Daniher said shortly, "so I'll listen."

"It's the goddamned state office complex. He's determined to build the fucking thing. And so far I can't talk him out of it." Charlie's air was offhand, one pro to another, as though he knew Daniher would sympathize with his problem. "He thinks he's got a way to finance it. But we're going to need your help."

Daniher lifted an incredulous eyebrow. "You're smoking something, Charlie. That's dream stuff. The law says . . ."

"I know what the law says," Charlie said impatiently. "So the voters won't build Stewart's playhouse for him. Right? Wrong. Because I'm tellin' you there *is* a way."

"That's horseshit, Charlie, and you know it."

Bishop lifted a hand in protest. "Now just a damn minute. You're going too fast. You haven't heard it all yet." Bishop drew a deep breath. "There's a lot of things you should know before you blow your fuse. I don't think you understand the situation, Des. Maybe I better lay it out for you." He reached down to the briefcase at his feet, took out a fat folder labeled Insurance Policies and handed it to Daniher.

Daniher opened the folder and slowly turned page after page, although it took only the first few to tell him what he held in his hands.

It was all there, the death knell of the Democratic party machine. Forty years of painstaking labor, all the compromises, the deals, the winnowing out—the winnowing in, for that matter—all of it out the window. Page after page the record was there, spelling out the stupidity, chicanery and greed of men who should have known better. Men who had grown so smugly safe in their positions that they had taken not even elmentary precautions. Key legislators in both houses, county and local chairmen, health-department officials, the attorney general's office, the cream of Daniher's particular crop.

Well, Daniher thought tiredly, *it had to come sometime*. Daniher closed Charlie Bishop's folder and turned his swivel chair to face the window. The trees outside were showing autumn colors and would soon be dropping their leaves on the streets of the City. His City. The City that would hold his heart for all of time.

He turned back to face Charlie Bishop. "How many, all told?"

"Two probables, four possibles . . . and twenty-one sure kills. Out of those twenty-one, say sixteen would be a cinch to make the jailhouse. Conspiracy, bribes, whatever. That's just the state. I don't know what the feds would do to 'em. But they'd sure want a shot."

"That's it, then." Daniher's voice sounded old even to him. "You've got more than enough to break our backs, Charlie. Put us out of business for good. If that's what you want. . . ."

"It doesn't have to be that way, Des. It's not what we really want—to bust up the organization. I figure if these guys know what we got, it should be enough to swing 'em our way. No need for a bloodbath.''

Today's enemy, tomorrow's friend, Daniher thought again. *So Charlie wasn't going to drop the axe. That was foolish of Charlie. Once you got 'em down, never let 'em up. Like the man said, Don't look back. Something might be gaining on you.* ''You're right, there, Charlie,'' Daniher said despondently. ''The kind of people you seem to have locked up could swing a lot of votes your way.'' Daniher closed the folder and started to hand it back. ''What do you want from me, Charlie?''

Bishop seemed almost apologetic. ''Look, Des, we don't want to bust anybody. I only showed you all this stuff so's you could see we got it locked up. What you got to do, Des, is persuade the county an' the City to put out a bond issue so's Stewart can build his fucking dream house, the goddamn state government complex. That's what you got to do. An' that's all you got to do. Come to maybe two or three hundred million. No more.''

Daniher began to laugh. He laughed until he had to wipe the tears from his eyes.

After a moment Charlie Bishop began to laugh, too, ruefully. ''I know,'' Bishop said at last. ''It's crazy. But that's what the man wants. An' that's what the man says he's gonna get. Or else.''

''And all because of the girl,'' Daniher marveled. ''Jesus Christ. Is that the way of it?'' He couldn't believe the sheer gall of the man, the outrageous arrogance, the thoughtless immorality.

After a while Daniher said, ''Charlie, you know it can't be done. There's just no way I could get the county and the City to float a couple of hundred million, even if I wanted to. Which, right now, I don't.''

''Yes, there is. I'm telling you it can be done. Legally. There's one key to the whole thing.''

''What's that?''

''The county an' the City don't have to have a referendum.'' Charlie pulled it out like a magician's rabbit. ''They can issue bonds on their own. Never has to come to a general vote.''

Daniher was blandly skeptical.

''True. But even then...''

448

"All the *state* has to do is guarantee the bonds. So the City an' the county can't lose. Stewart takes care of that when he's governor. Don't you see it?"

"No," Daniher said. "Frankly I don't. That can't be all there is to it."

"Well, no." Charlie was uncomfortable. "There's more. You better listen good, Des, while I lay it out for you. It gets a little complicated. But I swear to God it will work."

In the end they came to an agreement, there being no mortal enemies in politics. "That's it, then." Charlie closed his briefcase and got to his feet. "I'll get you all the facts and figures you'll need. Day or so. Glad you're with us, Des. Like old times."

He put out his hand. Daniher took it and held on.

"You know," he said thoughtfully, "it occurs to me you're going to be pouring a hell of a lot of cement in the next few years...."

Bishop took back his hand and laughed aloud.

"Jesus, Des, you never let up, do you. I'll bear it in mind."

Which meant to Daniher that the cement company in which he was a major stockholder would get top priority. Within reason. He let Charlie Bishop get almost to the door before he spoke again. "There's one other thing."

Bishop turned around slowly, showing his wariness.

"Since poor Johnny Kerrigan is no longer with us, we'll be needin' a new police commissioner. You couldn't find a better man than Gavin, now, could you?"

The muscles around Bishop's mouth tightened, and for a moment Daniher thought he had pushed his luck too far. Then Charlie nodded, a quick jerk of his head, and Daniher thought distractedly that he could have asked for a half-share in the Gansvoort fortune. And maybe gotten it. He gave Bishop one extra nudge, just to nail it down.

"If Stewart was to ask the mayor... especially with Stewart's strongest recommendation, the good man could hardly refuse, now, could he? With Gavin such a fine lad and all."

Daniher was perfectly capable of doing his own asking, but he wanted the request to come from the new governor. Just to show the mayor that his solidarity with Stewart Gansvoort was still firm. He watched Charlie Bishop turn this over, knowing that Charlie knew exactly what was in his mind. Charlie shrugged his shoulders lightly and smiled.

"When the time comes, Des. Like you said, he ain't governor yet. You got anything else on your mind? Before I go?"

"No," Daniher said gently. "Not today."

Charlie was motionless, the smile gone. Daniher met his look with bland innocence. They held their positions for a long moment, each busy with his thoughts of what had happened in the past half hour. Who had won? And who had lost?

Then, with a brief lifting of his hand, Charlie Bishop turned and left.

27

Time: 1970
NAN KENNICOTT

Demolition hadn't reached Deacy Street as yet, although the area between Deacy and the state capitol at the top of Schuyler Heights would have seemed familiar to Neil Armstrong after his recent walk on the moon. That same moon now cast an eerie light over the devastation of the Pit. Only the stark silhouettes of the giant cranes indicated the presence of man and his endeavors.

Chief Inspector Riordan was on a last sentimental journey through the Twelfth Ward. Most of the north side of Deacy had already been evacuated, store fronts dark and empty, houses bleak and abandoned. The south side of the street still had electricity and water, and a few of the sin spots of the Pit were doggedly hanging on. The neon sign of O'Dowd's Tavern cast a purple sheen on the sidewalk, and Riordan knew that Paddy O'Dowd was still taking illegal bets on sporting events in the back room and would until the wheels of progress rolled over him. Annie Gorman's bordello had long since gone out of business. The ground floor was now a pinball emporium.

Riordan remembered the night he had taken a naked Stewart Gansvoort out of Annie's backyard and how drunk they got later. "I'd like to tear the town down and build it all over again," Stewart had said. Well, there was consistency in Stewart. A man would have to give him that.

Gavin Riordan had been seven years away from the Third Precinct, six of them working for three-star Chief Inspector Kevin O'Boyle in Internal Affairs. He had settled into a life that wasn't exactly unhappy. He had long since given up his weekly visits to Birdie. Birdie no longer recognized him. He saw a good deal of Des Daniher and Daniher's friends and watched with some amusement how Daniher ran his kingdom: the endless maneuvering for advantage, favors given and returned, deals made and deals failed. Aside from that, he had few friends. His love life was casual and haphazard, except for Serena.

Serena spent about half of each year at home, and there was no pattern to her comings and goings. At times he didn't think of her for weeks. At others he missed her poignantly. She could still excite him in bed more than any other woman, but he had learned to accept both the companionship, sporadic as it was, and the deprivation of it.

Loneliness was at the bone of Gavin's existence and long had been. Now he puzzled over it, recalling his popularity in school, feeling in himself no hostility to fellow beings. But something set him apart, made him a loner. His marriage had been bad luck, but the rest seemed fated. He had been at odds with the Army and later with the Department. As a cop playing the scourge to bad cops, he was of course disliked, but here in the Third he had been disliked too, by fellow cops. This had driven him to learn the district itself better than any other cop assigned to it. Now Gavin

Riordan, pacing Deacy Street, was at the same time retracing the pathways of his life.

Riordan, lost in reminiscence, heard a woman scream. Once and then again, farther up Deacy, where St. Thomas's loomed against the sky—the only building in the Pit not scheduled for destruction. Riordan ran toward the sound, Beretta in hand.

Just at the edge of the light cast by one of the few remaining street lamps, he saw two figures struggling on the sidewalk by an overturned wheelchair, a woman holding on to a black boy who was struggling hard to get loose. The boy was clutching the woman's handbag in one hand and striking at her face with the other. Riordan brought the Beretta down on his head with enough force to deck him.

The woman was breathing hard. She sat up awkwardly and reached for the handbag, which had dropped.

"Son of a bitch thought I was easy," the woman said. "I wasn't about to let him get away with it."

Riordan bent to frisk the boy and came up with a switchblade. He put it into his own pocket. "Foolish, lady," Riordan said. "Nothing in that bag is worth your life. You all right?"

"Yes," the woman said shortly, and then, "I can take care of myself. But thanks, anyway." Riordan noted the broad shoulders and the muscular forearms common to so many paraplegics. The woman tossed the hair back from her face, and Riordan recognized her.

"Don't I know you?" the woman said uncertainly. "Weren't you . . . ?"

"Yes," he answered. "I'm Gavin Riordan. I'm a policeman. Can you . . . ?"

"I can if you'll move the chair where I can reach it."

The boy was thinking of getting up, so Gavin pressed his foot firmly on his shoulder, forcing him facedown on the sidewalk. "This is a gun I'm holding, so stay right where you are. I'm not through with you."

From close behind him a deep voice said, "You gonna blow away his knee, Cap'm?"

Riordan whirled, going into an instinctive crouch, the Beretta before him.

"Too slow," the black man said. "I could have taken you." He was both tall and wide, smartly dressed in a tailored uniform and green beret. Across the broad chest were rows of combat ribbons; there were sergeant's chevrons on one sleeve. "You don' know me, do you?"

"No. Should I?"

The soldier threw his shoulders back and gave an exaggerated salute. "Sergeant Leroy Biggs of the US Army. *Re*-tired. As of now, on terminal leave." Gavin made nothing of this introduction, so the black said, "I was gonna fix you like you did my brother. In the garage behind your house."

The boy in the garage. The homemade gun. "My, how you've grown, Leroy," Riordan said gently, and then, "Sergeant Biggs, meet Miss Nan Kennicott. Another old . . . acquaintance."

Riordan holstered his gun and righted the wheelchair. One wheel had been bent and was binding against the frame.

"I got a wagon up the street," Biggs offered.

"Thanks for the help. I guess the Pit has seen its last taxi. Of course, I could whistle up a squad car. . . ."

"No," Nan Kennicott said, "I'll take the gentleman's offer, if you don't mind."

Leroy Biggs hesitated, nodded toward the black boy still flat on the pavement. "What about him?"

It was Riordan's turn to hesitate, and Biggs said, "Maybe he's got a mother who scrubs floors in the statehouse."

Riordan looked down at Nan Kennicott. "You want to press charges?" He thought she would say, "You're goddamn right I do," but Nan Kennicott shook her head.

"What's the point? I work in the statehouse myself. In the governor's office. I'd just as soon not make the papers."

It figures, Riordan thought. *The Gansvoort payoff.* He prodded the boy in the ribs with his toe. "Get the hell out of here."

The boy got slowly to his feet.

"But first thank Sergeant Biggs for saving your ass. You owe him one. And don't forget it."

Biggs flashed his wide grin. "Gettin' soft in y'old age, Cap'm?"

"It would be a mistake to count on it, and it's chief inspector now. Now, about that car, Leroy?"

"Yassuh, yassuh, comin' right up," Biggs clowned. "Chief inspector now? My, my."

When he had left, Riordan said, "If it's not asking too much, what the devil are you doing in the Pit?"

"I *live* here," she said. "One of the old houses. It's close to the statehouse, where I work. Easy commute. Until they tear it down."

She looked at the damaged wheelchair. Gavin dragged it close to her.

"Why don't we get you into this?" He moved behind her and put his arms under hers to lift her, but she pushed him away. "You better just hold the chair steady," she said. "I'll make it on my own."

He did as he was told, watched her grasp the arms of the chair, pull herself up like a gymnast on parallel bars and, with a quick twist of her body, seat herself firmly on the padded seat. He heard the faint clink of the braces she wore under her slacks. It was an impressive performance. "You sure you're all right?" he asked.

"Except for a broken fingernail. It hurts."

She looked at the middle finger of her left hand. She had nice hands, long graceful fingers, carefully manicured. She put the injured finger in her mouth and sucked on it.

"I know your father. . . ." he said awkwardly.

"I know." She, too, was remembering their last meeting and was completely aware of what he was thinking. This embarrassed Riordan, but her self-possession was perfect. She was an odd creature, apparently fearless. He was relieved when Leroy Biggs brought his shiny new Chrysler station wagon to a halt at the curb.

Nan Kennicott's house was one of the graceful old federals still standing among the shabby three-deckers that had taken over in the Pit. Beside the steps leading to the first floor was a gently sloping ramp. *The Gansvoort touch*, Gavin thought. *Spare no expense. Nothing too good for our victims.*

Leroy Biggs lifted the girl from the front seat, carried her up the steps and held her easily in his arms as she took keys from her bag

454

and opened the door. Gavin manhandled the wheelchair up the ramp.

In the living room of the ground-floor flat, Leroy Biggs deposited the girl in a straight-backed chair and looked admiringly around the room. It was comfortably tasteful, fresh flowers everywhere. When Riordan put down the wheelchair, Biggs examined it critically. "You got a hammer? Screwdriver? See what I can do to get it to work."

"Kitchen cabinet," she said. "Tool box under the sink. It's down the hall at the back." She sounded tired and Gavin saw the lines of fatigue around her mouth. "I could use the bathroom, if it's not too much trouble." She gestured to a door on the other side of the room.

Gavin picked her up and carried her into a compact dressing room with waist-high rails along the walls. Tucked into the frame of the dressing-table mirror was a snapshot of Stewart Gansvoort.

Through another door was a Spartan bedroom, more rails, open shelves chest-high along the walls. The bed was queen-sized. At its head was a console nest with a clock radio, telephone, record player, water carafe, ashtrays and a small TV set on a retractable arm. From the ceiling was suspended a trapezelike affair. Metal crutches lay across the foot of the bed. She followed his look. "If you'll prop those outside the bathroom, I can manage from there."

He turned sideways to ease her through the bathroom door, and she snapped on the light. More metal tubing had been set into the tiles on floor and walls. At her gesture he sat her down on the toilet seat and she leaned back exhaustedly, looking suddenly much older than she could possibly be. There were deep shadows under her eyes and a thin white line around her mouth, a fine beading of perspiration at her hairline.

"Will you be all right?" Riordan asked.

She closed her eyes and nodded.

Gavin backed out and closed the door. When he turned around he could see across the bedroom Leroy rifling the vanity in the dressing room. Leroy glanced up and put a finger to his lips. Gavin crossed over to him and looked into the open drawer of the dressing table.

"Found this in the garbage in the kitchen." Leroy was holding a disposable hypodermic syringe. "Thought there was something odd about her. Look here."

In the drawer was a pharmacist's carton that held another dozen disposable syringes. Beside it was a battery-operated vibrator, and beside that a sizeable flesh-pink dildo with harness attached. Leroy Jones gave a low whistle. "This chick really into it, man. Kinky."

Gavin gave his attention to the soldier. "What were you looking for in her things?" he asked.

"I can spot a user," Leroy said. "Street boy like me, time in Vietnam? It's written all over her. Just made me curious." Leroy smiled sunnily.

"You want to be a witness if I bust her?"

"Somethin' 'bout a courtroom strikes me dumb," Leroy said. When Gavin said nothing, Leroy shrugged. "Better get back to fixing that wheelchair," he said.

Leroy Biggs had gone, silently as ever, when Nan yelled from the bathroom. "Where the hell are those crutches?"

Gavin pushed the drawer shut with his hip and went back into the bedroom. She had changed into a clinging silk robe that outlined her body, softly molding good breasts. She held herself propped up in the bathroom doorway. Her face had a clean scrubbed look, all tiredness gone now, in its place a kind of expectant animation. She was smiling, her eyes lit with an inner excitement, and Gavin knew that she had had her fix.

Gavin handed her the crutches. She tucked them expertly under her arms and set out across the room. They reached the living room as Leroy was pushing the wheelchair in from the kitchen.

"Should do till you get a new wheel," Leroy said. "This one's never going to be exactly right."

She maneuvered herself to the chair, reached to set the hand brakes that would hold it steady and, with an athlete's grace swung her body into the seat. "Thank you, Mr. Biggs. And speaking of thanks, rescuers always deserve a drink. What's your pleasure?"

"Well, I don't . . ." Leroy began and, at Gavin's look, changed it to, "That'd be jes' fine. Little touch of Scotch, very nice."

Nan Kennicott began to hum gently to herself as she got out ice and prepared three drinks with a maximum of efficiency. "This is fun," she called over her shoulder. "Lots better than an evening alone."

"What I tell you?" Leroy Biggs whispered. "She ain't even touching the ground."

Nan placed the glasses on a small tray, balanced the tray in her lap and wheeled herself to each of them in turn. When they had tasted the whiskey, she raised her glass, smiling brightly. "Here's to crime. Without it I wouldn't have met you gentlemen. And we wouldn't be having a party. This *is* nice, isn't it?" She took two long swallows of the whiskey and put her glass on a table. "You know, I think I'd like some music. Won't take a minute."

They watched as she wheeled herself swiftly toward the bedroom. "You gonna bust her?" Biggs asked.

"No," Gavin said. "Not yet. I'm curious where she gets it."

Leroy Biggs was relieved. "Then you sure don' need me. I'm gonna split soon's she gets back."

"What's your hurry? Aren't you having fun?"

Leroy reacted seriously to Gavin's sarcasm. "Not my idea of fun, Chief Inspector. Not how I get my kicks. Seems like a good lady to me."

"Where are you staying, Leroy?" Gavin asked. "Just in case I need you."

"Here and there right now." Biggs was blandly smiling. "Let you know when I get settled. If that's what you want."

"Old times' sake," Riordan said. "Keep in touch."

The strains of an old Fred Astaire recording came from hidden speakers. "They Can't Take That Away from Me." Leroy downed his drink and stood up as Nan came back. "Got to be going, Miss Kennicott. Thanks for the drink."

"So soon? I haven't had a chance to really thank you. I was hoping you'd stay." Her head turned toward Gavin. "Both of you." Her tone startled them both. Her smile was openly provocative.

"Sorry," Leroy Biggs said. "Things to do. Nice meeting you." He nodded to Gavin expressionlessly. "Have fun, Chief Inspector. I'll keep in touch."

They listened to the soft click of the front door as he closed it.

"Another drink?" she asked. Without waiting for an answer, she replenished both his drink and her own and wheeled back in front of him. "I haven't thanked you properly, either."

From the exertion of handling the wheelchair her robe now gaped open. He could see the soft undercurve of one breast. She saw where he was looking and made no move to cover herself. Gavin was filled with a sense of unreality; everything seemed slightly askew. "What did you put into it?" He waved his half-empty glass at her.

She was smiling brightly. "Just a tiny, tiny bit of acid. Not enough to trip. Just to loosen up."

He knew he should walk away from this, but he no longer cared. "What are you on?" he asked.

"Morphine, if it's any of your business," she said. "And... other things."

"Addict?"

"No...." She appeared genuinely uncertain. "At least I don't think so. I don't really know. I'd miss it like hell if I didn't have it. It helps with the pain."

"But I thought...?" He looked at her legs.

"They're not dead, you know. There's some feeling. And pain. I just can't move them, that's all."

"Where do you get it? Stewart?"

There was sudden alarm in her eyes. "I have prescriptions."

"That figures. The Gansvoorts' tame doctors. Always good for a fix. Any kind of fix."

"You'll never prove it." Her eyes sparkled, pupils alarmingly dilated. The smile was childish. "I'd like to go to bed now. Will you take me, please?"

He stood up. "I'll get your crutches."

"No. I want you to take me." The smile was almost a pout.

Why the hell not? Gavin thought. *It's better than a goddamn vibrator.* He lifted her from the wheelchair. Her arms went around his neck and she sighed dreamily. Her body now seemed weightless. So did his.

He carried her into the bedroom.

"Sit me up on the bed." She sat much as she had on the

sidewalk, legs straight out in front of her. She threw aside her robe, exposing the leather and aluminum braces, leaned forward and began to unbuckle them. With one arm she reached for the horizontal bar over the bed, shrugged out of the left side of her robe, switched hands expertly, got out of the other side and pulled the garment from under her.

Fascinated, Gavin watched the play of muscles in the wide shoulders and long arms. Her breasts, even when she was lying flat, were erect and firm; the nipples were long and stood like tiny fingers. Her legs showed little atrophy; the skin was alive and creamy. Her eyes were hot with excitement. She thrust her pelvis up at him. "Hurry up. Don't cripples turn you on?"

Gavin began to undress slowly. Time seemed to have no meaning. "*You* turn me on," he said.

Her lips were wet and parted, her voice as seductive as a siren. "I've got some surprises for you."

He lay down beside her and let his hand trail over the ridged muscles of her belly until he found her. She gasped and stiffened, her body taut as a bowstring. She reached up, grasped the bar above her and flipped herself over him. She held herself suspended, just touching his erection.

"Don't move!"

Slowly she lowered herself and he felt her hot wetness engulf him. With her arms hooked over the bar she began to rotate her hips. He could feel the contraction of vaginal muscles as though they were separate fingers caressing him. He held himself motionless, captured by the extraordinary sensation.

She seemed to know that he was about to climax. She lifted herself from him, dexterously changed hands on the bar and dropped to the bed on her back. He spread her legs with his and rolled on top of her. Once more he could feel the undulating grasp as she bucked under him. As he came he was conscious of the faint crunch of breaking glass under his nose. His next breath sent him to the ceiling.

His head told him that it was an amyl nitrite ampule. His body was wracked with an orgasm that seemed to go on and on. When his brain cleared she was moving frantically, trying to achieve her own climax. Suddenly he felt her legs clamp against his thighs, once and then again. He began to lose his erection.

"Christ! Don't stop!" she screamed.

He moved hard against her, and it was enough. He waited until her gasping shudders stopped, and she began to take long deep breaths. He rolled off her and sat up, cross-legged.

"You moved your legs," he said. "Both of them."

She looked at him unbelievingly.

"Goddamnit, you did. I felt it. Try it again."

She looked down at herself. Her legs were still spread wide. He saw her stomach muscles contract with effort as she tried to move them together. Nothing happened.

"You did it once. You can do it again. Try, damnit! Try!"

There were faint ripples on the flesh of her inner thighs, a twitching as though the skin were irritated. She was holding her breath as she strained, her stomach rigid with effort. Beads of sweat sprang out on her upper lip. Slowly one leg moved a fraction. Then the other. Her second effort brought another movement, more pronounced. Her breath came out in a loud rush of air.

"Ever do that before?" Gavin asked.

She shook her head, eyes closed. She began to weep.

"Well," Gavin said, "it's a beginning. All you've got to do is keep at it."

He reached out and gently brushed the tears from her cheeks. "Want to tell me about it? It might help."

She gave a long shuddering sigh and opened her eyes. For an instant she looked like the girl he had first seen, her eyes wide with pain and bewilderment.

"Yes," she said very slowly, the words tremulous and uncertain. "I think I do. . . . Oh, Jesus, Riordan."

He wasn't sure whether she swore to meet a present pain or the pain of remembering.

"You know what happened?" she asked.

"I had a good idea. Stewart raped you. Nothing to do about it once you decided to clam up."

"It wasn't . . . quite like that. But near enough. I made a bargain,

460

you see. And I kept it. So did Stewart. Everything a girl could want." She laughed sharply, a short bitter sound. "Except my legs."

After the days of healing Nan was allowed to sit up. At that point the endless tests began. She was X-rayed, her legs pricked regularly each day; she was submitted to every kind of analysis known to medicine. Stewart spared no expense. He hired the best men in the field. And still nothing. Her legs refused to respond.

It wasn't until they sent her to Rehab that she began to realize that she might be permanently crippled. She had a period of deep depression before the resilience of youth took over, and she threw herself into the Rehab routine with frightening single-mindedness.

She spent weekdays at the Rehab center, but as soon as she had mastered the transfer from bed to wheelchair and back again, she was allowed to go home for weekends. At Putnam House there were moveable ramps everywhere now. Her bedroom was now on the ground floor, with its own bath, with every conceivable gadget to make things easier for the paraplegic patient. All courtesy of Stewart Gansvoort.

After the first few weekends she found home unbearably depressing. It was the unfailing cheerfulness of her parents and the looks of pity they tried to hide and couldn't. She resented their instant attention when they thought she needed help, their embarrassed guilt when she refused it.

Not so with Stewart. He seemed to sense her need to do things for herself and never intruded. He visited her twice a week at the center and every weekend at Putnam House. He went with her on long excursions and pushed her chair only when she tired of pushing it herself.

They never spoke of the boathouse. Stewart talked of politics, his campaign for reelection, the strange and often amusing realities of political life. Stewart had a way with words. He never talked down to her. He treated her as the woman she now felt herself to be. It was flattering that this busy man of the world would spend so much time with her. And money. Her treatment and care cost Stewart thousands. But then, nothing he could ever do could make up for what he had already done. She could only think of Stewart's attention as her due.

Put Kennicott welcomed Stewart's visits. He was working at Gansvoort Associates now, in a job in which he could use his considerable abilities. He was pathetically grateful for Stewart's attention to Nan and accepted Stewart's financial outlays as the expression of a genuine desire to see Nan recover. Nan's mother watched Nan's developing relationship with Stewart with cool speculation, reserving judgment.

And there was a relationship, a strange one, founded on mutual guilt, a shared and dangerous secret and gratitude for what each was doing for the other. For Nan it was a confusing split. Part of her could hate and condemn this man. He had put her in this wheelchair, perhaps for the rest of her life. On the other hand, what exactly had he done? Could she really blame him when she couldn't remember? Her dreams of him, and she dreamed of Stewart constantly, were of lovemaking.

Stewart's unfailing kindness, his intuitive understanding, disarmed and charmed her. So she found herself trapped in a love-hate dilemma. She was beginning to realize that the love was definitely there, perhaps stronger than the hate.

Dr. Moomjii considered carefully before attempting to answer Stewart's question.

"She has no dysfunction of the bowel or the urinary tract. Ordinarily, in such a case, one would expect . . . But there is none. Therefore I would venture an opinion that there is no sexual inhibition—of the sexual *organs*, that is. She should be able to bear offspring."

"That's not exactly what I asked," Stewart said. "Would she enjoy fucking like the rest of us?"

"My dear sir, it is beyond me to answer such a question."

"Come on, Doctor. Quit stalling."

"There is no *physical* reason why she should not. However . . ." Dr. Moomjii seemed to be experiencing extreme reluctance. "As we both know . . . Unfortunately there were circumstances surrounding

462

her injury . . . of which we are both aware . . . that might inhibit sexual gratification."

Stewart smiled at him. "Something else of which we are both aware is that I can have you back on the streets of Calcutta in forty-eight hours if you don't stop this double-talk."

Dr. Moomjii sighed. His doelike eyes showed distress. "My dear Mr. Gansvoort, you must understand. To all intents the young lady is completely recovered. The hairline lumbar fracture has healed cleanly. And yet, she cannot move her legs."

"What are you trying to tell me?"

"Bear with me, sir. Consider a young girl of fifteen who has suffered a severe trauma. One of the most severe, at that age. The violation of her body against her will . . ."

Stewart snorted. "Not entirely."

"But nevertheless, to her, a shameful thing. The mind would do what it could to hide that shame. In short, a self-induced paralysis. Confinement to a wheelchair where she would be safe from further . . . attacks."

"She's faking it?" Stewart asked.

"Not at all, dear sir. Her paralysis is very real—as long as her mind believes it is. We know it as conversion hysteria, acute anxiety converted into dysfunction of parts of the body. In this case her legs."

"What are the chances?"

Dr. Moomjii was looking at him with great earnestness. "If you could . . . If the young person could be persuaded to undergo psychiatric treatment, perhaps . . ."

Stewart was instantly wary. "Could she come out of it herself?"

"It is possible," Moomjii said doubtfully. "In time."

"Well, thanks for the information, Doctor. I'll see what I can do."

Stewart left the hospital thinking, *Why take a chance that it might all come out in the open? Better to leave things as they are.*

Stewart didn't know any psychiatrists as malleable as Dr. Moomjii.

Two years later Nan entered Holyoke. Her tuition was paid by her family, but her living arrangements were provided by a grant from the Gansvoort Associates. She lived just at the edge of campus, in a house that had been converted into a sort of paraplegic heaven. A local woman came each day to both clean and cook. There was a succession of roommates—again arranged by Stewart—who doubled as companions and general bottle washers.

She followed Stewart's career avidly and wrote him long, rambling letters about her life and her thoughts, which he answered sporadically. He became many things to her, part benevolent, affectionate uncle, part glamorous political knight-in-armor, part the brother she never had—and always the object of her sexual fantasies. Since Stewart was the only sexual partner she would probably ever have, it seemed appropriate that she lavish her dream-love on him.

Over the years she became alienated from her family. She found it impossible to bury her resentment against them. If she hadn't tried to help them, she would be a two-legged Nan Kennicott; if they had been able to cope with life on their own, there would have been no need for her sacrifice.

In her junior year her mother died, and Nan was overwhelmed with guilt. It should have brought her closer to her father, but Putnam Kennicott, never demonstrative, became remote in his grief, as though with the death of the woman he had loved with such passion, he had no more love to give to anyone else. Or so it seemed to Nan. So in her mind Stewart was given one more role to play, along with all the rest.

Nan's roommate in her senior year was not the usual student helper. Marcie Dant was a dropout from nursing school and a friend of Stewart Gansvoort. From Stewart's letter of explanation Nan learned that Marcie was marking time until her fiancé got out of the Army and returned to his job at Riverhaven.

"They'll be married then," Stewart had written.

> In the meantime there's a problem. Marcie is pregnant. She wants to keep the baby, and her family would never understand. There would be one hell of a row. Never darken my door, and all that. So Holyoke and you seem an ideal solution. There will

464

be doctors and everything else that's needed, so it shouldn't be any trouble for you. Just a hideaway until the baby is born— which should be about the end of the school year.

You'll be doing everyone a favor. She's a sweet child, and I'm sure you'll like each other. . . .

Nan was delighted to be of help, and intrigued at the thought of being a part of gestation from start to finish, even though it was someone else's.

Stewart was right. They did like each other from the beginning. Marcie was a small bouncy girl with the figure of a belly dancer. She had a wide mischievous smile and eyes that seemed to know more than they should. Early in her stay she said, "What do you do for sex around here? No men. I don't think I can stand it."

Nan, with only half-formed ideas about marriage and fidelity, mentioned the absent father-to-be.

"Oh, him," Marcie grinned. "A million miles away. Sex is sex, honey. And should be enjoyed whenever and however possible." In sudden embarrassment she looked at Nan's useless legs. "Gee, I'm sorry. I didn't think. How about you? Do you . . . ? I mean, can you . . . ?"

"Fat chance. Who would want a cripple?" And then, "I don't really know. . . . I . . ."

Marcie's eyes widened in astonishment. "You mean you're a virgin?" She made it sound like a rare disease.

"Well, not exactly," Nan said slowly. "It was just once." She gestured to her wheelchair. "I don't get many offers."

Marcie was intrigued by Nan's condition. She marveled at how Nan managed, how she got herself into and out of her leg braces, the way she moved herself about on the bar over her bed. To Nan's dismay she insisted on watching how she went to the bathroom, offered to wash her back in the shower. When Marcie found that part of the job was to massage Nan's legs daily, she took that on with enthusiasm. "If I didn't learn anything else at nursing school," Marcie said, "I learned how to do a back rub." With Marcie the massage became a delight. Marcie went at it as though she expected

465

each treatment to restore life; her high merriment and optimism were infectious.

"You know," Marcie said, giving a leg a final pat, "they don't look crippled. They look great. Like you could just get up and walk away if you wanted to."

When Marcie found that Nan awoke in the night in pain, she introduced her to pot. It didn't kill the pain, but the delightful high helped her ignore it. "Didn't they give you anything at the hospital?"

"I've got a prescription. But it doesn't work most of the time."

"Maybe something stronger." Marcie was thoughtful. "I'll see what I can do." She returned the next day from a shopping expedition with a dark-green unlabeled bottle that contained a hundred slim capsules. "Go easy on those. They're dynamite," Marcie warned.

She was right. The pills not only banished her pain, they gave her a lovely euphoria. She smiled a lot and never asked Marcie what was in them.

Marcie's fiancé's name was Bob, and in a matter of days Nan knew all about Bob. Bob was tall, blond and a terrific lay. He was some years older and had worked as a mechanic at the Riverhaven farm since he was a boy. He knew Stewart very well indeed. "I think they used to whore around together. Not now, now that Stewart's such a big shot."

Marcie stopped when she saw the look on Nan's face. It wasn't really shock; it was more a sadness that she knew so little of Stewart's life except where it touched her own. Stewart whoring around? She knew Stewart was married. That was different. She never let herself picture it. But *whores*?

"You've got something going for him," Marcie guessed shrewdly.

Nan gave it some thought before she answered. "I guess I have."

"It's a no-win proposition, hon. Take it from me. I know."

Up to now Nan had allowed herself certain assumptions about that. Stewart's friendship with Marcie was because of his friendship with Bob. Now she wondered if she was being naive.

On the tenth day of her stay, Marcie had a miscarriage.

When she returned from classes, Nan found her in the bathroom, trying to clean up. There seemed to be an inordinate amount of blood. Nan panicked and called the doctor before Marcie had a chance to stop her. Marcie's principal reaction seemed to be anger. "For Christ's sake, Nan, miscarriage is no big deal. It was only a couple of months. Stop fidgeting."

The doctor came and went, seeming to treat the affair as casually as Marcie. "A few days in bed and she'll be fit again."

Marcie lay in the twin bed next to Nan's, silently staring at the ceiling, her face tight-lipped and closed. When Nan hesitantly suggested that Bob should be told, Marcie blew up.

"Fuck Bob! It wasn't his, anyway. It was probably Stewart. At least *he* thinks so. I'm not so sure. What the hell difference does it make? It's the baby. I wanted that goddamned baby. Jesus, I wanted that baby! It was my life insurance."

Nan's expression must have given her away.

"Quit looking at me like that. You'd probably have found out, anyway. Sorry about Stewart, but that's what fucking life is all about. So get used to it. And get off my back!"

Marcie flopped over and buried her face in her pillow.

After a moment Nan wheeled herself to the bathroom and took two capsules from the green bottle. In a short time she floated off to sleep in a sea of conflicting thoughts. The last one she remembered was how much she wanted Stewart's baby for herself.

In the middle of the night she woke up to find her cheeks wet with tears. She must have been sobbing, because she heard Marcie get out of bed. Then Marcie's arms were around her and Marcie was crooning to her, "Don't cry, baby. I'm sorry life is such a stinking lousy business. . . ." She drifted off again in the comfort of Marcie's gentle rocking.

In the morning things were back to normal; Marcie was her cheerful self. She apologized again for the things she had said and asked once more to be forgiven.

That was easy. But things were not the same for Nan. She watched the sway of Marcie's naked bottom as she bent over the washbowl to brush her teeth. She had seen this many times before, but now Marcie's body had a new significance. Because it had been coupled with Stewart's.

467

She was filled with a poignant sadness. Poor dead baby. Poor Marcie. Poor Stewart. And poor Nan. Most of all, poor Nan.

A few nights later Nan awoke to a strange buzzing noise that seemed to be coming from the next bed. Without thinking, she said, "What's that?"

"Shh!" Marcie hissed.

She was abruptly aware of Marcie's stertorous breathing and knew immediately what was happening. But she didn't know *how* it was happening. Marcie gave a shuddering groan, then a small yelp, and her breathing began to slow. "It's a vibrator. Haven't you ever used one?"

"No . . . I didn't know . . ."

"Don't tell me you don't masturbate."

"Well, yes, but . . ." She left it there, feeling that she was invading Marcie's privacy. Or Marcie was invading hers. She wasn't quite sure which. There was a silence, then she heard Marcie throw back the covers and sit up. "Maybe I better show you," Marcie said softly.

Nan slept nude to avoid the nuisance of getting in and out of nightgowns, but she was surprised by Marcie's nakedness as Marcie slid into bed beside her. She felt Marcie move her flaccid legs apart. She wasn't sure she wanted this, but she didn't know how to stop it. Marcie's large breasts pressed against hers, then Marcie's finger found her clitoris, and she *was* sure. Marcie felt her quivering reaction.

"Maybe we won't need the vibrator after all," Marcie whispered, and moved her mouth to cover Nan's.

Nothing in Nan's experience had prepared her for the next few hours. Marcie made love to her with an expertise that left her mindless with pleasure and treated each new orgasm as a personal triumph. When at last they lay exhausted in each other's arms, Nan said, "I never knew. . . ." and then, "Does this mean we are lesbians?"

Marcie burst out laughing. "Jesus, you don't have to be a lesbian to enjoy balling another woman. Sex is sex, honey. If it feels good, do it. That's my motto."

"But . . ."

468

"This was great. But men are better. The right man, that is. Oh, baby! Maybe we better find you a man."

But they never did, until much later.

By the time Nan was graduated in June, she had found a whole new life-style. Sex with Marcie remained good and, once she had adopted Marcie's attitude about it, became fantastic. For Marcie life was one long sexual experiment. When Nan asked her if she didn't miss men, Marcie's merry eyes lighted up. "Hell, yes, I miss 'em," she said. "But they have their drawbacks. Most of them are bastards. Besides, this way you don't get pregnant, which right now has got to to be a plus." Marcie was suddenly serious. "Look, Nan. I took this job in good faith. You took me in the same way. I figure we owe each other. So I'll stay until you graduate. I can use a vacation from men right now." Then grinning again, "Besides, what would you do without me? Vibrators can get awful lonesome."

Nan became a confirmed user of pot, and the two girls stayed pleasantly high much of the time. Nan learned that the pills she was taking were a morphine derivative. Because of Marcie's warnings about addiction, she adjusted her life to their rhythm and took them only when the need became acute. Marcie kept them supplied from some mysterious source she refused to reveal.

Lieutenant Governor Stewart Gansvoort gave the valedictory address to the graduating class, while Putnam Kennicott sat proudly by his daughter's wheelchair. She was surprised and touched when he held her hand.

Marcie refused to go to commencement, saying she wasn't ready for Stewart Gansvoort just yet. She was gone when Nan and her father returned to the house for Nan's things. There was only a brief note that ended with, "Lots of luck. I'll be seeing you."

Nan spent the summer at Putnam House with her father. She had hoped their relationship would improve, but it didn't. There just didn't seem to be anything they could talk about. By midsummer she was crawling the walls and wishing she were back at school. With Marcie.

She saw Stewart only twice, both times at parties at Riverhaven. Stewart was in the midst of a campaign for governor and hadn't much time for her. She did accomplish two partly satisfactory things. She got his promise of a job if he was elected. And when she told him of her misery at Putnam House, he gave her a smile and said, "That should be simple enough. I'll see what I can do." She hadn't a clue to what he had in mind.

What he had in mind became a reality the day after Stewart won the governorship in a landslide. Both the job in his office and the charming old house in the Pit. It turned out that he had already arranged things with her father, persuading him that, since she would be working in the statehouse, it would be impossible for her to commute all the way from Putnam House. The job was to start early in January.

One wintry afternoon, before she had quite settled in, the doorbell rang and she was delighted to find it was Marcie Dant who was shivering on her doorstep. Marcie shook the snow from an expensive fur coat and dropped it carelessly on the hall table.

Nan grinned. "Okay. Where'd you get it?"

"From a very nice gentleman," Marcie said with a wicked smile, "who shall remain nameless. Now—how about you. I want to know everything."

"You're a godsend, Marcie. I'm almost out of pills. And I miss pot terribly. I couldn't light up around my father, of course. But now that I'm alone . . . Will you break down and tell me how to get some?"

"No sweat," Marcie said. "I'll give you the name of a guy. But first . . ." She reached into her bag and produced a flat silver case. "Look what I brought you."

The case was packed with neatly rolled joints.

The two girls lit up and smoked for a while in silence. When the drug had a chance to take hold, Marcie reached out a foot and poked at Nan's braces. "Miss me?"

"You know I do," Nan said.

It was a memorable afternoon in more ways than one. At its end Nan was mindlessly stoned, lost in Marcie's ingenious ministrations.

Somewhere in her drugged brain she was conscious of the front door's opening. And closing. There were faint alarm bells, but she was too wrapped up in what was happening to her to do anything about it. Then Stewart Gansvoort was standing in the bedroom door, a look of mild amusement on his face. "My, my," Stewart said. "Room for one more?"

Marcie giggled.

Nan watched Stewart take off his clothes. It was the dream she had had a thousand times before. This time it was real.

It was weeks later, when Stewart asked for a key to her house, that Nan realized that Marcie must have left the front door unlocked on purpose. By that time it didn't matter.

"That son of a bitch," Gavin said.

"You can't blame Stewart," Nan said. "At least not entirely. If I hadn't wanted it, it wouldn't have happened." She took a slow drag at her cigarette. "At first it was great. I couldn't get enough of them both. There's something very attractive about lust—and depravity. But then . . . when he started bringing others into it . . . I don't know. I guess I'm really into sex. I'm good at it. The one thing I can do as well or better than the rest of you. It's the only way I can join the party. . . ."

"Bullshit," Gavin said. "The sex is one thing. It's the drugs. How far are you into that? What are you taking?"

"A little bit of everything. Uppers, downers, in-betweeners. Some LSD. Coke. Morphine."

"Heroin?"

"No. At least not yet." Her voice was bitter. "It helps, you know. A great little substitute for thinking. Thinking is a real downer."

Gavin considered her thoughtfully, weighing how much straight talk she could take, wondering if he was wasting his time on a thankless mission. He decided to give it a try, because if he could save her, it was somehow getting back at Stewart. He felt a cold rage when he thought of Stewart. Stewart the invulnerable, the untouchable. There had to be a way to stop Stewart.

"You know, I think you're hooked. Or as near as may be. And thinking is what you'll have to do if you're going to kick it. That is, if you want to kick it? Do you?"

She wouldn't look at him. He reached out, lifted her chin and forced her to meet his gaze. Her eyes were full of fear and uncertainty. "I don't know if I can. Stewart . . ."

"I can handle Stewart. I can take him off your back for good. It's the other. You've got to want it. A lot."

"I'm not sure. . . ." There was a look of pleading in her eyes. "Riordan, you don't know what it is to be alone. With Stewart and Marcie . . . and the others, at least I'm not alone. And the stuff I take helps. Oh, God, how it helps. . . ."

"Think!" Gavin said roughly. "What if you can get your legs back? You moved them, you know. What if you can walk again? Is this the kind of life you want to live?"

Slowly her face began to change until there was a look of hope, heartbreakingly hesitant at first, and Gavin thought, *Who am I to hold out hope? I'm playing God—and I don't know what the hell I'm doing. But if I can at least get her to try.* "Do you want to be Stewart's puppet for the rest of your life?" he asked roughly. "Dance—or screw—every time he yanks the strings? Because that's what it'll be. As long as he wants it."

"No." Her voice broke on the word. "I don't want that." Tears rolled slowly down her cheeks. She made no effort to brush them away. "No," she said again, "I don't want that."

Gavin knew he had her. For better or worse.

"I know a guy," he said softly. "At Veterans Hospital. Lots of experience with addicts. If anybody can help, he can. You can't do it alone, you know. We'll go see him tomorrow."

She closed her eyes. Her hand searched for his. He held her hand until she went to sleep.

Gavin's friend was a career colonel in the Army medical corps named Liam Rooney.

"She qualifies for treatment," Rooney said. "We've already booked her in."

"Does her father have to know?" Gavin asked.

"Maybe not. I'll see if I can short-circuit the paperwork."

Gavin had delivered Nan to the Vets Hospital at nine sharp. He had spent an hour giving Liam Rooney the background on Nan, holding back nothing except Stewart's involvement. Now it was early evening, and they were in a local bar at Rooney's invitation. Rooney was a short florid man, going slightly to fat in his middle years. He had twinkling Irish eyes and a lazy smile, both of which were deceptive. "Drugs are no real problem," Rooney said. "Fairly standard treatment, if she cooperates. It's the other."

"She damn well moved her legs. I saw it. If she did it once, why can't she do it again?"

"Know anything about paralysis?"

"Not much."

"Then shut up and listen. There are three possibilities here." Rooney ticked them off on his fingers. "One is conversion hysteria. It's a form of hysterical neurosis. Which means that acute anxiety is causing her head to tell her she can't move her legs. It's a tough psychiatric problem. Nothing much we can do about it physically. Strictly shrink territory. Two: Her X rays show she had a fracture of the second and third lumbar vertebrae. Beautifully healed and no apparent nerve damage. But..."—Rooney paused to light a cigarette, offered the pack to Gavin and shrugged when Gavin shook his head impatiently—"but it's possible that her fall gave her an acute lumbosacral luxation. To you that's a slight twist of the spinal column." Rooney illustrated by placing one thumb over the other and turning the top thumb away from him. "Which could have caused one vertebra to rotate over the next one and press on a nerve, which would impair its function. So you get a paralysis."

Gavin snorted. "Come on. She had the best doctors in the world. How the hell could they have missed that?"

Rooney shrugged again. "It's easy, baby. It wouldn't have to be much of a twist. An X ray is a two-dimensional thing. They could have X-rayed her every day for a month and still not picked it up. Unless they were lucky enough to get her in exactly the right position. So if she didn't have real pain, they wouldn't want to do an exploratory. Spinal operations are too tricky."

"Then how do you explain how she moved her legs, when...?"

Rooney grinned at him. "You were banging her, baby. I wasn't. Maybe you don't know your own strength. Figure it out. If counter-pressure were applied to the original twist in the spine, the vertebrae could snap back into place and some function would return."

"Okay. What's the third possibility?"

"Combination of both the above. Look, Riordan, you ever consider the possibility she wouldn't *want* to recover?"

Gavin looked at him uncomprehendingly.

"Think about it for a minute. Kid gives her all for dear old Dad. And succeeds. Dear old Dad happy as a clam in his job. Sure, the guy raped her. And that's bad. But the same guy is paying the rent, giving her everything she wants, including a job for the rest of her life. Clothes, money—and a little dandy fucking on the side. And that's good. Like the old joke, it should happen to your sister. There are a lot of reasons she might want to keep it that way. Consciously or unconsciously. So what do we do?"

"I guess it's up to her," Gavin said slowly.

The interview with Stewart Gansvoort took place in Stewart's hideaway suite in the Rensselaer Arms. It started with Gavin's saying, "I ought to kick the shit out of you, Stewart. But what the hell good would it do," and ended with, "Nothing changes for Nan. Except just stay the hell away from her. Unless she decides different. I'll know if she does. Otherwise, hands off."

As he was leaving, Gavin turned back. "By the way, the whole story is in my personal file in my lawyer's safe. With instructions. Just in case I should drop dead. Or something."

Stewart hadn't got up to see him out. He had been silent throughout the confrontation. Now he said, "And what will you do if I don't go along? Newspapers?"

Gavin eyed him contemptuously. "For starters I'd tell your wife. Then see how it plays."

He closed the door softly on Stewart's furious face.

28

Time: 1970
GAVIN RIORDAN

The next time Gavin met Leroy Biggs, it was broad daylight on Sugar Knob. It was Riordan's habit to walk his City on weekends. On a lovely Saturday morning in late March he left his car near the Blauvelt Reservoir and strolled uptown through Blauvelt Park. The sun, still with winter's pallor, cast dappled shadows through trees in first bud, on lawns not quite greening. The clear air held a last frosty bite and an invigorating promise of summer to come.

Riordan was headed for Sugar Knob, at the northern edge of the park. Sugar Knob was a ten-block area carved by developers out of the edge of the City's largest black ghetto. It was a place of new residential apartments and street-level shops, its affluence contrasting sharply with the black and Puerto Rican poverty abutting it on three sides. Its residents were about equally divided between middle-class blacks and whites.

Gavin took these walks in plain clothes. Today he was dressed in slacks, a blue shirt open at the neck and a heavy cable-knit sweater. He wore no hat, and his red hair flamed like a beacon. Being out of harness was part of his pleasure on these rambles.

Pedestrian traffic was as usual on a Saturday morning. Shoppers thronged; boutiques, delicatessens and a supermarket were doing brisk business. To Riordan's knowing eye, attuned to the pulse of the streets, it was a peaceful scene.

Coming toward him through the crowd was a man dressed in casual elegance, knife-creased fawn-colored slacks, a heather tweed jacket over a white cashmere turtleneck, cordovan loafers. The man was carrying groceries. Riordan watched him make his way through a knot of people surrounding a street peddler. He moved with the sure grace of a jungle cat, avoiding contact wherever possible.

"Hello, Leroy," Riordan said. "What you doing up here?"

Leroy Biggs smiled nicely. "I *live* here, man. You still walkin' the beat?"

"Just cruising," Riordan said. "Getting the feel of things. I thought you were going to keep in touch?"

"Been busy. You know how it is, man. This an' that."

Riordan looked him up and down appreciatively. "You are sure one handsome dude. You doing all right?"

Leroy waved a deprecating hand. "Po'k chops on the table an' steak on Saturday night. Can't complain." He looked at Riordan unsurely a moment, then made his decision.

"You want some java? Come on up to my pad. Meet the Big Mama."

Rioradn was curious. "Sure thing," he agreed, and followed Leroy down the street to an apartment house and into a spotless modern lobby.

Leroy Biggs's living room had a magnificent view of Blauvelt Park through a picture window, all the way down to the government offices at the south end and the capitol building on the hill beyond.

The room was white, walls and ceiling, and covered with a deep-pile white rug. On one wall there was a spectacular painting of an African warrior holding an assagai. One of the other walls held excellent examples of African primitive art.

Riordan was impressed and more curious than ever.

"Got company, hon," Leroy called. "Man could use some coffee."

From the kitchen at the far end of a hallway came the sound of dishes rattling and then a pleasant contralto voice.

"On the stove."

476

Leroy jiggled his bag of groceries.

"Jes' get rid of this. Back in a minute." Leroy padded down the hall, turned left and disappeared.

Riordan could hear the low murmur of voices and wondered how Leroy was explaining him. Instead of sitting, he wandered to a low bookcase and examined titles long enough to see that much of Leroy's reading was protest literature: Eldridge Cleaver, Bobby Seale, Huey Newton and others.

To his left, at the far end of the room, was an archway leading into what he supposed was a dining room. There were no lights, just shadowy space beyond the arch. And then, in one heart-stopping moment, he realized that the shadows were figures, people watching him. At least two. Possibly more.

Riordan moved swiftly to the shelter of the wall beside the arch. At this point he heard Leroy's soft chuckle.

Leroy, standing in the doorway, moved to the wall where Riordan stood and flipped a switch. "You seein' ghosts, man? Jes' dress models. Riana is a dress designer. That's the workroom."

Riordan felt foolish, not sure of how long Biggs had been watching him. Even in the light the two half-draped dress forms looked remarkably lifelike. "Ought to be a sign. Thought for a minute you had me covered there."

Leroy was suddenly serious. "Sorry about that. I know the feeling from 'Nam. Never know what's comin' at you."

Riordan stepped into the workroom. The windows were covered with heavy curtains. Along the far wall was a long cutting table, shears and scissors neatly arranged at one end, overhead a bank of work lights. To his left were shelves with stacked bolts of cloth, boxes filled with buttons and ornaments and pins; to his immediate right was a tilted drawing board, an unfinished line drawing still fixed to its surface. The other walls were covered with thumbtacked sketches, fashion magazine layouts. Among these, standing out incongruously from the other wall ornaments, was a poem in a black frame. Or at least Riordan thought it was a poem until he took a closer look. Leroy stood silently in the archway while he read.

1. No party member can have narcotics or weed in his possession while doing party work.
2. Any member found shooting narcotics will be expelled from this party.
3. No party member can be drunk while doing daily party work.
4. No party member will violate rules relating to office work and general meetings of the Black Panther party, or meetings of the Black Panther party anywhere.
5. No party member will point or fire a weapon unnecessarily at anyone other than the enemy.
6. No party member can join any other army or force other than the Black Liberation Army.
7. No party member can have a weapon in his possession while drunk or loaded on narcotics or weed.
8. No party member will commit any crimes against other black people at all, and cannot steal or take from the people, not even a needle and a piece of thread.
9. When arrested, Black Panther party members will give only name and address and will sign nothing. Legal first aid must be understood by all party members.
10. The Ten Point Program and platform of the Black Panther party must be known and understood by each party member.

Finished, Riordan looked at Biggs, eyebrows raised. "You really into this, Leroy?"

"All the way," Leroy said steadily. "All the way."

"What's the Ten Point Program? And just who the hell is the enemy?"

"If you don't know, man, I can't tell you." Biggs's eyes held something close to contempt. "Ten Point Program? Must be a copy in Headquarters's files."

"Don't know," Riordan said. "I'll have a look."

"You do that. Pass it around when you're done. Maybe somebody will get smart enough to listen to what's going down—before it's too late."

"Here's coffee." The contralto voice came from the living room. Leroy stood aside so that Riordan could go first and then followed him through the archway.

"Riana, this is Inspector Riordan. We go back a long way." She was tall, almost as tall as Biggs, with such a willowy grace that it was impossible to imagine her making an awkward movement. She was in a long caftan in tans and whites and blacks, swirling patterns as African as the art on the apartment walls. Her straight black hair was piled in a knot on top of her head, accentuating the long patrician face, with its high cheekbones, narrow high-bridged nose and almond-shaped eyes of deep brown. Her skin was the color of weathered cedar, a faint dusting of rose on her cheeks.

"Inspector." She held out her hand and Riordan took it. Her fingers were impossibly long, tipped with scarlet. When they were seated and Riordan had his coffee, Leroy turned to the girl.

"Mr. Riordan was asking about the Ten Points, hon."

"As I understand it," Riordan said softly, "you guys carry guns. I hate violence. Besides being against the law."

"Your law." Leroy put down his cup. "What about the inalienable right of every citizen to bear arms in his own defense? You got a war on your hands, Mr. Riordan. If you only knew it. You beat on people long enough, they gonna fight back. Only natural."

In a cool, matter-of-fact voice Riana said, "Martin Luther King tried nonviolence. It didn't work. It's hard to be nonviolent when the police go out of their way to spit on you and throw you in jail. For little more than existing, for merely being black and poor. And angry. We've suffered enough. What else can we do when you people have the guns and the law and the will to use them to keep us in our place? A place and an existence forced on us by you, Mr. Riordan. You and your Establishment."

Riordan looked around at the obvious opulence of the apartment. "You haven't done so bad."

"No, Mr. Riordan, I've been fortunate." Her great almond eyes held steadily on his. There was no heat in them, just a calm awareness of the unbridgeable difference between them. "But I'm

479

one of the few. Believe me, there are a lot of committed black people out there who won't take it anymore, who have gone beyond the slogans of the counterculture, into the realm of total violence. They've come to believe that terror is their only weapon. The ultimate weapon. Someday they'll use it. Can you honestly say they're wrong?"

"Yes," Riordan said. "Because I don't want violence to happen. Stopping it is my job. Well," he said, looking at his watch, "we won't solve anything today."

It was eleven-thirty. He had just an hour to pick up his car and meet Ericka Ullman for lunch. He put his cup on a low table and got to his feet. "Thanks for the coffee, Leroy. It's been . . . interesting. Maybe again some time, okay?" He held out his hand to the girl. "Nice meeting you . . ." He hesitated, not quite sure of her status, and settled on ". . . Riana."

She took his hand gravely, serenely, with utter surety of the rightness of what she believed. He felt a prick of irritation, because it wasn't all that simple. Nothing was. Nothing in the goddamn world.

Leroy saw him to the door.

Gavin wanted to say something more to Leroy. Sympathy? Reassurance? Warning? Tell him to watch his ass? Instead he gripped his hand in silence. Flesh to flesh, the age-old gesture of peace and friendship.

There was the ghost of a smile on Leroy Biggs's black face.

"Power to the people," Leroy said. "Panther power. Man, you better believe it."

Riordan shrugged. "If you say so, Leroy. See you around."

Gavin reached across Ericka's nakedness to answer the telephone and learned from his Uncle Des that he had just been appointed police commissioner. Under the circumstances the news didn't really register.

Daniher, puzzled by Gavin's lack of response, said, "Am I interrupting something?"

480

"Yes. No. . . . Look, Des, I'll have to call you back." He hung up and lay back on his side.

Ericka said, "I can go if you . . ."

Gavin pulled her to him. "Jesus, no."

"Hold me, Gavin," she whispered. "I feel so . . . safe."

Over her shoulder, in its place on the far wall, he could see the thing that had triggered what had just happened to them both: the framed watercolor portrait that George Barnstable had so proudly called *The Warrior.* A stranger stared back at him, a lean, rugged young soldier with a red beard covering half his face, cigarette smoke curling upward past squinted eyes. Another time. Another place.

He shivered involuntarily. He could almost feel the numbing cold of a Berlin Christmas so long ago. And then the warmth of the fire in the Ullman house, the close companionship, the promise the future held for all of them. The first smile of an enchanting child as she marveled over the gift of a box of colored chalks.

And now this.

In the three years since the reunion lunch with Ericka and George Barnstable, when Stewart had been so obviously smitten, Gavin had been a dinner guest of Barnstable's at the Gramercy Park house on a number of occasions. Cases he had been working on had brought him to New York with some frequency. He was genuinely fond of George and enjoyed being with him, and the Gramercy Park house was a warm and friendly place.

He took Ericka out alone for a mixture of reasons: duty dates to the concerts he knew she liked, in repayment for their hospitality; for the snide enjoyment he got from irritating Stewart, whom he knew was seeing her with all the frequency she would allow; and increasingly because he found her a fascinating enigma. She could enjoy the pop concerts in Central Park with all the spontaneous enthusiasm of a teen-ager, yet he knew from George that she was a serious and dedicated architect with a growing reputation who commanded top fees. The one time he picked her up at the offices of Barnstable-Ullman, he was hugely impressed by the deference with which she was treated by the staff.

She showed an intense interest in the work he did, a fascination with police procedure and all it entailed. Her interest wasn't superficial; she seemed to have a real desire to learn. At times he felt their relationship verged on that of teacher and pupil. It was immensely flattering until his policeman's mind, with its ingrained suspiciousness, forced him to ask himself why. That led him to pull Ten Tabard's nine-year-old letter from his files. The letter told him little more than the bare facts of the case. Two men dead and no way to prove who was responsible. He found it almost impossible to believe that this lovely woman was capable of any sort of violence. A lifetime of experience should have told him how wrong he could be. Somehow, with Ericka, it didn't.

When Ericka accepted Stewart's commission to build a house and stables for Olivia Gansvoort, Ericka took a suite at the Renssalaer Arms in the City, and Gavin began to see much more of her. Gavin had no current involvements, and Serena was away on one of her frequent safaris. So Ericka provided him a welcome companionship. There were lunches and dinners, an occasional evening listening to the hot bands in the nightclubs of the Pit.

At first Gavin suspected Ericka was using him to offset Stewart's importunities and accepted that as a legitimate obligation of friendship. For Stewart refused to give up. He wooed her in every way he could devise, from daily deliveries of flowers, to expensive gifts, to weekend invitations for a cruise on the Gansvoort yacht. They discussed Stewart frequently, treating Stewart's extravagances as a shared joke. Ericka seemed to find Stewart's attentions no more than a mild nuisance. Gavin tried to warn her that Stewart couldn't be taken so lightly.

It was during this time that Gavin gradually felt a subtle change in their relationship. The warmth and easy comfort of a good friendship turned into something more, a heightened awareness of each other that hadn't been there before. Sometimes he would catch her looking at him and she would drop her eyes.

Then Stewart won the governorship, and Barnstable & Ullman got the commission to build Stewart's state complex. George Barnstable threw himself into the project with all the fervor of a messiah. Ericka seemed unaffected by all the publicity, the furor pro and con.

Gavin expected her to be proud, excited, thrilled at having the biggest architectural assignment the state had ever undertaken. She showed none of these emotions.

Ericka saw Stewart's grandiose dream for what it was. At least in part. One more impossibly extravagant gift from Stewart in his determination to break down her barriers. She was concerned about George Barnstable's total commitment. Increasingly he seemed to see the state complex as the culmination of his career, something of everlasting beauty, the only kind of signature he wanted to leave.

When Gavin questioned her, she said, "Stewart thinks I'm part of the package he's hired. I'm not. It's George's project, not mine. Of course, I'll help as long as George needs me. But that's all. If it weren't so important to George, I'd turn it down. I've got work of my own I want to do."

It didn't reassure him. Gavin felt that Stewart was drawing them both much too far into something whose danger neither of them realized. Stewart needed the whip hand, and if the complex gave him power over them, he wouldn't hesitate to use it.

Ericka laughed at his warnings.

For Gavin it had ceased to be amusing. Stewart's constant attentions to her became unreasonably irritating. So much so that Gavin began to examine his own feelings. And found them confusing.

He was suddenly conscious of his age. The weight of the fifteen years between them seemed more like a lifetime. He speculated on what would happen if he made a move toward her and knew he never would. Because he couldn't bear it if she laughed.

In the loneliness of his nights he had unbidden pictures of Ericka in someone else's arms. Jean-Baptiste Moreau he knew about. But there were others, strangers, golden boys, handsome men—and finally, disturbingly, Stewart Gansvoort. He was filled with resentment that she could so occupy his thoughts, and increasingly he began to take it out on her.

It was the remembrance of that last fantasy that triggered things between them.

They were lunching after Gavin's visit to Leroy Biggs, and Ericka had just shown him an exquisite antique brooch that had come that morning with Stewart's daily offering of flowers. Her pleasure in it seemed to him as ingenuous as a child's and just as thoughtless. It irritated him almost beyond speech.

"Why the hell do you keep taking things from him? Why don't you just tie the can on the bastard? You keep taking things and you owe him. He knows that. I know it. And you ought to know it, too. Stewart collects on his debts. Or is that what you have in mind?"

"What's that supposed to mean?"

The sharpness of her tone matched his and took him by surprise.

"You seem to treat all men as if they owed *you* something. Can't you understand that with Stewart it's the other way around? You can't keep on accepting gifts from Stewart and..."

"Oh, yes, I can. Exactly as long as I choose to."

He had never seen her angry. Her face seemed composed, but there was a thin white line around her upper lip, and her jaw was rigidly clenched. The green of her eyes had turned murky, clouded with what she was feeling. Her indignation intimidated him, and he was on the point of apologizing for his temper. "No one can tell me what I can or can't do. Not even you, Gavin. If you think you can, you don't know me."

There was a cutting edge to what she said, and his anger flared again. "I know you a hell of a lot better than you think I do. I know about Paris, for instance."

He knew the instant he heard the words that he was wrong to say them. He had no smallest right to intrude on her past.

Her voice, when it came, was low and controlled. "What about Paris?"

He would have given anything to retrieve his words. But he had gone past the point of no return, trapped by his own foolish anger.

"A letter. From Ten Tabard. I read it again not long ago."

"You still have it? What did it say?"

There was an accusation in her eyes, as though *he* were somehow responsible for whatever had happened in Paris—in a way perhaps justified, for he had resurrected something better left buried. The thought sharpened his remorse. He couldn't force himself to tell her what Tabard had said. If there were to be accusations and suspicion, let it be in Ten Tabard's words, not his.

"Yes, I still have it. Perhaps you'd better read it for yourself."

484

*   *   *

They were silent on the ride to Gavin's apartment. She sat pressed against the passenger door, as far from him as she could get. Again, in the elevator, she chose a corner while he pressed the button for his floor. He was saddened by the conviction that his thoughtless anger had spoiled a relationship that had become very dear to him. It embarrassed him when he bent to remove the burnt paper match tucked between the lintel and the door, a cautious habit he had formed because of the sensitive information in his personal files and because it was important to know if he had uninvited visitors. Now it seemed childish, something out of cheap detective fiction.

Gavin's apartment was designed for utility and comfort. The walls were lined with bookcases, which held a sizeable law library and other books related to his trade. There were no-nonsense armchairs, a sofa in tan Naugahyde, small tables, ashtrays. There were only two pictures, one an oil of the French Riviera, the other a Vertes original of a girl stretched out on a sandy dune, something Serena had "borrowed" from the Gansvoort collection. Against the far wall were two low file cabinets flanking a wide desk that held three phones of different colors.

Built into the bookcases was a police-band radio that allowed Gavin to tune in on the ceasless chatter of police business throughout the city. From long habit he moved to switch it on, then changed direction and stooped before a file cabinet to find the thing she had come to see. He stayed crouched, holding Ten Tabard's letter, wondering if there were some way he could spare her and knowing there wasn't. He finally rose and faced her.

Ericka had dropped her coat and was sitting on the edge of the couch, head erect, back rigid, knees together. There was something so lonely, so indomitable, about her look, like a prisoner awaiting sentence, that he had the temptation to tear up the letter and take her in his arms. "You sure you want to do this?"

She took the letter from him and began to read. He sat beside her, feeling that someone should be close. It was a long letter. He watched as her eyes traveled page after page, seeing in his mind the words she was reading. Ten Tabard's view of her affair with Jean-Baptiste Moreau, who in Tabard's book was a Communist agitator, and so beyond the pale. Her pregnancy, the loss of her baby, the murder of Moreau, whom she must have loved. Top that with a brutal rape—if it was rape. The death of two men. Killed by Moreau? Before he himself was killed? And if not Moreau, then . . . ?

She put the letter in her lap, face expressionless. A ray of light caught her eyes, sent them far away across an ocean.

He didn't know what to say. He didn't know what he wanted her to say. And then, without volition, a lifetime of training took over. He asked the question he had asked before, times without number. The cop's question. "Did you do it?"

She turned toward him. Her face was still closed, a pale alabaster mask, her eyes remote and cool. She made a small gesture to the letter in her lap. "If you believe that, why do you ask?"

"Because, God help me, I need to know."

"Then you'll have to find the answer in yourself."

He looked closely at her, willing himself to find an answer. The pale oval of her face, thin bridge of a nose so delicately formed, only the cheekbones showing a faint blush of color. Darkly arched brows framing jade-green eyes full of grief. *Oh, God,* Gavin thought. *All the sad-eyed women. And why am I such a fool for them?*

Her eyes were fixed on his, so steadfast, calm, clearly incapable of deceit, watiting for his answer with the age-old compelling patience of women. What she was asking was an act of faith. To trust what was in his heart. His decision came with a sudden swift clarity that took him by surprise. "It doesn't matter," he said wonderingly. "It simply doesn't matter. Who the hell am I to sit in judgment? You know, I just don't give a damn."

She came to him as naturally as a child, presenting him with the gift of herself. She got out of her clothes with unstudied grace. First the sweater, which bared her breasts; then, breasts swinging free, the tweed skirt fell in a circle at her feet. She danced a step on one foot to get out of her panties, stepped away from the little mound of garments and raised her arms to him.

He picked her up and carried her into the bedroom.

She lay back on the pillows of his bed, one hand behind her head, legs flung apart, smiling at him as he undressed. So serene and gladly willing in the giving of herself. He kneeled beside her, one hand cupping the softness of her breast, the other gliding down her smooth stomach to find her wetness waiting for him. She arched herself to him and drew in her breath sharply as he found her. After a while he moved between her legs, propped on knees and elbows. Their hands met as both of them reached to guide him into her. It was she who led him, placed him at the entrance of her body and thrust up at him with a muted cry. She lifted her knees high to take in more of him, her hands pulling strongly on his buttocks. She came almost immediately with a long, sustained shudder. Then they began the give and take of love in slow knowing rhythm.

Gavin first was aware of the change in her breathing. He thought she was about to climax again and increased the power of his thrusting. Then her nails dug painfully deep into his back. Her body grew rigid and then convulsed in a scream so piercing it hurt his eardrums. She squirmed out from under him, her hands beating at his face, crouched on her knees on the far side of the bed, back pressed against the wall. Her face was a mask of outrage and terror. Her arm lifted, one quivering finger pointing at something behind him. Her voice, when it came, was a hoarse croak.

"It was you! You're the one who raped me!"

Bewildered, Gavin looked over his shoulder and saw George Barnstable's portrait of him.

Her eyes held the blank madness he had seen once before, unseeing, or seeing something no one else could see. A low animal sound began to come from deep inside her. It had all happened before, and Birdie had nearly killed him.

On hands and knees, she tried to scuttle past him and he grabbed her. She struggled wildly, mindlessly. He couldn't hold her, so he did instinctively the only thing he could think of. He clipped her sharply on the jaw. Her body went limp. Gavin cradled her in his arms, rocking her gently.

What had the portrait done to her?

She began to stir and after a moment opened her eyes. He saw with relief that her eyes were again alive, no longer empty, squinted now with faint puzzlement, staring wonderingly on his.

"It couldn't have been you...." Her voice was childlike, reminding him of the first time he had heard her speak. "You were with George. You were so kind. . . ."

"No. It wasn't me. . . ." He wasn't sure how he should handle the situation. "Ericka . . . what do you remember?"

Memory clouded her eyes. "The bearded man . . . and being chained. He hurt me, Gavin. . . ."

She lifted a tentative hand to her jaw and winced when she touched it.

"Just a lump. It'll be gone tomorrow."

Ericka moved restlessly and sat up beside him. She seemed completely recovered and asked in her normal voice, "What happened to me?"

"I had to . . ." For a moment he thought she was talking about the blow to her jaw.

She shook her head. "No. Back there. George told me I was raped . . . and I've blocked it all out. I've had dreams. All my life. And then just now, when I knew who you were . . . it started to come back. Just pieces of it. Was it so terrible, Gavin? Was it, Gavin? Don't you see that I want to know? It's time I knew. It can't hurt me now."

So he told her. Because it seemed to him he had no choice.

Dust motes danced in a shaft of afternoon sunlight that came through the bedroom window and touched her hair. They were talking of someone else. A child who seemed never to have existed in real life. A case history from one of his textbooks. Yet he knew by the strength of her grip on his hand that it was real enough to her. That and the rise and fall of her breasts, the rigidity of her nipples.

She was getting something out of it. He didn't know just what, but a subtle undercurrent of excitement began to come from her to him, a heat that was almost physical. His unbidden erection seemed a violation of its own.

She released his hand and kneeled in front of him, sitting back on her haunches, looking up at him, the sunlight full on her face.

"I want you to do it to me, Gavin. Everything *he* did. All of it. I want to know."

He listened to the words, but they had no meaning for him.

"Don't you see?" she whispered. "It's a sort of exorcism. I want to know what it was like. To get rid of nightmares once and for all. . . . Please, Gavin." Her voice held something close to entreaty. "If it's done with love—then it will be all right."

Later, during the catalog of coupling that followed, there came a point when Ericka screamed. "You're hurting me. I can't stand it!" But she wouldn't release him. She screamed again. But now he had crossed the threshold into lust and no longer cared. Her hips gyrated wildly; her screams became soft and panting. Then came a low-pitched monolog of lewdities, mindless exhortations, urging him on.

When it was over, conscious of his weight, he withdrew and rolled on his side. She turned her head, eyes clouded. And smiled at him.

"There's never been anything like that. For me. Something new happened. I don't know what it was. Except that it was you. Everything is all right now. I won't be afraid again. Not ever."

"I love you," Gavin heard himself say, wondering at the words. He hadn't meant to say them.

She looked away from him to some distant place of her own. "I don't know what love is, Gavin."

It was at that moment that Des Daniher's phone call came.

As police commissioner, Gavin Riordan rated a place on the platform with the notables. He had refused to wear morning clothes, as had George Barnstable. The rest of the governor's party was replete with swallowtail coats and shiny silk hats, including Desmond Daniher.

Stewart Gansvoort, before the speakers' rostrum, had removed his topper to address the crowd. He stood, his hand raised for quiet, tall, handsome, distinguished, his hair ruffled by the light summer breeze. "Now, isn't he the kiss-me-ass, with the striped pants, the carnation and all," Daniher murmured.

Barnstable, standing next to Gavin, chuckled. "Ah, the glory that was Greece. The grandeur that was Rome."

As if reading his mind, Stewart boomed out of the microphones: "As Augustus Caesar said, 'I found Rome a city of bricks. I will leave it a city of marble.' Not quite that, but what we do want is a capitol city that people can visit and be proud of. The most electrifying capitol in the world, brilliant, beautiful and efficient. And that's what we'll get. Look at it. Isn't it grand?''

Stewart waved his hands at the long table in front of the platform, which gave the public its first view of what Stewart had in mind, a huge model of what the Mall would look like when it was completed.

There it stood in all its pristine whiteness, the spire of the Bell Tower rising to the sky like a prophetic finger, the long stretch of the administration building faced by the four tall agency buildings, the state museum and library and the oyster-shaped meeting hall, in its center the placid length of two huge reflecting pools, which would someday mirror some of the world's greatest sculpture.

The sheer scope of the complex was breathtaking.

The wreckers had taken the whole of the Pit down to street level. Looking out over 103.5 acres of dirt and rubble, Gavin found it hard to connect the empty barren space with what would eventually stand there, just as he found it difficult to remember with any real clarity the Pit as it had been a few short months before. He thought the model was one of the most beautiful and impressive things he had ever seen, but translating it to the finished product seemed to him an impossible task.

"Jesus, George, it's absolutely magnificent! Never anything like it. I'm flabbergasted.''

Barnstable smiled at him. "It is, isn't it. Best thing I've ever done. Maybe the *only* thing I was ever completely proud of.''

Gavin turned away in embarrassment, for there were sudden tears in Barnstable's eyes. Gavin had the uneasy feeling that his friend was giving too much of himself to something that might turn out to be an impossibility. He didn't want to see George Barnstable hurt.

They listened in silence as Governor Gansvoort completed his speech, watched Stewart being escorted to the lone bulldozer that stood before the platform. Stewart mounted the cab. There was a sudden staccato roar of the motor; the shining blade rose and then dipped to bite into the loose soil, the first scoop, at least symbolically, in the excavation for the Mall.

It had taken Gavin Riordan no more than a month in his new job to confirm his opinion that the eight-thousand-man force he commanded was rotting slowly from the top down. The reforms of the Belding commission had cut neither widely nor deeply enough, and, in the thirteen years since, all the old abuses were back again. As head of Internal Affairs, he had had the knowledge but not the power to correct them.

Now he did.

Because he wanted to know exactly where he stood, he put his new authority to the test immediately by demanding the resignation of Police Chief P. J. Hairns. Hairns, who had a house in Florida and a stock portfolio that topped one million dollars and a numbered account in Switzerland just under that figure, took one look at the file Riordan had compiled on him over the years and put in his papers. Riordan sat back to await the repercussions.

Nothing happened, so Gavin knew that the word was out; he was safe in his job, at least for the time being. So he moved with all deliberate haste to replace the men who had grown fat under Chief Hairns, persuaded others to accept early retirement, shifted men from one precinct to another.

The shakeup was quiet but effective. As younger men moved into key jobs there was a stir of excitement throughout the force. For the first time in years there was competition, a chance to get ahead through ability and hard work rather than favoritism. The men began to see that the new commissioner was relentless in weeding out the rascals and at the same time quick to recognize good work. Riordan soon found he had the reputation of being fair, honest and, above all, tough.

Riordan nurtured that reputation because it helped enormously to free him from the pressures of city hall, the governor's office, district attorneys and all the endless special-interest groups of the City. It soon became clear to all that there was to be no "business as usual" in the commissioner's office.

That made him even more of a loner than before. The only man in the force he could consider a friend was his driver, Sergeant Marvin Barry, whom he had known since his days in the Third Precinct. But even Riordan couldn't completely bridge the gap between Barry's blackness and his own Irish whiteness.

Riordan found the semiofficial social duties of the commissioner both onerous and unavoidable. All policemen are confirmed joiners, so there were the balls and dinners of the PBA, the Erin Society, the various veterans' organizations, the Detectives Association, communion breakfasts, Hanukkah festivals, the Pulaski Club and a dozen others, each of which required his presence. Add to that the obligatory speaking engagements before women's clubs, League of Women Voters, Kiwanis, all kinds and shapes of civic organizations, and it left him little time to himself.

And little time for Ericka Ullman.

Their relationship was a strange one, brief meetings over lunch, rarely dinner, even less often a stolen evening of lovemaking, which left them both unsatisfied. He wanted more. Much more. He tried to tell himself that there was no room in his life for the complexities she brought to him. She was little more than half his age. He was saddled with a wife who was incurably ill. The difficulties involved in solving *that* problem were appalling. Yet he desperately wanted marriage with Ericka; his need for her was constant and unceasing.

Ericka, too, was deeply involved in her work. It took precedence over everything else. Gavin felt that she loved him, but her ability to love was surrounded by a tortured complex of emotions, and pushing her might blow it all apart. So he waited, letting her make her own pace.

Inevitably, because they both wanted to avoid commitment, the Mall became their main point of contact. It sometimes seemed to Gavin that it was the only thing that kept them together. The Mall increasingly became as much a part of his life as it was of hers, because from day one the Mall was a police problem. Small things at first, but over the years the whole of the City was to be threatened by the Mall's corruption.

The first incident that was officially recorded in police files was the theft of an excavation foreman's car. Riordan had formed the habit of "night riding," calling unexpectedly on precincts, talking to desk sergeants, signing the blotter with time and date to record his visits. It was at the new station house of the Third Precinct that he noticed the entry and the subsequent disposition of the complaint: Referred Auto Theft: Ptl. A. Guthrie.

492

Looking back, he remembered it well, because that was the day Serena surprised him at lunch with Ericka.

Serena had returned the week before from wherever she had been. Gavin's secretary had logged two calls from her during that week, and Gavin had returned neither of them. He knew he'd have to, but he wasn't ready for Serena just yet. He and Ericka were at a rather obscure waterfront restaurant, not because they had anything to hide, but because they both enjoyed the view of the river. It wasn't a place Serena would ordinarily have frequented. And certainly not alone. He watched her walk through the crowded restaurant, moving her long legs with that special assurance, the easy grace, the trim body still beautiful.

The two women exchanged the conventional peck on the cheek and Serena straightened. There was no avoiding an invitation to join them, because Serena obviously wasn't going anywhere.

When she had ordered a drink she turned to Ericka. "How's the great lover? I haven't seen him since I got back, but Olivia says he's rarely home, now that he's governor."

"Much as usual, I suppose." Ericka was noncommittal, but Gavin knew she was seeing more of Stewart than she was of him. Stewart's interest in the Mall made him impossible to avoid.

"Oh. I thought you'd know, from what I read in the columns."

Ericka got coolly to her feet. "Forgive me. I won't be long."

Gavin watched her go toward the ladies' room.

"I do hope I haven't offended her," Serena said sweetly.

"The hell you do. Jesus, Serena. It's not her fault Stewart's got ants in his pants."

"If it were only ants. From what I hear, she's not doing a hell of a lot to discourage him."

Gavin was exasperated. He had no answer to that. It was too close to what he felt himself.

"You've changed, Gavin." It wasn't a question, but her voice had a hint of speculation.

"Have I? How?"

"Hard to describe. You're tuned into *her* somehow. Larger than life. Of course, you two together *are* larger than life. In a way. Two beautiful people. Tell me, Gavin. Are you in love with her?"

There was no point in dissembling. He'd have had to tell Serena sooner or later. He owed her that. "Yes," he said slowly. "I think I am."

"Really in love? Or just . . . ?"

"No. Really in love."

Serena got up and leaned to put a hand gently on his cheek. "You poor bastard," she said. Her hand caressed him once, and then she was gone.

Barnstable & Ullman had set up shop in a three-story building on a low bluff over the river, just north of the Upper Bridge. Gavin delivered Ericka there after lunch and accepted her invitation to come in.

He wasn't prepared for what he saw. The ground floor was one huge open space filled with drafting tables covered with plans and blueprints. The river wall was entirely of glass, but most of the illumination came from banks of fluorescent tubes suspended from the ceiling. To the left the wall was windowless, forming a background for the enormous scale model of the Mall. There were at least a hundred people moving about in a sort of organized chaos.

"My God," Gavin exclaimed. "All yours?"

"Oh, no. The job's much too big for one firm. There are three other architectural outfits involved. We're in charge overall, but there's no way we could handle it alone."

A small, compact man wearing thick-lensed glasses laid an urgent hand on Ericka's arm. "Problem. Can you spare a minute? Sorry to interrupt."

Ericka looked at Gavin apologetically. "George's office is on the top floor. End of the corridor. Why don't you take the elevator up, and I'll meet you there in a few minutes?"

She was gone before he could say that he really hadn't the time. He did as he was told. On the third floor he walked down a hallway lined with glass-walled offices, each one housing the inevitable mark of the architectural trade, a drafting table, along with more conventional furniture. All the offices were occupied. No one looked up as he passed. At the end of the corridor was a heavy door of rough wood partially ajar. Gavin pushed through it and found himself in a large room, part office, part studio. River sounds came faintly from open windows. George Barnstable's desk was a simple white Formica shelf extending the length of one wall; beneath it other shelves held rolled up plans and drawings. Barnstable swiveled as he heard Gavin come in.

"Very impressive, George," said Gavin. "How many people do you have working here?"

"Gavin." Barnstable got up to shake hands. "Good to see you. People? Damned if I know. Ericka could tell you, I expect. What brings you here?"

"Ericka. We had lunch. Somebody grabbed her downstairs. She said she'd join us, but from what I could see of your menagerie, I doubt it. I've only got a minute. Just came up to say hello."

Gavin looked at the sketches, computer printouts, handwritten notes, a soggy half-empty coffee container and the remains of a sandwich that cluttered Barnstable's desk, and shook his head. "What a way to run a railroad. Much less to build a building. Seriously, where do you start?"

There was an amused twinkle in Barnstable's eyes.

"Well, first . . . you dig a hole."

"No, I mean it. I've got a feeling that I'm going to be spending a lot of time and effort on your Mall. I want to know what kind of impact it's going to have on the City. What's involved in building something this big? New people, new money, new business, whatever. I don't want to be caught short by something I don't really understand. How *do* you go about building the damned thing?"

Barnstable was immediately thoughtful. "I hadn't thought of it quite like that. Architects are more concerned with the site, the materials, space and form, the light itself—which really determines the style of a building. And, of course, the people who will use it. We tend to lose sight of the men of the building trades, the ant army that puts the whole thing together. We are really only choreographers.

"But I suppose you're right. From your point of view. If you really want to know what's involved, you should get in touch with the general contractor, the Moore-Liggett Company. See a man named Archie Ogden. He's their clerk of the works, responsible for everything that goes on. He'll tell you what you want to know a lot better than I can."

Gavin looked at his watch, conscious of the hundred and one details that waited for him at Headquarters. Ericka's "few minutes" had long since gone.

"George, I wish I could spend more time, but I've got to go. Say good-bye for me, will you, in case I miss her on the way out."

Barnstable held his hand longer than necessary. He seemed about to say something, then decided not to.

"Sure. We don't see enough of you, Gavin. . . ."

There seemed to be a sort of appeal in Barnstable's eyes, and Gavin hesitated. But George merely gave him a vague sort of wave and turned back to his desk. On the return trip down the corridor Gavin wondered briefly what was on Barnstable's mind and hoped it didn't concern his relationship with Ericka. He couldn't get over his feeling of guilt about George Barnstable.

In the huge workroom he looked for Ericka for a moment, but she was nowhere to be seen.

29

Time: 1973–1977
STEWART GANSVOORT

From the tall windows of the governor's suite Stewart could watch the progress of the Mall week by week. He saw the excavation take shape, and then the steady influx of more and more workers, until the site resembled some giant teeming ant complex. If he opened a window he could listen to the steady thudding of the massive pile drivers, catch the blue flare of welders' torches, the flash of sunlight on bright plastic hardhats, hear the shouted commands and instructions to the stream of truck traffic that arrived and departed as though on some endless conveyor belt. Any halt in the ceaseless activity was sure to bring a phone call from the governor's secretary demanding to know the cause.

The hours spent in George Barnstable's Manhattan offices, watching Barnstable's flying pencil create the original concept of the state office complex, had done a curious thing to Stewart Gansvoort. It had made him a compulsive builder of things great and small, from public tennis courts and children's playgrounds to immense power dams, schools, hospitals and thousands of miles of state highways. It filled him with a sense of power above and beyond that of great wealth. He wanted to change the face of the land. He saw himself as a creator.

During his years as governor, Stewart Gansvoort was to build more things than any individual in the history of the state. His only rival was perhaps Robert Moses, the master builder of New York. Stewart built big, grand, visible things—monuments, schools, parks, education complexes, museums and, finally, the Mall. His pyramid of bricks and mortar included 3 model towns, 29 mental-health facilities, 60 parks, 84 hospitals, 32 waste-disposal plants, a university system with facilities for almost a quarter of a million students on 67 campuses, more than 800 miles of multiple-lane highways and 120,000 units of new housing.

Unfortunately this last involved taking land away from the poor and giving it to the rich. Or at least to the middle classes. It was the beginning of the breakdown of the City's morale and the underlying cause of the trouble that was to come.

Charlie Bishop encouraged Stewart in all this because construction meant jobs, not only in the building trades but in all the surrounding areas needed to support such a massive program, office workers, teachers, doctors and nurses, manufacturers and middlemen.

To Charlie Bishop, jobs meant only one thing. Votes and more votes.

Charlie's legal advisors introduced Charlie and Stewart to the staggering power hidden behind the innocuous name *public authorities*. Public authorities, such as the Tunnel and Bridge Commission, the Parks Commission, the Transportation and Transit Commission, the State Power Authority, the Highway Commission, were supposedly above and outside of politics, since their funds were to be used solely in the interests of the public welfare. Mark Epstein pointed out that, since the projects of all public authorities were financed through the sale of revenue bonds to private investors, it could safely be contended by the governor that the cost to the taxpayers was nothing at all. At least, that was one way of looking at it.

There was an added advantage. The records of public government agencies are open to examination and subject to legislative scrutiny. Not so with public authorities. Under state law the records of public authorities were to be regarded just as any private corporation would be. Their records were immune to the prying eyes of the public and the press.

For Charlie Bishop it was a license to steal. For Governor Stewart Gansvoort it was merely an affirmation of his godlike power to create.

Until his father's death Stewart had had no real idea of the true extent of the Gansvoort wealth. He was to find that the Gansvoort international empire was one of the richest on earth, estimated in billions of dollars. More important to Stewart Gansvoort was the fact that there was not a bank in the state with which Gansvoort interests didn't have a link, either hidden or direct. Gansvoort controlled all the state's public utilities; its real-estate holdings rivaled those of the Catholic Church itself; Gansvoort oil companies kept the driving public on the highways and supplied the fuel for factories and families alike. As governor, Stewart had the use of not only his own vast resources but also the millions generated by the public authorities and matching federal funds.

Charlie Bishop set out to turn these endless dollars into an unbeatable political asset. He began by wooing the business power structure with legal fees, insurance commissions, real-estate plums, public-relations retainers, advertising fees. Charlie parceled out his largesse as Desmond Daniher had passed out turkeys and baskets of coal at Christmastime. Next, Charlie went after city and state political leaders with fees, commissions, retainers and profitable favors. In very short order he formed an alliance of strange bedfellows, banks, unions, Wall Street underwriters, insurance companies, real-estate impresarios, because they all had something to gain from state spending.

As Des Daniher was to say later to a member of the press, "They gave everybody involved exactly what they wanted. Everybody had a stake in keeping Stewart governor. No one in the political system could stand up against Stewart's pressure, because the pressure came from the system itself. The son of a bitch bought one political party outright—and took a long-term lease on the other one. He would have been governor for the rest of his life if . . ."

Charlie Bishop successfully kept himself out of the limelight, except for those in the know. Charlie took considerable satisfaction from the reputation he had acquired as a man who never forgot a friend—nor forgave an enemy. Charlie's backstage maneuvering resulted in the creation of a reputation-once-removed for Stewart as well, that of a ruthless man who got exactly what he wanted exactly when he wanted it. As one politician put it, "Put your bets on money. Not just any money. Old money. New money buys things; old money calls in all the due bills."

It was Charlie, rather than Stewart, who held all the notes. But hardly anyone knew that.

During Stewart Gansvoort's first term as governor, Charlie Bishop kept him carefully away from national issues. In the years when the nation shook with Cambodia, Kent State, Palestinian hijacks, attacks on police by black terrorists, Watergate and the Arab oil embargo, Charlie Bishop carefully steered Stewart down the middle of the road. The governor deplored (when it was safe), praised (when everyone else did), condemned (only when it was politically comfortable) and otherwise rode the fence. The electorate as a whole demanded no more in a state booming with prosperity—and no end in sight.

True, there were rumblings, faint at first, because in order to accommodate the endless building projects, something had to give. Space had to be found. Things had to come down before other, newer things could go up. Stewart's highway program alone dispossessed 150,000 people. His urban renewal, public housing, parks and playgrounds evicted another 50,000 or more. The problem was that too many of these people were black or Puerto Rican and poor. Especially in the City itself, there was no place for them to go except into already overcrowded areas—slums, which rapidly became ghettos. And the pot began to boil.

In the summer of Stewart Gansvoort's fourth year in office, the City had the nearest thing to a riot it had seen in 110 years. The better part of three slum blocks were destroyed by fire by angry blacks. The looting and burning went on for one whole night. Sixteen people were arrested. Luckily there were no fatalities. It was only Commissioner Gavin Riordan's training in riot control that put the lid back on.

Riordan reported personally to the governor that there was a desperate need for more jobs, housing, health care, schools and a thousand other things among the City's minorities. And that what had just happened would surely happen again if something wasn't done about it.

The governor seemed genuinely puzzled. "Why would they burn down their own buildings? I don't understand it."

Riordan was momentarily stopped by his inability to describe the situation to a man who had never seen, heard or tasted poverty.

"A lot of 'em would rather sleep in the streets than live the way they have to live. Can't say I blame them, either. Maybe you ought to take a look. In person."

"Of course," Stewart Gansvoort said. "I will. I had no idea."

Police Commissioner Gavin Riordan instituted a basic course in riot and crowd control for all active police under his command. He persuaded Desmond Daniher to persuade Charlie Bishop to make available enough state and City funds to train and equip a 300-man elite battalion devoted to coping with civil unrest.

"I think it's a waste of money," Daniher had advised. "Because, Gavin me boy, if you ever have to use it, it'll be far and away too late."

"Then you better get 'em the jobs and the housing they need," Gavin said angrily.

"Easy to say," was Daniher's rejoinder. "But blacks don't vote. A fact of life. And a thing to remember."

*　　*　　*

Early in the game Riordan had had a talk with Patsy Pavane. It had not gone well. At Gavin's insistence the meeting had taken place in the offices of the commissioner. Gavin needed the official surroundings to lend weight to what he had to say to a man he had known all his life.

Pavane's handshake was firm, his demeanor unruffled, as he looked around Riordan's inner sanctum, waiting for what was to come. Riordan let him look, hoping that what he saw would impress him.

Police Headquarters dated from 1895, and Riordan's present office was a small museum. The walls held old photographs and prints, mute witnesses to generations of law enforcement. With the pictures were other memorabilia, old billies, nightsticks, helmets, a 1903 map of the City showing the perimeters of each of its precincts, sets of ancient brass handcuffs and a framed citation for bravery above and beyond the call of duty for Patrolman Gavin Riordan, Third Precinct.

"You know why you're here, Patsy." Pavane met his eyes with a gentle smile, his eyebrows lifted in a barely perceived question, and Riordan knew that he wasn't going to get any help.

"I've got a problem with the Mall. Two problems, really. The workers are stealing everything that isn't nailed down, from trucks to steel H-beams. They're robbing the state blind, and there isn't a hell of a lot I can do about it. The O'Hare Detective Agency is responsible for security on the site, and I have no real jurisdiction unless I'm called in. But that's another story."

Pavane's face showed no more than a polite interest.

"It's the other problem that concerns me," Riordan went on. "There will be a hell of a lot of men working on that Mall off and on. The boys are beginning to move in on all that easy money. Numbers, narcotics, whores, floating crap games—you name it, it's all there. It's lousing up my town, and I want it stopped."

He waited for Pavane's reaction and got another smile.

"Aren't you asking a lot of your fellow man, Gavin?" Pavane asked reasonably. "People are going to screw. And they're going to gamble. And a lot of other things. Nothing you can do to stop them. It's the nature of the beast. Neither you nor I can change that."

"I can try," Riordan said. "I've formed a special squad for the Mall. Sort of a conglomerate. There'll be guys in it from Vice, Loft and Burglary, Narcotics, Auto Theft—the works. Any familiar face they see within a mile of the site is going to be rousted like they were never rousted before. It will get to be very discouraging."

Pavane considered this briefly and then shrugged his acceptance. "You'll do what you have to do, Gavin." He got up and smoothed the wrinkles of his expensive jacket. "Is that all?"

For a moment Riordan wished for the old days, when he could have taken this assured hoodlum into the back room of the station house and knocked off some of the polish. There was a lot to be said for the old times.

Gavin knew he would have to give Pavane's boys a certain leeway. Within reason. To avoid something worse. Pavane wanted things quiet so that his rackets could function without trouble. He would do his best to keep it that way. One more delicate accommodation between cops and crooks. *Well, better the devil you know* . . . It seemed to Riordan that his job was becoming one compromise after another in things both great and small. And that compromise became easier as time went on.

He sighed again. "Yes. That's about it."

"Then I'll be going," Pavane said pleasantly. "Nice seeing you, Gavin."

Neither of them offered to shake hands.

So much for Patsy Pavane. That meeting had been almost two years ago. Nothing had changed. Despite Riordan's tough policy, the bars near the Mall were still crawling with whores, policy and gambling flourished, you could buy narcotics on the street, the loan sharks were doing land-office business, the stealing and pilferage on the job had reached almost laughable proportions, an accepted way of life.

"Look at Jimmy Carter," Charlie Bishop said. "What is the guy actually saying? He's against Big Government, is all. What's that supposed to mean? He's gonna restore the people's confidence in their government? Fat fuckin' chance, after Watergate and Nixon's pardon. But he's gonna win in November. You can bet on it. Fuck issues. Who wants to hear about issues? He's gonna win it on *style*, is what. They're gonna vote for what they *think* they see on the boob tube. An' you better believe it. Because that's what *we're* gonna do for the last few weeks. We hit maybe a few more soft spots in person, and then it's straight TV with all the film we've already made. And the thirty-second spots.''

"Best news I've heard." Stewart sighed in relief. "If I see another chicken dinner, I'll crow like a rooster. And cheese blintzes. There's something about a cheese blintz that can make a strong man cry. How do you see it going, Charlie? Any real problems?''

"There's always problems," Bishop said morosely. "*No* election is ever a sure thing.''

The two men were in the governor's office, Charlie Bishop on the long red leather couch below the Gilbert Stuart portrait of George Washington, Stewart standing at the windows, looking out over the Mall site, as he did so often.

The campaign was nearing the end, close to that magic day in November when the electorate would go to the polls, secure in the belief that it actually mattered which lever they pulled, that they were voting for someone, from whichever party, who was devoted to their best interests, someone who would listen to their voices, right their wrongs.

Charlie Bishop knew better.

Charlie Bishop left nothing to chance. He had staffed the campaign with experts to prepare studies on every problem that could possibly come up. He had position papers on everything from the gypsy moth menace to matching federal funds. For the past months he had had his candidate on an endless merry-to-round from one end of the state to the other. Stewart had used his considerable charm on farmers in their fields, factory workers on lunch break, office clerks at street corners. He had traveled 9,000 miles and visited every county in the state at least once. He had raged against bossism, endorsed more money for mass transit, state aid to schools, mental institutions, summer jobs for young people. In a state whose rural areas were full of hunters, he had come out strongly against gun control. Because of an astronomical rise in the crime rate in the cities, he had urged the restoration of the death penalty.

"You can't tag 'em with labels anymore," Charlie Bishop seemed personally aggrieved. "Hardhats and students used to be on the same side. Not anymore. Since the war. Blacks and blue-collar ethnics voted together back in Johnson's time. Now they hate each other. How you gonna predict busing, amnesty for vets, women's lib, an' the gay fuckin' liberation nuts. Everybody's got long hair. Can't hardly tell the boys from the girls without you do a chest X ray. How you gonna figure these cats are gonna vote? There is just no fuckin' way. I tell you, the independent voter is fuckin' up the whole fuckin' country."

Stewart, looking out at the Mall, was only half listening. He had heard Charlie inveigh against the independent voter before. To Charlie the breed was a hobgoblin menace, if only because he couldn't get a handle on it. There was nobody in charge, nobody to sweet-talk, bribe, blackmail or bludgeon into delivering votes. The independent voter was a source of deep frustration to Charlie Bishop.

There were other things on Stewart's mind. He had his own frustrations. The Mall was only one of them. From where he stood he could see the beginnings of what would be the sharp clean marble lines of the Bell Tower, now only bare steel up to its seventh story. Opposite, the agency buildings hadn't progressed beyond two levels, the museum and the library were still holes in the ground. Where the reflecting pools would be was now a jumble of monster cranes, bulldozers, backhoes, generators, huge cement mixers, stacks of lumber, steel reinforcing rods, all 103 acres of the site overrun with hopelessly confused worker ants.

The slowness of the project was agonizing to him because it all led back to Ericka Ullman. With a patience of which he wouldn't have believed himself capable, Stewart still kept up his relentless pursuit of the woman he was determined to have. He had believed for a long time that his gift of the Mall to her—for that's what it really was—would do the trick. But she accepted that with the same cool gratitude with which she received all his other gifts. She never turned him down, even when some of his presents were ridiculously extravagant. It was what confirmed his certainty that she would

eventually give in. Nothing in his life had led him to think differently, because nothing in his life had proved to be unattainable.

It was the Mall she used now as an unspoken excuse for refusing
most of his invitations. She had no time for anything but her work.
So he wanted the Mall finished. As soon as humanly possible.

"You know," Stewart said slowly, "that thing is a monstrosity.
An eyesore."

"What thing?" Charlie Bishop came to stand beside him at the
window.

"That." Stewart pointed. "The church."

They both looked out over the quarter-mile rectangle that was to
be the Mall. The symmetry of the area was broken at one corner by
the two tall spires and Gothic facade of St. Thomas Cathedral,
which dated from 1848. The church was of local red sandstone and
an excellent example of the architecture of its time.

"I know we told the cardinal we'd leave it, but I didn't realize
how silly it would look. It's outmoded. It doesn't belong there. It
spoils the whole concept. There should be open space, landscaping,
beautiful gardens. Charlie, that thing has got to go. I want you to
take care of it. Tell him we'll help him build somewhere else."

Bishop was aghast.

"Jesus! You realize how many Catholics in this town? Hundreds
of thousands, is what. You can't be serious, Stewart. Those people
vote like they're told, if the cardinal says so. You'd be tossing away
every one of those fucking votes. For what? A lousy flower bed?
You already knocked down the Catholic high school, the rectory, the
Convent of St. Cecilia. You fuck around with the cathedral and they
hand you your hat."

Stewart laughed, and the laugh had a bad sound. "Catholics scare
you, Charlie? You think they'll scream if I take the cathedral purely
for aesthetics? Well, you better figure out how to sell them on what
I'm planning right after election. I'm going to divorce my wife,
Charlie. What does that do to your plans?"

Charlie Bishop drew a deep breath and said pleadingly, "You got
to be kidding, Stewart. . . ."

"Don't look so stricken, Charlie." Stewart smiled. "Your political expertise is running away with you. You're stuck with political

stereotypes going back to Al Smith's derby. Things are different now. What's divorce? People no longer think of divorce as . . ."

Charlie exploded. "What the fuck you know about what people think? *I* tell you what people think. Stewart, you are a goddamned freak. Your head is somewhere else. You are off in some cloudland the rest of us can't get into. There's a screw missing somewhere, because you don't have a clue as to what's really out there. Your only frame of reference is Stewart fucking Gansvoort, and that is a piss-poor thing to make book on. The odds would kill you."

Stewart was seeing a Charlie Bishop he had never seen before, and it bewildered him. It was as if some familiar object had suddenly come alive and turned on him. He could see the naked rage in Charlie's eyes, mixed with something close to contempt. For an instant Stewart was once again a boy, remembering, lonely as only the very rich can be, desperately yearning for a friend, any friend.

The moment slipped past, and he wanted to say something like "You can't talk that way to me. . . ." But Charlie already *had* talked that way, and there was no going back. Stewart felt the hurt of it deep inside him in that small place that was still vulnerable to what people thought.

Charlie must have seen something in Stewart's face. It brought him up short. His anger faded, and something like pity took its place. "You poor bastard," Charlie said softly. "You'll never know what it is to be like the rest of us. It's not your fault, I guess. No way you could help it. But you're missing one hell of a lot, and it's a fucking shame. Because you could be quite a guy . . . if you only knew how."

Charlie put his hand on Stewart's arm as gently as a feather, but Stewart felt the warmth of it and was obscurely grateful.

"I'm sorry, Stewart. I didn't mean to hurt you. Maybe we both better give the whole thing some thought. Call me at Calley's Bar if you change your mind. I'll be the drunk in the last booth on the left. The one that's cryin' in his Budweiser."

What Stewart hadn't gotten the chance to tell Charlie Bishop was that it was too late for any mind changing. Stewart had already made his deal with his wife. Olivia had agreed to go to Mexico for a quiet uncontested divorce. Just after the coming election. Olivia hadn't had much choice.

Olivia Minot entered the marriage with Stewart Gansvoort determined to make him the best of all possible wives. She set out to turn herself into a political asset. She was bright, charming, and there was a glow about her, a mixture of superb health and good intentions that Stewart's mixed bag of political friends found irresistible. She never revealed how the vulgarities of the politicians she entertained appalled her—the forced pleasantries of reception lines and official dinners. She joined women's clubs; she spoke before ethnic societies; she was on the boards of the Cancer Foundation, Children's Relief and the Bidwell Orphanage. She became a fund raiser of notable ability. In point of fact, she was so good at what she was determined to be that, inevitably, Stewart heard someone say, "She's marvelous. She'd make a better candidate than *he* would. . . ."

So after Stewart's second campaign for the assembly, Olivia was quietly asked by Charlie Bishop to cool it, keep a somewhat lower profile. Which she did, with considerable relief, never questioning Stewart's motives in asking.

For Olivia Minot Gansvoort was madly, hopelessly, mindlessly in love with her husband. Sex had burst on her like a fireworks display. She found she was gifted with the ability to have multiple orgasms, and that it needed little more than the touch of Stewart's lips on her nipples to bring her to climax.

Stewart at first was both flattered and delighted. It amused him to come up behind her as she sat in her negligee at her dressing table, reach over her shoulders, fondle her breasts briefly and watch in the mirror as her eyes grew cloudy and she panted to her summit.

For the first months he kept her in an embarrassing sea of breathless wetness. Always the bedroom innovator, Stewart taught her all the endless variations of sex. Olivia learned joyfully and well. Pleasure seemed infinite. Everything Stewart asked of her seemed right and good, because it was Stewart. It never occurred to her that it could be sex itself that sounded the siren call.

Until Stewart got bored.

It was all too easy. Stewart missed the chase, the excitement of unexplored vaginas, virgin territory. Or if not virgin, at least new and different. He showed it by moving to the adjoining bedroom and granting her his favors only when he felt like it.

It took Olivia weeks of sleepless nights, tossing and turning, with a heat between her legs that couldn't be assuaged even by Stewart's too infrequent visits, before she realized the honeymoon was over. Just as her older friends had warned her (and she had never believed), the first sweet blush of love was gone. Marriage had become merely an accommodation. Polite talk over the breakfast table—the dinner table as well while August Gansvoort was still alive. The old man insisted on at least the appearance of a family.

And family was another thing. Despite all her hopes, at the end of the first year Olivia hadn't become pregnant. Her doctor spoke of certain imbalances in the way her body functioned and suggested a regimen of temperature taking, regular sex in certain positions, warm baths, hormones and the like. All of which required the willing cooperation of a spouse. Which Olivia didn't have.

It was five years before Olivia took a lover. Five years of Stewart's intermittent forays into her bedroom, when he used her like a two-dollar whore. Although Stewart could still turn her on at a touch and bring on her orgasms as long as he was willing to stay, the demands of her body weren't proof against Stewart's absences. So, ever so discreetly, she accepted the attentions of a young man named Jason March Everett, who owned a stud farm twenty miles north of Riverhaven. She tried, with only moderate success, to teach him the things Stewart had taught her about sex and its myriad gratifications. Everett was the first of a number of lovers over the years, some satisfactory, some not, but all of them better than lonely longing.

The seeds of Olivia's destruction were sown innocently enough. In an exercise class at a health spa she attended along with other fashionable matrons was a masseuse named Irene, a tall, willowy, silent girl whose fingers could be both steel and velvet. Irene could turn corded muscles and aching backs into bliss.

At dinner one evening Stewart complimented Olivia on how glowing she looked, and Olivia described Irene's expertise.

"I could use some of that myself." Stewart had just returned from a six-stop upstate trip in his executive jet. "Short hops do me in. What did you say her name was?"

"Irene," Olivia said.

"Why don't you get her up here sometime? Take the kinks out of my back. Next trip, maybe. I suppose she'll make house calls?"

"I'll ask."

Some days later, again at dinner, Stewart finished the last of his coffee, patted his lips with his napkin and said, "By the way, I called the health spa. Your friend Irene does make house calls. She's coming in later to give us both a workout. About nine. Okay with you?"

Since Stewart hadn't made any more plane trips, something should have warned her. It didn't. Irene arrived on the dot, complete with portable massage table and a carryall of unguents and lotions. She set up the table in Olivia's bedroom. Olivia disrobed in her dressing room, wrapped herself in a fluffy bath towel and returned.

With her usual efficiency Irene had set out her potions on a small side table. She had removed her dress. Under it she wore her working costume of pale green hotpants and halter bra. Her long legs were bare, her feet in shower slippers. Above the band of her shorts her small, perfectly round belly button was a Cyclops's eye. She motioned silently for Olivia to take her place on the massage table. Everything Irene did was graceful, and, in a strange way, seductive.

Olivia dropped her towel, got on the table face down and gave herself up with closed eyes to Irene's ministrations.

Olivia, luxuriating in exquisite sensations, was on that fine edge between sleep and waking; Irene's hands were moving toward where her thighs widened, fingers gently probing, manipulating each separate muscle, relaxing, easing tension. For the first time she was conscious of Irene's hands as something personal. In her half-awake state part of her wanted to tell Irene to stop, that what she was doing was not part of the treatment and very close to naughtiness . . . but Olivia did not speak. Then she felt two knowing lubricated fingers slip into her. In and out.

Her eyes snapped widely open. The first thing she saw was Stewart standing beside her, his penis erect.

"Relax," Stewart said.

She turned her head to see Irene clad only in an encouraging

509

smile, the nipples of her small round breasts as rigid as soldiers on parade. Very gradually her body began to lose its tension as Irene's fingers found her clitoris. She couldn't have stopped if she had wanted to. And she didn't. Stewart moved close, his penis huge before her face.

It was the beginning of a long and curious night.

In the ensuing months Irene Wells became a frequent visitor to Riverhaven, and Stewart's sexual interest in his wife underwent a gratifying revival. A ménage à trois wasn't exactly what Olivia expected of her marriage. But it was sensually sensational, wickedly exciting, and in the long run Stewart shared was better than no Stewart at all.

Until Stewart got bored again. This time with Irene, despite her expertise in and out of bed. When the silent Irene finally talked, it was with a nasal Brooklyn accent that grated on the nerves. As Stewart put it, ''She opens her mouth and out come toads and serpents. She's as common as pig tracks.''

There followed a brief hiatus in their sex life, until Stewart introduced Olivia to a remarkable girl named Nan Kennicott—if *introduced* is the proper word for an acrobatic evening of alcohol, pot and wildly entwined bodies.

Stewart's enjoyment was heightened because both women were so obviously well bred, so clearly upper-class, so coolly assured and unapproachable in the everyday daylight world. True intimacy terrified Stewart because he had never experienced it. Stewart wanted a safe distance between himself and all others. His world had a population of one, whose need was to coerce, persuade, manipulate and in the end degrade, to make others smaller than himself. Watching these two sleek sensuous animals—whom in a sense he had created—rutting together for his pleasure gave him an immense gratification, a confirmation of his power.

Olivia began to understand some of this only when, one pot-filled afternoon alone together, she heard from Nan the story of Nan's relationship with Stewart. The two women had become friends, drawn to each other more by their inner loneliness than their sharing of Stewart.

510

Olivia gave a lot of thought to Nan's revelation, and to an examination of her own situation, and at last came up for air. She realized that she still loved Stewart—not Stewart as he was, but a Stewart who was a product of her own desires and needs, a Stewart who didn't really exist outside of her head. With her new insight she could now look at Stewart with some degree of objectivity. What she saw frightened her. Stewart was a danger to himself and, more important, a danger to others. There were no limits on Stewart, no restraints, no morality to hold him back, no code of ethics to curb him. Stewart had no sense of right and wrong. And it wasn't really his fault. There was no helping him, because he could never be made to see that he needed help.

Painfully Olivia decided she wanted no more of marriage to Stewart. And yet, she shrank from hurting him—and divorce would certainly injure him politically. Besides, she wasn't at all sure that Stewart's possessiveness would allow him to release her. It was a dilemma.

It was at this point that Stewart told her he wanted a divorce. Olivia was so surprised and blessedly relieved that Stewart himself was solving her problem that she could find nothing to say.

It was early in the morning. Olivia was still in negligee at her dressing table when Stewart entered, dressed for the day, carrying a briefcase under one arm. His demand had come baldly, with no preliminaries. He took her silence as opposition because it didn't occur to him that she wouldn't oppose divorce.

"If you've some idea of fighting me," Stewart said brusquely, "you'd better take a look at this."

He opened his briefcase, took out a sheaf of photographs and threw them on the mirrored tabletop, where they spread out like a fan. The top one showed Olivia and Nan Kennicott comforting each other in what some artists would have called a charming tableau. Their heads were turned toward each other on a single pillow, lips barely touching, eyes closed, their naked bodies firmly molded each to the other from breast to knee.

Olivia was shocked to her toes. She couldn't believe that even Stewart would stoop to something so degrading. She could only shake her head wordlessly. Stewart took this for more resistance.

"What do you suppose your father would say to these if they arrived with the morning mail?"

Stewart used Olivia's father as a threat because, given his relationship with his own father, he couldn't imagine anything worse.

Olivia began to laugh uncontrollably. She finally stopped long enough to gasp, "Oh, Stewart. He'd probably frame them."

Granted, there was something of hysteria in Olivia's laughter; it hardly called for Stewart's angry open-handed slap.

Olivia stiffened. Her eyes grew cold. One hand rose slowly to her cheek.

"What a pity." She reached forward to gather up the photographs. "You could have saved yourself the trouble. The only reason I haven't filed for divorce already is because of your career. Thanks for relieving me of that worry." She lifted the pictures toward him. "Tell me, Stewart, did Nan . . . know?"

"No." Stewart was torn between relief that he had gotten what he wanted and anger that she had given in so readily. "What the hell difference does it make?"

"That's good," Olivia said calmly. "I hardly thought she would lend herself to something as despicable as this. And now, Stewart, get out. Thank God, I'll never have to see you again. I'll be gone by this afternoon."

"Not so damned fast! I want you to go to Mexico. It's all arranged. . . ."

Olivia laughed again, this time in derision.

"You'll get your divorce, Stewart. On my terms. But don't worry, I'm as anxious as you are to get it over and done quickly. You'll have to be satisfied with that."

Olivia got her divorce. Not in Mexico, but in Puerto Rico, where she spent six lonely anonymous weeks in the seclusion of a friend's estate near Ponce. She spent those weeks wondering how to go about becoming her own person again.

512

30

Time: 1978
GAVIN RIORDAN

Birdie Connors Riordan died quietly in her sleep at St. Malachy's. There was no wake or laying out. She was buried in the Good Shepherd Cemetery on a gray Sunday morning. There were few mourners: Desmond Daniher's small entourage of Mary Margaret and Donnie Shay; Meg O'Day and Connie McGurn, who waited quietly in the background to drive them all away; three nuns from St. Malachy's, somber in their black habits.

It began to snow as they stood by the graveside, large, heavy flakes that settled on the casket with a gentle hiss. Gavin, standing, touching Daniher's shoulder, felt him shiver in the cold and had the thought that Daniher was growing old too fast.

"...deliver the souls of all the faithful," the priest intoned, "let them not be swallowed up in darkness...."

The ceremony over, they walked down the hill to where the cars were parked. The snowfall had increased, huge flakes swirling against the leaden sky. Gavin turned up his coat collar.

There was a woman in a mink coat, her head protected by a tightly drawn scarf, standing next to Daniher's hired limousine. She had been there for some time, judging by the snow which mantled her shoulders.

It was Serena. Gavin wasn't surprised. The others fell back a little, leaving Gavin and Daniher to approach alone.

"Serena." Daniher showed her the warm courtliness he always reserved for her. "Nice of you. Unexpected but appreciated."

"I was around for the beginning," Serena said. "It seemed right to be in at the finish." She held out her hand and Gavin took it, cold and bloodless as ice itself. "I'm sorry, Gavin. Truly sorry. For everything."

Her eyes were troubled, cloudy with a deep sadness. There was a meaning beyond her words, and Gavin suddenly felt the old familiar pain of what might have been. *All the sad-eyed women . . .* he thought distractedly.

"Serena. I . . ."

Something in her look stopped him. That and the realization that he wasn't at all sure of what he wanted to say.

Serena withdrew her hand and turned away, walking toward her car, parked just behind Daniher's.

Gavin watched her go. He felt Daniher's hand on his shoulder, gently squeezing.

"And so am I, dear boy." Daniher's voice was husky with emotion. "More sorry than I can say."

Gavin turned down Daniher's invitation to join him for a drink and asked that Connie drop him at his apartment. A quiet talk with Daniher would inevitably concern Birdie, and the silences would be filled with Daniher's unspoken sorrow at how the marriage he had so confidently arranged had spoiled Gavin's life. He didn't relish the prospect of his empty rooms, either, so he took a cab to his office.

Although the staff was reduced on weekends, Police Headquarters had its usual air of bustle. Crime was no respecter of the Lord's day. The duty officer handed him two telephone messages, which he stuffed in his pocket as he took the elevator up. The commissioner's suite was quiet, an island of silence protected from the activity below by its heavy paneled walls. The sergeant on weekend watch was a black policewoman whose name for some reason Gavin had difficulty remembering. He concentrated hard as he waved a greeting and finally came up with it. Barlow. Betsy Barlow.

Sergeant Barlow stood up as he passed her desk. "Two messages, Commissioner."

Gavin pulled the telephone slips from his pocket and waved them at her.

"Thanks, but I got 'em downstairs."

Barlow looked slightly annoyed that someone had beaten her to the punch.

"A Mr. Barnstable. Seemed very anxious. Said it was important."

Gavin handed his overcoat to Barlow and, although he was perfectly able to read it himself, waited for Barlow to tell him what was on the second message slip, since he knew she would do it anyway.

"Sergeant Mulvey. Twenty-third Precinct," Barlow said. "Personal. He wouldn't say what it was about."

Now, that was a name Gavin knew very well indeed, although he hadn't heard it in years. Jake Mulvey went back a long time, all the way to the early days in the Third Precinct, and Gavin had thought him long since retired.

At his desk he tried Barnstable first on his private line, counted eight rings before he hung up and then called to Sergeant Barlow to get Mulvey for him.

Mulvey got right to the point. "An Ericka Ullman. Picked up at . . . let's see . . ."—Mulvey was obviously referring to his blotter—"eleven-ten A.M. Patrolmen Davillo and Harvey. Car three-one-twelve. Seneca Street and Hudson Boulevard. Narcotics related, according to the officers." There was a pause. Then Mulvey again, diffident, with a note of apology. "Thought you ought to know, Commissioner. Hope I did the right thing."

Through his panic Gavin had the fleeting thought that Jake Mulvey knew a lot more about his commissioner's private life than he should know. He heard a calm unruffled voice that didn't seem to be his say, "Is she all right?" And then, "What happened?"

"Far as I know," Mulvey said, "runnin' down Seneca neckid as a jaybird when the officers spotted her. Spaced out. Not a bit of sense to her. They put her under restraint and delivered her to the psycho ward at City General. Nothing else to do."

Gavin cringed. The psycho ward at City was for the town's flotsam.

He said, "Thank you, Jake. I appreciate your call."

"Nothing, Commissioner. I thought I ought to . . ."

"I understand. Thanks again."

He hung up, his mind awhirl with questions and speculations. Drugs? Ericka?

He found a quietly frantic George Barnstable in the reception area of the hospital, trying to talk his way past a buxom charge nurse who was much too experienced and formidable for him. She was used to importunate friends and relatives and controlled them with a sure hand. The patient was under observation, and no one, but no one, would see her until the doctor said so. George's relief at Gavin's appearance was pitiable.

The nurse wasn't proof against the authority of the commissioner of police, and within minutes they were questioning a bored bespectacled intern who was burdened with a wispy mustache and a bad case of acne. "LSD, I think," the young man told them. "She had a very bad trip."

"Impossible." Barnstable was indignant. "She's never touched drugs in her life."

"You tellin' me my business, mister?" The intern picked at a scab as he studied Barnstable. "We used to get 'em in here all the time. Not as much lately. The kids are on to different stuff now, ludes and angel dust. But this one is old enough to know better. An' believe me, I know acid when I see it."

"I want her out of here," Gavin said. "When?"

"Now. Provided you got a meat wagon with a couple husky attendants. She's still seeing ghosties and ghoulies. *And* you sign a release. You a relative?"

"I am," Barnstable said.

"This way, mister."

Barnstable went with him while Gavin found a telephone and called Colonel Liam Rooney at the Veterans Hospital.

"Can't admit her here," Rooney told him. "Have to be Good Samaritan. I've got privileges there. I'll arrange to have them pick her up. See you in about an hour."

When George Barnstable returned, Gavin sent him off to Ericka's apartment for her clothes and whatever else she would need. Barnstable was grateful for the chance to get away from the depressing atmosphere of City Hospital.

Liam Rooney, still in hospital whites, joined Gavin in the coffee shop at Good Sam.

"She's pretty much out of it now," Rooney told him. "That trip was certainly no vacation. Where do you get these girls? First the Kennicott woman—now this one. Addicts turn you on or something?"

"She's no addict. No way."

Rooney nodded agreeably. "That's what she says, too. Not that she's necessarily telling the truth. Claims she doesn't know how she got the stuff. Curious. She says she was alone when it hit her."

"Will she be all right?"

"Hard to say." Rooney shrugged. "LSD is unpredictable. People can go into deep depression who haven't touched the drug for months. It can do things to the head. Rare, though. Most people are none the worse from a single dose." Rooney blinked at Gavin's uncertain expression. "You trust me, Gav? I didn't do so well with the last one."

"I was warned," Gavin said. "You didn't give me any guarantees. And you were right. She didn't have the guts for it. Not your fault. All right to go up to see her now?"

"Sure. I'd like to hear what she has to say. To you."

Ericka was deathly pale. She seemed to have trouble focusing, but she smiled weakly at Gavin. Gavin took her hand.

"Feel well enough to tell us what happened?"

"I guess so. Except I'm not really sure...."

"Try," Gavin said.

Her eyes clouded with the effort. "I took a shower. I remember drying myself. I went to the closet to pick a dress...a blue dress, because... Oh, my. I was supposed to lunch with Stewart. Someone should call him. He'll be worried."

Gavin wanted to say "Fuck him. Let him worry." But he nodded.

"I had the dress over my arm. I walked over to the bureau to get some underwear.... That's when it started. The room began to go

517

around. I saw things . . . horrible things. I was lying on the rug . . . and all the little fibers were snakes reaching with their tongues . . . to put out my eyes."

She turned her head restlessly on the pillow and put an arm across her face to block out whatever she was seeing.

"It's all so confused. I was terrified. . . . I remember how cold the wind was. Goose bumps as big as apples on my skin, swelling up and bursting like boils." She pulled her arm away, her eyes now open and pleading for reassurance. "In the street . . . was I in the street, Gavin? Naked in the street? What happened to me!"

Liam Rooney moved to the bedside. "Take it easy. It's all over now. Nothing to be afraid of. We think what you got was a dose of LSD. It's highly hallucinatory—and it can be extremely frightening if you don't know what to expect. But it's all in your head. None of it really happened. You must try and remember that. All hallucination. Tell me, did you have anything to eat? Or drink? Before . . ."

"No, nothing." She hesitated. "Yes, a drink of brandy. Before I showered. . . ."

"Brandy?" Gavin asked sharply. "In the middle of the morning?"

"I had cramps. . . . Brandy helps sometimes. . . ."

"Where'd you get it? The brandy?"

"I . . . I don't remember. I think Stewart gave it to me. . . ."

Gavin felt a murderous rage building in his chest. "Tell me." Despite his tension his voice was even. "Was Stewart supposed to pick you up at the apartment?"

"Yes. . . . We were going to drive out to Riverhaven for lunch."

"And in the normal course of events, you'd offer him a drink before you left?"

"I suppose so." There was a puzzled look on her pale face. "If he wanted one. . . ."

"Brandy?" Gavin said levelly. "He'd have asked for brandy. And you'd have joined him. Can't let a man drink alone. Only he would have let *you* drink alone, the son of a bitch."

Her eyes widened. "What are you saying? Not Stewart. He couldn't . . ." It all came out in a rush of words, her tongue stumbling on her denial. "Why would he . . . ? Stewart wants me to marry him! He wouldn't . . ."

518

"What was it to be today?" Gavin asked furiously. "An engagement lunch? That what he had in mind?"

Rooney clamped a hand on Gavin's arm. "Cut it out. She isn't up to it."

Ericka was staring at him, her face cold and closed.

"At least we can suppose that she didn't ingest much of the stuff," Rooney said in his professional voice. "Given the circumstances. Your man wouldn't have wanted as strong a reaction as she obviously had, now, would he? Not for what he was planning. If there *was* a man, and he was planning anything at all. Which I find it hard to believe, if the man is who I think it is."

"Maybe you better call him yourself, Ericka. You wouldn't want him to worry." Gavin hated himself for what he was saying to her, but he couldn't stop. He wanted to hurt. He wanted her to feel the pain that he was feeling.

George Barnstable came through the door carrying an overnight bag and saved Gavin from making a worse fool of himself.

"Dr. Rooney, George Barnstable," Gavin said. "I'll leave you to it." He left the room without looking at her, remembering only her face as he had last seen it, his jealousy eating at him like an acid.

From a public phone in the lobby he called his office and asked Sergeant Barlow to have someone from the Twenty-third meet him at Ericka Ullman's apartment. Then he took a cab there.

Lieutenant Dan Ball was waiting for him alone at the entrance to the building, which was surprising. He had expected a detective sergeant and probably a patrolman. All he needed was someone to witness what he meant to do.

Dan Ball was young for his rank, one of the up-and-comers. He had a thin, sharp-nosed face, circles of red from the cold on his high cheekbones. His eyes were alive with interest. "Afternoon, Commissioner," Ball said. "Thought I'd best come alone, sir. I didn't know . . ." He stopped uncertainly.

Dan Ball obviously knew that Riordan's interest in Ericka Ullman was something more than academic. Either he'd been briefed by his sergeant, Jake Mulvey, or the information was truly out on the grapevine. Ball was alone because he wanted to save his commissioner any possible embarrassment. Riordan appreciated his thoughtfulness, approved of his caution and found himself irritated anyway. They rode the elevator in silence, each wrapped in his own thoughts. Lieutenant Ball stayed carefully one step behind as they walked down the corridor.

The door to Ericka's apartment swung easily to the touch. In the bedroom they saw a crumpled blue dress on the floor, a wisp of bra and panties. On the pile carpeting were long marks where her fingernails had dug into the nap. In the kitchen cabinet next to the refrigerator there was vodka, gin, Scotch and several liqueurs. But no brandy. No brandy anywhere. And no used glass. Everything carefully in its place on the proper shelves.

There wouldn't be a need for anyone to call Stewart to explain why he had been stood up for his luncheon date. Stewart already knew. Or somebody.

Dan Ball, who had asked no questions up until now, except to inquire what they were looking for, said diffidently, "Drop you somewhere, Commissioner?"

"No," Riordan said. "I'll walk. I need to do some thinking." He held out his hand and Ball gripped it. "And thanks, Dan."

Dan Ball watched him, high square military shoulders, long legs swinging, his red hair bright in the sunlight, something indomitable in his carriage, until he turned a corner.

Riordan had some thought of going to his apartment, calling Ericka, apologizing for his anger, somehow mending his fences, but decided that would have to be done in person—if it could be done at all. He owed her that. But it should wait until she was home from the hospital. On her own turf. In a hospital bed she was at too much of a disadvantage. He'd call Rooney instead. Find out when. Maybe tomorrow morning?

But tomorrow morning was too late. Because all hell broke loose overnight. And by morning Commissioner Gavin Riordan's City was up to its ears in trouble.

*   *   *

The Reverend Cecil Weems filled the visitors' chair to overflowing. His big body settled itself like a man who intended to stay a long time. His black face, under the crown of white hair, was unreadable except for its determination.

Under his desk, out of sight of the man, Riordan's hands were clenched, because they were trembling with the anger that threatened to betray him into physical violence.

"I want those officers released, Reverend. At once! Taking police hostages is no answer to the problem."

"Hostages? Hardly, Commissioner." Weems's deep tones held a calm assurance which infuriated Riordan even more. "Your men are being held for their own protection. At the moment, on the streets their lives wouldn't be worth a nickel."

"In your church. Against their will." Riordan said tensely. "Come off it, Reverend. The church is surrounded. Sixty police are surely protection enough. I want those two men released! Damnit, you don't seem to realize you're breaking the law!"

"Not I, Mr. Riordan. I'm merely a messenger. As for the law, there's a higher law. An eye for an eye, a tooth for a tooth. Your men shot down an innocent child. In cold blood. Or doesn't your law apply to that?"

"Your innocent child was in the process of committing a felony. Armed robbery. With a gun. Which he turned on an officer of the law. That's what the report says."

Weems's eyes held his, coldly implacable. There was a long moment of silence. Then Weems said softly, "Sound familiar, Commissioner? How many times has a black man been shot—and a convenient weapon found at the scene?"

Riordan found he couldn't meet those accusing eyes. He swiveled in his chair to face the window. He listened to the clanking of the ancient heating system, conscious that he was sweating in the warm air. Outside, the sun was pale and wintry. There were pigeons in the snow on the window ledge. Their cooing came faintly through the glass.

Riordan was all too aware of the backup weapon many street cops carried. Self-preservation. If a trigger-happy officer made a mistake, shot the wrong man, a convenient knife or cheap pistol dropped beside a victim provided justification.

It could have happened here. All he had so far was a preliminary report. A thirteen-year-old boy, running from a grocery store that had just been robbed, had produced a weapon that threatened the life of the officers, who had thereupon opened fire. Now one dead boy.

He was concerned now with what had happened subsequently. An angry mob had formed before anybody could respond to the cops' Code 1199. If he could believe the Reverend Weems, all that had saved the officers' lives was the intervention of Weems himself, who had given the two policemen the sanctuary of his church. There his men were now, along with about fifty black parishioners, who refused to give them up despite being surrounded by enough fire-power to take a fort.

Riordan sighed and turned to face Weems. "All right, Doctor. What is it you want?"

The Reverend Weems steepled his hands before his face, considering. "I am informed that you are a man who will listen, Commissioner. That's what I want. Your time and your attention for what I have to say. Then we can discuss what's to be done."

Weems put both hands on the arms of his chair, the long spatulate fingers digging into the dark leather, leaned forward and began to speak in his vibrant orator's voice.

" 'The dark ghetto's invisible walls have been erected by the white society, by those who have power, both to confine those who have *no* power and to perpetuate their powerlessness. Their inhabitants are subject peoples, victims of the greed, cruelty, insensitivity, guilt and fear of their masters.

" 'Their objective dimensions . . . are overcrowded and deteriorated housing, high infant mortality, crime and disease. The subjective dimensions are resentment, hostility, despair, apathy, self-depreciation.

" 'Those who are required to live in congested and rat-infested homes are aware that others are not so dehumanized. The residents of the ghetto are not themselves blind to life as it is outside of the ghetto. The Negro lives in part in the world of television and motion pictures, often believing as literal truth their pictures of

522

luxury and happiness, and yet at the same time confronted by a harsh world of reality where the dreams do not come true—or change into nightmares.'

"Do you know who wrote those words? A great black man. A psychologist named Kenneth Clark, an advisor to presidents. Nightmares, Mr. Riordan. More familiar to us than daydreams.

"That's how it is with us. In the hot summer nights we sit on the stoops for a breath of air. We have no air conditioning. A white policeman orders us to get inside, get off the streets. If we protest there is the nightstick—a jab in the stomach, a rap on the head. How do we deal with this man? There is no way we can make him listen—unless it's a rap or a jab from his own nightstick.

"Why are there so many white police standing over us, Commissioner? In a white neighborhood we don't see black officers keeping the peace. Why aren't there black captains, lieutenants, sergeants, in the ghetto, Mr. Riordan? Why are the streets never cleaned, the houses allowed to rot away? Why are rats allowed to attack our children? Why, Mr. Riordan? Why?

"Why is there no money for playgrounds, decent housing, schools—when a white governor is spending millions, possibly billions, on a monument to himself, the Gansvoort Mall?

"Can you understand a resentment so strong that it demands blood? Most of us don't want bloodshed if we can help it. But if blood has to flow to make you listen, then well and good. Let it flow. On your own heads be it. I would like to see my people live in pride and dignity, even if it takes bloodshed to bring it about."

The Reverend Weems leaned forward, his huge hands now clutching his knees, his voice heavy with portent.

"This is only a beginning. So far only black blood has been spilled. The riot of 1974 should have given you a warning. It brought us promises from the governor—better housing, jobs, relief from our 'intolerable agony' is the way he put it. But it took a riot to get even promises. And nothing has been done.

"You are like the mule who has first to be hit on the head to gain his attention. But, believe me, the trouble of 1974 was nothing. The spontaneous reaction of a mob. Leaderless and, in the face of your guns, powerless in the end."

The dark irises of Weems's eyes were in startling contrast to the whiteness of the corneas. There was something almost hypnotic about those eyes. They bored into Riordan, as though Weems were compelling him to believe, to see things as Weems saw them.

"There is a difference now. The beginnings of organization. The Black Power movement. Leaders who preach that violence is the only answer to oppression. The law of the gun. They find ready ears in a black society where there is no other hope.

"I tell you, you are now sitting on a volcano whose eruption will know no bounds, Mr. Riordan. What are you going to do about it?"

Riordan considered. He believed what Weems was saying. But what could he offer? What had he to bargain with?

Riordan made up his mind. He reached into the lower drawer of his desk and pulled out a manila folder.

"I'm not sure I should be doing this. But I think you have a right to know where I stand." He slid the folder across the desk and Weems reached out to take it. "My confidential report to the governor on the 1974 thing. Pretty much everything you've just said to me is in there. All the wrongs, all the warnings, all the projections of what might happen. Pissing in the wind, for all the good it did. It changed nothing.

"I can't change the nature of cops, either," Gavin went on. "Or their prejudices. You got crime in the ghettos, for whatever reasons, it's a cop's job to fight it. It's what he's paid to do. I can't change that, either. But what I can do is give you the black officers you want, on every level I think advisable. Although it's my personal opinion it won't help a hell of a lot. Black cops are paid to do the same things white cops are.

"But let me give *you* a warning, Reverend. I've got a force of three hundred men who have all completed training in riot control. If your people take to the streets again, I'll hit you with everything I've got. And I'll win. Because I've got the artillery. You know it. You better rule out that option."

With an effort Riordan forced himself to relax a little. "So what's left, Reverend? Talk is the only thing. It may not solve your problem, but it doesn't get anybody killed, either. You put together a representative group, and I'll guarantee you get to see the governor personally. Get the chance to lay it all on him—with TV cameras and all the hoopla. Who knows, it might even do some good. It's a chance you'll have to take. Because I want my two officers released. If they aren't, you force me to come in and get 'em. I don't think either of us wants that.

"Another thing I'll guarantee is a fair and honest hearing on this thing. I'll want you to be present—as a friend of the court, so to speak. If there is the slightest doubt about their innocence, I'll turn 'em both over to the civil authorities for trial. You have my word on that.

"How about it? We go down there together. Now. We make a joint statement to those press hyenas, on the steps of your church. And I get my men. It's the best I can do."

The Reverend Weems slowly leaned back in his chair. One long fingernail tapped Riordan's confidential report in his lap.

"And this?"

"Release it if you want. Long as you don't tell 'em where you got it." Riordan sighed deeply. "You know, Reverend, between us we just might get something accomplished. Just maybe. It's worth a try."

The Reverend Weems's leonine head began to nod slowly.

Gavin got his men back. The same day, through Des Daniher and Charlie Bishop, he arranged for Cecil Weems and seven other leaders of the black community to have an emergency meeting with the governor.

Gavin wasn't present, because he didn't trust himself to face Stewart right at this moment. His anger was still too close to the surface. A phone call from Charlie Bishop told him that it had gone well. Stewart was at his best—concerned, sympathetic and properly outraged at conditions in the ghetto, promising quick redress for all the complaints, suggesting that the Reverend Weems head a committee to draw up a plan for the rehabilitation of the City's depressed area. When Gavin asked if anything had really been accomplished, Charlie laughed.

"Look, Commissioner," Charlie said. "Don't push your luck.

Your two guys got us into this thing when they let an unarmed mob fake 'em into giving up their weapons. You got what you asked for. Meeting with the governor. Media exposure. Umpteen miles of publicity. If those people keep some pressure on, the legislature might even do something. Except what you got to remember is . . ."

"I know," Gavin interrupted wearily. "Black people don't vote. What *you* should remember, Charlie, is a crime rate in the ghettos that is going out of sight. Because people have to eat. If they can't get jobs, they'll try some other way to get a buck. I hope you sleep sound, Charlie, knowing there are more than a million unregistered handguns in the City. To say nothing of automatic weapons and shotguns. Give it some thought, Charlie. I know I do. And it scares the shit out of me."

It wasn't until Wednesday afternoon that Gavin found time to call Liam Rooney to find that Ericka had been discharged the day before.

"Don't worry, Gav," Rooney told him. "She was completely recovered. I don't anticipate any further complications. But LSD is something the lady should stay away from. She hasn't the head for it."

Rooney wouldn't listen to Gavin's thanks, so he hung up and called Ericka. There was no answer at her apartment, so he rang George Barnstable.

"I've been trying to get you," Barnstable said. "She asked me to tell you . . ."

"It's been a little busy around here, George. Tell me what?"

There was a hesitation, and Gavin had a premonition that something was coming that he wouldn't want to hear. "She's gone, Gavin. She went to the New York house to get her clothes. By now she should be on her way to Tokyo."

"Tokyo? What the hell is she doing in Tokyo!"

"She has a commission. Library at the University. They've been after her for a long time. . . ."

Her letter came special delivery as Gavin was shaving the next morning. He left it on the kitchen shelf next to the automatic coffee pot while he finished dressing. He didn't want to read the letter; he dreaded what was in it.

My dearest Gavin:

I hope you will understand and forgive me. I am doing what I know I must do. If it's any comfort to you, it's hurting dreadfully—leaving you. At least as much as I know it hurts you.

Bear with me, dear Gavin. There's a lot I want to say, and it's hard to put it down. I've always availed myself of the privilege of saying what I mean with you. Grant it to me now, when I need it most.

You know that my introduction to men—and sex—was traumatic, to say the least. It left its scars. The sex part straightened itself out. At least, I think so. It s the emotional side of the relationship that seems to be lacking. The *involvement*. The heights, the depths and the shared passion poets write about— which other people all around me seem to feel. For years I have used sex as I would an aspirin—whenever the need arises.

Looking back, there was a time when it might have been different. With Jean-Baptiste Moreau. But you know about that. And he is dead. His death, *how* he died—and what happened afterward—left me with the sure conviction that men, with a capital *M*, were my enemies. Men can hurt you in so many, many ways.

Then you came back into my life.

For the first time in years, all of my convictions were shaken. I was down at the bottom of me, looking at the darkness I lived in. And it began to seem just barely possible that there *was* a light at the tunnel's end. (That overused phrase never seems to lose its aptness.) There was always a special sense of self when I was with you. You who knew all the external things that had happened to me. Was it possible that you could share the black things inside as well? And not sit in judgment?

I didn't know, Gavin. I still don't. It will have to wait. Anything else wouldn't be fair to either of us.

I owe you an explanation about Stewart. First, you must understand that George is the exception to all this about men. Love is too pale a word for what I feel for George. Devotion, affection, adoration—of all the synonyms, perhaps *worship* is the closest. In the sense of creation, veneration. For George is in a way my creator. He gave me life. And, more importantly, he gave me my work. Because of George I, too, can create, in my small way. Build things for people, good sturdy things that with luck have a beauty, too. It seems to me a justification for living—and the only way I can repay George for the precious opportunity he gave me.

I'm sure you realize that part of my tolerating Stewart (believe me, it was no more than that) was to protect what George wanted more than anything in the world. The chance to build the Mall. I don't suppose you can know the lure of building, using light, space, cadence, form and your own vision of the rightness of what you are creating. For an architect it's a thing of the soul, the ultimate in beauty. And in George that sense of beauty and rightness is stronger than in most architects. It's what he lives for. Perhaps the only thing he lives for.

And so, at first, Stewart had to be kept happy. Like any client. It seemed so little to do to protect George's dream. But Stewart is not insensitive. He *is* intuitive. He began to probe, gently in the beginning, trying to find out just how far I would go—for George's sake.

I know you were puzzled, and angry, over my relationship with Stewart. All the gifts—and what you called the "strings" attached to them. My acceptance, which seemed "easy" to you, *was* easy. You were right. You see, my life taught me that men were the enemy—the enemy of everything I ever wanted for myself—and the lesson seemed irrevocable. Why shouldn't I take Stewart's gifts, or anything else Stewart had to offer? Poor enough payment for what men owed me. I could handle Stewart, for, after all, the ultimate choice was mine. That feeling lulled me. My guard was down. I almost forgot what cruelty men are capable of.

I tried to make a friend of Stewart, to bring out the best in him. And there is a lot of good in Stewart, although I know you won't agree. I think I succeeded in a way. Stewart and I did become friends. I sometimes wonder if perhaps I have been the only friend he ever had. He was a stranger to friendship— but then, so was I. Both our lives in different ways have been so terribly lonely.

I might have gone to bed with Stewart, because it seemed so important to him—and so meaningless to me. But I didn't. I could say that it was because of you and, of course, Olivia. And in part it was. But not all. If I am to be truthful, there were deeper reasons. A lifetime of conditioning, the knowledge that if I withheld myself from men, I could cause them pain, extract a satisfying payment for the pain they have caused me. Not very admirable, is it? Also it gave me power. That dark yearning for power that is hidden in all of us. What I didn't realize was that my power over Stewart was a sham. The absolute power was Stewart's, not mine. And with it went absolute corruption.

Stewart made it clear that marrying him was the price for letting George finish the Mall. He couldn't know that that kind of force was the one thing I would resist the hardest. A sort of psychological rape—too close to the real thing.

Besides, I didn't believe him. I thought I knew him better than he did himself. I didn't understand the perverted, exquisite pleasure Stewart felt in exerting his absolute power.

And so we come to the LSD episode. I think he would have perferred it that way, to take me in helplessness rather than consent.

And so I'm running away. From circumstances I can't control. There are many reasons, not the least of which is my career, and you know how important that is to me. Also I don't think Stewart could stand it—you and me together. He never gives up, you know. Because he's never been denied.

Forgive me, if you can.

Perhaps in time . . .

*   *   *

There was no signature. Gavin folded the pages carefully and put them into the same file that held Ten Tabard's letter. It seemed an appropriate place, part of a past that now seemed dead and buried.

Officers Brian Emmett and Carlo Bonini were tried in the supreme court of the state on a charge of justifiable homicide (reduced from murder one) by an all-white jury of nine men and three women. The trial lasted six days. Despite the testimony of four eyewitnesses who claimed to have seen Officer Emmett drop a Saturday-night special beside the dead body of Bozeman Tate aged thirteen, the jury returned a verdict of not guilty. At a subsequent departmental proceeding both officers were found guilty of grave misconduct and allowed to resign from the force.

The day after the acquittal Governor Stewart Gansvoort presided over the dedication ceremonies for the Mall's Bell Tower, which had just been sheathed. People from all over the state had gathered on this chill and wintry day—officials, politicians, clergy, dignitaries— to witness the miracle of construction that had replaced miserable slums. There it stood in all its grandeur, eight buildings of various heights and conformities, huge, starkly white, clad in Italian marble. Gone at last were most of the cranes and scaffolding, the chugging motors, the staccato clang of pneumatic drills, the antlike activity of the work force. The complex was far from habitable as yet. All of the interior work was still to come, the landscaping, placing of the sculptures, the filling of the reflecting pools with their spectacular fountains of spray. But it was there in its final form, an edifice for all mankind to admire and wonder at, a monument to resist the inroads of time forever. The personal signature of Stewart Gansvoort.

"Isn't it grand!" Stewart Gansvoort cried, and clapped his hands. "Just grand!"

The microphone on the podium picked up his voice and boomed it out over the assembled multitude. The crowd laughed at his enthusiasm. On this great day, what did it matter that newspapers were headlining charges of gross mismanagement, unparalleled extravagance, unethical financing, criminal waste, dark tales of organized crime, FBI investigations and the specter of not one but five grand-jury hearings? What did it matter that a project originally budgeted at $550,000,000 was now approaching two billion dollars of the taxpayers' money? Was anyone listening to the Reverend Cecil Weems, who was quoted as saying, "This obscene monument is built on a foundation of human misery and degradation. Billions of dollars spent on cold marble and not one cent for the betterment of the poor and helpless. More than eight thousand workers to build this monstrosity, many of them imported from other states. And how many blacks? A grand total of one hundred and fifty-four—when black people are crowding our welfare rolls, forced, literally forced, to go on relief because there are no jobs, no money to buy food and shelter."

Commissioner Gavin Riordan, standing with Archie Ogden just below the speakers' platform, looked upward at the slim, graceful spire of the Bell Tower standing atop its forty-eight stories, pointing like a finger to the gray sky.

"By God, when all's said and done, it *is* magnificent, isn't it?"

Ogden began to laugh softly, so as not to be heard by the people around them.

"You can't notice it from here, an' you wouldn't believe it—but that ringtailed son of a bitch is almost two feet out of true. The boys call it Gansvoort's Leaning Tower."

"Jesus!" Riordan gasped. "How the hell . . . ?"

"Put it down to pilot error," Ogden said. "The easy way out for the manufacturer."

"How could it happen?"

"Simple. The bastard is really two separate buildings. . . ." Ogden stopped and then said, "Jesus Christ! Will you look at that." His face was a study in amazement.

Riordan turned to where Ogden was pointing. A squad of some twenty or thirty black men were marching in military precision down the long shallow steps on the north end of the Plaza. They were dressed in black leather jackets and black berets. Each man carried an M-1 rifle slung over his shoulder, chest crossed with bandoliers of .30 caliber cartridges. As they watched, the formation broke up and the men dissolved into the crowd, only the muzzles of their weapons showing above the heads of the spectators.

The speeches still droned over the loudspeaker system, the politi-

531

cians and dignitaries on the rostrum seemingly unaware of what was happening. Riordan started forward, but there were hundreds of people between him and the black invasion, if that's what it was.

Suddenly from overhead came the clatter of a helicopter. Faces turned skyward to see a bundle pushed out of the plane's open doorway. Riordan's first impulse was to hit the ground, but the bundle blossomed like a white shellburst. Thousands of leaflets filled the air and floated earthward.

Riordan could see now that the blacks in the crowd seemed to be passing out leaflets as well. It all seemed very orderly. Next to him Ogden speared a spiraling paper and Riordan read the large black type over his shoulder.

WHEN MURDERERS GO FREE IT IS TIME FOR CITIZENS TO ACT

> The Black Power party calls on all concerned, and black people in particular, to rebel against the racist police who are intensifying the terror, brutality, murder and intimidation of black people everywhere.
>
> We have begged, prayed, petitioned, to get the racist power structure to right the wrongs perpetrated against black people— to no avail.
>
> The time has come to arm.
>
> Power is the Gun.
>
> Every citizen has the right to bear arms in his own defense.
>
> The Constitution gives you that right.
>
> Use it NOW!
>
> Fight back against repression!

Riordan left at a run for the radio in his car.

"Get the first company of the strike battalion here. On the double. Don't arrest *anybody*! Just get them here fast."

He listened to the protests that flooded the police channel and then shouted, "No arrests! They haven't done anything to arrest 'em for. Until they do, the law protects them like anybody else. Get that through your head. And make sure my order goes out. No goddamned arrests!"

As he made his way back to the speakers' platform he could hear the sirens in the distance. He had time to pray that no one got trigger-happy, because one shot fired could blow the whole thing sky-high.

The speeches went on and on, and at a certain point Gavin Riordan knew the moment had passed for a bad confrontation. *Not this time,* he thought. *Thank God, not this time.*

31

Time: 1979–1980
THE MALL

Putnam Herkimer Kennicott looked at the grand-jury subpoena on the desk before him and then at the blank piece of paper in his typewriter.

The historic old house was full of creaks and groans, the night sounds of advancing age. The fire in the stone fireplace built by his great-great-grandfather had long since grown cold. In the light of his desk lamp the old gentleman's portrait looked down at him from above the mantle, a stolid Dutch burgher holding a long curved clay pipe, his eyes stern and uncompromising.

Put Kennocott lifted his hands and began to type.

> I am the last of the line. Little hope for Nan. My daughter's a hopeless cripple. And a drug addict. Am I to blame? I never meant it to be this way. . . . She is coming to dinner tomorrow night. What can I say to her?

*　*　*

He stared at what he had written and sighed deeply. Then he ripped the paper from the machine, crumpled it into the wastebasket and inserted another sheet. He headed it "Notes on the Mall for the Grand-Jury Hearing" and began to type at good speed.

"I told you!" Charlie Bishop said, "I told you the fucking thing would be a nightmare. But no, you had to have it. An' what have you got? Just more fucking trouble than you're ever gonna need. What the hell you think *this* is gonna do to you next election!" Bishop's hand hit the papers in front of him with a loud slap. "It's gonna bury you in shit, that's what! Unless I can think of something an' I don't know what."

The papers on the desk were a preliminary confidential report of the current Mall audit, from one of Charlie's spies in the comptroller's office. Charlie slapped the papers once more in his agitation. "There's stuff in here you could go to jail for if it ever comes out. Yeah, *you*, Stewart! All the fuckin' Gansvoort muscle can't buy out of this one. Because it's gonna hit the press and the networks. The whole fuckin' world! Even *you* can't buy the whole fuckin' world!"

Charlie Bishop was sitting in the visitors' chair next to the governor's desk. Stewart had his back to Charlie, standing at the tall windows, looking out over the expanse of the Mall. Without turning, Stewart said, "You'll think of something, Charlie."

Stewart's bland assurance paralyzed Bishop. He stared at Stewart, who in turn stared out at his creation.

"Look at it," Stewart said. "Isn't it grand? It takes your breath away. Nothing like it anywhere. Ever."

The words brought Charlie up short. Charlie reflected that he was dealing with something with which he was totally familiar— and understood not at all. Over the years he had learned to anticipate and manipulate Stewart's outward actions and reactions. If you pushed the right button *here,* then you got the predictable response *there*. Most of the time. The whys of Stewart were a mystery to him. It was a chancy business, manipulating Stewart, because in his guts Charlie knew that Stewart was not playing with a full deck.

"You know," Stewart said ruminatively, "Cheops built the Great Pyramid, one of the Seven Wonders of the World." He waved a hand at what was spread out before them. "You could put ten of it there. Maybe they'll call it the Eighth Wonder. And they'd be right. It's glorious."

The sun shimmered on the two reflecting pools, just recently filled with water. To their right, running the full length of the Mall, stretched the quarter-mile-long agency building complex, looking like rectangular boxes all in a row. Along both sides of the open platform, workmen were still putting in the landscaping, evergreens and flowering shrubs, impossibly green against the marble flatness of the Plaza. Interspersed with the formal plantings were imposing sculptures, many of which Stewart had purchased with his own money. At the far end of the Plaza a wide graceful flight of steps led up to the cultural center, which housed the museum and library, its multiple stories like flat square pancakes placed one on top of the other.

To the left was the skyscraper Bell Tower. The tall slender structure had a kind of startling immediacy, as though it had sprung up moments before in all its pristine marble whiteness. Almost a feeling of suspended motion, as if it were still quivering and settling after its rise. The thin needle of the Bell Tower itself soared like a rapier, clean and sharp against the sky, and cast a shadow that fell across the shimmering water and sliced the reflecting pools in half.

Again to the left, closer to them, only the squat oyster shape of the Edifice was still incomplete. Its lines were there, in gently flowing curves, its function still mysterious, as though it could open up and disclose some gigantic pearl.

Against the background of industrial smoke, mean, discolored buildings, dim, faded colors of the adjacent City, the Mall seemed to float on its foundations like some Camelot born of Merlin's magic visions.

"A long time ago, a king named Suleiman the Magnificent built such a tower. His people called it the Finger of God." There was awe in Stewart's voice.

"They'll call it shit if you don't pay attention to what I'm trying to tell you, Stewart. Because we're in the shit, good buddy. Deep, deep shit. You got to listen to me. . . ." Charlie was trying to sound reasonable, practical. "Nobody is gonna say you did any stealing yourself. Who's gonna think a thing like that? But you knew about a lot of other people with their hand in the till." He waved toward the report on Stewart's desk. "When that stuff hits the fan, they're gonna scream cover-up, collusion, conspiracy, cronyism, intent to defraud an' a lot of other things that could turn your stomach.

"Jesus Christ, Stewart! It's *two billion dollars* we're talking about! For two billion dollars you could buy Costa Rica! You think they're gonna give you a pat on the ass and send you back in the game? No fuckin' way. We gotta come up with something more than a kiss-me-ass an' a sweet smile, else we're deader than Kelsey's nuts."

"Can't you bury it? The report? Or the comptroller, for that matter." Stewart was still engrossed with the Mall.

Charlie took a deep breath, trying to figure out how to focus Stewart's attention where he wanted it. "The comptroller's elected. So you can't fire him without all sorts of legal horseshit. He is also a man who hates your guts. No way to get rid of him unless he dies from laughing when you fall in the shit. You got to remember you are not the most popular man in town. We hadda put the squeeze on a lot of people along the way. Like elephants, they remember."

Stewart at last turned toward him. There was something curiously chilling in Stewart's smile.

"Charlie, I've never met a man I couldn't break. Or a man I couldn't force to do exactly as I chose. That's what power really means. You once told me that I was an amoral man and that, because of it, I was missing a lot of things in life. You even had the gall to feel sorry for me. Well, Charlie, I don't think I've missed a hell of a lot. I'm not sure the things you *say* I missed even exist."

536

The words were ominous. Charlie had an involuntary shiver and felt the prickle of goosebumps on the back of his neck. Stewart in this mood was something Charlie feared and dreaded: The dark side of Stewart, always so close to the surface, could go out of control without warning.

"Sure, Stewart, you could bust this guy's chops. Easy. But it's just not practical. You deep-six this one an' there's always another. The fucking report won't just go away. No way."

Charlie let Stewart have his thoughtful look. He had had something in mind all along, but he wasn't sure Stewart would go for it. Stewart had to be led. Very gently. "You know," Charlie said, "what we need is a beard, a fall guy, somebody to take the heat. Anybody come to mind?"

Charlie saw that he now had Stewart's attention. He watched Stewart's eyes narrow as he thought about it.

"Several guys would fit. How about your friend Kennicott?"

Charlie knew immediately that he had guessed wrong. Kennicott wasn't who was in Stewart's thoughts.

"Or maybe . . ." Charlie began, and Stewart stopped him.

"Why Kennicott? He's honest if nothing else. How would you pin anything on him?" Stewart was interested now.

Charlie did another about-face. "Why? Because he's out front, is why. It's his office okays the money, sees everybody gets paid. Or paid off. A lot of phoney-baloney goes on in Plans and Services. Contracts and contractors, suppliers, insurance, the whole *schmeer*. You tell me half those guys aren't on the arm, I wouldn't believe it. So maybe we could channel that report his way."

"How?" Stewart persisted. And Charlie knew he was back on track. Stewart had no serious compunctions about sacrificing his friend.

Charlie Bishop allowed himself to grin. "Simple, baby. We wait till the report is about to come out. Then we fire Kennicott and call a press conference. Man, I can hear it now! 'It is with deep sadness . . . Misplaced confidence . . . He had my complete trust . . . I am as shocked as all of you at what this audit has revealed . . . It was I who made the mistake of appointing a man whose credentials seemed impeccable, a man who was my friend. . . .' Maybe you choke up a little here. Maybe the handkerchief. You blow your nose." Charlie wagged his head enthusiastically, warming to his scenario.

"Surely it would take more than a few sniffles to convince them," Stewart said. "They're not complete fools, you know."

"You think so?" Charlie said deadpan. "Well, they coulda fooled me. You won't be trying to *prove* anything, Mr. Governor. Just throw enough shit in their eyes to *confuse* things. Enough shit it could take years to figure out where all that money got to.

"Of course"—Charlie's voice went soft—"when the DA's office finds out about those couple or three hidden bank accounts in the name of Mr. Putnam Kennicott . . . Take a lot of explaining, wouldn't it?"

"That seems a little drastic," Stewart said slowly.

"Why stroke 'em with a feather when you got a meat axe?"

"You sure it would work?"

"Easy, greasy," Charlie said. "Piece of cake. Can't miss."

Stewart made up his mind. "All right," he said. "Do it."

On the way back to his own office, Charlie Bishop had his brief moment of compunction about Putnam Kennicott. It didn't last long. *What the hell,* he thought, *it's them or us. Just like always.*

Charlie had had an alternate for the frame in case he had missed with Kennicott. George Barnstable. Barnstable could have been tailored to fit almost as well. It was the architects who specified materials, everything from steel to toilet bowls. Lot of room there for preferential treatment, bribes, kickbacks and the like. And if there was room, you could be damned sure it had happened a time or two.

But Kennicott was better. A sitting duck. Charlie wasn't at all sure that Stewart would have stood still for chopping George Barnstable. After all, the guy was the girl's uncle. The girl was gone now—and there was something there he didn't know about. And things he didn't know worried Charlie. No, Kennicott was better all around. Best not fool with Barnstable. It wasn't like Stewart to give

538

up on anything he wanted. Charlie was sure they hadn't seen the last of the girl.

Charlie couldn't know how right he was.

The Grand Concourse of the Mall, one level below the Plaza, was scheduled to be opened to the public the following day. George Barnstable was taking a last walk-through along its quarter-mile length. Even without the crowds that would throng it on the morrow, there was a subdued bustle of activity as the various merchants got ready for the big day—bookstores, newsstands, travel agencies, boutiques, food stores and bakeries, cafeterias, restaurants, information booths, everything imaginable for the comfort and convenience of the thousands of state workers who would inhabit the Mall complex. Even with the dozens of businesses spotted along the vast cavernous Concourse, there were, by his own design, spacious areas of wall space, now filled with artwork, most of it by the world's best modern artists.

Barnstable stopped before a massive canvas acrylic that according to the official art collection guidebook he carried, measured ten by sixty feet and was entitled *Sky Train*. The title puzzled him. It seemed unrelated to the subject, which looked to him more like a tubular snake with neither head nor tail. George's membership on the Committee for the Arts was more honorary than practical. Because of the pressure of his own work, he had left the actual task of commissioning and purchasing to Serena Percival and the other distinguished members of her panel. While he himself preferred less contemporary work, he considered Serena had done an excellent job. Serena had surprised him by the seriousness with which she had attacked the job her brother had so casually handed to her. Serena had traveled the world, searching out the best that the world's artists and sculptors had to offer in modern art. The results were quite spectacular, a truly important collection.

George moved on and turned a corner, attracted by the smell of coffee coming from one of the eight cafeterias the Concourse boasted. Alone on the wall just in front of him was one of the few photographic exhibits he had seen. It seemed to be an abstract in black and white, an exaggerated closeup of something textured, the only portion of which he could identify was what looked like a flower in the very middle of it. Another glance at his guidebook told him it was called *Rosebud*. The photographer was anonymous.

His eyes shifted to the framed plaque below the picture, and he read slowly.

> The arts are for everyone. Hence we must constantly seek new ways to explore the potential for human awareness and perception, and so enhance the enjoyment of the world around us.
>
> The eternal confirmation of commitment to hard work, faith, patience, imagination and aesthetic integrity—all those factors that cause the act of creation and assure the survival of human values. The paintings and sculpture in this collection symbolize the spirit of free inquiry and creative integrity that are so vital to modern society—and the duty of governments everywhere to protect and promote the right of the creative individual to live and work in freedom.
>
> This collection of contemporary art makes the Mall a place that is not only an important center for government but also a living gallery for the art of our time. It is a place in which art and architecture work together to bring about an urban environment designed to meet the needs of its citizens. Many of the paintings and sculptures were commissioned and made for a particular site. All were chosen for their ability to stimulate the hearts and minds of the spectator.

Perfectly willing to have either heart or mind stimulated, George stepped back, trying to puzzle out what the photograph was supposed to be saying to him. The mass was a sort of carapace shaped like a helmet, wrinkled in connecting hills and valleys like greatly magnified skin. The skin, if that's what it was, held transparent globules of water droplets. From a graceful ellipse that split the center protruded a tiny, perfectly formed rosebud, its stem disappearing into the elongated aperture.

Intrigued by the composition and puzzled by his inability to figure it out, although the picture seemed to have a certain familiarity, George took two paces backward and cocked his head to one side. "Well, I'll be damned!" George said aloud, and began to grin.

From his new angle what he was seeing was surely a closeup, front view, of the head of a noble penis magnificently engorged. The tiny bud rising from the dewy background of its emission hole had a delicious poignancy, once you realized its symbolism.

"Oh, dear, I didn't think many people would catch on," said a low voice behind him. He turned to find Serena examining the picture over his shoulder, her head on one side, just as his had been.

"I hope you're not going to be stuffy about it. You won't tell on me, will you?" Serena cocked her head the other way. "I'm surprised you figured it out. Most people . . ."

"The trained eye," George said, still grinning. "Although I don't think I've ever seen many from this, ah . . . perspective before."

Still studying the photogograph, Serena appeared to give this some thought.

"Hmmm. I suppose you're right. Men tend to look *down*, don't they? Depends on the angle. Or the sex. Different points of view, so to speak. How about it? You going to yell copper?"

George laughed aloud.

"Never! I'll defend to the death your right to . . . express yourself. If that's what you were doing."

"The whole art project got so *serious*," Serena said plaintively. "Just trying to jolly up the place a bit." She stepped farther back a pace. "I do hope no one will recognize it. It's Gavin, you know. One rainy afternoon at the beach. A long time ago. . . . How is the dear boy?"

There was a certain wistfulness in her question that she was unable to disguise, and George had the quick intuition that she wanted to talk. He had been aware of her relationship with Gavin for a long time. Gavin hadn't taken any particular pains to hide it from him. He had been curious about its lack of resolution, but much too sensitive to question his friend. Then there had been Ericka . . . and Gavin. He hadn't asked questions about that, either. Now, because he liked and respected Serena and felt vaguely sorry for her, he decided to give her what little information he had.

"I was headed for some coffee. Why don't we see what the new restaurant off the Plaza can provide?"

They took the stairs to the platform above. Once in the open, Serena paused and took a deep breath, looking out over the expanse before them. The wind ruffled her dark hair and she tossed her head to bring it back in place. The air was redolent with earth smell and the sweet scent of the newly planted trees and flowering shrubs along the length of the reflecting pools, a promise of springtime fulfilled. It was a day to treasure, bright with sunshine, a breeze that seemed a gentle kiss. A day that would never die, like a dream remembered. Serena shaded her eyes against the light.

"You must be very proud, George. Most big buildings are cold, impersonal. At least to me. But this . . . I think what I feel most is a kind of joy that such beauty exists. That I have the privilege of seeing it. How sad that you've cast your pearls before swine."

"I can't buy that kind of cynicism," George said quietly. "If I had thought that in the beginning, I'd never have attempted it. If I thought it now, I would destroy it. Somehow."

"You'll forgive my arrogance, I hope. I want to keep on feeling it was built just for my enjoyment."

"Whatever you wish. I'm powerless against anyone who sees what you see in the Mall. It's reward enough."

He took her hand and they walked in silence over the inlaid glazed-brick pathway that led to the restaurant. George seated Serena at a table on the window wall that looked out over the Plaza and went off to see if he could promote some coffee from the harried staff, busy with preparations for tomorrow's opening day.

Serena, already regretting the impulse that had led her to accept George's invitation, was surprised to see him run down the steps outside her window. He headed toward a group of workmen who were in the process of transferring a large tree from a flatbed truck to a deep hole waiting to receive it. The tree was suspended from a hoist on the truck. All activity stopped as George arrived with a waving of hands, obviously issuing instructions.

At that moment a shirt-sleeved headwaiter arrived at her table

542

with a large pot of coffee and some tired-looking Danish pastry. By the time Serena had coped with that, George reappeared and sat down beside her.

To her unspoken question, George, who was breathing hard, said disgustedly, "Damn fools know that the hole has to be flooded with water. Otherwise the tree will die. Just too lazy to do it.

"You know, of all the weird things that have happened, those trees are about as ridiculous as any. They were bought way too early because the state thought it was getting a bargain. So the contractor had to store them somewhere else for three years. First thing was that the idiot planted them on property that didn't belong to him. We only heard about that when the owner of the land threatened to chop 'em all down. All thirty-four trees, if we didn't get 'em the hell off his property. Which he had a perfect right to do. It cost the state an arm and a leg to get a temporary lease from him.

"By the time we were ready for them, they'd had three years to grow and were so big there was no earthly way to move them from where they were stored across the river to where we wanted them here. Would you believe we had to *invent* a tree digger big enough to cut 'em out of the ground, bag them and transplant them? I'd hate to tell you how much each of those trees has cost so far.

"To top it all off, a lot of them contracted versicilum wilt somewhere along the way. And unless we can cure that, most of them will probably die."

He shook his head sadly. "One of the more bizarre things that have happened."

"I've heard some of the problems. . . . George, if you had it all to do over again, would you?"

He looked at her as though she were something from another planet, alien to everything he thought or believed.

"I'm sorry," Serena apologized. "Of course you would. It's just that it's hard for a layman to understand. The commitment. The dedication." She waved a hand. "It's magnificent, George. Truly. That kind of creativity is hard to get my head around. I puzzle why it's in some people and not in others."

George was silenced by the impossibility of explaining what he felt about his work and specifically the Mall. He had no words to describe it, not even to himself.

Serena felt something of what he was feeling. "Does it mean so much?" she asked curiously.

"Everything," George said simply. "There isn't anything else."

Serena was pensive. "I wish I could live in a magic garden like yours, George. Things would be so uncomplicated. As it is, I get trapped by traffic tickets, plane reservations, lost baggage . . . and lost loves. Speaking of which, you were going to tell me about Gavin. I haven't seen him in months."

"He's fine," George said, "if fine is harried, overworked, underfed, and overly worried about what's happening in the City—which for some reason he seems to believe is his sole responsibility. He gives the impression that the whole metropolis is about to come crashing down around our ears if somebody doesn't do something about it soon. Specifically your brother Stewart."

"Nothing new," Serena said lightly. "Stewart can be a trial to anybody. Lifetime habit." And then, suddenly serious, "About Ericka . . . what happened? If you can tell me."

George was uncomfortable. "I don't really know. . . . I don't ask questions. . . ."

"And I do? Women's prerogative, George. We do take advantage of our sex, don't we? I shouldn't have asked."

"She's in Tokyo," George said brightly, dissembling because he didn't feel he had the right to tell her what had sent Ericka there.

"Permanently I hope."

There was acid in the words. George ignored it and went determinedly on. "She's doing a library for the University. Fascinating project. You know, the client usually works up a list of what its needs are, relationship between space and usage. It's the architect's job then to reduce that to a physical form—drawings, renderings. That's where Ericka is so good. She's such a damned fine artist. She gave them a lovely idea of what the finished product would look like. They fell all over themselves buying it."

"How nice," Serena said. "And how long?"

"What?"

"How long will she be there?"

"Well . . . I don't really know."

"You're not exactly up to your ass in information, George. Something happened between those two. I'd like to know what the hell it was. It's not just idle curiosity—as you must have guessed."

Nettled and pushed harder than he cared to be, George hit back. "I don't think it's any of my business. Or yours. I don't ask you why you didn't grab him long ago, when you had the chance. Something I've been curious about for a long time. Why didn't you, Serena?"

The question seemed to surprise her. She considered it briefly, looking away from him. "Because I was a snob," she said at last. "Reverse order. I didn't think I was good enough for him."

Book Three

32

Time: THE PRESENT
NAN KENNICOTT

Early in the year, because he felt that it was high time for Stewart to get into the international act, Charlie Bishop let the word go out that Governor Gansvoort was about to embark on a visit to China. Press releases described the trip as an old-fashioned goodwill tour. The idea was received in Washington with something less than enthusiasm. The State Department was careful to point out that there was nothing official in the junket. From the Office of the President, Stewart got a mild pat on the back. What else could they say? After all, goodwill was something in very short supply in the White House.

For local consumption Charlie's PR people came down heavily that the primary purpose of the tour was to promote new business opportunities for Oriental capital to invest in the state and, conversely, to open new avenues for trade between the Far East and the richest state in the Union.

Governor Gansvoort got tremendous publicity mileage out of it, which Charlie kept alive and winging with an avalanche of releases and announcements. Charlie thought it was a hell of an idea. There was even a good chance that it might accomplish its avowed purpose. The Gansvoort influence assured Stewart of meetings with heads of state along the way—the Philippines, Japan and South Korea. All of it was first-class exposure for a man who was already being talked about as a possible candidate for the highest office in the land.

Charlie Bishop didn't make the trip. Reluctantly Charlie decided that it was better for him to stay home and keep the media pot boiling. With only a few misgivings he sent Stewart off, accompanied by a press corps that would have graced a president. With so many eager watchdogs Charlie figured that Stewart would have very little opportunity for chasing skirts. Everything would be before the public eye, high-visibility situations where Stewart was more than able to take care of himself. Before an audience Stewart was a sure winner. His charm and sincerity always came over the boob tube like gangbusters. After all, the trip was scheduled for only sixteen days. So what would happen in sixteen days?

The trip was a resounding success. Charlie watched the satellite film relays with intense satisfaction. Stewart saw all the right people and said all the right things for the folks back home, and he did it with considerable panache. He was photographed at the Great Wall, wined and dined with the chairman, talked to the Man in the Street with wit and grace, held serious conversations with representatives of both science and industry. In short, Stewart was at his very best, and he was being seen on the networks from coast to coast.

As each day went happily by, Charlie knew his man was catching the fancy of the nation. The image was forming, and it was a good one. Charlie began to smell the cherry blossoms along the Potomac. The odor was sweeter than wine and twice as heady.

Until the last day but one of the return leg of the journey.

What happened then was a media event that Charlie couldn't have imagined in his wildest dreams.

In Tokyo, Governor Stewart Gansvoort took to himself a new wife and overnight became the romantic darling of the nation. Possibly the world.

He was married by an Anglican bishop in the small Church of All Souls to Ericka Ullman, famous architect.

The bride was more beautiful than tongue could tell, and Stewart's boyish joy popped out of television screens all over the world like the promise of tomorrow. In a time full of troubles and fraught with perils, the marriage seemed an affirmation that God was still in His heaven after all.

Charlie Bishop was ecstatic. And at the same time apprehensive. To him the bride didn't look quite as happy as the bridegroom. His antennae quivered at the possibility of trouble ahead.

Serena wanted to call Gavin Riordan and thought better of it. Consumed with curiosity, she picked up the phone to call George Barnstable and decided against that, too. She left for Bermuda within two hours of the first broadcast in order to avoid the media, which had already begun to bay at her.

Riordan heard the news on his car radio. He didn't see pictures of the happy couple until much later. From his office he got George Barnstable and found he was equally shocked and bewildered.

"I don't understand it," George said distractedly. "It isn't like her at all. After what happened with him . . . I can't believe that she . . . There must be something more. . . ."

Gavin thought so, too. Something much more. Something very wrong. Something that frightened him. There was nothing he could do about it, so he tried to put it out of his mind. He had troubles of his own. Big troubles. Which were about to become bigger.

The incident that had triggered Riordan's problems had happened two months before. Two officers killed and one seriously wounded by a black militant or militants on a cold, miserable New Year's Eve.

What really happened as joyous bells rang in the New Year would probably never be known. There were twenty-one witnesses to the crime, twenty blacks and one white, the injured patrolman, Gilbert Teague. The testimony varied widely. According to the sworn depositions of four men and one woman who had been absorbing good cheer in the comfort of the Chattanooga Lounge, the officers had engaged in a shootout among themselves. No one from the black community had been involved.

Officer Teague, a twenty-four-year-old rookie on his first beat assignment, dictated his version from a hospital emergency room where interns were still trying to patch him up. His report was clear and concise—up to a point. After that it was strangely detached, lacking any of the heat and emotion one could have expected from someone in great pain who had just been told that he might never walk again because both of his kneecaps had been shattered. The last part of the taped report was couched in police argot, shot through with words like *perpetrator, proceeded forthwith, attempted to restrain* and *apprehended.* It was as impersonal as a hooker's response and sounded as if someone with far more experience than the young officer had fed him the words.

Riordan had both read the transcription and listened to the master tape a dozen times until he thought he could pick the precise point at which someone had started feeding words to Officer Gilbert Teague.

The question was why. Teague's voice was strong and he seemed perfectly capable of functioning coherently on his own, despite the acute pain he must have felt.

Riordan had made his own notes from the accumulated evidence, and it boiled down to this: Young Teague, walking his cold and lonely beat—and probably resenting like hell the year's-end celebration everyone else was enjoying—had come upon a male black (six feet or over, two hundred pounds or more, wearing a black leather jacket) who was committing a public nuisance by pissing all over the door of the Rib Joint restaurant. When Teague asked the man politely (according to Teague) to cease and desist, the man not only became abusive but turned a stream of urine on Teague's leg. Teague, whose intention had not been to arrest but merely to put a stop to what the man was doing (again, according to Teague), then became incensed and rapped the pisser in the stomach with his nightstick. The black man took Teague's stick away from him, knocked him down with it, ran the few paces to the Chattanooga Lounge and disappeared inside. Teague decided that he needed assistance to recover his nightstick, ran to the call box at the corner of Day and Delancy and called his precinct house for help. He waited by the box until the arrival of Officers Toon and Marino in squad car number 201. Teague and Marino then proceeded on foot back to the Chattanooga Lounge while Toon followed in the cruiser. Teague related to Marino what had happened (no verbatim record of this conversation).

When the men arrived, there was a group of blacks—estimated at twenty persons, both male and female—on the sidewalk outside the bar. The man who had fouled Teague's trousers was among them. The crowd seemed in an ugly mood and all three officers drew their weapons. Teague identified the man as the one who had taken his nightstick, and Marino and Toon, both considerably older and more experienced than Teague, charged through the crowd to arrest him. Teague followed more slowly.

It was at this point that Officer Teague was hit on the head by someone he didn't see and was knocked to the ground. He dropped his weapon, but, dazed and bleeding, he managed to crawl to the far side of the police cruiser, away from the action. It was his intention to radio for more help, but he was unable to get to his feet to open the door. It was from this position (flat on his stomach on the street) that Teague watched the ensuing action.

He saw the muzzle flash of a weapon fired by someone in the crowd. (Teague was positive the first shot was *not* fired by either officer.) The bullet hit Marino, who dropped to his knees. Both Marino and Toon fired into the crowd. Toon, slightly ahead of Marino, was hit and fell to the sidewalk. A number of shots were fired almost immediately by both sides. Teague recognized his original assailant. Because of his height, he stood out over the crowd. Teague had the *impression* that this man fired at both officers, although he did not actually see a weapon in the suspect's possession.

By this time Officer Teague had recovered sufficiently to get the door of the cruiser open and radio a 940 B emergency. He was trying to get at the shotgun mounted over the windshield when he was dragged from the car by several men and beaten unconscious.

The further report, from six officers of the Eighth Precinct who answered the emergency call, stated that all three officers were unconscious. The men from the Eighth radioed for an ambulance, and subsequently the three wounded men were rushed to Gansvoort Emergency. Both Toon and Marino were either dead already or succumbed before they could receive medical attention. Teague had no further recollection until he regained consciousness in Emergency.

Sergeant James Delgado of the Eighth stated that there was no man wearing a black leather jacket among the twenty witnesses who were held for questioning, nor were any weapons found other than those of the three officers.

The encounter took place between the hours of 1:40 and 1:55 A.M. on January 1.

Later, as he was being wheeled from the emergency room down the corridor to an operating room, Teague, now fully conscious, saw lying on a gurney the man in the black jacket who had pissed on his pants. Three black men were demanding medical attention for him. Teague called this to the attention of Sergeant Ernest Fessler of the Eighth and made an identification on the spot. The three companions of the suspect claimed that he and they had been there before Teague had been brought in and had been unable to get medical help. Since the suspect had not yet been logged in by the emergency admitting nurse, there was no clear evidence to show exactly *when* he had arrived. Subsequent examination by Dr. Morris Abelman revealed a gunshot wound that had perforated the lower intestine. The suspect claimed to be Abu Talib (a.k.a. Marcus Garvey Hopkins, later confirmed by LAPD, California), former Black Muslim activist and presently national leader of the Black Power movement. Later interrogation (Acting Captain Loomis, Eighth Precinct) established the claim by Hopkins that he had no idea of who shot him. He testified that he had been on Delancy Street on business at Black Power headquarters and, upon emerging from the building, he had heard shots and that he had been hit by a stray bullet. The three men who had brought Hopkins to the hospital stated that Hopkins had been inside the Black Power building from 10:30 until he left, at approximately the time of the shooting.

Despite this, Loomis read Hopkins his rights and placed him under arrest for assault on a police officer (Teague)—with knowledge that he *was* a police officer—and first-degree murder (Toon and Marino, either or both).

Hopkins was at present under detention at Ephesus State Prison Hospital, awaiting trial.

On the last page of the notes, in Riordan's neat hand, was the word *Questions* underlined three times.

*   *   *

1. Autopsy showed bullet that killed Toon entered from *back* and perforated heart. (Three other wounds from front.) Possible that Marino fired that one? Mistake? Or what? (No spent bullet available for ident.)

2. How could Teague have seen what he claimed from flat on his face on the side of the car *away* from the action?

3. The disparities in Teague's testimony. Explain?

4. Why no weapons found? Why the hell did the whole crowd stick around in the first place? Plenty of time to fade out before Eighth arrived. Atypical. Makes no sense.

5. *Three* cartridges fired from weapon Teague *claims* to have lost in scuffle. Why was it left on scene?

6. Why *no* spent shells at site? Except one taken from Hopkins which Ballistics thinks came from Teague's gun. (Ident. only tentative.) *Teague's* gun? Jesus Christ!

7. Hopkins. Place lousy with black leather jackets. No way to establish actual arrival time at ER. Three witnesses' word against Teague's? Teague only ident. Mistaken ident.? Or lying? If so, why? (Subsequent interrogation Int. Affairs unable shake Teague's story.)

8. Why Loomis so fucking quick with charges? No proper investigation? (Loomis real asshole. Permanent hard-on for anyone not Irish. Should have lowered boom on him long ago.)

9. Why Teague's kneecaps? Somebody sending me a message? Who? Leroy Biggs?

At the time it was the last entry that bothered Riordan most. It was too sharp a reminder of things he preferred to forget.

Ten days later a county grand jury returned an indictment against Marcus Garvey Hopkins (a.k.a. Abu Talib) on the original charges filed by Acting Captain Gerald Loomis, felonious assault of Gilbert Teague and the murder of Casey Toon and Rudy Marino.

The jurymen devoted all of thirty-one minutes to their deliberations.

The following day a crusade was launched which spread like a California forest fire. Disparate groups such as Weathermen, Urban Union, Christian Front Force, American Peace Party and Conference of Southern Blacks formed ranks in a drive to protest the arrest of Marcus Hopkins. FREE MARCUS signs sprouted everywhere, lapel buttons, bumper stickers, posters on building fronts and telephone poles. Rallies and protest marches were formed overnight. Slogans were born, black legislators protested. It was a remarkable piece of organization in the short time available, and it got the kind of media coverage Charlie Bishop would have envied.

The trial promised to be a three-ring circus, and although Riordan couldn't imagine anything short of acquittal, in view of the questions that were sure to be raised, he decided the time had come for a talk with Leroy Biggs. The devastating swiftness with which the crusade had built up appalled him and filled him with fear of what the black reaction might become if anything were to go wrong.

Wanting to talk to Leroy and actually getting him on the other end of the wire proved to be two different things. A call to the apartment where he had last seen Biggs revealed that Biggs and his startling girl friend had long since moved. Another try at her business address got the information, in person from Riana, that she had no idea of Biggs's present whereabouts—and the impression that she didn't really give a damn. No curiosity and no apparent interest. So Riordan put out the word to his own people. He wanted Leroy Biggs located—quietly.

At the end of five days Riordan was raging. Negative reports all the way. The network of police informers, which Riordan knew from his own experience had tentacles that reached into every remote corner of the City, was unable to produce what he wanted. The black community seemed to have swallowed Leroy without a trace.

Sergeant Marvin Barry, his driver, seemed to find it amusing.

"Why don't you try an ad in the *Times*?" Barry asked. "Something like, say, 'Baby, won't you please come home. 'Cause your Daddy's all alone . . .'?"

"So what do you suggest?" Riordan said morosely. "I refuse to believe that the whole fucking force can't find one man, who's only wanted for conversation."

"Biggs don't want to be found, you ain't gonna find him." Barry gave it a moment's thought. "Lemme see what I can do."

That same evening, as Riordan was having a drink before turning in at his own apartment, his private line buzzed.

"Hear you been lookin' for me." The deep voice had an amused chuckle in it. "What was it you wanted?"

Riordan was too relieved to be angry. "Help. I want to talk. I'm worried and I need information."

"Sounds sensible." Biggs was cautious. "What about?"

"Don't waltz me, Leroy. You know damn well what about. Can you come over here? Now?"

"Your turf? No way."

"Where, then?"

"How 'bout the Chattanooga Lounge? Nice quiet neighborhood."

"Quit it, Leroy. Goddamn it, just name a place."

"Okay," Biggs agreed. "Rensselaer Park. In half an hour. I'll be the guy with the M-1 rifle. Can't miss it."

"Hey," Riordan stopped him before he could hang up. "Why so hard to get? You're not wanted for anything that I know of."

"Big man now." There was a portentous seriousness in Biggs's voice. "Defense minister of the Black Power Party. Got responsibilities."

"Yeah," Riordan said slowly. "I see what you mean."

The night was heavy with the promise of rain. Garbage choked the gutters and fitful gusts of wind filled the air with dust and litter. Leroy Biggs was waiting for Riordan at the entrance to the small park. He was dressed in worn jeans, leather jacket, black beret, with its unobtrusive red badge, cocked with military precision over one eye.

When he saw Riordan, Biggs turned away down Amherst Street, and Riordan followed fifty feet behind. It went this way for half a dozen blocks before Biggs entered a dingy bar. There was no sign of him when Riordan pushed through the door. He was faced with nothing but black faces, a dozen men lined up along the bar, a dozen more in several booths along the wall. The bartender jerked his head toward a door in the rear wall, and Riordan walked the length of the place, feeling the hostility like a tangible thing.

The room he entered was lit by a single hooded bulb suspended from the ceiling. There were a table and five chairs, nothing more. On the wall in front of him was a king-size version of the famous Huey Newton poster, Huey in a large wicker chair placed on a zebra skin rug, flanked by two tall African shields. In one hand Huey held a slim sharp assagai, in the other a sawed-off shotgun. Huey's baby face scowled convincingly.

"Scares you, don't it." Leroy, seated at the table, waved at the poster. "Kid like that with all that power."

"Yeah," Riordan said. "Good thing they never got really organized, the Black Panthers."

"Different now."

It was a flat statement. Riordan gave himself a moment to think about it. He looked around at the bare room. Curiously the walls were covered with white calendar pop art, willowy blondes, smiling brunettes, slim legs, thrusting, impossibly pneumatic bosoms whose heavily ringed nipples looked back at him sorrowfully like spaniels' eyes.

"What do you mean by that?" asked Gavin.

"I mean they had the right idea. They just never could get it off the ground. Black Power party got it all together now. Up to now, Whitey had all the firepower. Not anymore. Your pigs come into the ghetto kick ass a little, an' your guns are gonna face our guns. Even things up some, won't it."

"You're talking about armed insurrection. A complete contravention of established law and order. You can't get away with that."

Biggs laughed shortly.

"You just won't listen. You just won't believe that every day of the year, an' twice on Sunday, your pigs come down on us, bustin' in doors without warrants, knockin' woolly heads without your due process, backin' cats against the wall for a quick frisk—for no reason except we're there, man. An' we're just animals, after all. Nobody really believes that kids are gettin' shot for stealing a pound of hamburger because they got no money to buy it. No money because they got no jobs, no jobs because no training, no chance to learn anything because their mama don't care and their daddy is long gone, because *he* can't get no jobs in this City. What the hell, they all jes' good-for-nothing niggers anyway. An' who gives a rat's ass.

558

Guns gonna change things, man. Some white motherfuckers gonna get blown away. Then you gotta believe. No other way."

"How in Christ's name do we stop it?"

"No 'we' about it. Strictly up to you, baby. Don't know's I *want* to stop it. Tell you one thing, though: The jury convict Marcus Hopkins an' the lid comes off. Governor got the death penalty back on the books for cop killin', so they convict him, they sure as shit gonna burn him. An' if they do, what is gonna happen here will make the Watts riots look like a Saturday-night barbecue. 'Burn, baby, burn' all over again. Only this time it will be organized like a military operation."

"They *can't* convict. Any good lawyer... Case simply doesn't stand up. What really happened on Delancy Street, Leroy? If you know."

Biggs grinned at him, white teeth gleaming in his handsome face.

"You mean you don't?"

"Come on," Riordan said impatiently.

"Brother pissin' up against a wall. Just standing there like anybody, shakin' the dew off his lily. Your kid pig jerks him around—an' he's right, he did get pissed on. Man can't turn off his pissin' just like that, you know. So your motherfucker raps him with his nightstick, and Hopkins takes it away from him an' raps him back.

"Lotta bad talk starts goin' down about then, pushin' an' shovin', and it draws a crowd. They tryin' to argue this young kid to quit leanin' on Hopkins. Kid gets scared and pulls his gun. Before you know it, the kid shoots Hopkins, holds the crowd with his piece, an' then runs off to the call box. Three of the brothers tote Hopkins off to the hospital. The rest stick around to make sure the rescue squad gets to hear what *really* happened.

"Didn't work out quite like that. Rescue squad comes in like gangbusters, guns out an' all. There's some hard words and one of your pigs fires a shot. Don't know what at. Too late by then, because everybody was bangin' away. No tellin' who offed who. That's about it."

"For Christ's sake! Won't anybody testify?"

Biggs shrugged. "Not likely. They waitin' to see what goes down at the trial. Hopkins gets acquitted, no need to testify as to who *really* did it. Can't say I blame 'em.''

''No,'' Riordan said. ''Understandable. We'll keep looking, you know. How about you, Leroy? What the hell does defense minister mean?''

''Just what it says, man. We're organizing black defense groups to protect ourselves against police brutality and oppression. Since the Second Amendment of the Constitution gives the right to all people to bear arms, that's what we're doing. All black people should arm in their own defense. You got your guns. We got ours.

''Look, man''—Biggs's voice was suddenly taut with suppressed anger—''something's got to give! You know it and I know it. I don't want blood in the streets any more than you—I've seen too much of it. But something's gotta give. You got to *listen*, man, before it's too late!''

''You know I've been trying,'' Riordan said slowly. ''Everything I could think of.''

''I hear. And nothin' gets done.''

''No. Nothing gets done.''

Biggs put both hands flat on the table. ''That's it, then. Nice talkin' to you, Commissioner.''

''Leroy . . .''

Biggs slapped the table sharply. ''That's *it,* man! Forget it.''

Leroy Biggs left the room without looking back. Riordan sat for a moment and then made his way down the long bar past all the closed hostile faces and out into a night as depressing as his meeting had been.

Early on, Nan Kennicott had established a good relationship with Oscar Renata, the manager of the Promenade Française, just off the Mall Plaza. With his instinct for the power structure, Oscar had discreetly determined that the charming woman in the wheelchair was the confidential secretary to the governor, so Oscar went out of his way to accommodate her.

There were three first-class restaurants in the Mall complex, and the Promenade Française was the best. Its location, just off the Plaza, with its shimmering pools surrounded by greenery, gave the diners fortunate enough to rate a window booth a breathtaking view of the whole Mall. The tables on the opposite side looked out over the City and the broad expanse of the river and its traffic.

Nan had merely to wheel herself to the elevator from the governor's suite in the capitol building, down three floors to the Concourse level of the Mall, a hundred-yard journey to the next elevator, up two floors, and the elevator doors opened directly into the restaurant itself. The booth just behind the elevator shaft, her favorite, gave her a sweeping view of the inner Mall.

Of all the thousands of workers and visitors, Nan felt that hers was a special relationship to the Mall. Almost from the time the wreckers swung the first ball against the old buildings of the Pit, Nan had been Stewart's designated liaison with day-to-day progress. She had suffered through all its tribulations, bled with all its wounds, shared each victory, agonized over each defeat.

One benefit of her preoccupation with the Mall had been a developing closeness with her father. For the first time in years their shared interest in the project allowed them to carry on more than polite conversation. Nan discovered that her father was full of unexpected qualities: wit, a wry humor, an unspoken but deeply felt sympathy for the problems he knew she had.

Her one effort to escape with Gavin Riordan's help had ended almost before it had begun. She had found that the life-style she was being asked to give up was in the end preferable to facing up to the harsh realities of going straight—with no friends, no easy retreat into the surcease of drugs, and none of the sex she had come to depend on as her only real contact with her fellow human beings.

To leave all that would take courage she knew she didn't have. It was easier to live from day to day, knowing that she could bring it all to an end anytime she chose with a simple overdose. In the meantime she functioned very well. She had the Mall and her job to fill the days—and who knew what the nights might bring.

Nan had given her order to the always attentive Oscar Renata and was trying to interest herself in a popular novel and finding that thoughts of her father wouldn't go away when a voice she recognized as Charlie Bishop's said, "Kennicott will stand still for it.

561

What the hell's he gonna say? It's a sort of 'Have you stopped beating your wife?' situation. He'll never know what hit him.''

One of the reasons Nan preferred her table in back of the elevator bank was that there, through some quirk of acoustics, one heard anything said in the three booths on the opposite side of the elevator shaft. Even whispers came through as clearly as though the speakers were sitting next to her. She shared the secret with Oscar Renata and would often signal him to join her when anything particularly juicy was in the acoustical pipeline. They had giggled over secretaries' confessions, discovered that the sexual preferences of a prominent lawmaker were for members of his own sex, and on one occasion listened to the sad ending of an affair between a senator and the wife of one of his colleagues—complete with tearful recriminations.

Now, when she heard her father's name, Nan went rigid with alarm. She knew Charlie Bishop very well indeed and distrusted him completely. Charlie was one of the few people who knew of her relationship with Stewart, and he never let her forget it. It was in his eyes every time he looked at her.

The clink of a glass came clearly to her, and then another voice. "He never struck me as a man who would take the boot lying down. Even from Stewart. I've an idea he'll fight back.''

"The guy's a *gentleman*.'' There was contempt in Bishop's voice. "What's he gonna say? That Stewart is deliberately giving him the shitty end of the stick? And if he did, who the hell would believe him?''

"Tell me, Charlie boy.'' The voice was gently amused. "Does your conscience ever trouble you in the long reaches of the night? Ever give a thought to what you'll say when you face your Maker? It would trouble me were I you, as God be thanked I'm not.''

"Well, Jesus,'' Bishop said defensively, "you can't expect *Stewart* to take the heat. Kennicott's as much to blame as anybody. As long as there's got to be a goat—an' you can bet your ass there has to be—why not feed 'em Kennicott? He's tailor-made for it. Have you seen the whole report?''

"Indeed I have.'' The answer was laconic. "It boggles the mind.''

"That's the point. There's enough dynamite in there to rock half the City. How's anybody to know who's responsible? *Really* responsible. Unless you direct all them pointy noses where to look? They find Kennicott, an' who's gonna look any further? Be one hell of a long time before anybody cuts through the shit we can throw up. Maybe never. At least it gets us past the election. An' that's what counts, Des."

"Oh, indeed. You know it, Charlie boy. Who better? No 'Women and children first' for you, is there? Let each man keep a firm eye on his own ass, and the Devil take the rest of 'em."

To Nan's ears Charlie Bishop's chuckle was chillingly evil. "Look who's talkin'. I owe it all to you, Des."

"Hmmm, yes. I suppose you do. It's a thought that troubles me from time to time."

There was only one "Des" to Nan. Desmond Daniher. It couldn't be anyone else. The whole scene began to grow fuzzy in her mind. She was sitting here in this pleasant restaurant, waiting to be served a fruit salad—or was it shrimp? She couldn't really be sure. And these disembodied voices were rattling around in her head like some half-remembered *Late Late Show* peopled with actors whose names were now reduced to trivia quizzes for film buffs. It all had the quality of dreams, which of course would go away when she woke up.

But it wasn't a dream. It was two very real people who were calmly discussing her father's ruin. It couldn't be a dream, because dreams couldn't hurt you, couldn't produce the twisting pain in her stomach that brought cold clammy sweat to her forehead. No, dreams are peaceful. It was reality that was the nightmare.

Nan slid across the leather banquette, manhandled herself into her wheelchair, hoping she could reach the protection of the elevator before she began to scream.

Desmond Daniher, looking up as he wiped his lips, saw her face as she jabbed urgently at the elevator button and wondered what on earth had spooked her.

"Of course I believe you," Putnam Kennicott told his daughter. "I'm appalled that Stewart would deliberately do such a thing. But there's damned little I can do about it. After all, the facts speak for themselves. I *am* to blame. In a way. Oh, there are a million reasons why the whole project disintegrated. It simply fed on itself, got bigger and bigger until it was beyond the power of anybody to stop it. God knows I tried. But nobody really *cared*. All that endless money, and everyone scrambling for a share of it. Nobody wanted to see it end. In hindsight there's a certain inevitability about that." Kennicott shrugged dejectedly. "Well, it's done now."

They were sitting over coffee in Kennicott's study in Putnam House. Nan had been unable to reach her father during the day, so dinner at his house had been her first opportunity to tell him what she had heard. Her afternoon had been a nightmare. She had first thought of facing Stewart with her information, threatening him with . . . what? Exposure of Stewart's secret life? He would have laughed at her. Next she thought of Gavin Riordan, who seemed to have a kind of influence with Stewart and who had continued to be her friend. But what could Gavin really do against Stewart's power? Perhaps if her father were warned, there might be some way he could protect himself. Get his side of the story out in the open before Stewart could . . .

Now, as she watched his tired drawn face, she knew suddenly there was nothing. Nothing at all that anyone could do. And she was devastated by her own guilt. All the devils of what might have been were riding her with bloody spurs. It all went back to what she had allowed to happen so long ago in the boathouse at Riverhaven. If it hadn't been for the bargain with Stewart, then her father would never have gone to work . . . would not be so helpless now.

"Of course, it will all have to come out now," her father was saying. "All the shady dealings, the bribes, the outright stealing—and, most damning of all, the fact that nobody *did* anything about it. I won't be the only casualty, you know. A lot of people will be tarred with the brush. Both the guilty *and* the innocent. That's the tragic part."

"Then there's nothing . . ." Nan heard herself say.

Putnam Kennicott passed a hand wearily over his eyes.

"Nothing. Oh, I suppose I could fight back. Perhaps even bring Stewart down with me. God knows he should share in the guilt. But why? Revenge? It seems a paltry, mean reason. It's somehow . . .

564

offensive to me. Demeaning, really. After all, Stewart is only playing by the rules. As he knows them. As I know them, too. Unfortunately they're not *my* rules. And it's too late to change.''

Nan felt the first twitching of her stomach muscles, the familiar dryness of her mouth that told her that it was time for what she still thought of as her medication. Those lovely calming pills that could float her oh so gently away from reality. Without really thinking, she rummaged in the bag that hung from the arm of her wheelchair, found the small plastic container, shook out a yellow Percodan and washed it down with what remained of her coffee. Twenty minutes to wait for the pleasant unthinking euphoria that would hold her together, at least until she was alone and could take something stronger.

Her father was watching her, and she saw the concern on his tired face, the pity in the single blue eye.

"Are you all right, Nan? Are you still in pain?"

"Headache," she said, "just aspirin," and saw from his face that that wouldn't do.

"I worry, you know. About . . . that." He gestured to her bag, and Nan realized that he knew at least *something* about her narcotics problems. She had a moment of panic that he was about to probe further. She wasn't sure that she could lie to him successfully.

His lone eye held her two eyes steadily. Somehow his single eye held more power, more intensity, than two eyes ever could.

"Don't worry about *me*," she said more sharply than she intended, and was relieved that it stopped whatever it was that he was about to say. She should have known that Putnam Kennicott would never invade anyone else's privacy without permission. "I mean . . . there are a lot worse things to worry about."

He was instantly concerned. "Stewart? This thing shouldn't affect you, you know. It's disgrace, yes, but there's nothing *criminal* in it. I'll weather it in the end."

Her own eyes filled with tears: In the middle of his troubles his thoughts were for her rather than himself. When none of it was *his* fault. Only hers. She was filled with a guilt that overwhelmed her, a terrible conviction of her own worthlessness. If only she could tell him, beg for his forgiveness. . . . But she knew she never could. It would be too cowardly to burden him with confession because she knew he would blame himself rather than her. No, the only thing she could do for him now was to stay silent.

"You know," he said, "I have known it was coming. Although not from Stewart. I put it all down—as I saw it. For the grand jury."

He went to his desk, opened the center drawer, took out a compact sheaf of papers and laid them in her lap.

"It's all there, if you'd care to read it. Not a pretty story. You know most of it. But not, I think, the extent of my involvement. Perhaps you'll understand why I choose not to fight Stewart."

He bowed his back and stretched tiredly with a faint grimace.

"Old bones," he said ruefully, and moved to stand beside her. She felt his hand gently on her head. "Look, my dear, nothing is ever as bad as it seems. In other words, this too shall pass. For both of us. Believe it.

"And now it's time for bed. I'll see you in the morning. Things always seem better then." He leaned as though to kiss her. But he didn't.

She heard his "Goodnight, my dear" and listened as his footsteps took him out of the room. Her eyes were fixed on the desk drawer, which he had left open. She saw the glint of lamplight on the blue steel of the revolver that had been kept in that drawer ever since she could remember.

She sat quietly for a long time before she wheeled herself forward. The weapon felt cold in her hand, and she dropped it quickly into her bag. She wasn't quite sure why she did this, but revolvers could be a solution. At least they had a certain finality about them.

In her old bedroom, which still held all the aids for the handicapped that Stewart had so thoughtfully provided, she prepared a hypodermic and gave herself an injection, secure in the knowledge that there would soon be a welcome oblivion.

33

Time: THE PRESENT. TOKYO
ERICKA

The door was opened by an old woman with steel-gray hair piled high on her head. She was dressed in a heavy silk kimono the color of wood ash. Her black eyes sparkled with interest and intelligence as she took in first Stewart, the American foreignness of him, next the wooden box he held and then the official car behind him on the narrow street.

"Miss Ullman?" the man asked. The woman pressed long, slim fingers together before her breasts and bowed to him.

"Please to come in. Miss Ullman is working." Her voice was thin and reedy. She backed away from him and gestured for him to enter.

He entered a room of waxed paper and bamboo. The glistening floor was partly masked by *tatamis,* the traditional reed mats. The room was furnished with low lacquered tables, flat cushioned stools. There were formal flower arrangements everywhere. Folding screens of exquisite beauty stood before *fusuma,* opaque sliding panels. The woman crossed the floor, opened a silent panel, went through it and closed it after her.

Stewart remained standing, awkwardly holding the package in his arms, feeling a little like a schoolboy bearing a bouquet, waiting for his first date. The feeling brought with it an instant irritation. This was no time for doubts or insecurities. Abruptly he sat down on one of the impossibly delicate stools and placed his box on the mat beside him. He heard voices from somewhere in the house. Words indistinguishable. Then there was silence.

He waited.

He thought of all the years of waiting. What did a few more minutes matter? Because this time he had an offer she couldn't refuse.

It was curious, the hold Ericka Ullman had on him. The only woman he had ever really wanted. And couldn't have. Until now. At first it had been just that. He wanted her because he couldn't have her. He couldn't believe her indifference was real. He was convinced there was some key to her that he was missing, something that would trigger acceptance on her part. He had tried them all: first his own charm, then wealth, power, position, the bribery of gifts, the ultimate bribery of the Mall and with it the chance to reach the very top in the work she loved. He was literally unable to believe that he could fail. His whole life had conditioned him to that.

At first he had unquestioningly accepted that what he felt for her was love, which, until he had met Ericka, had been a stranger to him. It was an emotion new to him. Something other people talked about. What else could it be but love? Now he knew it for something more. It had its elements of anger, resentment, frustration—yes, of hate, to give it its true label. An unreasoning rage that gnawed at his guts like the Spartan fox. At times he wanted to crush her. But more than that he wanted to possess her, to put his mark on her, break down an opposition that was beyond his understanding. It had become over the years an obsession over which he had no control. If he couldn't succeed, it would become a negation of his very manhood, a destruction of Stewart Gansvoort as he saw himself.

It never occurred to him that what he felt bordered on madness, a sickness of the soul as well as of the mind. He knew only that this time, if he failed, there was no choice but to cut off her life, remove permanently an opposition he could no longer tolerate.

He heard footsteps, and the *fusuma* panel slid open. She stood there, arrested like a wary animal poised for flight, her eyes going wide at the sight of him. She was dressed in jeans and a paint-smeared shirt tied at the waist. Her ash-blond hair was pulled

568

straight back, caught in a ponytail by a wisp of ribbon. She looked exquisitely beautiful, and it took his breath away. He fumbled for the bamboo box at his feet, got it open and put its contents on the low table by his stool.

"I brought you this. . . ."

They were both silent, each caught by the beauty of the small figurine. What Stewart's people had found for him was a priceless piece of jade carved by some ancient master in the form of a rearing horse. The animal had the strong heavy hindquarters and impossibly delicate legs, the exaggeratedly large eyes and gaping mouth so typical of Oriental equine art.

"T'ang Dynasty," Stewart said as if by rote, "about a thousand years before Christ. Note the typical oily luster, the pale translucent green of the stone, the exquisite musculature. A famous scholar, T'ang Jung-Tso, said, 'The magic powers of heaven and earth are ever combined to form perfect results. So the pure essence of hill and water became solidified into precious jade. . . .'" He broke off, smiling. "Listen," he said.

He took a small metal hammer from the box and struck the jade horse lightly. The figurine emitted a sound like the sweet ringing of tiny bells, mysterious and wonderful. "It's how you can tell it's the real thing. Lovely, isn't it?"

The music of the bells seemed to hang in the air like a ghostly memory. She moved toward him, and he could tell by her face that his gift was exactly right. It at least had served to get him back into her consciousness, destroyed her indifference. Because no one could be indifferent to the exquisite beauty of the little animal—or its giver. It wasn't forgiveness of things past. But it was a start. He wondered if she would ever forgive what he was about to do to her. And found that he didn't care—as long as he won.

"Sit down, Ericka. There's something I have to tell you." His voice was as emotionless as though he were discussing a business proposition. Which in a way he was. An offer she couldn't refuse. The thought gave him a wry amusement. He watched her seat herself wordlessly on a stool, her eyes still on the jade horse. "It won't come as any surprise to you that I want you to be my wife. I'm asking you again now. I don't think you'll refuse this time."

Now she was looking at him, and he was struck by the fact that the color of her eyes was like the color of the figurine, translucent green and as hard as the stone.

"Because I don't think you could live with the alternative. It's George, you see. Marry me—or George goes down the drain. All the way. Maybe even prison. It's as simple as that. I want you to believe me, Ericka. Because I will do exactly what I say. But I think you know that."

She held up her hand to stop him, using it like a shield between them. Her voice was low and controlled.

"Stewart, you are like a dangerous child deprived of his toys. A child in a man's body. Because something has been left out of you. Some basic human quality that comes to most of us in the process of growing up. You don't have it. Which makes it impossible to reason with you. There's no frame of reference, no *basis* for understanding.

"But you force me to try. You have an unerring instinct for the vulnerable area. You know that George is mine, so you think you can use that knowledge to make me do something that is totally foreign to everything I am. How can I make you see that, even if your blackmail worked, you wouldn't be getting what you think you want? You can't make someone be what she isn't. Especially against their will.

"Give it up, Stewart. It just won't work. I don't want to see George hurt, but I can't believe that he would leave himself open to whatever you're suggesting. George do something criminal? Never."

"Of course not," Stewart said calmly. "But you haven't let me finish. You see, in politics it's the appearance that counts. Not the reality. I think you'd better listen."

She saw that nothing she had said had changed anything for Stewart. She was right. There *was* no frame of reference. No way to get through to that twisted mind that fed only on its own desires, its own needs. She began to be afraid.

"You see, it's like this," Stewart said, and proceeded to lay out

Charlie Bishop's plan to hang the responsibility for the Mall's disasters on Putnam Kennicott.

Which would work just as well to destroy George Barnstable.

The trial of Marcus Garvey Hopkins (a.k.a. Abu Talib) for the murder of Officer Rudy Marino began six weeks to the day after Governor and Mrs. Stewart Stuyvesant Gansvoort returned from an extended honeymoon on the governor's private island off the Georgia coast.

Hopkins was represented by the famous civil-rights lawyer Leonard Harris, whose first move was to ask for the dismissal of the murder charge on the grounds of insufficient evidence. (The charge for the killing of Officer Toon had been dropped because of the autopsy finding that the projectile that killed Toon had come from the rear.) With biting logic Harris drummed home the fact that only the testimony of Officer Gilbert Teague placed Marcus Hopkins at the scene of the crime. At least six other witnesses contradicted this. The prosecution could produce no murder weapon, or any explanation for its absence, and failed to show that Hopkins possessed such a weapon, much less fired any shots. "It's just as reasonable to assume that Marino was killed by his fellow officer as to *assume* that Hopkins did it. The charge itself is merely an assumption, and before the law an *assumption* in no way constitutes proof. In addition," Attorney Harris trumpeted, "the bullet that wounded Hopkins has been tentatively identified as coming from the weapon of Officer Teague—something that cannot be *assumed* away. . . ."

All of Harris's motions for dismissal were denied in succession by the county superior court, the state district court of appeals and the state supreme court. There were last-minute efforts to slow down the unprecedented steamroller speed of the mechanism of the law, all of which failed.

The trial of Marcus Garvey Hopkins, before an all-white jury of his peers (ten men and two women), began on the first Monday of the month of June at eleven A.M., the Honorable Justice Patrick Foyles presiding. The crowds began arriving as early as six A.M. Although the sun had hardly risen, the temperature outside the rococo county courthouse had reached eighty-two degrees.

They came in the hundreds and then in the thousands. By ten-thirty, police estimates reached four thousand. They came on foot, by car, roller skates and bicycle. Mothers with small children, men and women of all ages, they brought their banners, their signs, their loud hailers, and they marched to the sound of tribal chants:

Black is beautiful!
Free Marcus!
Marcus is innocent!
Power to the People!
Off the pigs!

The early comers were predominantly black, but then came those who were looking only for the spectacle. And last came the nigger-haters, the hardhats, white teen-agers braced for trouble.

Police Commissioner Gavin Riordan had detailed only the First Company of his special strike force, with orders to keep a low profile, do nothing to excite the crowd. Unfortunately their shiny white space helmets, spick-and-span uniforms, gave them a high visibility, especially since compact squads of six men each guarded every entrance to the courthouse and nervously ranged the perimeter of the crowd. It was a question of how long these officers could stand the abuse shouted at them from every side. By the noon recess Riordan withdrew half his force and held them in strategic enclaves in the blocks adjacent to Courthouse Square, ready to move in at the first sign of trouble.

It was to be like this for the eleven days the trial lasted. Miraculously there were few incidents, none of them serious. Riordan was beginning to hope that they could get away with it without violence when, at three-thirty on the eleventh day, the jury of ten good men and true (and two women presumably the same) brought in a verdict of guilty of murder in the first degree against Marcus Garvey Hopkins.

Even the complacency of Judge Foyles was outraged. He excoriated the jury with a stinging rebuke, but he had no choice other than to sentence a convicted cop-killer to die in the electric chair.

Legislative Bill No. 431, Section 12, Paragraph 6, as signed into law by Governor Stewart Gansvoort just eight months previously, made the death sentence mandatory.

Attorney Harris immediately appealed the verdict.

Commissioner Riordan moved in his full strike force as soon as he heard the verdict, with orders to stop any demonstrations swiftly and firmly before they could gather steam.

Strangely the crowd didn't react. As the news spread through the packed square there was at first a muffled groan. And then silence, a silence more ominous to Riordan than screams of rape. From his command truck on the hill to the left of the courthouse, he watched his men move in to disperse the people. They went quietly, still in stunned silence, until all that was left in the deserted square was the untidy detritus of four thousand spectators. By six o'clock the Sanitation Department had taken over, and Courthouse Square was once again clean and peaceful under the torrid summer sun.

By that time Riordan was in the statehouse, demanding to see the governor. He intended to ask Stewart Gansvoort for a full and immediate pardon for Marcus Hopkins. In his opinion, waiting for a higher court to throw out the outrageous conviction was an extremely high-risk proposition.

While he cooled his heels in Stewart's outer office, he called his chief executive officer to schedule a meeting of all senior officers later in the evening to put in motion his contingency plan for controlling a major riot, a plan he had worked out in meticulous detail months before.

The governor received him with an outstretched hand that Riordan had to force himself to take. To Riordan's eye Stewart's broad grin held the knowledge of all that had happened between them over the years. Events passed through his mind like a badly edited newsreel filmed by some mad cameraman. And all the time Stewart kept grinning. It was the winner's grin of triumph, with no faintest sympathy for the loser. And it galled Riordan almost beyond endurance.

It didn't help that Stewart rejected his warning with a practiced politician's ease. "Why don't we wait and see what happens?"

Stewart said, as though talking to a precipitous child. Riordan should have known he was wasting his time. Firm courageous decisions were total strangers to the statehouse.

It seemed to him that his Irish gremlins were determined to spare him nothing when, on his way out, he saw Ericka Ullman Gansvoort coming toward him down the long corridor.

She paused and raised a tentative hand, as though to detain him. After his first heart-stopping look, he kept his eyes firmly ahead. They passed each other without speaking.

The media had kept Stewart's romantic marriage before the public during the short honeymoon by press helicopter overflights of the governor's private island. Telephoto lenses captured shots of the happy couple swimming in the warm Gulf Stream waters, fishing from the decks of a cabin cruiser and waving from the sixth green of the nine-hole golf course. The viewers ate it up. And Charlie Bishop saw that there were plenty of backgrounders to feed to doting audiences.

Gavin Riordan soon found he was avoiding both newspapers and television sets whenever possible. The TV coverage of the island where he and Serena had spent their few happy days discovering each other so long ago brought back too many images of tangled bedclothes, slippery bodies, bouts of passion on the hot sands.

Gavin and George Barnstable had a few awkward and unsatisfactory luncheons at which speculations were soon exhausted, leaving them with very little to say to one another.

The return of America's Sweethearts, as the media had dubbed them, produced everything except a ticker tape parade. Charlie Bishop had quietly axed that idea. Nevertheless, *open-armed* was a pale phrase to describe the welcome the City gave its governor and his new bride. It was weeks before the bride's insistence on at least a modicum of privacy caused the story to lose some of its momentum. By the fourth week the couple had settled in at Riverhaven for something resembling a normal life.

Knowing that George Barnstable had seen Ericka a number of times since her return, Gavin had waited with growing impatience for Barnstable to call him with some answers to the questions that plagued them both. But there was no word from Barnstable. In the end Gavin gave in and called George Barnstable.

Barnstable was apologetic. "I'm sorry, Gav. But there was just nothing to say. That you'd want to hear. Unforgivable, not calling. But there's nothing I can tell you. . . ."

"Come on, George. What the hell is that supposed to mean? There's got to be some reason she did it. I can't believe . . ."

"That's just it. Her reasons are her own. It was her decision. I can't argue with that. You can't, either. And, Gavin . . . she seems happy enough. And contented. I'm sorry. I know what she means to you. But there it is. What can I say . . . ?"

Barnstable's obvious sympathy was galling. Gavin said, "Well, fuck it!" and hung up with a bang. Taking his anger out on George wasn't much help. There was no course of action to follow, no decisions to make. The decisions had been made for him.

For a man of action his frustration was intolerable. It seemed to him that he was no longer in command of his own destiny. Circumstances were running him.

He could put Ericka out of his life. He found it impossible to put her out of his mind.

In a way the Marcus Garvey Hopkins affair was a relief. It allowed him little time to think of anything else.

In the wake of Hopkins's shocking conviction, Commissioner Riordan expected an immediate reaction from the black community. He was surprised and uneasy when it didn't come. At first there was nothing. Life in the ghettos seemed to go on much as usual. Arrest reports didn't increase significantly. The number of street incidents, minor clashes between police and individual blacks, seemed more frequent. But that was to be expected in a hot, dry summer.

The groundswell built slowly. In the early stages it seemed to come from outside organizations rather than from the ghetto people themselves. They descended on the City from everywhere—Mothers for Peace, Western Mobilization Against War, Iranian Students Association, Asian-American Political Alliance, Black Muslims, Black Panthers, Black Southern Conference, Right to Lifers and Gay

Liberation people. The cause of Marcus Garvey Hopkins exercised an appeal that for the life of him Riordan couldn't understand. The glaring injustice of it brought the kooks and the crazies together with the legitimate protestors in an uneasy alliance. Posters, placards and bumper stickers proliferated until the City seemed plastered with them. There were committees calling on the mayor and the governor. Street rallies were frequent but surprisingly peaceful. In short it seemed that the community had somehow decided that the ridiculous miscarriage of justice would soon be righted. Even the Establishment could be brought to see the logic of that. All it needed was a little prodding.

Riordan didn't believe it for a minute. It was against the nature of the beast. And Riordan knew what the beast could do once it was aroused.

His first move was to take twenty black cops out of uniform and send them into the streets for a firsthand report. The results were puzzling. The ghetto did indeed seem calm, although street corner talk was about little else but Marcus Hopkins. Resentment against Whitey was as strong as ever, but that was nothing new.

Riordan's black driver, Sergeant Barry, showed his apprehension.

"I don't parade around in my uniform down there," Barry said. "Take it off before I go home. Black or white look the same in blue. Folks got a real hard-on for a badge. You better hope it don't get hotter. Heat gonna angry-up the blood—an' something's gonna give. I can feel it in my bones."

Riordan had trained and prepared his riot control unit as best he could on a woefully inadequate budget. But he knew the preparation was rudimentary compared to, say, the superbly trained Japanese police or the Paris Guardiens de la Paix, with their motto of "Force applied with speed and vigor." Riordan's men had never really seen the real thing, never been tested under fire. There was no knowing how they would perform in a crisis.

He began to long for the expertise of the Paris riot battalions, with their disciplined cohesion, their matchless communications systems, which permitted each unit to be patched into the others as well as to the command control. Riordan's patrol cars couldn't talk to each other except by relay through the central police switchboard. When instant communications could be vital, his antiquated system was about as useful as a hooped skirt. The shortcomings of his troops filled him with foreboding. He felt he was sitting on some sort of time bomb that any small incident could explode.

The incident was so small that at first no one recognized it for what it was.

Reverend Cecil Weems's First Baptist Church of the Ascension held its yearly carnival and street fair, to raise money for black charities, in Anthony Wayne Park. One side of the park was still residential: neat, well-kept federal structures that had once housed the City's well-to-do middle class now sheltered affluent black families. The other three sides were strictly ghetto. Most of the year the park was controlled by street gangs, which considered it their private turf. The third week in August was the exception—carnival time. The carnival consisted of a short midway housing the usual fortune-tellers, fat ladies, Jo-Jo the Elephant Boy, the sword swallower, various games of dubious chance, shooting galleries and like attractions. At the end of the midway, in a baseball diamond long since denuded of its grass, were a number of sleazy rides, Dodgems, a creaking Ferris wheel and the ubiquitous fun house. There were hot dogs and hamburgers, candy apples, corn on the cob and fried pork skin, beer and soda pop and ice cream. No hard liquor, in deference to the sponsors, but there were three package stores within easy walking distance. There were bare-chested young bloods on the make for nubile girls in hotpants and halters or loose summer dresses. Children ran everywhere, chasing each other, throwing foodstuffs—and the occasional stone—screaming their delight.

Commissioner Riordan briefly considered banning the affair. Gatherings of more than three people represented a clear and present danger to him under the present tensions. Then he decided a cancellation might trigger the very thing he feared. He put the first two companies of his riot force on standby alert and ordered the third to establish a staging area in an empty lot three blocks away from the park itself.

If things had worked as planned, there would have been ten squad cars, a hundred police officers equipped with tear gas and protective

577

riot gear, as well as the pumper from the nearest firehouse—all ready to move in within minutes.

As it happened, the order to set up the staging area got lost in the bureaucratic shuffle at police headquarters, and as a consequence the carnival was covered only by the routine patrol that had sufficed in past years—eight uniformed footsloggers and a pair of two-man cruisers.

By five-thirty in the afternoon the temperature in the park had reached ninety-four degrees. The late sun beat down with a merciless glare on the bare tan dirt of the ballfield. Around the park, people sweltered on stoops, sat on curbstones, illegally opened fire hydrants and generally sweated and bitched about the weather. The mood of the crowd was mellow. Everybody was out and having a good time. The elders of the church were happily anticipating a record take. Even the presence of the cops was tolerated.

At five-thirty-four, according to the report of Probationary Officer Eugene Butts, an altercation started between a large black male (six foot one, two hundred and ten pounds, medium Afro, cutoff jeans, red tennis shoes, heavy medallion on gold chain, knife scar on left breast) and the white proprietor of one of the games along the Midway.

The black man claimed he had been cheated. Officer Butts, some distance away, saw the black pick up his smaller opponent, turn him upside down and begin to shake the loose change and bills from the man's pockets. The incident had its humor and drew a small crowd, which shouted good-natured encouragement. Up to this time the attitude of the crowd was still festive, and as Officer Butts arrived on the scene, his sympathies were with the black man, not only because he himself was black, but because he knew the reputation of games of chance. The suckers were seldom allowed to win. Butts felt he had things in control, and the incident might have passed for what it was, a one-on-one argument easily settled.

Unfortunately the carny people didn't see it that way. Roustabouts carrying tent stakes and pinch bars quickly surrounded the combatants, and before Officer Butts could react, someone laid a tent stake alongside the black man's head. His roar of rage surmounted the wheeze of calliope music and turned heads a hundred yards away.

578

The crowd instantly lost its festive air and became alert, with the wariness of a jungle animal that smells the hunters. For a long pregnant moment all sound seemed to cease—except for the tinny beat of the calliope.

Car number 116, manned by Officers Tatum and Principe, forced its way down the Midway through the press of bodies to come to the assistance of Officer Butts. The ominously silent crowd watched tensely as the three officers arrested both combatants and forced them into the rear section of the squad car. Butts remained on the scene as the cruiser made its slow way toward one of the park exits.

The incident might have ended there, except that someone (Butts was under the impression that it was a small boy) threw a pop bottle, which shattered against the rear window of the car.

The sound of that explosion seemed to trigger another explosion. The crowd, so peaceful moments before, found its own release. Tensions, which had lain just under the surface for so long, erupted with shocking, mindless violence.

They proceeded to destroy the carnival. The cry of "Burn, baby, burn" was heard for the first time. Within an hour the carnival was a raging inferno. Dried out and brittle from the drought, most of the trees and shrubbery of Anthony Wayne Park went up with it. An unexpected breeze sprang off the river and helped the fire to spread. The beautiful old federal houses, now full of black families who had made it up the ladder, were the first to go.

That was the first night of the riots. Despite the headquarters foul-up that had allowed the whole thing to get the jump on Riordan's people, his full task force was deployed within forty minutes of the first alarms, and by four in the morning Riordan felt that, barring something unforeseen, he had the thing under control, at least temporarily. There were still fires burning in parts of the ghetto, and sporadic incidents of looting, but the mob had had a long day, and people began to want some sleep.

Back in his office Riordan picked up the phone to report to the command post that had been established in the governor's office in the capitol building. He got Charlie Bishop on the other end of the line. He could hear the babble of voices in the background and was thankful that not he, but Charlie, had the chore of handling the press.

"You mean it's really over?" Charlie sounded harried.

"How the hell do I know?" Riordan snapped, and then wearily, "I think so, Charlie. At least the worst of it. I'm waiting for damage and casualty reports now. It'll be awhile. But I think we were lucky. This time. If something new doesn't start it up again. If the fucking TV crews don't rile 'em up again—we've had to rescue two units already. If nobody does anything stupid. If that bastard Stewart will get off his ass and *do* something. Lot of ifs, Charlie. And it doesn't give me a hell of a lot of pleasure to say I told you so."

"Stay in touch, Gav," Charlie pleaded. "I need all you can give me—for the press."

"Tell 'em to go home, Charlie. If we're lucky, things are buttoned up. At least for tonight."

Riordan hung up, left his desk to go to the leather couch on the far side of his office. He wanted to rest his aching back, but in moments he was asleep.

In the governor's suite, where the outer rooms had been turned into an impromptu press headquarters during the long night, the reporters dispersed slowly. By four-thirty most of them had left. Charlie Bishop was passing out the last of the free liquor from the office supply and distributing the final press releases his staff in the next room had prepared. Down the hall the formal conference room, where the television crews were wrapping it up for the night, was still a mass of snakelike cables and mobile cameras. Most of the equipment would stay in place for the early meeting Charlie had scheduled for the governor.

"No more until morning," Charlie said loudly. "Soon as we get damage reports the governor will have a statement. Why don't you bastards go home. The booze has run out, anyway."

They wouldn't go home, of course. Most of them would spend what was left of the night in the official press room on the floor below, raiding the coffee and sandwich machines, waiting for late-breaking news. But at least Stewart's private suite would be cleared, and the endless questions would stop for a few hours.

580

Charlie was eager to get rid of the crowd and join Stewart. He had a lot of straight-talking to do to his governor. Gavin Riordan and the night's violence had at last made a believer out of Charlie. Something had to be done. And fast.

Stewart, tieless and in his shirt-sleeves, was seated at his desk, dictating a memo to Nan Kennicott, when Charlie finally got free. There was a drink in his hand and one on the edge of the desk for Nan. The only outsider left was Colonel Roger Macklin, the deputy commander of the state National Guard. He, too, had a drink, which he finished as Charlie entered. Colonel Macklin had stayed glued to Stewart's elbow during the all-night vigil. He had a battalion of the Guard on full alert twelve miles up the river, and Bishop had had a hard time restraining him. Macklin was a gung-ho warrior and had wanted to move his troops in early on to maintain order and "break a few woolly heads," as he put it. Riordan had threatened to resign on the spot if Stewart permitted it.

"That's it, Colonel," Bishop said more briskly than he felt. "Looks like it's all buttoned up for the night. You and your boys can go home now. Come on, I'll see you to the elevator. We could all use some sleep."

The colonel put down his empty glass. Charlie took him firmly by the arm and steered him through the door, overcoming the colonel's obvious desire to say something more about the situation.

Left alone, Nan closed her steno pad and sighed wearily. "It's a long way down the hall. Mind if I use your private facilities?"

"Be my guest." Stewart watched her wheel herself through the oak door into the corner room, which held both toilet facilities and the sauna that he had had installed in his first term. When she had gone, he went to stand at the window looking out over the City.

Isolated fires were still burning in the ghetto, but the frantic sounds of fire engines and police sirens had stopped. Things did indeed seem under control. Stewart was a prey to mixed feelings. The night's action had produced a strange exhilaration in him. He felt a little as Nero must have felt watching Rome burn, and at the same time he was filled with an unreasoning anger that *they* should have dared to try to destroy *his* City. He had wanted badly to let Colonel Macklin have his way. And more than break a few heads.

He wanted retaliation, punishment, a punishment to fit the crime. Charlie Bishop would never know how close he had come to letting Macklin loose. The thought of the kind of force Macklin would have used filled him with a savage joy. The rioting bastards deserved everything Macklin would have given them.

Below Stewart's window the Mall Plaza was deserted, lit now only by small spotlight lamps cleverly concealed in the shrubbery that flanked the walk around the reflecting pool—just enough to show a late-night stroller his way along the mosaic paths. The huge searchlights at the corners of the Plaza had been dark now for several years, victims of the energy shortage. Once they had thrown their powerful beams upward to bathe the Bell Tower and its companion structures in stark beauty. The Mall at night had been a never-ending delight to Stewart, and he bitterly resented the public pressures that had forced him to darken the searchlights.

Now, in each building, only the utility floors were lit at night, rings of light that graced each structure like necklaces of jewels. Those, and the lights needed by the cleaning force that moved from floor to floor from darkness to dawn, so that the Mall buildings were ever-changing, light patterns never the same.

Some vaguely remembered line from the Bible found its way into Stewart's head: "And the Lord looked on what he had made, and found it good. . . ."

It *was* good. In a way he, Stewart Gansvoort, was the Lord, for he had created it.

Beyond the Mall, down the hill near the waterfront, flames suddenly flared, sending a shower of sparks upward, lighting up the sky for a moment, and as quickly gone.

"Burn it, you bastards!" Stewart whispered. "Burn it all! And I'll build it up again. In my own image."

The mental picture of the whole ugly City going up in smoke and flame, consuming the quick and the dead alike, gave him a stab of sensual pleasure. He felt the beginning of an erection, and that brought the thought of Nan Kennicott in his private bathroom with its adjacent sauna, which was always kept ready for him at the proper temperature. Nan Kennicott and the hot lazy release of the sauna. Why not? Charlie would know enough not to interrupt when he returned.

Stewart crossed the room quickly and pushed through the bathroom door without bothering to knock.

Nan had reached the end of her tether. Her pills had got her through the long night with less and less efficiency. Now she was swallowing the last of them, longing for the safety of her apartment, where she could take something stronger to produce the oblivion that had been her refuge since she had learned what Stewart planned to do to her father. She had passed the days since then in a trance. Her daytime job she did by rote, the nights she could block out with drugs. The object was not to think, because thinking meant the onslaught of guilt. Drugs, alcohol and guilt were causing a dangerous depression in Nan, which she hadn't the will or the character to combat. She knew only that living had become a burden, not living infinitely more appealing. She was beginning to think of ways. Not an overdose. They would think an overdose could be a mistake. Something more meaningful. A positive protest to tell them her act was deliberate, an expiation for her sins.

She still kept her father's revolver in the carryall hanging from the arm of her wheelchair. She wondered if she'd ever have the courage to use it.

Stewart was smiling as he came through the door, already unbuttoning his shirt.

"How about a sauna, baby? I think we could both use one right now. Relax the muscles and ease the mind. Come on, I'll help you get out of your braces."

Nan said the thing uppermost in her mind. "Stewart, you can't do that to Put. You can't hurt him like that. It isn't fair. . . ."

Stewart dropped his shirt and stared at her. "Who the hell told you about that?"

"It doesn't matter. But I do know. You've got to stop it."

"Come on, baby," Stewart said impatiently. "If you know, then you know it's just politics. The way the game is played. Somebody always has to take the blame when things go wrong. But don't

583

worry. Put will be all right when it's all over. Nothing will happen to him. I'll see to that.''

Stewart unzipped his trousers and stepped out of them, his erection already pushing at his shorts. "Come on, lift that beautiful ass so I can slide off your slacks. I need you, baby. Right now. We'll talk about the other later.''

It had a sick familiarity for Nan. Stewart was once again offering to deal. "First let's get laid, then we'll take care of your father's problems.'' Why not? It had become so easy with time, to do what Stewart wanted.

With no will of her own, she did as she was told. She let him remove her pants and held herself away from the seat of the wheelchair while he unstrapped her braces and pushed them aside. She didn't help him as he unbuttoned her blouse, unclasped her brassiere, until she sat naked, the metal of the chair cold against her skin.

Stewart lifted her in his arms, carried her in and sat her down on the bare plank bench against the wall. The heat from the steaming stones in their squat container hit her like a fist. It was hard to breathe, and her chest labored in the heavy air, her breasts rising and falling with effort.

Stewart stood before her, legs spread, his penis like a club. It pulsed before her face, the head with its Cyclops's eye already tearing. Slowly she reached for him.

At that precise instant Nan's mind rebelled.

Stewart screamed in agony and instinctively tried to jerk away, then hit her jaw with all the outraged force he could muster. The blow knocked her off her perch, and as she fell her outflung arm came in contact with the red-hot stones of the heating container. The pain was instant and excruciating.

It was Nan's screaming that Charlie Bishop heard as he returned from seeing Colonel Macklin off. Bishop burst into the bathroom and pushed open the door of the sauna. Nan was crouched in a corner, cradling one arm with the other, still screaming. Stewart was bent over, holding himself with cupped hands, saying "You bitch! You bitch!'' over and over again.

"Jesus!'' Charlie said. "What happened?''

"She *bit* me! The bitch bit me! Get her out of here! Get rid of her!" His voice was hoarse with pain. "Get her out—before I kill her!"

Still holding himself, Stewart brushed past him, and instants later Bishop heard water running into the hand-basin in the bathroom.

Charlie was already sweating from the heat of the sauna; he could feel the rivulets running down his back. He went toward Nan, wondering how the hell to get her up and into her clothes. When he touched her she began to swear at him, mindless obscenities pouring out of her in a repetitious stream. He got behind her, hooked his hands under her arms and dragged her out into the other room. Stewart was at the washbasin, running cold water on his lacerated member.

"Get her dressed and get rid of her," Stewart grated. "And keep her away from me. I never want to see the bitch again."

Nan had stopped screaming now. She sat propped up on her hands, legs extended while Charlie slid her into her slacks and then got her into her shirt. He didn't bother with panties, bra or braces, piling these in her lap when at last he lifted her into the wheelchair. She made no sound except to moan once when the shirt scraped against her burned arm. Stewart, on the other hand, let his pain be known in a series of groans and the whistling of his breath through clenched teeth as he bathed his groin.

"I'll go now," Nan said slowly. "I'm all right now."

Charlie looked at her closely. Her eyes were dull and lifeless, pupils unnaturally dilated, but otherwise she seemed to have recovered. "I'll see you down to your car," Charlie said doubtfully. And then to Stewart, "You need a doctor? Or what?"

"Christ, no!" Stewart snarled. "Just get her out of here."

Charlie wheeled her across Stewart's office to the small concealed private elevator installed during the Harding administration to give the governor a secret way in and out.

On the street, when he got her to her car, Nan said, "I'm all right. I can make it from here. You can leave me now."

"You sure?"

When she nodded he left her.

Nan waited until the sound of his footsteps died away. Then she began to wheel herself around the corner of the statehouse. She was heading for the Mall, which had become so much a part of her life. It seemed a fitting place for what she had at last made up her mind to do.

She reached the ramp beside the shallow steps that led down to the Plaza and, using her brakes, let herself slowly down. The ramp was part of the new attention to the needs of the handicapped, part of Barnstable's concept of a Mall for everyone's use. Nan was the most regular beneficiary.

It was dim beside the reflecting pool. The night-lights concealed in the shrubbery cast shimmering patterns across the placid expanse of water. Enough light for her to get a clear look at the revolver she took from her carryall. She had to be sure she knew exactly how it worked. After she had reassured herself that there was nothing complicated about the mechanism, that all she need do was pull the trigger, she sat there looking about her at the beauty of the place she had come to love—a last long look. After all, there was no hurry. How long does it take to pull a trigger?

There was a simple first-aid kit behind the bathroom mirror, containing sterile gauze pads and adhesive tape. Stewart had covered his lacerations with one of the pads and was holding it in place with one hand. He thrust the container of adhesive tape at Charlie Bishop.

"Either hold the fucking pad in place," Stewart snarled, "or put the fucking tape around it. I can't, for Christ's sake, do both."

Charlie, who had a certain reluctance about handling Stewart's pecker, said, "I'll tape it. Lift it up so's I can get at it."

Gingerly Stewart lifted his penis and Charlie awkwardly passed a strip of tape around the pad.

"Jesus! Not so tight. Goddamnit, that hurts."

"Sorry," Charlie mumbled. "Maybe you need a doctor after all."

"What I need is a drink. As soon as I can get my pants on." Stewart pulled up his pants, not bothering with his shorts, and carefully settled his injured member. The gauze pad made a noticeable lump in the light tropical slacks.

Charlie did the honors. Stewart took his drink and went to stand by the window. Standing was less painful than sitting down.

586

"Seriously," Charlie said, "you should really see a doctor. Suppose it got infected?"

"Jesus! You're a big help."

"Well, it could happen." Charlie said. "Lots of germs on teeth. The human bite is supposed to be the dirtiest..."

"Goddamnit. Quit it, Charlie. Quit sounding like you were enjoying it."

Looking down at the reflecting pool, Stewart saw on the pathway a puzzling stationary object that shouldn't be there at this time of night. After a moment he realized that it was Nan Kennicott in her wheelchair.

"What the hell is that crazy bitch doing down there?"

Charlie moved to his side and looked down at the tiny woman in the tiny wheelchair. "I left her by her car. I thought she was headed for home."

"Well, what's she doing down there?"

"How the hell would I know?"

As they watched, another figure started down the steps to the Plaza. It was a woman who walked idly down the path toward Nan Kennicott. The woman hesitated as though she had just discovered another presence and then went slowly on and finally stopped beside the wheelchair.

"By God," Stewart said wonderingly, "that's my wife! What the hell is going on?"

Charlie was silent. The combination of the two women spelled nothing but trouble to him.

"Well, I'll damned well find out!" Stewart walked awkwardly, legs well apart, toward the private elevator and pressed the call button.

"I think I'll sit this one out," Charlie said softly. Stewart didn't seem to hear him.

The ancient cage, whose performance was erratic at best, picked that time to cease functioning. So they had to walk down the hall, wait for the night operator to bring up the main elevator, then talk their way past the night guard at the main entrance.

On the deserted street Charlie took a deep breath of clean air, which had at last lost some of its oppressive heat. He felt unbearably weary. "You sure it was Ericka?"

Stewart answered him with a withering look. Charlie began to relent.

"You want me to go with you?"

"Go home, Charlie. I'll take care of this myself."

"Well . . ." Charlie said uncertainly. He watched Stewart limp off.

So it was a good fifteen minutes before Stewart reached the head of the steps leading to the Plaza. The two women were still there, and Stewart made his way crabwise down the steps, wincing in pain as he moved, his anger increasing at every step.

"I know it's none of my business," Serena said, "and you'll undoubtedly tell me so. But I've kept myself from asking for the last two weeks. And there's a limit. It's obvious to me, at least, you don't love him. So why the hell did you marry him?"

"No, I don't love him."

Ericka stopped there, and Serena sighed. "Well, if you won't talk, you won't. Knowing my dear brother, it's my guess he had you where the hair is short. I hope you got what you wanted out of him. And that it's worth it. From what I see, it's not exactly a marriage made in heaven."

"I thought I had. . . ." Ericka said slowly. "Now I'm not so sure."

Serena waited for more and, when she decided that it wasn't coming, turned back to the TV set.

"My God! Look at that!"

The sound was turned down to a murmur, but the picture was surely more graphic than a thousand words. Two policemen, looking like something out of *Star Wars* in their riot gear, were mercilessly beating a young black man with nightsticks. The blood streaming down the man's face glinted in the red light from nearby burning buildings. As they watched, the camera suddenly tilted, its image crazily upside down, and then the screen went momentarily dark. It came to life again on the professionally cool face of a studio announcer.

"Turn it up," Serena said, and when Ericka twisted the volume control, the rich voice came through: "Units of the Guard are on full alert. So far the governor has refused to call them in. The worst of the violence seems to have subsided. So far, we are told, there have been at least four deaths, all of them looters. There has been no official casualty report as yet, but Gansvoort Hospital, in the heart of the ghetto, has been swamped with the wounded. Other hospitals, farther from the rioting, are reporting gravely strained facilities. We take you to Gansvoort now, where our reporter is standing by. . . ."

Ericka reached forward and turned off the set.

"I picked a hell of a time to come home, didn't I," Serena said.

Ericka didn't answer. She moved to the window and stood looking out across the river. The red glare of burning buildings cast flickering shadows on her pale composed face. Too composed, Serena thought. Ericka had aged. There were new faint lines at the corners of her mouth, deeper shadows that served only to accent the remarkable green eyes. She was strung out like a wire—a wire that could snap at any moment. Her tension communicated itself and made Serena decidedly uncomfortable, a little like living under a volcano, waiting for it to explode. Serena was staying at Riverhaven only because her own duplex in the City was being repainted. Two more days before she could move in. She looked forward to it with relief.

But because she felt a strong sympathy for this troubled woman who was holding on to herself with such rigid control, Serena decided to give it one more try. For whatever her reasons, Ericka had got herself into something she obviously regretted. Perhaps if she could let Ericka know that there was at least one other person who was aware of exactly what kind of person Stewart was . . . Well, it might help. Just to know there was a sympathetic and understanding ear around if needed.

"You know," Serena said slowly, "there's not much excuse for Stewart. But there *is* a sort of explanation. I think you ought to hear it."

Ericka didn't turn, but Serena saw the slight stiffening of her shoulders. Was it because she didn't want to hear? Resented Serena's meddling? *What the hell*, Serena thought. *I'm stoned. I might as well finish it.*

"It's hard for anyone to understand what a terrifying temptation it

589

is to be able to buy anything you want. *Anything*—from people to whole countries. Small ones, of course.

"Most of the rich never discover the full extent of this kind of power or, if they do, are unwilling to use it. Because even rich kids usually have the kind of childhood and teen-agery where there are built-in constraints—the opinions of their peers, or their parents, or maybe teachers.

"Stewart missed out on all that. For a lot of reasons. He really doesn't understand the limits and controls most people are brought up to impose upon themselves. Parents? Forget it. He never met a teacher who could guide him. He had no religion, no moral preceptor. Stewart was impressed by nothing, influenced by nothing. Certainly not people, because he found out early on that anyone could be bought, or at least bent, if the price was right. Certainly not morality. He once told me that moral precepts were something dreamed up by authority to protect itself from the mob.

"Let's face it. There's nothing *inside* Stewart to prevent him from doing exactly what he wants. A lot of people can get hurt that way. I just hope you're not one of them."

There was no response from the woman by the window. Serena sighed and gave it up.

"I should have gone to a hotel." Serena's thought came out unexpectedly. "The silence around here is oppressive. I feel like I want to break something. Just to hear the crash. Look, honey, I wish I could do something to help. I hate to see dumb animals suffer. But you don't give me much chance. So what the hell, I think I'll go to bed. It's been one hell of a long night."

Ericka turned her head. "I'm sorry, Serena. It's something I have to work out for myself. And your being here *has* been . . . a help. I'm glad you came home."

"Thanks for nothing," Serena said. "I'd never have guessed. Well, I'll see you in the morning."

Left alone, Ericka drifted restlessly about the room, absently touching things, moving small objects, rearranging. It *had* been a long night, the two of them watching the appalling violence that swept the City just across the river. And yet she wasn't tired. She was filled with a kind of electric tension, as though each muscle

590

were controlled by an unseen dynamo. She was faced with a problem that had no solution and yet had to be solved. Her marriage to Stewart had to end. And if it did, it all had been for nothing. . . .

In the beginning Ericka had honestly tried to keep her bargain with Stewart. She had given a lot of thought to what Stewart wanted of her, tried to apply logic and reasonableness to a situation she felt she had no choice but to accept. First she must conquer her outrage, sublimate her anger. After all, she was by no means the first woman to enter into a loveless marriage contract. Throughout all history there were countless millions of women in the same position, and there would be millions more. Sex was easy, a mechanical thing. She could respond to a man, any attractive man. And if she couldn't, then she could fake it. Again she was not alone. How many more millions of women did the same.

But beyond sex, Stewart wanted a possession, something he could control and manipulate. She found that harder but not insurmountable. As long as she could anticipate him, stay one jump ahead of Stewart's mind, she found she could do considerable manipulating herself. At first it became a kind of game and had its own satisfactions.

The real difficulty was that Stewart wanted to be loved. Stewart's version of love was something peculiar to Stewart and beyond her capacity to understand. That was something she couldn't fake. And Stewart had found it out soon enough.

Stewart crossed, Stewart denied something he felt he had bought and paid for, was frighteningly different from anything she could have imagined. Stewart's resentment took the form of cruelty, the desire to hurt both physically and mentally. His lovemaking turned violent and kinky. He demanded the kind of sex from her she wasn't prepared to give, because it seemed to be designed only to hurt and humiliate. Each sexual encounter turned into a kind of rape, the one thing she couldn't stomach.

By the time they returned from the honeymoon, which for Ericka had ended in something close to nightmare, she was cringing at his touch. Yet she put up with it for two long months on the theory that the human being could stand anything as long as the reasons were strong enough. But she couldn't hide what she felt from Stewart. His finely tuned intuition where she was concerned told him that his bargain had gone sour. He divined that she had come to hate his attentions. It seemed to give him pleasure to push his lovemaking to its limits, as though he were trying to find just how much of his demands she could take, what it would take to break her.

Her innate honesty forced her to make one last appeal to Stewart's reason. In an effort to save something from the disaster, she told him that she couldn't and wouldn't be a wife to him anymore, trying to make him understand that sex not freely given couldn't possibly satisfy his needs. She offered, for the sake of his career, to keep up the pretense of marriage for as long as he wanted—if he would spare George Barnstable.

Stewart laughed at her.

In that chilling laugh, and in Stewart's hot excited eyes, she saw that what she had said merely confirmed what he had known for some time. And that in his perverse way he was enjoying the situation. He had no slightest intention of letting her out of what he considered her obligations as his wife—any of them.

That same day she moved her things into one of the guest suites, one that seemed to have an adequate lock on its door. It was false security. Stewart had duplicate keys. The first she knew of his presence was when he pulled down the sheet that covered her, lifted her nightgown and forced his naked body between her legs. It wasn't exactly rape, because after her first frightened struggles, she didn't resist him. She lay inert with a curious detachment while Stewart pumped away at her body. She was thinking that whatever traumas rape had held for her were surely gone now. She felt none of the terror, the outrage, she would have expected, because she knew that she had only herself to blame for what was happening to her. She had made a decision she now realized was unforgivably, stupidly arrogant. How could she have been so blindly naive as to think that she could control another human being? Especially Stewart, who played by his own rules and in another social stratum might well have been certifiably mad.

Stewart reached his climax and slowly left her body. He stood looking down at her. Her legs were still apart; she hadn't bothered to move them. She was conscious of her own wetness. It surprised her that she should be wet under the circumstances.

"Indifference won't work, you know," Stewart said tightly. "There are lots of ways to stimulate reaction. We'll try some next time."

"There won't be any 'next time.' I'm leaving you, Stewart."

"I think not." Stewart's tone was coldly matter-of-fact. "I'll see you dead first."

She realized with the beginnings of real terror that Stewart was capable of doing exactly what he said.

The next day Serena arrived, and she was temporarily safe with Serena in the house. She could put off any decisions until she could figure out how to protect herself. From a man who wielded limitless power and who, she now knew without any doubt, was truly insane. Serena would soon leave to move back into her own apartment, so there wasn't much time. Despite her lack of response, she had listened carefully to what Serena had said. It confirmed everything she herself had come to see in Stewart. But explanations didn't help. There was still the *fact* of Stewart. And explanations wouldn't take it away.

Ericka found herself standing by the window again. The fires were beginning to die down now. As she watched, the moon came briefly through a break in the smoke pall that hung over the City. For a few seconds moonlight bathed the tall Bell Tower in silver. Suddenly Ericka felt she had to get out of this house she so hated and immerse herself in the clean beauty of the thing George Barnstable had created. She slipped quietly through the front door and made her way to the garage.

In the fifteen minutes it had taken Stewart to get from his office to the Mall Plaza, Ericka had learned the full extent of what Stewart had done to Nan and to her. The monstrousness of Stewart's plotting had left her in a state bordering on shock.

As she had approached Nan's wheelchair, she had seen Nan raise a revolver to her temple. There was no mistaking her intention. Ericka covered the last few steps between them at a run. She hadn't wanted to shout for fear of startling Nan into pulling the trigger.

"Don't," she said, hoping her voice was calm and controlled. She reached out and gently pushed the gun away from Nan's head, exerting only the slightest pressure. She didn't try to take it away. It was a squat and evil-looking thing. It clinked against the metal of the braces that lay across Nan's knees.

"You mustn't, you know. Nothing can be that bad."

"Yes, it can." Nan spoke like a petulant child. Her eyes were huge, hurt and bewildered. There was no surprise in her recognition of Ericka, no questioning. "You must know what he is. You're married to him."

"Stewart? What . . . ?"

There was a sudden hope in Nan's wide eyes. "You can stop him, Ericka." Her free hand reached out, hesitant as a sleepwalker's, to take hold of Ericka's arm. "Oh, please, Ericka. Make him stop. Please, please . . ."

"Tell me," Ericka said slowly. "Tell me. . . ."

It came out disjointedly. Some of it made no sense to Ericka, but there was enough. As the careless cruelty of Stewart's manipulating began to sink in, Ericka was gripped by an anger so deep that it set up an almost uncontrollable trembling in her muscles. Her breath was shallow, and there was a lightness in her head, as though she were on the verge of fainting.

"Old-home week?" There was a biting edge to Stewart's voice behind her. "You two cutting up the carcass?"

Stewart moved awkwardly around the wheelchair and saw immediately the gun Nan held loosely in her lap. "Here, give me that." Stewart wanted no suicides on his personal doorstep. He reached for the weapon. His hand closed over the stubby barrel.

There was just enough tension in Nan's grip to make Stewart's grab miss its purpose. The gun seemed to leap in the air to fall between them. Stewart was bending over, trying to catch it, when the revolver hit the mosaic walk, butt first, and exploded.

The slug entered Stewart's chest and came out his back. Ericka saw the exit hole and the bloody flecks on Stewart's white shirt in the instant before he jerked upright. Stewart's mouth was open, the surprise on his face almost comical.

Stewart staggered back. The low wall that surrounded the reflecting pool caught him just behind the knees and tipped him over into the shallow water.

"Jesus!" Stewart said. He put one hand behind him and sat up, blood now staining the front of his shirt.

"Help me," Stewart said, and held out his free hand. Ericka picked up the revolver and fired it point blank into Stewart's body. The impact turned him around so that he was facedown in the water. He convulsed once and then was still.

The sound of the shot seemed to echo forever.

After a moment Ericka placed the gun back in Nan's lap, and again it clinked against her braces.

"We'd better go. . . ." She wanted only to be somewhere else. Anywhere. To get away from the obscene thing in the pool. "They'll want to talk to us, you know. We'll have to tell them. . . . But not here. Not here. . . ."

"No," Nan said in her child's voice. "I love it here. When the sun comes up. I come here often when the sun comes up. It's the very best time." Her eyes were cloudy, seeing something far away. She seemed unaware that anything had happened. After a moment Ericka left her there.

There was nothing she could do for either of them.

34

Time: THE AFTERMATH
GAVIN FRANCIS RIORDAN

> Take counsel, execute judgment; make thy shadow as the night
> in the midst of the noonday. . . . In mercy shall the throne be
> established: And he shall sit upon it in truth.
>
> *Isaiah XVI: 3, 5*

Nan Kennicott's recital of her history and of the events by the
reflecting pool that morning had somehow for the first time made
Gavin Riordan fully aware of the sheer viciousness of Stewart
Stuyvesant Gansvoort. He had known Nan's story, or most of it, and
only the details of Stewart's death had come as a surprise—that
Ericka was involved surely had not—yet it had shocked Gavin, and
he couldn't think why. That Nan should have to present it to her
father, perhaps.

Gavin sat now in the back of his official car, traveling through the
devastated area between Gansvoort Hospital and his office. The
conviction was growing in him that the riots had burned themselves
out for now, that it might be weeks or even a year before the
pressure would build again to the point of explosion. For their one
night so far, this had been the most violent and destructive he had
ever seen or heard of; worse than Watts, worse than Detroit, worse
than Miami.

There were, of course, conscious forces working here, unlike all those other outbursts; Leroy Biggs and his people might be able to keep them going a night longer than their natural force would ordinarily sustain. But there seemed to be a natural law at work in these things: When a certain amount of rage had been vented, depression set in. Gavin thought that point had been reached last night.

The issue remained, of course. Marcus Garvey Hopkins, a.k.a. Abu Talib, was still in jail, still convicted. But the issue was never the issue in the final analysis; it was only the trigger. Riots of this kind, Gavin had learned, were utterly unlike the consciously directed, politically motivated upheavals he had learned to deal with in Paris.

The force driving the destruction was old and it was huge and it would express itself soon or late. It wasn't ideology, it was plain rage. It might remain quiescent as sullen resentment for years, but it would inevitably develop into uncontainable fury. It was anger and it was justified. Not the results, the destruction, the killing—Gavin Riordan was profoundly offended by disorder so total. But the anger was justified, the grievances were real, and the infuriating arrogant stupidity of this people's governors—and not only the office holders, not only Stewart Gansvoort and his predecessors, but also, Gavin realized with angry regret, also Desmond Daniher and his minions. The blindness was almost as enraging to Gavin as it was to its victims.

Still, if Ten Tabard's precious "Force applied with speed and vigor" would have been effective, Gavin would have used it; his job was his job, and in any case he was as much offended by the disorder as outraged by its causes. But it would have been a cork only, and what was needed was a valve—for the moment; for the long run, a banking of the fires of grievance.

So, for now, let them riot.

It was a decision that astounded Gavin as he heard himself make it in his mind. Let them riot.

His orders would be for his men to be present where they could, to protect as much of life as they could, and even some property, if that was also possible. But it would have to blow itself out: Gavin

Riordan could not relieve the pressure from below and he would not put a stopper on it from above.

And anyway, the worst was over. The appeals process would proceed for Hopkins/Talib, respectable opinion would express itself in newspaper editorials and television commentary—it would deplore the rioting, but it would also deplore Hopkins's conviction—and calm would descend.

It would, that is, if Leroy Biggs and his force could be defused somehow. Gavin thought they could be. The killing of Stewart Gansvoort would not be a matter of indifference to Leroy; Leroy would see that for the moment at least Gavin Riordan was The Man. *For the moment and,* Gavin realized with a profound shock, *for as long as I choose.*

The car was now a block from police headquarters. Gavin suddenly said to his driver, "Sergeant Barry, hold it." He saw Barry's alert brown eyes in the rearview mirror, questioning. "We're going to Riverhaven," Gavin said, not knowing precisely why, but knowing there were questions more pressing than those about the riots, and that Riverhaven was where the answers were.

The limousine's siren made a belching sound as Barry made a sudden turn against traffic and then fell silent again as the car moved smoothly toward its real destination. It would retrace its path, past Gansvoort Hospital, through the Pit—through areas of devastation as terrible as those Gavin had lived in after the war in Europe. Too much of the Pit looked that way before the riot, for sure, but last night the wasteland had claimed much more ground.

But Gavin Riordan scarcely saw it anymore. What he saw was the Mall; what his mind was fixed on was Stewart Gansvoort. And Ericka.

Nan Kennicott's story had horrified Gavin so profoundly, he recognized finally, because of Ericka. Stewart had made Ericka a killer.

There was that in Gavin that knew that she had been a killer before, in Paris. She had been driven to it then, as she surely had been this time. This was as surely self-defense as that had been, and at the same time it was just as surely vengeance.

And it had, then as now, left her as cold and unrepentant as a Mafia hit man.

As Gavin could once coldly blast kneecaps, Ericka could kill. Yet there was a difference: Gavin had long since come to feel horror at his ruthless younger self. That capacity was lost in Ericka. It tore at his heart to know it, but it could not be denied: Something vitally human had been destroyed in Ericka, and George and Melinda Barnstable had not been able to replace it. They had never known it was gone.

Stewart had found that cold, empty space in her and exposed it, and Gavin hated him for it.

She had not, of course, killed Stewart really. The doctor had been clear about that: Either wound was fatal alone. But Nan's recollections seemed crystalline, and according to her, Stewart was not dead when Ericka picked up the pistol and fired the second bullet into his body.

She had believed she was killing him.

Ericka was a killer. Not only because she was capable of killing in extreme situations; she was not so rare in that. But because she did it coldly, matter-of-factly, when it suited her.

Ericka was a killer and Gavin was a policeman.

Ericka was a Gansvoort, and the Gansvoorts had always had those around them whose job it was to clean up after them. Gavin Riordan, though it enraged him to know it, had been one of those at times.

Ericka was Ericka, and Gavin had loved and wanted her beyond all else in the world.

Desmond Daniher's gray fedora sat firmly in its accustomed place on Des's head. Daniher sat at the scarred, massive old desk that had served him since his days as a young attorney—it had been second-hand when he acquired it. He sat in a tall swivel chair whose leather was cracked; it was not as old as the desk, but it was old and it knew Des Daniher's buttocks in their subtlest contours. Its back had rarely felt Des's back; Des worked in this chair, he did not lounge.

He sat forward now, his chin cradled in his right hand, right elbow on the desk; his left hand stretched toward the telephone, but rested just short of it. The desk and chair were not in the big office–sitting room in which he received petitioners but in the den just off it. It was his real workplace, and it had seen little of Des Daniher in recent months—indeed, it had begun to see less of him soon after the ascension of Stewart Gansvoort. He thought now that he might be spending more time there.

He was surprised at the memory of how invigorating a place this was to him. It was a serious place in a way that the luxurious receiving room was not, quite. The work he did out there was serious, to be sure—the listening and talking, mediating, conciliating, occasionally the bullying, the laying down of the law according to Daniher. But something attached to this place, this sanctum, of his work as an attorney seemed to him to be more serious still. Here he accomplished things himself. For himself and by himself. Though God knew he could do nothing without his telephone.

He had now made today's necessary calls, just two. He had left a message for Gavin Riordan. He had reached Charlie Bishop, surprisingly, at his home number. Always the last place to try for Charlie, and especially, Des would have thought, today. The call to Charlie was to express condolences, but really to take Charlie's pulse. Des had expected Charlie to be short of his feisty best, but Charlie had sounded shockingly bad. Sullen drunk, to begin with, lost and frightened. Far worse than Des had expected.

Charlie had better be given a little time and some bolstering. His unresistant cooperation would be required, but so would a modicum of alertness and that charade of toughness Charlie was capable of.

If anything at all was to be salvaged from this mess, if Des Daniher was to have anything to say about what rushed into the vacuum Stewart had left behind, Charlie Bishop would have to call in some very large favors. It galled Des to know it, but Charlie owned more of them now than Des did.

What do they call that nasty little fish that attaches itself to a shark? And what happens to it when its host is dead? Does it grieve unto death? Not very likely. It might be lost momentarily, but another great and powerful swimmer will presently come into view. It gave Des Daniher no pleasure at all to know that Charlie Bishop was in large measure Daniher's creature. *What*, he had thought more than once since Charlie had attached himself to Stewart Gansvoort, *what have I set loose on the world? Not just Charlie but Stewart Gansvoort himself.*

Pilot fish, Des thought, associating them with Charlie's relationship with Stewart. *Charlie was Stewart's pilot, and those nasty little creatures are called pilot fish. Well, this one must be put to use for a time again. But this time I'll know better than to allow him swimming room of his own. This time, when I'm finished with him, he's finished.*

Des was waiting for a telephone call that he knew would come soon, now. It would be Gavin Riordan. No other call would pass Meg O'Day. Not even the cardinal, whom Meg had unhappily put off once today already.

Des would return the cardinal's call, and soon, but not just yet. The stream of power had been catastrophically confused in its flow this morning, and it was Desmond Daniher's hope that it might very soon return to its old, secure bed; the cardinal, then, would once again be further from its channel than would Des Daniher. The cardinal was not, because of his position, which Des genuinely revered, to be slighted and in any event was not to be trifled with, because he was no fool and by no means lacking in the skill and the will to wield the power he did have.

So his call would be returned, but not just yet. Which of them needed the other more was still to be determined. It would be determined by the telephone call Des was now expecting. Or, more likely, by a face-to-face meeting with Gavin just a bit later in the day. For Gavin (though if Des knew him, he wouldn't yet be aware of it) was now suddenly the master of sharks in this ocean. What Gavin Riordan meant to do would decide just where the power would flow.

And what would be done with it. For Daniher, in spite of his reputation, did not love power for its own sake. He wanted his city to be liveable, and not only for himself and his Irish. Des did not blame Stewart Gansvoort alone for the decline of the quality of life in his city; Des himself had made mistakes, had failed to take some people seriously enough.

Cecil Weems was pompous, stentorian, arrogant in his unforgiveness of those who had gone before him, callow in his refusal to allow for what was genuinely possible and what was not—he was all of this, but he was not frivolous and he was by no means without substance. And there must be others among the blacks. Some of them must be accommodated, given a voice of some sort.

The blacks who had succeeded in Des's organization fell into two groups: faithful retainers, ward pluggers who had been from time to time rewarded with positions of visibility but little power; and flamboyant figureheads who had lined their own pockets all the while they were charming their constituents with panache. It was no longer enough.

Gavin could be made to see that. Gavin's political instincts were those of a policeman, not those of a politician, and he would have to be led to some extent. He would likely have to be told that he held the power at the moment and then be guided to place it where it belonged.

What would Gavin do? It was apparent from the news reports that Stewart had not been assassinated but murdered: It was personal, not political. Nan Kennicott, the crippled girl, was there. Charlie Bishop, with sardonic, half-hysterical laughter, had seemed to hint that Stewart's new wife was involved. Ericka. The woman Gavin had so long been involved with in one way or another. An architect involved with the Mall. That tumor, that cancer on Des Daniher's state.

Nan Kennicott was the daughter of the man Stewart had evidently thrown to the wolves—or to the grand jury at least—over the Mall corruption. But she was also private secretary, or some-such, to the governor. Charlie had hinted that she was more some-such than secretary. Des shook his head.

Des Daniher was not used to knowing only what the public knew. He knew, in fact, considerably more of this case than the public, but not nearly enough.

What would Gavin do? What he had always done was clean up. That was his policeman's reflex, for one thing, but then it was his relationship with the Gansvoorts as well. *He won't want to clean this one up,* Des thought, *and I don't believe he will. Though if Ericka's involved . . .*

602

Gavin could be mayor of this City, in time; not a position of maximum power, the way the state and City were constituted—the state government's vastly larger taxing authority made the governor the real power, even in the City. Perhaps he could even be governor—but Des Daniher would not, he thought with a pang of real regret, live to see that. There was much that Des wouldn't live to see.

It occurred to him now, though, that he had not felt even a touch of that closeness in his chest that had become his increasingly constant companion. Not once since Connie McGurn had burst into his reception room with this morning's news.

Des glared at the telephone. He was not used to waiting long for a return telephone call. It had happened with increasing regularity in recent years, and he had come almost to accept it. But not today. And never, he thought, again.

Serena stood in the door of Ericka's studio, looking in at Ericka with a kind of uneasy awe. Ericka sat at a drafting table on a high stool, studied a thick report, made notes on foolscap with a draftsman's pencil. Business as usual? Or putting her affairs in order?

"Ericka?"

Ericka nodded and raised her left index finger to acknowledge Serena's presence, but went on writing on her yellow pad.

When Ericka finished her note and raised her head to look up calmly, Serena went on. "I've been watching television. Nothing on but news, you know. Some about the riots, but mostly about Stewart. Retrospectives of his career. Cut down at the apex, that sort of thing. But they are becoming downright peevish about the lack of solid information about his death."

Ericka had no reaction at all. Serena went on, "He was shot twice, they know that. Nan Kennicott was there, but there was no evidence that the gun was fired by Nan. There was someone else there, they seem to think. A woman."

Ericka's expression did not change.

"Ericka—Ericka, God*damn*it, there *will* be an accounting. Gavin can't just pretend nothing happened at the Mall this morning, and he can't just let Nan . . . take the rap. Even if he wanted to."

"I know, Serena. It doesn't matter."

603

"It doesn't—" Serena took a deep breath. "Look, Ericka, if there were a God in heaven, there would be no retribution—there'd probably be a reward—for stamping out Stewart. There is scarcely anyone on earth whose death would so improve the world. There's no telling what damage won't be done because he's gone once and for all. But there is no God, there's only cops and reporters and judges and juries."

"It doesn't matter, Serena. Stewart's death was an accident. Nan was going to shoot herself. Stewart and I attempted to stop her."

Serena stared at her. It could actually be true, of course. But it wasn't credible, nevertheless. "Gavin won't buy that."

Ericka nodded, still as calm as if they were discussing an excuse to stand up a lunch date. "He will. He'll want to and he'll be able to."

"He won't, but let that pass. The press won't."

Ericka's eyebrows rose just a little. She was faintly surprised, perhaps even a touch amused, that Serena would think that mattered. *Good God,* Serena thought, *she is a Gansvoort . . . no. That's her own. She had that always.*

"Serena, look," Ericka brought herself to say, "I'm sorry about all this. Stewart was a beast, but I am not blameless, and I'm not as indifferent to that fact as I might seem. I . . . I even suspect that you're not as indifferent to your brother's death as you pretend, and I'm sorry for that, too. But . . ."—she shook her head—"I am going to go on with George's work. Gavin will help me—us—because Gavin is Gavin. I'll—I suppose I'll do at least some of what's expected of me in public. And soon it'll be over, and life will go on."

Serena found to her surprise that there was indeed a tiny seed of sorrow in herself for Stewart. For his life, though, not for his death. "So," she said, "you do have feelings. Rather faint ones, not intolerably intense, luckily, but still . . . Or was that just a speech?"

Ericka didn't answer.

A houseman appeared then and announced Gavin at the gate.

"Bring him to Mrs. Gansvoort, please, Brooks," Serena instructed him. "And see that he stops by my room before he leaves."

* * *

Serena's room was actually a considerable apartment, of course. Not only bedroom, sitting room, dressing room, but a gallery-library and even a solarium and porch.

Gavin found her in the sitting room looking, uncharacteristically, every inch the lady—dressed and made up conservatively, strikingly beautiful.

She rose and came to him, kissed his cheek, held his hand. "Come sit down, Gavin. Would you like some tea?"

Gavin looked bone weary, eyes haggard. When could he have slept last? And angry. Coldly angry. She could see that in the millimeter's tilt of his chin. "How was the widow?" she said.

"Serena, I haven't time. Is there something—?"

"Gavin, she . . . there isn't much there, is there?" She spoke sympathetically.

He let out a great breath.

"Will the riots go on? The news people seem to think so."

He shook his head. "There's no telling for certain, but I don't think so, at least not at the same level, not for long." He sat down at last. "I will have some tea. Plain."

She smiled almost undetectably and did not say, don't you suppose I remember? She poured and handed him the cup.

He sipped and some of the tension seemed to leave his body. He allowed the chair to feel comfortable to him. "No," he said, "there isn't much there." This was a new Serena to him. He had known several, and none of them prepared him for this lady. This lady of the house, in fact. She seemed for the first time to belong there.

What was this? Did she have some sense of succession? Had Stewart's death made her grow up suddenly, made her the reigning Gansvoort?

He shook his head slowly, remembering where he was and when, and what was expected of him outside this great house. He glanced at a window, as if expecting to see ravening hordes of reporters, policemen, politicians.

Serena said, "There've been dozens of calls for you here. A Sergeant Macy first, but then the mayor, the lieutenant governor, two network anchormen, the *Times*, *Time*, *Newsweek*, others. Mr.

Kaplan, the DA, several times." She looked at a little table beside her, on which rested a pile of small slips of formal notepaper.

Gavin wondered at the serenity of this place. No telephones were jangling, there was no running about and shouting; yet those calls must still be coming in. He nodded. "Brooks told me as he was showing me in." He sipped his tea and did not move.

"What will you do, Gavin?"

"She didn't kill him."

She didn't look startled, but as if to answer his silent question about how completely transformed she was, she said, "Bullshit."

He smiled momentarily, in spite of himself. "No, it's true. It actually was an accident."

She looked hard at him. "Gavin, I don't suppose that you're a fool, but neither am I. I've talked to her. She didn't say to me that she'd shot him, but her manner, her . . . Gavin, I am not mistaken. She killed him. Are you lying to me for some reason?"

He shook his head. "She probably does think she killed him. She did shoot him. But he was already dead. Shot through the heart by accident, taking the gun from Nan."

Gavin found the irony monstrous, insupportable. It gave him no relief. If Ericka had fired the first shot, he'd have had no decision to make. He'd simply have delivered her to the prosecutor. That would sear his soul, but scarcely more than his knowledge that she was a killer already did.

He was no philosopher, and he suspected that a philosopher would find the distinction trivial: Ericka had believed that she was shooting a living man. Yet, the fact that Stewart would be no more alive if she had never fired at all gave him, or so it felt, a choice: He could, without utterly destroying his sense of himself, either accuse her of homicide or accept her version of the story and put an end to it.

He did not doubt that he could, by calling on Des Daniher and Charlie Bishop to pressure the appropriate coroners and prosecutors, put a reasonably clean end to it.

"You have a choice to make, then," Serena said. "If she had actually killed him you'd have had no choice, but now you have."

Gavin was startled. It was as if his mind had just been read. "You know me very well," he said.

She nodded. "I do. What will you do, Gavin?"

"You tell me."

After a thoughtful pause she said, "All right. I'll try. If you arrest her, present Nan's version. . . ."

"Which happens to be the truth."

"Yes. If you arrest Ericka and present that to the district attorney, you'll have done your job as a policeman. . . ."

"Serena, that's the first time you've ever admitted that I've been a policeman."

"What?"

"Oh, yes. I've been your lover, or a Gansvoort family retainer, or a *potential* something—I've never been sure what—*dressed up* as a policeman for some eccentric reason of my own, or *serving time* as a policeman until I come to my senses. You've never referred to me as a policeman before, except sarcastically."

"Well. In any case. You'll have—yes, very well, you're right. So you'll have done your job as a policeman and won't have played God. Which there's been intolerably too much of. You're a fastidious man, Gavin, and that would be the fastidious thing to do. Clean hands."

She doesn't know me quite as well as she thinks, Gavin thought with some satisfaction. "Sounds as though you wouldn't approve," he said.

Ignoring that, she went on. "There would probably be a trial, though not necessarily. Can there be enough real evidence to indict, or arraign, or whatever it is? Still, it would be a public issue for months. Shot by his wife in the presence of another woman. The whole cesspool of Stewart's filthy leavings would be uncovered. God alone knows how many showgirls and cocktail waitresses would get book contracts. And there's a certain rough justice in that, isn't there? It's only a shame Stewart wouldn't be around to breathe his own stink."

Gavin finished his tea and nodded.

"Whereas," Serena continued, "if you quash it . . . there'd still be a mess. Coroner's inquest or whatever—grand jury? There'd be no trial, surely. There'd be editorials about Mall corruption, though, just the same. Stewart's name would still be tainted, but just a little human-after-all kind of thing. Some always did say he was overbearing. They'll crow, but not too loud, now he's dead. Died preventing a suicide. Cut off at the apex. Not everyone will buy it, but everyone never does. There'll be gossip, but hell, there already is.

"So it'll be over soon and life will go on."

Gavin nodded. "And which way will I choose?"

"That depends on whether you really are a policeman after all, or a . . . governor."

Gavin's eyes rose a little, and Serena smiled.

"I mean whether you mean to police, or whether you mean to govern, to run things. If you want to run things, you want Stewart dead and gone, once and for all, now."

Gavin smiled a little. "Is Stewart's secretary in?"

Serena nodded. "Do you want to use his office?" But without waiting for an answer, she picked up the pile of phone messages, rose with Gavin and took his arm. They walked together to the mansion's south wing.

They walked through an outer office, where a young man and a young woman sat at desks, listening to telephones, writing messages. In the next office Miss Ann Schuyler sat at a desk rather grander than Gavin's in the commissioner's office. She said "Just a moment" into her phone and peremptorily punched the hold button. "Mr. Riordan," she said.

"Miss Schuyler, get this message to my driver, outside: Tell him to set up a meeting with Leroy Biggs. Wherever he likes, but today. Then let's make some calls."

The little buzzer on Des Daniher's telephone sounded at last. Not much of a wait, he noted with satisfaction. He began to speak as he raised the reciever to his ear. "Gavin, me boy—"

"Just a moment for Mr. Riordan, please," said a businesslike woman's voice, and Des was at once off-balance. Meg O'Day didn't often lose one of those "put him on" tussles.

"Hello, Des."

"Gavin, thank you for calling—"

608

"Des, where's Charlie Bishop?" But he did not wait for an answer. "I want some leaning done. I want you to do it, but unless I'm mistaken, you'll need Bishop's help for the time being. That's up to you, but I want it done. I want this business of Stewart's death cleaned up. Now." He paused.

"Well, Gavin. Suppose you tell me what happened, and we'll see what's to be done with it." Des was stalling for time, to sort out just what was happening here to Desmond Patrick Daniher.

"I'll tell you what happened, Des, and I'll tell you what's to be done with it. Then we'll discuss some other matters of mutual interest. Can the mayor be beaten next fall?"

"He can be beaten if we want him beaten, but, Gavin, he's ours." *My God, does he want it so soon?*

"He's a miserable, useless hack, Des. He'll be happier out to pasture. Could Cecil Weems be induced to run?"

That took Des's breath away. "The Reverend Cecil Lovewell *Weems?*"

There was a moment's silence. It sounded to Des like impatient silence. Recovering, he asked, "What do you have in mind, Gavin?"

"I have in mind making this goddamned state and this goddamned city run, Des. Now, are you going to help me?"

Des Daniher sighed. *Another thing I am not used to*, he thought, *is impatient silences. He can bloody well wait for me to stew a minute.*

"Des," Gavin said finally, in a voice of infinite gentleness.

By God! Des thought, *I'm being patronized!*

"Des, we'll make it run together, you and I. Get Bishop or whoever you need to get Stewart's shit covered up so it'll finally stop fouling the air."

"Gavin . . . what happened at the Mall, Gavin? And what's to be done with it?"

Serena had left Gavin in the governor's office, but she stopped by Miss Schuyler's desk, from where she could hear his voice through the door she'd left open. After a moment she nodded, said softly to no one, "I believe he's ready," and walked away.

Bestsellers from
WARNER BOOKS

___**CELEBRITY**
by Thomas Thompson   *(A30-238, $3.95, U.S.A.)*
                                (A30-660, $4.95, Canada)
They were princes...the royalty of their 1950 high school
graduating class—three promising young men who were,
without a doubt, most likely to succeed. And they did succeed. In films, in journalism and in charismatic religion,
they reached that dazzling, dangerous pinnacle called
CELEBRITY...only to be haunted by memories of a dark
night of violence and a shared secret guilt that could destroy them all.

___**RAGE OF ANGELS**
by Sidney Sheldon   *(A36-214, $3.95, U.S.A.)*
                               (A30-655, $4.95, Canada)
A breath-taking novel that takes you behind the doors of
the law and inside the heart and mind of Jennifer Parker.
She rises from the ashes of her own courtroom disaster to
become one of America's most brilliant attorneys. Her
story is interwoven with that of two very different men of
enormous power. As Jennifer inspires both men to passion,
each is determined to destroy the other—and Jennifer,
caught in the crossfire, becomes the ultimate victim.

___**CHANCES**
by Jackie Collins   *(A30-268, $3.95)*
Handsome, hot-blooded, hard-to-handle Gino Santangelo
took chances on the city streets where he staked his guts
and brains to build an empire. He used women, discarded
them at will...until he met the woman of his dreams. The
greatest chance he ever took led him to America to escape
prosecution when he entrusted his empire to Lucky Santangelo. Jackie Collins' latest is a real sizzling, sexy, action-
packed national bestseller!

BEST OF BESTSELLERS FROM WARNER BOOKS

BESTSELLERS FROM WARNER BOOKS

___**THE OFFICERS' WIVES**
by Thomas Fleming   *(A90-920, $3.95)*
This is a book you will never forget. It is about the U.S.
Army, the huge unwieldy organism on which much of the
nation's survival depends. It is about Americans trying to
live personal lives, to cling to touchstones of faith and
hope in the grip of the blind, blunderous history of the last
25 years. It is about marriage, the illusions and hopes that
people bring to it, the struggle to maintain and renew commitment.

___**BELLEFLEUR**
by Joyce Carol Oates   *(A30-732, $4.50)*
A swirl of fantasy, history, family feuds, love affairs and
dreams, this is the saga of the Bellefleurs who live like feu-
dal barons in a mythical place that might perhaps be the
Adirondacks. A strange curse, it is said, hovers over the
family, causing magical and horrible events to occur. Past
and present appear to live side-by-side, as the fantastic
reality of the Bellefleurs unfolds.

___**RICH DREAMS**
by Ben and Norma Barzman   *(F90-034, $3.50)*
He's the world's sex novel king with a personal life to
match. He's rolling in royalties, champagne and mis-
tresses. He's a Bel Air baron—the Boston slum kind who
hustled his way through Hollywood orgies, poured out a
bestseller at age 23, and operates with mob connections.

Best Of Bestsellers
from WARNER BOOKS

___**PALOVERDE**
by Jacqueline Briskin　　　　　　　*(A30-345, $3.95)*
The love story of Amelie—the sensitive, ardent, young girl
whose uncompromising code of honor leads her to choices
that will reverberate for generations, plus the chronicle of a
unique city, Los Angeles, wrestling with the power of railroads, discovery of oil, and growing into the fabulous capital of filmdom, makes this one of the most talked-about
novels of the year.

___**DAZZLE**
by Elinor Klein & Dora Landey　　　　*(A93-476, $2.95)*
Only one man can make every fantasy come true—
entertainers, industrialists, politicians, and society
leaders all need Costigan. Costigan, the man with the
power of PR, whose past is a mystery, whose present is
hidden in hype, and whose future may be out of his own
hands. In a few hours, a marriage will end, a love affair
begin, a new star will be created, and an old score settled.
And Costigan will know whether or not he has won or lost in
the gamble of life.

___**SCRUPLES**
by Judith Krantz　　　　　　　　　*(A30-531, $3.95)*
The ultimate romance! The spellbinding story of the rise of
a fascinating woman from fat, unhappy "poor relative" of
an aristocratic Boston family to a unique position among
the super-beautiful and super-rich, a woman who got
everything she wanted—fame, wealth, power and love.

The BEST Of JACKIE COLLINS

The Best OF Bestsellers
From WARNER BOOKS